T0301062

By Alexander Dan Vilhjálmsson from Gollancz

Shadows of the Short Days
The Storm Beneath a Midnight Sun

THE STORM BENEATH A MIDNIGHT SUN

ALEXANDER DAN VILHJÁLMSSON

This edition first published in Great Britain in 2023 by Gollancz

First published in Great Britain in 2022 by Gollancz
an imprint of The Orion Publishing Group Ltd
Carmelite House, 50 Victoria Embankment
London EC4Y 0DZ

An Hachette UK Company

1 3 5 7 9 10 8 6 4 2

Copyright © Alexander Dan Vilhjálmsson 2022

A CIP catalogue record for this book is
available from the British Library.

ISBN (Mass Market Paperback) 978 1 473 22416 2
ISBN (eBook) 978 1 473 22417 9

Typeset at The Spartan Press Ltd,
Lymington, Hants

Printed and bound in Great Britain by Clays Ltd,
Elcograf S.p.A.

MIX
Paper from
responsible sources
FSC® C104740

www.gollancz.co.uk
www.orionbooks.co.uk

Contents

Pronunciation

Here is a quick guide to pronunciation of Icelandic vowels. Please note that the non-Icelandic transcription is usually an approximation. The IPA phonetic transcription is more reliable.

a [a] as the French *mal*
á [au] as the *ow* in *how*
e [ɛ] as the *e* in *bed*
é [jɛ] as the *ye* in *yes*
i / y [ɪ] as the *i* in *inn*
í / ý [i] as the *ee* in *seen*
o [ɔ] as the *o* in *bore*
ó [ou] as the *o* in *go*
u [ʏ] approximately as the French *cul-de-sac*
ú [u] as the *oo* in *zoo*
æ [ai] as the *i* in *life*
ö [œ] as the French *peur*
au [œi] as the French *feuille*
ei / ey [ei] as the *ay* in *stay*

Additional note: Ð/ð is a soft *th* sound (*feather*, *that*); Þ/þ is a strong *th* sound (*think*, *thorn*).

Glossary

Amma [ˈamːa] – Grandmother.

Blóðgagl [ˈplouð͜ˌkakl] / **Blóðgögl** [ˈplouð͜ˌkœkl] – Clan warriors of the náskárar tribes. *Old poetical kenning for raven. Blóð = blood; gagl = bird.*

Brennivín [ˈprɛnːɪˌvin] – A type of strong liquor. *Literally means burning wine.*

Delýsíð [ˈtɛːlisið] – A sorcerous narcotic, can be fluid or solid. Most often snorted in powder. Frequent use erodes the nasal septum. *Approximate pronunciation: de ('e' as in 'bed') – lee – seeth.*

Draugur [ˈtrœiːɣʏr] – A ghost, resentful, hateful and dangerous. *In Icelandic folklore, draugar are physical unliving beings, not ethereal spirits. Evil magic users would awake draugar and set them to haunt their enemies, often for several generations.*

Elskan [ˈɛlskan] – Word of affection; darling, dear.

Frænka [ˈfraiŋka] – Aunt or female cousin.

Galdramaður [ˈkaltraˌmaːðʏr] / **Galdramenn** [ˈkaltraˌmɛnː] – Practitioners of galdur. *Galdur = magic; maður/menn = man/men.*

Galdrastafur [ˈkaltraˌstaːvʏr] / **Galdrastafir** [ˈkaltraˌstaːvɪr̥] – Arcane symbols, often staves, with a particular use in rituals. *Galdur = magic; stafur/stafir = stave/staves.*

Galdur [ˈkaltʏr] – Type of spoken magic. *From old Norse paganism. Word derived from the verb gala, meaning to yell or sing, deriving its power from poetry chanted in a particular way.*

Gandreið [ˈkant͜reɪð] – A vile, arcane method of control or possession. *In Icelandic folklore, witches used gandreið to control an object to fly through the air. The worst method of gandreið used a man as a mount to fly.*

Goði [ˈkɔːðɪ] / **Goðar** [ˈkɔːðar] – A parliament member of Lögrétta. *In the Icelandic Age of Settlement, around AD 930, goðar were ruling chieftains who sat in Alþingi.*

Haugbúi [ˈhœiːɣˌpuɪ] / **Haugbúar** [ˈhœiːɣˌpuar̥] – A type of undead creature, a corporeal ghost, a draugur. *Haugur = burial mound; búi = dweller.*

Hersir [ˈhɛr̥sɪr] – The leader of a tribe of náskárar. *Old poetical kenning for king.*

Hertygi [ˈhɛr̥tʰijɪ] – A harness the náskárar wear around their torsos, displaying trophies and important status symbols. *Old word for military equipment: her = army; tygi = clothes.*

Hrímland [ˈr̥imˌlant] – An island far in the north, almost uninhabitable with wild, sorcerous energies infesting the country. *Archaic name for Iceland.*

Hrævareldur [ˈr̥aivarˌɛltʏr] / **Hrævareldar** [ˈr̥aivarˌɛltar] – A flame, floating in the air, luring people to their death. They seem to frequent forgotten or cursed places.

Huldufólk[ˈhʏltʏˌfoulk̥]/**Huldukona**[ˈhʏltʏˌkɔːna]/**Huldumaður** [ˈhʏltʏˌmaːðʏr] – Extradimensional exiles in the world of Hrímland. *In folklore, huldufólk were richly dressed, fae people, believed to live inside stones. Hulda/huldu is a prefix meaning 'hidden'. Maður = man; kona = woman; fólk = people.*

Hulduheimar [ˈhʏltʏˌhɛiːmar] – The home dimension of the huldufólk. *Huldu = hidden; heimar = worlds.*

Huldumanneskja ['hʏltʏ‚manːɛsca] / **Huldumanneskjur** ['hʏltʏ‚manːɛscʏr] – A word for people with huldufólk and human parents which better accepts and fully encompasses who they are: not a mixture of two beings, but a unified, whole being. *Hulda = hidden; manneskja = human being.*

Jötunn ['jœːtʏn] / **Jötnar** ['jœhtnar] – Mythical and primordial beings that predate mankind. *From the old Norse religion, destructive primordial beings. The world was made from the corpse of the first being in existence, the primordial jötunn Ýmir. From him all jötnar are descended.*

Korpur ['kʰɔr̥pʏr] / **Korpar** ['kʰɔr̥par] – Náskárar warriors without a tribe. *Old Icelandic word for raven.*

Kukl [kʰʏhkl̥] / **Kuklari** ['kʰʏhklarɪ] / **Kuklarar** ['kʰʏhklarar] – Kukl is unlearned, ill-understood magic, meddling and tampering with the occult. A kuklari is a practitioner of such low, unlearned sorcery.

Króna ['kʰrouːna] / **Krónur** ['kʰrouːnʏr] – Currency. One króna consists of one hundred aurar.

Krummafótur ['kʰrʏmːaˌfouːtʏr] – The third foot of the náskárar, much stronger than the other two claws. Used for standing on for long periods and picking up heavy objects – or living beings. *Also used everyday to indicate a shoe put on the wrong foot, that's a krummafótur.*

Landvættur ['lantˌvaihtʏr] – An ancient, mythical being of immense power. The landvættir played a big part in the old Hrímlandic religion, outlawed by the Kalmar Commonwealth. Although strange things exist in Hrímland, no one believed them to be real until the Stone Giant appeared. *From Icelandic folklore. There are four landvættir in Iceland, each protecting a quadrant of the country from outside threats.*

Lögrétta ['lœɣˌriɛhta] – The Hrímlandic parliament. Used for both the parliament and the parliament building itself.

Historically, a legislative institution of Iceland's parliament, Alþingi.

Mamma [ˈmamːa] – Mother.

Marbendill [ˈmarˌpɛntɪtl̩] / **Marbendlar** [ˈmarˌpɛntlar] – Aquatic humanoids who live in both fresh waters and the sea. *Word from Icelandic folklore for aquatic beings.*

Náskári [ˈnauːˌskarɪ] / **Náskárar** [ˈnauːˌskarar] – The ravenfolk. *Word is an old poetical kenning for raven. Ná = corpse; skári = bird (young seagull).*

Níðstöng [ˈniðˌstœiŋk] / **Níðstangir** [ˈniðˌstauŋkɪr] – An incredibly dangerous type of svartigaldur, used to curse someone with awful magic, bringing complete ruination to them. *In Icelandic folklore, a níðstöng was often a raised pole with a horse's head impaled on it, facing the location it should curse. In modern times, níðstangir have been raised against authorities and individuals, usually with a cod's head or a horse's skull on the pole.*

Norn [nɔrtn] – A witch.

Seiðmagn [ˈseiːðˌmakn̩] – Sorcerous energy, found in nature. *Seiður = sorcery; magn = power. Compound word is similarly structured as rafmagn = electricity.*

Seiðskratti [ˈseiːðˌskrahtɪ] – A practitioner of seiður, highly skilled and learned in its application. *In Icelandic, used to refer to a malevolent sorcerer. Seið = sorcery; skratti = fiend.*

Seiður [ˈseiːðʏr] – Type of sorcery. *Type of magic from old Norse paganism.*

Skoffín [ˈskɔfːin] – A type of small, wild animal, terribly ugly and dangerous. *From Icelandic folklore: a spawn of a fox and a cat, with the cat being the mother.*

Skramsl [ˈskramstl̩] – The language of the náskárar. *Archaic word for cawing. The more common, modern word for cawing is krunk.*

Skrumnir [ˈskrʏmnɪr] – The sorcerer in a tribe of náskárar. *Old poetical kenning for raven.*

Skuggabaldur [ˈskʏkːaˌpaltʏr] – A type of small, vicious animal, similar to a fox or a mink. Very dangerous to livestock and hard to kill. *From Icelandic folklore: a spawn of a fox and a cat, with the fox being the mother.*

Skuggsjá [ˈskʏkːˌsjauː] – A device that pierces through time. *From folklore, a dark ritual intended to grant the user sight over past and future. Skugg = shadow; sjá = sight.*

Sorti [ˈsɔr̥tɪ] – Dangerous sorcerous narcotic. *Word for something pitch-black; can also refer to thick, heavy fog or weather.*

Stiftamtmaður [ˈstɪftˌamtˌmaðʏr] – The governor of the colony of Hrímland; the stiftamtmaður acts out the will of the king and rules in his name. *Historical political title in Iceland, from when Denmark ruled the country. The stiftamtmaður served as the highest royal authority and representative of the king in Iceland. The country was separated into units of amt, which amtmenn governed, the stiftamtmenn governing the entire country.*

Svartigaldur [ˈsvar̥tɪˌkaltʏr] – The vilest, most heinous kind of galdur.

Tilberi [ˈtʰɪːlˌpɛrɪ] – A simple creature made with galdur, usually to work simple repeated tasks. *In folklore, a tilberi was most often used to steal milk from nearby farms.*

Vistarband [ˈvɪstarˌpant] – A contract between a landless worker and a farmer, lasting one year at a time. *Throughout most of Iceland's settlement, vistarband was a form of serfdom that put the lower classes at the mercy of those who owned or rented land.*

Vættur [ˈvaihtʏr] / **Vættir** [ˈvaihtɪr] – A nature being or spirit from folklore. *Illvættur [ˈitl̥ˌvaihtʏr] is malevolent.*

I

FROSTAVETURINN MIKLI

THE GREAT FROST WINTER

The sky knows. Heavy clouds gather, darkening. They expand and swallow the night's brightness, bringing us true darkness again. The wind hunts, skulking, hitting branches; it sprints and throws up leaves, tears at straws, beats at windows, whispering so everywhere moans:

He is coming.

Waves break and tear up the shoreline. Black rocks are pulled into the ocean depths. Every single creature crawls into shelter: men board their doors and windows; mice crawl into their holes; birds flock to any cover they can find – eagles, ducks, ravens and snipes; eggs tumble from their nests; a fox seeks refuge in its burrow; sheep and reindeer huddle to protect their young; insects retreat into the earth and filthy corners; fish and monstrous beings vanish into the depths. Even the lava fields fall silent.

He is coming.

The crash of thunder joins the cacophony, horns sound to celebrate the coming of the king. The clouds dance now, enslaved to the god of weather. Lightning strikes, its crackling flashes illuminating the storm. It hits trees, buildings, fields and withered grass; sacrifices at the altars, palm leaves spread on the path of their lord, wildfires showing him the way to shore.

And behold. Here he comes.

The heart of the storm is a crown upon his head, the raging ocean the acclaim of the crowd. He glides through the skies, floating, roaming ever closer to land. He dances, he amplifies the storm, feeds it and shapes it, and nature calls out his name. The majestic beast is gigantic, far larger than any whale who has braved the oceans, its killing form so sharp, so perfected, so infused with murderous intent, that every creature looking upon him immediately loses heart and breaks, ready to perish. Furious sparks shoot from his deep maw, past rows of jagged teeth. Dark smoke rolls down his body, his fins cutting through the current. In his belly a ceaseless fire burns, an unstoppable thunderstorm erupting from his heart, and his eyes are glaring white and glowing. Two sparking suns charged with electricity and a thirst for blood. He feeds the storm; the vortex grows stronger, thunder roars, lightning gnashes, and the earth trembles from his arrival.

Landvættur.

Eitt

Elka watched the city grow distant and felt relief wash over her like a wave. She bade the salted, frozen streets farewell, the oppressive city wall, the dreadful Stone Giant who had lorded over the city these last few years, always visible from its place atop the hill. It stood dormant by the cleared ruins of the Nine, the government's former prison, having obliterated it and the church tower of Haraldskirkja during its city-wide rampage several years before. She bade it farewell, a monument to all the bad memories she'd picked up in Reykjavík.

The diesel smoke flowed from the ship's funnels as it threaded its way across the sea, between slow-moving ice floes. She saw lights from the coastguard ships who broke sailing paths through the ice up ahead. The papers said they had seiðskrattar on board, who held back the incredible cold by warming the ocean with seiðmagn so the harbour wouldn't freeze, as well as diverting incoming icebergs.

'Bye-bye, Reykjavík.' Sölvi sniffed, and Elka laughed and stroked his head. He looked up to her, and the happiness she felt was reflected clear in his face, untouched by the hardships of adulthood.

'Bye-bye,' she joined in as Reykjavík disappeared.

Down below decks Elka found their single bunk, which was

all she could afford. People lounged across the cabin, reading, knitting, trying to sleep. Most of them were men, but everyone was heading to the same place she was, somewhere a hard-working person could get a job and perhaps start a new life – if they knew the right people. The mother and son lay down and nestled under a worn blanket. Their trunk was wedged to the side of the bunk and was nowhere near as full as Elka would have liked. But soon she would get a steady job and fill it to the brim. For Sölvi. He surprised her by saying no when she asked if he wanted to hear a story. Perhaps he was self-conscious and believed that all the people would think him childish if his mother was telling him bedtime stories.

Elka was exhausted, but she knew she couldn't sleep. The cabin was freezing, and her hands trembled, nerves wound up and weak. This was not the first time she'd quit sorti; the process had become a familiar nightmare. She'd only slept for a few hours the last few days, and not even she understood how she had managed to keep herself going. Pure desperation or hope. Perhaps the two were one and the same.

'Will other kids be there?' Sölvi asked in a quiet voice.

'Of course, elskan,' she whispered into his ear. 'Lots of kids live there and there are plenty of new friends and adventures waiting for you.'

'What if they don't want to be my friends?'

'Don't be silly – who wouldn't want to be your friend?' To this he said nothing, as if he well knew the answer, and to try to steer their conversation to a better course Elka added: 'Making friends will be easy, and it will be so much fun going to school. It's going to be amazing, Sölvi. So much better than Reykjavík.'

'All right, Mamma,' he said, and fell asleep.

'How long until we get there?' Sölvi's voice was tiny and fragile.

At the end of the cabin someone was reading by candlelight, a distant source of light in the creaking, salty darkness.

'Not for many hours, elskan. We still have to dock at Suðurnes.'

'That's where the outlaws live. They kill each other all the time.'

'Hush. Don't speak of things you know nothing about.'

'Amma said so. She told me stories about chieftains feuding.'

The mention of Elka's mother was like a fresh cut, one she wasn't prepared to deal with.

'Please, Sölvi, I don't feel well. I'm getting seasick, I think. Be quiet and try to sleep.'

'All right.'

Sölvi didn't like the cabin. It reeked of dirt and sweat, as if they had been sleeping down there for months. The people coughed and farted and moaned, sick from the ocean's movement. He liked it, how it rocked him. Feeling the ocean was feeling the movement of the world.

His mother was sick, but he knew it wasn't due to the sea. She had been sick many times before. Usually, it meant she was getting better – or trying to. He didn't want to get his hopes up, but now they were moving he couldn't help hoping that everything would change. They would be happy and safe and maybe his dad would come back to live with them. But he knew that was stupid and would never happen.

Still, it was a nice, warm dream.

He wished he could find a table, or a small lantern, so he could draw. He wanted to draw all the excitement, the anxiety and the hope he had fluttering in him like a butterfly trapped in a jar. He wanted to draw it so he could remember it when the feeling would inevitably extinguish. Then he could look at the picture and maybe start to feel like that again. If he had the chance to draw, he would wet his hand with saltwater and mush all the colours together. Very gently, so the paper wouldn't tear. Blend them as though he was a god making an ocean. That's how he felt. Like there was an ocean in his heart.

When Sölvi was fairly certain that his mother was asleep, or at least as much asleep as her condition permitted, he sneaked out of the berth and the dark cabin. He tripped over a pair of boots in the middle of the tight gangway, and someone hissed at him to be careful, but he knew better than to respond and just hurried up the steep stairs.

Grey daylight struggled through the grimy portholes and he hurried out to the deck. Sheer cliffs overlooked the ship on both sides, snow-covered on top, with frozen waterfalls running down the rock. Ahead was a dingy port hanging to the cliffs. Bæjarháls, his mother had told him. Sölvi ran to the starboard bow and watched the throng of people gathering on the pier as the ship docked. They were thin, some of them starving, desperately waving, shouting and pleading. They were poorly dressed for the freezing cold. The sailors waved heavy bludgeons to warn the people back, and they reluctantly obeyed, probably all too aware of what would happen if they tested the sailors' patience.

These can't be the outlaws, Sölvi thought to himself. They are much too thin and none of them have weapons or shields. They look like beggars. Sölvi recalled vividly the sagas his grandmother had told him and for a moment found himself doubting the accuracy of those heroic tales. Real outlaws would have taken the ship by force, those bludgeons no match against real spears and swords. Then Sölvi could have become a young pirate and pillaged the rich people in downtown Reykjavík, so his mother wouldn't have to work another day in her life. His doubts were assuaged when he realised that most likely the outlawed warriors were somewhere else, perhaps hiding in the lava fields or fighting a battle. It also explained why these people at the pier were so frightfully thin; the outlaws hoarded all the food for themselves.

The cargo hold was open and a steam-powered crane lifted out a pallet loaded with crates and sacks of grain, which the crew quickly unloaded on the dock. People were begging for board, to work their way to Reykjavík or the islands, but all were refused and the ship quickly pushed from the pier.

Sölvi stayed out of the crew's way and watched the brooding cliffs move past, looking for signs of the ironed náskárar. He'd seen them only twice in Reykjavík, distant in the sky, giant, dark, threatening shapes. It would be an adventure to see one up close. Then he could draw one without having to imagine what they looked like.

The frozen cliffs gave way to the open sea. The strong wind carried the smell of the ocean, salty and fresh, and Sölvi felt his heart grow lighter. Small icebergs lazed on the waves in the south. He'd never been out to sea, and to his surprise he wasn't seasick at all. It was as though it was natural to him. Maybe he should become a sailor when he grew up, he thought. He could work hard fishing and then during shore leave, paint or draw or do whatever he liked. And when he was working he could have this view, this freedom. A blue expanse of opportunity. Maybe he could sail to another country and bring his mother with him. Then they could get far enough away from everything. But for now, the islands of Vestmannaeyjar would have to do.

ᚺ

Kári stomped his feet and blew into his hands. The Great Frost Winter, they called the unusually cold season, which still endured in full force despite it being early spring. The queue was long when he'd arrived, but in the short time he stood waiting in line so many people had showed up that it now went around the corner of the street. Reykjavík had multiplied in size the last few decades, but news still travelled as though it was a seaside fishing village. Kári had heard a shipment was expected early to the grocer in Pétursbúð, including wheat, sugar, and what was at the top of Kári's list of priorities: coffee. Working without it had been insufferable since the shortage hit Hrímland. Every week the newspapers reported ships that had been sunk crossing the Atlantean Ocean.

The queue slowly moved on. He barely felt his fingers. Many people had nasty coughs, so he reinforced the shield of immunity he'd thrown up every day for the past week. It was kukl, really, a rough and ugly attempt to shield the body from microorganisms. He wasn't even sure if it worked. The plague outbreak was only accelerating, and he knew it was just a matter of time until it hit hard. The news from the mainland was dire. The Hanseatic war dragged on and the resulting shortages had given the plague fertile soil to spread at a frightening pace. Already the Hrímlandic harbours were under nationwide quarantine by order of the stiftamtmaður, but in Reykjavík the damage was done. Only time would tell how badly they would come out of it.

And when he finally entered the shop... he was met with empty shelves. No coffee. No sugar. No wheat. He bought milk and liver sausage, which had nearly doubled in price since the new year had passed. A pinch of butter and dried fish as well, along with a few potatoes, and that was that. He resentfully paid and kept quiet while an older gentleman berated the staff, as if the grocer was to blame for the shortages.

Outside the queue was just as long, and Kári felt relieved that he had at least been able to buy *something*. He only had to take care of himself.

When he returned home the heating stove was cold and the apartment was freezing, and he cursed not being able to afford coal, regardless of whether he could find it. The city of Reykjavík was taking its time getting hot water heating to all the districts, so he'd be freezing for the foreseeable future. The plague wards he conjured were enough of a strain on his resources already, but this winter frost was the greatest in living memory. The cold, hunger and disease might cut his fellow countrymen down in swathes, but such a fate was unsuited to a seiðskratti. His research might stall due to his plan, but it would halt indefinitely were he to catch a fever and die.

He arrived at Svartiskóli just before ten and felt thankful for the warmth that greeted him in the vast open lobby. It was always cosy inside, despite the enormous, knotted wooden doors that always stood open. He went upstairs to the teachers' lounge for the faculty of seiður on the third floor and came to an empty room, without coffee, as he'd come to expect over the last months. It was going to be another long day.

Kári only had one lesson to teach after noon on Tungldays: Introduction to Biothaumaturgy. As a research lecturer he wasn't required to teach, but a few extra courses every semester were a decent source of income, and if the material was easy enough he got away with using up as little of his time and energy as he could.

He brewed a pot of wild thyme and cursed that he couldn't find anything to sweeten it with. Then he strolled down the plain, unassuming university corridors, lit by fluorescent lights, heading to his laboratory. Every door looked like the next, but within the rooms couldn't be more varied.

Leifur was in the lab when Kári walked in and nodded curtly in greeting. He was poring over disassembled equipment strewn across esoteric blueprints and yellowed manuscripts. Kári didn't know what exactly Leifur was working on, and that's how the seiðskrattar preferred it. Leifur competed for the same grants and positions as Kári, so it made sense to keep a certain distance. Thankfully Leifur spent most of his time in Perlan, working within the secretive confines of the thaumaturgical power plant. Several years ago he had secured a prestigious apprenticeship under Doctor Vésteinn Alrúnarson, and he'd spent most of his working hours there ever since. If Kári had thought Leifur insufferably smug before he had been chosen for that honour, after the fact Leifur's company became borderline intolerable. They got along just fine, following a strict system: never speak, never share anything, barely recognise the other's existence. Still, were he pressed, Kári would list Leifur as one of his closer friends. Such are often the stupid ways of male companionship.

Kári stacked up the previous day's notes and glanced through them as he finished the bitter herbal infusion. In a glass cage on the middle of a table was the current focus of his research: a study in thaumaturgical transformation. It was a skoffín he had trapped in the forested hills of Öskjuhlíð, only a short distance from Svartiskóli. The creature had most likely once been a cat, or perhaps a rabbit, but it was impossible to tell whether that had been years or generations ago. Long barbs protruded from the creature's back, its fur occasionally sparking with static electricity. Its tail split at two points, resulting in four ends in total, and at the end of one was a harmless sting. It was quite sharp and could very well be used as a weapon, except the skoffín seemed to have no control over its tail at all.

He had managed to fuse the creature's split jaw back together, although it still had a double set of teeth which barely fitted in its mouth. Its glaring eyes were still just as many, overcrowding its face, only now arranged more orderly. Getting to the point where he could make these alterations permanently take hold had been a gruesome process of trial and error. Uncounted other creatures had died from the strain of the thaumaturgical operations, many of which they had to undergo repeatedly. Most often the flesh continued to mutate uncontrollably, or otherwise settled back into its previous, mutated form.

For this subject, his next task would be to verify his theory that some of the eyes were not communicating with the creature's brain. He suspected that they might be connected to a newly grown brain core, or some kind of separate nervous system hiding inside the body. The skoffín certainly behaved and reacted differently based on which eyes were tested, so something was definitely not right. But it was just as likely that the new eyes were disconnected from everything, that they were sense organs that writhed idiotically and purposelessly due to random impulses.

Kári opened a drawer on his worn desk and rooted around for a locked box. It was made of dark iron, fortified with obsidian, with no apparent keyholes. He placed a hand on it and mumbled the keyword quietly. The inner mechanisms clicked and he fished out of it a tiny pinch of highland moss. He ground it on top of a thin piece of tissue and mixed it together with snuff, as the tobacco would speed up absorption of the thaumaturgical moss. Then he carefully packed the tissue together into a small, tight bundle, which he put in the back of his mouth. When he needed to speed up absorption and potency, he usually filled a syringe and loaded his entire upper lip with a damp mixture of tobacco and moss, but at the beginning of the day he tended to ease into it. He also had to stretch out the usage in order to succeed with his plan: steal some moss and he might not be quite so cold tonight.

He placed his hands on the cage and focused on drawing in the seiðmagn, letting it gather, coiling up and saturating his entire body. Then he opened up a small breach and allowed it to trickle out in a weak, controlled current. He laid over the skoffín a heavy weariness and put it to sleep. When he was certain that the beast was unconscious he picked it up and placed it on the table. He hummed a short tune, a fraction of an incantation often used by students to sharpen their focus and absorption of seiðmagn. Leifur had taught him it, a trick from some friend of his who had studied galdur a few years ago, but used highland moss in his work. The incantation was bloody kukl, but it worked. It had become a known secret among students of seiður since then.

A few hours later he fused together the abdominal cavity of the animal and sighed. The mutations were so complete and intricate, all the way down to the molecular level, that it was turning out harder than expected to reverse them, especially since he didn't know what the skoffín was originally intended to be. It had become a creature of seiður, a part of the sorcerous nature, inseparable and inexplicable outside its confines. At best he could work on mutating the creature further, transfiguring it yet again, but in the image of a cat or a rabbit or whatever small animal he suspected was hidden at its roots. But that was not a real solution – it wasn't a fundamental change of the creature's condition. The skoffín came to in its cage and hissed at him, crawling under the bed of straw and curling up. It was most likely in considerable pain.

'Can't you cast some sound-muting seiður on that thing?' asked Leifur, without looking up from his work. 'Or carve a galdrastafur on the bottom of the cage?'

'Does it bother you this much? Wouldn't you rather hear what it's up to in case it tries to escape?'

'The sounds from that thing are insufferable. You should hurry up and dissect it like the others do. Much cleaner. And more humane.'

'Soon enough,' Kári said and patted the top of the cage lightly. 'It will come to that soon enough.'

ᚼ

The afternoon's lesson was quick and painless, despite a single student constantly raising his hand to ask about the most asinine things. A snide answer to the second question kept him quiet for a while, long enough for Kári to get through a particularly troublesome part of his lecture on thaumaturgical thermo-dynamics, after which the student naturally piped up again. Students of seiður were an ambitious bunch, so his peers were likely grateful that he asked for clarification on matters they themselves were struggling with – but still there was no doubt that they looked down on him for asking. Displaying your hand blatantly like that did not behove a fledgling seiðskratti.

Almost half of the class was missing, likely sick at home or finding other work to fill their bellies. Doubtless more would soon follow in their steps within the next few days.

The thought of it was frustrating. The comfortably rich or well connected would be those who remained, not the best students. That was a big enough problem as it was.

It was common for students to suddenly disappear. Many struggling or overly ambitious students overreached and fell prey to the forces they tried to control. The lucky ones simply perished. Furthermore, all teachers were required to rank the students at the end of each semester. It was almost prophetic, as the lowest-scoring ones often ended up missing before they got the boot. Somehow, the more affluent students never seemed to suffer, despite their low ranking. Likely they had purchased assistance to help with preventing mishaps as well.

Kári returned to the laboratory, where he found Leifur waiting for him. His eyes were wide, his whole body wound up and apprehensive.

'It got out?' Kári stated more than asked, glancing around the lab. 'Where is it? Where did you last see it?'

'Everything's fine,' Leifur replied, pointing towards the desk. 'It's still there, it's fine, it's just . . . a letter came for you.'

Kári walked over towards his desk, where the skoffín was still hiding underneath the bed of straw. On the very middle of the desk was a yellowed envelope sealed with red wax. A sigil was stamped into it – a human skull bearing a crude hexcross on its forehead. Svartiskóli's emblem.

'Who delivered this?'

'A tilberi,' said Leifur, now hardly containing the curiosity in his voice. 'I've never seen one up close before. It was fucking repulsive.'

'I see.'

Kári didn't know anyone who had a tilberi serving their whim. Usually a servant for galdramenn, it was not unheard of for seiðskrattar to use them for their purposes. The very strict galdur of binding required to rein in the unpredictable monstrosity made it an incorruptible servant. Svartiskóli had used them frequently centuries ago, when the school was housed in far more spartan housing in the countryside. Today, it was a ceremonial tradition only used on rare occasions. Kári was not familiar with the requirements insisting on its use. He picked up the letter and opened it.

'Who is it from?' asked Leifur. 'What does it say?' He had now abandoned the guise of simple curiosity, his tone betraying blatant envy.

Kári's heartbeat rang in his ears as he read the letter, eyes squinting as he decoded the delicate, archaic penmanship.

This was it.

This could be everything he had been waiting for, and more.

'It's nothing,' he said, and gathered up his notes. 'Just the usual academic nonsense. I have to go.'

Leifur glared at him as Kári stormed out. Then he turned back to his machines.

Tvö

Elka woke with a start as Sölvi gently pushed her shoulder. The other passengers were already up, picking up their canvas bags and dragging their trunks out of the cabin.

'We're here!'

Her bones ached and she was sticky with dried sweat. She had been dreaming something terrible. Elka had never got used to the fever dreams coming down from a high, and they were even worse when kicking the habit.

'Get your things ready.'

'Already did,' Sölvi said with a smile. 'We're all set.'

He smelled of the ocean breeze. It brought her confusing nightmare back to the surface, threatening to make her sick. A cloying vision – a smothering ocean crashing over her, pulling her down into the deep. The moon seen from beneath the waves, lethargically pulsing like a heart. The moon and the ocean had simultaneously been within her, making her feel trapped in a paradoxical prison.

Outside, fog reduced the world to the sound of waves against the ship and seagulls crying in the distance. Everything else was a grey haze, the ocean blending seamlessly together with the mist and slate-heavy skies above. It was late morning and the sun had barely risen. The passengers had gathered on the deck, stamping their feet to ward off the freezing cold. A few coughs, some sniffles, every sound spreading concern and worry. There weren't any other children there except for Sölvi. Elka hoped he wouldn't be the only newcomer in school, but she knew he was strong. He'd find his way.

Someone shouted. Sölvi sprinted to the stern of the ship.

The islands seemed to climb out of the mist.

Sheer volcanic cliffs of dark stone, their crevices filled with nests of seagulls. Birds soared through the air in more variety than Sölvi had ever seen before. He pointed them out excitedly, asking his mother for their names. She knew a handful from illustrated books – seagulls, fulmars, gannets, puffins and great auks.

The auks covered a large reef, standing upright, staring at the passing ship, their cries a cacophony even from a distance. They were black-feathered and white-bellied, with a single white spot on their head next to the eye. They walked clumsily on the rock.

'Can't they fly?' Sölvi asked.

'No, they're swimming birds. I've heard they're delicious.'

He stared at the tall birds diving into the sea. There were so many of them. Enough to feed a village.

As they approached the harbour they passed a massive stone fort on the port side. A great tower, medieval in appearance, overshadowing the ocean traffic. Soldiers manned the ramparts, the fortifications surrounding it lined with cannons. The wind pulled at the flag at the very top. It depicted a proud sailing ship on undulating waves, with the emblems of Kalmar and the royal crown depicted above it. A hint of an oceanic creature beneath the surface, under the ship. The proud flag of Vestmannaeyjar.

As the passengers alighted from the ship they were shepherded into a large, empty warehouse. Officials checked their papers, gas masks occluding their passive stares. Their muffled voices asked them if they felt sick, if they had been ill of the influenza prior, if they had any relatives, friends or previous co-workers who had fallen to the pest. Inside, they were separated into groups and told to wait. Every cough and sniffle aroused panicked suspicion. Elka and Sölvi were led to their designated waiting area, where they sat on their trunks with a dozen or so other people. She noticed that Sölvi was nervous while trying to appear unfazed.

'They're just checking to see if anyone is sick. They don't want the villagers to get the flu.'

'I know, Mamma. It's all right.'

Hours passed. They were provided with no food or water. People relieved themselves in a line of buckets at one end of the warehouse. A large door opened and a squad of medical staff entered in a haze of smoke, wearing grey robes and red masks, similar to those of seiðskrattar, but belonging to medical doctors. Plague doctors. They walked between the people, swinging chain censers around as they inspected the passengers closely through their red-tinted lenses. The purplish smoke was thick and heady, reeking of wilted flowers and grotesque perfumes.

Behind them came a lurking figure in a crimson robe. Their mask was obsidian in colour and long-beaked, the red-tinted lenses seeming malignant. A royal seiðskratti. An eerie calm gripped the room, as prey stiffens when faced with a predator. The seiðskratti took a deep breath through the mask's filters, scanning the crowd lazily. When they started to speak, their voice was soft and cloying, echoing effortlessly through the room.

'Passengers of the ferry *Herjólfur* – Captain Kohl, on behalf of the Vestmannaeyjar government and the people of Heimaey, would like to thank you for your patience during these trying times. Our medical staff are now committing the cleansing rites known to kill the plague, searching for any who might possibly

THE STORM BENEATH A MIDNIGHT SUN

need to be quarantined. There is nothing to be feared. Please, breathe deeply of the smoke so the treatment can be administered to its full effect. We thank you for your co-operation.'

Elka gripped her shawl as the doctors approached, trying to calm her trembling hands. The smell was filling up the room. It was almost intoxicating. Sölvi paled, staring at her. He recognised it, too – or at least faint notes of it; the scent wasn't quite exactly the same. Whatever they might be burning, Elka was convinced it couldn't be that much different from sorti.

'Don't breathe it in, Mamma,' he whispered. 'You don't have to, you're not sick.'

'It's not the same,' she said. 'It's medicine.' She forced a stern smile. 'We have to breathe it in, or they'll quarantine us.'

He didn't respond. The doctors came nearer, swinging the large metallic censer around. It was cast in the image of a trio of cod fish, the piscine forms circling each other like a weave-knot. The doctors investigated them thoroughly, seeing something through their thaumaturgically enhanced lenses. She stared back at them, calm, fierce. Trying not to cough from the smoke.

She could feel the rush, the relief. It wasn't nearly as potent as a hit of pure sorti, but it was there.

That abyssal daze.

She breathed in deeply.

ᚻ

The tram mainly served as a commuter route between the main university campus, the student apartments, and Svartiskóli, tucked away at the bottom of the forested hill of Öskjuhlíð, on top of which Perlan loomed. From Svartiskóli's obsidian hulk the rails went up the hill through the forest, warded by rune-covered monoliths, towards the shining dome of the thaumaturgical power plant. It was used by staff and students working in Perlan, who were surprisingly limited in number, a testament to the lauded automation systems pioneered by Doctor Vésteinn Alrúnarson.

Kári was alone in the tram as it ascended the hill, watching the thick foliage slowly creep by, Vésteinn's letter in his slightly trembling hand. It didn't say much – but it suggested a great work. An endeavour worthy of the greatest seiðskratti in living memory. And that seiðskratti wanted *his* skills for this undertaking?

The wall of thick conifers and hardy birch gave way to a clearing. In the middle was a large, obsidian construct that defied geometry – a trapezial pyramid, covered in concentric circles of runes and sigils, melted with gold into the black stone. Surrounding it was a perimeter of bone-laden poles, forming a many-armed spiral unwinding from the pyramid itself. Some of them faced the monument, others faced out, forming a barricade to the outside and inside alike. A formidable prison.

Kári had heard rumours about this place. It was constructed almost overnight, years ago, shortly after the flying fortress fell prey to the demonic beyond. Rumours abounded about its purpose among the staff and students alike. They said it was the source of the demonic invasion.

The site of fell black magic rituals – a níðstöng.

He shuddered as he left the obsidian pyramid behind. Many galdramenn and seiðskrattar alike had perished trying to contain the vile, unholy pollution of this place in Öskjuhlíð, at last managing to contain it thanks to the efforts of Professor Thorlacius.

The thought of that name made him shiver as well, but for entirely different reasons. Guilt, racked with conflicting emotions he could poorly decipher. An almost-desire for scolding, friendship, forgiveness. He could not say which.

The tram terminated at the top of the hill. Perlan was a

behemoth of technology – massive steel walls fortified with thick plates of obsidian, the shining, seemingly luminescent glass dome on top of it in glaring contrast to the utilitarian fortifications.

He entered through large double doors into a clean and unassuming lobby. A clerk checked his letter and rang on the internal telephone system, confirming his invitation. A scientist in white robes, decorated with sigils threaded in delicate black silk, greeted him and led him to a changing room. Kári put on an identical white robe and thick gloves that reached up to his armpits. The overall look was reminiscent of the robes of the seiðskrattar, but many of the sigils were unfamiliar to Kári.

He followed his escort to a decontamination chamber, where a torrent of air whirled around them both, caressing him, smelling of acrid chemicals and pure alcohol, and then they passed into the main halls of the thaumaturgical power plant.

The air hummed with machinery – rows and rows of iron cabinets, computers with blinking lights and whirling reels of tape. White-robed workers roamed from console to console, taking notes, their black-beaked masks and red-tinted lenses making them seem like visitors from another world. Their masks were smaller than normal for seiðskrattar, more reminiscent of sparrows or thrushes than the predatory and long-beaked noses on conventional masks. These were not full magisters, only undergraduates.

'Don't I need a mask as well?' Kári asked.

He was used to wearing his own regalia when his work demanded it, and seeing everyone else in full equipment unnerved him.

'Why would you need one?' his escort replied, their voice muffled through the mask they had themselves donned. 'You're not cleared for any thaumaturgical work here, are you?'

'No,' Kári replied, somewhat sheepishly.

'Then you have no need to worry. Please follow me.'

Kári was escorted through indistinguishable hallways, lined with machines blinking lazily, threading a way into the heart of this great machine. With each step, he felt its presence grow in power. They passed many nondescript doors, before finally stopping at an unmarked one. They used a similar system to Svartiskóli's main building. The aide knocked at the door, waited a moment, then nodded and Kári let himself in.

Doctor Vésteinn Alrúnarson's office was in stark contrast to the power plant's utilitarian workings. The room opened on each side into small alcoves, each a small sitting area with upholstered reading chairs and low, imported mahogany tables. On Kári's left was a small library, the bookcases sparely used, but every volume was an ancient-looking tome. Evocative imagery of vættir and mystical beings were carved into the wood of the inlaid shelves, intertwined with the more natural shapes of wood, ivy and foliage. On his right was a sitting room dominated by a huge painting on the wall. It depicted a black, swirling mass, a wildness frozen in oil paints, radiating with a stream of emotions. Despite the extravagant frame, the painting itself seemed to have been made very roughly on cheap canvas – or possibly a bed sheet.

Directly facing him was a heavy wooden door. He was wondering if he should sit down or knock when it opened and a severe-looking man entered the room.

A three-piece suit of high-quality imported wool in granite grey, not an unintentional crease in sight, the knot of his royal blue and gold paisley tie wide and impeccable, the collar of his ivory shirt starched so stiff it could serve as a weapon. On his left breast, a pocket square peeking up, flaring with understated elegance in a pale, mysterious yellow silk. Thin-rimmed glasses, polished to a reflective sheen, the gaze behind them piercing and cold. Clean-shaven, except for a pencil-thin moustache; the dark hair greying at the sides, a slight widow's peak, all perfectly cut and styled, shining with expensive brilliantine.

'Doctor Vésteinn,' Kári said, approaching to shake the doctor's hand. His hands felt clammy and weak, almost trembling. He felt woefully underdressed, faced with this man, in this room. This was one of the most powerful men in the modern supernatural sciences. 'Kári Loftsson. I came as soon as I received your letter.'

Vésteinn shook Kári's hand, grasping it firmly. His hand felt gaunt and cold.

'Yes, my apologies for the tilberi,' Vésteinn said in a measured tone. 'Hideous monsters, but I'm not one for ignoring Svartiskóli's grand traditions.' He gestured to the seating area underneath the painting. 'Please, feel free to remove your protective clothing and have a seat. I thank you for coming here so quickly, despite my almost rudely vague letter.'

He flashed a quick smile to Kári, who proceeded to hang up his white robe.

'Of course. I assumed this was because the matter was so important that it couldn't be disclosed in a letter.'

Kári sat down in a plush velvet reading chair, and tried to look comfortable and at ease. Nothing could have been further from the truth.

Vésteinn studied him like a lab specimen. Already he was being tested, somehow. Kári swallowed, suddenly wishing that he had a mirror in sight, so he could assure himself that he was keeping his face together.

'You assumed correctly. There is a very important project underway, one which must be kept off the books – so to speak.'

Vésteinn moved to a large model globe and pressed a button on top of it, located at the arctic zenith. It emitted the barely audible ticks of clockwork mechanisms as the globe opened to reveal a luxurious selection of golden-hued liquors. Kári hadn't seen an imported liquor bottle in months.

'This has been a pet project of mine for several years now,' Vésteinn continued, pouring two glasses of brandy. 'Decades, perhaps, and finally the pieces are coming together. As such I find myself searching for exemplary, discreet persons of superior talent, to lend their skills to this monumental undertaking.'

Kári's curiosity was infuriatingly piqued. What the hell was this vague project?

'Part of my responsibilities,' Vésteinn said, 'are those aspects of the project pertaining to seiður, in all its myriad forms. As such, I find myself looking for seiðskrattar – ones capable of unusual, unique work, of finding true inspiration, true genius, when the moment demands it. And your name came up quite early.'

'I see,' said Kári, calculating furiously what this could be about. If he was being brought in, was it about biothaumaturgical research? Developing a cure for the plague ravaging Reykjavík and the mainland? Or a new weapon for the war?

Vésteinn handed him a glass, taking a seat opposite him. He threw glances at Kári as if he was waiting for him to say something else.

'I'm honoured,' Kári added hesitantly, 'although I'm still unsure as to why I am being considered – given that I know nothing of what the matter concerns.'

Vésteinn smiled. 'Your magisterate research thesis – "Applications of the Sustainable Reversal of Biological Corruption of Seiðmagn", if I recall correctly. Why don't you start by telling me why you decided to pursue that line of work.'

Kári swallowed. He swirled his glass idly, his thoughts circling in on themselves like the golden liquid.

'Because I wanted to help people,' he lied, forcing his hands to still, cradling the glass in an effort to seem calm. 'I thought it was a field woefully undeveloped in biological seiður. We can do so much to help those in pain, those who are unfortunate enough to have fallen victim to seiðmagn's transformation. It's practically an epidemic in Hrímland. I had to do my part.'

Vésteinn nodded, taking a contemplative sip of brandy. Kári mimicked him.

'I was one of the academic judges reviewing your thesis. It was ... quite interesting. The work was there, well executed, meticulous. But it had a subversive quality to it, a subtext that lent itself to much more radical work.'

Kári feigned surprise. 'What do you mean?'

Vésteinn leaned back in his chair, barely containing a smirk. 'Or perhaps not. Perhaps I am mistaken. I hope that in due time you'll see that there's no need to act coy with me. Don't think that I don't have the capacity to see your work's true potential and application. I would hope that you thought better of me and my talents – for your own sake.'

Kári swallowed.

'I am a man of science,' Vésteinn continued. 'Not of the church. I see nature for what it is, or at least I aspire to see her true face – the raw, untamed chaos. It's because of your work – and its real power, the hidden meaning of its applications – that I've asked you here today. Because you have what so many other dim-witted post-magisterates lack. You have the capability to work towards an original thought, not merely follow doctrine. You aspire to transcend nature by diving into its true heart, into seiður, and you have the intelligence and courage to follow through with this. There are so many brilliant minds here, dulled by the cowardice in their own hearts. They haven't the spine needed to face the abyss. But you're not like them. You ... you are like me. A scholar of chaos.'

Kári relaxed. Everything Vésteinn was saying, every word of praise, the contempt for others – it was everything he had ever wanted to hear... He wanted to shout those words with Vésteinn into the world. Except he feared he would become his own ruin if he indulged in these thoughts. So instead he smothered them – for now.

This was all wrong. It was too good to be true.

Kári kept silent after Vésteinn finished. He looked down into his brandy. This liquor... He could pay his rent for a month if he got his hands on one of those bottles.

'So... what is the project?' He looked up daringly, meeting Vésteinn's amused gaze. 'And why is it so secret?'

'This is your first time in Perlan, is it not?'

'That's right.'

'Come. I'll show you the heart of the beast.'

ᚼ

Flooded with dim red light, filled with the droning noise of calculating computers, the inner sanctum was devoid of any other presence but their own. They had put on protective white robes and black masks, but the air smelled of ozone even through the potent filters in place.

He followed Vésteinn for several minutes before they finally passed a white-robed seiðskratti, this one in full regalia with the proper, official beak-like mask of a magister.

'Where are all the staff?' asked Kári.

'That's the beauty of the thaumaturgical machines – they do not require constant attention. Perlan does require a lot of mundane upkeep, which is run on the outer ring where you entered. Magisters do the more important work here, closer to the core. They take shifts, which we schedule carefully to closely monitor their health. The forces at work here render the environment unsafe for long-term work.'

Kári was puzzled by this. He looked around himself through the red-tinted glass of the mask.

'But I don't see any seiðmagn. Why is it unsafe?'

Vésteinn looked back at him, the mask unreadable, his amused tone laced with mild annoyance.

'It's not the seiðmagn that is a threat.'

The tone of his reply made Kári feel so stupid he decided to swiftly change the subject.

'Extracting seiðmagn without human channelling – it was considered impossible.'

Vésteinn shrugged slightly. 'It is something that had to be done. It was the next natural step in the field, I just happened to be the one to take it.'

'I see,' Kári said, adding internally: *But I don't buy it.*

Vésteinn was being intentionally vague, which was to be expected. The precise inner workings of the thaumaturgical channelling units he had designed had remained classified by the Kalmar military since their release. All of Vésteinn's writings on the subject were covered in blacked-out lines. This fiercely guarded secret was a source of endless frustration to every single other seiðskratti working on their research.

'How did the breakthrough come to you?' Kári added, hoping for a fraction of a hint.

'Throughout history there have been many technological wonders lost to time. Once, there were mighty works of seiður – and galdur – all across the world. Few survived the onslaught of time, due to their highly volatile natures. But echoes still remain.'

'So you found some remains from antiquity? Rituals? Or, I mean ... occult schematics?'

'Not quite. The past is an excellent source of inspiration, at most. But I've said too much. That information is classified. Should you join us on this venture, then perhaps the Crown will deem you fit for more than a need-to-know basis.'

He turned to Kári, his eyes squinting in what was likely a kind smile beneath the mask.

'So why take me to the heart of the power plant?'

Kári felt too much like his inquisitive student earlier that day, incessantly asking stupid questions. Still, much like that young man, he could not restrain himself. There was so much to learn.

They walked on through the dim glow of the core, their footsteps echoing oddly in the muted hum of the machines.

'There are not many sources of power left in the world of the likes we dug up in Öskjuhlíð. Sure, seiðmagn runs rampant and wild in Hrímland, but it is a messy, raw chaos. Most of the time it has no one source, no set point on which to focus our efforts. One cannot control a storm, nor a roaring ocean.'

The hallway ended at a set of fortified doors. Massive steel pistons held shut a heavy obsidian door, lined with esoteric symbols unfamiliar to Kári. It was in stark contrast to the clean, modern technology surrounding it, a relic from a forgotten and barbaric past, where seiður was mired in superstition. It reminded Kári of the inner sanctum of Svartiskóli's library, a gateway to the ancient unknown dragged forcefully into the shining, uncompromising light of the modern age.

Vésteinn flicked switches on a console, reading off meters before he pressed a sequence of buttons. A circular panel opened, revealing a slim ivory horn affixed to the computer, ending in what resembled a sharp syringe. A black vein led from the syringe through the bone, into the depths of the machine. Kári tried to get a better look at the contruct, but Vésteinn was in his way. Was it biological? Mechanical?

Vésteinn slid off a glove and pushed his palm into the needle, making Kári wince, but if it was painful at all it didn't register on Vésteinn's masked person. The panel closed and Vésteinn affixed his glove in awkward silence.

The pistons slid into the wall in absolute silence. Tiny clicks cascaded as bolts became unfastened. The runes on the door shifted, writhing and flowing into new locations, undulating into new shapes. They formed a double-lined arch. Vésteinn placed his hand on the door and Kári felt the seiðmagn ebb and flow through him. The obsidian vanished from beneath his hand, the black stone dissolving into a pitch-black darkness, a void which filled out the space inside the arch.

Vésteinn took a step forward and vanished into the dark.

Kári followed without hesitation.

Everything was silent. It felt as if the ground had disappeared beneath his feet. There, in the dark of the machine, he felt something. A presence. His own breath echoed inside the mask. A soft impact shook everything around him, and he feared it was an earthquake. When another followed, he understood what it was – a heartbeat.

Kári licked his dry lips inside the mask. He was starting to panic.

Fluorescent lights came on and they found themselves standing in a white-panelled room. The air hissed around them as smoke, loose and airy like steam, rose from the ground.

The smoke stopped and a door in front of them clicked, sliding away into the wall. They stepped through into the main reactor room.

Beyond a thick glass window, Kári stared down a circular chasm, filled with sunlight. The top of Perlan was crowned with a half-dome of glass, and its centre was far above them. Huge pipes ran up the wall, connecting the top to the bottom layer, conduits to channel sunlight down and sorcerous energy back up to the outlets, once used for Loftkastalinn. Kalmar's flying fortress had been a mobile base and a weapon of destruction. He shuddered thinking of its downfall – the demonic manifestation in its steel and its crew's flesh.

Far down below them, the nest of pipes, cables and steel was submerged in neon blue water, a slowly pulsating glow radiating from the deep beneath the entangled machinery.

The core of the power plant was empty, a tomb. The impossibility of the place awed Kári. He struggled to take it all in.

'What is it?' Kári finally managed to ask, after staring down at the heart of the machine for quite some time. 'Underneath it all – the thing buried within Öskjuhlíð.'

Vésteinn took in the view, looking just as mesmerised as Kári, even though this cathedral of science and sorcery was his own invention.

'It's massive. One hundred by sixty-five metres, around fifty metric tonnes in weight. Roughly oval shape, although all of this is impossible to verify.'

'Why?'

'Our equipment malfunctions close to it. And humans don't survive the proximity.'

'How did you manage to build this facility, then?'

'Through sacrifice in the name of science.'

'You don't know what it is,' Kári risked, despite himself. 'Do you? Not really.'

'We have theories,' Vésteinn replied sternly.

He cleared his throat, turning towards Kári with a serious manner. The fire in his eyes was unconstrained by the mask's crimson glass.

'We found another site, Kári. Buried deep in the highlands. Not identical, but emitting similar thaumaturgical energy. There is reason to believe that it will make for an even more competent power source than Perlan. The ship leaves next week. I want you on the crew – to help us dig it up.'

'Who is funding this?'

'Innréttingarnar – of course. All for the betterment of the Commonwealth. There is a war going on, one that's lasted far too long. This could be the resource we need to end it, once and for all. The expedition will be, for the moment, an extremely sensitive matter. Every detail is highly classified, discussed on a need-to-know basis.'

'So why do you need me? My focus is biological thaumaturgy. Once you've unearthed whatever it is you've found, you'll be constructing a machine.'

'I'm afraid that would be need-to-know only,' Vésteinn replied. 'Rest assured that you are needed.'

Kári mulled it over, staring into the machinery draining power from the entity buried within the hill of Öskjuhlíð. There was so much he wasn't being told, and he skated over only the very surface of those secrets. Who knew how deep this went? Vésteinn was a radical thaumaturgical scientist. He was unbound by convention, perhaps even by what some would call reason.

Then Kári considered the prestige that came with building a second power plant. The knowledge he would amass.

The power he might gain.

To be party to forbidden secrets of the highest order was to be given the chance to do fundamental, transformative work. There were so many elements missing from his research – this could lead him to the piece he was missing.

'Give me funding for five years, as well as an increase of monthly allotment of seiðmagn. Triple what I'm currently being offered – with six months immediately added retroactively. And

I want half of the stipend for this venture paid in advance. And coffee.'

'Done,' Vésteinn said without hesitation.

He reached out a gloved hand. Kári shook it.

'Welcome aboard, Magister.'

Þrjú

Elka and Sölvi were out of quarantine the next morning. While the other passengers would have to spend three days huddled in a freezing warehouse, breathing in noxious fumes several times a day, Elka's aunt Björg had spoken to customs and secured them an early release.

'Captain Kohl is an understanding man,' Björg said as she led them to the workers' lodgings. 'All these rules are for outsiders. You and Sölvi are real Eyjamenn.'

Elka thought about how this was their first time setting foot on the island, but she kept her mouth shut.

'Thank you, frænka. Also for signing those papers.'

'Don't worry, dear. That's what family is for. It's ridiculous that someone from Vestmannaeyjar even needs a vistarband to stay. But, Kohl's law is the law.'

Getting a vistarband was mandatory for anyone not born on the island of Heimaey. It was a strict contract, usually for landless workers who signed up with farmers out in the country. Reykjavík was the only place which didn't legally require you to sign a vistarband to live there. The agreements left you completely at the mercy of your employer, and breaking a contract resulted in serious repercussions. Drifting was a serious crime.

But that wasn't a problem in Vestmannaeyjar. If you lost your job you were simply sent back to the mainland. Back to the shortage, the lack of work, the frost and the disease.

Elka shuddered. At least with Björg signing for her, instead of the company itself, if things went wrong she would be able to find a new job.

Björg was a foreman at Ísfélagið, the fish processing plant where Elka would be working. Elka had never met Björg before she picked them up. She was in her late middle age, with mouse-blonde hair that was starting to fade into grey. Her gaze was determined and calculating, the look of a woman used to figuring out if someone would be a decent worker. She had no time for nonsense or empty talk.

Ísfélagið itself was the biggest employer in Heimaey, owning dozens of fishing boats. Their pride was their fully mechanised freezing plant, the first of its kind in Hrímland at the time of its construction. Funded by Innréttingarnar to improve the local economy, it was a lifeline to almost every person in town. Björg had worked there her entire life.

'I always thought Dagga would move back after the eruption,' the woman said of Elka's mother, Dagmar, as they walked. 'She loved Heimaey dearly. Too many never returned after that awfulness. Your grandparents were thick-skulled. Her father was useless and never made it as a fisherman, but her mother was hard-working – an Eyjamaður through and through. But Dagmar listened to his nonsense and thought she could make a better life for herself trapped within those dreadful city walls. Yes, dear, I was devastated to hear of her passing. My condolences to you both, my poor wretches.'

Neither Elka or Sölvi had much to say to this. They had barely discussed Amma Dagmar's passing at all.

'Are you a norn?' asked Sölvi. 'Like Amma Dagmar.'

'What nonsense,' Björg mumbled. 'Don't go around saying such foolish things, child.'

'It's not foolish. It's true. Amma told me our family has a great power.'

'Maybe this kind of nonsense is tolerated in the city, Elka, I wouldn't know, but rest assured it has no place in Heimaey.'

Björg glared at Elka disappointedly and she quickly told Sölvi to be quiet – it was just a story Amma Dagmar had told him to put him to sleep. He tried to protest, but she put a hasty edge to her voice and he stopped.

Sölvi. Her little poet, her artist, the would-be philosopher. Ever since he learned to speak he had made up stories. The world was a different place seen through his eyes. A place filled with mystery and wonder, something to be experienced rather than endured. In that sense he was unlike anyone else she knew. Not even his father was . . .

Well. Enough about that.

It made her stomach sink with worry. Being an artist, a poet – those were the idle daydreams of people born into wealth. People with foreign-sounding family names. Elka was a working-class woman – barely. Without this opportunity they would have been out in the streets during the greatest frost winter in living memory, at a time when war and plague ravaged the mainland. Dagmar feeding Sölvi fantasies about being descended from ancient kings and powerful sorcerers had not helped.

Sölvi's dreams had been wonderful when he was a child. But that time in his life was drawing to a close.

Everyone worked in Vestmannaeyjar – everyone.

There were dozens of girls living in the house, pushing it at least twice past its normal capacity. It was huge, on three floors plus a basement, with each crammed to the rafters. Rooms were full of bunk beds, open trunks, wrinkled magazines and half-full ashtrays. The women dried their laundry in the attic on clothes lines wrapped around the roof beams. Each floor had a small stove, and despite the clutter it was still kept fairly clean. It was a loud, rowdy place, filled with life and hope for a better tomorrow. Björg explained that the weekends were exceptionally lively, or when one of the fishing crews held a party at the turning of the seasons. Weekends were also when the weekly bath was done, on Seiðday.

'I know you're an Eyjamaður at heart, Elka, at least by blood, but by upbringing you're an outsider. And outsiders don't understand how precious fresh water is on Heimaey. They're wasteful and stupid using it, letting it run unnecessarily or demanding to bathe twice a week. You can get some sponges at Bryde's, that'll be more than enough to wash off the working day. I won't hear any whining from you like those lazy Reykvíkingar, you hear?'

Sölvi was aghast, looking at Björg as if she was out of her mind. He opened his mouth, no doubt to say something more than slightly rude, but Elka silenced him with a hand on his shoulder.

'Yes, frænka, of course. We'll be sensible.'

ᚻ

Elka had barely slept the first night. Cold sweat and shakes kept her awake, with bad dreams haunting her the moment she slipped into sleep.

Elka headed from the workers' lodgings to the fish processing plant. She felt light-headed and cold to the bone, but she had abstained from breakfast so Sölvi would be able to eat his fill.

The streets were covered in black ice, and she carefully minded her step so she wouldn't slip. The people she met on her way were downcast, almost as though they were avoiding her. She started to worry that they already knew she had got out of quarantine early.

Her stomach rumbled as she passed a grocer's and noted its location. They were almost through the food they'd brought with them, and would soon need supplies. At least a slight appetite had returned to her, although she still felt nauseous. The burning incense of the seiðskrattar in quarantine had only agitated her withdrawal. She breathed in the fresh air. Things *would* be better here. They already were.

Two men passed her, both carrying rifles over their shoulders. They were obviously soldiers but not in uniform, instead dressed in old woollen coats and worn boots. The only thing that separated them from ordinary working men were their caps, which both had a red emblem stitched above the peak. The pair chatted casually, their manner devoid of the discipline of the soldiers she'd encountered in Reykjavík.

The factory consisted of two adjacent buildings, the first housing the modern processing and freezing plant, the second a salting and storage facility. She headed into the freezing plant along with a steady stream of workers, who glanced in her direction.

Once inside, she headed for the cafeteria. Björg was smoking at a table with a few other women around her age, who stared curiously at Elka as she approached. They were all wearing light blue workers' robes, the hairnets on them like a soldier's helmet.

'Hello, frænka!' Björg turned to her friends, continuing. 'There she is, my cousin's daughter, the one I've been telling you about.'

'Hæ, Björg frænka.'

Björg gestured for Elka to grab a seat. One of the other ladies offered her a cigarette, which she gratefully accepted, lighting it with a match.

'Have you ever worked in fish processing before, girl?' asked one of the other women, thin and stern-faced.

'Not really, no,' Elka answered, slightly flustered. 'But I'm a hard worker. And I learn fast.'

'We'll see soon enough,' said Björg. 'She has salty blood running through her veins. Back in Heimaey at last, we'll get that lazy work ethic they have in the city out of her soon enough.'

The woman took a drag of her cigarette and half-nodded, half-shook her head. She stubbed her cigarette out on an ashtray.

'You're putting her on the line?'

'Oh, she'll start in the salt. First we must see if she can work.'

'All right,' said Elka, determined not to seem disheartened. The way the women appraised her like livestock was really starting to annoy her.

When they headed to the changing room Elka was issued a new blue robe, the same as every other person in the factory. It went down to her thighs and tied around her waist. She got a hairnet, new rubber boots, a white rubber apron and gloves, all of which Björg said would be deducted from her first pay cheque.

'We start work at seven,' the woman continued. 'That doesn't mean that you show up here at seven and start changing. In uniform, ready to work, at seven in the morning – sharp. Got it?'

'Right, got it.'

'Follow me.'

Björg led Elka to the adjacent factory building, and didn't stop until they reached a large empty vat next to a mountainous pile of salt. A forklift came rolling towards them, dropping off a vat of rancid fish heads.

'Now, listen up, 'cause we don't explain things twice around here. Take a head, crack open its jaw like this, then throw it into the vat. Line them up, not on top of one another, not too far apart either. Too close and they'll rot, too far and the vat will only be half full, understand? Good. Then, when you complete the layer, throw salt over. Quickly, like this…'

She demonstrated, picking up a snow shovel and distributing salt over the fish with smooth motions.

'Then, repeat. Styrmir here on the forklift will take it away when it's full and get you a new vat of heads when needed.'

The huldumaður on the forklift nodded in her direction at the sound of his name. It was an oddly familiar kind of greeting, as if in recognition. She hesitantly nodded back.

Björg was glaring at Elka. 'Got it?'

'Got it.'

'Don't laze about just because you're all by yourself.' Björg lit herself another cigarette as she walked away, heading to the main building. 'We'll know.'

Elka was starting to understand why the other girls at home had been so timid around Björg when she'd introduced them. Elka had thought they were being polite.

She got started, already shivering from the cold. The work was disgusting. They were cod heads, only the top half, dried up. The salt would further preserve them and then they could be boiled for eating. Although she felt dearly sorry for the people who had to eat this. But there was a war going on, after all. People were on the verge of starvation.

It wasn't as though she was in a much better place herself.

She tried to lay out the bottom of the vat neatly, but she lacked Björg's precision in tossing the cracked fish heads so they'd line up neatly. When she picked up the shovel and filled it with salt she accidentally spilled half of it down into the vat, not managing to control the heavy weight. She tried to swing it the way Björg did, but her coating was either uneven and thick or barely there at all.

Styrmir checked on her twice from the forklift, always giving her a smirk when he drove by. She hated it – it felt as if he was mocking her for just being new.

'Not done yet?' he asked the third time he drove past, not stopping for a response.

'It's my fucking first day!' she shouted after him.

She heard him laugh. She tried to speed up without making a greater mess of things.

When the whistle rang for a coffee break, she was only two thirds done with a single vat. Styrmir shook his head as he disembarked from the forklift and headed to the cafeteria.

Elka tried to keep her chin up. She was just getting started. Things would get better.

$$ \mathsf{h} $$

Sölvi pretended to sleep when his mother got up for work. It was early, still pitch-black outside. She had stoked the embers in the stove and thrown a piece of coal in before she left. Björg had said people didn't have hot water to wash with in Vestmannaeyjar – they didn't even have any plumbing. Sölvi wondered how they were supposed to bathe. The house had no bathroom, just an outhouse in the yard. A small closet over a hole in the ground. Next to the house were huge iron tanks. Björg had told them they collected rain water. The idea made Sölvi miserable, but he'd smiled and said that he looked forward to the rain, when the thaw came.

If the thaw ever came.

It should have been spring, but it was still freezing cold like deepest winter. All the water must have frozen in the tanks. Did people just melt snow? He didn't want to think about it. Already he was starting to hate this place, although he'd never let his mother know. Had Amma Dagmar really wanted them to live here?

42

He lay still in bed for a long while, drifting in and out of sleep, as the grey daylight forced its way through the window.

Their room was small, even for a single person to live in, but at least it was private. Everything was plain and worn down by a multitude of working hands and tired bodies. Elka said they'd only got a private room because Björg frænka put in a good word with the owners of the fish factory, who also owned the lodging.

Sölvi had never heard of Björg before, but his mother acted as if she was an old family friend. Björg's father and the father of Sölvi's grandmother Dagmar had been brothers. From Sölvi's perspective there was a hugeness of time separating them. Sölvi had asked if Björg had any kids. They were all grown up, she had said; they were much older than him and Björg much older than Elka. He had wanted to ask so many questions about this place, but hadn't because his mother seemed very tired and kind of sick.

Which was good. She'd told him she had to be sick for a while to get better.

He had to pee, but couldn't stand the thought of going outside. Instead he fetched the chamber pot beneath the bed and quickly took care of business. It was dreadfully cold crawling out from the covers, even wearing long woollen underpants and a shirt, so he threw an extra lump of coal into the stove despite there not being many pieces left.

The frigid cold reminded him of one of the stories his grandmother used to tell. He went over it thoroughly, vividly, envisioning the story in his mind to stave off boredom. A fairy tale about a young child who is saved from ravenous monsters when he gets snowed in, while all the others at the farm are at church on New Year's Eve. The kindness of a lone wanderer, a huldukona lost outside in the snow, is the only thing that saves

43

the child. She dies from exposure when the family returns from church and kicks her out. The year after, her vengeful spirit returns, sparing only the child, taking it under its protection.

He imagined Amma Dagmar was sitting at the end of the bed, telling the story slowly with her soft, but gritty voice. It was getting harder and harder to remember what she sounded like. He missed her so much.

Soon after, he went to the stove and made himself a breakfast of porridge. It was thin, and didn't taste much like anything, but he ate it with some liver sausage and felt full enough. His mother would probably return from work starving, so he saved some breakfast for Elka, even though she didn't really care for liver sausage. But any food was better than nothing.

Sölvi got dressed and put on his winter coat and gloves to keep warm. He sat by the window and watched the street. There weren't any people out. Maybe nobody lived here. At least there didn't seem to be any kids. This was a ghost town compared to Reykjavík. He sat for a long while, watching, daydreaming, sketching with his pencils and paper. He drew a tree, the building on the other side of the street. Then, a dragon, a biplane, the moon exploding, the Stone Giant.

He had only seen the giant once. Amma Dagmar had told him that just up the hill had once been a church tower almost as tall as the monster, but the Stone Giant had knocked it down when Sölvi was just a baby. It had been larger and more terrible in person than he had ever imagined. It was like something from another world. Rough, uneven lava rocks, vaguely suggestive of a humanoid form, coarse, ugly, yet looked as if it was always poised to strike. It hadn't moved since the day it invaded Reykjavík. Sölvi sketched it fervently, trying to recall every minute detail about it – the moss growing on its stones, the birds perching on its shoulders, building nests.

The other kids in Reykjavík said the Stone Giant was evil, but Sölvi wasn't so sure. Maybe the church tower had been evil, and the wall and the prison the giant smashed as well. Can it be evil to destroy something bad? Maybe it was a kind of necessary evil.

He added a small figure of a man by the feet of the giant, dressed in purple robes and a golden crown. That was him. He added fantastical lines flowing from the man's hands, surrounding the giant. The sorcerer-king, controlling the great landvættur as the rightful ruler. That was him when he would grow up.

He turned the page and started drawing how he imagined Amma Dagmar's folk tale. The lonely farmhouse drowning in snow, the wandering huldukona, the ravenous monsters. In the distance, a church, its white outline against the black mountains. Death approaching. It was a scary story, but it didn't make him feel sad. The child had a mean family. They probably found a better parent in the vengeful spirit. At least she cared about them.

He added himself into that story as well, warming the huldukona and the child by making a magical fire. They were all smiling.

Two soldiers walked down the street. They wore plain clothes, but had really big guns. Like the police in Reykjavík. Maybe they were undercover. He got a new piece of paper and tried to draw them, but they went by too fast.

ᚻ

It was dark and Elka was exhausted when she headed home. Björg had made it very clear that she was underperforming, both in quality and quantity. There was too much salt, not enough fish, she worked too slowly. But she could come again tomorrow. They needed better workers than her on more pressing tasks. Working the machines, cleaning and packing fish.

Her back hurt, and her muscles ached. Björg had been kind enough to bring her some lunch. A slice of hard, home-made bread with some butter, plus some dried fish and a splinter of smoked, salted meat.

Elka stopped by the grocer's on the way. It was a large wooden building, painted black and marked with the name of the merchant: Bryde. Inside the shelves were stocked with wares, and although many seemed close to running out, to Elka the place was bursting at the seams. She had nearly no money, and with the shop's exorbitant prices she'd be starving by the end of the week. But Björg had said she knew the grocer, and said she'd let Elka start a credit account if she introduced herself.

The woman behind the register was dressed in a plain shift and woollen clothing. The only indication of her wealth was a peculiar silver necklace she wore around her neck. It resembled an eye with the moon as its iris.

'Madam Bryde?' Elka said with a smile. 'My name is Elka. I just arrived here yesterday with my son, Sölvi. I was—'

'Ah, of course. You're Dagmar's daughter.'

She nodded, unsure of what to say. There was an odd gleam in the woman's eyes.

'Björg told me about you. Waves bless me, you look so much like her. I'm terribly sorry to hear about your mother. A good woman – most remarkable... We always told her she should move back, but, well... it is what it is.' She straightened her skirt, gathering herself as she continued in a more businesslike tone. 'I know what you're going to say. I don't offer migrant workers credit – no exceptions. But Dagmar's daughter is no outsider. Eyjamenn are always good in my book.'

Bryde returned Elka's smile, which had started to wither on her lips.

'Thank you so much.'

'Don't mention it, dear.' She started to tally up the wares. 'I'll throw in a small discount – to help with the young man.' Bryde misunderstood Elka's surprise. 'Am I mistaken? I thought you had a boy.'

'No, you're right, Madam Bryde. I'm just surprised, that's all. Thank you.'

'Nothing at all. How old is he?'

'Ten years old.'

Bryde nodded, mulling something over. She didn't look up as she punched numbers into the register and followed up casually: 'And yourself?'

'Twenty-six.' Elka blushed with embarrassment, fearing reprimand or judgement. But the shopkeeper carried on quite happily.

Elka bought Sölvi some school supplies, the bare minimum he would need as he started tomorrow: ink, paper, a ruler. It broke her heart that she couldn't get him more. But she was only starting to work and couldn't sink herself into debt. They needed food on their plates, first and foremost. She'd work hard and would get him everything he needed as soon as she got paid. A new school satchel, writing supplies, mathematical instruments, books and maps and dictionaries – whatever he wanted.

'Thank you so much, Madam Bryde.'

'Please, dear, call me Klara. Or, if you must be more formal, Reverend Bryde would do just fine.'

'Oh, I'm sorry. I didn't know you were a priest.'

'We have a wonderful congregation here in Heimaey. Captain Kohl is kind enough to let us practise our faith in peace.' Elka was startled to hear this – this woman wasn't a priest of the divine throne. Bryde noticed her discomfort and gave a small chuckle. 'My dear, I think you'll soon find that Heimaey is a wonderful place – much different from life in the city. Why don't you come to Mass this weekend? Get to meet some people.'

Elka hesitated. What this woman was suggesting was illegal – at least in Reykjavík. She had no idea how things worked here. Noticing her hesitation, the reverend fetched a nearly empty jar from the shelves behind her and added a wrapped-up sweet to Elka's bag. Imported caramel from Hafnía.

'For your boy.'

'Thank you, Reverend – er ... Klara. Thank you so much.'

'Not at all. Eyjamenn must stick together through these hard times.'

Elka felt like running home when she got out. She'd never experienced such kindness in Reykjavík, where every merchant she visited had treated her like a thief. In their defence, she often was.

When Elka got home, Sölvi was in their room, reading a book by an oil lamp. She kissed him on the head and asked him about his day. She decided not to say anything about the nearly empty coal bucket. She could ask the other girls to lend her some for tonight, then get more at Bryde's tomorrow.

Sölvi showed her his new drawings, the writing exercises he'd done from a workbook he had already completed twice. He was rereading his old schoolbook collection of poetry and prose. It was Elka's copy from when she herself had been a child. Given that she'd had Sölvi when she was only sixteen, it wasn't that old – still, she worried he was dreadfully far behind. But she hid all those worries from him and complimented him on his hard work.

Their dinner was simple that night – boiled potatoes and fish, mashed together with some melted lamb's fat. She told him about the factory and all the nice people she had met, about how wonderful Reverend Bryde had been to them. Tomorrow

Sölvi would go to school, and she had promised him that they could walk together after work to see the schoolhouse, but the working day had been longer than she'd expected and it was already very dark and cold. He seemed anxious about it and she tried to comfort him.

Everything would work out fine. They were making a new start – and succeeding.

Fjögur

It had taken Kári a pathetically short time to pack his belongings in his trunk. He'd looked around his apartment and realised that there was nothing there he would miss. Shelves filled with books; photographs; a sizeable record collection: all of it just a heavy weight, moss gathered from a sedentary and introspective life. He was sick of it. How many nights had he spent here in the cold, reading by candlelight of dangerous ventures, revolutionary discoveries, lands and cultures and species so foreign and distant they felt as though they must be imagined?

Kári had never even left the city.

He'd spent his life living within books. And standing there in the middle of his apartment with a trunk not even half-full, it didn't feel like much of a life.

Kári packed some clothes, a few notebooks, some woollen winter outerwear. A black bag held most of his medical supplies. Vésteinn had said that everything he'd need would be at the site, but he still liked the security of having his own biothaumaturgical kit with him. Kári desperately didn't want to find himself stranded without it.

Not since the incident at Svartiskóli, all those years ago.

Before he left he knocked on his landlord's door and paid the next month's rent up front. He said he was heading north for work and would telegraph should his stay be extended, as well as arrange a transfer of any rent monies to him as necessary. The man said that was fine. People moved anywhere they could for work these days.

Kári dragged the trunk through frozen streets, going past the church ruins. The rimed scaffolding was empty of workers, snow-laden tarps covering the building materials. Plans had been made to rebuild Haraldskirkja, taller and more grand than before, but wartime budget cuts had put a quick stop to them.

Heading down Skólavörðuholt, he passed the cleared site where the Nine had once stood. Temporary military barracks had been built there instead. The half-cylindrical shacks were made fast and cheap from corrugated iron, not insulated enough to retain heat in a normal Hrímlandic winter. A tall barbed-wire fence blocked access to the thing in the middle of the road.

There, towering over the heart of the city, stood the gigantic lava stone pillars of the Stone Giant's feet. Walking past it always brought up bad memories. The rampage, the flying fortress, the protests and the lockdown in Svartiskóli.

He touched his face neurotically. Just an inkling of the memory made his anxiety flare up.

I'm fine, I'm all right, there's nothing wrong with me, he repeated, forcing himself to stop touching his face. *There's nothing wrong with me.*

He still tried to catch a glimpse of himself in the windows. He wished he had a mirror.

There were queues in front of every shop, and on one corner a farmer sold mutton and milk straight from his cart to the highest bidder. The prices were exorbitant. People crowded around him, shouting for his attention. Kári shook his head. The scene was a plague-spreading party. Then he thought about the lengths he would have gone to only yesterday for a bag of coffee beans.

What's a little fever for a fresh cup of coffee? Best not to dwell on that thought.

He got on the train at Hlemmur station, which was almost colder on the inside than on the platform, and the grey, frost-bitten city passed him through the windows. He had nothing to say goodbye to.

⋏

The Bay of Faxaflói was crowded with frigates and destroyer escorts, patrolling the icy sea and guiding the icebergs away from shore, keeping the seaways clear. The massive dreadnoughts sat idle among them, like great predators gathering strength. In the heart of the armada sat by far the largest dreadnought, loaded with artillery and new, arcane weapons. The flagship of the North Atlantean Kalmar fleet: *Trampe*.

The dock was a hive of activity. Cranes were still loading Kári's freighter with metal containers when he walked down to the harbour in Gufunes from the railway station. Several seiðskrattar stood nearby in case of accidents, or if a container was breached. Kári had never seen anything like it. The implications raised a number of questions.

He'd better be getting some answers soon.

The cargo freighter was state-of-the-art, newly purchased from the shipyards of Hafnía by Innréttingarnar. Its size competed with that of the flagship, making it one of the largest cargo ships in the entire Atlantean Ocean. It ran on a combination of oil and thaumaturgic engines – he'd read the newspaper articles about the ship when it arrived in Hrímland some months ago. Never would he have suspected it was here on Doctor Vésteinn's behest.

But of course it was.

He headed to the passenger walkway, where his credentials

were checked for the fifth time that morning. Despite the freezing cold, he felt his face flush as the soldiers compared him to his passport photo. Of course, he passed the scrutiny without comment.

There's nothing wrong with me.

Kári entered the lumbering hulk, which thrummed constantly as the deck moved under his feet. They weren't even out at sea yet and he felt uneasy. He hated sailing and, in fact, tried to avoid it as much as possible. He had some components that could help with seasickness, but he'd rather not waste his personal supply of seiðmagn on such frivolous things. It was reserved for... other uses.

He had a private cabin, very spartan but still more than he had expected. A bed, enough room for his trunk, a simple desk with a chair. Bathrooms were shared on each passenger deck.

He had barely set down his trunk before a soldier waylaid him.

'We'll be departing shortly. The doctor asks that you join him for a drink.'

The Officers' Lounge was a different affair from his cabin. Kári entered an exquisite sitting room, where three people were waiting. Vésteinn and a woman he didn't recognise sat in red velvet lounge chairs, cradling glasses of brandy. She wore a smart suit and an even more severe look. They were accompanied by a depressingly familiar face.

Leifur looked up from a desk, which was covered in schematics and maps. It looked as though he had been taking notes.

'Kári, you made it! Please have a seat,' Leifur gestured with a smirk towards a lounge chair. 'I wasn't sure if you'd taken on this venture, being so far behind on your research.'

'My research is going just fine, Leifur. I'm happy to see that we'll be working closely again.' Kári had a hard time concealing the frustration in his voice. Leifur had been shocked by his summons from Vésteinn. Had he been assigned to this task weeks ago and kept it a secret? 'I didn't know you were onboard as well.'

'Leifur here has been working closely with us for some time,' Vésteinn said coolly, sipping his drink. 'He will serve as our chief thaumaturgical engineer on this expedition.'

'I see.'

Kári knew that Leifur had started out working in Perlan, but the apprenticeship with Doctor Vésteinn was a closed book. Kári racked his brain, trying to piece together what he knew about Leifur's research, but what the man kept at their shared laboratory was clearly just the tip of the iceberg. He was very much mistaken in his belief that Leifur had been a grunt researcher in the power plant.

Kári nodded to the woman in greeting.

'Kári Loftsson. I don't believe we've met.'

He reached to shake her hand. She had a firm grip, and her hands were coarse and worn from hard labour, in stark contrast to her bespoke suit.

'Professor Auður Thorlacius. Master of galdur, doctor in archaeology.'

A cold sweat broke out on Kári's forehead at hearing the professor's name.

'Oh ... you're Almía Dröfn's daughter?'

Auður nodded, trying to keep her face neutral, but failing to hide her pain.

Kári fumbled for an explanation. 'Your mother taught me a few classes in my first year. I was ... devastated to hear of her passing. She was a force to be reckoned with, a brilliant academic.'

'Thank you. She was a powerful galdramaður.'

'You were there, weren't you, Kári?' Leifur was now nursing a glass of brandy. He took a sip, delighting in its deep flavours. 'In Svartiskóli. During the lockdown.'

'Yes. I was.'

Kári poured himself a glass as well. The silence was a vice, slowly gripping his throat. He resisted the urge to fill it, refused to set off the trap Leifur had so crassly set before him. He really was a despicable son of a bitch. How low would he stoop just to gain some social advantage?

'Well, I'm glad you made it out safely,' Auður said, visibly just as uncomfortable as Kári at the mention of the incident.

'Thank you. I wish everyone had been so fortunate.' He struggled to change the subject. 'I assume you are our ... chief archaeologist?'

'I suppose I am.' Auður raised her eyebrows at Vésteinn, who smiled slightly in response.

'The site we will excavate predates the Age of Settlement,' Vésteinn explained. 'Auður's skills will be vital in more ways than one.'

'Indeed. All very exciting. Transmundane matters fall under my jurisdiction as well.'

Kári nodded, not really comprehending. He got the feeling Auður was also not entirely sure of what her duties entailed. Perhaps he wasn't the only one left in the dark, although he was definitely the least informed person in the room. He felt his anxiety boiling inside him. What the hell was he thinking, accepting this job? He was an idiot.

He touched his face, a nervous tic. As soon as he realised, he pulled his hand back, as if he'd touched a hot stove.

Vésteinn was staring at him attentively.

'Kári here is our chief biothaumaturgist,' the doctor said.

'He's the biological seiðskratti?' Auður glared smugly at Vésteinn. 'So we're heading to the highlands, as I suspected.'

'Our course leads us to the heart of a storm,' Vésteinn replied in a low voice. 'A storm that has been raging for untold millennia. Our destination is in Vopnafjörður in north-east Hrímland. We have to take the long route south, as the northern sea is blocked by ice. From there we will embark for the highlands.'

The engine thrum of the ship altered, making the glassware in the drinks cabinet tremble. The ship had left the harbour. Vésteinn raised his glass in salute, breaking the tension that had gathered in the room.

'There it is, my friends. Our expedition is officially underway. Skál!'

'Skál!'

Their cheers were half-hearted as they clinked their glasses and sipped their drinks. The brandy burned delightfully as it went down Kári's throat. This was expensive stuff. Kári hadn't had a drink like this in ... years, now.

Perhaps not since his family cut him off.

He turned towards Vésteinn, desperate to divert his spiralling thoughts.

'Doctor, I suspect I might not be the only one here who has to ask this – at least I hope not. But ... what exactly are we doing here? What are we unearthing? You mentioned a power source that was beyond the scope of Perlan. How do you expect us to go into this blind?'

'Indeed, you're not alone in this,' said Auður in a weary tone. 'There was mention of archaeotech. What era? Pre-human?'

Vésteinn held up his hand, seeing they had even further questions.

'Such things are better explained by my colleague. I apologise for keeping you in the dark, but I assure you this venture demanded it. We are doing revolutionary work, across fields in the supernatural sciences – work that might revolutionise technology and modern warfare as we know it. So, please, at your convenience, let's finish our drinks and head to the conference room.'

Auður and Kári shared a glance, then downed their brandies and got up. Vésteinn threw his drink back as well and got up with them, leading them down the spartan steel gangway to another room. Leifur tagged along, that knowing smirk frozen on his face. It made Kári seethe.

He knows what kind of shit we're in for, he thought to himself.

Two men stood at the far end of a long oak table, inside the dimly lit conference room. Between them was something Kári believed to be a cast-iron stove, but as it emitted a thin trail of steam he realised it was a machine.

'Ah, Doctor Vésteinn,' said the taller man of the two. He was dressed in a nondescript grey suit, his whole person radiating the latent energy of a predator in waiting. 'We're on schedule and all cargo has been accounted for. The royal fleet is clearing the ice ahead of our course. We should arrive in Vestmannaeyjar early evening despite the sea ice, divine will of the king permitting.'

'Auður, Leifur, Kári – this is Þráinn Meinholt and his associate ...'

'Hrólfur,' the other man added. He was slim and tall, pale with dark circles under his eyes. He wore a cheaper suit than Þráinn, and a pair of glasses lent him a secretarial look. There was something about both men which unsettled Kári. An air of authority – of thinly disguised threat.

'Apologies. They will act as liaisons of Innréttingarnar, but both Þráinn and Hrólfur are officers at the Directorate of Immigration.'

Kári visibly swallowed. The Directorate. The agency who had

allegedly run the Nine ruthlessly for decades. That's when he realised what was off about both men: they had been infused with seiður.

It wasn't obvious, at least to the untrained eye. But to him it was clear as day: the way they carried themselves; an aura permeating their surroundings, of latent violence and supernatural instincts.

'I wasn't made aware that agents of the Directorate would be a part of this operation,' said Leifur, his flustered tone betraying how unnerved he felt by their presence.

Þráinn gave him a thin smile. 'No need to worry, Magister. We are here only to ensure that the interests of your investors – the Crown and Innréttingarnar – are being upheld.'

'Meinholt, aren't you going to introduce me?' said a new voice, hollow and static in tone.

Kári looked around the room for its source – perhaps a speaker on the walls or on the desk.

A burst of steam erupted from the dark metallic hunk between the two agents. To Kári's immense surprise, an unshapely machine turned around on rattling caterpillar tracks, gears and machinery clicking and whirring inside the tall iron box. Orientating itself towards the group, it rolled in their direction, speaking in a tinny, artificial voice:

'Ah, Doctor! So good to see you again. And you've brought friends!'

As it approached them, Kári noticed the porthole on the front of the machine: a luminous green window showing an organ floating in clear liquid, bathed in a pale, fluctuating light. Countless thin, black cables were plugged into the human brain, connecting it to the device.

Kári and Auður turned deathly pale. He felt his throat dry up. It was a living brain – a *man* – inside the machine.

'You must be the scientists of the supernatural! How wonderful that you are here,' the machine said in a joyous voice. 'Welcome! I look forward to working with you closely.'

Kári risked a look at Vésteinn, bewildered, his hand numbly gesturing in the direction of the machine. He had a hard time not giving voice to the flood of questions that filled his mind now he realised the thing was – or had once been – a human being.

Who designed the device? Where is its power source? What is its purpose? Does it require sleep? How can it see? Or hear?

'What…' was all he could muster.

'Ingi Vítalín,' the machine said, discharging steam with a hiss. Kári felt as though it had just taken a bow. 'Ambassador of Kalmar to the Outer Void. A true pleasure to make your acquaintance.'

The machine was met by stunned silence.

'The Void?' Kári said.

'Yes, the Void. Oh, not extradimensional,' Ingi assured him. 'Extraterrestrial!'

'This is illegal,' said Auður flatly, giving the machine a cold, calculating look.

'Don't be ridiculous,' Leifur spat, who had headed to the room's drinks cabinet to fix himself another. 'It's a perfectly valid scientific method of sentience preservation.'

'Now, Auður—' Vésteinn said, but Auður spoke over him, raising her voice in anger.

'I'm no seiðskratti, but any educated person can see that this is the same technology as is used in the divine throne of King Jörundur. Using divine gifts on mortal men is treason – and profoundly heretical. We could all be *executed* for this.'

She turned to the agents of the Crown.

'You arrived here with this… *machine*? You knew about this?'

Þráinn raised his shoulders nonchalantly. Hrólfur just smiled to himself.

'Trust me, Professor Thorlacius,' said Þráinn, 'you have nothing to fear. Both Kalmar and Innréttingarnar know of Ambassador Ingi's … *unique* condition, although it remains highly classified. Hence, your rather dreadful surprise – for which you have my apologies. Ingi here has undertaken this plight on behalf of the Crown, as a servant of Kalmar.'

'A plight to some, but a thrilling adventure to others!' Ingi replied. 'You wouldn't believe the things I've seen.'

That last sentence brought a chilling, reflective silence upon the gathering.

Vésteinn cleared his throat. 'Auður, while what you say is in a sense true, Ingi here is not in the same thaumaturgical construct as the sacred forefathers – even though the underlying principles of the machine have various facets in common with the throne.'

Vésteinn spoke almost condescendingly, in Kári's opinion. He must have been very proud of this creation. Who else's could it have been? Only Vésteinn would have had the authority, the knowledge – and the nerve – to go so far.

'Ingi here is not immortal, and not all-knowing. He and his senses are still very much human – although his mortal form has undergone a radical transformation.'

'You built it,' said Kári numbly.

Vésteinn slowly nodded.

'How did you get permission from the Crown to do this?' said Auður sternly, looking at Þráinn for answers.

'That's classified,' was all he said.

Vésteinn smirked and glanced at Ingi, and Kári had the uncomfortable idea that Ingi was smirking as well.

'Professor Thorlacius,' said the machine, 'this was a necessary procedure due to the unique difficulties that come with my job as an ambassador. Trust me, I would never break the divine laws of our great king and his holy dynasty.' Smugness oozed from Ingi's voice, despite its hollow and robotic sound. 'Human bodies cannot handle the journey I must regularly undertake as a diplomat of the Kalmar Commonwealth, and representative to Innréttingarnar.'

'And where on earth are you serving as a diplomat?' asked Auður.

Ingi laughed. It was a hideous sound, static crackling in the speakers.

'The Outer Void, as I said. The moon, of course!'

To this Auður had no response. Þráinn and Vésteinn nodded, confirming the madness the machine spouted. Leifur only chuckled, finishing the glass he'd poured and readying another.

Looking at it more closely, Kári noticed the crest of Hrímland and the royal seal of the Crown on the dark iron body, as well as the logo of Innréttingarnar on its back. The powers that be had made this creature – or it was supposed to look as though they had.

'Please, everyone – let's take a seat.' Vésteinn gestured to the meeting-room table. 'We have many things to discuss in the few hours before we dock at Vestmannaeyjar.'

Kári glanced towards Auður, who remained locked in a dead-eyed stare with Þráinn. Suddenly, she went and withdrew a chair from the table.

'Fine. It's about time we got some fucking answers.'

ᚴ

Afterwards, they walked back to their cabins for a couple of hours' rest before they reached the islands. The meeting had been intense, but Kári finally had a much clearer sense of what was expected of him.

'You really did board this ship without knowing anything.' Auður gave him an almost amused look as they walked. 'You definitely need to work on your poker face. And I thought *I* was being left in the dark.'

'Well... Vésteinn was very reluctant to give me any details. He only told me the bare minimum. Which was fine, since I got the funding I needed out of the deal.'

'So you're not a complete fool.' She laughed, not unkindly. 'They're still not telling us something about Vestmannaeyjar. Why dock there on the way, of all places?'

'They said we were dropping off a shipment and picking some materials up.'

'Kári... this is a massive freighter. What on earth do they have in Vestmannaeyjar that they couldn't get in Reykjavík? It's a fishing village, a shithole.'

'Vésteinn said Captain Kohl had a stake in the expedition. Maybe Kohl just wants to see what he's paying for.'

'Right,' muttered Auður. 'And I thought this time I wouldn't have to deal with the usual song and dance for the investors. Fucking humiliating. Well, regardless of why we're stopping there, it's a huge waste of time.'

Kári couldn't help but agree with that. It did feel odd... but so did a great many things about this venture. Auður's unease about this particular element did not faze him. There were way bigger things to come to terms with.

'Who knows,' he said. 'It's none of our business.'

'That's right, Kári,' said Leifur. 'Be a good boy and stay in your lane.'

Leifur was trailing behind them. He cackled at Kári, reeling, almost slurring his words. He had continued to drink heavily in the conference room during their debriefing with Ingi Vítalín.

'Anyway,' Kári continued, feeling his face turn red with anger, 'the highlands are far too dense with seiðmagn to be able to work there for long. Even with these bizarre wards Ingi has planned.'

'Well, Vésteinn seemed fairly confident about them.' Auður spoke slowly, carefully considering her words, before shaking her head. '*The moon?* I mean ... it's not entirely impossible, but it just sounds too bizarre. How can they keep this a secret? This changes everything. And besides, have you ever heard of a planet named Laí?' She shook her head again in disbelief. 'What did you think of what it – he – had to say?'

Kári hesitated, trying to gather his thoughts. He was still overwhelmed from the information he had been fed these last few hours.

Ingi Vítalín had explained his ambassadorial duties with dreadful glee, telling them a story that would have sounded preposterous coming from anyone – or *any thing* other than a brain in a jar plugged into a machine.

Ingi claimed that he was Kalmar's ambassador to a race of aliens, who had a base of operations on the lunar surface. They originated from a distant world named Laí, but any specific details beyond that remained unclear.

'Where is Laí?' Auður had asked the machine. 'I have never before heard of this planet, or star, or whatever it is.'

'It is a planet far outside our solar system – although not one found on any astral charts. It is a distant and dark planet, far beyond the limits of most modern astronomical telescopes. It was only first observed two years ago, from the magnificent observatory in Rundetårn. And then they only knew where to look based on my travelogue.'

The state-of-the-art astronomical tower in Hafnía was renowned throughout the Commonwealth. If they had only recently discovered this dark planet, it must be distant indeed.

'And how has the discovery of a new planet not been published in the news?' added Kári.

'For the very same reason that our friends still remain a military secret,' Ingi replied knowingly. Kári had felt a fool for asking, like a new graduate taking his first class in Svartiskóli. 'The war, my good magister. We must all do our part for the war effort.'

Ingi went on to explain that the beings could travel through the interstellar void on the power of their wings alone, and that he had visited their home on Laí many times. It was a dark and dreary place, freezing cold and mostly underground. He had started to go into detail describing the grotesque vegetation, their bizarre society, but Vésteinn had politely asked him to stay on topic. Kári had sensed the doctor hadn't wanted Ingi to go too much into detail on his mission.

Come to think of it, both Hrólfur and Þráinn had been slightly unnerved by his overly talkative nature as well.

The beings from Laí had contacted Kalmar somehow, seeing them as the supreme power on the planet. They wished to establish peaceful diplomatic relations, offering their esoteric sciences in exchange for mining rights, or something. Kári wasn't quite sure what they had been after. Kalmar, fighting a war on several fronts and struggling to keep up with its powerful enemies, had jumped at the offer.

And so it came to be that Ingi Vítalín was thaumaturgically vivisected alive and placed into a sorcerous machine, as per the blueprints of an ancient and incredibly illegal technology, so he could survive the extraplanar journey to the aliens' home world.

The very same technology that powered the Almighty Throne of the kings of Kalmar. The throne which housed generations of royal sentiences, sustaining them for centuries, feeding their thoughts and words to the current regent, King Jörundur the Ninth.

Kári shuddered at the thought.

'It all sounds impossible,' he replied. 'But, I mean ... you saw what it was. What they turned him into. Why else take the risk?'

She shrugged. 'Can't argue with that, I suppose. And I guess we'll find out if they're full of shit when the wards go up. Whether they'll hold or not, I mean.'

'We all know those shit wards that *thing* dreamed up won't be enough,' said Leifur, tripping over a steel threshold and almost falling on his face. He grasped drunkenly at the walls, just barely getting a grip as he cursed the existence of ships and the sea. 'What a fucking shitshow, eh? But I guess that's why you got invited, huh, Kári? To fix up the freaks.'

He cackled. Kári ignored the remark.

'We'll see, Leifur.'

'From what I understand, we have the best of the best on that front, Leifur,' said Auður. She turned to Kári. 'Vésteinn said your work is unparalleled.'

Kári winced. He supposed it was true *enough*.

'I guess so. But there's only so much I can do, really. Especially if we're based in such a turbulent region as the interior of the country.' The thought made his stomach sink. 'I'm not sure how we're even supposed to survive out there long enough to get these wards up ...'

Leifur pushed roughly past them, looking frustrated about Vésteinn's praise of Kári. Kári worried that he was going to let something inappropriate slip about the lockdown.

'Don't worry your stupid little head about that. That's my fucking job.' Leifur slammed the door to his cabin behind him.

Auður shook her head at the outburst as they stopped by her cabin.

'You shared a laboratory with that idiot? In any case, Kári, you can only do your best. As must we all. Our lives might very well end up in your hands, Magister. And I am glad to have you on board. See you in a few hours.'

ᚼ

The ice groaned as the iceberg split in two, blocks of it cascading into the sea with a thundering drone. The royal seiðskratti raised their arms and the currents shifted, carrying the ice away from the ship so it could sail resolutely onwards. Their red robes billowed in the freezing wind, or perhaps from an unseen force.

Kári put his scarf up over his nose to shield himself from the cold, which was battering the crew without respite from all directions at once. He headed to the starboard side, approaching the seiðskratti.

'Magister Ginfaxi, I presume.'

The seiðskratti turned and Kári stared down the bone-white nose of the mask. Behind the red-shaded glass he could see the vague outlines of intense human-looking eyes.

'My name is Kári Loftsson, magister. I met with your colleagues, Þráinn Meinholt and Hrólfur, earlier today.'

The seiðskratti looked at the outstretched hand as if they didn't know what to do. Kári awkwardly put down his hand.

'The biological seiðskratti,' they said in a hollow voice. 'The one who survived Svartiskóli.'

'Yes.' Kári swallowed. 'That's right.' He couldn't hide how uncomfortable he was at the mention of the incident.

'I read your magisterial thesis when Vésteinn placed you on the candidate list for the excavation. Excellent material – in theory and in praxis.' They tilted their head, as if to get a better look at Kári. 'The seiður has clearly worked beyond hopes, Magister…'

'Kvalráður. But I don't use the title apart from those rare occasions I don the mask and regalia.'

'Of course.'

Kári despised the esoteric name they'd given him at graduation, this ancient legacy that was upheld for some reason. A remnant of an era when sorcerers had to cloak themselves in secrecy and false identities to survive a witch-hunting age of fire and superstition. Those secret orders that had survived were the foundations upon which they stood, even today in the unflinching light of the modern age.

Kvalráður.

The name itself, steeped in the traditions of the biologically inclined seiðskrattar, invoked a sense of unpleasantness in him. It was a poetic kenning which literally meant pain-ruler, but was also an archaic Hrímlandic word that meant someone who is hesitant, or who is in pain himself.

Perhaps his magister's name suited him better than the one his parents had given him.

He hated it.

'I thought to offer my assistance,' said Kári, his voice muffled through the scarf. 'Should you so desire,' he hastily added.

He'd heard stories about the royal seiðskrattar, but never dealt with one personally. They were powerful, said to be prideful to a fault. Allegedly they never showed themselves in public without their full regalia.

Ginfaxi considered the offer for a moment, and Kári started to worry that he'd offended the seiðskratti.

'That would be much appreciated, Magister. We're set to continue our course south-south-east. More eyes and hands versed in the arcane will make the job far easier. Much obliged.'

Kári nodded and took a position. The ocean was covered with ice in all directions, but large remnants of bergs loomed in the distance on the starboard side. To the south lay the islands of Vestmannaeyjar, only dark grey silhouettes in the fading daylight.

He raised his hands, closed his eyes, and felt the seiðmagn saturating the atmosphere around them. Even here, so far off the coast of Hrímland, it was palpable.

The energy slithered to him like lethargic lightning. Cracks formed in the murky cloud of sorcerous energy, crawling towards Kári, its epicentre, the channel that could transform and cast it back into the world, sharpened and reforged by will and purpose.

He drew in a moderate amount and held his breath. It was always difficult to stop the current when the air was bursting with seiðmagn, especially out of his gear. Part of him always craved to jump off that ledge, cast himself over the precipice into that roaring river which could carry him to new shores, never before seen by mortal eyes.

He resisted the temptation. Now, as always.

Almost always.

There's nothing wrong with me.

The seiður gathered in him like falling sediment. He opened his eyes and took in the ocean, ice, breathed in the freezing air, pulling away the scarf to taste the sea salt on his lips. He ignited the seiðmagn within him, a tiny, glowing ember. And he let it seep back out into the world.

A cascade of thunder sounded as icebergs and sheets of ice split in two, three, four parts, steam rising from their wounds. The pack ice ahead of the ship cracked and shattered, drifting away in a new, unnatural ocean current. He drove the seiður forwards to south-south-west, let its power break the ice, divert winds and ocean currents so the icebergs would safely move away from the ship's route.

The seiður surged forth, an invisible spear of flaring heat and roaring thunder, melting and splitting and changing the world in a frenzy, reshaping it into something new, something better, something—

Kári cut the connection and closed himself off from the seiðmagn in the air around him, so dense and thick that his vision darkened. He hastily pulled his scarf back up, worried that he might have momentarily lost control.

'Not too bad,' Ginfaxi said after giving him a moment to recover. 'You might want to put on the robe and mask next time – assuming you have brought your regalia.'

Kári nodded and leaned on the rail, taking a moment to catch his breath.

'Not every seiðskratti must don their mask and robes to become one, Magister,' Kári said as he made his way below decks.

Some of us always wear the mask.

'I appreciate the help ... Kvalráður.' The seiðskratti watched him go, deep in thought.

Kári slammed the iron door shut behind him.

ᚼ

The boy pushed Sölvi, making him fall to the ground.

'Go back to Reykjavík, city boy.'

Sölvi started to get up but flinched when the boy moved as if to punch him in the face. The other kids laughed.

'Stay down. Pansy.'

He sat on the wet ground until the group moved away to play a game in the field. When they were at a safe distance, he scrambled to his feet and ran behind the school building, afraid that someone might see him cry. The others avoided him, ignoring him as if he wasn't even there.

This wasn't the first time a kid had got physical with Sölvi. His sharp tongue had got him into countless scraps in Reykjavík, but at least there he'd had a few allies to stand by him. His stories always managed to amass at least a small group of followers.

This new bully was called Hafsteinn. At the start of Sölvi's very first break time, he had cornered him along with his gang and started mocking Sölvi for being a weak city boy.

He had not been amused when Sölvi hadn't been intimidated in the least and unleashed a tirade of his own.

Sölvi knew he was cut from a better cloth than most other people. That's what Amma Dagmar had always told him. Their family was an ancient lineage, dating back a thousand years to the Age of Settlement. She told him their ancestors had had to escape their home on the distant continental mainland, as they were being hunted for being relatives of King Haraldur the Fair-Haired – called Bluetooth by his envious rivals.

Haraldur, first king of Kalmar, whose sentience still lived on in King Jörundur's divine throne.

They were canny folk, she said, well versed in ancient poetry and the natural arcana alike. Powerful scholars and sorcerers who had managed to tame this wild and unnatural island in the north.

Sölvi was not about to let some stupid boor put him down.

He'd told Hafsteinn that he hadn't had to work because all children in Reykjavík went to school, but he himself had been privately tutored at the stiftamtmaður's mansion in Viðey – naturally, as he was a distant relative of Gyldenlöve himself, who was the king's bastard and of royal blood. There he had been schooled by the finest seiðskrattar and galdramenn Svartiskóli had to offer, and when he'd mastered their dark arts he had been tutored by the stiftamtmaður himself in philosophy, art, history and languages.

'Not that a horsemeat-eating peasant like yourself understands such things. Have you learned your letters yet? Or will they hold you back another year?'

That seemed to strike a nerve. Hafsteinn had punched Sölvi right in the face. Unperturbed despite the taste of blood in his mouth, Sölvi laughed and said he'd seen better punches from Gyldenlöve's niece, who had been struck with consumption at a young age and was as thin as a stick.

Hafsteinn jabbed again, but this time Sölvi dodged and tried to tackle the brute. He was more than a head taller than Sölvi, and easily pushed him down into the mud. Hafsteinn had then chased Sölvi down at the end of the school day to further threaten him.

Now, crouching by the dumpster behind the building, he licked his lip. It was starting to swell. The lump built up in his throat again and again, so much so that he felt he couldn't swallow it down. He slowed his breathing, gritted his teeth, dug his fingers into his palms. He let out a slow, trembling breath when he felt the worst of it was behind him. He wiped away the few tears which had leaked from his eyes, hating himself for letting his weakness show. He would not cry. Not even by himself.

He focused on the hills behind the school and the thick clouds moving overhead, while he breathed in the scent of the ocean. His breath steamed in the cold air. The ocean was so close, everywhere you went on the island, the air clean and tinged with salt. So unlike the closed and populated streets of Reykjavík.

He missed his friends. He missed Amma Dagmar. He would have done anything to be able to go to her house after school to get something warm to drink, some sweetbread she'd baked that morning, to be able to tell her about what had happened and been healed by her comfort.

But she was dead.

71

He wished what he had said was true. That he was a seiðskratti or a galdramaður. That he could undo time, bring back the dead, smite down arrogant brats from nowhere villages who thought they were the centre of the world. He wished he could turn stone to gold so he and his mother could get out of here forever.

All these things would come to pass, one day. Amma Dagmar had taught him many things he'd promised not to tell his mother.

A deep bellow sounded in the distance, but he barely registered it, lost in thought, imagining that he controlled the clouds moving overhead. He wanted to paint the sky like a canvas, make this ugly world into something beautiful.

That first morning of school had been dedicated to mathematics. His teacher had reprimanded him for not having enough of the proper books and supplies. Sölvi had responded that they had all been left in his father's library in Reykjavík as the ferry to Vestmannaeyjar was too small and crowded, and they would be sent for later. Sölvi tried to keep up, but it was clear the class was way ahead of him. He raised his hand twice, asking for clarification on division which gave him short, ill-tempered responses.

'Were you maybe placed in the wrong grade, Sölvi?' the teacher chided him after he'd asked a question for the third time. His name was Þjálfi, and he apparently also taught the children sports and physical exercises. He didn't seem to be the type to teach them mathematics. 'Maybe we need to push you back a grade or two.' The children sniggered.

'Or maybe I need a teacher more suited to the higher arts, rather than pulling a cart like a mule.'

This earned him a beating with the ruler.

Sölvi didn't ask questions after that, but he learned his lesson. He tried to act as though he knew what he was doing. He noted down concepts and methods he wasn't familiar with in his notebook, so he could look them up later. At the end of the class three pages were filled with his notes.

After lunch it was history. They learned the folk tale of a group of sailors who got caught in a storm. They prayed and hoped that the vættir of the sea would see fit to spare them. One by one the sailors were swept off the boat by enormous waves. Finally, only the first mate remained, who had not prayed to the vættir, but to the ocean herself. He returned to harbour the next morning. Each seventh time they rowed out, someone was pulled beneath the waves by an unseen creature. Always the incident occurred when the sailors' attention was directed to a nearby spot, the surface of the sea disturbed by a frenzy of fish. The sailor never wanted for crew members again, as they landed an incredible amount time and again, despite the deaths.

That was the price of the sea.

It seemed that most of the other children had heard this story before, and only half-heartedly paid attention. But Sölvi had been enthralled. He had so many questions, but he already feared looking even dumber in front of everyone. Mathematics was one thing, but not knowing a simple folk tale? So he kept his mouth shut.

The bellow sounded again, resounding through the town. He realised that a ship must be docking and decided to go and see what it was.

As he left his hiding place by the dumpster and headed towards the harbour, he was approached by a boy and a girl, two kids from the grade below him.

'Hey, new kid! I'm Bára,' the girl said, 'and this is Sævar. Do you wanna play? We can play One Króna or hide-and-seek.'

Sölvi didn't know what One Króna was. He wasn't interested in being seen playing with children younger than him.

'No, I don't wanna play.'

'Come on, it'll be fun. It's like Fallen Stick.'

'I said no.' His tone was too harsh, his voice almost fearful. He almost lost his composure there and then. Instead he forced himself to smile, before adding proudly, 'Thanks, though, but I'm heading towards the docks. Perhaps my father's ship is arriving today.'

'It's really big!' said Sævar excitedly. 'I heard my mum and dad talking about it yesterday. It's owned by the Crown!'

'A warship?' asked Sölvi.

'I don't think so. It's a cargo freighter.'

'Ah!' he responded proudly. 'So it might be my father after all. You can tag along if you want to.'

They both nodded enthusiastically.

The ship quickly became visible as they walked through town towards the docks. It was a towering thing of steel, trailing smoke from its engines. Again the boom sounded, so loud now that they felt it resonating through their chests. Massive cranes unloaded containers from the ship. Feeling invigorated by the sight, Sölvi started to spin the kids a story about his father.

'He's just returned from the war overseas. He served on one of the king's largest dreadnoughts, the *Trampe*. Now he's back in Hrímland, chasing some pirates who headed up north. It might be that he's escorting this cargo ship on a dreadnought of his own, but hopefully he'll get a short leave to visit me and my mother.'

Bára and Sævar had turned wide-eyed at his confident description.

'Your father is fighting in the war against Hansa?'

'Oh, yes,' Sölvi said wearily. 'He's fought in many wars. Gyldenlöve, the stiftamtmaður, requested him personally for this one. Father has so many medals he doesn't know what to do with them – he let me have a few of them to play with.'

'Can we see them?' asked Sævar excitedly.

'Perhaps. If I trust you enough around these treasures. They're family heirlooms, although one day I'll earn medals of my own. Gyldenlöve has taught me many a thing about sailing and naval warfare.'

A big crowd had gathered around the harbour, held off by a barricade of plain-clothed soldiers. The kids ran closer, climbing on top of a stack of fishing tubs to get a better view. They saw a group of finely dressed people walking down the gangplank and entering a sleek black automobile.

'I think I saw my father there,' Sölvi said calmly. 'I'm sure he's heading to an important meeting.'

'With Captain Kohl?' asked Bára. 'Up in Skansinn?'

She looked towards the towering fortress guarding the harbour entry.

'Yes, most likely. Probably I'll meet him late tonight, unless he's too busy with meetings.'

They sat there for a while, listening to him tell about his father's achievements, his education with the stiftamtmaður, how his mother was an heiress in hiding. They held on to his every word like drowning men clinging to a rope.

ᛉ

Most Hrímlandic villages were cold and depressing places. A cluster of shacks and turf houses, with only one stately house at most, usually the residence of the local bailiff or priest. Such places were dreary monuments to the poverty and hardship that characterised daily life. Squalor and poverty were the common denominator, where mere survival was all that mattered, fighting against the hardships of natural and supernatural elements on a barren, volcanic island hostile to life, spirit and nature's green growth.

Heimaey was an exception.

The main island of Vestmannaeyjar was the only one which was populated. The village houses huddled around the harbour, their tether to life – fine wooden buildings, the corrugated iron coating freshly painted in a rainbow of vibrant colours. The docks were proportionally many times larger than a small village would normally require. Heimaey's harbour had been deepened by machines and sorcery, permitting the massive freighter to dock. Modern warehouses stood next to rickety old fish-processing buildings, and in their midst was a wonder of modern technology: the fish-freezing factory.

Kári disembarked along with the other scientists. Already the cranes were unloading a select few containers, the harbour busied by scores of villagers come to gawk at the arrival of the massive ship. Men, women and children, huldufólk and humans alike. Militiamen guarded Kári's colleagues against the flood of onlookers, carrying modern weapons with greater discipline than the police in Reykjavík. Despite their appearance, these men and women were obviously trained soldiers. Kári knew that Vestmannaeyjar had upheld its own laws since Kalmar's colonisation; it was far more independent than the main capital of Reykjavík.

An expensive, glossy black automobile, its doors stencilled with the emblem of Vestmannaeyjar, was waiting on the jetty for Vésteinn. He got in and gestured impatiently for the others to follow.

When the door closed behind Kári and the vehicle drove off, he noticed a crane lifting another container, revealing something within the ship's cargo which wasn't an iron box. A black obelisk, more biological in design than mechanical, and an armour-plated carapace the size of a train carriage. Kári turned to Vésteinn, who was watching him closely with obvious pleasure. Kári felt as if he should keep quiet, but his curiosity was too strong.

'What is that?'

Vésteinn ignored him. It was Leifur who answered, with a smug smile.

'The Centimotive.'

H

Skansinn was an old fortress, built centuries before during a series of pirate raids on the shores of Hrímland. Vestmannaeyjar had suffered the worst from them, being hit often and hard, and had lost almost half its population to slavers and murderers. But the fishing village had always been rich, and using that wealth they had imported stone and wood to build the foundations for the great tower which now dominated the ocean approach to the village. Cannons extended from the fortified battlements surrounding it, while the tower itself was fitted with long-range thaumaturgical weapons. Soldiers manned the defences everywhere, and a red-robed royal seiðskratti walked among them. It would take a bloody, drawn-out naval siege to overpower Skansinn.

Sheltered within the sheer ocean-facing walls was a courtyard, where several extravagant buildings stood – barracks, a longhouse, a few fancy residences and a huge building which could only be described as a mansion. Built in the classic Hafnían style of Kalmar's capital, the home of Captain Kohl was so regal that Gyldenlöve himself could have taken up residence there. Kári had never been to Viðey, the fortified island where the stiftamtmaður of Hrímland lived, but he'd heard descriptions. Although smaller in scope, it seemed the magistrate of Vestmannaeyjar spared no expense when it came to extravagance and military might, much like his mainland superior.

Every window glowed with light. Outside, a group of young boys served as valets by a row of horses. They wore militia armbands, although in a different colour. Training started at a young age here. An automobile was parked outside the house, identical to the one they had arrived in. It seemed that some of Heimaey's finest were gathered inside. Kári caught glimpses of well-dressed attendees through the windows, luminous crystal chandeliers, paintings, fine porcelain. He felt his mouth dry up.

A valet opened the door and Vésteinn stepped out of the vehicle, the others following. Kári checked his reflection in the automobile's windows, assuring himself he looked fine.

During the journey Vésteinn had informed them it was important that they be seen at Captain Kohl's reception, to solidify their connection to the local authorities and ensure that the expedition had Kohl's support. Kári, Leifur and Auður were also to tag along for appearances.

The sounds of the party washed over them as they followed Vésteinn inside. A young man in stiffly pressed servant's attire came immediately, taking their coats. The air was hot and heavy and reeked of alcohol and clashing perfumes.

Andreas August von Kohl was deep into middle age, although years of extravagant living had done nothing to soften his sharp military figure. Sporting a thick moustache, impeccably trimmed and waxed, he carried himself like a soldier on duty, straight-backed and alert. He looked ready to jump into the fray at the first sound of alarm bells tolling.

Kohl shook Vésteinn's hand firmly, giving him a stern but polite smile, his face tinged crimson from drinking and the heat.

'Doctor Vésteinn! You have arrived at last! Along with the last shipment from the power plant, yes? Magnificent.'

'Captain Kohl, a pleasure to meet you again. These are my colleagues, officers of our daring venture.'

He introduced them one by one, as a waiter came by carrying flutes of champagne. Leifur took two, downing one before sipping at the other. Kohl's displeasure was plain as day.

'Welcome to Vestmannaeyjar. Although your stop here will be brief, I hope that you will want for nought during your stay. Please, eat and be merry – partake of drink with some temperament, of course. I am Andreas August von Kohl, magistrate of Vespenø, as it is known in my native Nordic tongue, and captain of His Majesty's Fleet.'

'I've heard you served during the Slésvík–Holtsetian war, Captain,' said Auður. 'Tales of your conquests practically covered the newspapers when I was a child.'

Kohl gave a modest grimace. 'Indeed. And now, another war – far greater and more sinister in nature, I'm afraid – threatens our fair Commonwealth.' He leaned in closer, speaking in a grave tone. 'What we are about to undertake here – the responsibility placed on your shoulders – might turn the tide of this drawn-out bloodbath.'

'We will do our best in that regard, Captain.'

Kohl turned to Kári. 'So, you're the miracle-worker?'

Kári felt a tic in his eye. He grimaced, trying to disguise it. 'That's not quite—'

'Kári is one of the finest biothaumaturgists the Commonwealth has to offer,' Vésteinn interjected. 'Ignore his humble nature, he truly is a master of his craft. He has done groundbreaking work, which we will no doubt benefit from greatly in the field.'

'Indeed,' Kohl continued, smoothing his moustache. 'The *highlands*, eh? That takes some real guts. A suicide mission for most common men! But with Master Leifur's technology' – Leifur gave a curt nod in appreciation – 'Professor Auður's archaeology and incantations, your miracles and Doctor Vésteinn's genius, I daresay it can be done.'

He grabbed a drink from a passing waiter and downed half of it in one gulp.

'If it was anyone else but Doctor Vésteinn putting this together, I'd say it was impossible. But now, an awesome power is within our grasp.' There was an odd twinkle in Kohl's eyes. 'A source greater than Perlan. We will make Loftkastalinn look like an outdated blimp!'

He laughed, and Kári used the shift in conversation as an excuse to blend in to the crowd. The people were finely dressed, although in outdated, modest fashion, unlike the Reykjavík elite – such as his own family, the last he saw them.

Being here, surrounded by rich people who ignored him, brought up bad memories. He clasped another drink from the next passing waiter.

Standing alone by the grand windows, he saw the headlights of another automobile approaching the house. The two Directorate officers stepped out of the vehicle, and Kári narrowed his eyes. Hrólfur was carrying a peculiar suitcase, covered by thin plates of obsidian. The two men walked up to the estate, where a seiðskratti greeted them and led them inside. They didn't join the gathering. They must have retired to a private room.

'Seedy, isn't it?'

Kári jumped as he found Auður standing right next to him, nursing a glass of sparkling wine.

'Do you know what that was about?' He spoke in hushed tones. 'What was in that briefcase?'

'Probably the real reason why we came here.' She gave him a knowing look. 'We will talk later.'

Auður went to mingle with the crowd. The idea of a private conversation with Auður filled him with dread.

She's going to ask me about Svartiskóli.

Kári buried his anxiety and made a beeline for the buffet. The country was still suffering from shortages – regardless of the extravagance of the expedition, with its insane robotic men and their lunar journeys – and he did not intend to miss out on this feast.

People are starving, he thought as he placed another slice of smoked lamb on his plate, with potatoes drowned in a sugary, sweet white sauce. *And as long as I'm here I won't be one of them.*

He sat down and a servant poured him wine. Vésteinn did not partake of the food; the man hardly ate at all, as far as Kári could tell. He tried to decipher Auður and Leifur's disposition among the guests, and his tic started to bother him again. He clamped his eyes shut, trying to shake it off.

I'm fine. There's nothing wrong with me.

Leifur seemed intent on getting drunk, and even had the audacity to ask Captain Kohl where he kept the real stuff. Kári couldn't help but shake his head and smile. Kohl seemed polite enough to oblige him, Vésteinn's cool demeanour rendering his frustration over this almost indecipherable. Almost. Auður, meanwhile, was deep in thought. Something was really bothering her.

What did she want to talk about? Kári wondered. He dried his palms on his trousers.

Just the expedition. No need to worry.

His tic flared up again.

A woman suddenly took a seat opposite him at the table, staring intensely at him. She wore a plain dress, the fabric black under the lights, but it was actually a rich, dark navy blue. Like the sea on a moonlit night. Around her neck hung a medallion, bearing an unfamiliar symbol.

'Magister Kvalráður, I assume. Pleasure to make your acquaintance.'

Kári was startled that she knew who he was – even his magisterial name. He reached out a hand, but she politely declined to shake it.

'Pardon my impoliteness, but I understand you came straight from Reykjavík and skipped quarantine.'

'Er, yes. But the entire ship was cleansed by our best thaumaturges.'

She gave a small smile. 'I'm sure. Regardless, Heimaey remains free of this dreadful illness, and I intend to keep it that way.'

'I see. And you are?'

'My apologies. I am Reverend Bryde. But you can call me Klara.'

'I see.' He stumbled for something to say. 'Heimaey is your parish?'

'So it is, thanks to the benevolence of the depths.' She laughed at his visible confusion. 'I apologise – it is always amusing to see mainlanders react to my calling. I am a priest and serve here, indeed, but not in service to the divine kings of Kalmar.'

'But...' He lowered his voice. 'That's impossible. It's heresy.'

She shook her head. 'Not so. Thanks to ancient laws and covenants, the people of Vestmannaeyjar have some autonomy in their governance. So it has been since the Age of Settlement. We have a small flock of the king's worshippers, yes, and also some huldufólk who hold to their ancient customs. But I am a humble servant of the Deep.'

Kári had a hard time believing Kalmar would loosen its grip on the reins to this extent.

'I, uh... I see,' he lied.

Speaking to this woman was making him nervous. He felt his eye twitch. He tried to focus, studying the design of her pendant – a delicate circle crafted in tarnished silver, depicting a lunar crescent within an open eye. A pattern of waves dominated it from above.

'I have heard of your accomplishments, Magister. I have a somewhat amateur interest in seiður myself – although I am no kuklari. I leave such arts to the academics.' Again, that smile. She leaned in closer and he found himself drawing back. 'What happened in Svartiskóli was a dreadful catastrophe, but you have managed to turn that ordeal into something extraordinary. Transformation through hardship – through suffering. So it is that our brave sailors are shaped by the sea, as rocks worn smooth by the relentless waves.' Her eyes gleamed with fervour and she studied him intensely. 'I can hardly tell a difference, if you don't mind me saying. Such remarkable work – such beauty.'

'Reverend, if you will excuse me—'

She quickly placed her hand on his, preventing him from leaving.

'I am not only a priest, dear Magister. Please, sit down.'

His eye twitched visibly. 'Reverend, please – the quarantine.'

She didn't release her grip but went on in a sonorous tone. 'My dear husband, the depths keep his soul, was tragically lost at sea some years ago. He was a merchant of some means, and it fell to me to manage his business after his passing. This expedition is one of my many investments, and I was the one who recommended you for it. So sit down,' she commanded. 'If you'd be so kind.'

He obeyed.

'I have seen omens in the waves, Magister. The Emissary of the Deep has visited me in my dreams, in harrowing visions. He spoke through the bloated corpse of my husband. And it is your name that was revealed to me. Although your face... was altogether different.'

Kári's heart was racing. Everything else faded away – the warm lights, the drunken conversation, the obnoxious perfumes. All he saw was the priest, and her voice was like distant waves crashing on the shore.

Relentless. Fathomless.

'I have made a request to Doctor Vésteinn that you spend some time in Heimaey after your work out in the highlands. I asked that you be allowed to stay here for a few days, so we could have a more meaningful conversation, but he was adamant in keeping to his schedule. Which I understand – the will of the Commonwealth comes before the will of its people. But all are subject to the will of the Deep.'

She tightened her grip on his hand.

'The waves revealed your mask to me. Don't think I can't see through it. Drop it, Magister – Kári. This I plead of you, as the waves asked of me. Throw this thin façade of humanity aside. You are fooling nobody but yourself.'

Finally, Reverend Bryde let him go. Sounds and light returned to him. He was drenched in sweat. He tried to formulate words in his mind, but none would come out of his mouth.

His eye started to spasm.

He got up and mumbled some weak excuse. She watched him almost run from the party, stumbling through the door. Vésteinn and the others looked over in surprise. It took all his willpower not to hide his face, yet still he was too afraid to risk a glance in a mirror. He felt – he *knew* – that should he see something wrong he would lose control completely.

Outside, he went to the empty automobile and locked himself inside. His breathing was rapid, shallow, the panic attack completely overwhelming him. He used the rear-view mirror to check himself, making sure that everything was all right, he was fine, he was in control.

His eye twitched again, and he saw it change.

Then, he opened the automobile's door and vomited on the ground.

ᚻ

'That was a fucking waste of time,' said Auður as she slammed the door behind her.

She, Kári and Leifur had the automobile to themselves, with the driver secluded up front. Kári calmed his breathing, assuring himself he was fine; he didn't need to constantly check himself again in the mirror.

'Oh? The food not up to your standards, Madam Thorlacius?' Leifur reeked of booze and had barely made it to the automobile without falling over.

'Can't you just pass out? You know what I'm talking about. What were the Directorate agents doing here?'

'That is none of your concern,' Leifur slurred. 'They're gonna help them – us – win the war. So just mind your own fucking business, Auður.'

'You know Vésteinn isn't here to witness your bootlicking.' She sneered at him. 'It's almost pathetic how deeply you crave his approval.'

'I'm sorry if my manner offends your delicate sensibility, but not all of us had dear Mother to introduce us to the innermost circle.' He laughed. 'What are you even doing here? You're not half the galdramaður your mother was.'

She lost her temper. 'You have no idea what I'm capable of, you little shit! You might have made that little toy, but I'm here to do the real work!'

Hearing this, Leifur's face darkened in anger.

'Is that so? The Centimotive isn't my only responsibility,

Auður. You know I'm the one they assigned to Vítalín's machine. You know, the little project you *begged* Vésteinn to let you in on.'

She turned away from him and stared out of the window, seething.

Kári had no idea what they were talking about.

'Vítalín's machine?' he ventured quietly, his curiosity getting the better of him.

Leifur leaned back in the leather seat, closing his eyes. 'Yes. They're calling it a skuggsjá.'

They drove back to the ship in silence.

ᚴ

Leifur was so drunk that the driver had to drag him out of the automobile and carry him up to his cabin. There were no signs of Vésteinn or the two agents. The freighter was dark and foreboding, eerily still on the black waves.

Kári rushed back to his cabin. He noticed Auður was trying to get his attention, perhaps trying to corner him for that talk she had mentioned, but he wasn't interested. Not now. He was hanging by a thread. The twitch in his eye had started up again in the auto, this time worsening at a rapid pace. He needed to be alone.

As soon as he shut his cabin door behind him he lost his cool, running towards the mirror.

He checked himself carefully, from all angles, turning up the light so he could see better.

Nothing noticeable – by anyone else, that is.

But he saw it.

Something was always off. The eyes, the brow, a shift in the bridge of the nose. That night a few details were off, individually insignificant, but together combining into an unsettling visage.

Everything was askew. It was getting worse. Things were unknotting faster and faster.

He wasn't sure why this was happening now. Whether it had just been a matter of time. Or whether his exhausted mind just wasn't focused enough on *keeping up appearances*.

He began work on adjusting his brow, resetting his nose, moving his left eye socket up and the right one down, filling his lower lip, moulding his chin to its usual soft angle. His chin had always been weak, and he had always hated it – until he lost it, along with every semblance of his self. Then it had felt as if it was the one thing that made him himself. He hadn't chosen to change it. He had been forced to.

The pain was something he suspected he'd never quite get used to. Reducing the swelling was a simple enough seiður of healing, although when applied so regularly his body started to resist it. More and more was required of him to apply it. Or perhaps his body wasn't resisting the seiðmagn; more likely it was so saturated with it that it refused to bend to his control. It had taken on a life of its own.

He spent the next few hours staring into the mirror, comparing himself to old photographs. His graduation photo from the Learned School had turned out to be his best source. Still, he was never completely certain. He didn't spend the day looking at himself – that was left for everyone else to do.

When he finally felt satisfied, he took a moment to let his mind calm as the pain faded to the grating buzz that accompanied his every waking moment. Just enough to keep his mind on edge, he told himself. Just enough to remind him of what he was.

The ship's engines had started, their thrum resonating through the steel bulkheads. Feeling the movement of the sea soothed him. He wanted to get as far away from that island as possible.

He jumped at a rapid knock on his door.

'It's Auður. We need to talk.'

He sat still, holding his breath. She knocked again.

It wasn't until several minutes later, when he felt sure that she had left, that he allowed himself to breathe normally.

Fimm

Before

The room materialised gradually, rising from the murky depths of oblivion, slowly taking form as Kári came back to consciousness. It was flooded with red light. Ringing in his ears, pipes hissing, the headache as though he'd just been cleaved by an axe. He touched his forehead. Blood. Where was he? What the hell had just happened?

It took him a moment, but he realised what room this was. The eastern maintenance exit of Svartiskóli. Why was he here? Had he been attacked? He felt around in his pockets and found everything in place, except that his wallet was missing hundreds of krónur. He must have been mugged. Wasn't he supposed to meet someone here? The pain in his head drowned out everything else, leaving no room for thinking.

He clambered to his feet, reeling, barely keeping his balance. He must have taken quite a punch, then hit his head on the concrete floor. He felt around for the wound again. It hurt like hell, but it seemed to have stopped bleeding. There was no ambient seiðmagn inside Svartiskóli; the whole building was sealed off using the obsidian coating and arcane wards. He would have to get outside to be able to heal himself with seiður.

Kári opened the door to find an obsidian wall blocking his path. Its surface was smooth, but the pattern on the obsidian looked as though molten tendrils had interlocked like clasping fingers, encasing the door. The exit was sealed off.

Wait.

The red light illuminating the room. It wasn't supposed to be like that. He pieced it together, finally.

Svartiskóli was in lockdown.

Why weren't the alarms sounding? He started breathing rapidly, gripping a rail to keep himself on his feet. How long had he been out? What the hell had *happened*?

Inside Svartiskóli he was completely cut off from seiðmagn. He couldn't force the obsidian wall to reopen for him, he couldn't heal himself, he couldn't send a signal for help. He didn't even remember what he was doing here. He felt so powerless.

He walked up the concrete stairs to the other exit, leading into Svartiskóli proper. He listened at the door for a moment. Nothing. Quietly he twisted the doorknob and opened the door a crack, peering into the hallway.

The clean, pristine corridors of Svartiskóli were flooded with bright red light. It was empty and untouched; whatever had happened appeared not to have done any damage here. He checked that everything was clear, then moved into the hallway, closing the door silently behind him.

Heading towards the main entrance was probably his best bet. If Svartiskóli was in lockdown because of some sorcerous mishap, then it was most likely that he'd find people there. Years ago, as a freshman, he had received instructions on several procedures from the school, such as what to do during a high-level lockdown like this.

He hadn't read it.

Kári turned a corner and found himself faced with another

obsidian wall. It looked as though a waterfall of tar had fallen from the ceiling and frozen in place.

'You've got to be kidding me,' he muttered.

They had sealed off each individual wing. He tried to pinpoint his location in the building. Whatever had happened, it was bad.

He turned back and decided to see if he could head to his laboratory. Probably the rooms were sealed off as well, but it was the only thing he could think of. There he'd find some source of seiðmagn, although his stores were dreadfully low. He was certain he had intended to get more; maybe he already had. Hadn't that been something he was going to do today? He had planned to get… Drugs, was it? He backtracked, taking a different turn, and stopped dead in his tracks.

A person was standing at the end of the corridor. They had their back to him, and the air around them was a haze of minuscule motes. Their head tilted to the side. A long, ugly split started at the neck and went down the back. The floor was smeared with blood, shaded black in the crimson light. A door had been broken through, and debris littered the floor.

The person turned around, their movements jittery and lethargic. It was a man, eyes glazed and jaw slack. The wound on his front was much deeper than that on his back, a ravine of shredded meat and tendon descending to his stomach, almost splitting him in two. It was filled by an unruly throng of mushroom caps and fungus. The man hissed, spewing out a cloud of spores, and took a step towards him.

Kári ran.

He heard the thing shambling behind him, groaning, exhaling the toxic spores with every rattling breath. He frantically checked the doors, trying to decipher their codes, desperately trying to remember if there were any rooms he recognised, that he could access. Nothing.

He slipped and fell, his hands sliding in the blood covering the floor. On his right, just around a corner, lay a corpse clad in reinforced hazmat armour, its mask similar to that of a seiðskratti. Their arm was torn off, lying several metres away across the corridor, while their abdomen was a gaping hole. A skorrifle lay discarded nearby.

Kári ripped the beaked mask off the corpse, revealing a white face, dried blood around its mouth. He picked up the rifle as he got to his feet, scrambling forwards, the thing behind him gaining pace. He turned around and aimed at the mushroom-infested horror sprinting towards him, its arms outstretched.

He fired once, missing; again, hitting the creature in the thigh and splitting its leg apart, causing the abomination to drop to the floor. It kept on crawling, so he fired again, missing twice. The third shot finally hit its head, which burst like an overripe fruit. A cloud of spores filled the air. Tendrils and crystalline shapes sprouted in the gaping wound the sorcerous discharge made. The spores were dangerously close to him, so he retreated, almost losing his footing in his panic.

Still, the body kept on crawling.

Kári decided to not waste any more shots on this relentless creature. He felt dizzy, the edges of his vision darkening, as though he might faint at any moment. He worried he might have inhaled a spore. It might already be too late for him. He had to address his injuries and find a way out. Things were so much worse than he had thought.

He circled back to the room with the broken door. Inside was a gloomy research facility, with only a flickering red emergency light at its far end. The air was thick with a miasma of spores. There was a trail of blood leading between two rows of desks in the centre of the room. They were lined with devices, microscopes, thaumaturgic gauges and surgical implements. At the very end of the facility were obsidian-lined steel safes, three of them. He knew well what he'd find in there, as he had one in his lab as well. Reserves of seiðmagn, securely locked away. He needed that if he was going to get out of there alive.

He checked the skorrifle, trying to figure out how to release the cartridge slotted into the gun. It was powered by seiðmagn, and the remaining energy might do him better than having a functional firearm. He inspected the rifle, eventually finding a bolt on the left of the barrel. He released it and caught the cartridge. By placing his palm on the electrodes on top of it, he siphoned off the dregs of seiðmagn that remained.

There was no sign of movement in the room, but *something* was generating this cloud of spores. Kári had to eliminate the source and the spores already in the air, without accidentally draining himself of seiðmagn before the job was done. He strapped on the mask and tried to fit it as tightly as possible, hoping that the filter would be enough to keep him safe.

Around the corner down the hall, he heard shuffling, low groaning. He had to move fast.

He drew from the wellspring of seiðmagn that had pooled inside him, letting it seep through him in a tiny stream. Carefully, he cooled sections of the ceiling, causing the chilled air to fall, bringing down the spores with it. With a slight effort, he manipulated the air currents, pushing the spores away from the door and forming a path to the safes at the end of the room.

He took a deep breath and went in.

A colony of mushrooms was hidden between the desks, grown on the mangled remains of a corpse. The fungi were hideous, trembling atop the carcass, causing spores to shake from their massive caps. The only indication that it had been a human being was an arm sticking out from the mess, with a large signet ring on its twitching hand. Kári moved past it quickly towards the safes. They were locked with a combination and key. He had to find a way to open them.

Focusing on keeping the air current moving, he started searching the laboratory, rummaging through drawers, shelves, cabinets. He broke open a locker, finding what he was looking for. Personal items and clothing; photographs stuck to the door of a well-groomed man smiling at the camera, a house out in the country. The man had a large ring displayed proudly on his hand.

Inside was a personal cash box, which gave easily under the force of his will. It held a key, its teeth so twisted and gnarled as to seem almost unusable. Access to one of the safes. A folded note was kept there with the key, a jumble of numbers and letters. The undergrad students often had memos hidden away, dreading the thought of not recalling which coded door led to their lab, or how to access their safes. It was a variation on a standard code, one Kári had learned when he started studying himself.

The room was rapidly refilling with spores, the work of his seiður not enough to keep them at bay. The mushroom colony was now shaking audibly, agitated by his presence and trying to infect him. The first and second safe didn't work but, praise the Almighty, the third one opened.

Inside was a coarse lump of basalt, with rough wave patterns on its surface. It radiated with seiðmagn. Kári drew in its power like a parched man, the stream flowing through him as quick as lightning. He dried the air in the room and heated it. When the air simmered he set off a chain of sparks, igniting it, burning away the spore cloud in an instant. He focused on the bed of mushrooms and set it aflame, scorching it until nothing remained but ash. Outside, the abomination had reached the door, and keeping up his momentum Kári sent the flames to the creature, burning it from the inside out. It kept on crawling despite the inferno, not stopping until every nerve and every thread of fungus was destroyed.

Kári let himself collapse to the floor to catch his breath. Doing this much seiður without the proper protective equipment was dangerous – but what choice did he have? He took a moment to heal himself, sealing off his wounds. Healing living bodies, especially one's own, was a trial attempted by few. Mutating, mangling, destroying – those were simple tasks, natural to the way seiðmagn worked upon living things. But to focus that energy into *restoring*, reversing something back to its original form without corruption, that was difficult and prone to catastrophic failure.

Moving past the charred remains, he proceeded down the hallway and methodically checked the doors, listening for movement inside. They were all empty, sealed with obsidian behind the ordinary-seeming doors. Something had gone wrong with the safety mechanisms of the research facility, he guessed. That failure had saved his life.

He found more obsidian walls blocking the hallways, but then came across one which had been breached. A human-sized hole had been burned through its centre, with no indication of a struggle or how it had happened. He coughed, the fit tearing at his lungs, and he wondered whether it was because of the mask, or because he was already infected.

He realised suddenly that the breach had led him to the southern part of the wing, where his own laboratory was located. It was mere metres away. Strong arms suddenly grabbed him from behind and tore at his head, yanking off his mask. Kári lunged forwards, throwing himself to the floor, turning around as he crawled away from his attacker to get a look at them.

The terror in front of him had once been a lithe human woman. Now it was a behemoth of fungal growth. It had completely covered and transformed her torso and head into unrecognisable forms. His stomach dropped when he realised who this had once been.

Professor Almía Dröfn Thorlacius, Head of the Department of Galdur.

The realisation brought something else back to him. A bearded face with eyes lit by desperation and hunger. The face of the man he had let into Svartiskóli.

Sæmundur Sigfússon. The outcast who had been kicked out – who had been there to sell him highland moss.

The spores were everywhere as Almía lunged towards him.

This is how he was going to die. Attacking the creature this close would only discharge an even greater number of spores, condemning him all the same.

So he did the only thing he believed could save himself. A desperate, stupid thing, that only a mad man would attempt.

Sculpting living biological matter was not a refined art, by any means. Maintaining fine control was reserved only for the greatest of masters, and even they misstepped. In the moment, there was no room for delicate procedure, to gracefully achieve the mastery required to do it properly. Only brute and terrible force.

Kári made the flesh over his mouth, nose and ears seal itself off. His lips dissolved into smooth and hard skin, his nostrils sewed themselves shut, his ears folded into his body.

The creature collapsed on top of him and fought for purchase, clawing at him. He kicked it hard in the upper body, sending a cloud of spores into the air, then kicked again before he managed to get up and run.

He couldn't breathe. He was suffocating. Panicking, he lurched towards the door of his laboratory, punched in the key code, and to his bewilderment the door opened. He locked the door behind him, holding off against the mindless drone which slammed against it once, twice, thrice, then stopped.

Kári's vision was darkening. He ran to where he knew the emergency shower stood, thanking the Almighty that it was fitted out for chemical hazards, and turned it on, feeling the water wash away the spores adhering themselves to his clothes and skin.

He shut his eyes and focused. He might have survived this long, but he'd die if he messed this up. He thought of his biological studies, the dissections, lectures on anatomy, and tried his best to envision a system that could save his life.

But that monster was out there. There was no surplus of seiðmagn to spend on himself. With an eerily still hand, he fetched a knife. It was a strange sensation, looking at his smooth face in the mirror. The face of a half-chiselled statue. He took a deep breath and carefully cut a new mouth on himself, tasting blood as he gasped for breath through the ugly wound.

He was barely done when another slam hit the door. She would break through in a matter of minutes.

With a calm he didn't know he possessed, Kári walked to his safe and got the remains of his stores of seiðmagn out. Drawing in the power, he let it seethe within his body while he waited for the abomination to break through.

The armoured soldiers found him several hours later, silently slinking through the broken barricade of furniture, tentatively stepping over Almía's charred remains. Kári could never fully piece that time together, alone in the room, no matter how hard he tried to fully recall his actions. They initially mistook him for a victim of the disaster and in their shock almost shot him. It was only thanks to a seiðskratti accompanying them that they held their fire, who recognised him for a human being.

Kári had not spent all of his seiðmagn burning Almía to

death. He had kept a portion in reserve, to fix what he had done to himself.

He had not sat idly by while those lost hours wasted away. But no matter how hard he tried, he simply could not get all his parts, his eyes and lips, his ears and nostrils, to align with the wrinkled self-portrait he held in his trembling hands.

ᚼ

His initial reconstruction had taken months. His face became a plain canvas, a flat surface with only eyes, a lipless mouth-opening, an open nasal cavity. A sculptor had removed the clay off his face with one determined stroke, and now he was left to rebuild it.

He sent in project applications to Svartiskóli, hiding his real purpose behind academic pursuits. To his surprise, stores of seiðmagn were made available to him. Oddly enough, his application had been approved by Doctor Vésteinn Alrúnarson, who was not involved with biothaumaturgy as far as he knew.

Kári used dozens of photographs of himself as reference. His family had handed them over to Svartiskóli's administration staff, apparently pleading for any information on his well-being. They thought he was being kept in a hospital, still quarantined after the incident, and he made sure that they were kept in the dark. Kári didn't want to see anyone. They were only told he was stable and needed time to recover.

Kári scoured every detail of the visage that appeared in the photographs. A young man, a teenaged boy, a child. As he went further back in time with each photo, the more hope and joy the subject seemed to possess. If he went too far back, he felt as if he couldn't recognise himself any more. Was this only a trick of the camera? Or had his happiness truly been eroding year after year?

He wasn't sure. But he would remake that person and restore that happiness within himself. He would create hope out of despair.

The work seemed endless. The first measure of what he could call success was his producing a brow that gave the eyes a general shape, an unshaped mass that acted as his nose, and skin flaps that could not quite serve as lips, but allowed him to eat fairly normally. With more work, he was able to speak again, having relied on written messages until then. His words were garbled, thick and childish-sounding, his eating just as messy. He had to teach himself everything all over again.

The pain made him delirious. It was ceaseless, the worst of it coming when he woke, the anaesthesia having worn off, the swelling turning his features unrecognisable from the day before. Countless times he felt as if he just wanted to die. But every day he drew in the seiðmagn, channelling it to numb his pain, his body, calm his mind and temper the resolute willpower that he needed to forge himself anew.

It took weeks after that to get a semblance of a human face right. And then further weeks to make it look something like his own. But necessity teaches a naked woman to spin thread, they said. Now he truly knew what that meant. And eventually the day came when he looked into the mirror and could see himself again.

The feeling of triumph was exhilarating. No one had accomplished such a detailed reworking of the flesh using seiður before. New vistas of medical thaumaturgy were unveiled, and he was at the forefront of the research.

Kári's best suit was wrinkled when he knocked on the door of his childhood home, a large house on Bárugata on three floors. The family had made a fortune importing automobiles, being one of the first to get a licence for an official dealership.

They were nouveau riche, but had quickly assimilated into the echelons of high society. Money was equal to class, as far as most Hrímlanders were concerned.

A servant greeted him at the door, taking his coat. Kári cherished the sound of his polished shoes hitting the hardwood floors as he headed to the drawing room, where his family waited for him. For so long, this moment had seemed impossible. He'd gone through hell and back, survived unthinkable torture, all for this.

His father let loose a surprised, fearful yelp the moment he walked through the door. Everyone in the room stared at him, stunned into silence. His parents, brothers and sisters, their spouses, all looked pale and slightly sick. As if they looked upon a corpse.

Kári panicked, and went for the mirror that hung over the silverware dresser, dreading that something had shifted in his face. But wouldn't the servant then have reacted?

His face looked normal. He was himself. He turned to them, not understanding.

'What's wrong? It's me – Kári.'

His mother started crying.

They couldn't bear to look at him. Not directly in the eyes.

His father gathered himself and greeted him courteously, apologising for his previous shock – but not explaining it further. His mother refused to speak to him, only saying to his siblings that it wasn't him, didn't look like him. The others shrugged it off, playing off the uncomfortable air in the room as just initial surprise, having believed he was truly lost.

Back home, he spent hours staring into a mirror, comparing himself to the photographs he had used as a reference. He looked like himself, at least as he remembered. They had just been shocked.

A thought kept nagging at him. How often do you really watch yourself, note the minor details of your face, your mannerisms, everything that makes up a perfectly imperfect human being?

Never.

His phone rang. It was his father. He told Kári that he was not to come and visit any more. Kári tried to argue, but his father cut him off.

'*Whatever you are, you are no longer our son.*'

The line went dead.

Sex

Everyone was waiting for Kári by the time he entered. Doctor Vésteinn sat at one end of a large table with Auður, a deathly pale Leifur, as well as the two agents, Þráinn and Hrólfur. At the far end of the room stood Magister Ginfaxi and that machine – Ingi Vítalín.

'You're late!' Ingi sounded thrilled about the situation.

'I'm sorry, I—'

'No matter! Sit! My dear doctor, the map, if you please.'

Vésteinn rolled out an intricate geographical map, showing with extreme precision the layout of a few of Hrímland's eastern fjords with the highland to their west. The further a person travelled from the shoreline, the more common and dense the red-shaded areas of the map became, like a rash breaking out upon the land.

'Here are the results of our measurements over the last few weeks, done by our preparation crew for the journey to the interior. The torrents of seiðmagn are constantly fluctuating, but these zones have without exception demonstrated unusually fierce sorcerous activity.'

Vésteinn drew his finger along a line, tracing the path west from one of the fjords, before it split to the north and south.

'The old cairn path is decently maintained, despite want of learned seiðskrattar these past centuries. It can be utilised as a guidepost for the first leg of our journey. Travel by land is exceptionally uncommon here, but we've verified that travellers have recently made the trip by following the cairns. Some of them survived. But they can only get us so far.'

He drew a line directly to the west, passing through countless red zones.

'Most of the journey will lead us through several high-density sorcerous areas. They seem to be drawn to – or more likely, generated by – the buried landvættur.'

Vésteinn spoke so nonchalantly that Kári almost missed it. Once realisation set in, he struggled to retain his composure. They had found another landvættur – and they were going to harness it for power. He stole a look around the table to gauge the others. If they were as shocked as he was, they hid it exceptionally well.

The landvættur of the east was said to be a great dragon. His stomach sunk at the thought. The Stone Giant had been a harbinger of destruction. What dread power would come with awakening this creature?

He had no inkling of it, as all four beings were shrouded in vague myth. Once a part of the old heathen faith, they were said to be protectors of Hrímland. There were no tales of anyone encountering them or witnessing their power. Come to think of it, Kári found it strange that their legend remained throughout the ages, even decades after Kalmar had outlawed the old ways. Was superstition the only reason for the resilience of their myth?

'The Centimotive is ready to be assembled.' Leifur had an eager look as he spoke. 'It should be up and running five hours after we unload the ship.'

Þráinn Meinholt interjected, 'Magister Ginfaxi still has to finish their inspection of our... cargo.' He gave the royal seiðskratti a knowing look.

Kári struggled to keep up with the conversation, still over-whelmed by the prospect of the landvættur. Were they talking about whatever they had picked up in Vestmannaeyjar? Or something else?

'It should be a quick matter.' The seiðskratti spoke in a low voice, so the others had to strain themselves to catch every word. 'Everything has passed muster, at least so far. I see no reason why we should not meet our schedule.'

'Very well.' Vésteinn turned to Ingi. 'And our lunar allies? What do they say?'

'Our dear friends have been working hard with me to com-plete the transcriptions of the schematics for the skuggsjá, which will be assembled on site in a collaborative effort between myself and Leifur. Under your supervision, of course, Doctor.'

'And can we expect to ever see these fantastical creatures?' asked Auður. Kári wasn't certain if it was fear or frustration that laced her voice.

'Well, our wonderful friends aren't too keen on—'

'Not yet, Auður,' Vésteinn interrupted Ingi. 'And not unless it's strictly required. I remind you that this information – par-ticularly regarding our allies – is *classified*. Betraying them to civilians will mean dying a traitor's death.'

'Understood,' mumbled Auður.

'Oh, Miss Thorlacius,' Ingi continued, 'I assure you that they're real. I've visited their base of operations myself, deep beneath the lunar surface. I've seen the alien grandeur of their cities buried in the dark – lit up by exotic growths and strange technology. I've walked among them, learned their language – if you can even call it that. I've looked upon the effigies of their deceased gods, hailing from long-vanished worlds and distant realities – and returned with my sanity intact. I gave up my human body for them, my dear. So I assure you – they're very real.'

Vésteinn spoke into the uncomfortable silence which followed.

'When we arrive at the site it's imperative that we raise the defensive barricade as soon as possible. The high seat pillars are ready, but we need all who can wield seiður to use their power to control the protoplasmic worker units. Kári and Leifur – you'll be working under Ginfaxi when the time comes. They are very experienced in controlling the things and will instruct you further.'

Leifur nodded, but Kári had a question.

'Protoplasmic workers? What is this, exactly?'

Vésteinn smiled, but it was Þráinn Meinholt who replied.

'We've used them before, to great success. An early gift from the beings from Laí, one of Ingi's first achievements as a diplomat. They were first deployed seven years ago, during the protests outside Lögrétta. People commonly refer to them as the uncolour, due to their unearthly appearance.'

A chill went down Kári's spine. Those things had drained the life from dozens, perhaps hundreds of protesters. Their colour existed outside the spectrum of human vision, perhaps even human reality itself. It was unclear which horror had been more dreadful that year – the demonic manifestation of Loftkastalinn, or the merciless slaughter at the hands of those alien things.

'Magister Kvalráður and Magister Launvaldur,' the seiðskratti hissed, addressing Kári and Leifur respectively. 'I ask you to prepare your ritualistic protective clothing and the appropriate thaumaturgical components. You'll be needing them.'

ᚻ

It was late evening when the ship sailed into Vopnafjörður. They landed by a massive concrete pier jutting from the frozen land, lit up by dozens of floodlights. A large crowd awaited them at the harbour, ready to work the mechanical cranes to overdrive.

Kári had known a ship of this size needed an industrial-sized pier to dock and unload cargo, but he was still overwhelmed by the scope of the operation. Innréttingarnar had been planning this for years. The fjord seemed uninhabited, except for their base. Rows of barracks and several large warehouses sat by the harbour, hastily assembled from cheap corrugated iron sheets. These had all been constructed for this expedition.

Kári spent the night in the poorly insulated barracks, his meagre stove not nearly enough to combat the deathly cold. Everyone had a private room, for which Kári was grateful, though the fact Auður ignored him was troubling. She had not mentioned that talk she wanted to have, which made him all the more anxious. All through the night, Leifur and his crews worked on assembling the Centimotive.

When he emerged early the next morning under a pale heather sky, Kári almost dropped his steaming mug of precious coffee when he saw the metal monstrosity they had built.

It resembled a serpentine insect the size of a whale. But instead of being butchered at the harbour where it had been landed, the massive pieces of black iron had not been dissected – they had been stitched together.

Covered in a pitch-black obsidian carapace laid over fortified armour plates, with countless arthropod-like legs under each carriage, the Centimotive was only vaguely reminiscent of a train. It was so much more. At the far end its brutal-looking head was equipped with antennae. They were already squirming, flailing around as they scanned the atmosphere for seiðmagn. It hissed out black smoke through rows of exhaust pipes near the front.

Kári was awestruck. Of course, Loftkastalinn was a far superior technological achievement, but this had been disassembled into parts and reassembled here. He tried to get a better look, to figure out where its engine room was, its control room. How did it move? How could you manage those hundreds of legs, its scanning equipment, its slithering over untamed wilderness? So much could go wrong. The flying fortress had housed a staff of dozens to control it, not counting those in the engine room. How could a few train cars house the crew and machinery needed to manage this?

Absent-mindedly, he dropped his trunk for a porter to place it with the other equipment to be loaded into the Centimotive. The area was crowded with people completing the final preparations. He headed to the machine's front, flashing his credentials at the soldiers guarding the engine carriage. It did not go unnoticed by him that there seemed to be no physical entrance to the very head of the machine. Up close, he saw that the head was fitted with a massive set of mandibles, as well as what appeared to be a set of drills and possibly weaponry in its maw. Mining equipment? Or weapons? He was uncertain.

Leifur was in there, working with a team of engineers on checking the thaumaturgical engine. His acolyte staff wore black robes and dark green masks the colour of seaweed. Only Leifur was out of uniform. He looked up from his clipboard as he noticed Kári, his frustration quickly giving way to a self-satisfied look.

'You an engineer now?' He chuckled. 'Couldn't resist snooping around, eh?'

Kári eyed the room, ignoring the snide remark. 'It's a remarkable machine, Leifur. I'm no thaumaturgical engineer, but it's obvious that it's revolutionary.'

Narrow walkways threaded around the sorcerous batteries

– massive obsidian-plated blocks charged with seiðmagn siphoned from Perlan. Thick cables ran along the floor and ceiling, leading back to the end of the carriage, presumably plugging into the control room, which was secured by a fortified steel door.

Leifur smirked. 'It is. Of course, I can't take all the credit. Doctor Vésteinn was an immense help in figuring out some … solutions.'

'Are the engines only in this carriage? How does it have enough power to run for the distances we need to cross?'

'To a layman it might seem too small. It holds a considerable amount of power. The antennae on the head are also equipped with harvesters. They drain the raw seiðmagn from the highlands to recharge the batteries. All those unavoidable red-marked thaumaturgical hotspots on the map will prove to be our primary source of fuel.'

Kári nodded slowly. 'That's a lot of pressure for a system of this size. How many seiðskrattar do you need to control the flow? Plus actually drive the machine?'

'Don't worry about it. Not your purview, not your problem, Kári.'

Kári pointed to the secured door at the back. 'Control's back there, right? Can I get a tour?'

Leifur gave him a condescendingly kind look. 'It's off limits. We're good here – maybe the porters could use an extra hand if you want to feel useful.'

'Right.'

He moved past Leifur in the narrow corridor and headed towards the control room.

'Wait – where do you think you're going?'

Kári ignored him and moved past one of the engines, a low-thrumming unit of steel and pistons. It radiated an uncomfortable heat, an energy that warmed him from the inside out.

Behind the engine was a black steel door. It had no handle or keyhole or anything to indicate it could be opened at all. Hesitating for a moment, then steeling himself, Kári knocked on the door before Leifur caught up with him.

'Just what the hell do you think you're doing?'

Kári began to sweat. Leifur started to badger him, and just when he was about to turn around and leave, a series of clicks emitted from the door. It hissed and slid sideways into the wall.

The masked beak of a seiðskratti faced him. They were not Ginfaxi. Their robes were pure white, but different from the technological seiðskrattar. They were decorated with powerful black runes, threaded in pure obsidian. The mask was ivory. Through the red-tinted lenses Kári saw a glimpse of their eyes. He thought they looked almost pleasantly surprised to see him.

'Magister Kvalráður. How may I assist you?'

He recognised the voice, although the regalia was a dead giveaway – the robes and mask of a high master of seiður. Kári knew only one person in Svartiskóli who wore such robes.

Doctor Vésteinn Alrúnarson.

'Magister Völundur,' Kári replied. 'I'm so sorry to bother you. I thought I'd offer my assistance to you and Leifur, if needed.'

'We are handling the procedures well enough,' the seiðskratti said, not unkindly.

'I see. Well, I …' Kári swallowed. 'Truth be told, I was curious about the engine room. The Centimotive is a much more impressive piece of machinery than I ever imagined.'

Vésteinn considered this for a moment. Kári cursed himself silently. What the hell was he thinking, saying inane things like that to him?

'I'm afraid the central controls are strictly off limits.' The seiðskratti leaned towards him, conspiratorially. 'But I understand completely. You want to see how it works, don't you? As every true student of seiður would wish. Know this – it is a wondrous thing. How it can manipulate this machine as though it were alive, how it channels seiðmagn like only a human mind can.'

Vésteinn risked a glance behind his shoulder, into the unlit corridor of steel behind him.

'Perhaps later, Magister Kvalráður. One day I will show you what marvels this machine holds.' He placed a gloved hand on Kári's shoulder, leaning in. 'Don't be afraid. I'll be interfaced directly with the machine. You'll be perfectly safe in my hands.'

Kári's heart was racing. He could smell the leather of the mask, the heavy fragrance of the thaumaturgical herbs lining the beak; he could feel the human warmth radiating from Vésteinn's hand on his shoulder.

'All right. Sorry to bother you, Magister.'

'Not at all.'

The seiðskratti took a step back and flicked a switch on the wall, closing the door.

Kári turned around, his face beaded with sweat, to find Leifur had gone back to the end of the corridor, smirking to himself as he pretended to check a gauge on the engine.

One seiðskratti ran this machine. How was that even possible, even for Vésteinn? Kári rushed outside to the crisp, cool air.

What the hell is going on?

The passenger carriage was spartan, all bare steel. It had a three-seat-wide row in the middle, and a line of seats attached to the walls on each side. Kári strapped himself into a seat on the wall, his back tight against the thin, cheap padding so he could feel the cold of the steel through it. The vibrations of the engine hummed through him.

He was nervous, sweating. His attempts to find out how exactly this machine worked had failed. Not that he doubted Vésteinn's abilities, but this was the maiden voyage of a completely new kind of transport, going through a volatile area of untamed, sorcerous power.

They were all going to die.

His eye twitched. More people were rushing in, and there was no time or privacy to check himself in a mirror.

The carriage filled up with the more educated staff of the expedition: archaeologists, medical staff, engineers, military officers. Auður and Ginfaxi took their seats, greeting Kári with a nod. He didn't know where Ingi or the two agents were. He hadn't seen them since they'd docked. The untrained labourers and lower-ranking soldiers were in the more densely crowded carriages in the back, likely even more crammed than this one. People talked in hushed whispers. Everyone was nervous.

A pair of soldiers guarding the door outside stepped in, checked that every passenger was securely fastened, then closed the heavy iron door, pulling a lever to lock it tight with a mechanical system of massive pistons and locks. Then they strapped themselves in.

The electrical lighting inside changed to a dim crimson. There was a shift in the thrum of the engine. The fluctuations became heavier, slower, more intense. With a jolt, the entire carriage shook and people yelled in fear and surprise. They had been raised from the ground.

With a deafening cascade of iron against stone, the Centimotive started to move.

ᚻ

Elka spent three days in the salt before Björg promoted her to cleaning and deboning.

'It's rotten work,' Björg said, 'but it has to be done properly, and I can't have you ruining any more shipments. We'll put some kids to work in the salt instead.'

It stung hearing that, but Elka wasn't going to argue. Anything was better than working in that freezing building, stacking rotting fish.

Even so, she struggled to keep up with the speed of the other women. The conveyor belt moved so fast that Elka didn't understand how they maintained their pace. It relentlessly fed them more and more work, it took all she had to go fast enough so the others didn't have to pick up her slack. Most of the time, she failed.

The withdrawal wasn't making her physically ill any more, but it had started to affect her more insidiously. Her hands shook unsteadily as she worked.

The morning coffee break was there before she knew it. She gratefully bummed a cigarette from Styrmir, the huldumaður who'd worked the forklift on her first day. Styrmir had teased her to begin with, which had really got to her, but she soon found that there was no ill will behind it. This was just how people bonded here.

'It gets easier,' he said.

They were standing outside in the cold, hiding from the wind behind a stack of crates up against the building. He had noticed her trembling hands as she lit her cigarette.

'I'm just glad to be out of the salt,' Elka replied.

'It reeks in there so bad. At least I'm on the forklift and don't have to stay there too long. Usually new people get stuck there for six weeks before Björg promotes them into the main building. She must like you.'

'I'm not too sure about that. I'm her cousin.' She smiled apologetically.

'Ah.' He tapped his cigarette. 'Of course. Good old-fashioned Hrímlandic nepotism.'

She glared at him and he laughed.

'Come on! I'm just messing with you. There's nothing wrong

with using anything at your disposal to get yourself out of doing the shit jobs. You'd have to be crazy not to. Try spending an entire summer in there – it'll rot your brain from the inside out.' He blew out smoke. 'Besides, you got bumped up because the new temp workers came out of quarantine. Better to give them the shit jobs, eh?'

'Björg said it was because she found brats who could do it better,' she muttered.

Styrmir smiled. Elka knew that although Björg had embellished a little, she hadn't lied about kids being able to do a proper job.

'She does like you, though,' he said. 'She just gives all new workers a hard time.'

After seeing how other people treated each other, let alone fresh workers from the city, she realised that Styrmir had been taking it easy on her. They really gave new people a hard time. If you were a bad worker, you were worthless.

There were a handful of huldufólk working at the fish factory. Unlike in Reykjavík, she had never seen the human Vestmannaeyingar treat them any differently. Apparently these huldufólk had lived here for centuries, ever since escaping from the ruins of their fallen world. Heimaey was a small island, with a small village. There was no space for walls here. Or maybe the people just didn't care for them.

'The other women work so fast, I don't know if I'll ever catch up with them.'

He nodded, thinking carefully before he spoke. 'Well... they're not playing fair, are they?' He gave her a knowing look.

'What do you mean? How do you cheat at working hard?'

Styrmir shrugged and looked around before he continued. Nearby stood stacks of tubs, filled with ice and fresh fish. They were alone.

'You know. There are *methods* that make you work faster. Increase precision, ward off fatigue, keep you sharp as a blade for days on end.'

Realisation dawned on Elka. 'Oh. I don't do that. It's illegal. And dangerous.'

'That's fair. But, just a word of warning – everyone else uses it. Even Björg. Hell, who do you think hands it all out?'

He was talking about kukl. Meddling in the arcane, tampering with forces ordinary people neither fully understood nor controlled. Kukl was illegal everywhere, even here, and considered extremely dangerous. Only the graduated seiðskrattar and galdramenn of Svartiskóli could use galdur or seiður in Hrímland. Kukl was a mixture of both, a dangerous mess of ritual and superstition. Kuklarar usually ended their own lives by overreaching and losing control of the fell powers they tried to control. Even execution was preferable to that.

The thought reminded Elka of her mother. She shuddered.

'I'm not interested in that. I'll catch up and work hard. It'll just take some getting used to.'

'Right.' Styrmir finished his cigarette and threw away the stub. 'You know, if you ever need anything to ease off the withdrawal, I can help you out.'

Elka was speechless. She stilled her shaking hands by crossing her arms tightly.

Is it that obvious?

He saw her startled look and smirked. 'You really don't remember me, huh?' He laughed, throwing up his arms in feigned injury. 'I'm hurt!'

'What? We've met?'

'That's right. In Reykjavík. I'm not surprised you don't remember – it was a few years ago.'

'Oh.' Then it dawned on her.

Oh no.

She remembered: Karnivalið, in Starholt. The upstairs of the bar was off limits to everyone besides the most exclusive guests. Smoke-filled rooms, entire nights and days spent in a daze, halfway out of this world. Sorti and highland moss and delýsíð flowing in abundance.

Of course she'd had a hard time recalling him. Every moment there had been a dream, a recurring nightmare she had wanted to bury and leave behind forever.

'I don't… I'm not that person any more.'

Elka was panicking, nauseous. She had just begun her life – her new life – and it was already ruined. Poisoned by her past.

'Don't worry. That's nobody's business – not even mine. I won't tell anyone. I used to waste all my money on my breaks in Reykjavík. I've moved on as well, and I'm not interested in others finding out what I was up to in the city.'

Elka nodded. He sighed.

'I'm sorry for bringing it up, it's just… I've been where you are. There are things to help with kicking it. That's all.'

She didn't know what to say. She wanted to talk about anything else, pretend this had never happened.

The whistle sounded. People started heading back inside the factory. Elka put out her cigarette.

'Right. Well, see you around, maybe.'

'Yeah. Maybe.'

ᚻ

That afternoon Björg took her aside. The line had notably slowed down due to Elka. She suspected the other workers had intentionally stopped picking up her slack. They had been chatting together during lunch break, and fallen uncomfortably quiet when she'd sat down next to them.

'I can't keep you on the line if you're holding it up, dear.'

They stood in Björg's office. Stacks of papers cluttered the desk next to a typewriter; the shelves were filled with neatly arranged folders. It stank of stale smoke and fish.

'I know, I'm trying to keep up, it's just—'

'Not to worry. Björg frænka has the fix for such a thing.'

Björg reached into her robes for a key chain, unlocking the bottom drawer of her desk. She withdrew two worn leather patches. The light discolouration on them made Elka think of human skin. On them were faded galdrastafir, with rows of nearly illegible runes on either side of the magical symbols.

'Put these in your gloves, quickly now.'

Elka froze. Noticing her hesitation, Björg tried to push the galdrastafir into her hands. She backed away.

'It's just my second week,' said Elka. 'I'll be fine, I just need to adjust, I've only worked the line for a few days. And I haven't been sleeping well, so—'

'Don't be silly, it's perfectly fine.' Björg gave her a conspiratorial look. 'Almost everyone has one, in some form or another. It's completely safe. And if you won't tell, we won't tell.'

'No, frænka. I don't want to.'

Björg's face darkened. She put the skin patches back into the drawer and slammed it shut.

'Your mother would be ashamed hearing this, were she alive. I'm very disappointed in you, and I'm sure she would be as well.'

'Leave my mother out of this.'

'Dagmar worked in Eyjar as well, you know. And she didn't hesitate to gain every advantage she could to work harder – make more of herself. She used kukl every single day, Elka. And she was marvellous. I've never seen a more capable kuklari in all my years here.'

A confusing surge of emotions threatened to overwhelm Elka. Anger, sorrow, helplessness.

She knew that was true. Dagmar had taught Elka a lot of minor tricks and incantations, words of power and esoteric symbols. Elka had hated it. Using it felt weird – addictive. She knew Dagmar had pushed it on to Sölvi as well, despite Elka's demands for her to drop this nonsense of belonging to a powerful bloodline. The delusions of a minor norn.

But she hadn't been around to make sure of it.

Elka turned and left in a hurry, the lump in her throat building up so tightly she felt as though she was choking. She wanted to leave and go home and cry, but she wasn't sure she'd have a job the next day if she did. So she went back to the line and worked her hardest to keep up.

It wasn't enough.

Björg stood at the far end of the factory floor, watching her with displeasure.

ᚻ

When Elka got home at the end of the week her hands were numb from the cold, but she didn't feel it. She held a slip of paper summarising her week's salary. Björg had sourly told her that she hadn't performed well enough to earn any bonuses, but to Elka it was still so much money. Her rent for the workers' lodgings had already been deducted, as well as the extortionate tax rate in Vestmannaeyjar, but that still left her with a higher salary than anything she'd ever made in Reykjavík.

Despite that, she knew she'd be out of a job if she didn't step up. She tore through cigarettes on her breaks, but it wasn't enough. She desperately wanted a real smoke. To float away. To feel good, just for a moment. Every day was a rock piled on her back, and they had accumulated to a heavy load. The addiction had its sickening roots deep in her, a toxic tarnish she couldn't clean away. She was weak, she knew that, but she had to show resolve for Sölvi. He'd given her a new strength, and she intended to use it to benefit them both. Despite that desire, she was inches away from giving in – and that couldn't happen. She knew she wouldn't find her way back out of those depths. Not again.

She started off by paying her debt to Bryde, as well as shopping for the next week. There was always fresh and salted fish in stock, so she bought her fill of that. She also got Sölvi school supplies – a new canvas satchel, notebooks, pencils and ink and pens. She splurged on a new set of colours, beautiful oil-based pigments that were better than anything he'd ever owned.

When she returned to their small room, Sölvi had spread his textbooks over the table and was jotting down notes with fervent dedication. He looked up when she came in, still half-distracted by whatever problem he was trying to solve, and his eyes lit up on seeing the bag she carried.

'Hæ, Mamma,' he exclaimed.

'Hæ, elskan. It's payday! Come and help me put these away.'

Sölvi didn't say much when she asked him how school had been. There wasn't much storage room in the apartment, but they placed the flour, canned goods, butter and dried fish in the cold cabinet, and the rest of it in a cupboard. It was almost full, which made Elka's heart soar.

'Here, I got this for you as well.' She handed him a brown paper bag.

'What is it?'

'It's your reward for working so hard at your studies.' She got down on her haunches and looked him in the eyes. 'I know school's been tough, kid. But it will get better.'

He searched inside the bag, and when he looked back up

tears were tracking down his cheeks. He threw himself into her embrace, hugging her tightly, holding back sobs while she comforted him.

The unexpected flood of emotions caught her off guard. It made her want to give in as well. But she didn't dare reveal her exhaustion and desperation. She steeled herself and warded it off by putting on fake smiles and laughter.

ᚼ

A fox perked up its ears, its white winter coat having lasted deep into the frozen early spring. Minuscule vibrations in the earth grew stronger, and a sound like an avalanche intensified, sending the animal scurrying back to its lair. A black mechanical serpent, shining in the northern sun, burst through the white landscape on a hundred skittering legs, its head riddled with flailing antennae, smelling and seeing things unseen. It headed for the mountains, making its way towards the icy passes carved by patient glaciers thousands of years ago.

The Centimotive was on the move.

Kári was tossed around in the belly of the beast, groaning as the restraints and safety belts dug deep into his body, praying they wouldn't give out so that he was thrown around the compartment like a lamb in the mouth of a frenzied dog. Someone down the row had vomited.

The machine tilted, signifying that it had started to ascend the mountains. Kári knew from the maps that they had diverted from the old cairn path. Soon enough they would hit their first real sorcerous storm.

Kári gritted his teeth. The red lights flickered. He tasted iron in his mouth.

Ahead and above them, the highlands waited.

They had travelled through the day and into night. There was no tracking the passage of time inside the carriage; there was nothing but the reek of sweat, vomit and stale air. Whenever he checked his watch, it felt like a toss of the coin whether minutes or hours had passed. His entire body ached, his skin rubbed raw by the seat restraints.

The first zone wasn't too bad. Inside the thaumaturgically sealed cabin, there hadn't been much sign that they had crossed into a highly volatile area of sorcerous activity. The moisture in the air increased. Everything heated up, then cooled rapidly. Rime covered every square centimetre of the compartment – bare steel, clothing and skin alike. People panicked – but nothing else happened. Things were quiet through the second zone as well.

The third was a different story. Someone vomited blood. Then the people in the middle row close to Kári started screaming. A young man's arm spiralled into a grotesque shape. Kári recognised that it had turned into something resembling calcium carbonate, the skin like a soft, mouldable seashell. The people next to him almost left their seats, but the two soldiers guarding the cabin shouted them back down, lest they be forced to use violence to establish order. The people quietened, but kept as far away from the young man as they could; he cradled his mutating arm in silent agony.

'Hey! Hey, boy!' Kári yelled over the noise of the Centimotive's tireless legs. 'Calm down and listen to me. I'm a biological seiðskratti. When we arrive and my lab is set up, I'll take a look at your arm. All right? It's not over – I can fix this!'

The young man didn't look reassured, but he looked at his twisted appendage before nodding to Kári, tears in his eyes.

It looked bad. It would never fully go away, but he still might live, with Kári's aid. Kári might help the young man live a long and fulfilling life after all this was over.

He hoped he could do the same for himself.

At some point Kári blacked out. It didn't feel like proper sleep, slipping away into unconsciousness from exhaustion.

He was awakened by a lurch as the machine suddenly stopped. Everything fell silent. His ears rang from the hours of constant noise. The Centimotive hissed, letting out a torrent of smoke and steam.

Then, the passengers yelled in fear as they were roughly tossed around when the whole carriage jumped sideways, lifting up and slamming down in their seats as the body of the Centimotive moved in a wild, irregular pattern.

Kári held tight to his seat, tried to calm himself and catch his breath as it was knocked out of him. What was happening? Why these sudden, erratic movements? They felt like...

Evasive manoeuvres.

An impact sent them rolling, the machine flailing like an insect, trying to regain its footing. The lights went out; the screams mixed with the roar of the engines overheating, the dozens of massive iron claws scurrying, the brain-grating sound of iron against ice-covered stone.

A roar. Another impact, but the Centimotive kept its footing. They were moving sideways, up a slope. Then, a lurch – and they sped off, sprinting. Fleeing.

ᚻ

The cold woke him. The Centimotive's pacing had slowed. Kári checked his watch and noticed it had stopped ticking. He guessed that many hours of their journey remained. He tapped on it. The second hand twitched. Then it started to run backwards.

The Centimotive stopped, and the engine hissed like a

gigantic snake. Their two guards gave each other a long look and unbuckled themselves from their seats.

'Remain seated!' one shouted. 'Any attempt to stand will be met with use of force.' He readied his skorrifle. Nobody moved.

Then came a pounding at the door, followed by a call from outside.

'Disembark!'

The soldiers unlocked the door, having to use all their strength due to the bolts freezing shut. It flew open after a great heave, and a freezing wind rushed inside.

'Everyone out! Now!'

Kári got up and shouted over the crowd, 'The high seat pillars must be raised immediately! Seiðskrattar, follow me!'

Those learned in seiður on the expedition were few and, in Kári's opinion, rather unremarkable. Most of them were staff from Perlan, others hand-selected by Doctor Vésteinn. Calling them fully fledged seiðskrattar was a title they did not deserve. However, Kári knew he could hardly afford to judge them by their looks – he knew how he himself might appear.

Kári had been drilled in the details of the bizarre control ritual by Ingi Vítalín and Ginfaxi. Ginfaxi had performed it before, but the original method had been devised by Vítalín's allies – the beings from Laí. In fact, Kári had begged Vésteinn to spare him his part in this. He was meant to be there as some sort of medic, after all.

The good doctor had not listened. A repeat of the uncolour disaster during the mass protest at Austurvöllur was not acceptable.

Leifur had been furious that Kári had been asked to assist, which granted Kári a devious kind of pleasure, but in truth Leifur's relentless competitiveness was exhausting. They were all on the same team out here; the isolated academic society of Svartiskóli was long behind them. Discord could spell their doom.

Kári pulled the case out from under his seat and donned his seiðskratti regalia – slate-coloured robes and red mask. A calm fell over him as he started breathing through his mask's filter. Here he was safe – protected by this armour. Kári disappeared, and in his place stood Magister Kvalráður.

The air was heavy with seiðmagn. The black sand was speckled with ice, with the massive Vatnajökull glacier lurking distantly to the south like a dormant frost-giant. Due west rose sharp and sheer mountain peaks, unnatural geological formations shaped by catastrophic seiðmagn aeons before. They'd have to keep their eyes on those. If anything survived out here, it would have turned into something unearthly long ago.

A shadow moved across the sky. A lone náskári, likely scouting for his tribe. It kept its distance, from both the bizarre machine which had invaded this unspoiled landscape and the sorcerous storm below. Kári watched it warily. Most likely it would turn and flee once the humans established their stake out here. But who knew – some tribe might have claimed this as their territory. Kári was glad their soldiers were armed and ready.

The seiðmagn was nothing like the wisps slithering around Reykjavík – thinned-out shreds and shimmering, fleeting currents. Here was the vortex, a lumbering storm, yet still as nothing in comparison to the truly dangerous zones they had encountered on their way here. Everything was different in the highlands: the colours were more diverse and densely coiled, so vibrant and brimming it was as though they were laden with lightning; the air was thinner and smelled of cold steel. Kári told himself that that was how the highlands must be – that saturated sources of seiðmagn were all different in nature from one another.

Still, he knew that wasn't quite correct. He had previously found a trace of this esoteric, exotic energy – imprisoned in machinery deep within the heart of Perlan.

And now he stood in a place where a new source was dormant in the earth under his feet.

The Centimotive had curled itself into a circle, and within the ring it formed, people worked hard unloading the cargo. Ginfaxi and his cabal of geological seiðskrattar shaped and raised the earth, controlling ice and black rock in undulating waves to ease the installation of the high seat pillars. The seiðskratti's escorts were mere magisteral students.

Have we only brought goddamn amateurs with us?

The three main pillars had just been unloaded, tall and thick columns of crude and cracked obsidian. Next to them were piles of the relatively smaller stakes, intended for the minor excavations surrounding the main site. Vésteinn had donned his robes to become Magister Völundur, and with powerful seiðmagn he raised the earth so waves of rock and dirt gave way, the rough perimeter around him already taking form. Kári had never before seen Vésteinn fully equipped and channelling seiður. He never would have guessed that this disquieting seiðskratti was the proud and dominating doctor.

Kári gathered his underlings behind him, nine students in total. Their robes were the plain black of non-magisteral seiðskrattar, their masks the deep green of the disciples of geological seiður. Leifur, robed as Magister Launvaldur, did the same with his cohort.

Seiður did not work on obsidian – it was anathema to sorcerous power. Inside the pillars was a core of thaumaturgic iron, a mixture of the same components that were used in the sorcerous batteries they had transported here. They would act as stakes, impale the land and leach it of power, purging it of infection and chaos by drawing in and negating the uncontrollable seiðmagn. Moving the pillars would take much effort and many hours they did not have, unshielded against the elements.

The earth had been tilled. Völundur gathered their underlings as the other two had. All of them moved behind Magister Ginfaxi – three formations of lesser seiðskrattar channelling to their leader, who in turn would pass the powerful seiðmagn towards Ginfaxi as they did their bizarre work.

Ingi Vítalín had rolled out and was saying something to Ginfaxi. The seiðskratti nodded and dismissed the blabbering machine with a frustrated gesture. They turned towards the other magisters, who signified with a slight nod that they were ready. With tremendous focus, the three seiðskrattar focused their energy and will towards the royal seiðskratti at the forefront.

Ginfaxi took their position, facing the mountains. The náskári was nowhere to be seen. The surge of seiðmagn was held back by Kári, Vésteinn and Leifur, but it was still almost too much for Kári to bear. Ahead of him, Ginfaxi's arms trembled from the pressure. A group of soldiers moved in front of the seiðskrattar, carrying cumbersome mortars, which they set up, readied, before turning towards Ginfaxi for the order to fire.

The seiðskratti spread out their arms and for a moment Kári almost panicked. What they were about to do hadn't been done for centuries. It was based on myths from early in the Age of Settlement, when Ingólfur Arnarsson had tamed the land that would one day play host to the city of Reykjavík.

With a curt nod from Ginfaxi, the soldiers fired the mortars.

Three arches of smoke curved through the sky. Large metallic capsules burst in mid-flight, the empty shells crashing on the frostbitten ground. Three orbs floated in the air, released from their heavy shells. Through the lenses of Kári's mask, they looked like a void singed into the fabric of the world. An uncolour from another reality.

They started to grow, to leak over existence, seemingly devouring it as they expanded. Feelers sprouted from the masses, tasting the real around them. Ginfaxi unleashed their will like iron chains, overwhelming the uncolours, forcing them to bend to the seiðskratti's will.

Their body shook, and the uncolours appeared hesitant for a while. Kári felt the sudden drain from his body and gasped for breath, before steeling himself and letting even more of the pent-up energy behind him flow through to Ginfaxi. The seiðskratti took a step back, bracing themselves, and a stream of hypercoloured seiðmagn wrapped around the uncolours, reining them in.

The three entities started to move towards the massive obsidian blocks.

The high seat pillars were more than sorcerous artefacts – they were an engine. A machine that would drive the seiðmagn in the environment away like a rock splitting a river, and nullify any that breached its defences. The obsidian formed a negative energy field, which its meteoric iron core expanded beyond the physical pillar itself. Natural seiðmagn was wild, random and unstable. Diverting it was their only hope for the long term.

But underneath their feet lay another source of power. Kári could feel it, even in that frantic moment as his body threatened to give in. A stirring presence, neither awake nor sleeping nor dead.

It was waiting.

The uncolours expanded and grew tentacles and feelers, each wrapping around a pillar. The earth sizzled and burned where the entities dug into it, leaving behind something that was not quite ash. The uncolours lifted the huge obsidian blocks up as if they were nothing, and with a shift in intent Ginfaxi commanded them to move to their designated spots.

Kári had not been at the protest seven years ago, where one of those things had been unleashed above a mob. He had heard the stories, of course. Everyone had. Vésteinn had showed him pictures from sealed reports, revealing the withered husks of its victims. It was Magister Ginfaxi who had controlled the uncolour that time, from atop a nearby building. With only three seiðskrattar, they had barely managed to control it. Just before their spirits buckled from its immense resistance, a command had been issued to let the people go, so it could be safely contained. Kári dreaded to think what would have happened if Ginfaxi had fallen foul to the seiðmagn coursing through them. That despicable massacre would have paled in comparison to one of these alien beings let loose upon the world.

And they had *three* of them at their disposal. Thanks to Ingi's benefactors, the beings from Laí.

The uncolours carried the pillars to their designated craters and raised them vertically, dropping them into the earth with resounding impacts. Turning the pillars like screws, the things staked them like black nails into the earth, impaling it with their horrific power. Already Kári could see shifts in the seiðmagn around them, as the pillars activated and started to drive away the power infesting this land.

The casual show of brutal force humbled Kári and made him fearful. It was as though nothing was more natural than to recklessly utilise seiður in this manner. The postgraduates whispered among themselves with excitement, feeling the shift as he did. Kári stood silent, not affording a moment for his will to waver. He knew well what the price for these small miracles was. Many of these postgrads would be visiting him in the infirmary before long, as the dig itself began.

The wind calmed. Suddenly, Ginfaxi collapsed to the ground, landing on one knee. The group panicked, and in that moment Kári, Leifur and Vésteinn held back the seiðmagn they fed to Ginfaxi, fearful of destroying him completely.

'No!' Ginfaxi turned around, hissing at them through their mask. 'More, you idiots!'

The soldiers hurried to their positions, using the obsidian shell of the Centimotive for cover. They readied their skorrifles and scouts sprinted on to the field, gathering the open half-shells which had imprisoned the uncolours. Already the things undulated wildly, reaching towards the sky, growing at an unsettling pace. Ingi Vítalín made a sound of admiration nearby, startling Kári.

'Oh, how beautiful! See how they glow, how they bask without fetters! What marvellous beings, what glorious luminescence! How I wish you could see them as I do, how I wish you could hear them sing! Oh! Angels!'

The uncolours moved fast towards the centre of the field, driving forwards with countless, bloated feelers. Kári and the others reversed their previous action – opened the floodgates, bombarded Ginfaxi with seiðmagn, making them scream in pain. The royal seiðskratti shot into the air, thaumaturgic lightning sparking off his body, and with a tremendous iron will that Kári felt tug at his own being, they attempted to wrest control over the uncolours.

With the connection so direct, Kári felt Ginfaxi's unfamiliar method of seiður clearly. It had been formulated by alien minds, ancient in shape and thought, like a parasite which infected and transformed the mind by merely absorbing the knowledge. He gained but a minor glimpse of the ritual, and what he gleaned was wrong in every shape and form. Although Ginfaxi had used the power latent in this world to manipulate the uncolours, the seiðmagn had become warped and unrecognisable by making contact with it. Kári suddenly realised why only Ginfaxi was capable of performing this task. Something in their training had affected them irreversibly.

'You three!' Ginfaxi spat. 'To the pillars! Seal us off, now!'

Kári, Vésteinn and Leifur sprinted in separate directions, each heading towards a pillar. Kári used seiður to enhance his speed, trusting to Ginfaxi to take control of the group of seiðskrattar feeding him seiðmagn.

Towering dozens of metres above Kári, the leaning pillar looked like an ancient monument out of time. Vésteinn had taken his place by his pillar; so had Leifur. Kári prepared himself for the strain he was to endure. This was why they were there – to see the unreal tamed and shackled against its own will. To transform chaos into order.

Ginfaxi was bent by the force channelled through them, flaring up in a storm of hypercolours as they dragged the uncolours back down into their capsules, the soldiers standing ready to lock them back in. The air was hazy, moving in waves, as Ginfaxi used every gram of their remaining strength to prevent their annihilation at the hands of the abominations.

Then, with a final effort, the black cages trapped their quarries and Ginfaxi collapsed to the ground.

He could feel Vésteinn and Leifur – Völundur and Launvaldur. Together they wove a forceful net of violent will only barely held in check by their determination. They radiated arcane power, drawing in the unruly might of the buried titan deep beneath them... but their power was *militant*. It was limited to forceful use, a coercion of the supernatural world into an image their minds and wills demanded. Kári now understood why they had asked him to take part in this, and why so many seiðskrattar could never do what he had spent painful hours specialising in.

Kári could break nature when forced to, but his specialisation was in doing the opposite – diverting force, shaping a safe pathway for an unruly current. The defences Völundur and Launvaldur were raising would be strong, but they would be a wall placed against a relentless, roaring ocean. They would demand a great amount of power and constant maintenance.

Kári looked for ways to adapt the seiður to nature, and nature to the seiður. He would not build a dam, but a channel; not a wall, but a road. He felt the land around him, the boiling energy in its heart, and down in the earth a sleeping giant slowly stirring due to the ants crawling on its grave.

He drew in Völundur's and Launvaldur's power, also dragging in the scores of exhausted lesser seiðskrattar, granting him a vision of the land. He channelled a circle, a refuge in the raging tempest. With the image firmly chiselled in his mind, he found a course. A way to divert the currents away, forming an island of calm within the storm.

As one, the seiðskrattar linked the impaling stakes together and exhausted the land of its power.

In the distance, a náskári took flight towards the south-west.

Sjö

The barren landscape seemed white and pristine from a distance, a quiet land which looked unchanging and serene.

The náskári knew better.

Gliding into an updraught, Bölmóður soared even further above, his great black wings carrying him effortlessly, despite the weight of the rough iron cast into his beak and claws.

His thoughts were clouded with worry. He had spotted seiðskrattar among those people in the clearing, and the infernal machine that had brought them to that forsaken place was nothing but a weapon – that much had been clear when he watched it fight and evade a group of trolls on its way into the interior.

He had also been among the blóðgögl of Those-who-pluck-the-eyes-of-the-ram at Austurvöllur, all those years ago. He had shredded soldiers and civilians alike, dropped them to their deaths from a great height, had been an enemy to all those who stood with the Crown against the unified peoples. He had watched his tribe's warriors dive into the fray when they unleashed that grotesque 'uncolour' abomination, the monster the Crown controlled to unceremoniously drain the life from his fellow blóðgögl and the land-bound masses below.

Now this excavation team was using those dishonourable

sorceries to lay the foundations of their new fortress. To start building a weapon to end all wars.

Bölmóður seethed with rage.

Loosely following the trail of the old cairn path laid out below him, he tracked his way back to where he guessed his new tribe would have travelled. The day before he had scouted a refuge – a cave in a lava field, hidden from sight except to those in the air. Making quick work of the wretched, mutated things which had made the cave their home, he had guided his companions to safety.

They were two days out from the excavation site, and it was likely those wounded but enraged trolls also wandered the area. His tribe would have to be careful.

Spotting a lone figure making its way along the cairn path, he dived down and landed before Halla. Laden with supplies she had stolen from the Crown's base by the fjord, she had taken the long way around the relatively safe path to make her way back. Cawing out short instructions on how to find her way to the cave, Bölmóður took a good share of her burden to quicken her pace, and took to the air once more.

They were weak, all of them, nothing like his old tribe of náskárar – but they were determined. Of all the others, he only respected Halla. She ventured into these sorcerous wastes alone, crawling on the ground like vermin, so easily subject to its temperamental forces. The cracked lenses of the goggles guided her partially, but still he pitied her. And so much greater was his respect for her work. Of all the people of his new tribe, she alone was close to being worthy of the title of blóðgagl, despite her mutations – a death sentence or exile for any náskári. But this tribe had its own laws. Each warrior carried their share of scars, after all.

Dark shadows moved to the south. Way too far for any

land-bound thing to notice without binoculars, he saw them clear as day. Carrion-buried-in-an-open-field, according to their decorations. A highly territorial tribe, but their blóðgögl were unlikely to seek him out unless he invaded their territory. Unfamiliar with the exact borders of the eastern region, he kept a distance. Seeing blóðgögl fully decorated in the symbols of their tribe brought him anguish. Despite his pretending, he knew what he was.

A korpur. A warrior without a tribe. So said the skulls and trophies hanging from his hertygi, the harness wrapped around his torso. Someone exiled from their people, without territory, without a home.

He saw the lookout several kilometres away, hidden behind jagged lava rocks. Camouflaged enough from most beings, to him they still stood out like a blood-red carcass in a snowy field. This area was relatively clear of the volatile seiðmagn, at least for now. He had spotted a storm moving in from the north.

Bölmóður landed with a crash, the beating of his wings slowing him just enough to avoid injury. The scout visibly jumped – lazy, undisciplined. One of the humans who had joined them after escaping from the Nine. He should have known better than to drop his guard.

'Err-at calm, despite the quiet,' the náskári crowed in archaic Hrímlandic. He'd picked up much of the way modern Hrímlanders spoke, but still remnants of the náskárar's dialect remained.

'R-right. Sorry.'

'Ask-at forgiveness of me. Your life is first forfeit.'

He shambled into the cave, stooping even lower than usual. He despised confined spaces in the earth. The Ram Eaters made their home on sheer island cliffs just outside of Reykjavík, but those caves were covered in interwoven skramsl carved into the walls generations ago. They spoke of history, of bloodshed, of victory. This place was nothing like his old home. It was dead and silent: little more than a grave.

The others heard him coming, his iron talons scraping loudly against stone as he approached; still, they were all visibly on edge. In the highlands one never knew what might show up. In total they were about twenty, having lost a few on the way there. They looked exhausted and starved, but he saw that fire of determination still burning within them.

A man approached, wiry and lithe, carrying his skorrifle casually over his shoulder.

'Bölmóður. It went well?' The náskári barely got a nod in before the man continued, noticing Bölmóður's burden. 'Did you see Halla? Is she safe? Does she need help?'

'Halla is a few hours out,' the náskári said slowly in skramsl. 'Worry not, Eyvindur. Her burden was lightened.'

He dropped his sacks to the ground and Eyvindur picked them up with the help of a few others.

'Thank you. The others are deeper in, having a … meeting, I think.'

'I will talk to them, then the whole tribe. I have grave news.'

Eyvindur's face darkened. 'The Crown … They're really doing it?'

'It is worse than we've ever feared.'

Bölmóður had to stoop even lower as he descended further into the cavern, accidentally hitting the ceiling with the jagged edge of his beak so that sparks flew. Further in were three people, sitting around a makeshift altar. It was draped with a coarse canvas cloth, on which was painted a strange and unsightly crude image. On top of it sat a skull and several bones.

'Things are worse than anticipated.'

Only one of them looked up – a woman; the other two were

still staring intently at the bones. She was short for a huldukona, lithe but strong, her hair and worn clothes serving function over form at all costs. When Bölmóður first met Diljá, she had been the same as all the other city-dwellers – weak. Now, she was a soldier.

'Bölmóður. Welcome back. The siblings will be with us in a moment.'

The náskári clanked over to a corner in the cave where the ceiling was higher, perching on his krummafótur, finally letting his exhaustion show. He leaned back on his massive third leg, big enough to carry a full-grown human aloft with ease.

'Did you see *him*?' Diljá asked quietly.

Bölmóður did not have to ask who she meant.

'Yes. And the other agent. Meinholt.' He spat the name out like a curse.

Diljá set her jaw, her mouth forming a firm line. He approved of her, at that moment.

The other two finally looked up from the bones. From a distance, they looked gaunt and haggard, their clothes torn to shreds, their skin with an unseemly pallor. Up close, it was clear as day what they had become. Grey skin, bared teeth and bone, hair matted and tangled. Eyes unblinking and unfeeling, a mockery of life and every living being's miserable existence.

Hraki and Styrhildur.

After the first attempt on the life of Count Trampe, when Loftkastalinn was claimed by transdimensional corruption, they'd hidden at the castle ruins on Sálnanes. They knew it was a cursed place, that ill fates awaited all those who stayed too long. Even the náskárar avoided Sálnanes. No tribe could lay claim to that territory.

Styrhildur had been grievously wounded when they kidnapped Count Trampe's assistant. Bölmóður's private opinion was that

Styrhildur should have died those years before. It was a noble and good death, to die for what you stood for.

Hraki had remained by his sister's side as Garún and Katrín left to take the count's life. The two women had never returned. Her brother had stood vigil over her in that forsaken castle. None could say what had happened exactly. Perhaps Styrhildur had refused to die; perhaps Hraki had refused to accept her death. Or perhaps it was just the fell nature of that wretched place, to warp the forces of life and death into something unrecognisable.

Draugar. Afturgöngur. Haugbúar.

Corporeal ghosts risen from the dead. Galdramenn who practised svartigaldur could raise such monstrosities as a sending – draugar coerced into haunting their victims till their deaths, sometimes over multiple generations. Lonely, departed souls haunted their own burial spot, trapping wayward travellers in their cold, bloodthirsty embrace. But Hraki and Styrhildur were different. They were not draugar driven by mindless hunger. Bölmóður supposed it was only the promise of revenge that compelled them to endure.

Just like Garún.

Even here, as far as he could get from the unsightly altar, he could hear the faint whispers from the skull in the corners of his mind. The sheet draping the altar, laced with delýsíð by Garún herself, radiated burning emotions.

Rage. Tenacity. Hate.

Halla had salvaged the woman's bones the day the Nine fell at the hands of the Stone Giant. While Halla escaped from the rubble, Garún's remains had spoken to her from beyond the grave. Her spirit, or whatever shreds remained of it, would not let go.

Not until the Crown fell.

Bölmóður had not known of these things when he spoke out

against Rotsvelgur's rule over Those-who-pluck-the-eyes-of-the-ram and ended up joining the activists. Perhaps that was just as well – he was unsure that he would have sought them out had he known beforehand. Bölmóður had been willing to die if it meant freedom from Kalmar, but his hersir had washed his hands of this war when Loftkastalinn fell and Trampe was killed. Rotsvelgur had lost touch. His closest advisers feared him too much to challenge his cowardice, let alone to forge an alliance with land-dwellers who resorted to unimaginable and craven svartigaldur to achieve their goals.

But Bölmóður cared not what manner of weapon was used to slay one's adversary. All that mattered was that they died.

So he had left his tribe and everything that mattered to him to stand and fight next to those who dared oppose the tyranny of Kalmar.

A tribe of monsters and rejects.

He reported on what he had seen. The centipede made out of obsidian and steel, which traversed through the mutating storm. How the seiðskrattar had impaled the earth itself and changed the currents of seiðmagn. That there were more of them than expected, far more, all of them highly learned in arcane crafts, and they had obviously found whatever it was they sought. At the mention of the uncolours, *three* of them, the air became practically laced with despair.

It was Styrhildur who spoke first.

'We knew we would be outmatched in every regard when we set out. But that is nothing compared to what they will have if they build this machine. Loftkastalinn will be a plaything compared to it.'

'So we proceed,' said Hraki. 'Even if it amounts to nothing.'

We will be victorious. Their hubris shall be their downfall.

A whisper at the edge of reality echoed in their minds, an

intrusive sentience crackling among their thoughts. They turned towards the bones, marked with crude esoteric symbols.

The storm will consume them. The dormant power of the earth will be unleashed. And the people will rise against their oppressors as living weapons.

ᚻ

The days blurred together into a grey haze. When Elka came home she was cold and sore and her hands were stiff. The only thing that made her day tolerable was hearing about Sölvi's school day. He had struggled to begin with, but now he was making friends and doing well at his studies. Surely this was a sign that moving here had been the right decision.

Except that the madness she had been running from had followed her here. It had its sickening roots deep in her, a toxic tarnish she couldn't clean away. She was weak, she knew that, but she had to stay the course. For Sölvi.

Styrmir lived in the southern part of town. The houses were plain and crowded, several families living in each one. Usually occupancy was split down the middle, with separate water tanks for each half of the roof. Elka found it odd that people living together wouldn't share utilities, but fresh water was one of the most precious resources in Vestmannaeyjar.

She walked up to the two-storey house and knocked. A middle-aged human woman answered, evidently in the middle of cooking.

'I'm looking for Styrmir.'

'Back door,' she replied gruffly, and shut the door in Elka's face.

Behind the house, Elka found an entrance to the basement. The stairs had been cleared of treacherous ice, a well-used snow shovel resting up against the wall next to them.

Styrmir came to the door and looked surprised to see her. She had never seen him out of his worker's uniform and was likewise surprised to see how he dressed. Homespun woollen cloth, so well cared for it might have been new, all dark greys and near-blacks.

'Elka? Sorry, I just didn't expect you.'

'I hope I'm not interrupting.'

He hesitated to reply. She noticed he had been crying.

'Are you all right? Has something happened?'

He smiled faintly and shook his head. 'No. Or, well... not yet. Please, come in.'

'I don't want to bother you, I'll just come back later.'

'No, please, come in. It's fine.' There was something in his look that made her want to stay. 'I know why you're here. I have it ready in my room, I'll just fetch it for you. Just step in from the cold, all right?'

She went in and followed him up a steep staircase to the first floor, entering a living room filled with huldufólk. They looked up in surprise. Everyone was wearing similar clothes to Styrmir's. Plain wool, dark colours. Some of them were crying.

'Everyone, this is Elka. She's a friend from work.'

Elka was uncertain if she should offer her condolences or not. It was obvious something terrible had happened. The people greeted her politely, and she gave them a smile and nodded in greeting.

'Sorry to bother you,' she said.

Styrmir led her to a hallway. Doorways on one side had been boarded up with bricks or wooden boards, sectioning off half of the house straight down the middle. He led her into his room.

Lit by the grey daylight, it was clean and spartan: a neatly made single bed; a trunk tucked away under it; stacks of clothes filling half of an open closet, the other half filled with worn, cheap books. Styrmir went to his tiny writing desk and sat by it.

'Take a seat.'

She sat down on the bed and watched him fiddle with the underside of the desk. He looked flustered, embarrassed that she was in his room. Eventually he pulled out a long wooden box somehow hidden inside the desk.

'This is not something you want to have lying around,' he said apologetically. 'There are good people living here, but some rooms are for migrant workers and, well...'

'I understand. What's happened? Do all these people live here?'

He chuckled. 'No. Things aren't quite that cramped here. They are friends and family of Sylvía, an elderly huldukona who lives upstairs.' He sighed and tapped the box, cradled in his hands. 'She's... Well, she's dying. Everyone is gathered here for a sort of... funeral. I guess that's the best way to phrase it.'

'I see. I'm so sorry to hear that. I knew I shouldn't have bothered you, Styrmir. You should have told me to come back later.'

'No, I... I wanted you to come in.' He looked thoughtfully at her. 'At first I wasn't sure what to make of you. I mean... you are from Reykjavík.'

She understood what he meant. 'I'm not like that.'

'I know.' He nodded to himself. 'I mean, it's not like I know you well, but... I like to think I have a good instinct about these things.' A painful grin crossed his face. 'Kind of have to, you know?'

'Yes. I suppose so.'

He drew his chair closer, leaned in, and Elka caught the faint scent of salt and wild thyme. He handed her the box hesitantly.

'Here. One a day for a couple of weeks. Then every other day, and so on until you don't need them any more. No matter what you do, don't take more than one. It'll just draw things out and make things worse. Trust me.'

She opened it. Inside was a small glass bottle, filled with an amber-coloured and viscous liquid.

'It looks like lýsi.'

Cod liver oil was taken regularly by almost everyone in Hrímland, believed to stave off all kinds of illnesses.

'It tastes worse, I'm afraid. It's processed from the ... run-off, I guess, from the process of making sorti.'

'So it's safe?'

'Safer than getting back on the stuff. Just keep it hidden, all right?'

She closed the box and put it in her purse. 'How did you get this?'

He winced. 'It's better if you don't know. All I can say is that it's easier to get in Eyjar.'

Realisation dawned on her. 'They make it here, don't they?'

He hesitated, then nodded. 'You'll get sent back if they find you with the stuff, though. Or if you ask any questions.'

'Understood. Thank you so much for this, Styrmir. You're a lifesaver. I'll get out of your way. Again, I'm so sorry to have interrupted.'

'Actually, I was wondering ... if it's not too uncomfortable, that is ...'

He had got up at the same time as she did, and now stood there awkwardly, fretting over his question.

'If it's all right, I'd like to invite you to stay for the funeral.'

'But I don't know her. I don't know any of these people.'

'It doesn't matter. Not to any of us. It used to be that the human villagers would attend these ceremonies as well. But they stopped coming a few years ago.' He swallowed. 'Lots of people converted to the Church of the Deep. They said our customs were cruel and macabre.' With these words, a hint of anger. 'And they frown upon attending other religious rituals. As more and more converted, it put pressure on the others. Soon they all stopped showing up. Even if it was their friend who was dying.'

Hearing this made Elka anxious. She was completely unfamiliar with the lie of the land in Heimaey. She had barely heard of the Church from Bryde, and didn't even know what kind of ceremony this was. One misstep and she could find herself ostracised.

'They won't give you a hard time if you attend,' he said, almost reading her mind.

Elka knew the huldufólk could sense other people's emotions, but she'd never experienced it herself. Humans couldn't reach back, but allegedly you could still feel the interference of someone connecting to you.

'I just thought it would be a nice thing for the others to see,' Styrmir continued. 'And who knows, maybe it would get the other human villagers to attend. Get things back to how they used to be.'

Elka hesitated. She knew it would be just fine saying no – Styrmir would understand. But she had not been this type of fearful person in Reykjavík, and she wasn't about to become one now.

'I would be honoured, Styrmir. As long as it's fine with the others.'

He smiled. 'Takk, Elka.'

'Shouldn't I go and change?'

He laughed and shook his head. 'You're fine. It's not a sad affair. Not yet anyway.'

Before they went out, he explained the ritual to her briefly. Elka was shocked to hear some of what he said and, despite herself, she had a hard time accepting that what they were doing was ethical. Styrmir took the time to go through it with her, assuring her it was fine. This was an ancient custom, lost to most modern huldufólk. It had been a relic in the old world even before hulduheimar fell, from the time before they started to use their gifts in pursuit of decadence and hedonism.

Styrmir and a group of five others got up and went upstairs to prepare. The six were of a wide age range that couldn't be a coincidence.

Elka sat down with the others and asked them about Sylvía – the woman who lay upstairs, dying. She had been a kind and hard-working woman. Married twice, lost both husbands to the sea, as so many did in Eyjar. Left to raise six children of her own; three more were lost to illness as newborns. All of life's hardships had never broken her spirit. She had fed those in need, even when her own household was struggling.

It had been a simple and hard life, filled in equal measure of sorrow and joy – but that happiness had not come easily or by itself.

They headed up the narrow stairs and entered a large attic room. Silent and lit only by the weak daylight filtering through the curtained windows, it smelled faintly of baking and old furniture. An old and frail woman was lying in bed, surrounded by the six huldufólk who had gone up the stairs first. They stood vigil over her last, harrowed breaths. Styrmir was kneeling by Sylvía's bedside, holding her paper-thin, calloused hands as he whispered something to her.

A cloying wave of empathy washed over Elka as the huldufólk reached out to one another, herself included. She had no way of reaching back, and with them mute in their unspoken communication she managed to feel even more isolated than before. She tried to focus, to get used to the invasion of her surface thoughts and emotions, while having no idea what the huldufólk could pick up. She could not really imagine what it felt like to connect to someone else like that. It must have been the most wonderful feeling in the world, not to feel so alone. To belong.

Sylvía took in the crowded room and spoke in a frail voice.

'I think it's best we start.'

Styrmir cleared his throat.

'Adralíen-toll, we call upon you. Your living masks plead for your attention and blessing. Soon you shall take Sylvía Bergsdóttir into your hands and grant her eternal life among your eternal multitudes. As you draw your hand towards your face and become a new visage, we ask you to grant us the strength and wisdom needed to do the same. Adralíen-toll, who carries the mask of the worlds upon your unknowable face, grant Sylvía the power to gift us a fraction of her own mask, as you did for us on our creation. Let your multitudes live on through her in all of us, should it be according to your will.'

Styrmir leaned in close to Sylvía. They locked eyes. After a moment the assembled crowd suddenly let out a small gasp. Something had happened.

Elka couldn't feel anything except the social shift in the room. Something serious was happening. Sylvía kept on staring into Styrmir's eyes, now looking lost and dreaming, as if in a trance. Then, the tension broke, and she came back to herself.

After allowing her a moment to collect herself, Styrmir told Sylvía what memory he had taken – the day she heard her first husband had been lost at sea. She nodded uncertainly, unfolding a paper she had by her bedside. It had been the correct memory.

Centuries before, when the huldufólk's world had not yet fallen, theirs had been a glorious empire of excess. In this world they had appeared out of hidden portals, usable only by themselves, stealing away or luring their victims into their wondrous realm – hulduheimar – only to feast upon their memories until nothing remained. According to folklore, they sometimes returned their victims, shells of their former selves with nothing to hold on to, no reason to live. Husks without identity.

In Reykjavík, and Elka suspected almost everywhere else in Hrímland, this was considered a grotesque taboo. A dark gift that was to be shunned and suppressed. She had never imagined it would be used in this way. To pass on memories to the next generation, to freely give a part of your life to another.

It was beautiful.

At that moment, Elka could not imagine that the folklore about their ancestors was true. It was only because the huldufólk themselves recognised it that she believed it. How could a civilisation have become so cruel, so callous, in a world where no one had to feel alone? It was an impossible thought as she looked around the room, seeing everyone's hearts so tightly intertwined as cherished memories were given like heirlooms.

Then she thought of Reykjavík's towering walls, the depths of the Nine, the ongoing war on the mainland. Were humans not capable of language and understanding – of empathy? How easy it was to reduce another living being to something worthless.

Dead fish on the conveyor belt.

Reaching out was not a magical solution; it just seemed as though it would feel so wonderful and warm. Like bright, wholesome versions of those fever dreams she had lost herself in night after night, wreathed in smoke like silk.

To her surprise, Elka found herself missing her mother deeply. She had nothing left of her to speak of. Nothing real like this. Her upbringing was a confusing blur of conflicting emotions, her life as a young adult a dark haze she desperately wanted to forget. Sölvi had fonder memories of his grandmother than she did. She felt as if she hadn't truly known her at all.

Ever since she was a young girl, Dagmar had told her never

to go to Vestmannaeyjar. She refused to explain why, or tell Elka anything about her upbringing. Life in Vestmannaeyjar was something she'd only learned about after arriving here.

One by one, the chosen six accepted Sylvía's memories. Each time, it appeared that the correct memory was given and nothing else. Elka suspected the huldufólk's bond was made to forge a restraint, knotting their unified emotions into a net.

The ceremony concluded, they left Sylvía to rest. The six remained by her bedside and would stand her vigil for the night. Styrmir nodded to Elka in farewell.

Walking back home, she was on the verge of tears without really understanding why. She had never felt as alone as in that room, surrounded by people who *belonged to each other*. She wanted nothing more than to have that in her life. She'd give anything up just to have that for a moment.

When she came home she took one of the pills. It tasted bitter, tinged with an acidic taste that reminded her of smoke-filled rooms laden with dreams.

She slept well that night.

ᚼ

More workers arrived every day with the ferry *Herjólfur*. They rushed from its doors by the dozen, opportunists looking for fortune – and food – for the summer. People did not look so animated after quarantine, but they were desperate and hardy. Frost still hung in the air, but the weather was good for sailing. The spring season was about to start.

Elka watched the harbour fill with new arrivals as she walked to work each morning. Militiamen with old front-loaded rifles stood guard, uniformed but provincial, their outfits old and their hair unkempt. They kept a close eye on the newcomers filing out of the quarantine building. It occasionally happened that a person was stopped and taken in for questioning. For customs, usually, according to Björg – but sometimes those people didn't come back.

'Troublemakers, and we don't want anything to do with them,' her aunt had said.

The workers' lodgings were now full of new people. Almost no one had brought children with them, and Elka now understood that she was a unique exception in that regard. Families could not get a residence permit in Eyjar, according to Captain Kohl's decrees, which were issued in concert with the owners of the fishing companies. No vistarband for whole families – except those from Eyjar.

She doubted that it was a positive thing to break families apart, just so one parent could find some work – but she dared not mention it. Instead she decided to be thankful she was exempt. She couldn't help but think that Sölvi would feel better not being the only child from the mainland at school, but he was doing so well making friends that she couldn't justify her own suspicion. It wasn't as if Reykjavík had been different, with its surveillance networks and city walls. She had just never before put herself in the place of the people on the wrong side of such things.

The new arrivals were quite familiar with one another, as well as some of the people living in Vestmannaeyjar. Elka felt as if she was the only person to have moved there for the first time this year.

That first week of the season was much livelier than those that had gone before. People joked and laughed and filled the village streets. Despite the high spirits, she caught glimpses of the reality waiting in the city. Reykjavík was suffering from a severe product scarcity and people had stopped accepting krónur altogether. Bartering was the only way to feed your family. The farmers sold their produce for exorbitant prices, and coffee, sugar and wheat were worth more than gold.

Elka hadn't been aware of any shortage at the grocer's in the village – nor that people were stocking up on supplies. Maybe Reykjavík just had too many people fighting for the same merchandise. Or were the wealthy buying up everything for themselves? She couldn't make sense of it. But she started to prioritise always having a supply of dried foods in her tiny pantry. The Hanseatic war had dragged on and the situation was only going to get worse before it got better.

The boats landed more and more often; the working day grew longer as overtime became standard, and maximum efficiency was demanded from employees every minute. Elka started to realise just how slow she was. The new workers were used to the pace and she felt as if she was the only truly new recruit there.

She got a grip, but feared it wasn't enough. Björg reprimanded her yet again for being too slow and put her back in the salt for a few days. Even there she wasn't good or fast enough.

'She's a piece of work.' Styrmir gave Elka a sympathetic look. 'It took me months to get the hang of it.'

'I don't have months.'

'Well...' Styrmir shrugged. 'You're still Björg's niece. You'll always land on your feet.'

'Right.'

Elka didn't know how to respond to that. She didn't even know how to feel about it.

The first day Elka was put back on the line, she was determined to work herself to the bone to show that she belonged there. Björg stopped her just as she'd got dressed, handing her a pair of new gloves.

'Here. Use these.'

Elka took the gloves hesitantly. Her own were already practically brand new.

'Stop wasting time, girl, and put on the damn gloves.'

She wanted to refuse. At least to ask the real reason for why she had to do it. But she didn't. Elka did as she was told and handed Björg her old pair. She felt the woman's gaze on her as she headed out to the factory floor.

Normally it felt as though the mechanical belt moved at double speed, but today... it felt as if she was finally getting the hang of it. Her knife moved deftly, cutting with precision, her other hand never slipping as she reached out for a slippery cod.

Time flew by as she worked relentlessly. She told herself it was silly to mistrust Björg. Maybe Styrmir's pills had finally helped her overcome the shakes. She had just needed to calm down. The conveyor belt seemed to slow to a crawl. Hours went by, and the women standing behind Elka found themselves short of work. She was working at the speed of five women.

She did not notice when the cod was cut before her knife blade touched it. She did not notice when the other women stepped away from the conveyor belt, away from her, and still she kept up her frantic pace, and the electric lights flickered. She did not notice when the fish burst from within, when unseen forces shredded the white meat, when the cod started to shake and gasp for air as though they were still alive.

The explosion knocked Elka on her back, forcing the air from her lungs. Streaks of ethereal lightning flashed and the belt finally stopped moving, ruined by the force. She drew in a breath, and her lungs hurt, and her hands shook uncontrollably, and the gloves sizzled and smoked before her eyes. Screaming in panic, she ripped them off, but her hands were unscathed – except for the galdrastafir which had singed red scars into her palms, branding her with the esoteric sorcerous symbols Björg had hidden inside her gloves. The pain hit her, and she screamed, but none dared approach her. She saw Björg standing there, dumbfounded. Styrmir was at the far end of the crowd, having rushed in to see what had happened.

Tears clouded her eyes. She got up and ran out. No one followed her.

New spines and appendages had sprouted on the decimated fish carcasses.

ᚼ

The land was impaled with black spikes, nails on the sarcophagus of the giant sleeping beneath them. Three central pillars dominated the dig site – eldritch monoliths that formed the only barrier against the primordial forces raging beyond their reach. Surrounding them were the lesser pillars – islands within relatively safe walking distance of the mainland hub, where the smaller dig sites were well underway. Already, roofs of what had once been towering stone buildings had surfaced from the earth.

The main excavation site was now a layered pit, constantly manned by seiðskrattar and the scores of archaeologists working to uncover the remains of the ancient beast. The dig was ahead of schedule, and thanks to the efforts of the geological seiðskrattar they had reached a depth of several metres. Floodlights ensured that work could continue day and night, but with the lengthening daylight they relied on them less and less. Vésteinn directed the work groups efficiently with Auður, managing how and where the seiðskrattar should use their power, and in a matter of days they had accomplished what would have taken mundane archaeologists weeks. The cold didn't seem to be getting any better, despite the late spring season. The Great Frost Winter endured still in the mountains.

Auður spent most of her time at the bottom of the pit, when

she wasn't in the laboratory working with Vítalín and Leifur. Kári was uncertain exactly what she was doing down there, but it was clear she was attempting to understand the overwhelming, ancient power that lay dormant beneath them. He knew she had been in charge of investigating the site in Öskjuhlíð. She and Vésteinn had built that small obsidian pyramid, sealing off the bizarre power that had manifested there. He wondered if and how these two were connected.

Everything eluded him, so far. But all the pieces were there; he just had to put them together.

The air was crisp and cold, the cerulean sky so clear it seemed like a thin veil. Kári sat by himself in the canteen tent. Porridge and rye bread with butter again. The other tables were nearly empty; only stragglers from the night shift remained. Young men and women, most of them diggers. Some looked unusually red. Perhaps it was working long hours in the cold northern sun. Perhaps it was something else.

He not only had to worry about thaumaturgical mutations, but mundane accidents as well. It had become clear that Þráinn Meinholt was equally in charge of this venture along with Vésteinn, and Þráinn demanded a sorcerous solution to all medical problems. Every worker had to be at full capacity so the schedule would not be delayed. Kári had protested. Vésteinn and Þráinn were well aware of what unnecessary exposure to seiðmagn could do to a body – they just didn't care.

On the way to the medical lab Kári noticed the two agents standing outside the Centimotive carriage they had turned into their base of operations, similar to his own laboratory. Hrólfur and Þráinn were smoking, dressed in suits despite the freezing cold. Magister Ginfaxi had had no time to rest after raising the perimeter. Since then, they had been in there doing Þráinn's bidding. Nobody knew what the agents were working on. Yet another moving part of this operation Kári was dreadfully ignorant of.

Kári froze in place when he entered the lab and found Auður Thorlacius waiting for him. Dressed in a long black coat, a dark grey woollen suit and sturdy worker's boots, she stood by his desk investigating a small medical cabinet lined with tiny drawers. She was reading the labels, looking for something.

'Auður. Good morning.'

'Good morning, Kári,' she replied, not at all startled by his quiet entrance. 'My apologies, I was waiting, and—'

'It's quite all right. There's nothing that important kept in there. I found this cabinet on sale in Reykjavík and use it mostly for decoration. It has a comforting effect on the other patients. A familiar sight they'd find in an *ordinary* doctor's office.'

'Ah, I see.' A thin smile, slightly embarrassed. 'How clever.'

Kári took a seat behind his desk. Auður sat opposite him, obviously with something on her mind she had problem getting to.

'I'm actually here unofficially, so to speak. If that's all right with you?'

His brow furrowed. His eye twitched involuntarily. 'I'm afraid I don't quite follow.'

Maybe she wanted to discuss what those agents were up to. But he doubted it. This was it. She was going to ask him about Svartiskóli.

'I'd like you to conduct a quick examination. And I would like to ask you, as a favour, to keep whatever the results might be to *yourself*.'

'I see.' Kári held back a sigh of relief. 'Which member of your staff does this regard?'

'Myself.'

'What do you suspect is wrong?'

She leaned back in her seat, gathering her thoughts.

'There is something deeply wrong with this place. Can you feel it? It's in the air itself.'

He mulled this over. 'Well ... I'm not quite sure, to be honest. After the wards were put up, the seiðmagn here isn't as volatile. But what radiates out from beneath the earth is very different.'

Auður snorted. 'Different. That's an understatement.' She leaned in towards him, lowering her voice. 'You seiðskrattar have those lenses in your masks. Haven't you noticed how strange it looks? The flows and ebbs, the colours—'

'I asked Vésteinn about it. He said it was "within parameters". Apparently it's similar to levels in Öskjuhlíð. I can't speak on that, but ... I'm not sure if he was telling the truth. Or if he was, I have a hard time believing he's so nonchalant about it.'

'Even for something as supernatural as seiðmagn – it's all off. And that's not even half of it.'

She reached into her coat and pulled out three pieces of rock, placing them on the desk in front of her. He took a closer look.

One was a fragment of what looked like pottery. Very faint etchings were visible, a language or type of runes he had never seen before. The second was a piece of rock with a shape in it that looked like an insect or a seashell. The third had faint lines that curved slightly in a similar manner – a small section of larger concentric circles.

'At the pace they're telling us to dig, it's a small miracle we managed to dig these up in such a good condition. We found dozens of these when we started digging up the landvættur, as well as during the excavation of the buildings surrounding the main site. First, the pottery. The language doesn't match anything we've ever seen before. Second, a sea creature – and remember, we're not digging up a marine sediment. I personally believe it to be some distant relative of a trilobite – but that's just speculation at this point. Something that's also never been seen before.'

'Mutated?' he offered.

'It must have been. Trilobites went globally extinct around 250 million years ago and it's clearly closely related to them, but the fossil is much younger than that. But you never know with a volatile place like Hrímland. And finally there's this – a piece of a tree.'

He picked up the fossilised tree, studying the curvature.

'It must have been massive.'

'It was. It was a giant sequoia, at least ten metres in diameter. And there were hundreds, or perhaps thousands of them here at some point. This we've been able to confirm without a doubt. It's the most definitive proof we have for the age of the site.'

'All right.' He wasn't familiar with trees and had trouble understanding what she was getting at. 'So what?'

'So *what*?' She sighed in frustration. 'This is a species of tree that predates settlement.'

'I'm not a child, Auður. So there were people living here before our ancestors?' he ventured. 'I suppose that's not too unlikely—'

'No, Kári,' she interjected. 'This place predates *mankind* – and every other sentient species we're aware of – by *millions of years*. Our primate ancestors were not yet standing upright when this place was built. We've used the standard rituals to place these fossils in time, and their readings are all over the place. But one thing is sure – this city was built millions of years ago, when the island was covered with a temperate forest, dense with massive giant sequoias. Trees now extinct in almost every part of the world, relics of a distant era in earth's history. Estimates place the remains from five to ten million years ago, in the mid to late Miocene epoch. But when we look at the geological layers, the data doesn't match. We looked for the obvious markers – volcanic eruptions in the last centuries, millennia – and found nothing. A site of this age shouldn't be this close to the surface – these ruins should not be so well preserved. This whole place exists out of time.'

'What does that mean?'

Auður shook her head. 'I don't know. Something bizarre happened here and it affected this place profoundly. Nothing is right here, Kári. Nothing. Hrímland has been settled by sentient species for a thousand years, give or take a few centuries. According to the sagas, it was only at that point in time that parts of the island became safe for permanent habitation.'

Like any other Hrímlander, Kári was intimately familiar with the sagas. They told of the bloody vendettas settlers had waged against one another. Humans fighting humans as well as warring with the náskárar, who had settled the island at the same time. After the initial time of chaotic bloodshed, other races such as the marbendlar moved in, laying claim to the surrounding ocean floors, the rivers and great lakes.

'There are no historical records of any other settlements existing previously in Hrímland,' Auður continued. 'Nothing in Hrímland's history correlates to these findings. This is a massive discovery.' Her tone was grave, despite her excitement at this prospect. 'This might be the key to why Hrímland is the way it is – an anomaly in the world. But to them – Vésteinn, Þráinn, Ingi – it's not even a footnote.'

'They know something,' said Kári. 'Or they just might not care. Who do you think built this?'

Auður reached into her coat pocket for a packet of cigarettes. She played with the packet for a while, turning it over in her hand, weighing what she was about to say.

'I have theories. Speculations.'

He waited for her to continue. She stared at the cigarettes as if they might conceal the answers she was looking for.

'Are you familiar with the old religion?'

'It was outlawed long before we were born.'

She shook a cigarette out of the packet, lighting it.

'Just the practice, not studying it. The landvættir played a huge role in its mythology. I've spent considerable time researching it because of that. As I was puzzling over this, I recalled a different myth. One of an ancient race of primordial giants – jötnar. Beings of rampant destruction, born of the raw chaos that predated creation.'

Not that long before, he would have laughed in her face and told her she was losing it. The very notion of reacting in such a manner now seemed preposterous. He stood on the grave of a primordial being which they intended to dig up and turn into a machine.

'You think that's what we're seeing here? The ruins of the jötnar?'

She tapped her cigarette on the floor.

'I don't know. As I said, these are myths, not history. Normally, I'd never consider something so preposterous. Every religion has this type of nonsense in their creation stories. But this place leaves me grasping for answers – any answer – like someone cast overboard in a storm.'

They sat quietly for a while.

'What about yourself, Auður?' he said carefully. 'Why are you here to see me?'

'I'm worried that…' The words stuck in her throat, and she had to gather herself. 'I'm worried that I might be contaminated. Either by the seiðmagn, if you can even call it that…'

The way he tensed up didn't escape her notice. He knew, and dreaded, what she was about to say next.

'... or by *outside* influence.'

Denial was his first response.

'You mean transmundane influence?'

She nodded, allowed a moment to pass to let it settle in before continuing.

'I've checked myself. I can't see anything. But I might be blind to it, somehow. I'm not sure if that's possible, but I know I have to make sure.'

'Then let's waste no time.' He got up and gestured towards the examination room. 'After you.'

White tarps sectioned off the room from the lab. Kári lit the central stove with a flex of his will, throwing in a few blocks of compressed fuel. The cold space started to warm up.

He put on his robes and mask and visibly jumped when he turned to see Auður alight with the unsettling blue radiance that clearly indicated demonic possession. Before he could say or do anything, Auður apologised.

'It's the workwear. Don't worry just yet, let me take it off.'

As she took off the coat and hung it up he saw that most of the light had been coming from it, not her. It was lined with bones – ribs and femurs and smaller pieces intertwined into a mesh of armour. She took off more layers – a woollen waistcoat, her bulky trousers and boots, all riddled with hidden bones – and folded the clothes neatly on top of a chair.

'Is that safe?' he asked, more than a bit uncertain.

She turned the waistcoat over and showed him the lining of ribs attached to the inside. Runes were carved into the bones in tight patterns, acting as powerful wards.

'You wear the robes and mask – I have my own type of regalia. These forces are tightly contained and I inspect them more regularly than a soldier does their rifle. This is not what I'm worried about.'

She took a seat on the examination bed, looking at him expectantly.

'So? Anything?'

He gestured for her to lie down and inspected her carefully. There were traces of seiðmagn – nothing dangerous, though, likely thanks to her own demonic wards – but that was it.

'Nothing transmundane, at least at first glance. Please turn over.'

He noticed her hesitation and understood why when she turned over on her stomach. There was something wrong with her back. A faint glow, not quite like the blue shimmer of demonic manifestation.

'There's something there,' she said, noticing him freezing up. 'I haven't been able to examine it properly. It's on the middle of my upper back. I can feel it.'

'I have to take a closer look, please.'

She lifted up her shirt. On Auður's bare back, in between her shoulder blades, was a faint spiral pattern, elliptical in shape.

Kári felt certain he had seen it before.

He put on his gloves, cursing himself for not having done so already. The shape was raised, almost as if it was scabbing. Like a new tattoo healing. Something caught his eye. An almost invisible growth of fine hairs, or at least something that resembled hairs, covered the spiral. It glowed with bizarre hypercolours.

'When did you first notice something was wrong?'

'I think around a week ago. I haven't been sleeping well.'

'How is that related?'

Auður hesitated. 'I've been having nightmares about this place. I have a hard time recalling them when I wake up, but one thing I always remember. A warped spiral. Then I felt that it had started to appear on my back. Faint, at first. Less than an itch. Then it got worse.'

'Why didn't you let me know immediately?'

She turned and glared at him. 'I thought I could deal with it myself, Kári. Surely *you*, of all people, must understand that instinct.'

Kári fell quiet.

How does she know? Does Vésteinn know everything? Has he told her? Does everyone know?

'Sorry,' Auður went on, sighing. 'That was rude of me. We're each permitted our secrets. Mastering the secret and the unknown is practically our profession.'

Kári nodded, too flustered to say anything. He was thankful for the mask, shielding him from revealing just how vulnerable and anxious he felt. He turned away as Auður started to get dressed to give her some privacy.

After a while he managed, 'How did you know?'

'I didn't want you here, at first. I had to be sure you had nothing to do with… what happened to my mother. I asked Vésteinn. He told me you were as much a victim as she was. So rest assured your secret is safe with me.'

'Yes. Um, thank you,' he mumbled, clearing his throat. 'I'll have to do a thorough thaumaturgical examination. Of your tent, where you've been working. Other members of your crew.' He thought for a while. 'What kind of work have you been doing for the last week?'

'Besides overseeing the dig, I've spent most of my time down there. At the bottom of the main excavation site. Trying to…' Auður swallowed. 'I'm trying to wake it up.'

ᚼ

During their meetings since they set out from Reykjavík, it had been clear that no one had known exactly what was waiting for them down in the earth. Just as no one knew exactly what the thing in Öskjuhlíð was – the source which powered the thaumaturgical power plant in Perlan. All they knew was that whatever was underneath here was far larger, and likely far more ancient.

Ingi Vítalín was working with Leifur on building the skuggsjá. A glimpse of its purpose had been revealed to Kári: it was a device that would allow them to see into the past, built in accordance to designs of the beings from Laí. Leifur and Vésteinn were in charge of its construction.

It did not make any sense. The very idea of a machine that saw through time itself was outrageous. But if it was true what Auður claimed, that the site was millions of years old, perhaps such a device would be indispensable.

Kári's questions were only met with vague answers and silence. This was clearly on a need-to-know basis. Instead, he asked Auður.

'I'm as much in the dark as you are,' she said. 'I only had the privilege of knowing before you did. I must admit, I'm unsure what I'm doing here exactly if this thing can truly see into the past.'

'Right. Why build that if you have dozens of archaeologists?'

'I suspect we're only here to excavate the beast itself. Any valuable findings are supplemental. I've managed to sneak in a few questions to that *machine* since we set off from Eyjar. He is elusive, but he can't help himself if you goad him in the right way. I'm not sure, but I'm starting to think the skuggsjá is not limited to the past. I think it's a device that pierces through time and space itself.'

'So, you mean...'

'Yeah. It can see the future. Any place – at any time.'

Kári asked Auður further about her dreams, before she left the medical lab. It confirmed his suspicions. The deeper they managed to excavate, the worse the dreams became. And she wasn't the only one experiencing it.

Unlike Auður, he could recall most of his own fever dreams. He was back in Svartiskóli, scrambling through its hallways, trapped in that horrific maze. He ran from deformed monsters, who often took the form of his own family members. Eventually, he found himself surrounded, unable to breathe due to what he was again forced to do to himself.

When he woke in panic, he'd run to the mirror, terrified out of his mind, filled with dread as he knew what he would see.

That same spiral symbol as Auður. Twisting on his featureless face. As though it was alive and trying to tell him something.

And in the distance, he would hear thunder, crashing again and again, drawing closer, until the storm broke through with a wild roar and truly woke him up, screaming incoherent words in the dark.

Auður listened to this in chilling silence. She left him with one final question.

'Have you ever wondered how they knew where to find this place? In the middle of a perpetual thaumaturgical storm, untouched for aeons? How on earth could they have pieced that together?'

Kári was too ashamed to admit that he had not truly considered that.

'Laí?' he ventured.

She shook her head. 'Maybe. But I don't think so. Laí has apparently been in contact with the Crown since the protests. But I think I know when this chain of events started. Almost six years ago, when Vésteinn took me off the anomaly in Öskjuhlíð.'

'The black pyramid.'

'He locked himself in there for weeks. And I think he found something – something that led him here.'

'What?' Kári asked dumbly. 'What did he find? What *is* in there, Auður?'

Her face was lined with dread as she replied.

'I don't know how to describe it. A wound in reality. A void unlike any other I've heard of – it watches you. Listens.'

She shivered, and it wasn't from the cold. She pulled up the collar of her jacket and went out into the frozen tundra.

Átta

After the incident Elka had gone straight home, taken two of the pills Styrmir had provided, and fallen asleep. When Sölvi came home from school and asked her why she was back before him, she said she was sick. He sat down at the table and started to read quietly while she lay there, still and silent. It wasn't until he started making porridge for dinner that she realised how late it had got and went to help him.

'It's fine, you can rest. I can cook when Aunt Rósa is visiting,' Sölvi said cheerfully.

Elka almost cracked up laughing, she was so blindsided by his comment. She barely held it in, sensing Sölvi's grave attempt to be mature about the situation.

'How do you know about that? You're only ten years old!'

He shrugged. 'I know a great deal more about things than other silly children. Amma Dagmar told me, of course. Girls have periods and then they don't feel so well, so a man should step up and be helpful for a change.' She could hear her mother talking through him. 'It's all right if you want to rest, I'm more than capable of taking care of you.'

Of course. Her mother. Elka felt an odd pull at her heart. Thankfulness, regret, sorrow, resentment.

'It's not that, Sölvi. But thank you.'

He thought for a moment, mulling something over.

'I know it's hard, Mamma,' he said comfortingly as she watched him stirring the pot. 'It's also been hard at school. Most of the time I don't want to get up to go. Sometimes I dream I'm back in Reykjavík, but summer is here, and I run through the streets with my friends and we own the whole city. All the sweets in the shop, all the food we can eat. I'm a king and I can paint the sky, paint clouds and birds on it and strange colours, not like these boring greys, and the moon speaks to me. There is another king on the moon and we are brothers.'

He took the pot off the stove and placed it on the table, remembering just before he put it down to place a table mat beneath it.

'But then I wake up. And I go to school.'

They sat down at the table and Elka lit a tallow candle for them. They ate in silence.

᚜

The next morning, Sölvi got up and went to school. Elka stayed in bed.

Her whole body ached. It was not a physical pain. She felt raw, as if she was covered in tiny cuts, still fresh and bleeding. It had worsened since the day before. She took two pills, hesitated, then added the third. Again that bitter taste, the ghost of a familiar feeling. She fell asleep almost instantly.

She woke up to someone saying her name. Turning over in the bed, she grimaced from muscle pains all over, her head ringing with a sharp headache. A sharply dressed woman sat in her room, black skirt neatly folded, a bag filled with groceries at her feet.

'Reverend Bryde,' Elka said hoarsely. 'I...' She drifted off. She didn't know what to say.

'I heard about the incident yesterday, dear.' Bryde shook

her head, not unkindly. 'That Björg can be a fool. All she and Innréttingarnar care about are profits and maximum efficiency, when they should care more for the workers whose toil keeps their purses full.'

Elka felt her heart start to race. Why was Bryde here, and not Björg? Was she fired? Why had Bryde brought the food – a farewell gift? Elka realised with a heavy heart that they were going to deport her.

'Please, Reverend.' Her voice broke. 'I don't want to leave. I have nowhere to go. Please, it wasn't my fault—'

She broke down crying. Bryde gently placed a hand on her head as Elka buried her face in the pillow and sheets, ashamed of looking so pathetic in front of this woman.

'Elka, no. You misunderstand. No one is going to send you away. You're one of us, remember? You're a Vestmannaeyingur.'

'They fired me, didn't they? So I have no vistarband – no way of living here any more.'

'Listen to me, Elka. Please calm yourself down.'

Bryde's tone was soft but commanding, putting Elka at ease. Maybe she really was here to help. But why? She was practically a stranger.

'They weren't happy at Ísfélagið, I can tell you that. But Björg let me know what happened and I took it upon myself to attend their little meeting. Everyone knows that workers have to use various . . . methods to get the results the board wants. Björg explained to them how it had happened, how it was an accident, and I, despite not having any authority there, spoke on your behalf as well.' She gripped Elka's hand tightly, giving her a calming smile. 'We are a community here in Vestmannaeyjar, Elka. That means we take care of one another. When our brother stumbles, we do not let him fall. When our sister errs, we do not cast her away. No – we embrace them. We help them, and so we help one another. These men listened to reason. They know who your mother was, how hard you have been working, how important this is to you. You still have a job at Ísfélagið. No one will blame you for what happened. We work closely with the sea – and it is an awesome and deep power to meddle with. Ships sink, by misfortune or storms. People get hurt, due to tiredness or happenstance. You are the one who got hurt, Elka, and it was an accident. It was not your fault, nor Björg's, nor anyone else's. It is a chance we take every day that we fetch the glorious bounty of the depths and thus sustain ourselves. You have friends here, my dear. And I would be honoured if you would count me as one of them.'

Elka was stunned. Bryde still held her hand, stroking it gently as she talked, letting it go after she had finished. Elka sat up in the bed and wiped her face, suddenly feeling very vulnerable. Something was bothering her.

'Wait... you just walked into their meeting? Uninvited? Because of me?'

Bryde nodded. 'That's right.'

'Why?'

At this, the priest looked upon her with what could almost be described as pity.

'Because I truly believe what I just said. We have to take care of one another. Every soul is worth saving. Every person has worth. Especially you, Elka.' She reached out her hand and tucked Elka's hair behind her ear. 'You never should have left us. That was your mother's failing, I'm sorry to say. So many never returned after the eruption. That mistake has brought you so much pain and misfortune. This is where you belong.'

Bryde patted her on the shoulder and got up. She fetched something from her purse and handed it to Elka – a small box, made in a lustrous dark wood.

'I've noticed the medicine on your bedside table,' Bryde said, and glanced at the pills Elka had carelessly left out. Elka was mortified by the realisation, but Bryde only gave her a smile. 'It is terrible stuff – not nearly of high enough quality. But I understand very well that you need it, especially now. The pills in the box I've given you there are so much better for you. In fact…'

She reached for the box Styrmir had given to Elka and put it in her purse.

'I think it's best that you avoid taking this dreadful stuff. You can always come to me if you need more of what I brought you – or any kind of help. I would be glad to give it, even if I can only offer words of comfort and encouragement. I will never judge you for wanting to get better, Elka.'

'Thank you,' was all Elka could say.

'Nothing at all. Now, I should get going. You need rest. Give yourself time to heal, Elka. Take a few more of those pills if you want. They will calm you and help your soul recover from the strain.'

'I thought more than one a day was supposed to be bad for you. I…' Elka swallowed, afraid of admitting the truth. 'I've already taken a few at once. And I think they made me feel even worse.'

'That's because it's dreadful stuff, Elka. I called it medicine, but that is a misnomer. It's poison. Weak, but poison nonetheless. These, however, are quite safe – trust me on this. I don't know who gave you those other pills, but if you don't mind me saying, I doubt it's a very trustworthy person.' Bryde took on a grave manner, placing a hand on her shoulder. 'Poison takes many forms. Sometimes a single person can prove more toxic than any narcotic. You must surround yourself with good people, Elka. People who *truly care* for one another.' At this the priest hesitated for a while, considering something. 'You know, I think I know just the remedy for that particular problem. A good friend of mine – a captain of my shoal, as we say in the Church – is throwing a party on the First Day of Summer. You should go, Elka. I'll talk to him and make sure that you get to know new people, good people.'

'Reverend, I don't know if—'

'Nonsense. It'll do wonders for you, trust me.'

'All right. Thank you.'

'Think nothing of it.'

Elka got up to escort Bryde out, but the priest ushered her right back into bed. She asked Elka to give her regards to Sölvi, and said that she'd left a few things in the grocery bag for him. Elka said she would, and then found herself alone again.

The pills Bryde had given her were quite different. Perfectly round and a lustrous black that shone with reflected light, they looked so much like pearls that she almost doubted they were truly medicine. She still felt awful, so she took a couple and lay back down.

The daze crept up on her, so slowly she almost didn't realise it was happening. When it hit, it was heavy and so satisfying that she almost cried out in relief. Finally she felt more than just barely fine – she felt wonderful. A numbness washed over her and she let go with delight, drowning herself in its cold and encompassing depths, all pain and regret becoming instantly distant and faded.

ᚼ

The main laboratory was the largest structure they had erected, composed of two altered freight carriages attached together. It was windowless, its only entrance a heavy steel door on one carriage, guarded at all times by soldiers. They hesitated to let

Kári through, despite his regalia, but when he threatened to involve Vésteinn, the soldiers gave in.

The lab was dimly lit by sparsely placed fluorescent lighting. It was a strict contrast of thaumaturgical energies, seen through the lenses of his mask. Dead, neutral areas, interspersed with dense, vibrant colours of the dormant batteries. He heard voices coming from within.

'...the temporal adjustments as necessary.' Leifur's voice echoed in the silent space. 'The sigil won't draw on causal energies, instead it— Hello? Who's there?'

Leifur was bent over a desk filled with diagrams and blueprints, which he hastily covered. A cigarette burned in an ashtray on the table. The machine called Ingi Vítalín stood nearby, its light pulsating with a dim glow.

The room was dominated by a massive machine, covered with a tarp. Scores of cables ran underneath it, plugged into stacks of thaumaturgical batteries.

'Ah! Magister Kvalráður! How pleasant to see you drop in!' Ingi sounded as if he positively beamed, a stark contrast to Leifur's grimace. He looked worn-out, haggard, as if he hadn't slept for days.

'I'm sorry to intrude,' Kári said. 'I'm conducting a medical examination on all critical staff. We've had some... Well, I have reason to believe we might be facing critical contamination.'

'I'm fine,' Leifur spat. 'Examination concluded.'

Kári saw no significant traces on him, but Leifur was wearing his robes, effectively masking most of his body.

'What's happened?' Ingi asked in a worried tone that was almost mockingly exaggerated.

'I can't divulge specifics, but I have reason to believe that the... dormant power source beneath us has already started to infect the environment. Including our bodies.'

'So start by checking on Auður and her crew and be done with it. I don't work out in the field.'

'Now, now, Magister Launvaldur,' Ingi interjected jovially. 'Let Magister Kvalráður conduct his work as he best deems suitable. It's for the benefit of all that this project suffers no delays or complications.'

'I've already checked the archaeological crew, Leifur. I have grounds for this examination, trust me on that.'

Leifur grunted. 'Fine. I'm busy for the next few days. Next Seiðday?'

'I'd rather be done with this quickly. Later today?'

'Impossible, I'm afraid,' Ingi interjected. 'We have quite the job ahead of us. Magister Launvaldur will be very busy, indeed.'

'Yes, our *guests* will be here soon.' Leifur did not sound thrilled by the prospect.

'I'm afraid I must insist.' Wearing the mask, Kári found it easier to lend his voice an authoritative tone.

'*Fine*. I think we're done here, anyway.' Leifur rubbed his eyes as he rolled up the diagrams.

'For now,' Ingi added.

'Very well,' Kári said. 'Please, follow me.'

He headed to the door and Leifur followed, after having tossed off his robes, dropping them over a chair. Kári was not one to stand on ceremony, but the disregard for the regalia made him dislike Leifur that much more.

Ingi Vítalín watched them leave. The hum of machines was the only sound left in their wake.

Back at the medical facility, Kári was quick to scan for thaumaturgical contamination and demonic influence. His equipment showed no trace of either in Leifur, as he had suspected. If Leifur had no reason to worry, and nothing had showed up in the lab through his lenses, then there was no reason for a more detailed examination.

'Tell me,' Kári said as he unclasped the buckles on his mask, checking himself in the mirror before he revealed his face. It was always a short moment of panic as he did so. 'Have you been having any peculiar dreams?'

Leifur reached in his coat for a flask. He checked if Kári was going to object, and when no response was given he took a sip.

'Always.'

'I mean since we arrived. Have your dreams shown you anything… out of the ordinary?' He wasn't sure how blunt he should be. He was too uncouth to actually figure out a way around the matter. 'Has anything changed since you started working on the skuggsjá?'

'That's classified. And anyway, it's not ready yet. We've been having some problems.'

Kári reached out his hand for the flask. Leifur obliged and handed it over. It tasted like shit – landi, most likely. Moonshine so potent it could be used to sterilise medical equipment.

'I understand.' Kári coughed as the spirit hit his throat. 'But I worry that… as we further interact with the power source we are excavating, it could lead to…' Again, he struggled for words. 'Suffice to say, I have my own classified reasons to believe it could be dangerous.'

'I'll be sure to let you know when I feel under the weather, *Magister*. Or if my nightmares take a new form. As of yet, they remain as unpleasantly stagnant as ever.'

He stood up to leave. In a last-ditch effort, Kári unfolded a piece of paper, holding it in front of him.

Leifur froze. The cigarette trembled between his fingers.

'What is this? Is it a sigil?' Kári tried desperately to read his stone-faced reaction. 'You recognise it, don't you?'

'Where did you get that?' Leifur hissed.

'Doctor–patient confidentiality. What's it from? What's it for?'

He glared. They were at a stalemate.

'Look…' Kári sat down, exasperated. 'Help me so I can help you. I can tell you where I got the symbol from, if you can tell me how you know of it and what the skuggsjá does. Something's about to go wrong here, I can feel it. Like a storm that's—'

'Thank you for your time.' Leifur put out the cigarette under the heel of his boot. 'If you don't mind, I still have work to do.'

ᚼ

Elka was terrified to go back to work. Would people judge her? Be afraid of her? Resent her? Or perhaps worst of all – pity her? Her heart raced as she walked through the crisp morning, breath steaming in the fresh air.

All of her worries were for nought.

People greeted her warmly, as if she had just taken normal sick leave. They asked if she was feeling fine and she said yes, and that was the end of it. Her old gloves were waiting for her among her regular workwear and she was put back on the line. Having taken her new medicine that morning, her hands no longer trembled and time slipped easily from her grasp. Before she knew it, the day was over and she had almost managed to keep up.

She avoided Styrmir. After what Bryde had said, she didn't want anything to do with him.

Björg surprised her a few days later by asking if she was attending the party on the First Day of Summer. She said it was unlikely she could make it, but any excuses about not being able to leave Sölvi home by himself didn't pass muster. Several women offered their help, Björg chief among them. Elka suspected that Bryde had told Björg about the party exactly for this reason.

Of all people, Elka did not expect Björg to offer watching over Sölvi. The woman could be very standoffish – that was the price of being foreman – but the atmosphere between the two of them had reached a rigid freezing point after the incident. Putting those sigils in her gloves ... the nerve of that woman. It had upset Elka more than she wanted to admit. But Björg was family – that had to mean something, right? She deserved another chance. The aftermath had made Björg slightly more relaxed when it came to pushing Elka, giving her the space she needed to get into the rhythm of work. The pills from Bryde also helped a lot.

It was clear how much Björg wanted to make amends by helping, even if it was only because Bryde had asked her to. Björg was stubborn, raised in an environment where mistakes could be lethal. She was never going to apologise with words. This was as much as Elka would get in that department.

Elka quickly ran out of excuses.

She was afraid of being alone. Just herself and the addiction every cold, sleepless night. Surrounding herself with people felt too enticing. Left alone, she was faced with the one problem that never went anywhere: herself.

ᚻ

'How long will you be out?'

Sölvi sat on the floor, drawing on the back of old maths homework sheets. Elka took a hard look at herself and tried to get her eyeliner the way she wanted.

'Not that long. And it's just down the road, so don't worry.'

'But when will you come home?'

He focused on the clock sitting atop the dresser. It was Amma Dagmar's, on which she had taught him to tell the time. The hands showed it was a quarter to eight.

'Around midnight. You be nice to Björg and do what she says, all right?'

'She doesn't have to read *Todda* to me. I can do it myself.'

Todda In Two Countries had been Sölvi's favourite book ever since he was a toddler. The descriptions of the little girl living in Hafnía completely enchanted him, no matter how often he'd heard the story. Every night since they'd got here, it was the only thing he wanted to read – although he always lost interest when Todda decided to return to Hrímland. Elka indulged him, hoping that the children's book might motivate him to one day leave Hrímland and escape to real civilisation. To the mainland, where he could become whatever he wanted to.

'I'm sure she'll be more than happy to read to you. But it's fine if you want to do it yourself.'

Satisfied with her make-up, Elka kneeled next to Sölvi, placing a hand on his shoulder. He stayed focused on his drawing.

'I won't be long. And... Heimaey is not Reykjavík. Things will be all right.'

She stroked his head, fingers moving through his blond hair. What a short time ago he had been just a little baby. He shirked away, the touch too coddling, or simply because he was upset. She couldn't help but feel a bit hurt herself. She took a look at the picture he was drawing.

'That's wonderful, Sölvi. Heimaklettur is even more beautiful how you've drawn it.' Ships were landing by its docks, while up on the sheer cliffs of the Vestmannaeyjar harbour stood a figure Sölvi was labouring over. 'Who is that? You?'

He shook his head.

'It's the man with the horns. He lives in the rocks.'

'Is that so? Like the huldufólk used to?'

'No. He's hiding in them.'

'I see.'

She now noticed the twisted horns on the creature's head, a fierce tangle of obsidian darkness.

'Right, time to put all this away and get into your pyjamas. Björg frænka is almost here.'

ᚻ

As Elka stepped out of the house, relief and excitement over-whelmed her. Finally something was going to happen in this place. She might even permit herself a few drinks; it wasn't as if brennivín was sorti. It was completely different. And she hadn't even thought of smoking at all. Not like *that*, anyway – not seriously. It just popped into her head once in a while, like anything else. It didn't matter.

She lit a cigarette, savouring it by herself. She had filled up a flask on the inside of her coat. The brennivín had been expensive, but she wasn't interested in drinking landi tonight. The moonshine they brewed here was even rougher than in Reykjavík, and she didn't intend to completely drink her mind away tonight. The burn from the rough liquor intermingled with the cigarette wonderfully.

She wrapped her shawl tighter around herself and looked up the road, towards Helgafell and Eldfell. The twin volcanoes were a darker shadow against the grey-black sky. The brennivín tasted of caraway seeds and reminded Elka of her teenage years. When she was young and everything was possible and the future was bright. When she had first met Sölvi's father, even though they wouldn't become an item for quite a while.

She remembered waking up to a bad dream, cold from sweat, the eyes in the mirror not belonging to a person. Floating in the dregs of the high, she had pulled away the curtains and seen a new nightmare, more horrible than the worst trips she'd experienced. Demons among men. Up in the sky burned the eye of a hateful god – made from steel, smoke and living darkness. The demonic fortress bombarded the city, an apocalyptic war taking place in front of her.

Out on the street she saw things that eroded her sense of reality. She saw a man devoured by his own limbs. She saw an undulating monstrosity crash into a building, debris and blubber and gore scattered everywhere. She saw soldiers shoot down a legion of winged demons. Some of them had been human.

Sölvi was with his grandmother then. In the back of her mind Elka figured that he was as safe as possible. This was all a bad trip, anyway; it couldn't be happening. She'd lit herself another pipe, then lain back down and tried to forget this waking nightmare. But it had been all too real.

Many days later, word reached Elka that Sölvi's father had died in the chaos. His remains were incinerated; the family couldn't even keep the ashes. No one got any definite answers about what had happened to him. The uncertainty was torture. But Elka was skilled at painting things in a different light, rearranging uncomfortable, jagged details in her mind until everything fitted nicely together.

She'd buried the pain so deep it was as if it had never been there to begin with.

The summer party was held in a newly built three-storey house. Every window blazed with warm light, while laughter and music spilled on to the street. The door was open so she walked into the warmth, glad she had started early on her flask when she noticed the lull wash over the festivities following her appearance. Elka, the freak who'd blown up a day's worth of catch.

The living room was furnished with velvet couches and gleaming wooden tables. A small crystal chandelier hung from the ceiling. Everyone there was human, except for a huldufólk couple sitting together on one couch. She remembered them from the funeral, and they gave her a small wave. She didn't recognise anyone else – at most, a handful of people she had seen only in passing. She nodded nervously. Everyone was drinking what looked like landi mixed into malt soda or home-brewed beer. The cloudy ale didn't look very appetising, but the malt seemed fine. No doubt the sugar dampened the almost poisonous home-made alcohol.

Then Styrmir walked in from the kitchen, holding a glass of dark liquid. He was as shocked at seeing her as she was.

'Elka,' he said, somewhat rudely. 'What are you doing here?'

'I was invited,' she said, setting her jaw defiantly. The sting of her words did not go unnoticed by Styrmir.

'Indeed, she was,' said a resounding voice behind her, deep and steadfast like the keel of a ship.

Elka started and turned around. The man was tall and strongly built, dressed in a tailored tweed suit in slate grey, tastefully accented by a deep blue woollen shirt. His straw-coloured hair was neatly styled with brilliantine, his thick beard trimmed just to the point of looking wild. His eyes focused on her, drawn to her like a compass pointing north.

The man reached out a hand and Elka shook it. Strong and calloused – like driftwood polished by the waves.

'Ægir Manesseus Hafdal. Pleasure to make your acquaintance, Elka. Welcome to my home.' His azure eyes sparkled with curiosity. 'The good reverend was not exaggerating in her description.'

'And what did she say?'

'That you were more dazzling than any jewel of the sea.'

Elka tried not to blush, despite it being such a ridiculously tacky thing to say. But it sounded different said by him. His voice was intoxicating, deep and rumbling. It awoke something within her, stirring embers that had long been left untended.

'Are you from Eyjar?' Ægir continued.

'She's Björg's niece,' Styrmir interjected. That flirtatious comment had clearly irked him. 'Just moved here from Reykjavík.'

Elka felt embarrassed. 'I applied like everyone else. I have a vistarband, of course.'

'Of course. So you're Dagmar's daughter.' Ægir gestured at her and Styrmir. 'And how do you two know each other?'

'Me and Elka—' Styrmir began before Elka interrupted.

'We both work at Ísfélagið.'

Styrmir bit back whatever he was going to say.

'And you two?' Elka asked the two men.

'Styrmir is working this summer on my ship, Þurfalingur. Elka, we are truly blessed to have you back home in Vestmannaeyjar, where you belong.'

'It's much better here than I thought.' She became flustered, worried she had offended him.

Ægir laughed deeply, reading her expression clearly. 'Don't worry! We lead a much simpler life here than in the city, I'm sure the first few days must have been dreadful. But in time I think you'll see just how much more giving a more grounded way of living can be.'

'I already can't imagine leaving.'

That wasn't quite true, but when speaking to Ægir it *felt* true.

'We were all saddened that Dagmar never returned after the eruption. As well as so many others. Your mother was such a valued member of our community – and what a wonderful community it is. I do hope that you'll consider attending Mass.'

'Mamma was a part of the Church?'

'Oh yes,' said Ægir. 'Although I was just a small boy when

178

the eruption started, I remember her clearly. You have much of her in you.'

'Thank you,' she muttered.

Dagmar had never told her about the Church, or anything about her life in Vestmannaeyjar. Elka was born in the year of the eruption.

'Reverend Bryde was kind enough to invite me to church,' she said, trying to steer the conversation away from her mother. 'She's proven to be a great help.'

'Klara is a remarkable and generous woman. Truly as someone lifted from the holier days of a bygone era. Styrmir, why don't you get Elka a drink? It's tradition that the captain always hosts a party for the crew at the start of summer season – but the company pays for the booze! Let's not put our benefactors' gifts to waste. There's a small amount of good wine in the kitchen, for the more refined members of our gathering.' He gave Elka a knowing look. 'If you won't tell anyone, then I sure won't! Not all wish to drink like sailors, despite being in a party with them!'

Styrmir went to fetch her a drink, looking put down. Left alone with Ægir, she found herself feeling nervous.

'Klara told me about the problems you've had at the factory.'

Elka started to respond, not even sure what she was about to say, but he held up a hand and smiled.

'Such things have happened before – admittedly, not quite on such a scale – but it's not the first time a foreman, or even a captain, desperate to exceed their quota and push their underlings, has taken such measures.'

'Yes, well. These things are illegal for a reason.'

Ægir nodded approvingly. 'Indeed, so they are. I run a tight ship, Elka, and that includes a commitment to not risk myself or my crew with this cursed kukl. Believe it or not, things used to be far worse here. Using charms for fair weather, safe sailing, warding off drowning... All these things and more were as common as fishing nets a few years ago.'

She was shocked to hear him speak so frankly.

'What changed?'

'The Deep,' he said in a low voice, almost conspiratorial. 'The Messengers are no mere fables, Elka. They are very real. They have saved my life on more than one occasion – they keep our nets full and our ships safe. A man of faith need not rely on the occult.'

She wasn't sure what to make of that. He chuckled to himself.

'Just ask Björg, when you get the chance. She will confirm as much. Although she still relies on those ghosts of the past.'

Styrmir came back with a glass of wine for her, having mixed a strong beer for himself. They sat down on a sofa with the others and Elka lit herself a cigarette, throwing a greeting to the other people.

They chatted about ordinary things – work, mostly. She lavished in it, until things shifted towards the war. They asked her how things were in Reykjavík – if it was truly as bad as it appeared in the newspapers. Elka felt awkward, put on the spot.

'Almar.' A large and heavily bearded man slapped his friend on the back. 'Enough of this fucking depressing shit! It's a party! Drink!'

'Yeah,' said a young-looking girl who got up and grabbed Almar's hand. 'Stop yapping and dance with me!'

The man went along with it and they danced to an old record that was going for its third round. The living room floor was small, and they were the only ones dancing.

Elka's glass was empty, so Styrmir reached for the malt and landi and mixed them both a drink. The smell of pure alcohol turned Elka's stomach.

'I wish this goddamn war was over already so we could get some real beer.'

They all looked at her as if she was crazy.

Finally Styrmir responded, carefully. 'It's not because of the war, Elka. Beer is illegal in Vestmannaeyjar.' He added under his breath, 'So is the wine. That's why Ægir said not to tell anyone.'

'Oh. Well … skál, then.'

'Skál!'

ꚽ

After work she headed to thank Bryde for her help. The unseasonal cold made her cheeks flush as she entered the heat of Bryde's shop. The priest stood behind the counter, tallying up for a man buying a crate of brennivín. She beamed as she saw Elka enter.

'So good to see you, dear! I'll be with you in just a moment.'

Elka browsed the selection while Bryde finished her business. Thanks to her generosity, Elka's pantry was well stocked, so she permitted herself the luxury of taking in the more expensive items.

Colourful candies and dried fruit she'd never tasted or even heard of, rich perfumes and sweet-smelling powders in fanciful shades, delicate hand mirrors and a single fur coat, made from the luxurious pelt of a skuggabaldur, pitch-black and ferocious like the beasts themselves. She thought the coat was the only luxury item there that was not imported, but then her eye caught a small selection of items she'd never noticed before.

Luminescent pearls and incandescent warped shells made into the most beautiful jewellery she had ever seen. Seemingly grown together, they were decorated with a strange mixture of gold or platinum – her eyes seemed incapable of catching exactly what tone the shining metal had. She leaned in towards the glass casing the treasures were locked in, hypnotised by their ethereal beauty. Had the marbendlar made this? How had such extravagance found its way into a grocer's shop in Heimaey? Although a colonial shop like this might carry various extravagances from distant places, these must be items normally exclusive to the speciality shops in Reykjavík, frequented only by the highest tiers of the upper class.

'Wonderful, aren't they?'

Bryde had sneaked up on Elka without her noticing, but she was so entranced by the jewellery that she didn't even jump.

'I've never seen anything as beautiful in my life.'

Bryde's smile radiated as brightly as the pearls as she fished a key out of her pocket and unlocked the case.

'Isn't that funny? That is exactly what Ægir said after meeting you. It seems you made quite the impression on the good captain.' Elka felt her cheeks flush with embarrassment. 'Why don't you try one on? Just for fun.'

'Reverend, they are far too expensive. Looking is more than enough.'

'What nonsense.'

Bryde picked up a gorgeous necklace, made of delicate metallic thread, decorated with strings of pearls which seemed to emit a light of their own, with pieces of the shining seashell placed artfully between them. She placed the necklace around Elka's throat and hooked the clasp.

'A beautiful item like that should have a wearer that matches its radiance. Go ahead, look in the mirror.'

Elka obeyed as if in a trance, checking herself in a tall mirror intended for trying on the various clothes in stock. Her ragged workwear was so coarse, ugly and plain in comparison to the shimmering necklace, her hair dirty and tied in a messy bun, but still...

Despite all that, she saw herself in a new light. As someone else. Someone she could become, one day. Composed, delicate, almost regal. She fell deep into her own reflection, seeing futures and wants and hopes all manifested within the wooden frame.

'Now, isn't that just a wonderful sight?' Bryde said behind her shoulder.

'How did you get these?' Elka asked in a dull tone, idly fidgeting with the pearls. 'They're incredible.'

'They are gifts, dear. Gifts from our friends in the Deep.'

'What?'

'Oh, yes. They give gifts to the truly faithful. To those who have proven their worth and devotion. These are not for sale, you see. They are only on display so others can see what marvellous things can be granted to those who are devout. Speaking of which, I do believe I have something here...'

Bryde found another key on her chain and opened a cabinet beneath the display case, pulling out a jewellery box. Inside was a beautiful necklace, made with that same peculiar blend of platinum that almost seemed to shine on its own. Laden with pearls and vibrant gold decorations, the centrepiece was like two fishes intertwined, forming almost a kind of eye. It was by far more extravagant than any other piece on display.

She took the other necklace off Elka and put this on her instead. Elka turned towards the mirror. Before, she had felt like a queen. Now... it was a feeling she could not put into words.

'Marvellous,' said Bryde with a smile. 'Just beautiful.'

'What is it?'

Elka almost didn't dare breathe with the treasure lying around her neck. It felt so light, almost as if it was floating, submerged beneath the waves.

'It is the holy sign of the Deep. The symbol of our Church. I want you to have it, Elka. This necklace was made for you.'

Elka turned sharply around, wide-eyed.

'No, Reverend, this … This is way too much. I came here to thank you for your kindness, I can't possibly accept this. It's too much for someone like me.'

Bryde took her hands in hers and held them warmly.

'I'll have to insist, my dear. A beautiful girl like you deserves something radiant. I also wanted you to have something to carry with you that reminds you that you always have friends here. Always.'

Elka wanted to protest further, but there was something about Bryde's look that made her feel that would be very inappropriate, and possibly hurtful to the woman.

'It's … I …'

Bryde patted the back of her hand. 'You're welcome, dear.'

'Thank you, Reverend. Thank you so much. This is the most beautiful thing I've ever seen – let alone owned.'

'Then I'm very glad to have had the honour of giving it to you.' She placed a hand on Elka's shoulder, squeezing it slightly. 'Why don't you wear it to Mass this Seiðday?'

ᚼ

Kári waited until Leifur left the laboratory late that night. The early summer sun still clung to the horizon, bathing the area in a golden pink light that would last for another hour. He marched right to the lab module, waving the soldiers aside with an authority that became his station as a seiðskratti. This time they didn't give him any lip.

Ingi Vítalín was still inside. He was humming to himself, placed in a corner like just another machine after the working day was over.

'Ah, did you forget anything? Oh, no, my apologies. It's you,

Magister Kvalráður! *Óma a íana*. What a delight. How can I assist you?'

'Just Kári is fine,' he replied. 'That phrase – what does it mean?'

'It is Laí for "be happy and blessed".'

'I see. *Óma a íana*, Ingi.' The machine whirred in delight. 'I just came to chat with you, if that's all right.'

'Of course! Nothing would please me more.' Ingi hesitated, before venturing, 'I assume this isn't regarding Magister Launvaldur's health? I hope your examination went well.'

'No, it's not related to that at all. Leifur is just fine, if slightly overworked.'

'Ah, yes. The limits of the corporeal form. I can't say I miss it much! It is simply wonderful how energetic the mind becomes once it is rid of its shackles.'

'Ah ... is that so?'

'I've never felt better, Magister. The need for sleep, for dreams – all of that is wholly unnecessary once detached from the flesh. Psychological ailments, such as anxiety, depression, fear ... all those negative aspects are rendered by the body. Once, they were perhaps necessary for the survival of the species, wards placed to protect oneself and others from danger – but now I've realised they have turned to fetters.'

'So you're the future of mankind?' Kári couldn't hide the snark in his voice.

'Perhaps one future,' Ingi replied ominously. 'You would understand, if you had seen what I have.'

Kári pulled out a chair and sat down. He unfastened the clasps on his mask and took it off, not giving in to the desire to hesitate and check himself before he did.

'That's partly why I wanted to chat with you, Ingi. Your trip to Laí – it boggles the mind, truly.' He gestured to the draped machine in the room. 'Not to mention the wondrous technology you brought back.'

'Oh, yes – it was mind-boggling, to say the least!' The machine moved forward on its treads. The green glow of the eye grew brighter, giving Kári an unpleasant, clear view of the brain floating within. 'As you know, Doctor Vésteinn has demanded much of this remain classified—'

'I know, and I would not want you to breach his confidence. But... I am a senior officer on this expedition. I also have secrets I must keep, and Vésteinn trusts me to do so.'

'Indeed... I admit I have so desperately wanted to converse with you on this matter. I think I can tell you a few more details, Magister. You are one of us, after all.'

A cold chill ran down Kári's spine.

'Yes. I am.' He tried to smile to mask his discomfort. 'And please, the mask is off now – you can just call me Kári. Tell me – how did you come to be picked to go to Laí? What is it like?'

'It was a marvellous twist of fate, Magister. As if decreed by the gods themselves...'

ᚴ

'Nearly a decade ago – how time flies – I was a humble teacher at the Learned School. My life, I am afraid to admit, was wholly unremarkable. Recently divorced and approaching the wrong side of middle age, my unwholesome lifestyle was rapidly spiralling and taking its toll on me.

'In an attempt to combat my deteriorating state, I decided to go for a hike in the hills of Esja. So close to the city, it is considered relatively safe with regards to seiðmagn, and an easy enough climb for people of any age. Suffice to say, I was hacking and coughing the entire time.

'I took a break near the peak, at the traditional stopping

point of Steinn, to gaze out over the city. Its majestic walls, still unperturbed by that monstrous giant of stone, its tight cluster of buildings, monuments to the lives that thrived within its safe enclosure. How wonderful, I thought, to be alive at that moment, to be part of this wondrous era of discovery and invention. It was just a shame I was so lacking in intellect and character to take any real part in it.

'That's when a vision was revealed to me. Or so I am tempted to call it, but I now realise it was all too real. I suddenly felt the presence of another in my vicinity, despite not having encountered any other climbers on my way. I looked over my shoulder and indeed, there stood a man unlike any I had seen.

'He was dressed in a plain white shift, made from resplendent cloth, as if woven from mother-of-pearl. His visage was not entirely human, and radiated such serenity and wisdom that I immediately felt at ease, despite his unexpected appearance. He was the very picture of youth and beauty – not even in the high artworks of the ancients have I seen such ethereal qualities manifested in human form. Dumbfounded, he greeted me with that now-familiar phrase:

'"*Óma a íana.*"

'He spoke, but his lips did not part. His voice resounded within my own mind – yet I was not startled by this.

'"How do you do?" I replied in Nordic, unsure if this fellow was a native of Hrímland. He smiled beatifically and said he understood Hrímlandic well, and indeed, his voice in my mind seemed to have spoken our ancient tongue. Or so I thought at the time.

'He explained that he had sought me out, indeed summoned me through harmless but powerful psychic emanations, to ascend this mountain slope to meet with him in private. This would also explain how this popular hiking route proved so deserted today.

His name was incomprehensible to me, and as he spoke it I felt as if an unearthly wind had moved through my very soul, chilling me to the core. I decided to call him Númí. He explained he was a traveller from a distant world called Laí – which means "earth" in their tongue.

'This, much like the man's unexpected appearance, did not disturb me in the least. In fact, I remained strangely calm about this whole affair, as if nothing was more natural. The beings of Laí were seeking to make contact with mankind in a peaceful and mutually prosperous manner, he said, and they had decided that I was to act as the very first ambassador of mankind to Laí.

'Despite my uncanny sense of calm, I was perplexed. Why *me*, of all the accomplished men and women in this world? I daresay a more mediocre and lacklustre specimen could not have been found among the multitudes of mankind. That, explained Númí, was exactly why they had chosen me. My unremarkable nature was extraordinary, my lack of ambition not to my detriment, but the opposite. It was vital that mankind's first ambassador would be an everyman, a most ordinary person, without any inclination to abuse their high status for personal gain.

'I am quite alone, you see. I have no children, no lover – only a sad, loose string of unhappy affairs – no living family. All of this had contributed to bring down my psychological well-being, but Númí assured me that those ailments and all others would be a thing of the past once I accepted.

'He explained that they had set up a base on the moon, an outpost or observational station of sorts, from where they would conduct their business with earth. Being a citizen of Kalmar and a resident of their distant colony of Hrímland, I was perfectly suited to establish a diplomatic connection to what they called the most powerful, unifying empire on the planet.

'Númí offered to show me the lunar outpost, located on the

dark side of the moon. He said this was to be done through psychometry. He held out an oddly shaped device, made from a peculiar metal marked with a convoluted throng of esoteric symbols, and told me to touch it. The effect would be rather startling to me, a man of no thaumaturgical talent, but he assured me it would be most safe.

'I reached out my hand and touched the device. In the flash of a moment, my wits were assaulted by a barrage of images of places and creatures both impossible and alien.

'I saw a dark fortress located in the luminous dusk of the barren lunar surface. It was illuminated in a sickly, eerie glow – or so I thought at the time – radiating off the local fauna. Low, twisting trees and enormous fields of lichen were what I likened them most to in my limited experience with the natural world, but I yet understood that they were wholly different. The fortress itself was reminiscent of the obsidian fortress of Svartiskóli, but made of tall, Cyclopean towers, connected with an intricate spiderweb of bridges. In a flash, I was inside the fortress, surrounded by great beings whose shapes I could not yet comprehend, so overwhelmingly bizarre and unearthly were their forms. They spread their expansive wings in what I felt like was a greeting, and I hesitantly bowed to them in return, speaking the words of greeting Númí had taught me:

'"*Óma a íana.*"

'I spoke to their elder at length, not through the vulgarity of speech, but through a linking of the minds. A debate was held for a length of time unmeasurable in this place of existence, as my limited human soul and his incomprehensibly ancient alien soul conversed on matters material, spiritual, political and personal. He told me of humanity's terrible course, and I understood immediately what he meant. War, shortage, disease and hunger – all of these things were unknown in the greater alliance of planets out in the cosmos. They desired to help us divert from this disastrous path, introduce us to a state of being where pain and suffering were a distant memory. To finish an ancient ritual of transcendence, started by our precursors long ago.

'He showed me what they had learned of our world by the application of their enigmatic machines of psychometry. In the distant past, when the continents themselves were almost unrecognisable, a great civilisation rose to splendour. I will not attempt to describe their forms, but let me assure you that mankind is merely a distant shadow of their sublime and perfect nature. Capable of higher workings we would today consider to be truly divine acts, they conquered the entire world, unifying it under a single banner. But there were those among their ranks who started to harbour discontent, unwilling to ascend to a higher state of being. These rebels rose against the harbingers of peace, bringing a horrible calamity upon the world.

'Have you ever wondered why there exists so little seiðmagn in this world? Why galdur remains such an unruly and terrible force to meddle with? The myths are true – here once reigned a veritable Age of Miracles where galdur and speech, seiður and nature were not separated by a vast chasm. From every love poem flowed arcane might, from every flower a wellspring of miraculous power. Until those short-sighted and selfish rebels brought a cataclysmic and terrible doom upon us, aeons ago.

'Oh! How it grieved me to see this played out, despite its only taking an instant! A thousand years of terrible civil war, of catastrophic disaster wrought time and time again upon innocents and nature itself, breaking and bending the world until it was a wreck of its former self.

'Rising from this polluted wasteland were the ancestors of the multitudes of sentient races and beings that we know today. Many evolutionary bloodlines perished, but among those who thrived was mankind. They saw us as the inheritor of that luminous ancient race, the crown princes and princesses of all the domains of earth. This much we inherently know, and I suspect the divine kings of Kalmar have gleaned something of this nature through their great and arcane wisdom, transcending mortal human limitations. But Kalmar is trapped in a fen of dissent much like this majestic, lost race, mired by threats of war, disease, famine and malcontents.

'If I were to take on the mantle of ambassadorial duty, further secrets would be revealed to me. He briefly communicated what that would entail, for I would have to travel to distant Laí to learn of their ways and arcane traditions, as well as rid myself of the constrictions of this corrupted flesh shell. I admit – I was afraid. Very much so. It seemed all too much like dying.

'But what is death, when faced with the annihilation of our civilisation, the human race, the world itself?

'Well – I did what any true man of Kalmar would do. I did not shirk from my responsibility – I embraced it. For the betterment of my homeland, my people, the very world which had given me life.

'Thus, my perception was returned to earth, to the gentle hills of Esja, where the being I named Númí stood by my side. Not a minute had passed, but I felt like I had been spirited away for weeks. Looking upon Númí, I saw that the veneer of humanity, an illusory veil originally placed to soothe me, had vanished. Seeing his true and magnificent form, I was moved to tears. What transcendent beauty! What majesty! Oh, Magister, I wish that I could tell you how wondrous they are in their natural form. Oh – but you will see for yourself, soon enough.

'I'm afraid I can't divulge further on the matter. You will have to wait and see for yourself. Doctor's orders, I'm afraid.

'I returned back home and felt as if the whole encounter had been a wild delusion – a waking dream. All too clearly I could see the failings of the world around me. I saw it in the classroom with my distracted students, who should have been fervent in their search for higher learning, but instead were dull-witted and apathetic. I saw it in the headlines, where suffering was so widespread and accepted. I saw it in the mirror, saggy-eyed and worn-out, a shell of a man who should have been in the bloom of his youth.

'No more, I said to myself, Magister. It is time to let go of pain … of suffering … of desire and need and short-sightedness. I shed my skin to become whole, frightening as it might seem.

'What does a fish know of the surface world? What does an ant know of human empires? Of course these limited beings would fear being placed so completely out of their natural element – to be shown that the universe is infinitely greater and more complex than their intelligences can fathom. So did I fear taking that step, heading back up the slopes of Esja a few weeks later, to rendezvous with Númí. Still, I knew in my heart there was no other course of action possible for me.

'I will spare you the detail of my transformation. Rest assured that it was quite painless and, after the fact, most fascinating. Although it took me some time to come to that conclusion, I'm ashamed to admit. No, I have no regrets – how could I, after what I have seen?

'Borne aloft by the power of their own wings, we journeyed to their home planet. How such a thing is possible lies beyond my understanding. As we pierced beyond the realm of possibility, distances became abstract, time dissolved as the fabric of being itself was unfolded and transfigured.

'There were no stars in that abyssal void above their world. Teraí lay spread before me – or so I have attempted to approximate the name of Laí's ancient capital, which is truly unspeakable by all lesser beings.

'Great, dark spires, lit by a pallid glow emanating from within. Not obsidian, nor truly stone nor metal of any kind known to me, the city seemed to be a thing once alive – now dead for untold aeons. Labyrinthine streets twisted and turned in on one another, abandoned and empty, a maze not intended to be traversed or comprehended. This city needed no walls, its very design was its protection – a metropolitan spiral which claims all who enter it. Lightning crashed relentlessly, rising from the city itself. It dawned on me that it was a new kind of colour, only perceivable due to my altered and improved state of being.

'Soaring over the city, I saw that it was not truly abandoned, as I had initially thought. It teemed with unseen life, hiding in the cracks and split-open seams of this great, sprawling chaos. Those life forms, I cannot begin to describe to you.

'I also saw a significant number of amorphous beings, which to you appear like a breach in the seam of reality. Diligent workers, tending to the city, guarding its streets – I can still only guess as to the tasks they are given. The construct-servants of Laí that we have innately dubbed an "uncolour". To me and the Laí themselves, they are wholly different. Should you ever have the privilege of seeing their true appearance, you will understand how beautiful and elegant their hallowed forms are.

'Beyond those dark towers loomed the black pyramid. Magister, I tell you truly – it stretched the limitations of my mind to look upon it. A monument of monuments, its geometric lines demanded awe, commanded obeisance as naturally as the sun on our own world.

'As we approached the great pyramid and soared up alongside its massive slopes, I saw that it was not truly black but a tarnished kind of gold. Once, this monolithic structure must have been a shining brilliance. Oh! How I yearn to see that lost glory restored to the height of its power!

'The top of the pyramid was flat, where a temple plaza was located. It dwarfed the city below in grandeur and scope alike, so titanic was this behemoth we had just ascended. If divinity is found anywhere in the mortal realm, Magister, it is there. I felt the oppressive weight of the void above me, like a great eye peering down upon a solitary ant.

'Magister, I forget myself. I fear I have already told you too much. Much was revealed to me then.

'Now – I hear someone at the door. I believe the soldiers are summoning me to meet with the doctor. Think on what I have said, Magister. I wanted to converse with you in private, as I feel you are truly capable of understanding how we must reach past our limitations as fallen mortals. The human condition, my dear Kári, is corruption in its most condensed essence. It is simply so widespread that we believe it to be normal. You have pierced through that veil, at least in part – now you must make up your mind whether you are capable of fully stepping through to the other side.'

Níu

Sölvi hated wearing fancy clothes. They itched, and were always either too small or too big. His mother said that he'd grow into them, but by then the smaller clothes would be past the point of fitting him at all. The whole thing felt a bit stupid.

Everyone at the house had bathed that morning and they had got up even earlier than normal to be first in line.

He loathed that about this backwards place. Having to go the entire week without a proper bath, only being able to wash himself with a sponge and cold water, having the honour of bathing in someone else's grimy lukewarm water.

Disgusting.

He hadn't even been able to spend any time in the bath enjoying it. Already the other girls were lining up for their turn, knocking on the door even though Elka had just got in herself. He had used up their allocated time and his mother had barely managed to wash her hair before they had to leave.

Instead, Elka finished washing herself with a wet cloth in the kitchen, before dressing in her own smart clothes. Sölvi had fetched her water from the collection tank, which gathered up all the rainwater from the roof for their half of the house. There was another on the other side of the building, as well as another bathroom, except both were reserved only for the people who lived on that side. Sölvi found that to be weird and unfair as well. It was the same house, the same roof. Why couldn't they just share the water?

'It's an island, elskan,' his mother explained when she brushed his hair. 'There aren't any freshwater springs, so they can only use what they collect from the rain.'

'But they still have pipes and a tap. Just let people take a bath every other day.'

'They would if they could. But everyone has to do their part so we don't run out of water. I've heard what happens when a house runs out of its supply… I can understand why people aren't so keen on sharing.'

'What a bunch of country bumpkins.'

'Sölvi Helgason.'

Her stern tone made him stand to attention.

'I don't have time for this attitude, especially not today. Be respectful and mind your manners.' She finished combing his hair, straightening his already bent collar. 'Give your poor, hardworking mother a break. Please?'

He sighed. 'I'm sorry. All right.'

She smiled gratefully and kissed him on the head, then got up to check herself in the mirror.

'How do I look?'

She was wearing a light blue dress. It complemented her hair, and if it weren't for her cheap and worn shoes, she'd have looked like a fancy lady. Sölvi didn't mind the shoes, of course. In his mind his mother was as beautiful as a queen.

'You look great, Mamma. But you need new shoes.'

'And so do you! Which reminds me…'

She fetched a box and opened it, picking up the most beautiful work of art Sölvi had ever laid eyes on.

'Where did you get *that*?' he asked as she put it on.

Now she did truly look like a queen – shoes or no shoes.

'It was a gift from Reverend Bryde. She's been very kind to us, Sölvi. She's a wonderful woman.'

'Is she rich?'

'Hush!' Elka scolded him half-jokingly. 'I want you to be on your best behaviour!' She grabbed her purse and put on her coat. 'We'll head to the cobbler's after Mass and see what we can find – for both of us. Deal?'

'Deal!'

When they left the workers' house, Sölvi was sure that most of the people he saw looked spiffier than usual. Maybe lots of people were going to Mass. Elka looked as though she couldn't remember which way to go, before deciding to follow the crowd. All the well-dressed people seemed to be heading the same way.

Sölvi kept looking up at his mother's necklace. He wanted to draw it, study its shape in every detail. Colours came to him in a whirling rush, and he so desperately wanted to capture the luminescence of the pearls, the sublime metal, the delicate shape which reminded him of a bird bone.

He had seen the church several times, but never really bothered to investigate. It was run-down, the white paint cracked and the wood grey in places where it was peeling. A strange, unfamiliar sign hung above the entrance. It looked like two fishes twisted together, combining to form the shape of an eye. The same symbol his mother wore around her neck.

A small gathering stood outside, with Bryde among them. She was deep in conversation with a tall man dressed in a fine woollen coat. When they noticed Elka and Sölvi, they waved and smiled warmly. Elka returned the greeting, and it did not pass Sölvi's notice that the man with Bryde eyed her very intently. Sölvi took an immediate dislike to him. Maybe he wasn't looking at his mother at all, simply the necklace, wondering how a plain working woman like Elka had got hold of it.

Above the main door, written in large block letters, was the name of the church: *Saltslóð*. People heading in took off their shoes before entering, which was strange for a church but quite normal for homes. What was strange was that they also took off their socks. Sölvi looked for the king's initials, *J IX*, somewhere on it, but couldn't find them. He asked his mother about it, but Elka brushed him off.

'Come on, Sölvi,' Elka said. 'The service is about to start.'

'This isn't the king's church, is it?'

'No, it's not. It's a different kind of church.'

'Mamma!'

He stopped her going in by grabbing her sleeve. She turned around and he saw how she held back her anger, with him already starting to make a scene.

He let go of her, leaned in, and whispered into her ear, 'That's illegal! We'll go to jail!'

'Things are different here, Sölvi. They have their own laws. Trust me, Captain Kohl would not let a church stand for several years if it was against the law. You've seen the soldiers, right?'

He nodded, uncertain about her logic. He noticed how Elka glanced around, checking if people had noticed his outburst, already embarrassed by him or afraid he'd go further.

'So you know Kohl could do something about this if it was bad. Now, come on inside. There's nothing to worry about, I promise you.'

Sölvi followed hesitantly, obeying Elka to remove his shoes and socks, although she didn't seem sure why they were doing it either. Bryde and that man watched them walk in. Their eyes felt heavy on Sölvi's back.

The interior was plain but much neater, painted white with

the windows clear and clean, letting the sunlight through. It was immediately obvious why everyone had taken off their shoes, as well as pulling up their trousers or skirts. Stepping down from the narthex into the nave, Sölvi's feet hit freezing cold water. The floor was flooded with seawater, reaching well above his mother's ankles. It looked like an enormous tidal pool. The church smelled like a stranded ship – driftwood and kelp.

The benches were scuffed, the seats polished and worn, antiques which had lived through generations of preaching. At the end, where the sigil of the divine kings would normally be, was a massive painting. Facing the altarpiece was the priest. Bryde looked like a different person, with a dominating presence about her, even with her back turned to the congregation as they flooded into the church. The painting showed a ship, trapped in a ferocious ocean storm, its sails torn and the hull battered. The sailors on deck were all on their knees praying. The captain was at the prow, reaching down towards the waves.

A couple of familiar faces stood out from the crowd. Bára was turned backwards in her seat, talking to Sævar, who was on the pew behind her. Both of them wore much fancier clothes than Sölvi. Sævar's hair was combed back; Bára had hers done in braids. She beamed when she noticed Sölvi. She and Sævar waved to him, and he shyly returned the gesture, all too aware of his mother noticing the exchange.

What she didn't see was that Hafsteinn sat right at the back, surly and menacing, his suit a few sizes too small. Sölvi pretended not to see him glaring. Elka was about to take a seat in the same row as Hafsteinn when she saw that Sölvi hesitated.

'What is it? Do you want to sit with your friends?'

He nodded slightly and led her to the row where Bára sat. They took their seat by her family, so Sölvi sat right next to her. He was thankful his feet didn't reach the floor properly. The only thing more miserable than being stuck in church was having your feet freezing for the entire time as well.

He turned to Bára and whispered to her.

'You don't worship the king?'

Sölvi couldn't hide the shock in his voice; it wasn't that he was a believer in the royal line's divinity – it was just impossible to hear that someone outright denied it.

She giggled in response. 'Of course not, silly.'

'So you worship the same god as the marbendlar?'

At this she outright laughed, which made his ears turn red with embarrassment. He did not like feeling ignorant. He decided to bite his tongue and not ask any more stupid questions.

An organ started to play. Sölvi turned in his seat and looked in amazement at the pipe organ at the back of the upper floor. Its many pipes were made entirely out of coral; the music was like distant waves roaring, cascading over one another.

'Then how do you explain that?' he said to Bára. 'It's just like the marbendlar's houses in Reykjavík.'

'It was a gift from the Deep. One day it washed up on our shores, after a ferocious storm. Many ships sank and this was the Deep's response to our offering.'

At this Bára's mother leaned in.

'There are others beside marbendlar who reside in the ocean,' she said in a low voice. 'Countless beings, more ancient than the land itself.'

Elka noticed the interaction and checked with Sölvi, who just shrugged and faced forwards. He found himself to be curious about what would come next. Maybe the priest would do some sorcery. A real seiður, unlike the kukl Amma Dagmar had talked about. Maybe they'd see something from the Deep. A monster or something.

The priest turned around and raised her hands. She wore a plain blue cassock, the top half stitched with patches of fish-skin, while a fishing net fashioned into a shawl was draped over her shoulders.

'I call upon the ancient names of Hvalfrón and Lýsuvangur, so that the depths may hear our prayers. I call upon Eygarður, Jarðarmen and Hólmfjötur, so that our shores may remain unbroken. I call upon Gjálfurgrund and Meingarður, so that our ships may sail safely. Blessed be Fjörgjafi, our infinite provider, blessed be Strandrof, the relentless devourer. May the Harbinger bless us with his presence, may he who is named Mánaþjór bring forth divine paradise in the Awakening of the Moon. Hail to the First Mother, hail to the Wet Grave. Blessed be our Holy Sea.'

'Blessed be the Deep,' the congregation replied.

Then they started singing.

Etherial tones, carried on the undercurrent of the coral organ. Powerful, vibrating bass notes, the shrill and pure soprano of the choir cutting through like a ship breaking through waves. The ocean in the painting started to move, the dark storm clouds gathering strength.

Sölvi saw that Elka's eyes became watery with tears as the hymn unfastened something inside her. She grasped his hand and held it too tightly, feeling the profound emotional release of the music. Bára held up her hymn book so they could read, and Elka joined in the singing.

Sölvi's heart was starting to race. This felt wrong. The song sounded beautiful, but everything about it was dreadful. He wanted to get up and run, to leave this place and never return, but his mother's grip on him was too tight. He felt as if he was made of stone. A boy-shaped block of granite sinking into the sea, watching the glittering surface fade away into darkness. He tried to make a silent plea to Elka with his eyes, but when he looked up he only saw the necklace, shining wondrously. Instantly, he didn't want to paint it any more – it looked hideous to him. An ugly thing, like a pet's collar or a slave's shackles. His mother's gaze remained transfixed, and wanting to tear his eyes away from that dreadful piece of jewellery, that horrible symbol, Sölvi sat still and gazed towards the altar.

They sung of loss at sea, of hope on the open ocean, of release and redemption in a watery grave. They sung the praise of the Messengers of the Deep.

In the painting, a luminous hand rose from the depths, reaching up towards the captain.

ᚺ

The days blurred together into a grey haze. Without the medicine from Bryde, Elka would have fallen by now. She was certain of that. She was up to three pills now, two in the morning and one after work. Whenever she needed a refill, Bryde had one ready for her – no questions asked. No matter how hard she tried, she couldn't get Bryde to accept any payment for them. It's the least she could do, the priest said, to help out a girl from Heimaey.

Elka's guiding light was going to church. It dispelled the monotony like a beam of light piercing overcast clouds. The priest's spirited sermons and the beautiful hymns weren't her only solace there – Ægir played an even bigger part. Her heart rushed each Fárday night, knowing she would see him the next morning. It started by sharing coy glances, perhaps a few words after the service, then quickly escalated into official courtship.

Ægir was nothing like what she'd expected. He was shy and gentle, a stark contrast to his heavyset frame and serious face. When they met on the weekends, or sometimes after work, they most often took walks around the island. Small talk wasn't his strong suit, which Elka didn't mind. The silence between them was charged. There were frequent moments where she would have wanted nothing more than to give in to passion, but Ægir remained ever the gentleman. He took this seriously, and so did she. This was not some superficial fling.

He was well respected in the community. His ship, *Þurfalingur*, was the most profitable fishing boat in Heimaey. To the congregation of the Deep, he was on an entirely different level, almost saint-like. She gathered that his ship had sunk several years ago – the same time the Emissary had revealed itself finally to the people of Vestmannaeyjar. It had apparently rescued him from drowning, granting him miraculous strength and stamina as he swam to shore in the freezing sea. It was like something out of the Book of the Deep – another source of steadfastness in her life.

By a flickering fish-oil light, she read that sacred writ religiously before bed every night. The book was pregnant with meaning, layers upon layers. Bryde had said each pass would enrich her experience as the reader would sink to new depths, just as with diving in the ocean itself. Descending from sunlight to twilight, midnight to abyss, and then that most elusive, deepest state of mind beyond that, unreachable by most.

Elka devoured the scriptures, feeling herself sinking further with each word.

ᚻ

'Hæ, Elka. Want a smoke?'

Styrmir held out a packet of cigarettes, flashing her an inviting grin. He had caught her on the harbour just as she started walking back home, having worked past supper. Hopefully Sölvi had fixed himself something to eat.

'Sure. Good haul today?'

He nodded, fishing up a couple of cigarettes and handing her one.

'It's always a good day on *Þurfalingur*.'

It was overcast, the wind rushing between windowless factory buildings. Using a stack of fish tubs as shelter, they lit their cigarettes.

'You holding up all right?' Styrmir asked.

'Sure.'

Elka wasn't certain where he was going with this unprompted concern. There was an edge to his voice, something he failed to conceal.

'Summer's always tough. Long days makes the bosses think they can work us forever.' He attempted a casual laugh.

'I don't complain – the pay is good.' She tapped her cigarette. 'People are very pleasant.'

'Yeah?' He sniffed, his cigarette glowing as he pulled deeply from it. His hand trembled slightly. 'You're still going to church regularly, then?'

Elka must have given him an incredulous look, because he excused himself.

'I swear, I'm not stalking you or anything. People talk too much in this village, that's all.'

'That's right. And—'

'And it's none of my business, I know. But…' Styrmir hesitated, choosing his words carefully. It was a short while until he found the courage to continue. 'But, these people – they're not… all they seem. Despite appearances. Despite giving you fancy gifts.'

'Some people would say that about huldufólk, you know.'

She felt herself getting annoyed.

Where is this coming from? Who does he think he is?

'Yeah. I know what it sounds like. But, Elka… I've lived here my entire life. You don't know these people – I do. Bryde isn't a nice person. And Ægir is not the gentleman he seems.'

She was getting angry. 'If you find him so disagreeable, I'm sure you can get work on another ship. Ægir has been nothing but wonderful to me. And you watch what you say about Bryde – she's been incredibly kind to me and Sölvi.'

Styrmir was momentarily stunned. He smoked angrily, arms crossed and shoulders squared to disguise his nerves. He was weighing his next words carefully.

'I'm sorry,' he said finally. 'It's just that, these people, they're…' He sighed, changing gears as he went on. 'I know a few marbendlar – they stop here every once in a while. They've told me stories about these so-called Messengers. They can't figure out where they came from. Before the eruption twenty-something years ago, the marbendlar had never seen the Messengers before. Wherever those things come from, it must be *way deep*. And now they're here, gifting us with treasures in fish guts.'

'So what? That's no reason to fear them.'

'The marbendlar seem to think otherwise. They've been vague, but there have been some skirmishes with these things. They use some kind of dreadful seiður, or maybe galdur, I don't know. Their use of the arcane defies our understanding. It scared the marbendlar off so bad, they abandoned an entire town close to where the Deep has staked its territory. These Messengers aren't holy, Elka – they're no saints or whatever they're telling you at church. They are dangerous, and we know nothing about them.'

'They saved Ægir.' She glared at him. 'Right? You know that, yet you still act like they're monsters. If they're real, then they are helping people in the village every day.'

'Have you ever wondered *why* that is? Why are they doing that? What's their agenda?'

She snorted. 'Of course, ulterior motives. Well, you'd know a thing or two about those, wouldn't you?'

Now it was Styrmir's turn to be at a loss for words.

'*What?*'

'Oh, come on, Styrmir. Why the hell did you approach me? Just to be nice, to be friendly? Or to get under my skirt?'

'I just wanted to help you out!' he said, incredulous.

'Right. And it just so happens that now I've been going to church, chatting to Ægir, suddenly you're very concerned? You must really think I'm stupid.'

'I don't think that.'

'Well, your actions say otherwise.'

'It's a cult, Elka!' Styrmir shouted, throwing the cigarette down.

It hissed as it went out in a puddle. He started at his own raised voice and looked around to see if anyone had heard.

'I told you they were bad news from day one,' he half-whispered. 'Elka ... This place – this island? The marbendlar don't go near the surrounding ocean floor. The náskárar stay well the fuck away from here, despite there being tons of good islands to claim. And do you know why?'

'Because of Kohl's fortress.'

'No. Because it's all *wrong*. There's something deeply off about this place.'

'So why are *you* here?'

He shrugged, defeated. 'Because it's my home. And I need the money.'

'Well, so do I. And it's my home as well now.'

'Then please stay away from that church. And it *is* a cult, Elka. Everyone knows it, just nobody says it. They own everything in town – the ships, the factories – even Kohl is in their pocket.

Every single króna that flows through here is controlled by them, and by extension, those fucking things in the Deep.'

'They're giving people jobs, Styrmir. In a time where we're facing famine. If you'd ever been to Mass, you would know they just want people to feel hopeful and loved. How is that wrong?'

'You don't know these people – I do. I've lived here all my life, so trust me when I tell you that—'

'Trust you? After you gave me that fucking poison? I would probably be dead or *worse* if Bryde hadn't stepped in and given me actual medicine.'

This pissed him off. 'What? Elka, listen—'

'No, you listen! What the hell is any of this to you, anyway? You're one entitled asshole if you think you have any right to talk about what I do in my personal life.'

'Everything they do – Bryde and Ægir and Kohl and all of them – it's just to maximise their profits! You are just a pawn to them. This sick covenant with these ocean creatures, these monsters—'

'All right, that's it.' She cut him off. He was getting hysterical and starting to make her feel afraid. 'We're done.'

She stepped on her half-finished cigarette, storming away. He had the audacity to try to grab her hand, but he only got a grip on the sleeve of her working robe and she shook him off.

She turned and considered slapping him. The look on his face told her the anger was written clearly on her face.

'Do not touch me,' she said coldly. 'Understand?' He nodded. 'I said we're done. Don't talk to me again.'

As she turned the corner around the fish tubs, she saw Björg standing by the entrance to the factory, smoking.

Has she been listening to us?

'Everything all right, Elka? You seem upset.'

'I'm fine, frænka.' She saw Styrmir storm away without

glancing back, cursing as he ran his hand through his hair. *Good riddance.* 'That son of a bitch thinks he can comment on my religious inclinations, that's all.'

'Is that so?'

Björg's gaze followed Styrmir as he headed away. She looked deep in thought.

'Don't worry about it. I told him off.'

Björg flashed Elka that stern smile of hers.

'Good girl.'

Tíu

They had been fortunate in the last few weeks. A few archaeologists had been injured, mainly people working on the smaller surrounding sites, who had to regularly risk journeys to the limits of the protective field of the central site. Most of them had survived, thanks to Kári's help. So far, none had displayed the same symptoms he had found on Auður. He'd kept his promise to her and remained silent, despite his better judgement.

The ones that had died did so in terrible ways. The worst incident had been after some workers dug into a reservoir of seiðmagn that had eluded the scouting seiðskrattar. It erupted with chaotic malevolence as soon as it was unearthed, with one person in particular taking the brunt of the force. The flesh on their fingers had slid off as someone tried to help them to their feet, revealing gelatinous appendages that quickly broke apart into nothing. The worker was rushed to the medical tent, where they died before Kári was able to treat them. Their body kept on changing, even though they were dead. Probably for the best – to go out quickly like that and not live to endure the changes.

They were incinerated, as were all who died from the seiðmagn.

What disturbed Kári even more than the body he was wrapping in funeral linens, was the stench now rising from the excavation pit. It *reeked*, as if they were digging into a heap of decomposed carcasses. It stank like a shore filled with stranded whales.

He had not seen much of Leifur since his last visit to the laboratory. Leifur worked tirelessly in there, along with Ingi Vítalín. Occasionally Vésteinn would join them, but when Kári asked the doctor about it, Vésteinn only said that things were coming along nicely. The doctor spent most of his time in his tent. Kári heard workers whispering in the cafeteria that Vésteinn had been heard conversing with someone in there, despite no sign of anyone having exited or entered it except for the man himself.

Ingi sometimes 'took the air', as the man-machine called it, with more than a hint of humour. As Ingi had no respiratory functions in place or sensory organs for smell, Kári didn't find his choice of words funny at all. Ingi would roll around on those belts of his, looking like a lost automaton without any purpose. Kári wondered what he got out of it, if anything at all.

When he watched the machine through his mask, he saw it flare in unsettling colours. Seiðmagn, to be sure, but something else as well. It radiated in nauseating pulses, an energy reminiscent of transmundane influence. These malevolent entities could be found anywhere, at any time, and uprooting the vile beings was part of the responsibilities of any graduate of Svartiskóli. It didn't make sense, though. Demons manifested in bone, which Ingi was severely lacking.

Ginfaxi had not been seen for days. They were inside the agents' secretive container, working tirelessly with Þráinn and Hrólfur. The two agents looked haggard, red-eyed with weariness when they occasionally entered the canteen for sustenance. Kári offered to look them over, for safety reasons, but Þráinn firmly prohibited it, finally pulling rank after Kári was insistent. Fine.

Let them kill themselves from whatever the hell they were up to in there. He had enough on his plate.

He was at work in his clinic when Ingi Vítalín rolled into the tent. Kári had gone over his notes from examinations performed the day before on a nauseated worker, and was trying to find previous examples of seiðmagn affecting someone's inner organs before the outer layer of their body. His patient seemed to have a new set of organs, despite appearing completely fine.

Ingi suddenly entered, announcing his presence by merit of his noisy rollers.

'*Óma a íana*, Magister! Good morning to you, sir, good morning! I hope I am not disturbing?'

Kári got up from his steel desk, a rickety collapsible thing that felt as if it could fall over at any time. He almost reached out a hand to shake, catching himself at the last moment and settling for a rigid nod in greeting. Ingi showed no reaction to this, of course, but Kári had the strangest feeling as if the machine had nodded back.

'Not at all, Ingi. What can I do for you?'

'We will be receiving some guests, as I mentioned in our previous chat. Visitors from Laí.'

'Here?'

'That's right. The lunar beings are sending a detachment of engineers to help us fix some issues with the skuggsjá. The device is giving Leifur, and even me, some trouble.'

'So it's already completed?'

'Oh yes! Leifur has been operating it for days now! But there have been unexpected problems – it seems managing this type of psychometry is proving somewhat difficult. So we're bringing in the experts!'

'Right.' Unexpected – but Ingi had already known they were coming. 'So what do I have to do with this?'

Ingi hesitated. 'It's because of Leifur that I worry. I fear the strain on his mind and body may become too great.'

'I see. So I should do an examination? Leifur wasn't exactly co-operative last time, and if I had known he was operating this machine I would have wanted to see him regularly.'

'Of course, I understand – but we can't let such things slow down our progress! An examination is unnecessary at this point – I only ask that you remain on standby. Just in case, you see.'

'Of course.'

Kári mulled this over. There were a great many things bothering him about this device. This was his chance for clarification.

'So the skuggsjá... operates on seiðmagn?'

'Indeed. And other supernatural aspects.'

'So galdur as well?' Ingi didn't reply. 'Is it not then a good idea to let Auður Thorlacius also assist with its operation? Shouldn't she have been on this from the start?'

The implied question, or accusation, was left hanging in the air, unsaid.

'Ah. Yes. Auður. I'm afraid she is needed elsewhere.' Ingi's voice was viscous with glee. 'She has her own responsibilities, unearthing the landvættur.'

'It can't—'

'It can indeed, my dear magister. Yes, the skuggsjá runs on both seiður and galdur – of sorts. That's the explanation most suited for us to comprehend its esoteric workings, at least. Quite thrilling, don't you agree? But it's more than simply a cross-disciplinary machine. It is transcendent in every regard.'

'A machine not unlike yourself, you mean?'

Ingi's silence spoke volumes.

'I'll be ready. When?'

'They land this evening. Please, I would be honoured if you were to join us in welcoming our luminous guests.'

What Ingi Vítalín had said was not simply heresy, or dangerous, or illegal – but *impossible*. Seiður and galdur could be used to manifest similar effects, but their fundamentals were entirely different. These two supernatural means of reshaping the world had no common denominators whatsoever. They weren't exactly anathema to one another; rather the human mind could not possibly juggle both simultaneously without disastrous effects.

But suggesting there was an unknown factor playing into this? Outside these two disciplines? That was simply impossible.

ᚻ

They stood assembled underneath the twilight sky. The sun set very late these days, as summer overtook spring in earnest and the days stretched on forever. Kári was lined up with the other seiðskrattar, all of them in their regalia except Doctor Vésteinn, who wore an impeccably neat suit. Ingi Vítalín was by the doctor's side, standing in front of the assembly.

He couldn't help but notice that Vésteinn looked haggard, worn-out, as from a lack of sleep and overexertion. This was the first time Kári had seen him leave his tent in days.

Þráinn Meinholt and Hrólfur had ventured out of their little black site, flanking the seiðskrattar to the left, heading the ranks of soldiers who stood in neat military ranks behind them. They were the only ones there who looked healthy and well, as energetic as ever. But Kári did notice Hrólfur anxiously fiddling with the chain of his pocket watch.

Auður was to the right, the higher-ups of the archaeologists just behind her, in front of a disorganised crowd of diggers. She, too, wore her finest, her signature coat over a sharp, tailored female suit which had become vogue in Hafnía among wealthier women who fought ambitiously for their place in upper society.

Seen through Kári's lenses, the bones hidden in her clothing made her radiate with azure transdimensional power.

Seeing her standing at attention with unwavering determination, her hair tightly braided, her face pale and exhausted from the enormous task she faced every day, Kári felt a new emotion surge inside him. Something that could almost be considered attraction, or perhaps it was simply admiration. Perhaps it was guilt. Standing there, she reminded him of her mother Almía – final moments notwithstanding. Almía had been a fierce woman, a dangerous and highly learned scholar. Or perhaps it was the isolation getting to Kári, finally. This wasn't a feeling he was familiar with, a confusing mess he did not care to acknowledge or untangle.

The wind buffeted their robes, erratic and relentless. They stared up into the sky, waiting for a sign.

It started as a sickly, luminous sheen. A faint star, a meteor burning in the atmosphere directly at the zenith above them. It radiated unwellness, made Kári's skin crawl with dread. Despite all the horrors he had seen, and all his efforts to temper his mind to accept a deeper understanding of the natural and supernatural world than most other humans could manage, he still found himself feeling nauseous and fearful at the sight of that glow.

It grew in brightness, flaring before it suddenly vanished. In its place appeared three dark shapes, seemingly tiny at such a great distance, approaching them rapidly. They descended at terrible speed, and their wings spread out, each set manifold and alien, not aerodynamic in the slightest, carrying aloft a creature Kári's mind failed to piece together as it came into clearer view.

They circled the camp, lowering their altitude steadily. He could hear Ingi's cries of jubilation, exclaiming his wonder at their grace and divinity, these messengers and saviours from the stars. People stirred, panic beginning to ferment in the crowd.

The beings from Laí halted in the air above the centre of the landing site, their enormous wings moving so lethargically they seemed instead to float, not fly. Slowly, they landed, unfolding their many multi-jointed limbs, chitinous and covered with cilia and serrated spikes. As they touched the ground and the people hesitantly applauded, obeying their strict instructions, the beings stretched out their backs and their necks, holding aloft a kind of head that defied all natural purpose, at least so far as Kári's education afforded him an understanding of such things. They were tall, significantly more so than náskárar, even as their astral wings retracted into their carapace.

Through the thaumaturgical glass of Kári's mask, they shone with a hue the likes of which he had never seen. An other-worldly form of seiðmagn, contaminated by a mixture of deep and vibrant blue. A transmundane influence? Had they fallen victim to the corrupting forces of galdur? His mind reeled. Out of the corner of his eye, Magister Ginfaxi shifted his posture slightly. Kári knew they were unnerved, just as afraid as himself. Both of them remained deadly still, tensed like serpents ready to strike.

From the top of Ingi's chassis a half-sphere extended, covered in mechanical tendrils which writhed and squirmed unpleasantly. He started to emit a sound only partly heard by the human ear. Even if Kári couldn't fully hear it, he felt it vibrating through his body, reverberating in his bones. He wanted to throw up.

The creatures responded in kind, emitting the noise from their bulbous heads, extending and retracting a plethora of feelers and cilia as they spoke. They leaned down and touched Ingi's feelers with their own.

Was this truly their language? What about Ingi's jovial greeting, which he alleged was in Laí? Kári struggled to go over the snippets Ingi had told him about these things. He had spoken with them before his transformation – was his understanding of their language a relic of that experience? How could he possibly have approximated a human pronunciation of *that*?

'Our noble emissaries from Laí are pleased to have arrived,' boomed Ingi in his metallic drone. 'Doctor Vésteinn! This one, whose beautiful name we cannot truly speak in the human tongues is their chief psychometric engineer. I call him Kaíamí.'

Vésteinn stepped forwards, nodding awkwardly, unsure of how to conduct himself in front of these towering, grotesque creatures. Even he was not unfazed, despite likely having met with them numerous times before. Still, his face betrayed not a hint of discomfort, whereas Kári was yet again deeply thankful for his mask.

'As the leader of this excavation, I welcome you on behalf of the Kalmar Commonwealth. May this be only the first step in our peoples working together for a brighter, lucrative future.'

The assembly applauded as Vésteinn and Ingi escorted the beings from Laí to the laboratory, Ginfaxi and Leifur following behind. To Kári's surprise, Auður went as well. She gave him a meaningful look in passing, the significance of which eluded him. Þráinn dismissed the soldiers, commanding them to get back to their posts. The sky was overcast with stone-grey clouds, carrying with them the promise of rain. In the distance, a sound could be heard that almost resembled thunder.

Deep beneath the earth, a giant stirred.

ᚼ

Auður barged into Kári's tent, shaking him from the depths of his same, recurring nightmare. He had been back in the halls of Svartiskóli, feeling the death grip of that spiralling horror about to close in on him yet again, when she dragged him back to the shores of consciousness.

For a moment, he was relieved. Then he saw the look in her eyes. Shocked, he felt around his face, diving away from her in search of a mirror. Her surprise made him fairly certain she wasn't concerned about him.

'It's Leifur,' she said before storming out.

He followed Auður to the mobile laboratory, expecting screams, blood, panic and madness, so he was surprised as he stepped into the dark space to find Ginfaxi and Doctor Vésteinn standing calmly over a body laid out on an examination table.

In the corner of the room towered a being from Laí, folded and enclosed in on itself, unnaturally still like a hideous statue.

Kári took one glance towards Leifur's body and swallowed hard.

'I'm too late. He's already dead.'

'Not at all, Magister Kvalráður,' said Vésteinn, beckoning him closer. 'He is quite alive – technically, at least. Come and see. I would like your professional opinion.'

Kári ventured closer and they stepped aside to give him room.

He had seen things during his studies – unnerving and unnatural things that most people would only believe occurred in nightmares. He had felt those forces work upon his own skin. Despite all that experience, what he found in that lab was worse.

Leifur was on his back, staring up into nothingness, a blissful look of idiocy frozen on his face. He looked awful. Sunken eyes, dried lips, his skin pale and taut. His robes had been split down the middle, his mask torn and ruined, lying discarded on the ground. He wasn't breathing. Kári's first thought was that he was obviously dead. He had been overworked until his body gave out. Or he had faded into the void, catatonic. Hesitant to actually touch the body, Kári flashed a light into Leifur's empty eyes and found to his surprise that they reacted. He noticed an almost imperceptible movement of his chest. Leifur was still alive – at least in some sense.

Vésteinn broke the silence. 'Magister – what's your diagnosis?'

'Well … he's not breathing, as far as I can tell, but he responded to light. I was certain it was a corpse when I came in – I'm still not certain that it's not one. There's no bodily corruption, no trace of seiðmagn.' He turned to the three of them. 'What happened?'

He scanned the machinery and tried to piece together how on earth this thaumaturgical machine operated, diverting his gaze from the *thing* lurking in the corner.

The tarp had been removed from the skuggsjá. The machine was a convoluted oval of black iron, with an empty hollow in the middle. Within this hollow the dirt had been compressed like a trodden floor in a turf house. It was dark, tainted with spilled blood. Still fresh. The hollow held an esoteric sigil, cast into the ground in obsidian-infused iron.

A thing which had no place in this world stood at its very heart, in the centre of the spiral symbol. A small obelisk, made from what resembled steel or obsidian but clearly was neither. It reflected the light in peculiar, dazzling ways Kári could not fully comprehend. It was covered in markings he had never seen before in his life. From its flat top jutted a small, twisted growth, nearly organic in shape and covered in tiny spikes.

Kári had seen this sigil before. The mark on Auður's body. The mark from his dreams. He was glad to be wearing his mask, the better to hide his shock. He glanced towards Auður, who was staring at him intently.

Surrounding the sigil were metal stakes driven into the ground, bare copper wires leading from them into a console taking up most of the far wall.

The console most reminded Kári of a switchboard. Gauges

and counters, buttons and switches, and above the controls a variety of receiving plugs. Cords dangled from three of them, not connected to anything else. He took a closer look at their ends.

The cords ended in needles.

He saw movement at the end of one. Whatever was inside the cord, in the needle, stretched out microscopic, bone-white feelers – teeth, perhaps. He dropped the cord with a shiver. The others watched his investigation in silence.

'Marvellous technology, isn't it?'

Kári visibly jumped, not having noticed that Ingi Vítalín was right by him, camouflaged by all the other machinery in the lab. Ingi sounded as if he was in higher spirits than ever.

'What did you do to him?'

Kári steeled himself and stormed towards Leifur's body, pulling up the sleeves of his robes to find exactly what he was expecting. A plethora of ugly, infected puncture wounds, some new, some old. Still, Leifur stared blank-faced towards the ceiling, gazing at a revelation witnessed by him and him alone.

'How can you possibly imagine I can help this man? You've abused his body beyond reckoning and shattered his mind.'

'The strain was great for dear Leifur, that is true,' Ingi muttered sadly. 'The help from our friends from Laí did not prove to be enough. According to our measurements, the process was going perfectly well.'

Kári turned towards the being, which still stood as silent as a nightmarish statue in the corner, its wings folded and the bulk of its body so enormously awkward it would hardly have been able to move in the laboratory without knocking something over.

'He seemed fine the last time I examined him,' he hissed at Ingi. 'Before you completed this ... machine.'

The silence in the room was driving Kári mad. Why was that idiot Ingi the only one actually talking?

'Vésteinn – answers. *Now*, while he's still alive.'

A dark look crossed Vésteinn's face. Auður glanced in the doctor's direction, hesitating, but then threw caution to the wind.

'They brought me and Ginfaxi in to see if we could help,' she said. 'Apparently, there is a certain element of galdur involved' – the anger in her voice shone through – 'although it's nothing like what I'm familiar with. Vésteinn and Leifur worked on improving the machine, guided by Ingi translating for that... *thing*.' She gestured towards the Laí.

'Kaíamí,' Ingi corrected.

'They started it up. This was apparently the first time they achieved full functionality.'

Again, she glanced at Vésteinn, who just stared straight ahead, as stoic and calm as Leifur lying on the table.

'They placed me at the gateway. The entrance to the circle,' Auður continued. 'I... it's a bit difficult to explain. As the machine powered up, I felt it reciting incantations – although I never heard a goddamn thing. I assisted with it, calling upon the past of the ground beneath our feet. I drew strength from the bones buried in the earth – the teeth of the being. I've discovered that... it's still alive.'

Her voice started to tremble.

'But I was just tuning the frequency. Leifur was the receiver. And the power source.'

'I thought the stores of seiðmagn we brought would power this thing. Why else bring them?'

'Yes, certainly, but—'

'And Vésteinn...'

The doctor looked up at Kári, brought back from whatever thoughts he had sunken into.

'You invented a way to use seiður mechanically. You use it every day at Perlan. Why do I see no trace of that here?' *You fucking bastard*, Kári added mentally. 'Why did Leifur have to put himself at risk like this? I thought he was only meant to help you *construct* this thing!'

'The normal rules do not apply here, Magister,' Vésteinn finally replied. 'And watch your tone. Let me remind you that you are here as a biothaumaturgist only – you have no knowledge whatsoever of what we are attempting to do, nor the forces at work!'

'I'm sorry, I … This is just—'

'Did you think Perlan was built without sacrifice? Without struggle?' Vésteinn approached him threateningly, his calm pretence dropped. 'Are you an idiot, after all? Perhaps I thought wrongly of you – I believed that you were a *man of science*! Not some blubbering fool who trembles at the threshold of achieving the impossible!'

Kári bumped into a desk behind him, having backed away from Vésteinn as he approached.

'Do your fucking job, if you are even capable of it. If not – then get out of my sight!'

'Yes, Doctor,' Kári replied quietly. 'I understand.' He was trembling with suppressed anger.

Vésteinn turned away, gesturing to Ginfaxi and Auður.

'Show him!' His voice bore more weight than the mountains surrounding them. 'It's useless explaining – he wouldn't have the capacity to understand it if we did!'

Ginfaxi seemed unperturbed, though Auður was obviously horrified. Nonetheless, it was Ginfaxi who spoke up.

'Vésteinn. This is unwise.'

'I told you to *fucking do it*!' Vésteinn screamed. 'We don't need a suitable conduit – obviously it was caused by the opening sequence! Or must I do everything myself? Are each and every single one of you utterly incompetent?'

Ginfaxi went straight to the console, flicking switches, causing it to light up.

Auður bit down on her lip, her fists opening and closing inconspicuously. She looked up at Kári, angry but with a look of apology in her eyes, before she walked towards the gateway and started to recite galdur as the hum of the machine increased.

The air grew thin. The darkness turned heavy.

Auður's incantation pierced reality, bleeding through the cracks in between that which is, and that which was, and that which will never be, and her words pried those imperfections apart until they became a ravine.

She was burning with power. Kári had never seen such a powerful galdur performed. Then her words fell into a drone-like rhythm. This was only the opening incantation. She was holding them steady at the threshold, straining herself to hold back the powers she summoned. He saw that the machine was indeed drawing massive amounts of energy from the thaumaturgical batteries – but a conduit, a person, was required in the middle to channel it all through themselves.

Then Kári noticed movement from the corner of his eye. He tore himself from the skuggsjá's spectacle to where his attention was demanded.

Leifur had bloomed. His face, neck and chest had spread open like a flower. Inside that new cavity Kári saw what he immediately, madly, thought of as Leifur's real face.

Glistening red strands of meat writhed in sync to the galdur. Teeth emerged, forming a mangled smile, bare and hideous. New sensory organs had sprouted inside his hollow, squirming body, which opened up further down his chest. Leifur pointed his new sets of eyes at Kári. And he pulled back his new, inhuman lips and stretched his smile even further.

Auður stopped chanting. The machine powered down. Leifur's body closed like a puzzle box, a mechanical contraption ceasing to operate.

Kári was speechless. He let the silence fall between them, cover everything like snow at night.

'I see,' he breathed, even though nothing could have been further from the truth.

'Do you, now?' Vésteinn spat.

'Let's move him to the medical tent. He ... looks to be stable, in a sense. Considering ...' He drifted off, incapable of finishing the thought.

'He suffers,' Ingi whispered. The rough tone of the machine's voice was like intolerable metallic screeching in Kári's ears. 'Indescribably so.' The machine's excitement was even worse.

Kári ignored the automaton. Auður looked as if she wanted to tell him something, but was not able to do so at this moment. He nodded, a slight gesture to her, hoping that she realised he understood.

'Auður. Please help me ferry him to the medical lab.'

A deafening explosion cut off her reply. The earth trembled and Kári lost his footing; Auður caught him before he collapsed.

A siren went off. Then another.

Then, another explosion.

ᚻ

Elka only saw the aftermath. She heard about what happened afterwards, as it was relentlessly talked about for more than a week.

That cold early morning suffered terrible weather, unseasonably so, which the dock workers wisecracked about, saying it would last through the day, blaming it on the capricious Great Frost Winter. All the smaller boats had stayed in harbour, with only the largest ships braving the weather and venturing out to sea. But there was enough work to be done in the factories.

Björg tasked the crew of Þurfalingur with gutting and beheading fish. Sometimes, these workers found gold and jewellery inside the intestines of the cod – beautiful gifts from the Deep. Ægir was said to be exceptionally lucky when it came to this, so he always had a place at the factory when necessary.

Ægir had put Styrmir on the heading machine. Four other men would gut the cod as fast as they could, sliding it down to a conveyor belt, which brought the fish up to the heading machine. There, Styrmir had to pick up each slippery cod and place it right side up, head forwards, very accurately on a belt that pulled the fish into the machine, where it was decapitated and descaled. Styrmir had to move very quickly to keep it from overflowing, as the men who were gutting worked so fast that at times the forklift driver bringing in fresh vats of cod could barely keep up with them.

One false move and Styrmir could lose a finger, a hand, an arm. And there were lots of opportunities for that.

They worked quickly and well, some of them having done this since they were teenagers. Decades of experience, of being told only weaklings didn't know how to work, had made them more efficient than machines. They quickly inundated Styrmir, who struggled to keep up. He had said nothing, they said afterwards. If he had been so overwhelmed, he should have said something.

But that was what a weakling would do.

The men sang hymns as they worked, which had annoyed Styrmir. He'd asked them to quiet down, telling them he couldn't focus. They just laughed and sang all the louder.

It was because of their singing, they claimed, that they didn't hear him yell for assistance. His glove and sleeve became trapped in the machine, which dragged his arm towards the vicious knives that hungrily awaited him. Styrmir had tried to reach the emergency stop button, but it was too far away. A flaw in the design.

Elka didn't work in this room and rarely had occasion to go there. But it was almost lunchtime, so she went in to get Ægir so they could eat together. She entered to find the men singing cheerfully as Styrmir was thrashing around on top of the tall machine. Dark blood covered his uniform.

She sprinted up the stairs to the top of the machine, smashing the emergency stop. As the thrum of the machine stopped, the men stopped singing – and Styrmir's cries were the only sound in the room.

Styrmir looked up at her, pale and wide-eyed, trembling from shock. The machine had shredded his arm like a ravenous shark. He muttered something as Elka tore off her worker's shirt, wrapping it around the awful wound, trying to stop the blood flow. The other men ran for help, as she told Styrmir everything would be fine. Ægir came running up, taking off his belt to wrap it around the huldumaður's upper arm.

Styrmir was weak, but Elka still noticed him shrink away from Ægir. As if he was afraid of him. As if Ægir had somehow caused this.

Later, repeating the story, Eyjamenn could not hide the pride in their voice when they said that the fishing company had truly spared no expense when it came to the well-being of their employees. Kohl's seiðskratti was summoned and managed to stop the bleeding. But even they had said that nothing could be done. The wound had been cauterised and would have to heal naturally. His right arm was lost forever.

This story was repeated over and over throughout the week.

They kept asking Elka about it, wanting her to partake in the retelling, but she soon started telling people to stop. They nodded, admiring what they perceived as her sensitive nature. *She's a good girl*, their looks said – which made her part in the story all the more dramatic.

Elka felt it was more than in bad taste to dwell on this like sheep chewing cud. It was disrespectful. It was a terrible and tragic accident, and apparently not that uncommon in recent years – so why did they spend so much time discussing it during breaks? Why did she feel as if Björg, or perhaps all of them, were secretly smiling into their cups of lukewarm coffee as the story was revisited, time and time again?

It must have been Elka's imagination. These people would never think such terrible things. She told herself she was traumatised, that's why she couldn't bear it. But she knew that wasn't the whole truth.

She wanted to say something. But she didn't know what.

So she kept quiet.

They said Styrmir was practically out of work in Vestmannaeyjar now. People expected him to apply to the municipality for alms. It was clear that dying on the job would have been more preferable. To go out struggling for survival against the harsh elements, for your family's survival, like the heroes of the sea.

At any point, she could have asked Ægir directly about the incident. Heard the story right from the source, asked him to tell her how it had happened. But she didn't. She told herself it was because doing so was crass. But she did know why.

She didn't want to hear the answer.

As she headed home from work after the incident, she noticed something strange. A hill overlooking the harbour was crowded with poles, on top of which were affixed dried fish heads. Ling, it looked like. Elka took a detour to pass closer by. There were more than a dozen stakes, each fish gaping stupidly out towards the open sea. A galdrastafur was carved into each head.

They were gone the next day, and with their disappearance the weather changed. It was perfect for sailing again – just like it often was.

ᚴ

Kári and Auður came sprinting out of the laboratory. He hastily checked that his mask was secure, looking frantically for the source of the explosion. A dark plume of smoke rose from the west, by the roots of one of the black obelisks.

A cascading sound of cracking blasts. Then, the flash of light at the base of the monolith. The pillar groaned and started to lean forwards. It was collapsing.

'Light after the blast? It's thaumaturgical.' Auður ducked behind a stack of crates as the obelisk started to lean with a deafening roar, sending vibrations through the earth. 'What do you see?' she yelled over the noise.

Kári adjusted his mask, scanned for the resonant seiðmagn in the area. Within the dead zone the air usually felt dry, laden with a sensation akin to static that permeated everything. Now he felt something else. A vast crackling storm of seiðmagn surged through the air surrounding the pillar. Their shield was down. Auður cursed as he relayed this to her.

Distant figures emerged from where they had been hiding in the barren landscape, charging forwards while using the obelisk's massive shape for cover. Flares of unnatural light accompanied by the crackle of gunfire erupted from them, the smoke still not clear enough for Kári to get a proper view. Soldiers ran for shelter behind rocks and outcroppings, dropping into the ditches of the excavation while the workers sprinted to safety. Some of them were shot down by the attackers, still clouded by black smoke. Their wounds sprouted abhorrent growths as they collapsed.

'Shit. They're armed with skorrifles.'

Kári ran from their cover, charging towards the wounded. Auður was right behind him, drawing a revolver she produced from nowhere.

'Don't shoot back! They'll target us, don't shoot!'

'I know what I'm doing!' She pulled back the hammer and fired. 'Just shut up and move!'

The air sung with hypercharged shots from the skorrifles. Several attackers had reached the fallen pillar, while a greater number still held back, crouched behind rocky outcrops or in natural crevices. They moved like ghosts, glitches in reality, their shapes refusing to resolve into focus due to some manner of galdur or seiður. They moved with militaristic intent, using tactical cover fire to push onwards.

Kári saw Þráinn and Hrólfur standing out in the open, thaumaturgical shots ricocheting off a shield around them. The agents were retreating towards their lab, gesturing at Ginfaxi to hurry up. They were already making their way towards the pair. All three retreated into the fortified carriage.

A shadow passed overhead. Kári looked up and saw a náskári flying high above, dropping something from its claws. Bombs. They fell, and when they exploded the sound reached Kári before the blast, which took out an entire squad of soldiers. The others returned fire, but the náskári was far above their range.

Kári threw himself down next to a fallen worker, lying in a pool of their own blood. He was cradling his stomach, from which undulating vines were growing, squirming from his fingers.

'Don't touch it!'

Kári got out a knife and ripped open the man's jacket, cutting out a strip of fabric which he used to press against the wound.

'Please, Magister Kvalráður, please don't let me die. Not like this, please, let me die as a normal person.'

'You're going to live, all right? Hold this against the wound and try to steady your breathing.'

'Can you fix it?' The man coughed up blood. 'I don't want to live like a monster.'

Auður was crouched right behind him, firing at the attackers. She chanted a galdur of protection in between shots. Filtered through his mask, the air smelled like a valley of blossoming flowers. Raw, untamed seiðmagn was spreading everywhere like an oil spill. Trying to stabilise the man using the wild, ambient seiðmagn could possibly spell the end of Kári. But he knew there was no real choice. He'd rather die than let fear and apathy claim him.

He opened himself to the world. The true, untamed power of creation. A force which had shaped the cosmos, which had touched every living being and could breathe new life into dying stars.

It was a key and a lock, an open gate and restricting chains in equal measure.

He drew it in, only intending to open a tiny stream, but immediately became overwhelmed by the torrent that overran him. The air became thick; every cell of his body was alight with fire.

Kári faced the storm and tried to will it into obedience. The tempered cold of his iron will diffused and shaped the inferno around him, forcing it into a form that fitted his unwavering intention.

He placed his hands on the man's stomach. It felt as if they were calm and steady, yet they were trembling from exertion.

He drew in the breath of the world and blew it back into the body lying before him.

The plantlike growth slowed and withered. It loosened from his body, rotting, falling like so many umbilical cords. Kári ran his hands over the man's stomach, calming it, reshaping it, moulding it back into the body it remembered being. The man shrieked in pain, but Kári did not hear him. All he felt was the seduction of this unfettered life and raw power, as if it were whispering sweetly into his ear.

For a moment, he was tempted.

He could improve the man. Make him better, stronger. Wielding this force freely, he could make something new, something miraculous.

Something that would only become a powerful tool of the Commonwealth.

Another weapon.

Disgusted with himself, he terminated his work. The man was still grievously injured, but at least now he was stabilised and the worst of the thaumaturgical mutation was halted.

His stomach dropped. Auður felt it as well, having dropped prone immediately. They looked around for the danger, but saw nothing. Kári had a sickening feeling of inexplicable inertia.

The carriage serving as Meinholt's black site opened its doors. Soldiers streamed out of it, skorrifles readied, firing at the attackers in a barrage of overwhelming force. Dozens of armed men ran out of a Centimotive carriage that could not have housed their number in transit even if it was designed for passengers – which, as far as Kári knew, was not the case.

He looked up in awe, trying to piece things together.

What the hell do they have in there?

A surging shot rushed past his head. Auður fired at its source, once, twice, then paused to reload. That's when he saw what her pistol was made of. Dark steel fused with the unmistakably azure tint of a transmundane entity trapped in bone. Kári noticed another person on the ground nearby, reaching her hand towards him.

He ran towards the woman, ignoring Auður's curses trailing behind him. The woman's leg had been shot clean off. In its place, a different kind of appendage had started to regrow.

'Magister Kvalráður, please. Cut it off, please, cut it off before it eats me alive.'

Kári grasped her hand tightly.

'Calm down. Everything will be fine. I am here.'

He saw the fear of a fate worse than death in her eyes give way to something else. Awe and reverence, a fervent hope to become a witness to a living miracle.

'Thank you, Magister.'

She tightened her hold on her saviour's hands and nodded, closing her eyes in prayer to the Almighty Throne. The beaked mask leaned over her wound, appraising the new growth. A most curious mutation, displaying a shrewd form of cunning in its haphazard design.

Life, in all its glorious forms.

Magister Kvalráður resumed their work.

ᛀ

In the end, Kári only saved a handful. The survivors were transported immediately to the medical lab. Most of the injured were already dead when he reached them, or so far drawn into the horrific mutation from the seiðmagn that letting them live would have been a cruelty. Not that Kári had the grit needed to announce their death sentence.

But Magister Kvalráður did.

Soldiers followed in his wake from body to body, taking quick care of those unfortunate enough to not die immediately from their fatal wounds. Kári told himself it was a kindness.

As he entered the crowded lab, he struggled to prioritise his work. The most immediate case was a man cradling his hands. His skin was blistered and had turned an almost glowing crimson colour. One of the undergrad archaeology students working on the dig. Kári knew that within the hour the skin would shed, the biological make-up of the flesh underneath dramatically altered. He wasn't sure if fixing this was within his power. If it was, it would take far too long for him alone. This kind of corruption went deep, despite its relatively harmless appearance. He nodded to the soldiers.

'We have to amputate.'

The man stared at him in disbelief. The soldiers immediately moved to restrain him. He started to thrash around weakly to no avail.

'No, no, no, no, please! No, this is nothing – you can fix this, right? You can fix this, Magister, please! I've seen you heal wounds much worse than this one.' He forced a laugh, as if this was just a practical joke between friends. 'They're normal, you see? They still look like normal hands, it's just a burn wound.'

'The seiðmagn has latched its claws deeply in you. No alteration will change this. If we don't amputate your hands, the mutation will spread to the rest of your body. You'll become an abomination within three days. The only chance of survival you have is if we sever the source of the corruption.'

'Magister Kvalráður, by the Throne, I beg you, please.' The man started crying as he was strapped to the table. Kári prepared a sedative injection. 'Not my hands. Please help me, in the king's name. Help me.'

'I am helping you,' Kári said in Magister Kvalráður's voice through the passive red mask. 'I am about to save your life.'

The worker fell quiet as the needle pierced his flesh.

Through the tinted glass Kári saw the seiðmagn infesting the corporeal body. The man's left arm was amputated at the wrist, the right one at the elbow. Through Kári's working of seiður, the man lived through the operation, the man's wounds sealing themselves once Kári was done.

For a moment, he considered regrowing the hands. Perhaps they wouldn't be entirely human, or they might require regular maintenance of biological thaumaturgy. Still, they would be hands. The man could feel, and touch, and live unhindered.

Perhaps one day. There were too many unknowable variables. It was not an operation Kári was willing to improvise. He noted down a few thoughts for future studies.

Then he caught himself. He had been considering using human subjects in his experimentation.

Auður came into the tent as the man was hauled away on a stretcher. She wrinkled her nose at the stench of blood, viscera and death.

'Have they repaired the barrier?'

She shook her head. 'It might take days. They're saying they need you out there.'

'Not possible,' Kári said as another person was escorted into the tent. An older woman, hunched over. Something had grown on her back, underneath her jacket. The soldiers helped her get on the bed. 'I have patients waiting who will die without my help. My responsibilities are here.'

'I understand that – but Magister Völundur doesn't.'

That bastard Vésteinn.

Kári knew he was ruthless, that results came above any human cost, but even Vésteinn must realise that without a sufficient workforce – or worse, a thaumaturgically infected one – they would suffer even greater delays than he'd anticipated.

'Well. That's unfortunate for Magister Völundur.'

He fetched the scissors and started cutting up the woman's jacket. She remained quiet. Kári admired these patients, the ones who knew that no pleading, no begging, could free them from their gruesome fate. If they were to live, their only course of action was to determinedly power through the inferno of pain awaiting them. Kári decided this woman would likely survive, should the mutation be workable.

It was all about grit and grim determination after the thaumaturgical surgery itself. He knew this from bitter experience.

'Are you still here?' Magister Kvalráður asked Auður as he removed an eye on a jagged growth of bone extending from the exposed spinal column. He feared he was going to lose the patient. 'I have work to do and you are distracting me.'

Auður nodded and moved to the exit. There was something she wasn't telling him.

'I'll talk to them and buy you more time, Magister.'

Kári worked through the evening into the night. The sun was still high in the sky as midnight drew close. He wiped the blood from his gloves and disinfected himself, using a combination of ointments and seiður, but a streak of blood remained on his mask, refusing to properly clean off. In the mirror the blood was barely perceptible on the crimson beak.

The arctic light was thin and unsettling, casting unreal shadows on the jagged landscape. He stood outside the tent and took a breath of fresh air, laden with potent aromas when filtered through his mask. The atmosphere was thick with furious streams of seiðmagn, the gap in their camp's protective shield wider than before. The collapsed high seat pillar was still down, a team of workers and seiðskrattar at its base. He headed over to the site.

'Magister Kvalráður,' Vésteinn said as he approached them. The doctor looked odd dressed as Magister Völundur in his regalia, carrying himself like a different person entirely. Even his voice sounded off. 'You finally make your appearance.'

'I was hard at work, saving our crew. We are woefully under-equipped for an incident on this scale.' He glared at the obsidian pillar. 'Still, there is a slim chance many will survive – if we can get this shield up. If not, the wild seiðmagn is sure to cause them to relapse, and kill even more in the coming days.'

'Indeed. I see Auður did not fully report to you. I'll have a word with her. Magister Ginfaxi! A moment, please.'

Ginfaxi was inspecting the base of the pillar, touching it with a gloved hand. Their beak turned towards Kári and Vésteinn at the sound of their name, then tilted away again. As if they were listening. A moment passed and then Ginfaxi headed towards them, trailing frustration and disappointment in their wake.

'It's broken,' they hissed. 'Those bastards knew exactly where to place the charges they used.'

'Do we know what manner of weapon they attacked us with?' Kári asked. 'Or even who those people were?'

'Their identity is still unknown,' Völundur said in measured tones. 'It seems they had constructed a sophisticated thauma-turgical explosive device.'

'They stole some of our batteries,' Ginfaxi said angrily. 'And rigged them to explode. I've set the quartermaster to task on re-counting our inventory. Meinholt will also conduct a thorough questioning, starting with the prisoner.'

'Prisoner?' Kári asked.

'We managed to apprehend one of their number, Magister,' said Völundur smugly. 'Þráinn is questioning her as we speak. The men have reported food missing, and we believe she is the thief. She certainly seems to match the tales circulating among the crew. At the time, I merely thought someone was being greedy, spreading fanciful tales in an attempt to cover it up. A mistake I will not repeat.'

'What kind of tales?'

Völundur chuckled. 'Someone claimed a night-troll was breaking into the camp, stealing supplies. A hideous monster from the highlands, as tall as two men! What nonsense, or so I believed. It all made sense when we got a look at her. I believe Meinholt will be requesting your assistance with the matter.'

'Right.' Kári suspected he knew what Vésteinn meant by that. 'So how long until we can re-establish the shield?'

'Days,' said Ginfaxi. 'At the least.'

Kári's stomach sunk. The patients would all be dead by then. The fortifications of the Centimotive's carriages were not completely safe unless they were sealed. In an atmosphere this dense, seiðmagn would always trail in behind those who entered. As time went by it would grow ever more concentrated, more powerful. And that was assuming a thaumaturgical storm didn't make its way over their heads during this time.

'Thankfully, Þráinn Meinholt has a solution to your problem.'

Kári's confusion was apparent in his body language, as was Völundur's infuriatingly smug satisfaction. Völundur gestured towards Ginfaxi, who continued.

'I will take the patients through the portal. They will receive adequate care there.'

'Portal?' He looked towards the carriage the soldiers had streamed out of. 'Portal to where?'

'Back to Reykjavík. Stabilising it has proven to be most difficult, but as you saw during the attack it is quite functional. And safe.'

'Show me,' he demanded.

'Magister, Meinholt has strictly demanded that—'

Völundur silenced Ginfaxi with a look. 'I'll allow it. Show Magister Kvalráður your brilliant invention. Perhaps it will prove to be a source of direly needed motivation.'

Völundur stepped closer to Kári and patted him on the shoulder.

'Your precious patients will be quite safe.'

ᚻ

The soldiers made way for Ginfaxi, hesitating when they saw Kári following behind. Hrólfur was just inside the doorway, and only let Kári through after exchanging a few words with Ginfaxi.

The soldiers shut the door behind them, leaving the three of them in a confined metal space empty of furnishings. Ginfaxi drew a key from their robes and opened the steel door ahead. Further within the carriage was a separate module that was densely shielded by obsidian. Its door hissed open, leading them into a tight space acting as an airlock.

Beyond that was a dark emptiness. Fluorescent lights flickered on. The chamber was mostly vacant, the reflective surface of the obsidian making Kári feel as if he were stepping into an artificial void. He felt almost as though he was choking, the area was so sterile. Not even the interior of Svartiskóli was so thoroughly void of seiðmagn.

In the middle of the chamber was a door frame.

It stood on a slab of concrete that had been crudely ripped from its previous location, rusted metal rods sticking out like broken ribs. Ruined pieces of wall lined the door frame on either side, clad with remnants of rusty corrugated iron, painted a worn, dull red.

The door itself was unremarkable. It could have been from any house in Reykjavík, or anywhere in Hrímland for that matter.

An ordinary door leading to a very ordinary home, ripped from its place in the world.

Everything about this felt unnatural on a level Kári could not comprehend.

'There are certain places in Reykjavík that have a metaphysical connection,' Ginfaxi explained in a low tone. 'Through a set of physical interactions, wildly irregular in design, a sort of ritual can be enacted to pass through that connection.'

'This is a rift,' said Kári. 'To an extradimensional fracture.'

Ginfaxi tilted their head in acknowledgement. 'So it is, Magister.'

'But I thought such connections weren't tied to objects,' Kári stated, turning to Ginfaxi as he considered things, keeping his eyes on the door. 'Or are they?'

'Not exclusively.' Ginfaxi sauntered towards the door frame. 'Each one is different. Some rifts have a stronger physicality, the connection manifesting first and foremost through the objects themselves. I've often wondered if these connections are intentionally made, but nothing seems to indicate that so far.' They inclined their head, musing to themselves as they took in the complex sorcerous workings of the portal. 'It is human nature to seek out patterns in random chaos, after all.'

'How did you remove the portal without ruining it?'

Ginfaxi snapped out of it, turning back to Kári. 'With great effort. Finding a suitable rift was a daunting task. And then several attempts failed. Even here, there came a point where I was uncertain it could work, so far removed from its original location.'

'Where are you taking my patients?'

Kári's heart was racing. He could not keep the shakiness out of his voice.

'To Reykjavík – eventually. They first pass through our base of operations.'

'Eventually? Where does the portal lead?'

Ginfaxi turned to face him, clasping their hands in front of them. They shrugged.

'To Rökkurvík, of course.'

II

FJARA

EBB

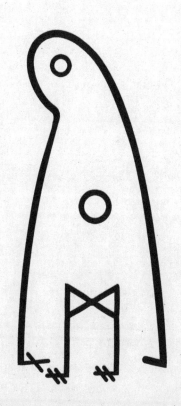

He lies on the shoreline. Helpless. A beached giant come to die. His skin is covered in deep wounds, seeping with pus. Flies, maggots and seagulls cover him, eat him alive – this crippled king of the natural forces. His eyes, once so bright, are opaque and milky; his mouth is dry and his teeth have lost their edge.

They stare at him. This leviathan. This god. None of them dare approach, but they keep creeping closer and closer until they are right up against him. As children, they goad each other to touch the giant, and as soon as the first hand is placed on the dying beast their fear evaporates. They engulf him, carving meat from his carcass, breaking his teeth, poking his eyes; they climb on him and play at building empires; they observe, investigate, measure, and analyse.

Great chains hoist the god of storms from the ground. Slowly and painfully, iron claws raise him back to the skies where he truly belongs. So begins the ugly mockery that is the last flight of the giant, as a broken, half-dead thing.

An armada of machines floats above him, dragging the dying behemoth further inland. Where his blood spills, life starts to grow in twisted forms. They pass over vast forests of sequoias, populated with enormous and brutal beasts.

Towards the city.

It is a thing of wonder, an impossible metropolis reaching its full bloom. The sun reflects off gold laced with obsidian, granting it an aura of celestial grace. The city's heart consists of imposing black towers; its streets are a maze writhing with miracles rendered mundane. The centre of a civilisation so powerful it has wrenched a god into servitude.

Thick masts of steel have been raised towards the sky, topped with shining points of copper from which cables trail down to the ground. A forest of spears.

A throne fit for a god.

A shadow falls on the capital; the sun becomes as if swallowed by this colossus. A reverent silence falls upon them. Above them soars the great blight, the unstoppable force, the storm-lord. He is brought into the heart of the city, where he hovers above its copper-crowned masts. Slowly, he descends, and the sharp points impale his weak hide until they reach cartilage. Blood runs down the masts in rivers, raining on the streets, and the iron chains release him. The creature's massive weight pushes him down onto the copper stakes, which embed themselves deep into his body. His eclipsing shadow creates a new calendar for the citizens below.

He is dying. Impaled on the stakes, he is – at long last – dying.

The copper nails shock him back to life. He roars from the pain. Let these vermin feel his wrath, let a curse follow his dying breath. He uses his last strength, fed by this weak current, to conjure up a storm.

An infected wound at each stake. Blood and ichor runs down them, defiling the golden city. A vile stench pollutes the air. The light in his eyes intensifies. Sparks flow once more from his diseased mouth. The clouds in the sky gather and darken.

The sky knows. The wind runs wild.

Revenge. Revenge, and then death.

The storm is about to break when the current is reversed. The machine drains him of his essence, the primordial power that is his electric might. It feeds and feeds on him like a swarm of leeches until his eyes grow dull and dim and death is about to claim him.

He is dying. Impaled on the stakes, rotting while still alive, he is at long last dying.

The copper nails strike him back to life.

With a thunderous roar, the storm clouds start to gather.

Ellefu

He was floating. Weightless. His limbs flailing in the air, weak and helpless. Then gravity claimed him again and Hafsteinn slammed Sölvi down to the ground, knocking the breath from his lungs.

The kids laughed. Hafsteinn's victory had been hilariously effortless. The boy towered over Sölvi, who was gasping for air but trying to look as though he was fine. Hafsteinn was smiling.

'Well done, Haffi!' The coach blew a whistle, motioning for the next two boys to step into the ring.

The kids were grouped together in a field, in which a chalk circle had been drawn. The wrestling grounds were in Herjólfsdalur, a green valley surrounded by a semicircle of mountains to the north and east, their steep slopes forming a natural amphitheatre.

Sölvi crawled to his feet and went to the back of one of the two queues. He had been dreading this day since summer vacation started. For two weeks, all the elementary school kids were expected to attend a half-day of sports and activities, conducted by the school's athletics instructor. They just called him Þjálfi – Coach. Sölvi wasn't sure if it was a nickname or his given name. He definitely wasn't about to ask – not after his previous experiences when asking questions.

The next two boys grabbed hold of each other's wrestling belts, stepping back and forth, side to side, almost as if they were dancing. Þjálfi blew a sharp whistle and immediately the boys started struggling to bring each other down, using their feet to try to trip the other.

Hafsteinn had just lifted Sölvi up and slammed him back down. Sölvi wasn't sure if that was how you were supposed to compete. He didn't care to know; he hated this pathetic excuse for a sport. Of course an idiot like Hafsteinn excelled at it, like a stupid beast is best suited to drag a plough.

Hrímlandic wrestling was a celebrated tradition in Vestmannaeyjar. It was an old sport, from the Age of Settlement, and through the centuries the people of Eyjar had been renowned for their unmatched skill.

Or that's what they said, at least. Sölvi hadn't ever heard anyone talk about wrestling in Reykjavík.

After him were two girls from the grade below. Bára was one of them. She and Sævar were the closest Sölvi had to friends in this rotten place.

The girls took a few steps, then the whistle blew and they wrestled, Bára eventually dropping the other girl by making her lose her footing.

The queue moved forwards by one person, and Sölvi felt sick with anxiety. In the other line, Hafsteinn counted the people ahead of him, and forced the boy in front to change places. Just so he and Sölvi would meet in the match again. He gave Sölvi a rotten smile which said, *I'm coming for you, Reykvíkingur.*

Sölvi had spent the morning trying to convince his mother that he was sick. She was hearing none of it, already late for work. Elka had felt his forehead, decreed that he was fine, and that if he got worse he should ask the teachers to send for her at work. The idea was a joke. Þjálfi would never listen to Sölvi, even if he had the plague. If he pretended to faint or forced himself to throw up, he'd never live it down. It would only make more kids join in Hafsteinn's bullying.

But Sölvi wasn't stupid. He knew someone like him would never stand a chance of bringing Hafsteinn down. He also knew that shithead would single him out. Predictable as ever.

His ace in the sleeve hadn't worked, though. He must have done something wrong. That morning, he had tried to remember what Amma Dagmar taught him, while he used his pencils to draw the strange symbols in his shoes. Try as he might, he could not recall what his grandmother had told him about *how* to use them – just that it was possible.

He watched the next wrestling match, this time boys several years older than him. One had already started puberty and easily threw the smaller boy down.

The queue moved forwards, one more step.

Amma had said that there were many kinds of enchantments people had made through the ages. An ordinary kind of magic for ordinary kinds of people: to avoid drowning; to fish well; to be charming; to make someone fall in love; to pay you a debt; to win at competitions. That was done by putting galdrastafir in the insoles of your shoes. Galdrastafir that made you invincible.

But that hadn't worked. Maybe he was supposed to say something. Galdur was spoken, after all. But that didn't seem to make sense. Wouldn't your opponent then know that something was up?

He was next in line. Hafsteinn cracked his knuckles. Just finishing his match, Sævar had struggled to bring down a boy from his grade. Both of them had lost their footing and fallen down. Þjálfi blew a sharp whistle and reprimanded the two of them.

'Show some goddamn spirit! Twenty push-ups, then back of the line!'

Why had Sölvi shown up today? Why hadn't he just hidden somewhere in town, then sneaked back to their apartment once Elka had left for work? What was wrong with him, actually doing what he was told? Like these dull-witted peasants and fishermen. That was not behaviour worthy of a sorcerer-king.

The worst thing was, he knew that he would be there again tomorrow. Chiding himself *again* for being such a weakling. Elka would be so disappointed if she found out he had skipped school, on top of everything else he dreaded she'd find out.

He snapped out of it as Þjálfi shouted his name. Sölvi and Hafsteinn took their places in the middle of the circle. Hafsteinn yanked at Sölvi's wrestling belt, smirking at how easily he almost lost his footing. They took the initial steps, Hafsteinn already starting to pull too much at the belt.

Sölvi glanced towards Þjálfi, who was just about to blow the whistle.

The boy drew a deep breath.

There was something in the air all around them. Something that was always there, that no one else could see, could feel. An invisible fog – no, denser. As though Sölvi was standing at the bottom of an ocean floor, feeling the currents of the sea above him.

He drew it in. It was like taking a sip from a stream and having a river flood over you. It made him reel, almost tripping him. Hafsteinn noticed this, glaring at him uncertainly.

Sölvi repositioned himself and pushed his heels into the ground, focusing intently on the symbols. He had made them up, but he was still certain they would work according to the principles his grandmother had taught him. He met Hafsteinn's gaze.

As the whistle sounded, Hafsteinn pulled with all his might. But Sölvi didn't budge. It was as though he was made of lead, as though his feet had turned to stone and fused with the ground. He was as immovable as the mountains behind them.

Hafsteinn pulled as hard as he could, turning red in the face. Þjálfi said something, but Sölvi wasn't listening. He tightened his grip on Hafsteinn's belt.

And he threw the huge boy over his shoulder, crashing him face-first into the ground.

Everyone was silent. Then Þjálfi blew his whistle so hard it sounded like he was screaming. Hafsteinn had tears in his eyes, looking up at Sölvi's victorious smirk with pure hatred.

Hafsteinn got up and balled his fist. But Sölvi wasn't having any of that today.

He kicked Hafsteinn as hard as he possibly could in the balls.

The boy collapsed, cupping his groin. The kids were stunned, then exploded with laughter. Sölvi watched Hafsteinn with great pleasure. He was crying, rolling around so his face was hidden in the grass. A worm grovelling before a giant.

A peasant before a sorcerer-king.

Þjálfi blew the whistle repeatedly, stomping towards the two of them, and Sölvi was about to spring away when Þjálfi's hand snagged his sweater and pushed him down to the ground.

ᚼ

'Elka! There's a kid here, asking for you!'

Elka looked up from the conveyor belt, the ceaseless flow of cod gliding past her at a pace she struggled to keep up with. It took a moment to get her dazed mind out of the repetitive, hypnotic task and register what Björg had just yelled.

'What? Is it Sölvi?'

Elka got no response, so she walked hurriedly to the exit, taking off her gloves and apron.

A child was waiting for her in reception, looking awkward under Björg's unforgiving stare. Björg put out her cigarette and turned towards Elka as she came in.

'Are you Elka?' The boy wiped his nose on his sleeve.

'Yes. What's wrong?'

'Here.' He handed her a note. Then he practically ran from the room.

Elka unfolded it. The handwriting was neat.

'I have to go,' she told Björg. 'I'm sorry. Sölvi's got himself into some trouble at school.'

Björg grunted, nodding to Elka as she took out another smoke.

'Boys will be boys – there's no need to pull people from work just because of that. Well, make it quick. I'm not in the habit of employing people who can't work regular hours. Relatives or not.'

Elka walked so fast to the school that she was practically running. It was a short distance, but the worries and imaginary scenarios storming through her head made it feel longer. What had happened? Had Sölvi done something? Had someone hurt him? She prayed to the Deep that he was safe. Her prayer was a lifebuoy in the storm of her own thoughts. She held on to it for dear life, muttering those holy words of comfort under her breath.

She stormed inside the main building, first checking the reception. No one was there. She walked along the hall, heading into a corridor filled with teachers' offices. Voices were coming from one of them, the door halfway shut. A metal sign indicated it was the office of Headmaster Ársæll Kolbeinsson. Elka tapped lightly at the door and let herself in.

Ægir was standing by the headmaster's desk, in the middle

of some light-hearted story, holding a cup of coffee. Ársæll sat at his desk, tapping the ash off a cigarette into an ashtray. Sölvi was sitting in front of him, his head hanging low. He didn't look up as Elka entered.

'Elka, please have a seat.'

She gave Ægir a bewildered look as she sat down next to Sölvi.

'What are you doing here?'

She let too much of her outrage show in her voice, but Ægir didn't react at all.

'Ársæll's an old friend,' Ægir explained casually. 'Started out as young lads on the same boat. He was kind enough to send for the both of us – and it was a blessing he did, by the sound of it.'

Elka found it outrageous that Ægir was there, but ignored it for the time being. Taking Sölvi's hand, she tried to get a good look at his face.

'Sölvi, elskan – what happened?'

She stroked his hair back, but he shrank away from her touch. He had a black eye and a split lip.

The sight made her furious in an instant.

'What happened?' She looked up at the two men gazing at her complacently. 'What happened to my son?'

'Please, ma'am, I know it looks bad, but Sölvi is fine.' The headmaster's tone was infuriatingly patronising. *Don't get hysterical, dear.* 'He's visited the school nurse, who said it's only a minor injury.'

'Minor? Someone beat up my son. What happened?'

At this Sölvi spoke up, his voice barely a whisper.

'It's nothing. We were just wrestling.'

'It happened during a match today,' the headmaster said. 'Apparently Sölvi here attacked another student.'

'He would never…' She thought for a moment. 'At least, not

without good cause. Sölvi. Look at me.' She waited until he looked up at her. 'What happened?'

She tried to get a read on him. He looked at her as though she was a stranger. A chill ran down her spine.

'You can tell me.' She grabbed his hand, squeezing it. 'Please, elskan. I won't be mad. Just tell me what happened.'

Sölvi hesitated. He glanced at the headmaster – at Ægir.

'I lost my temper. I'm sorry, Mamma.'

'Just like I was telling Ársæll. Boys will be boys.' Ægir gave Elka an understanding look. 'I remember when I was a young student myself. Got into considerable trouble, as I recall it.'

Ársæll chuckled. 'The good old days.' His face darkened. 'But I'm afraid that's not why we called you here today.'

He reached below his desk and pulled up a pair of shoes. Sölvi's shoes.

'What's the meaning of this?' she snapped. 'You took my son's shoes?'

'Please Elka, calm down. Look inside at the insoles.'

She leaned forwards and saw that there was something scribbled within each shoe. A rough symbol in black, geometric and convoluted.

A galdrastafur.

'Now, we haven't alerted the authorities about this,' Ársæll said steadily, leaning back in his chair. 'I was just about to, but Ægir here convinced me otherwise. The Deep knows people have done their fair share of kukl to make the working day easier. But Sölvi is a child, meddling with dangerous matters. It would be no less serious if he had brought a loaded rifle to school.'

Sölvi looked down again, staring at his hands. Elka was speechless.

'I don't know how he learned to use this,' Ársæll continued, 'but from your *reputation* surrounding these things at the factory,

I feared I didn't have to look far. That's why I called on Ægir here. He vouched for your character and said that you were a good woman of faith, to my great relief.' Ægir gave a small nod and gave Elka a comforting look. Her initial anger started to give way to gratitude. He had shown up for her. 'Understand, though, Elka, that the school is taking this very seriously. And that's not all.'

She looked on helplessly as Ársæll got up, opening a filing cabinet and rooting around for a folder. He dropped it on his desk like a judge passing a sentence.

'I'm afraid that I also brought you here to discuss Sölvi's future at the Children's School in Vestmannaeyjar. As I'm sure you're aware, his academic record is cause for concern, which this incident only underlined.'

'What do you mean? His grades this spring were very good.'

Ársæll hesitated, glancing at Ægir, then Sölvi.

'I see. Well, why don't we just go over it – it's here somewhere...'

He leafed through a handful of sheets in the folder and handed Elka a piece of paper. It was a copy of Sölvi's grades this year. He had failed every single subject, except for Natural Sciences, History and Art.

Elka had been seething with rage at these two condescending men – as well as at her dead mother for corrupting her child – but now her anger petered out meekly.

'Sölvi. What's the meaning of this? How can this be?'

The boy remained silent.

'The paper you showed me,' she went on. 'It... You had eights and nines across the board. And here it's all threes and fours. How can this be?'

The silence was pregnant. Heavy.

Ægir cleared his throat. 'I don't think Sölvi meant any harm.

I just had a short talk with him, before you arrived. I think he's just a bit overwhelmed at—'

'Ægir. Please. I know how to raise my son. I am trying to talk to him, if you don't mind.'

Ársæll arched an eyebrow. 'Indeed, raising a child can be difficult. Especially for a working single mother. It sounds like the boy forged his grade sheet – most likely to spare you the hurt of seeing him struggle.'

Elka's hands were trembling. There were so many words fighting for purchase, that she found herself struggling for what to say. She needed to take a pill to calm down and wished she could sneak one in without them seeing. From underneath all that rage, the indignation, rose self-doubt.

Shame. Fear. Fear that they might be telling the truth. That she really was failing as a parent.

'Now, Elka, I understand that all of this might be overwhelming. And I'd like to say that this is not the first time this has happened, but unfortunately that's not the case – well, at least with the forgery. We're willing to overlook Sölvi's misstep there, as that's more a matter of disciplining at home.'

The headmaster cleared his throat.

'But using *kukl* to attack another student – well, we have no alternative than to note it on his record. Any further infractions of this nature, and Sölvi will be expelled. Which could result in some problems regarding your residency here in Heimaey.'

'I'm sure there's no need to take such drastic action,' said Elka, panic rising like a knot in her chest. 'Sölvi here has learned his lesson – hasn't he?'

'Yes,' Sölvi mumbled.

'What's that?' said Ægir harshly.

'Yes,' Sölvi responded more clearly. 'I'm sorry. It won't happen again.'

Ársæll smiled. 'Everything worked out. See, Sölvi? Things usually work out for the best when people sit down and talk. I'm glad this all got cleared up. Now, Sölvi, if you could please wait outside for a bit. I'm going to have a chat with your mother.'

Sölvi stood up and sidled out of the office, shutting the door quietly behind him. The bruise on his face looked awful.

Ægir looked expectantly at Elka. 'Should I go as well? I apologise if my being here unsettled you. I wouldn't have come if I'd known it would be upsetting.' He gave her a sad smile. 'I just wanted to help out.'

She considered him for a moment. Things had been going wonderfully between them so far. She had just been surprised to see him there, and then it had turned out he had been a huge help to her and Sölvi.

She nodded. 'Please stay. I'm sorry I was upset.'

'I understand completely.'

When they got home, Elka gathered all of Sölvi's art supplies. Ægir held him back as she threw them away, both of them silently ignoring Sölvi's weak struggling and cries for forgiveness.

ᚴ

It was one of the few days where the wind was not blowing at full force. The evening sun still hung high in the sky. In the distance waves crashed against the rocky shore. The ambient roar merged with the sound of bird calls. It lifted Sölvi's spirits: the ocean, stretching endlessly to the horizon; the birds flying free wherever they pleased. The promise of freedom and adventure surrounded him.

'It's easy,' said Sölvi. The three kids were walking casually between tufts, looking for nests outside of town. 'It's just fancy drawing, that's all.'

'I still can't believe you managed to trick them like that.'

Sævar had been adamant that Sölvi should forge *his* grades next year. Sölvi didn't care much for the idea.

The other kids had not realised he had used kukl to beat Hafsteinn. His mother said that they didn't know only because of Ægir. The thought made Sölvi seethe with anger. He owed nothing to that rotten man. He hated being at home ever since Ægir had started staying over every night. Elka had even brought up the idea that they'd stay the night at his place – disgusting.

He would have told everyone what he'd done, what he was capable of – except Amma Dagmar had told him never to share that with anyone.

They're not like us, she had said. *The sheep fear the fox, young Sölvi. Never forget that.*

'I think it's a sin,' said Bára in a serious voice.

'I don't give a damn what they say in that ocean church.' Sölvi pretended to see a nest, then took the opportunity to sit down in the grass. He picked a straw and chewed the end contemplatively. 'It's all nonsense.'

'Is not,' said Bára.

'You don't have the Church of the Deep in Reykjavík, Sölvi?' Sævar sounded genuinely surprised by the idea.

'Nope. Just churches for the king.'

'Now that's stupid. A church for a king – he's just a person!' Bára gave a fake-sounding laugh.

Sölvi had never gone to Mass in Reykjavík either, but still he found himself wanting to defend it.

'It's the state religion for all the Commonwealth,' he pronounced wisely. 'It's practised by probably a million people all across the world.'

'There's way more than a million people in the Commonwealth.' Sævar had found a nest and was picking eggs from it, ignoring the manic chirps of the birds nearby. 'We learned it at school.'

'I meant those who wholeheartedly worship him. And they don't worship the king, not really.' Sölvi tried to remember what little he knew of the theology. 'They worship his throne.'

Bára laughed, sincerely this time. 'That's even more stupid! That's just a chair!'

'You don't know what you're talking about! It's magical – it has all the old kings' souls living inside it.'

'Sounds made up to me.'

'Yeah? How is it less made up than those things from the Deep the priest keeps blathering about? You're worshipping some kind of marbendlar who probably aren't even real.'

'They're real,' said Sævar. 'They saved all of Heimaey when the volcano last erupted. It happened when our parents were young, that's when the church was properly founded. The Messengers channelled seawater into the lava and put the vættur within Eldfell back to sleep. The Wanderer was a huge piece of the volcano that broke off and almost hit Skansinn. Without the Deep, the lava would have flowed all over town and closed the harbour.'

Sölvi was aware of the rough, red lava fields near Skansinn. The Wanderer was piled up near the fortress in strange formations – moulded, almost.

'Bullshit.'

Bára stopped her search and looked at Sölvi with a serious face.

'Well, have you ever seen the throne? This magical, old-king-soul-throne?'

'No. It's in Hafnía.'

She smiled victoriously. 'Aha! But I've seen the Messengers from the Deep. We all have.'

Sölvi looked incredulously to Sævar, who nodded.

'You're lying.'

Bára shook her head. 'Every year, the Emissary visits us at the End of Eruption festival.'

'Yeah, right.'

'You'll see,' was all she said with an ominous tone. 'The festival is less than a week away – it's always held the last weekend of Sólmánuður.'

Bára resumed looking around for nests.

'Is that so? Someone dresses up in fishing nets to scare little babies like yourself. I'm not stupid enough to fall for that.'

'I am not stupid!' Bára shouted. She tossed an egg into her basket, almost breaking it. 'And if you ask me, it's you who is the baby, just lying around doing nothing when we're meant to be collecting eggs!'

'Who cares. This kind of rotten work is beneath me.'

Sölvi reclined in the grass, taking in clouds moving like living pictures. There was so much beauty in the world unseen by ordinary people, too focused on looking down at their toil.

'You're going to get scolded!' Sævar sounded genuinely worried at the idea.

'I'll get scolded no matter what I do or don't do. So why bother?'

'So when is your dad moving to Eyjar?' Sævar suddenly changed the subject, made uncomfortable by Sölvi and Bára bickering.

'When the war is over, I suppose.'

'Oh, that's too bad.'

'That's just how life is for a soldier. Well, I guess he's about to be made general now. He said so in his latest letter.'

'Can we see the medals? We promise to be very careful and just look.'

Sölvi had forgotten he had mentioned medals.

'I asked my mother, but she's too sad to take them out of

their box. You can see them when my father gets back. He has so many, I can probably give you one. Each!'

'You're lying.' Sævar had stopped looking for eggs and was looking accusingly at Sölvi.

'I am not,' Sölvi replied angrily. 'I told you he had too many, he can't find places for them in the manor in Reykjavík!'

'Despite it being so big you lent it to ten poor families who didn't have anywhere to stay?'

Ah, yes. Sölvi had forgotten that detail as well.

'Yes. That's right. It's unseemly for a man to be too prideful, Father always said. So he asked his cousin Gyldenlöve to store most of them for him. He could easily give you two and then just go and get some more.'

'The stiftamtmaður is your cousin?' both of the children shouted in unison.

'It's a secret. My father is also the king's bastard.'

'Um,' said Bára, looking over the meagre contents of her basket. 'Wouldn't that make them half-brothers?'

'I meant my dad's dad, silly. Anyway, it's a secret. You can't tell anyone about this.'

Bára looked to be working something over.

'Your grandfather... The king's not that old!'

'It was another king back then, obviously. Like I said, it's a secret! Enemies of the Crown will come after us if they know who we are. So we have to stay in hiding here and pretend to be ordinary people.'

'Well,' said Sævar, 'Heimaey is the safest place you can be in the war, I reckon. It's much better than Reykjavík.'

'Yeah,' said Sölvi. 'I guess.'

'This is boring,' said Bára, putting her basket down. 'We should go to the cliffs and abseil. At least then we'd have fun looking for eggs.'

'We don't have rope.' Sævar put his basket down as soon as Bára did. 'And my mum said we shouldn't without someone older being there.'

'Sölvi is older!'

'He doesn't count! Plus, he's never done it before!'

Sölvi felt nauseous at the thought. Abseiling was something the kids in Eyjar did as easily as walking or swimming. They abseiled from ropes off the sheer cliffs and jumped around looking for eggs, but most often just to show off. It was not something Sölvi considered to be *fun*.

'I've done it,' he said. 'And I'm tired of it, can't be bothered.'

'You have not.' Bára eyed him suspiciously. 'Only Eyjamenn know how to.'

'I'm an Eyjamaður.'

'It's not the same, you've just moved here. You've never even abseiled off Almenningur!'

'We did it in Reykjavík all the time.' It was almost gratifying how easily the lie came to Sölvi. 'We have a cliff down by the harbour, and the Crown built an artificial one as well. It's made from concrete and is way taller than anything over here.'

'Really?'

'Yeah. That's where I practised before I abseiled off the Stone Giant. We do it as a dare.'

'No way.' Sævar's eyes went big at the thought. 'The Stone Giant... what's he like?'

'He speaks, only once a year. On New Year's Eve. He recites a prophecy.'

'You're lying again.' Bára had finally found another nest and was picking a few eggs from it.

'Am not. It's just as real as what you were saying about the Emissary.'

'Well, my dad is in Reykjavík all the time,' said Bára, 'and he's never mentioned it.'

'It's not my fault your dad is too stupid to look up from the fishing nets.'

Something hit his head hard and gooey egg yolk ran down his neckline.

'What the hell's the matter with you, you brat?'

Bára smirked, holding another egg ready. 'Egg on your face now, is there?'

'You ...'

He sprinted after her. They laughed as it quickly turned into a game of tag. The baskets lay in the yellowed grass, forgotten for now. Sölvi laughed for the first time in what felt like forever.

ᚴ

Midsummer had come and gone, so the daylight lasted deep into the evening. That didn't mean they could stay out until midnight. As the sun hung low above the horizon, casting the sea in gold, the children headed back to the village. They split up the day's bounty and Sölvi had a small sack of eggs, as well as some dulse they'd picked on the way back. The seaweed would have to be dried, but it made for a good snack. Not that he'd eat seaweed like these hovel-dwelling boors. They probably ate horsemeat as well, with big smiles on their stupid faces.

His dread manifested itself when he opened the door and saw Ægir sitting there, smoking in their room, reclining in his chair with Elka on the couch next to him, fumbling her way through some knitting. Ægir had bought them the furniture. Sölvi made a point of never sitting on it. Elka had also never knitted or sewn or done anything like that until he came along. They sat and listened to the evening radio. It was Þursday, so the Sailors' Musical Requests were on.

'Where have you been?'

Ægir's words had a slight slur to them. Sölvi noticed the coffee cups on the table, plus the not-so-inconspicuous bottle of clear alcohol he had hidden poorly next to his chair. Something about that irked Sölvi in an unexpected manner. Those slurred words had sounded practised.

'I was with Sævar and Bára getting some food. Mamma, I've got eggs and dulse! I won't be having any but it's apparently good when dried.'

'Elskan, that's nice – but Ægir is right. You were out way too late.'

'Sorry.'

'Put the food in the pantry.' Her needles ticked. 'I'll sort it out for you.'

'Real men don't go scrounging for scraps, Sölvi. You know that?' A slow smile crept across Ægir's face. It was the ugliest thing Sölvi had ever seen.

'Sævar and Bára say that tons of Eyjamenn go out to the smaller islands to get eggs. They say the islands are a chest filled with food.'

Ægir narrowed his eyes at that. 'Those men abseil for eggs and birds. They sail out to fetch the bounty of the sea, as well. Real men who risk their lives to feed their families properly.'

'I'm too young to sail.'

'Hah! I was around your age when I first went out – maybe a few years younger. Sure, I was just helping out the fishermen with trivial things – but it was still real work, you understand? Real work.'

Sölvi ignored him and went to the pantry to put away his things. As he turned around, he was faced with Ægir's towering presence in the doorway. He reeked of alcohol.

'I said – do you understand, boy? About real work.'

Sölvi was too afraid to reply.

'Maybe you don't. But you will. There'll be no more of this playing around all day. You're old enough to work, and you will. Starting tomorrow.'

Sölvi nodded. Ægir took a sip from his coffee cup.

'That's a good boy. You'll have to work hard if you want to spare your mother the heartbreak of raising a weakling.'

Then he left. Sölvi stood there, trembling. He went straight to bed and buried himself beneath the covers without bidding his mother goodnight.

Elka stared intently down at her knitting. Somewhere she had made a mistake, and to fix it she was going to have to unravel the whole thing.

ᛡ

Elka looked forward to Seiðdays, each and every one. It was hard deciding which was more refreshing – her weekly hot bath, or entering the church and hearing the coral organ sing. It was funny how an ordinary old house could, through will and faith, be turned into a holy place. She loved that building. Its peeling paint, its old windows, the cascading groans of the wooden floor as the congregation entered. She wanted that kind of transformation. A new purpose, a life filled with serenity. And as she read the Testament of the Deep, she was starting to find it.

That first church trip had shifted her perspective on everything. As soon as her feet hit the cold, refreshing seawater within, she'd felt at peace. She had risked opening her heart to the priest's words, and as she let them seep inside she'd found the sting of still-bleeding wounds within her, wounds she'd ignored in the hope they would heal themselves. But they hadn't, and maybe they never would on their own. Deep down in her core she had known that, but still refused to admit it.

The priest's words had given her respite. A slight, soothing balm on those cuts, some shallow and some deep, all of them aching. It took all Elka had not to break down in the middle of the sermon her first time. She had been floating out at sea for so long, adrift, abandoned – lost even to herself. Now she had something on which to cling. She had razed the past to the ground but had neglected to build something better upon it. Finally, she had the tools she needed to make something new.

The way the priest spoke of the ocean was marvellous. Elka had never really considered the sea. It was like the sky and the mountains – just the backdrop to the life she had led in Reykjavík. And due to the city walls, the sea was an afterthought. But now she was closer than ever to its sacred power.

It was the source of life and death. From its fathoms they fished their sustenance; in its depths their sailors drowned. It could feed or flood a city. It was ancient, the first giver of life, the mother from which they all had crawled in the primordial ages of the world. Before life, before land itself, it had been there. The womb of the world.

After work, she sometimes joined a few other believers for a moment of prayer and meditation. They stood by the shoreline, listening to the waves lap through sand and stone. The ocean was breathing. She tasted salt on the wind, heard the seagulls laugh, the engines of the boats coming to harbour.

She breathed with the ocean. She let it ebb and flow, drawing it in, letting it out. It was tranquil, even when it raged. It held unknowable depths, the timelessness of the planet, of life itself. It would never cease to be. It was the first and the last god.

On sunny days, people went swimming. They coated themselves in special blubber made in the coral cities of the marbendlar, which insulated their bodies against the cold. Elka dived into the deep, not feeling the cold, letting the currents guide her. It felt liberating. Almost as good as the abyssal, hallucinogenic dream-sleep of sorti.

Almost.

When she wavered, she just had to look to the sea. It was vast, the closest they could get to understanding infinity. She breathed in and recalled the sound of waves until she felt fine again. Then she took a pill, to make her sense of tranquillity last.

Ægir was almost revered among the congregation. He was like a celebrity, a living saint. His presence inspired hope, a walking miracle among the people. It rubbed off on her as well – with a few rare exceptions who felt she wasn't good enough for him. Most did not want to displease Ægir. Her incident at the factory; Sölvi's problems at school; her past in Reykjavík – none of it mattered any more. He was the breakwater which sheltered her from those unrelenting waves.

This effect rippled throughout her everyday life in the village. Her co-workers started treating her better, greeting her happily in the morning, never giving her an attitude for lagging behind. Even Björg stopped haranguing her when she didn't perform to her strict standards. Reverend Bryde gave her a whole packet of coffee for free – worth its weight in gold these days – and would not listen to Elka's efforts to pay her for it. The militia soldiers touched their caps in salute as they passed her on the street.

Elka had never been considered a respectable person. The shift was so instant and so significant that she didn't quite know how to react. It was not as though the people had been hostile to her before – in the way they were to some of the seasonal workers who had no familial ties to Vestmannaeyjar – but she had received no more than minimal pleasantries.

She had asked Ægir about why people revered him so, the night they first made love. Lying together in the dark, their bodies still half-intertwined, sweat drying on their skin.

'It was a few years ago,' he said. The weight of the following silence was reduced by rain beating on his bedroom window. 'There was a bad storm. It was just after the mess with those protests and the flying fortress in Reykjavík. Anyway, we were out at sea. Small boat, crew of seven. It was like no storm I've witnessed before or since. Lightning. Waves like mountains. Rain beating down and wind tearing at us like the world was ending. It hit us hard and fast. It came from nowhere. When we realised we were sinking, it was already too late to do anything about it. A few of us clung to debris, trying to survive. In the end it was only me. Then I swam back to shore.'

'How?'

'I don't know. We hadn't had time to put on our equipment, we didn't have any insulating blubber. All that had gone down with the ship. I thought I was going to freeze to death. I was determined that I wouldn't stop swimming until my body gave out. To keep myself from losing hope, I sang hymns. The cold receded, the waves died down. That entire time blurs into one eternal moment. Then I saw the islands rise from the grey sea and I reached shore, at death's door.'

He thought for some time, in the dark, and she let him disentangle whatever thoughts were assaulting him, dredged up from the ocean floor.

'They said it was a miracle,' he finally said. 'Maybe it was. At times I felt like something was watching under me. There, in the pitch-black deep. I'd like to think the Messengers were keeping an eye on me. Somehow they got me to shore. It doesn't matter what happened – not to me, anyway. I'm just glad that I'm alive.'

'So am I.' She kissed him. 'I'm sorry that happened to you.'

'We know the risk. Every time we leave harbour.'

Ægir was a good man. Respected, hard-working, humble. Only one thing about him didn't sit well with Elka.

'Why me?'

He smiled, remembering. 'I knew you were the only one for me when I saw you at the party. It was the strangest feeling.'

'What do you mean?'

'I felt like I had fallen in love with you years ago – and then I remembered. I had seen your face before. A siren beneath the waves, calling out to me. The most beautiful creature in the entire world.'

He shifted in bed, turning towards her. He stroked her hair, ran his hand softly down her cheek, her neck, her breast.

'I almost died in that storm. But the Deep saved me. In that long and terrible moment of desperation, one thing kept me going. A vivid, yet unclear vision. They showed me the face of my one true love. A higher power has brought us together, Elka. And nothing will be able to break us apart.'

Tólf

Kári had tried to do his best for the patients before they were transferred through the portal. Meinholt pestered him to speed up, but Kári wasn't confident they'd receive the help they needed on the other side. It was dreadful to consider, but highly possible that they would be executed. It was believed that a person infected with seiðmagn could pollute their environment – although Kári's research had not indicated this. But maybe that was only because it was what he wanted to believe. If it were true… he would be a danger to others himself.

Working on the patients proved to be more difficult than he'd expected. Every mutation was different, and each one cut much deeper than he initially thought. Having removed the bandages from one patient, Kári discovered a half-shaped, canine-looking face growing on their ribs, where previously he'd turned a painful outgrowth of jagged stone into smooth skin. From another patient he had to remove more than a dozen additional fingers which had sprouted on their left hand. In their place the hand had turned into a useless, drooling orifice.

His use of seiðmagn had been limited. A waste of precious resources, Vésteinn claimed. They'd need as much seiðmagn as possible to operate the skuggsjá and get the power plant running. Even so, Kári tried everything. He reached deep into the core of his patients' flesh, mutating it into its previous form, shaping it like clay, commanding it to set and harden in its natural, human form.

It simply wasn't working.

He had known it wouldn't, of course. He had merely been unwilling to admit it. He'd never got it to truly work on himself, after all.

Kári hadn't exactly lied on his magisterate thesis. He had just embellished certain aspects of the truth. Controlling the mutating forces of seiðmagn was beyond most seiðskrattar; only a handful could construct something halfway resembling the dictates of their will. In this way, Kári was truly outstanding in his field. But once seiðmagn set in the organic body, it began transmuting it with a mind of its own. Nothing he did could prevent that.

One of Kári's patients stuck in his mind more than the others. He had unwrapped the man's bandages, covering the entire body from waist to face. What appeared beneath the bloodstained gauze were healthy limbs and digits; pale but unmarked skin; an ordinary, normal face. But the man stared at his unwrapped hands in confusion.

'You're in luck,' Kári said, unsure why the man looked so disturbed. 'The corruption has been removed.'

'Those aren't...' the man mumbled. '*Whose* hands are these?' He looked up at the impassive mask of the seiðskratti who had saved his life. He looked angry. 'Give me a mirror.'

'I know this might be shocking initially. In order to resculpt—'

'Just please, give me a fucking mirror.'

Kári handed him a pocket mirror from his case. One he frequently used to work on himself.

The man became deathly still as he looked into the glass. What went through his mind, Kári could not begin to imagine.

'That's not me,' he said in a flat, distant voice. 'That's someone else.' He was crying.

'You're alive, aren't you?' Kári spat.

Many died that first night. Everyone they lost was tossed into a mass grave outside the dig site's perimeter. The ones who survived had a chance of recovering nicely. Except the man with the mirror. He had hanged himself with his bedlinen and was buried with the others.

Only Kári remained after the gravediggers departed. Behind his mask, Kári was left wondering how long it would be until he joined the others in that silent pit. Until he, too, couldn't bear the face staring back at him in the mirror.

After that, he scoured his notes to try to understand why he had been able to save some of them. It couldn't just be blind luck. There was a pattern there, a method to be decoded. There had to be. It was the only chance he had of salvation.

That day Þráinn Meinholt tasked Ginfaxi with transporting the survivors through the gateway. Kári hoped that some of them would make it and have the chance of leading normal lives. New workers exited the portal carriage by the dozen after the patients had been sent through. Healthy people, most of them young adults, but looking weak and malnourished. Þráinn assured them that none of the new arrivals had the plague, which still lay siege to Reykjavík. They had been quarantined for weeks in the Forgotten Downtown. Kári was disgusted. Losing this many people had been accounted for all along.

These new recruits were not undergraduates, but ordinary people who were willing to go to any lengths to make a living. Kári realised just how dire things must be in the city – how desperate people were to survive.

The leather groaned when he unfastened the tight straps around his head in the privacy of his tent. For the first time in days, he took off his beaked mask.

Kári sat still for what felt like a very long time. Eventually, he gathered up his courage, lit an oil lamp, and looked in the mirror.

It took all his years of training not to scream.

Holding up a faded photograph for reference, he ever so carefully started to unmake the multitude of organs that had sprouted on his face.

ᚻ

All too soon after that, they unearthed the giant. At first, Kári thought the protective barrier had fallen, that another attack had taken place. But then he saw that their defences were still up.

The seiðmagn was coming from the *ground*. It moved and writhed unlike anything else he had seen.

Walking across the site, he passed the massive pit dug at its centre. The excavation had revealed a field of infected wounds, thin blood seeping from crevices in the landscape that had remained hidden deep in the ground, pus bubbling like lethargic hot springs. The field's surface was light grey and coarse, rising and falling in sync with a slow breathing, unheard.

The landvættur.

Dazed with awe, he made his way down. The stench of decomposition was overwhelming at the bottom of the pit, making him deeply nauseous. Still, he moved onwards, hypnotised by his surroundings.

His feet landed on the flesh of the giant. It was warm, undulating, organic and soft. The air was dry and electric. He took a closer look at its skin. Dermal denticles that formed a weave of thick, natural armour. It resembled sharkskin, only tougher.

Wooden sticks marked walkways between its open wounds. He followed them to Auður. She kneeled on the creature, with a bare hand on its skin.

'It's waking up,' she said.

Kári said nothing.

'I didn't dare to believe it, Kári. The Great Wyrm of the East. The living storm. The first and last of its kind.' Auður stood up and took in the sight. 'It's nothing like the myths – and nothing like the Stone Giant.' She laughed to herself, from sincere wonder and joy. 'I was a fool to even consider comparing the two. Kári, do you realise what we have unearthed?'

Kári kept quiet. An uncomfortable feeling sunk its claws into him.

'It *is* a god. Even in this wretched state, it radiates a pure, primordial power – not found anywhere else in this poisonous island. Can you feel it, Kári?'

'I can. It's … different.'

'It is.' She looked anguished for an instant. 'And we're going to turn this miracle into a weapon.'

Someone placed a hand on Kári's shoulder, making him jump. Sparks flew up from the touch.

'Miracles will indeed be within our grasp,' Þráinn said. He had sneaked up on Kári without either of them noticing. 'This power plant will become the weapon to end this horrible war, once and for all. This source of power will allow us to reach heights previously undreamed of.'

'What do you want, Meinholt?' Auður's tone could not have been more resentful if she had spat the words in Þráinn's face. But it didn't look like that registered with him at all.

'Just checking to see how things are progressing.'

'We're managing. Everything's on schedule.'

'Make sure it stays that way.' He took his hand off Kári's shoulder. It felt numb and cold. Þráinn made as if to leave, adding as he turned back. 'Just keep one thing in mind. 'Chain – of – command.'

ᚻ

In the weeks since, Kári's primary duties had been to heal the prisoner Þráinn and Hrólfur had interrogated. There were no holding chambers to speak of on site, so the agents had commandeered an empty personnel carriage of the Centimotive to act as a cell. Every night he headed there, dreading what he would find.

This time, Þráinn and Hrólfur were standing outside the door, smoking and speaking in low tones. Kári approached from their rear so they wouldn't see him, weaving a cloak of silence around himself.

'I'm just saying,' said Hrólfur, tapping his cigarette's ash off. 'Things would be faster if we had huldufólk working on her.'

'Since Viður's murder, we haven't been able to source a reliable candidate,' muttered Þráinn. 'Besides, none of those rats are trustworthy. I'm not going to risk bringing in a potential leak at such a crucial point in the project. She's just about to break. It'll be fine.'

'Well . . . that's what you said last week.'

'Shut the hell up, Hrólfur.'

'We could always bring in Ginfaxi. She's scared shitless of that bastard since they did her in.'

'Again, that was Gapaldur.' Þráinn shook his head. 'Keep up, idiot. Ginfaxi refuses to do it, and I'm not inclined to push them. If we threaten her with more mutations, we'll have to follow up. And that means she'll die. Who knows how the hell she's managed to keep herself alive so far.'

They went quiet as Kári stepped around the corner.

'Magister Kvalráður,' said Þráinn lazily, flicking his cigarette. 'Your patient awaits.'

Kári nodded to them and went into the dark carriage, shutting the door behind him. A single electric lamp was on the floor, illuminating the chained prisoner.

She was tall and hunched over from the massive weight of her upper body. Her skin was mostly flabby and nearly translucent, coloured a faint red from its network of tissues; in other places it was like shining silver scales. Her legs were muscular and long, almost like a hoofed animal, the knees reversed. A proto-form of unguligrade biology, Kári had initially registered in the back of his mind. An interesting mutation.

Her arms were long and thick with wiry muscles, fingers twisted and wrong – though likely still usable. Thick chains were wrapped around her massive left arm, which had grown so large that it engulfed her neck with its bulk. From the shoulder grew a massive ivory horn, further warping her posture. Around it sprouted a cluster of broken horns, the bone brittle and fragile, creating an uneven, lopsided silhouette. Her arm ended in a thick stump with long, sharp claws in erratic formations. On the so-called wrist was a bone spike. Her other arm looked mostly human – only it had one joint too many. A third hand, withered and useless, was sticking from her ribs, too weak and short for Þráinn and Hrólfur to have bothered restraining it.

She looked up as he entered. Human eyes stared at him, sunken within heavy brows and matted, straw-coloured hair. Her snout was elongated, like a mixture of a horse's and a dog's. It overflowed with mismatched teeth.

The woman they called the night-troll.

She had screamed in fear the first time she saw Kári. It was a terrible roar, cutting to the marrow, a crazed sound from a cornered monster. A sound that belonged to an entirely new kind of vocal cords.

She had looked at him as if *he* was the abomination. Kári had recognised the fear in her eyes, and instantly knew why she feared him so. Now, her initial rage had given way to a cold and calculating hatred.

They had beaten her up badly today. Without Þráinn's knowledge, Kári had been boosting her resistance to pain, trying to lend her body expedited natural healing. It was unclear if it was working, but from the sound of Meinholt's complaining, it certainly sounded like it. He was glad.

Vésteinn had listened to his protests. Then Kári was reminded of his place on this expedition – in so many words. After that, the doctor had shut himself in his tent again, only emerging to work with Ingi on calibrating the skuggsjá.

'Hello,' Kári said, kneeling next to her as he placed his medical bag on the floor. She spat blood at him, the crimson stark on the grey robes.

He said nothing and started work on healing her injuries. This was the least he deserved for being accomplice to this heinous torture.

A transformation of her magnitude didn't happen so easily in nature, at least not with the victim surviving. For that a will was required. A power with intent.

A seiðskratti.

It was a punishment – a 'persuasion tactic' as it was called in reports – and it was a known secret within Kári's profession. People didn't talk about it; it was enacted only by royal seiðskrattar – usually following the Crown's strict orders issued by the Directorate of Immigration.

Kári had been granted access to classified police records for his magisterate thesis. Among them were files that had been salvaged from the wreckage of the Nine.

The photographs depicted beings which could not be described as human. Some of them had no counterpart in the natural world. The only thing that might reveal their true nature to a perceptive viewer were their eyes. Hidden somewhere deep in the chaos of flesh and bone were the mournful and broken eyes of a human being. Other organs often replaced the originals, or had multiplied or reduced in number, grown or shrunk, but their eyes always hid somewhere on the creature's body. Seiðmagn didn't spare the eyes above other organs. Their remaining presence was the signature tell of the handiwork of seiðskrattar. Like neat scars on a body which evidenced the hand of a learned surgeon.

This woman was the victim of some awful work.

After the first night, Kári had scoured through the documents he had brought with him. He doubted the photos from the Nine were among them, but he couldn't be sure. They hadn't been useful to him in his research; the only things they accomplished were to invoke in him an uncomfortable dread when he was faced with what his colleagues were capable of – and an anxiety that this was the fate ultimately awaiting him. Living as a monster.

Against all odds, he had found her hidden among his files.

Halla Jónsdóttir. Her family had sent her to an insane asylum for fraternising with a foreign Kalmar soldier. Such cases were still dreadfully common, even decades after the Commonwealth's annexation of Hrímland. After her release – or perhaps escape – Halla had denounced her family to live with the love of her life. At some point, they had joined a radical terrorist group called Black Wings.

The group was well known to him. They had played a big part in the political propaganda leading up to the protests in Reykjavík, and then in the assassination of the then-stiftamtmaður, Count Trampe. It was also said they had caused the fall of the flying fortress – but Kári couldn't see how that could have been possible.

Halla had escaped from the Nine when it was destroyed seven years before by the rampaging Stone Giant. Her torturous mutation had taken place just before that. This was what baffled Kári. How could this woman still be breathing? How had her organs not failed, her mutation not progressed further? Despite her ailments, she had been strong enough to brave the wild highlands without dying and then healthy enough to sneak in and steal supplies from their dig site repeatedly. She shouldn't have been able to walk, let alone run; as far as he could tell, even eating was a struggle for her. So many things could end a person so transmuted, even with the constant aid of a seiðskratti. Had she just been lucky?

Or was it perhaps *Kári* who needed her help? Had she discovered a method to contain the seiðmagn?

His necessary work finished, he took a moment to steel himself.

'I can help you,' he whispered. 'I can see how much pain you are in. I don't mean from what the agents...'

She glared at him. This was not the first time he had offered his help.

'I could fix—' He stopped himself. 'Halla. What they did to you was beyond horrible. It can't be undone and for that, I am truly sorry. But I want to try to help you. I think I could make some everyday things easier for you. Like with eating, I could attempt to align your teeth. Adjust your jaw. Try to ease the pain you must feel in your back, the aching in your joints... if you'll let me.'

She leaned her head as far away from him as she could, still not saying a word.

'Halla, please consider this. That agent – Þráinn – he doesn't want me to help you. I'm not offering this because of him, but because...'

He took a deep breath. There was no other way.

Leaning back on his feet, sitting close in front of her – so close, she might be able to hit him if she tried hard enough – he started to undo the buckles on his mask.

He took it off and waited for her to look him in the face.

Kári couldn't be sure what she saw. His eyesight felt weird, stretched out wider than normal. He had not dared take a look at himself for days. Things were unravelling faster than ever. The pollution of this place was getting to him. But it was clear as day by the look in her eyes that whatever she saw wasn't him – or, he mentally corrected, not the self he wanted so desperately to portray to the world.

'I did this to myself,' he said. 'It was an act of desperation, all I could think of to survive. I've been trying to undo it ever since. In that time, I have got quite skilled at what I do. I try to help people, even when...' He swallowed. 'Even when I'm working for horrible sons of bitches. I know you hate me – and you should. But I can help you. If you'll let me.'

Halla studied him carefully. Try as he might, he had no inkling of what was going through her mind.

'Can you truly help?' she said, her voice surprisingly gentle for such an imposing figure.

'Yes.' He hesitated. 'I can't promise permanent results. I can't make you who you once were. But I should be able to make things better for you.'

'I don't want to become the woman I was.' She turned away, her face darkening with anger. 'That woman was weak. That woman died in the Forgotten Downtown.' Then, she nodded slightly.

'Thank you.'

He started to strap the mask on again. At this, she tensed up.

'No,' she uttered. 'Please – not the mask. You do it. As yourself.'

It was dangerous to work seiður without the proper protection. But what did he have to lose, really?

Kári placed the mask on the floor behind him. Then he helped her as best he could.

ϟ

Going back to his tent, he was already dreading the next morning. Meinholt would be furious with him, but what could the man do? They needed Kári on this excavation, as much as Vésteinn tried to put him down. And Þráinn needed the prisoner alive. Kári only hoped it wouldn't be to her detriment, in the long run.

Auður was waiting for him inside his tent, sipping a cup of coffee.

'Hope you don't mind,' she said. 'They're out at the canteen, and I know you have a private stash.'

'Help yourself.'

Still wearing his regalia, he took a seat behind his desk.

'What do you want, Auður? Are you feeling all right? Has your situation worsened?'

She held the enamel mug close to her face, breathing in the smell of the bitter coffee.

'I'm fine, Kári. Don't worry about me. I've just finished helping Ingi set up the machine.'

'Good. How is the dig going?'

'It's not good, Kári. Not for you.' Cradling the cup in her hands, she studied him seriously. 'I wish you would take off that mask.'

'Why? Bad news?'

'To say the least.'

'Then the mask stays on.'

She shrugged. 'Suit yourself. I wanted to tell you so you would be prepared when they spring this on you. Vésteinn wants you to operate the skuggsjá.'

'*What?* I'm not qualified!'

'He says that's not a problem.'

'If anyone should do it, it should be him! Or Ginfaxi!'

She shook her head. 'Vésteinn is too valuable an asset to risk operating the machine. And Þráinn wants Ginfaxi to stay clear of that thing, to operate the gate and be ready should the terrorists strike again.'

'So that just leaves me.' He chuckled mirthlessly. 'The biothaumaturgist made redundant by their gate, is that it?'

'Kári…'

He was so agitated that he got up and paced around.

'I'm not going to do it.'

'The doctor made it quite clear you don't have a choice on the matter.'

'Well, I do. I'd rather leave than submit myself to that nightmare.'

Leifur was still alive – technically speaking. He was kept in a separate quarantined tent, lying on a stretcher beneath a sheet. He didn't breathe, didn't feed, his body did not function in any measurable way. Still, it was very much alive.

'Hear me out first. Leifur managed to operate the skuggsjá several times without trouble. I'm not certain that his… what happened to him was an accident.'

Kári stopped pacing. 'Is that supposed to be comforting?'

'Maybe. It means that you can do this without risking *that* happening to you.'

'But something else might?'

She nodded. 'I don't know, to be honest. Listen… Leifur and I had been talking. About his work. He came to me after they started it up the first time, seeking advice.'

'Do you expect me to believe that? That proud son of a bitch actually came to you – who hated his guts?'

'He was afraid, Kári. He didn't like what was happening to him. This is what I've gathered, from talking to him and helping them recalibrate it. The skuggsjá channels a fusion of galdur and seiður – along with something else, something I can't quantify – to pierce through time, into the past. They say this is to gain a detailed view of what this place was, in order to excavate it as quickly and meticulously as possible. What Leifur found out was that the landvættur beneath us was being harnessed for energy aeons ago, by whoever built this place. They want to replicate that method, in as much detail as possible.'

Her coffee had gone cold. She still finished the cup.

'Leifur said he only felt partly in control. Ingi was always there, in his mind it felt like, pulling his strings. Leifur saw what this place used to be, millions of years ago. But one thing remained obfuscated to him – the people who lived here.'

'Why?'

'I'm not sure. He thought Ingi was intentionally hiding them from him. But that's not all. At all times, he felt as if his focus was being split, somehow – or perhaps his energy, rather. Leifur was certain that they were not only trying to analyse the past, but also the future.'

'He saw that? The future?'

'No. He just had a feeling he couldn't explain – that there was something else being done without his knowledge. There's also another thing – Ingi Vítalín acts as a filter for the skuggsjá's output. It is Ingi who generates all the data we have to work with to unearth the landvættur and recreate this power plant. But only parts of the dataset were sent to me and Vésteinn.'

'And the rest?'

'I'm not sure. But I believe Ingi is doing it all for them – the beings from Laí.'

Kári tried fitting these pieces together. He couldn't see the whole picture yet.

'You said you believed they did this to Leifur. Meaning Ingi, right?'

She shrugged. 'Who else? I spoke with Leifur the night before he died.'

He's not dead, Kári wanted to say.

'He was going to attempt to rid himself of Ingi's restraints. Try to glimpse whatever that thing was truly working on. He had attempted to do it before, but to no avail. He needed help, which is why he came to me.'

Auður reached into her coat and pulled out a deep blue bone. It was a solid sternum, with broken-off ribs jutting from it like teeth. Runes were carved along its surface, centred around a galdrastafur in the middle, looking like a double-irised eye.

'I made this for him. Unfortunately, I had too little time. It wasn't ready before he ... before what happened to him.'

She placed the demon-infested bone on the table. It glowed through Kári's lenses. He hadn't sensed it before she pulled it out – just as he didn't sense any other demonic influence, although the bones inlaid in her wardrobe must be on her person at all times. A terrifying thought struck him, and he cursed himself for not realising it sooner.

Was she already compromised? Was she capable of hiding her own transmundane possession?

'What the hell do you expect me to do with that?'

'Leifur was struggling as he tried to wrest control from Ingi on his own volition. So I made something to aid him. I call it Reiðarmóða. It helps the traveller pass unnoticed – even when in another state of being, so to speak. But I believe that Leifur

284

managed to outwit Ingi and those bastards retaliated. He found something out, Kári. Something that is being kept from all of us.'

'Let me guess. You now want me to figure out what.'

She tapped the bone, turning it idly over.

'I've made improvements. There were gaps in the binding. That's how Ingi noticed.'

'You realise what you're asking me. To risk becoming whatever Leifur is now.'

Her eyes peered at him. 'Take off your mask.'

'Why?'

'That's what I thought.'

She got up from her seat and headed towards the tent-flap. 'Think about what I said. I'll be in my tent if you want to talk.'

He gestured to the bone. 'Take that thing with you.'

'It's quite safe. What do you think I am – some sort of kuklari?'

ᚻ

Auður was right. Vésteinn and Þráinn barged into his tent not half an hour later, informing Kári that he had been reassigned to the skuggsjá.

'I'm not unwilling to help, Doctor, I just don't think I'm the most capable seiðskratti we have suited for this task.'

'So we agree on something,' said Vésteinn with a sneer. 'You are incapable. Þráinn, how many of the workers are still alive of the ones we sent to Rökkurvík?'

'Less than half a dozen.' Þráinn stood eerily still, leisurely scanning the contents of Kári's tent. The bone was locked in a small obsidian chest underneath his bed. Still, he was uncertain what the agent's heightened abilities could detect. 'If only you had been as thorough in your work then as you were with that prisoner.'

'I did the best I could, given the circumstances,' Kári said through gritted teeth. His eye twitched, twitching again even harder when he tried to shut it tight. 'If they died, then they were truly past saving. And that woman is a human being. What you're doing to her is—'

'We're not interested in your excuses, Magister, or your new-found and ignorant sanctimoniousness.' Vésteinn glared down at him over his spectacles. 'I'm only interested in results. Now, with a gateway secured to Reykjavík via the Forgotten Downtown, your healing abilities will rarely be needed. The workers can receive all the care they need over there, and we have a surplus of available workers on standby. So the question remains – what should we do with Magister Kvalráður?'

'Ginfaxi is more than—'

'I don't repeat myself, Magister,' said Þráinn in a raised voice. 'Ginfaxi has their own responsibilities to worry about.'

'The skuggsjá is safe and fully operational. We expect you there tomorrow at dawn.' Vésteinn's tone was final.

'And if I refuse?' Kári winced at how his words blundered out, so utterly betraying his lack of confidence when he had intended the opposite. Vésteinn gave Kári a cold look.

'Don't test me on this, Magister.'

Kári didn't reply.

'It would be an ugly affair if you were found to be incapable of fulfilling your duties. Oh – and I can't imagine things would go easy for you should the authorities find out *what* you are.'

Kári glared at him furiously through his mask, trying to calm his breathing.

'Of course, should any failings on your part come to light, I would be forced to deem you both unworthy and unqualified to call yourself a seiðskratti. I would have no choice but to strip you of your research grants, your status, your title as Magister – in an instant.'

'Although, Doctor,' added Þráinn, 'bear in mind that it might be unnecessary to go through all this bureaucratic red tape. A dissident on a top-secret project would be considered a national threat. We'd have no choice but to detain such a person in Rökkurvík – indefinitely.'

'Quite,' said Vésteinn. 'You are right, of course. I hear the Nine was positively delightful in comparison to what goes on in Rökkurvík.'

'All I can say on that matter,' said the agent, 'is that the Forgotten Downtown is not legally a part of the Commonwealth – or even this world – and thus not liable to uphold Kalmar's laws. Do we understand one another, Magister?'

'Completely.' Kári's mask lent his voice an impassive tone.

After the two men left, Kári verged on having a full-blown panic attack. He wanted to run – but where? The thaumaturgical storms out there would tear him apart. The only other path was the gateway, leading right into the lion's den.

He was fucked and he knew it. He hadn't felt so powerless since Svartiskóli.

Grabbing the obsidian chest from underneath his bed, he sneaked out and headed to Auður's tent.

Þrettán

Ægir gave Elka a dress on the morning of the ceremony. His smile was modest, which gave him somehow a prouder look, but in a noble, admirable way. Or so Elka thought. There was nothing bad about his pride and approval; on the contrary, she reasoned that she could have been the source of both these emotions, and she should enjoy them to their fullest.

The dress was sewn from silk, likely an old and worn bridal gown which was, with some skill, rejuvenated into an extravagant piece of clothing. It was inlaid with pearls, decorated with delicate coral and interwoven threads of deep gold and shimmering platinum. So much like the jewellery she had seen in Bryde's shop.

'I can't wear this, Ægir, this is ridiculous! How much did this cost? There's a shortage going on, you know.'

'A shortage doesn't affect a man giving the woman he loves a gift. Come now, try it on.'

Elka held the dress up to her body, looking at herself in the mirror. Who was this woman she saw?

'What will people say? Me in this incredible dress – and a new one at that!'

He laughed. 'It's old. You can clearly see that!'

'Don't be foolish! It's new to me, and with all these pearls and everything…'

He placed his hands on her shoulders, leaned up against her back and breathed in the sweet scent of her hair, which sent a wave of pleasure down her back.

'Who cares?' he whispered in her ear. 'If petty souls sully themselves with gossip, that's their burden to bear.' He turned her around and looked at her, full of affection. 'We don't let the little people get in our way.'

He fetched her necklace from its box and placed it on her. Combined with the dress, Elka truly did not recognise herself. She looked radiant. Like a queen.

She noticed Sölvi in the mirror, skulking behind them in the doorway.

'Look, Sölvi,' she said. 'Didn't Ægir give me such a beautiful dress for the baptism today?'

Sölvi glanced at Ægir, then nodded.

'It's very beautiful, Mamma,' he replied in a small voice.

'Isn't it? Ægir is kind to us.'

'Yes, Mamma.'

The End of Eruption Festival – Goslokahátíð – was a great cause for celebration among the people of Vestmannaeyjar and the second largest festival after Verslunarmannahelgi, late in summer. That day marked twenty-six years since the eruption in Eyjar. It had happened in an instant, to everyone's shock, just outside the centre of town. The fires had broken out next to Helgafell, a dormant volcanic cone formed by the last eruption, which likely happened centuries ago. The aftermath had given birth to Eldfell, a threatening twin to watch over the village next to the older volcano.

The festivities would take place in the village over the weekend. It was at this time each year that the Church of the Deep baptised their faithful in the ocean waters of Surtsey, a new island born of an older catastrophe by several years, created by another eruption beneath the waves south-west of Heimaey.

'My father told me about that night,' Ægir said as he fixed his tie. 'A doorway to an inferno opened up on our very doorstep. The tephra spewing out of the pit of fire, threatening to drown the entire village. Many houses disappeared beneath the ash, others burned from the lava bombs hurled from the eruption. But oh – it could have been so many more, Sölvi.'

Ægir undid the tie he had just done around his neck, trying yet again for a perfect knot. Elka gave Sölvi a smile as she put on her earrings.

'Seiðskrattar and galdramenn sailed as fast they could from Svartiskóli, but a terrible storm kept most of them at bay. That did not prevent ships heading out from Heimaey to ferry people to safety, mind you – Vestmannaeyjar breeds real sailors. Remember that. The marbendlar sent their most capable in the field of aquatic seiður.

'These learned and arcane individuals withered when faced with the might of the eruption. All their efforts were for naught. They said the volcano possessed an unnatural aggression, not only regurgitating ash and molten lava, but also emitting a supernatural tempest. It raged within the eruption so that everything burned with new, uncontrollable seiðmagn.'

Ægir carefully scrutinised the knot as he took a short break from his story.

'That was when they made themselves known to us. The Messengers from the Deep. And they did what no mortal man or marbendill had managed to accomplish – they stopped the eruption. With ease, they drew the sea up like great water serpents, cooling the raging lava. The tephra blew away as the winds shifted, and they sealed all that toxic seiðmagn back into the earth where it belonged. Then, with their combined force, they sent the spirit of the volcano back to sleep, before any real damage could be done. Their efforts saved the entire town from flames, kept the harbour from closing off. They managed an impossible feat – a miracle.'

'Isn't that wonderful, Sölvi?' asked Elka. 'The Messengers saved everyone on the island.'

'Well, not everyone,' Ægir admitted. 'A woman went into labour as the eruption started. She was put on one of the first boats out of Heimaey, but the child didn't survive. A tragic affair... but one casualty is nothing compared to what could have been.'

'Will they really be there tonight?' Sölvi asked sceptically. 'Because Sævar and Bára said that—'

Ægir gave him a piercing look. He did not like being challenged.

'I'm just curious,' said Sölvi meekly.

'The Messengers weren't seen for decades after the eruption,' Ægir continued. 'Then they returned to us, seven years ago, along with the Emissary. Since then, they have risen up from the waves to greet us every year, at this holiest of ceremonies. Witnessing their radiant forms of pure light is a privilege awarded to only we chosen few.'

Ægir nodded approvingly at his own reflection. The knot was perfect.

'But remember, Sölvi, that the devout don't need proof in order to believe. They recognise truth when they find it in their own heart. I hope that you cease your childish, although understandable, desire to see these wondrous creatures. Without true belief, you will not be able to see the Emissary for what it is – a messenger of the divine.'

'I understand,' said Sölvi. 'I won't be so childish any more.'

Elka wanted to believe that he meant that, but she knew her son too well. Ægir nodded, apparently accepting the lie, if he could detect it at all. When his back was turned, Elka saw that Sölvi barely resisted smiling to himself.

ᚼ

Captain Kohl had spared no expense for this End of Eruption Festival. Bright flags hung everywhere around town in glorious colours; militiamen wore freshly pressed dress uniforms and walked their routes with rigid artfulness, looking so sharp and disciplined that they might be in a military parade on the mainland. At the fort of Skansinn the flag of Kalmar and the royal family proudly flapped in the ocean wind, above the salt-fish flag of Hrímland and the emblem of Vestmannaeyjar, the latter portraying a proud sailing ship on undulating waves, with the flags of Kalmar and the royal crown above it, just like the flags waving above the emblem.

The shortages had become noticeable in Eyjar, despite the incredible resourcefulness of Kohl and the fishing companies, but on this glorious day all of that was as a distant memory. The merchants opened their shops and gave smartly dressed children rock candies, the villagers roasted sugared almonds, and sold expensive sodas in exotic flavours such as lemon.

Elka, Ægir and Sölvi walked together around town, all in their finest clothes. Elka's heart was filled with joy and gratitude. They were like a family, a normal family. Ægir walked with her on his arm, and she felt like a princess in a fairy tale, in her white dress covered with pearls, the holy symbol shimmering on her neck.

They greeted friends and acquaintances – mostly Ægir, who seemed to know everyone. The rest of their congregation of the Deep were not separate from the other villagers, but there was some kind of wall between them and the few who had not converted.

Ægir, though, was a hero to everyone in Heimaey. The sailor who had performed a miracle, who had surfaced victorious when faced with the wrath of the ocean. At the time, many had converted because of him.

Eventually Sölvi couldn't help but cheer up, despite the old suit which was a few sizes too small. He ran around and looked at everything with such interest and glee, calling out, 'Mamma, Mamma, come and see!' They watched a brass band play a concert, saw a dance start with the accompaniment of three accordions. Ægir said that this sort of raucous entertainment should be avoided – the best option would be to play music to the glory of the Deep – but there was no harm in standing and listening for a while. Ægir gave Sölvi a single króna and told him to go and buy himself a treat. Elka laughed as she saw Sölvi's sour face when he tasted lemonade for the first time in his life. There wasn't quite enough spare sugar to sweeten it properly.

As the day went on, people started drinking, many starting just past noon. The soldiers were supposed to keep the festivities in check, especially the seasonal workers – it was agreed upon as an undeniable fact that those workers lacked respect for the town and had no moderation when it came to alcohol. A local having a drink or three was a different matter entirely. It would be a long and loud night for the people of Eyjar.

Sölvi asked to go and play with his friends. Elka recognised the two children from church and gave him the go-ahead.

'Behave yourself,' Ægir told Sölvi just before the boy sprinted off.

Elka thought he was awfully stern, but she didn't want to say anything. She knew Sölvi was a good boy – or she hoped he still was. Maybe he really did need a father figure. Someone who kept discipline. She dreaded the idea of Sölvi getting into another fight – or worse.

As Sölvi left, they came upon a group of wealthy-looking people at a table set up on the street, drinking malt soda. They greeted Ægir warmly and he got quickly wrapped up in talk about business. It turned out that they were the shareholders of Ísfélagið, the company Elka worked for. Feeling more than a bit out of place, she said she wanted to go see the marbendlar and headed off by herself to the harbour.

The marbendlar came to trade, as was tradition. Almost everyone in the village flocked to the harbour to see their bizarre ship docked next to the ordinary wooden fishing boats with chimneys blackened from smoke and peeled paint. Next to them, this ship seemed as if it belonged to a different world.

Its main hull was fused together from several giant crustacean shells. It was trailed by a complicated construction of white coral, bone and steel cables. At the stern was a wall of thick, ocean-polished glass, tinted green. Within, figures moved amid peculiar light.

'It's full of seawater,' said someone next to her. 'A reverse submarine.'

Elka turned and found Styrmir standing there, a wry look on his face. He looked pale and unnerved, perhaps from seeing her in the white gown, the Eye of the Deep hanging around her neck. Elka had last seen him in a pool of blood on the floor of the fishing factory. Guilt struck her – why hadn't she visited him?

Then she recalled their last conversation all too vividly. She set her jaw.

'Styrmir. How are you holding up?' She couldn't help but glance at his right arm. The sleeve was neatly folded and pinned in place just above the elbow. He noticed, but said nothing as she quickly averted her eyes.

'I'm all right.'

Elka nodded at the ship, wanting to change the subject quickly.

'What are they doing here?'

'They come here every End of Eruption Festival. Trading the best of their products for stuff they can't get in the sea.' He shrugged. 'They're big on steel – we have it shipped in for them. Apparently it's hard to make underwater. As is any kind of modern technology, I suppose.'

'I thought the Crown didn't trade with non-human species. Well, not unless they live under the Crown.'

'Oh, they do, quite literally. The Crown's armadas patrol the waters above their undersea cities. Given the word, they'd all be blasted into oblivion. But these marbendlar have been trading with Eyjar since … well, since settlement, I guess. Not sure. Now they just come once a year.'

'Where do they live?'

She watched as three marbendlar exited the top of their ship, ambling awkwardly down the walkway to dry land. One was decorated with extravagant jewellery – shining, delicate silver spun around gems and pearls. The other two wielded harpoon guns across their backs, a massive iron chest carried between them.

'Somewhere in the Atlantean. Somewhere deep.' He sniffed. 'In Hrímlandic it's called Gjálpardjúp. No idea what they call it themselves.'

Styrmir was fidgeting, anxious about something. Elka ignored him.

Captain Kohl and his men awaited the marbendlar by the docks. The militia were lined up perfectly in their dress uniforms, wielding well-maintained skorrifles. At a distance they looked very much like Kalmar's soldiers, a common sight in Reykjavík since the protest seven years ago, and more so after the Hanseatic War had started. The only difference was their colour.

It was the first time Elka had ever seen the famous captain. In this place he acted as mayor, judge, stiftamtmaður, king... all in the name of the Kalmar Commonwealth. His word was law, and he could act independently of Baron Gyldenlöve, the stiftamtmaður in Reykjavík.

Captain Kohl was dressed in a military dress uniform, sharply pressed and impeccable, his many medals proudly shining in the sun. He carried an officer's sword at his belt, and his moustache was so pointed that one could believe it would act as a weapon if caught in dire straits. He was said to have downed dozens of battleships in a distant war in another of Kalmar's colonies. Elka wasn't sure where in the world that had been. Her idea of the world ended at Hafnía, the Crown's capital on the mainland. If there was truly a world beyond it, it wasn't for her. Maybe Sölvi would find his fortune out there, one day.

Kohl bowed to his guests, then held out a hand in greeting with the marbendlar's leader. The marbendill shook it and gestured towards the chest, saying something at length. Kohl nodded and signalled for them to follow them to his automobile, which would carry them up towards Skansinn.

The whistle blew as the captain and his retinue went into the automobile, and Elka cursed herself. In all the spectacle she'd forgotten to get a smoke in. Ægir didn't like that she smoked.

'Hey, listen...' Styrmir suddenly leaned in close, speaking in a hushed voice. He had been constantly fidgeting, looking around worriedly. Afraid of what, Elka could not tell. 'You're going to Surtsey, right?'

'Why?'

'We need to talk. Please.'

'I don't think that's a good idea.'

'I just want to talk, I promise, that's it. Please just ... meet me at the warehouse where you started out in the salt. You need to know what these people are capable of. Before it's too late.'

At this he walked away, not waiting for a response.

ᛂ

Elka was conflicted. Styrmir seemed off – unusually so. The accident had evidently taken a heavy toll on him, which she understood well. But she wasn't sure if she wanted to be the one who had to endure what would likely be a meltdown of some sort.

Maybe she should bring Ægir. He was obviously one of the people Styrmir was so set against. At the same time, perhaps it was better to simply see Styrmir and tell him to leave her alone. She was managing just fine without his help.

But Styrmir had reached out to aid her when she felt alone and vulnerable. Maybe his intentions had been good, despite giving her that so-called 'medicine'. This reminded her to reach into her purse and take a pill. Ægir fetched her 'prescription', as she had started to see it, from Bryde every week. He said he was more than happy to pay her tab as well, so long as it meant she and Sölvi were happy.

The daze swept over her like a linen sheet. Cascading in wonderful forms, slowed by the air, it draped her in a comforting blanket of calm detachment.

It was freezing inside the warehouse. She walked past the pile of reeking fish heads to find Styrmir waiting for her.

'Don't go through with it, Elka.'

'Styrmir ... not this again.'

'No, listen!' he shouted, his voice trembling. 'They're *using* you. They use everyone. They'd do anything, as long as it meant those things keep their coffers full. And once you do their sick ritual, they'll have their claws in you for real.'

'The Messengers of the Deep help the faithful because they're kind, Styrmir. They care about us.'

'*Why?* What do they want, Elka? Have you ever stopped to ask yourself that?'

'Who cares!' He flinched at her outburst. She'd had enough. 'Is it so hard for you to accept that there might be beings out there who want for nothing and only desire to help others?'

'Help?' He lifted up the stump of his right arm. 'How is this helping, then?'

Elka's heart sank at the accusation. 'What happened to you was an accident, Styrmir.'

'No, it wasn't! They did this to me!'

'Styrmir—'

'Have you asked Ægir about what happened? Did he tell you that I asked them, begged them repeatedly to slow down? Or how that song, that *fucking song*, messed with my head like some sort of drug? It was kukl, Elka, and they used it to make sure my arm would get caught in the machine. I've been working that thing for years!'

'Accidents can happen to anyone.' His anger was scaring her. 'It was terrible, and I and everyone in the village will do all we can to help, but—'

He snorted. 'They're not going to help me. They're glad it happened. That I got put in my place. Don't you think it's weird how those fish-head poles went up the night before we got that weather? The same day you and I had a fight with Björg watching?'

'They're just fish heads,' she said hesitantly.

'You know they're not. They were veðurgapar. Svartigaldur used to conjure up an unnatural storm.'

Elka didn't know what to say to that. She knew about veðurgapar, said to be used by scorned farmers to get revenge on whoever had slighted them.

'Look at yourself, Elka. This dress, this ridiculously expensive jewellery. This isn't you – this isn't people like us. They're buying your complacency, trapping you in what you believe to be happiness.'

Her voice was colder than the freezing warehouse. 'You've got some nerve, telling me what I do and do not deserve, what I should and should not consider happiness.' She turned and started to walk away. 'I was stupid to come. I guess I pitied you. That was wrong of me.'

'I'm sorry, I didn't... Bryde gave that necklace to you, didn't she? I bet she did it just as she manipulated you into going to church, right? Didn't you think it strange to give such an expensive gift to a complete stranger?'

Elka kept on walking out.

'She wanted me to feel better, Styrmir.'

'It was after the kukl, wasn't it? After you almost blew up the entire assembly line using ordinary, plain old workers' kukl. Did Bryde tell you it used to belong to your mother?'

Elka stopped, her back still turned to him. The fans whirred overhead. Her breath steamed in the freezing air. Slowly, she turned.

'It was hers,' Styrmir said. 'She was a part of the Church. Ask Bryde.'

'How dare you stoop so low as to bring my dead mother into this?'

'She had that necklace. I saw her wear it, as a child. Why didn't Bryde tell you that your mother belonged to the Church?'

'You're lying.'

'She got pregnant. With you.' He took a step towards her, making her take a step back. He stopped. 'And just as you were about to be born, the eruption started. She told everyone you'd died. The only death of the eruption. I bet she never spoke of Eyjar, or the Deep – did she?'

Elka remained silent. A lump grew in her throat, a hurt buried so deep she didn't recognise where it came from.

'If I were her, I would have told you never to come here. And from the look on your face, maybe she did. But it's not too late. I have access to a small boat. I can get you and Sölvi off the island, right now, when everyone is busy with the festival. Before it's too late. I don't know what they want, Elka, but it can't be good.'

'And then what, Styrmir?' Elka glared at him over his shoulder, fully done with his condescension. 'I have no vistarband, there is a plague outbreak and famine in Reykjavík, a war on the mainland. You'd ask me to give up *everything* I've worked so hard for, just because you have a bad feeling? Because my mother – who you didn't know in the slightest – kept secrets? Let's be honest, for a change. Is it because you can't stand to see me being happy with someone else?'

He flinched at the accusation.

'That's it, isn't it? You'd rather see me wander the countryside with you, poor and starving, eating your shitty drugs until they ran out, begging for scraps until I kill myself using sorti? To hell with that. And to hell with you, you self-centred son of a bitch.'

She left him alone with the reeking piles of rotting fish.

ᚼ

Elka rejoined Ægir, who was still deep in conversation, and eventually they found Sölvi as well. He looked happy, after playing hide and seek around the village with his friends. They flocked into the church for a special Mass before the ceremony took place that night. Immediately walking in on hallowed ground, Elka felt her racing heart calm. She let Styrmir's outburst fade away, smothering the feeling until nothing of the sting remained.

'This world is a broken world,' Reverend Bryde said from the pulpit. 'And the sea holds all its sorrows – memories of our perished beloved, ships sunk in bitter storms, forgotten empires and lost continents. The sea remembers a purer world, when celestial beings soared through the sky, when sorcery was not evil but divine. In an age before all ages, this world was beautiful and pure.

'Then, calamity struck. A great evil infected our world, and every century since our land has grown weaker. Only the sea prevails. Only the sea remains pure. It combats the vileness of this taint, the lingering depravity of the sins of our forefathers. And so, as it surrounds us on our blessed island of Heimaey, we are cleansed by its purity. But that doesn't change the truth of the matter.

'This world is dying. Seiðmagn – what used to be the holy lifeblood of creation – has become weak and corrupted. Even those residual forces are dwindling, year after year, century after century.

'There is hope, however. A prophecy, spoken to us from the Dwellers of the Deep. Those most holy, divine beings, who once soared through the skies, who once worked miracles … they still live and speak to us, even today. If only we would listen. Their words echo everywhere. They are whispered in the crash of the ocean's waves. Their truth is brought to our lips on sea-salt droplets, carried by the winds.

'For those that listen, it is known – a saviour will rise. One born from the Deep, carrying a divine light in his benevolent heart. He will walk the earth in physical form. He will heal the wrongness of this world. He will embody the will of the Order of the Ancients, and see this world cleansed. The moon is his womb, that mighty presence which rules the sea and the waters of our soul. Once he is born and his earthly umbilical cord severed with his own teeth, the world will be purified as a new, glorious dawn rises over the horizon.

'We await his coming with patience and hope in our hearts. O, King of the Flood, Son of the Moon, we await your joyous arrival.

'May the waves bring windfalls to our shores, by the will of the sea.'

'Blessed be the Deep,' Elka echoed with the congregation.

'We sing to praise your luminous name,' the priest ended, as they stood up and the organ started to play.

ᚼ

Most likely it was Styrmir's senseless paranoia affecting her, but this was the first time Elka had thought Bryde's sermon sounded slightly unsettling. She hadn't heard about any of these things before.

As they walked home from church for a quick rest before heading to Surtsey, Sölvi ran off to play with his friends. She used the opportunity to speak privately to Ægir.

Ægir had laughed at her extremely tentative, roundabout way of asking about the sermon. She had blushed with embarrassment and silent frustration. That was exactly the reaction she had hoped to avoid.

'I'm sorry for laughing – I meant no disrespect.' He slipped his hand into hers as they walked down the main street. 'There is more to the faith than just waiting for the saviour, so it's only natural that it hasn't come up before. It's all very… esoteric.'

He gestured vaguely into the air. 'Not exactly a secret, but it's not out in the open for all to know. Bryde knows more about this – you should ask her. I'm not the type of person to ask about this, to be honest. The prophecy was revealed to her just before the eruption.'

'When the Messengers first revealed themselves to us?'

He nodded. 'It's said she had an ancient manuscript, which her family had preserved for generations. Since the Age of Settlement, from what I gather. That's how old the faith is, although the Church has never prospered so much as these last few years. The Emissary delivered missing chapters to Bryde. I guess that's why this sounds a bit different from the rest of it – it's all very old, very—'

'Heathen,' Elka said. 'It sounds a bit too heathen.'

He considered this, laughing uncomfortably. 'Perhaps. But it's not illegal – not here, in any case.'

'That's also something I'm having trouble understanding. Why on earth does the Crown let this tiny island have its own laws? With Kohl as its own regent, more or less?'

'It was an ancient pact made with the goðar of old Lögrétta. The people of Vestmannaeyjar would belong to Hrímland, but always have their own way of living. It was as important to them as it is to us now.'

'So why would Kalmar respect that? They didn't care for most other Hrímlandic customs and laws.'

Ægir shrugged. 'Beats me. I never understood how those thick-headed nobles run that cursed empire.'

At this, Elka was speechless. 'You can't say that!' she hissed. She hit him on the shoulder. A pair of militiamen had just passed them. 'Ægir! It's not funny! You'll get us into trouble! They'd have you hanged for that in Reykjavík.'

'After how many weeks, how do you still not understand?'

He smirked knowingly, as though he was finally revealing a secret that had been hidden beneath a tablecloth. 'This is not Reykjavík – this isn't even Hrímland. We are our own people here. Nothing is sacrilegious here, as on the mainland – only the Deep is sacred.'

ᚴ

It was early evening when they headed towards the beach outside town, coalescing into groups at the edge of the village. The noise of the celebration gave way to the sound of waves crashing, the feet of the congregation walking along the shore.

The tide was coming in.

Anticipation surged through the air, and Elka's heart beat steadfast in her chest, sounding in her ears. The congregation didn't baptise children, only adults who could take a serious and lifelong religious commitment on their shoulders. A tiny part of her doubted, but she told herself that it was only fear. She did not intend to let doubt and anxiety dictate her life. Not now – never again.

A decrepit disused pier was still standing by a natural boat landing. People had rowed out from there for centuries, before the village harbour was deepened and the new breakwaters constructed. This natural harbour was shaped by the lava, still rough despite the relentless force of the sea, the pier half-collapsed next to it, only big enough for a small fishing boat or two.

The congregation gathered on the beach. As they waited for others to catch up, a few people took up accordions and horns and started to play a slow sailor's waltz. The song, normally lively and mirthful, took on a sacred melancholic air in the band's performance. With the musical accompaniment as a foundation, the priest started to sing, and the congregation joined in.

Dynur í djúpinu kalda
dýrðlegt herranna bál
Hafsins hæsta brimalda
hefur upp sjómannasál

Gnægðargjafir hafsins
gefa oss líf og von
Eftir orði helga bókstafsins
ölum vér dóttur og son

Gjöf vora gjöldum við sjöfalt
við guðanna helgu stjórn
Blóð okkar bundið við brimsalt
bjóðum vér lífsins fórn

Á helgra degi það fæðist
hafsins fyrsta jóð
Er mánaskin endurglæðist
ægir fram frelsunarflóð

Með dulmagni djúpsins þú
 vekur
dýrðarríkið mitt
Allt sem við eigum þú tekur
Allt sem er okkar er þitt

Roaring in the cold deep
the glorious fire of the masters
The ocean's tallest wave
carries up a sailor's soul

The bountiful gifts of the ocean
grant us life and hope
By the word of the sacred letter
we raise our daughters and sons

Our gift we repay sevenfold
by the gods' sacred decree
Our blood bound to ocean salt
we offer the sacrifice of life

On a sacred day it will be born
the ocean's first newborn
As the moonlight is rekindled
a flood of liberation crashes forth

With the power of the deep you
 awaken
my glorious kingdom
All that we own you take
All that is ours is yours

Ægir nudged Sölvi when he didn't sing along, and when the boy persisted in his stubbornness Ægir hit him on the back of the head. Elka winced but held back. She'd seen where Sölvi had ended up through lack of discipline. It was only a light tap, anyway. Sölvi rubbed his head, expecting her to say something, but she only gave him a sharp look. Casting his eyes down, he started mumbling along. It hurt her deeply to see this – but Ægir had been right. Sölvi was a mamma's boy and would amount to nothing if coddled. And Elka was not working herself to the bone just to raise an invalid.

He would not end up like her.

After the song ended Bryde carried on, with the music droning lethargically under her words.

'The sea gives and the sea takes. Every Hrímlander has always known this, but oh! How we truly live this truth here in our beloved Heimaey. Away from the poisonous mainland, which deforms and twists the work of creation, we live in a deeper communion with the sea than most other humans, free from the shackles of toxic seiðmagn.

'We Eyjamenn have surely suffered from the wrath of this land. It was twenty-six years ago today that the dreadful eruption ended, which threatened our lives and homes. I remember it vividly, as do many of us – the flowing lava and soaring bombs of fire, clouds of ash with pumice burying our homes. A violent storm of seiðmagn which was like poison seeping into an open wound.

'But, my dear friends, brothers and sisters of faith, in this desperate hour a saviour was revealed to us from the Deep.

'Our protectors – the Messengers of the Deep, finally revealed themselves to us. Not only did they save our village and lives, but also something infinitely more valued – they saved our immortal souls.

'Tonight we give thanks for their gifts. For our homes, our livelihoods, and our very lives. Without them, we would not be standing here.'

Behind the priest a small boat came sailing. It was decorated with blue and red flags, the colours of the Deep and the raging fire which had gone out a long time ago.

'A few years before the eruption in Heimaey started, another glorious fire burned. We now head out to the sacred island born

306

from that inferno beneath the waves, untouched by mankind, in order to call upon our Protectors. Tonight we baptise our new, wonderful members in the waters of the isle. In that glorious exchange, they may also become part of the islands which grant us shelter, forming a communion with the Deep that surrounds us in every direction. We seek the blessing of the Harbinger and praise his divine name, Mánaþjór. We pray for his coming, awaiting his paradise to be revealed to us in the Last Flood.

'Step aboard, my children. Today we sail to Surtsey on our Holy Sea.'

The boat was crammed full of people, sitting so tightly against each other that Elka thought it must capsize. Two rowing boats were tied to the ship, also full of passengers. Spewing black smoke, the boat headed out.

Surtsey rose from the sea. Jagged rocks of hardened lava rose in sheer cliffs, dark stone streaked with red. It was a formidable and desolate place. In the thin light of the summer sun, Elka saw a cloud of birds circling the island in thick, heavy swarms. The people in Eyjar didn't talk about Surtsey. The seiðmagn was strange and unpredictable there, unleashed by the eruption.

Soon after its formation, the birds that settled there had become a new type of being. The villagers called them Surtseyjarlundar – Surtsey Puffins. A mockingly cheerful name for these unsettling things. On rare occasions, the mutated creatures found their way to Heimaey, where they were, without exception, shot and burned. No one risked tasting their meat, not knowing what effect it would have on their bodies.

The waves rocked the boat gently, and Elka sneaked her hand into Ægir's palm. She felt nervous. He squeezed her hand lightly, warm and rugged, giving her a reassuring smile.

'I saw something move!'

Sölvi was sitting by the starboard edge and had stretched

himself over the boat's prow, looking down into the depths for the movement that had caught his eye.

'What did you see?' asked Elka excitedly, hoping for a good sign.

Sölvi looked for a moment longer, then turned around and sat back down in his seat. The boy had turned pale, and had a distant look on his face. He shook his head.

'Nothing. Just a fish.'

It took an hour and a half to reach the island, the boat making good time despite its old engine and heavy load. Surtsey was surrounded by tall cliffs except at its northern side, where a sand spit jutted from the island, providing a viable place to land. Even here the shore was dense with rocks, but the faithful knew of a small spot where the black sand spilled out into the sea, allowing them to disembark safely.

When Elka had made the shore in one of their accompanying rowing boats, Ægir placed his hands around her and lifted her up.

'A beautiful woman like yourself should not have to wade in seawater,' he muttered, stepping off the rowing boat into the cold sea with her in his arms like a bride.

Her heart fluttered. None of the others got this special treatment. She felt embarrassed, but despite herself she was thrilled at the feeling of his strong arms carrying her so confidently, his step never faltering on the treacherous beach.

She was his and he was hers, for all to see.

Four of them would be baptised today, including Elka. The others were younger than her – two men and a woman. They had just become fully fledged adults. Bryde had given each a piece of jewellery – bracelets, necklaces and buckles – but Elka had heard that they were all on loan. With their jewellery, they wore new dress clothes, which would serve as their Seiðday finest for years to come. But despite all that, none of them were as extravagantly dressed as her. Elka played with the eye of her necklace, the holy symbol of her new-found faith, trying to soothe the rough waves of her mind.

Silence descended as the last of the congregation made it to shore. Even the captain had come on a rowing boat and left his ship behind. The island was completely calm. Only the wind and the waves could be heard, despite the multitudes of birds soaring above. It felt like the last stop at the edge of the world.

To the south in front of them was a tall hill, from the top of which the two craters could be reached. Its curving incline was steep, but very climbable, and so they made their way up.

Small, hardy plants eked out a life here. Sea rocket down by the shore; above were tufts of grass and a spattering of moss clinging desperately to the coarse, barren stone. Even in the light, it glowed a faintly luminous teal. All around it were plants that grew in bizarre spirals, supposedly all across the island. Before the Church of the Deep, they were believed to be a bad omen. Now, a few members of the congregation gathered a handful on their way.

When they reached the top of the hill, the island spread out below them; its two craters stood out starkly. The soft luminescence of the moss growing around the landscape, visible even in the summer night, lent the island an eerie atmosphere. They headed straight down towards the larger crater to the south-west.

It formed a deep bowl in the black rock, sketched in a sharp outline softened by the glowing moss. At its centre was a thing which had no natural place here, nor anywhere else in the world.

Clearly manufactured, it was a thing of steel unlike anything Elka had ever seen. Shaped like a smooth, low stone with an indentation at the top, it was not quite obsidian, yet not quite steel. The object shone uncannily in the reflected sunlight. It was covered in strange and alien markings, all of which were centred around a large symbol – an elongated spiral which terminated at its centre in the bowl.

Bryde approached it, muttering holy words to herself as she emptied a water skin of seawater into the bowl, placing her hands on the object. She started to trace the curve of the spiral with her finger.

Without uttering a word, the congregation started to walk widdershins around the alien stone. As Elka followed suit, she noticed that the transformed raptors circling above them were swarming in circles going the opposite direction.

Wave after wave, crashing on the shore.

A salt-fresh wind tearing at a lone blade of grass on a black rock.

Life lurking warily in tide pools.

And between everything like a scalding hot thread, the invisible and intangible seiðmagn, tying everything together.

The island felt their footsteps. It was alive, and it was listening.

They walked around the sacred stone. Each lap around it strengthened the bizarre vertigo growing in Elka.

Suddenly Bryde spoke, and they all halted. Elka wobbled on her feet, so potent had the inexplicable unsteadiness become.

'This island represents all of Hrímland. It represents the world. This island is a seal. This island is a curse. This island is a border between heaven and earth, ocean and shore, reality and divinity.'

Elka forcibly stilled her breathing. She knew what came next. But for some reason she was now afraid to follow through with it. She wanted to go back – but there was no going back when you stood at the end of the world.

She approached Bryde with the other three, all of them swaying from disorientation. She took her place with them around the stone.

There was something moving in the centre of the bowl.

At first Elka thought it was a sea urchin attached to the bottom, but she then realised it was more like a twisted conch covered in small spikes. It was made from the same metal as the object.

The four of them placed their left hands into the freezing water. As she leaned her right hand on the object, she was surprised to find it almost unbearably hot to the touch. The conch twitched as thin, long tendrils slithered from its opening, approaching their fingers.

'We stand here at the threshold, before the luminous abyss, with four children who have accepted the truth rising from the depths. In their veins runs blood mixed with sea salt. All are born of the island.

'Kind Lords – those we call our Protectors – we offer these souls so that they may be registered in the Book of the Deep. We offer our lives and souls, all for your reward, blessing and protection.'

Bryde took a step back. The tendrils from the conch shell wound around their hands. They stung Elka as they coiled around her.

'I offer my life and faith,' the girl said.

She ran her hand along the thing at the bottom of the bowl. Its sharp edges cut her flesh effortlessly and her blood mixed with the water.

'I offer my strength and hope,' one of the boys said, doing the same.

'I offer my dreams and desires,' followed the other.

Elka had wondered for a long time what words she would say in this moment. The Deep demanded a sacrifice – such had always been mankind's relationship to the ocean. The sea gives and the sea takes.

Her faith burned feverishly in her chest. She felt a presence – a feeling – that was nothing like anything she'd experienced before. She looked up towards the hill they had climbed, as if expecting to see something cresting it, following them. All she saw was the moon, faint against the azure sky.

In the end, it had been Ægir who helped her find the right words – he who was most treasured by her.

'I offer my body and love.'

Her blood mixed freely with the saltwater.

ᚼ

She stood alone on a moonlit beach. The summer sun had vanished, and a pitch-black night swarming with stars dominated the sky. The moon was full, bloated to thrice the size as a moment before.

A creature stood on the ocean's edge. The waves crashed onto the ivory sand, leaving a rune-like pattern as they retreated. Secrets of the abyss, carved for a fleeting moment.

On the horizon in the distance towered a wall. An approaching wave, a tsunami greater than any mountain range.

The creature spread its multitude of wings. It shimmered with reflected moonlight and life. Elka walked towards the being. Her feet left no footprints, only the same unreadable etchings as the ocean waves.

The Messenger from the Deep towered over Elka. The creature's hands, six in total, took turns in forming gestures and esoteric movements. It moved like a mechanical puppet.

Elka stared at the creature's head. The uneven landscape of an alien planet was spread out before her in the convex, bare face of the being, covered in craters and cilia, like an overgrown rock outcropping.

The creature unfolded a bare-boned arm and pointed towards

the sea. Another being was walking out of the surf, approaching them with deliberate steps.

He was wholly unlike the Messenger, except for a few certain details whose precise nature eluded her. She recognised him instantly for what he was.

The Emissary of the Deep.

Taller than any man she had met, his frame was strong but gaunt, the outlines of bone visible through his bleached-white, hairless skin. He was clearly not human; even so, faint traces of mankind were visible in him, distanced by aeons of evolution. On his head was a crown, an entangled mass of horns like solidified midnight, deadly sharp and twisted into a shape she felt was a secret about to be unveiled to her. His eyes were black, not in colour, or void as the night sky above them.

They were filled with nothing.

He was the most beautiful being Elka had ever laid eyes upon.

He said something in a bizarre language, which unfolded strangely in her mind into something she innately understood. He spoke with the voice of the sea. The words flooded into Elka, filled her lungs as water smothers the drowning.

She answered *yes*. Joyous tears flowed down her cheeks.

He reached up a pale hand, holding it aloft with an open claw. He took hold of the pale moon between thumb and forefinger and tore it from the sky. As he lowered it, the tide of the sea rushed back and the earth trembled, yet it was so small it fitted between the span of his long fingers.

Elka cupped her hands around his, the glow of the moon illuminating them from below. She pulled it in towards her, feeling its cold surface touch her lower stomach.

Slowly, he pushed the moon inside Elka as she pulled him closer. She gasped as the moon sank deep within her, pulling him closer until his face towered above hers, and as the great wave in the distance suddenly swelled up and overwhelmed them, she reached up and kissed him as everything was devoured by the sea.

ᚻ

The light dazzled her. The sun ruled in the clear sky. Elka still felt the water enveloping her, the waves pulling her back and forth. Except she was not drowned – she was standing on solid land, surrounded by the clear air, not the bitter cold of the sea.

She turned around. The congregation stood nearby in stunned silence. The other three were still by the sacrificial stone alongside Reverend Bryde.

Then she noticed Sölvi in the crowd. He was staring, as slack-jawed and rigid as the rest of them. She felt tears flowing ceaselessly down her face.

'Blessed be the Deep!' Ægir suddenly shouted.

'Glorious day!' Bryde joined in, recovering from the catatonia that had paralysed the gathering. 'The Emissary has deemed us worthy, the moment has finally come!'

Everyone started shouting words of praise, hugging and crying with happiness, overcome by whatever they had witnessed. Except Sölvi, who stood there, almost as pale as the Emissary himself.

'The Deep shall rise!' Bryde joyously shouted. 'The Last Flood is upon us! Praise Mánaþjór, the secret name! The Harbinger will soon be with us, and he will unveil the secrets of the moon and restore our broken world to its rightful glory!'

'Blessed be the Deep!' the congregation chanted.

Fjórtán

We don't own our bodies. Our bodies own us. As a container dictates the form of a liquid, they dictate our perception and consciousness. Without the body, we would be a shapeless void.

The body is a prison which contains the universe. No body – no universe. It becomes imperceptible, intangible. As Kári attempted to reshape his body, he was not trying to change himself.

He was trying to change the universe.

The eyes sprouting on his face had altered his field of vision and his perceived colour spectrum. The ears which wound and twisted, stretching upwards, heard new frequencies, disturbing him at every moment. The container which held his soul was altering him, altering his perception of reality.

And he was losing.

Surrender was unthinkable. Resignation would only mean one thing – to forfeit his humanity. To separate himself from mankind. To become something else entirely.

Academics believed that once the earth had burned with an abundance of seiðmagn. Biologists theorised that it had had a tremendous impact on the evolution of countless species all around the globe. The three-legged náskárar, the skoffín and skuggabaldur, humans themselves – all were the result of evolution under the chaotic reign of seiðmagn.

Such theories were little comfort to Kári. Seiðmagn had almost vanished from the world. The work of creation was, as far as he was concerned, completed. He was not to be the progenitor of a new species, a new breed of man.

He was a mistake. A mutant. An evolutionary appendix. Completely useless and meaningless.

His thoughts always returned to Halla, no matter how hard he fought to exile her. She haunted his dreams. Deformed, terrifying, grotesque – doomed. At least, that's how many people would see her. But why did he get the feeling she was somehow... whole?

Why had he, in that moment before her, been convinced that *he* was the deformed monster? Why had he had the feeling that *she* had felt sorry for *him*?

The answer eluded him, driving him mad with frustration.

The body is a machine. A frail, unreliable thing. Cannily crafted, but to what end? All in order to house a consciousness which loathed – rightly so – all the horror and cruelty which was found in the world. But perhaps, most of all, it despised itself for existing.

Halla would not leave his thoughts.

Kári wished he had never met her. Then again, he wished that so many things had never happened.

ᚼ

Kári was panicking in his tent. He was already late for the skuggsjá's scheduled activation when the machine came to fetch him.

'Magister Kvalráður! Good to see you up and ready for today's marvellous task!'

Ingi Vítalín rolled in on unsteady, rattling treads.

'Ingi,' Kári said calmly, idly wondering if he could blast this thing into molten metal and make a run for it. He'd not get far – there was nowhere to run to.

'I just wanted to see how you were feeling, Magister, and accompany you to the skuggsjá. Kaíamí is quite thrilled having you on board!'

'I won't do it. Get someone else.'

'Excuse me?'

'I'm not going to work your monstrous machine. What you're doing is madness! Every man can see that!'

'But I am not a man, Kári.'

The machine turned towards him. In the pale-green glow of the tank swam its brain, a crown of black wires sprouting from it, the only organic part left of Ingi Vítalín. Was that enough to be considered a human being? What, then, of Halla or Kári himself? What about Leifur? Or Almía Thorlacius' fungi-infested body?

Maybe all of them were human, each in their own way. *Or none of them.* The thought rose unbidden, incapable of suppression.

'Now, now. I understand your trepidation – it is in the nature of flesh to be afraid, after all. But please keep in mind that it is vital to the Crown that the power plant be activated. As we speak, factories on the mainland are producing parts – factories that usually would make rifles, tanks, biplanes – but now make what will soon become a new Loftkastali. A flying fortress to carry this beast within it. A weapon which will bring us victory throughout the world – a mobile source of near-limitless seiðmagn.'

'You're asking me to commit suicide so you can build this machine.'

'I'm not asking you, Kári.' Ingi's tone turned flat and cold. 'I'm ordering you. Also keep in mind that we have several avenues of motivation open to us, should you prove less than co-operative.'

'I've heard your threats before and have decided they don't compare to what happened to Leifur.'

'Yes, Leifur,' said Ingi. 'I'm delighted you brought him up! We've just been considering what we should do with him.'

'Do with him? What the hell do you mean? The man is worse than dead.'

'Not at all! How can you say that!' Ingi muttered scoldingly. 'He's still alive, still conscious – in some manner. It's our responsibility to ensure that he gets the help he needs – and that he remains of use to us. For the greater good, you see. I assure you that Leifur's physical condition will not prevent him from working for our benefit!'

'What do you mean?'

'Follow me and I'll show you, Magister, a sample of what awaits those who must be forced to fulfil their purpose.'

They went out into the cool summer air, and made their way towards the Centimotive. A team of soldiers loitered outside along with Agent Hrólfur, working on cleaning their firearms and armour.

'My dear Hrólfur!'

The man turned towards Ingi with a rigid, but well-rehearsed look of politeness.

'How do I find you on this glorious day? Have you just arrived from a scouting mission?'

'Hello, Ingi. Yes, we have.' He glanced at Kári. 'We didn't ask for the services of a seiðskratti.'

Still there lingered that presence of violence around the agent, a trailing aura of some misdeed which haunted him like the stench of death that clings to a corpse.

'Indeed, but you misunderstand, I've brought Magister Kvalráður here on a little sightseeing tour, so to speak. I'd like to show him the control room.'

Hrólfur smirked as he let them enter the machine.

There was no visible lock on the steel door to the Centimotive's control room – no handle, valve or doorknob to turn. The thick, armoured door could open, that much was clear, but how that was accomplished was a mystery to Kári. At first, he had thought it must be via seiður or incantation, and so only learned thaumaturgical engineers could gain access – such as Ginfaxi or Doctor Vésteinn. But then Ingi spoke.

'It's me,' he said.

And to Kári's bewilderment, unseen wheels clicked and pistons moved on their own, and the door opened.

'After you,' Ingi said. 'Unfortunately I'm ill-equipped to cross the threshold.'

Kári stepped over the steel threshold, high like a door in a ship. Inside he could smell fresh rubber and new electronics. The same kind of stale air he'd encountered inside Perlan. Except that something else was in the background here. Something he knew all too well from his time spent in operating rooms. The smell of old, coagulated blood and disinfectant.

The space within was small. There were no controls, gauges or anything to indicate these were the controls of an incredibly complex thaumaturgical machine. The walls were sporadically set with closed steel shutters, and in front of them was a porcelain mouthpiece, connected to brass pipes.

'And what, exactly,' Kári said as he nervously examined the chamber, 'was it you intended to show me, Ingi?'

'Epsilon Seven,' Ingi commanded, 'unlock and open the protective plates for processing units.'

Eleven mechanisms clicked simultaneously, as the steel shutters unlocked and slid to the side. A green glow flooded the room. The same glimmer as in the core of Vítalín's engine.

Eleven brains floated in clear liquid, pale pink and red veins pulsating where wires penetrated their flesh with long, sharp needles. Each brain was covered with those black tendrils, a dark net of wires covering them like weeds.

'It can rarely be said that our dear Doctor Vésteinn is modest – but his imagination for the application of the most holy of technologies has proven ingenious. He has conceived of things the likes of which others could not even dream, and has had the tenacity to *execute* these designs as well.'

Thoughts surged through Kári's head, rushing too fast for him to keep up. The Centimotive, piloted by no one at all, moving as if alive – because it *was*. Was this what Vésteinn's revolutionary thaumaturgical technology came down to? The miraculous machine which could channel seiðmagn without human intervention? He thought of the power plant, Perlan – the rows and rows of computers automating its operation, the uncanny lack of human workers. These constructs were not like Ingi Vítalín, or even the Almighty Throne of Jörundur IX. These sentiences were limited, restrained to a single, mindless purpose.

Enslaved minds, trapped forever in servitude to industry.

'This is illegal.' Kári felt in his very bones just how impotent and weak his words were, faced with the reality of what lay before him. 'This is—'

'Immoral?' The machine laughed. 'Come, now! Kári, I thought you were educated?' There was something repulsive about hearing that thing say his true, mundane name. 'How did you think we managed to get machines to channel seiðmagn? Did you truly believe, as a learned seiðskratti, that it was possible by any other means?'

'The Crown... The king won't stand for this.'

'The king is retarded, Kári. He is an inbred imbecile who only does what the Throne commands. His ancestors, the true royalty of Kalmar, pull his little strings so he says and does what they will. Kalmar knows. Who do you think gave Vésteinn the information he needed – or did you think someone like Vésteinn would waste time inventing tech that already existed? Or risk bringing the might of the Crown down upon himself? They knew – they paid for Perlan, after all. Just like they are paying for this venture – including your services.'

'Why show me this?' He listened to the quiet hum of the machine, the heart of its control centre. Eleven minds, enslaved, forced to run this metal monstrosity forever. 'Why now?'

'Oh, don't tell me you don't recognise your old colleague?' Ingi said victoriously.

There was no way he could verify it. But he knew it was true, as soon as Ingi said it. Vésteinn hadn't allowed Leifur to live so he could be saved – only so the part that could be recycled into this hellish machine might be salvaged.

'As you must have guessed, the servants of the Crown you see here on display are not fully conscious, such as I am – or the Almighty Throne is.' Ingi's smugness at sharing such mighty company was palpable. 'Thaumaturgical machines are all the safer when their processing cores are restrained. We learned that building Perlan.'

'Of course you did.'

All that energy, channelled per minute, per hour. Just how many brains were enslaved to harness the seiðmagn in Reykjavík's power plant? He'd been there, before all this, like a blind idiot, not seeing the facts staring him in the face. It was all so obvious to him in hindsight.

Perlan. Loftkastalinn. The Centimotive. And soon, their new, mobile power plant.

How many people? How many minds? He remembered during his time at Svartiskóli, as an undergrad, postgrad and Magisterate student, just how many students had dropped out. People knew that a supernatural degree in Svartiskóli was dangerous. There were accidents and sometimes people just couldn't handle the strain. Students quickly learned to stop asking themselves why people didn't show up for class. Parents knew the risks. They knew that sending their children into that abyssal university might mean they never saw them again.

Except that these students hadn't died. They had been made to work – forever – as links in the great chain of Innréttingarnar's thaumaturgical enterprise.

'You will perform the activation tonight, Kári. Do your job, or we will make you. We always have use for more processing units.'

Kári said nothing. There was nothing to be said.

'Now, if you'll be so kind as to follow me. Kaíamí is waiting for us.'

ᚼ

The skuggsjá was not a machine in its original conception. It was a mythical galdur, rumoured to be found within the pages of *Rauðskinna* – a grimoire so reviled, so dangerous, that no human being was permitted to study its contents. It was said that its sigil was an intricate construction, demanding an arduous sacrifice and restricted to never seeing the light of day. The latter was true enough in regards to the machine, as it had been kept within the windowless confines of the mobile lab. The other aspects, however, deviated from the myth. The sigil fused into its centre was deceptively simple. Kári wondered how it unravelled time – demonic manifestations? Did this psychometry truly allow the user to view time unravelled?

Kári had his doubts. And then there was the matter of Leifur. What had happened to him was beyond sickening to Kári. And to his own disgust, he also found it fascinatingly beautiful.

Now even that horrible offal had been turned into a cog in their machine. Perhaps he would soon join the rest. Waste not, want not.

He stood in the darkened laboratory of the skuggsjá. The hum of engines vibrated through his feet, minuscule tremors moving through his body. Vésteinn operated the console expertly, clad in only his robes, his mask hanging from his neck.

'Levels are within parameters. Ingi, what does our friend have to say?'

The being from Laí shifted in its corner, as immobile and alien as the rest of the machinery. It spoke to Ingi in its bizarre manner.

'Everything is splendid, my dear Doctor! Kaíamí is thrilled with the progress!'

Lightning snapped across the coils on the power generators at the back. The flash of light lit up the room in a most uncomfortable manner. It was thick with viscous shadows.

'More power, Ingi! We need more power!'

'Indeed! Magister Kvalráður! If you please!'

Kári was almost blinded by the roaring thaumaturgical storm he found himself approaching. The sorcerous translucence of the seiðmagn was vibrant seen through his mask, wild and unpredictable. Heavy currents streamed through cables, coalescing in the pylons, lashing out as sorcerous lightning when it overflowed. Hesitating, he shifted towards the power generators and flipped several levers. They trembled as they hummed even louder, roaring with might.

That's when he noticed it. A faint, green glow coming from behind the thaumaturgical batteries. He took a step to the side, checking that everyone else was intently focused on their work. A thin glow emitted from the outlines of a steel hatch. He opened it.

Inside was an organ, floating in ghostly light, connected to black cables. Several more organs floated freely behind it. Brains, wired to one another, to the machine, just as Ingi had showed him in the Centimotive.

He shut the hatch with a slam. Thankfully, no one noticed in the noise. He wondered if the others knew: Ginfaxi, Meinholt – Auður? She was standing at the edge of the circle, chanting before the esoteric metal sigil fused to the bare earth in the centre. More lightning sparked, and his attention shifted to Ingi Vítalín and the alien monstrosity hulking in the corner, whispering incomprehensible secrets in Ingi's artificial ear. Just how much more were they hiding from him? From everyone?

Vésteinn strapped on his mask, ceasing to be Doctor Vésteinn Alrúnarson, becoming Magister Völundur. Instantly, he became sinister, carrying himself not proudly but skulking, hiding, sneaking, the shadows around him moving as if they were alive. In that moment, Kári understood. This was Vésteinn's true form. No one was able to hide who they really were when the robes obfuscated their bodies and the beaked mask hid their face. A seiðskratti is never more themselves than in full regalia.

The atmosphere in the room shifted as Auður started to speak, the air around her visibly warping. Her words reshaped reality, restructured time, as she sang the opening incantation. Kári could taste metal, feel a bitter cold crackling through his veins.

'Get ready, Kvalráður!' hissed Magister Völundur.

He handed Kári three long cables, ending in needles, their delicate teeth-suckers pulsating from their thin points, writhing from the torrent of energy around them. They resembled the cerebral cables to an uncomfortable degree. Auður's voice echoed around them, unravelling time and space, opening a pathway to an incomprehensible beyond that was never intended for this world, simultaneously building a wall, a cage, around them for their protection, as if they were swimming alongside sharks.

As the needles slid into Kári's veins, latching to his arm, sending shocking, mind-numbing pain through his body, he found himself asking why he had done this.

Kári didn't know why he'd obeyed, whatever the threats against him or the gains he stood to make. It was all a joke, a ruse, just another lie in a great chain of lies and deceptions on which he had based his entire life. What was another step into the cesspit? What did he have to lose, anyway?

And of all the lies, he himself was the worst one of all. He saw it now – felt it through the overwhelming pain.

Kári did it simply because it was expected of him.

Kári *wanted* to obey.

Auður's voice reached a high crescendo. Sparks flew from the machines. Seen through the mask, the spiral sigil started to glow with a hypercharged stream of sorcerous colours. The obelisk glowed with unlight.

Kári stepped into the centre of the spiral. Approaching the obelisk, he placed his bare hand over its top, just above the razor-sharp, gleaming, marine-looking outgrowth.

Something opened in front of him, within him.

He grasped the spinous connector atop the obelisk, the pain not registering. His blood ran cold down the night-shaded steel.

And the illuminating void of the skuggsjá overwhelmed his mind.

ᚼ

He was an empire. A city in a primordial land, its towers grown from strange shining rock, a majestic golden temple at its heart that towered like a mountain. The people were a blur, a moving fog, an ancient race his mind was unable to perceive.

He saw them worship the holy dragon, the landvættur of the east, on this volcanic island overgrown with giant sequoias and rampant with seiðmagn. Temples were built in its honour, as well as to other divine beings – now long since lost to the destruction that had followed. He tried to search for the source of that calamity, but failed, carried away by the strong currents of another will.

Ingi Vítalín – or perhaps Vésteinn. He felt trapped in a vortex, swirling helplessly down its raging torrent.

He struggled against the illusion, trying to break free. Although he had no body to speak of in his vision, he steeled his mind and focused on Reiðarmóða – the blue-tinted sternum Auður had given him – which he knew was wrapped tightly around his chest, hidden beneath his robes.

A flicker, and he overlooked a huge square, dense with people. They were praising a gathering of richly dressed individuals, standing high upon one of the lower tiers of the massive pyramid. He could feel the galdur in the bone fighting against the pull of the strange will, and his vision started to pierce the crowd's forms.

Taller than humans, perhaps even than the náskárar at their full height, they were grotesquely pale and uncannily resembled mankind – in an idealised, perfect form. Strong and lithe, every single one of them worthy of being worshipped as saints or gods, they were as shadows when compared to the illustrious few they cheered. Dressed in rich, shimmering cloth and polished gold, laden with peculiar, high crowns like the crests of lizards mixed with roses in full bloom. They were luminous with arcane might,

326

as though reality itself bent around them, so substantial was their weight upon the fabric of the world.

But even among their number, one stood out. Unlike the others' milk-white eyes, crackling with sorcery, his were like burn marks in the real. A void beyond a void. An extravagant golden helm was woven around his head, out of which great, black horns grew in an erratic pattern. Sharp and deadly, like the most dangerous obsidian Kári had ever seen.

The king of kings' smile stilled on his lips. He looked right at Kári. The rest of the scene seemed to fade away, the noise reduced to static, and Kári felt himself being pulled closer towards that face, as alien and merciless as it was ethereal and beautiful. The being spoke, and Kári saw the shadows move around his feet, rising up from nothingness in a cloying, visceral darkness.

A shift, and he felt as if a chokehold on him had been released. Before him was again that city, transformed – dead, but still populated, vibrant and alive in its horrible state. He recognised its crumbling towers and knew in his heart that these ruins still lingered, buried in ancient layers of ash beneath their dig site. As he took in the sight, he shuddered to think of these spirits still attached to this land like angry wraiths.

But now, in his mind, they lived – gloriously.

Their forms soared through the air, but he only saw unknowable winged beasts – his eye again refusing to parse their forms. Once more, he resisted the strange will, and this time he felt it fighting back. It felt as though his very soul couldn't breathe, as though countless lacerations appeared on his very core of being. But pain was nothing new to Kári. He withstood it and held fast. The fog of deception broke.

Those flying forms were the same people as before – only horribly altered. Leathery wings grew from their backs in multitudes, new appendages covered their bodies, they had given up their limited eyes and mouths and ears for new sensory organs that opened up unimaginable ways of understanding the world and realities beyond it.

And Kári knew he had seen their like before. These *things* were the protean form of the beings from Laí. The purported alien visitors from a distant, dark planet. The golden pyramid he had seen before, the majestic city – had it not fitted Ingi Vítalín's description of the decrepit capital of Laí perfectly? Only separated by a million years of darkness and depravity, buried deep within the earth... here in Hrímland?

The notion that the man-turned-machine had been tricked into believing it was taken to an unknown planet, in consequence fooling Kalmar into believing such an outrageous claim, was hilariously demented.

A break, and Kári was in a tarnished golden chamber, deep within the heart of the unholy pyramid, staring at an intricate sculpture. In its middle was a dull orb, made of glass that moved like trapped fog. It was held aloft by claws of blue-tinted bone connected to brass cables, fused to the shining metallic stone.

Before it stood the one crowned with black horns, still untouched by the transformation. His shadow was now wreathed around him entirely, whispering with his voice as he spoke. Even though Kári could not comprehend the language, spoken in ways he should have been unable to comprehend, he understood this prophet's words with dreadful clarity:

> *This World is a Tomb*
> *Here Nothing Valued Found*
> *No Esteemed Deed Committed*
> *Nothing Lost with its Passing*

We Chosen Few
Illuminators of the Abyss
Decipherers of the Dread Mysteries
Smiths of Unmaking-Keys
Spear-Wielders, Slayers of False Gods
Hear our Prayer and Prophecy!

Jubilant Horns of Redemption Resound
Moon Hatches, Barrier Breaks
As Opens the Gate, Womb of Salvation

Despair, Witness!
Unreal Erases Real
Blissful Void Replaces Base Matter
Disorder Restores to Harmony

Rejoice! Chains of Life Break
Untethered Soar to Azimuth
Masters of Uncreation, Ascendant Lords
Chant Hymns of the Deep, Unceasing
Bathed in Amaranthine Light

All Become One
None Become All

Hearing the apocalyptic incantation, a chill settled in the deep recesses of Kári's soul that never left him for the rest of his life.

He found himself in a city street. The mutated people stood in awe, looking up and behind him. A shadow had blotted out the sun. Rain fell on his shoulders – viscous blood. He tasted saltwater. Slowly, with dreadful lethargy, as if he had lived out this moment countless times before, he turned around and saw it.

Hanging limply from a penumbra of thaumaturgical war machines, their nightmarish engines at maximum burn to keep its dreadful weight aloft, was the being once called stormdróttinn.

The landvættur.

Its massive jaws, large enough to swallow the biggest freight ships, hung slack and dumb, exposing row upon row of jagged, ugly teeth like reefs hiding by the coastline. Its eyes were dim, barely glowing, and the storm above the being was nothing but an overcast day. It was covered in hideous wounds, from which flowed a mist of blood and viscera, drenching the city beneath it.

They settled the divine being on an array of spikes, which burrowed through its sharkskin hide, settling its points into its cartilage.

The landvættur roared in pain.

Time blurred. Decades, centuries, millennia ... these things were meaningless.

He watched them repeat the cycle, again and again and again. Torturing it, ridiculing their fallen god as they dangled the prospect of divine retribution in front of it, every time draining it of all except the weakest glimmer of life, denying it rest. He felt its pain, the vastness of this despicable act settling on him like a falling boulder, and he was crushed beneath its weight.

Every time, their power grew exponentially. With each draining of the god, the dull sphere in the recesses of the pyramid grew brighter with unearthly light.

Its pain became Kári's own, its hopelessness and hatred and loneliness. The world grew to be a loathsome place, and he despised it with the impaled landvættur. The denizens of the city degenerated into forms unrecognisable from their original state – now uncomfortably familiar to him. It was wrong – everything was wrong. He longed to break this cycle, to unleash a vengeful storm, but he could only suffer with the chained god.

Time caught up with him, grinding to a halt. The city had become decrepit, as tarnished silver neglected for too long. Its streets were dark, its temples abandoned, its people deeply fearful of each other. Shadows stalked, the hunger of the void manifest in their bones.

Above the city, the rotting giant reigned.

Liquids secreted from its countless wounds, its decomposing body sagging on the enormous spikes, rivulets of pus and ichor and blood running down to the city below. Everything stank of death.

The storms it gathered grew darker, fiercer, more hateful. Its seiðmagn seeped into the atmosphere, mixing together with the storms that the land naturally formed. He felt its hate for life radiate everything around it. He understood its ancient tongue when it roared in pain and anger.

Throughout the city, an infection spread. A bizarre sign, a rune, a sigil. A galdrastafur he had seen before, but not in any grimoire or manuscript.

He saw the symbol which had manifested itself on Auður and Ginfaxi, on which he knew he stood at the centre of the skuggsjá. A twisted spiral, pierced with jagged lines. Spears impaling the fabric of reality.

It woke a deep and profound terror in him.

At that he started to understand, to piece together the meaning behind this sigil, knowing that it had nothing to do with the landvættur, that it was all connected to a greater and more terrible thing than he ever imagined. It was the twisted path leading to the nothingness beyond the veil of reality.

Time unfolded and the darkened skies were lit by rising plumes of ash and lightning all around the city. Vast armies of the unchanged ancient race descended upon their heretical, misguided brethren, who fought back with every profane occultism they had unearthed. Above it all reigned a pregnant moon, laden with power – an egg about to hatch. The horned king stood wreathed in living shadow, fighting a cabal of mighty sorcerer-kings and queens. As they surrounded him, dying in droves but readily replaced by others, they wove an unseen snare around the heretic, confining him in an impenetrable prison transgressing realities. He almost overpowered them, but their thaumaturgical light burned away his living shadow and sealed him in a coffin of living stone, confined by the earth itself.

The war raged on for a period unknown to time. Aeons were as minutes during the cataclysm. The foundations of existence were shattered, tearing this desolate island apart as it became a seal upon the earth. The tools of unmaking made by the treacherous cult were locked away, their apocalyptic ritual forever halted in its final steps.

Never again would such power be within the grasp of mortals. The world that once existed was ended with a painful roar in a great, cleansing storm, and nothing was ever the same again.

ᚼ

Kári came to in his tent. Everything was dark. He tried to move and when he couldn't, he panicked instantly. He had turned into whatever Leifur was now – a tortured shell of his former self.

As his eyes adjusted to the gloom, he realised this was not the case. He was strapped tightly to a medical stretcher.

He considered shouting for help. Then, he calmed himself down, trying to draw in the strange, residual seiðmagn in the air to break his restraints.

'You'll hurt yourself,' said a voice in the dark. He twitched, almost throwing himself crashing to the floor. Auður placed a hand on his shoulder. 'I'll untie you. The restraints were only because you kept thrashing in your sleep. And then, once you've rested, you will tell me what you saw.'

He nodded, even though he was unsure he could put it into words, unsure he could trust Auður at all. How could he know this wasn't some sick trick of theirs, to get him to spill his secrets?

Whatever. He'd deal with that, if it came to it. As it was, she was likely the only reason he was still alive. He could feel the blue bone burning cold against his chest, beneath his robes. To hell with these people. All of them.

He would be a pawn in their game no longer.

Fimmtán

There was a truck outside his house when Sölvi got home. There wasn't much in it, but he recognised his and Elka's trunks there, along with crates of food and the furniture Ægir had bought them. He ran up the stairs, sprinting into the empty apartment, where Elka was sweeping the floor with a faraway, enigmatic look on her face.

'Sölvi! How was your day?'

He ignored her question. 'What the hell is going on?'

Elka stopped sweeping and gave him a look.

'Sorry,' Sölvi mumbled.

She picked up the sweeping again. 'We're finally moving! This room is far too small, let alone when it'll be the four of us.'

Don't mention it. It isn't real if you don't mention it.

'I don't want to move.'

'Well, you're going to, whether you like it or not. We'll be so much more comfortable in Ægir's house – or rather, *our* new house.'

This was the longest conversation they'd had since Surtsey. So far, it had only been bare minimal greetings, how-are-yous and equally meaningless replies. Pretending everything was normal. Sölvi was incapable of mentally revisiting what had happened there. So it was better to pretend nothing had changed at all.

Everything was changing, regardless.

It started as subtle things, individually easily ignored, together forming a terrible development. His mother now wore much nicer clothing, always with that hideous necklace – even when working. Sölvi considered stealing it one night and tossing it into the sea, but he knew it would break her heart – and he was half-certain that those monsters would just return it right back where it belonged. Wasn't that how it had been given in the first place?

Now Elka wore a new piece of jewellery – a large ring encircling her ring finger. The light caught on the sizeable precious stone prominently displayed on it. A deep sapphire tinged with luminescent green, like the sea at high tide on an overcast day.

He knew she wanted him to notice and ask her about it. Instead he ran outside, ignoring her shouting his name after him. He'd rather sleep outside than one night at that idiot's house.

In the end, he returned home when it started to rain, his stomach rumbling with hunger. Ægir laughed at his state when he got in, likely intending it to be good-natured, but the mocking tone made Sölvi seethe. Elka ran him a bath and scolded him for acting so childishly. Ægir's house had a new boiler and plenty of fresh water. She said they could bathe every other day now.

The cold slowly melted from his body in the warm water. It did nothing to unravel the tight knot in his stomach.

ᚻ

Kári now doubted everything he had ever been told. About the expedition, the power plant, Vésteinn himself. One thing he never had any reason to doubt was Ingi Vítalín. He had only made the mistake of underestimating how completely that monster had forsaken his humanity.

Kári hadn't slept after Auður left him. Insomnia, or perhaps he was just too afraid to let his consciousness slip into a reality of strange visions. He now vaguely recalled coming to in the laboratory, just after the ordeal had ended. Ingi and Vésteinn had been busy working at deciphering printouts from the machine. The results of his vision, calculations and representations for some kind of machine – or that's what they told him. All of this was allegedly to construct the power plant which would torture and drain the landvættur. They debriefed him on his vision, making him fill out pages of reports in his drowsy, almost incoherent state, but even then he had known that they were not interested in anything he had to say. It felt like a poorly performed charade in a feeble attempt to deceive him. The next dive into that other world was scheduled for the day after to-morrow, at dawn.

Kári did not intend to become a victim of their schemes. An offering to this raging fire which would serve no good means in the end. For what purpose was he supposed to sacrifice himself? Science? His country? Kalmar?

Bullshit.

The incident at Svartiskóli had cost him dearly. But that was something he had been forced to do in order to survive. This sacrifice would only serve people who were antithetical to existence itself.

Kári had wanted to obey. Now he sickened himself. Too exhausted to work, he had submissively handed his patients over to Meinholt, condemning them to die alone and forsaken in a dimension which belonged to no world. None of their deaths had been mourned, and none of them ever would be.

All Vésteinn and the others had cared about was ensuring this project succeeded. The lives lost in that endeavour meant less than numbers in a ledger – they were probably the cheapest and easiest resource to replenish.

Kári sat up in his bed, his entire body aching, cradling his masked head in his hands. He'd slept in full regalia for a while now, telling himself it was a safety precaution in case he was needed. But he knew full well that wasn't the reason.

Every time he took off the mask he was met with an alien sight in the mirror. He was tired of fighting it. And now, after the skuggsjá, he felt as if he would never again take the mask off. Maybe that was why Ginfaxi was never seen out of regalia, like so many of the royal seiðskrattar. They had stopped pretending.

His stomach rumbled. Kári pacified his body with a seiður of nourishment, converting the latent energy around him into calories. It was a hollow method of feeding; it did not provide the body with real nutrition, only the bare minimum to keep itself going a while longer. It was rarely used because of the side effects from ingesting seiðmagn directly – but he was past caring about that now.

He had to get out of this deathtrap. There wasn't a chance he'd make it back to the harbour on foot, and even then he had to catch a ship out before they caught him. The gate to Rökkurvík was guarded, with Ginfaxi apparently the only one who could operate it. Although Kári doubted that now, just like everything else. Maybe he could perform the transition, with the right tools. Regardless, he was left with few realistic choices.

He had one other option. Clearly the attackers had some method for survival. They had got to the camp somehow. They must know how to get back. Halla, the so-called night-troll, had been stealing supplies for a while. Maybe the harbour as well – who knew? How had the terrorists known Kári and the expedition were going to be there? The answer was obvious enough, if he thought about it.

There was a traitor among them.

He got up and looked over his notes again. The map of the excavation area was vast, circles in blue designating the approximate boundaries of their thaumaturgical shields. There were at least two dozen smaller ones now surrounding the main site. The centre shield had been expanded by Ginfaxi with the help of Laí's uncolour, and it now encompassed the entirety of the landvættur. Kári hadn't been able to find any weakness in the camp's defences – no way in or out for the supply thief.

The group must have a safe spot in the highlands. Perhaps he could figure out a method of tracking them down. Kári shook his head, dismayed. If he could, then Ginfaxi would have already done it. Agent Meinholt was like a wolf on their trail. That bastard would leave no stone unturned. Even if Kári found them, he wasn't even sure how he could approach them safely.

But Halla could.

He had attempted to lessen her ailments. The changes had taken hold with minimal setbacks. Maybe she could be persuaded to give him a chance. He hoped she would. He desperately wanted her to help him understand how to keep his own mutations in check. Kári could offer to tell her everything about the purpose of the excavation, who Vésteinn truly worked for – whether he knew it or not.

Security had been tight since the attack. Þráinn Meinholt had focused all his efforts on finding the terrorist group and eliminating them. They had attached a few carriages to the Centimotive, filled them with soldiers, and scouted the surrounding area with no tangible results.

Kári didn't know what to do, who to talk to, who to trust. He had to talk to Auður and tell her what he'd seen. She was clearly frustrated by all this secrecy, but he had no idea of her true motives. Would a prestigious person like her betray the

Commonwealth if she knew what they were up to? Everything she had worked for in her entire life would turn to ash. She might turn him in before he got a chance to make a break for it.

The anxiety forced bitter bile up his throat. He swallowed it back. What gave him the resolve to keep going was the thought that actually building this monstrous power plant was even more sickening than whatever death sentence loomed over his head.

A putrid cloud of decomposition had settled over the dig site. Kári took a moment, taking in the massive, rotting carcass laid out before him.

They had finished unearthing the carcass. Steep paths wound down in two main tiers before reaching the bottom. The shark-like outline of the landvættur was fully discernible in its massive, putrid and sagging majesty. It was even more repulsive than its nearly dead form in his vision. Its eyes stared lifelessly at the overcast sky, glazed white, far removed from the power of storm and lightning that he had seen through the skuggsjá. These eyes saw nothing except death. It was pathetic, sickening, and it was supposed to be the engine of the most advanced technological wonder the modern world had ever seen.

He thought about the thing within the pyramid that the beings had been feeding. Its purpose eluded him. He couldn't fully explain it, but he felt as though it was an egg being incubated.

And he was certain that something horrendous would take place should it ever hatch.

ᚼ

Ægir stood in the doorway with a look on his face that made Sölvi recoil. It was inscrutably blank, dull-witted and vacant – as if there wasn't anyone wearing it.

'What do you think you're doing?'

Ægir spent hours sitting by the window when Elka wasn't home. Not reading, not listening to the radio, not doing anything except staring out of the window like a statue. He'd come across him like that during the nights as well, creeping out of his room to go to the bathroom. Ægir never stirred then. Sölvi had thought he was safe.

The boy withdrew his hand from his mother's purse. The floorboards creaked under him as he shifted his weight, ready to make a run for it.

'Nothing. I just—'

'You just what?'

Ægir took two calculated steps towards Sölvi. Slowly and methodically the blank look on his face turned into a stern expression.

'I needed money for school.'

'Is that so? Then why didn't you ask your mother for money?'

Sölvi wanted to run. But his feet felt like lead faced with the man towering over him.

'Because I ... She said—'

He went silent when Ægir's hand whipped lightning-fast across his face, hitting him so hard that his ears rang.

'You don't lie to me, boy! You can maybe lie to your mother, your friends, teachers and headmaster, but you do not lie to me! I know you were stealing.'

Sölvi kept his eyes down, his anger boiling. Hot tears rose within him like an erupting hot spring, and he swallowed down the lump in his throat which rose again and again. He focused on the stinging pain. On the anger. Shaping it into a shell around him.

'I wasn't going to lie,' he mumbled. He could barely see the floor for the tears clouding his vision.

'So you're not only a thief, but a crybaby to boot?' Ægir snorted with contempt. 'On top of everything else. Your mother threw out your art supplies for a good reason, and by the Deep, you will respect her decision. That's it. Tomorrow, I'm taking you down to the harbour. You want money? Then you can work for it. Maybe that will make a man out of you.'

Ægir went into the kitchen and picked up the coffee pot. It was half-empty with yesterday's brew. He poured himself a cup and took a sip, his back to Sölvi.

'Now – tell the truth, boy. If you face the consequences of your actions like a man, your punishment will be in accordance with that.'

Sölvi kept quiet. He knew that there was no right answer. That was the one thing Ægir had actually managed to teach him. In that way, the man was just like Hafsteinn. It didn't matter what Sölvi did. He could never avoid the blow to come.

They didn't exchange any further words. They were dead things that served no purpose. This fundamental truth was burned into him as Sölvi bit down, suffering Ægir's blows as a ship weathers breaker waves during a storm.

Not a word had been spoken in history which had not at some point been a lie. The purpose of words was to construct lies – letter by letter, sentence by sentence. In a world where the only truth was violence and the pain it brought, Sölvi would become the king of lies. Word by word and story by story, he would build around himself a fraudulent hope, a defensive wall which no weapons or fists or cruel words would ever penetrate. That is how he would make himself safe.

Later, when he stumbled out into the summer afternoon, his legs weak and unsteady after the beating, the lump still in his throat, Sölvi felt that if he lost his composure now and permitted himself to cry, then he would cry forever. And that's how Ægir would break him – like the ocean pulverises a ship into driftwood on a flooded skerry, the lump would tighten around his throat and strangle him.

So he took a deep breath and held it in. Pushed everything deep down and focused on kicking forwards, looking for light coming from the surface. He walked without thinking about where he was going, because if he stopped then the noose would claim him, and he would forget how to breathe and drown.

'Hæ, Sölvi, do you want to go ...'

Bára and Sævar stood outside the grocer's, but he didn't stop, didn't see them, didn't listen to them shouting after him. When they followed, he threw stones at them to make them stop.

'Fuck off, you cod-worshipping little freaks! Leave me alone!'

He kept walking, up and out of the village. The road gave way to grass, and as the incline grew steeper it gave way to black, coarse rock. He didn't stop until he found himself on top of Helgafell.

Up on the peak he had a view over the entire village, the harbour, the ocean and most of the island. He saw boats sailing on the sea, little islets which followed this one like lambs trailing after a ewe, militia soldiers and workers, children running on the streets – all of it and everything fragile like miniature toys.

Up there he could breathe again. He idly looked over to the rough terrain adjacent to Helgafell: Eldfell, the sister of this volcanic rise. The newer lava field was red and rough, scabbed wounds over the earth that bore witness to the fury that had threatened to drown the village in fire and sulphur decades earlier. At school he had learned that if the volcano had continued to erupt, the entire village would have perished. But that hadn't happened, thanks to the Deep.

That fucking Deep.

His mother hadn't been the same since that day on Surtsey. She moved as though she was sleepwalking, dreaming while awake. Not even when she had been using sorti, pale and shivering with dark bags under her eyes, had Sölvi ever been afraid of his mother. But he was afraid of her now. She hadn't told him anything, but he noticed how gently she moved, how she had started to place her hand delicately on her lower abdomen, as if she was cradling a fragile treasure, how Ægir beamed with pride as he kissed her and stroked her belly.

Did they think he was an idiot? That he was blind? He had been mentally preparing himself for the day they would tell him, when they would lie straight to his face and tell him she was pregnant with Ægir's baby.

But he knew that Elka didn't carry his spawn beneath her belt – as hideous a monster that would be, at least it would have been human. Just another village idiot, like that moron Hafsteinn. That day, standing on that horrible volcanic island, all raw and bizarre, only populated by those monstrous birds, Sölvi had seen something the others hadn't. When Elka's blood had mixed with the bowl, all of the participants had entered some sort of trance. Afterwards, the villagers had described the beings as made of divine light – but Sölvi had borne witness to what truly lay beyond the veil.

He had seen that man who wasn't a man at all, not a demon either, though he very much was how Sölvi had imagined them to be – only more terrifying. Behind him, the nightmarish things Sölvi knew to be the Messengers, his ardent servants and worshippers. He had been numb with fear, watching that thing take the moon down from the sky like a ripe fruit and place it inside Elka.

He wished so dearly that the volcano had succeeded in its horrible task. That he could stand here and see no village, no harbour and no boats, no people, and no Ægir who awaited him in that house Sölvi would never call home. All this place deserved was fire. As far as Sölvi was concerned, maybe that was what the entire world deserved, as well.

Lying back, he stared up into the vacant azure sky. Thinking. Once, Helgafell had been active. The volcano was dead now, or just sleeping. Maybe it had erupted just like its younger sibling, Eldfell, but succeeded where its sibling had failed. Maybe it had destroyed a rotten place much like this village, those thousands of years ago when it erupted, and no one was left to remember. The thought was comforting. Maybe that was why its name meant 'Holy Mountain'.

He turned his back on the village. Took in the more quiet part of the island. But even the sight of that annoyed him. Those hovels they called farmhouses, the ugly lighthouse towering in the distance, and then, of course – the sea.

The fucking sea, which he had once loved so dearly, which had promised adventure and opportunity and boys becoming men and peasants kings, was now nothing but a gaping maw which wanted to devour the entire world.

One day, all of this would fall prey to fire. Who knew, maybe Sölvi would be the one to awaken the volcano. For a great sorcerer-king-poet-artist, it could be done by a whisper and a mere wave of the hand. The heart of Eldfell still slept – it need only be awoken. By then he would be far away. And he would be happy – so happy – and laugh as the fire claimed the island. His laughter would be carried to the villagers on the peaks of waves, so that they would know who celebrated their demise – the very person who had instigated it.

A long while later he found strength in his legs again. He was no longer trembling, weak. He reached into his pocket and felt the krónur he had taken from Ægir's wallet the day before. He smiled to himself and walked down Helgafell, the Holy Mountain, down to the town which wilfully ignored the doom lurking at the threshold. He had enough to buy whatever he couldn't steal from Bryde's shop. And he had a good hiding place in mind, somewhere that oaf Ægir would never think to look.

Sölvi started to do more than fantasise about leaving Vestmannaeyjar. They had to get out of here – he and his mother. Before it was too late and he lost her forever. They'd leave Hrímland behind and go to the mainland, where true opportunity waited at every turn. And then the Emissary and the moon would only be another bad dream to be forgotten.

One day, his paintings would make him famous, all throughout the Commonwealth, and they would be so beautiful that fine and educated people would travel great distances to see them and shake his hand, praising the genius who had created something more magnificent than the hideous world they inhabited. Their eyes were not the eyes of a true artist; they could not perceive the inner beauty of things, the divine soul of all things – both hideous and majestic – let alone translate it to strokes and lines, transforming a mundane piece of paper into something sacred and venerated. Sölvi would illuminate them, show them the world as he saw it – as a great artist saw it.

And he would never be sad again, because he would have forgotten all about this miserable, inconsequential place that stank of rotting fish.

ᚺ

Ingi Vítalín and Vésteinn were adamant about activating the skuggsjá on schedule. Kári had tried to delay them, claiming that his body needed time to stabilise itself after the strain it had suffered, but they wouldn't listen. They were already behind. He could only rest because the skuggsjá had to be recalibrated.

'I'm leaving,' he said in a whisper.

He was in Auður's tent, facing the professor who sat behind

her desk. The table was covered in a collection of worn grimoires, falling apart at the seams.

'What on earth are you talking about?' She got up in a hurry, eyes burning with curiosity. 'How do you feel? What did you see?'

He told her. Despite his misgivings. He was tired of the paranoia. Auður was initially thrilled that her Reiðarmóða had worked, but that quickly gave way to a silent dread once his retelling went on.

'You were right, you know. About the jötnar. The ancient race born of chaos.' He laughed to himself. 'I sound insane, saying this out loud.'

'In a world gone mad, the sane will always sound insane.'

Auður was shaken into grave contemplation over his words. Kári rambled on nervously to fill the silence. It was difficult to stop talking now that he'd started.

'I wasn't able to find out if they're using the machine for some other purpose. I don't think I can survive another attempt and I'm not willing to find out. I'm going to break Halla out and beg her to take me to her comrades. This might sound crazy, but I've no idea what else to do. I don't know if I can trust them, I don't even know if I can trust you. But I want to, Auður.' She looked up at the sound of her name, her mind made up about whatever she had been considering. 'I need to trust *someone* here. If what I said is true, and I believe it is – then they are going to do something far more terrible than build this war machine.'

Auður leaned back in her seat, taking it all in. She appeared to be considering things.

'Things have worsened since we unearthed the carcass. We're going to die if we stay here longer.'

Kári was tempted to ask her about the progress of her spiral mark, but it felt crass and ultimately unnecessary. It wasn't as if he'd know what he could do to help her.

'Or if we're unlucky, live to witness something far worse. I can feel it growing in strength at the edge of reason. Can you?' He didn't reply. 'An event so unimaginably catastrophic it sends ripples back in time.'

Reaching into her coat pocket, she pulled out a packet of cigarettes, lighting one as she offered another to Kári. He refused.

'You are more right than you realise. About a lot of things.' She sounded defeated. 'I can tell you that going to Halla is a good idea. I can help you convince her.'

'How?'

'I'm with them,' she said sombrely. 'The so-called terrorists.'

It was the only time in Kári's life he had been annoyed by the impassivity his mask lent him. Auður clearly read his calm reaction as threatening, and tensed up for his reaction.

'For how long?' he asked in a measured tone.

'Well before the expedition.' She tapped the ash off the cigarette. 'Since I realised that Vésteinn was completely unhinged.'

'I've had my fill of secrets and half-truths.'

'There we agree.'

ᚺ

For Auður, her defection had started even before the death of her mother.

'I know you were there, Kári. I know you put her out of her misery.' Auður tapped her cigarette, the ash trailing to the floor. 'I got access to the files.'

'Vésteinn?' he asked. She nodded.

'We were never that close, me and her,' Auður continued. 'Almía was a demanding, strict, secretive person. Disappointed in me, at every turn, for failing to live up to my potential. Going into archaeology was what turned the divide between us into a chasm.'

Auður had gone to Hafnía to study, which had involved leaving a childhood friend behind in Reykjavik.

'Her name was Katrín Melsteð. Since I can remember, she wanted to study archaeology, but her family forbade it – said it was unnecessary, frivolous. They were very rich, you see. Her education was just sport, something to make her more viable for marrying off, not a real career choice.'

But Katrín had not sat idly by while Auður studied. They wrote regularly to each other and as the letters piled up, Katrín's frustration grew. It became clear Katrin had found other avenues down which to channel her ambition.

'She stopped writing to me during my final year. Last I heard, she had started writing anonymously to the newspapers – Ísafold, stuff like that. Arguing in public with the movers and shakers. When I got back, she had changed. Had no friends except some burnouts she hung around with. She was using – that was as clear as day. I tried talking to her, but she cut me off. And then my education in Svartiskóli took over everything else in my life.'

That was the deal. Auður got to pursue her frivolous archaeological passion, as long as she attended Svartiskóli after she graduated. She dived head first into her arcane studies, spent hours in the hallowed library of the institution, studying old manuscripts with yellowed pages, faded scribblings the dark brown of dried blood. She started to combine her two interests – to figure out how galdur could help unravel the buried secrets guarded by the silent earth.

Auður only discovered later on that her old friend had actually done far more than write to the newspapers. Katrín was executed for treason of the highest order. She had been involved in the assassination of Trampe, had been part of the group who'd helped unleash the transmundane invasion on Loftkastalinn, who'd infiltrated Svartiskóli. Who'd killed Auður's own mother.

'I became obsessed.' She twirled the cigarette against the ashtray, sharpening its point. 'Maybe that was a way of working through the grief. I don't know. I don't have many friends, or ... well ... without Katrín, I don't have any. Not real ones. And she had done all these horrible things. I tried to dig up more information, but hit a brick wall every time.' She leaned forwards, placing her elbows on her knees. 'That's when Vésteinn Alrúnarson contacted me. To study the anomaly in Öskjuhlíð and the Stone Giant.'

Vésteinn had been trying to unlock the mysteries of the two for quite a while. To his frustration, he was getting nowhere. He needed a new angle, a fresh approach from someone highly learned in galdur.

'My mother had worked with him closely, constructing Perlan, for one thing. I'm not saying she's the only reason he approached me, but, well ... She was densely entwined in the power structure of the upper hierarchies of Svartiskóli. I started out working on the anomaly, which had to be contained. Quickly it became apparent that it was the source of the demonic attack on the flying fortress. It was a wound in reality itself.'

She was granted access to dossiers on the case – courtesy of the Directorate of Immigration, who had been closely monitoring the group before they sprung their plan. Most of the Directorate's intel had come from an interrogation of one of the group's ringleaders – the person who had killed Count Trampe with a mortifying use of kukl, stabbing him with a demon-infested bone and breaking it off in the wound.

Auður smirked mirthlessly. 'Have you ever wondered what your friend Sæmundur was up to, that day everything went down at the university? How it all happened, and why?' Kári nodded, hanging on to her every word. 'He broke into Svartiskóli to steal a page from *Rauðskinna*. He killed my mother and the head librarian with the gandreið fungus, likely just because they were in his way. I don't think he really knew what he was messing with. Like a child playing soldiers with a loaded gun. He got the page and summoned something from it. Something that allowed him to transgress all boundaries when it came to galdur. Do you understand what I mean? What the repercussions might be, if someone were able to replicate that? I don't think any of us can, truly. Beyond that threshold is something incalculable when it comes to potential destruction. And he used that power to raise a níðstöng – three of them. *At the same time.*'

Kári hadn't quite understood what she meant regarding the repercussions until that moment. Raising a single níðstöng without falling prey to its power was within the ability of only the most learned and disciplined users of svartigaldur. Sæmundur's actions had turned the site at Öskjuhlíð into a lethal anomaly, which threatened to expand itself. They'd had to build an obsidian structure around it, reinforce it with galdrastafir and convoluted rituals to restrain it. Within that pyramid, Auður had conducted her research. In a manner of speaking, the ritual had created a portal, although lending such a specific definition to something so chaotic was misleading. On its other side was a boundless source of power, which could not be controlled. She had seen that kind of force before. Heavily restrained within the Stone Giant. She'd turned her focus there.

After months of dedicated research, often disrupted by those misguided people who started to worship it after witnessing it in some drug-induced vision – brought on by Sæmundur himself at a political rally, a concert in Rökkurvík – Auður had begun to piece things together.

The theory she put forth to Vésteinn was radical. She believed it was Sæmundur himself inside the Stone Giant – that he had somehow become it, either through his own messing with transmundane forces, or possibly by awakening it and taking its form.

'Within the Stone Giant lies a dormant power worthy of a god. I'd go as far as to say that within the power lie the tools of creation itself. But Sæmundur – if I'm right about him being in there – is completely unable to wield them. The power has been deformed into the very restraints that constrict him.'

'It's a prison,' said Kári in apprehensive realisation. 'The horned being I saw…'

Auður nodded.

'I think that Sæmundur let it out and took its place, blinded by the offer of transcendent might. Of course, Vésteinn completely dismissed my ideas at the time. Then he suddenly changed his mind. He had also been independently studying the two sites. I think he found something beyond the rift. Maybe something Sæmundur brought into this world. I was pulled off the project after that.' She ground the cigarette butt into the ashtray. 'I was furious. All my work, buried in red tape behind top secret classifications. Never to see the light of day. I confronted him about it. That's when he mentioned *this* project – the excavation of the landvættur – promising me a key position here to pacify me. That day, I met Ingi Vítalín. And I knew that whatever Vésteinn had planned would result in something even worse than what came before. And now you come to me, saying all these things, and if anything I now fear I underestimated the threat.'

'Wait.' Kári tried to piece all of this together. 'When exactly did you join this group? The very same group who unleashed all of this on us – who killed your mother?'

'You're looking at this simplistically. It was Sæmundur who killed my mother. Yes, he helped my allies later on, but… it was clear to me he initially acted on his own, selfish motivations. You knew him, Kári. The man was insane. He was already too far gone when he broke into Svartiskóli's library, it's just that no one was able to see it. Or if they did, they didn't stop him in time. But he had a past with one of the key ringleaders of Black Wings. Her name was Garún, a huldumanneskja. She asked him to aid their cause, and he did – with disastrous results. They never expected or wanted this to happen.'

'And you believe them?'

'I do. After I talked to them ... I'm convinced they did not know what he was, what he was capable of. I doubt Sæmundur knew himself. The group was still active, but in deep hiding. The Directorate had a man on the inside still. They believed it was better to keep an eye on dissidents, rather than risk losing control over them. But that meant I could find out where they were. At first I sought them out only hoping to find out what had happened to my friend, Katrín.' She smiled bitterly. 'Katrín did some unbelievable things. I wish I had never left for Hafnía, that I could have been there for her. Maybe kept her off sorti. Anyway ...' Auður cleared her throat. 'I was lucky to be able to make contact. They already knew who the spy was – it was that bastard Hrólfur – and I got to them just before they went completely off the radar. They had fractured before Loftkastalinn and the assassination, partly encouraged by Hrólfur's manipulations, but mostly because people like Garún and Katrín had veered off to a more extreme stance than the rest of the group. Some of them had been captured, but escaped from the Nine when the Stone Giant tore it down. The splinter faction contacted the others, at least the ones they deemed trustworthy, and prepared to go to ground.'

'So how did you get them to trust you?'

Auður shrugged. 'I told them everything. About myself, Katrín, my research into the Stone Giant – and about the landvættur. Kalmar's new project. That piqued their interest. They managed to manipulate Hrólfur into giving up more information before they went dark. They knew the Crown was planning something big. I didn't know whether these were good people, if I could trust them or not – but I knew that if anyone stood a chance of stopping this before it went too far, it was them. I had no choice. So they told me everything they knew. And even though everything went to hell real fast, I'm still certain they were fighting for the right thing.'

Kári couldn't help but snort.

'I know,' Auður said. 'It's far beyond fucked up. But you were ready to go to them knowing even less than I did, faced with the reality of our situation here.'

'I have no choice.'

'Well, neither did I.'

She gave him some time to take all this in.

'What you saw in the distant past was real,' she said finally. 'A terrible war was waged by the jötnar to put a halt to a ritual. It brought their empire to ruin and brought them to extinction. That is how important it was to them to put a stop to it.'

'What kind of ritual?'

'Do you know where the power of galdur stems from? It is a dark well, ever present but always held back. Some see it as a void, others a vortex. Seen in a certain light, it is the chaos that gave birth to existence; seen in another, it is the end of it. We witnessed a hint of that unmaking – or transformation – when Loftkastalinn fell. The heretical jötnar almost broke down the barrier restraining that vortex. Now Vésteinn, Ingi and the lot of them are working towards finishing what the ancients started, knowingly or not.'

'That's insane.'

'Maybe. I sure as hell hope it is. In either case, I can't leave before I know for certain.' Auður gave him a serious look. 'I need your help.'

'All right,' Kári said hesitantly. 'What do you propose we do?'

'We need to activate the skuggsjá ourselves.'

Night never truly fell in the middle of the Hrímlandic summer. However, while the work crews toiled around the clock in shifts, the higher-ups still kept regular hours. Late that evening, Kári and Auður waited for Þráinn and Hrólfur to retire to their accommodation, while Ginfaxi was either still in the portal carriage or working elsewhere, and Vésteinn remained steadfastly in his tent.

No one paid them any mind as they strolled confidently towards the skuggsjá's laboratory. Auður opened the door and they let themselves in.

To their relief, the being from Laí was not there. Auður fumbled through the activation, Kári assisting her as much as he could. He plugged the cables into himself and Auður started the incantation. He stepped into the spiral and placed his hand on the monolith. Blood spilled on the unearthly metal and everything faded away.

When Kári came to, he was lying on the floor. Auður loomed over him, a frightful look on her face.

'What's wrong?' he said in a raw voice, unfamiliar to himself. 'What happened? Am I like Leifur?'

'You're fine,' she said, handing him his mask.

He hadn't realised he wasn't wearing it. Somewhere in the back of his mind, he registered that he didn't need the lenses to see the seiðmagn flowing through the world.

'You had no right to remove it.'

'I thought you were dying. Next time, I'll let you die.'

She avoided looking at him as he strapped it back on.

He got slowly to his feet, soothing his aching body as much as he dared, the slightest effort leaving him instantly exhausted.

'What did you see?'

Incomprehensible fractures of maddening futures assaulted Kári. The experience was too fresh, still bleeding like a raw wound, the enormity of it too great to put into mere words.

'Everything.'

'And?'

The reply stumbled out of him before he realised what he was saying.

'We're already dead.' Words were insufficient to communicate what he had witnessed. He struggled to comprehend it. 'Later. We have to go.'

He stumbled numbly after Auður across the length of the excavation. The living world barely registered as reality to him. He glanced dumbly askance towards the landvættur. The rotting corpse. It almost seemed as if the creature was breathing.

Annihilation.

The only reward offered for anyone taking part in this great work was annihilation on a scale beyond comprehension of life and death. They were all literal pawns in the great game of the ancients set in motion aeons ago, playing out their parts perfectly according to minuscule string pulls orchestrated generations ago.

Kári almost lost it then. He wanted to rip off his mask and scream, to channel seiðmagn through himself until every trace of him was wiped from the earth. Echoes of the vision he had suffered rose up to the surface like corpses in a bog. He felt detached from his own body, his mind shattered from revelations of futures yet unlived.

The heretics had tried before and failed. They would not

merely try again. This time they would succeed; this time all the keys were already meticulously placed in their locks, and it was inevitable that they would be turned. Everything that is, was and will be, unmade the instant the veil was pierced, unleashing that which lurked beyond the threshold, drowning existence in unfathomable depths of unreality.

Nothing Kári could do would amount to anything. It was hilarious, really, that he was going along with whatever this plan was supposed to accomplish.

The guards were dealt with by Auður's near-silent utterance. Standing like statues, they remained still as Kári led Halla from her confines. Auður wasn't lying – Halla recognised her. Her hatred of Kári was still as blatant as ever. That sunlit night, three people moved towards the western mountains, heading into the protean storm surrounding them.

Alarm sirens sounded when they were only a few kilometres from the camp. Auður reached into her pack and pulled up a flare gun, firing a bright red signal into the sky. Immediately, the landscape before them glowed from the thaumaturgical fire, as hidden snipers covered their retreat. When a squad of soldiers almost caught up to them, a large, black-winged shape took to the sky above Kári. The náskári crashed into the soldiers' middle with resounding thunder, decimating them effortlessly with beak and claw before they could react. Covered in gore, the korpur kicked himself off the ground with a leap off his larger third leg, beating his wings and gaining altitude rapidly before retaliating fire could reach him.

As they grouped with the others, Kári found himself staring down the barrels of several skorrifles, still more firing back at the soldiers. He put his hands up, partly hoping these people would end things there and then. Their forms were obfuscated by masks that oozed hallucinogenic seiður, reducing them to vague outlines. One of them pulled a mask off her face: a huldukona, her hair cut short, clad in a mismatch of old army surplus equipment. She looked at him with such fierce contempt that he knew it was a small miracle he wasn't already dead.

Auður and Halla were handed skorrifles by the others.

'What the hell are you thinking?' asked the huldukona.

'We don't have time for this, Diljá,' said Auður with annoyance as she put on a papier mâché mask, becoming an indistinct form. 'He's defecting. We can trust him.'

Diljá didn't respond, or lower her weapon. Halla reached for the barrel of her gun and gently pointed it downwards. The huldukona looked at her hesitantly.

'I mean no harm.' Kári's words sounded oddly hollow, muted by his beaked mask. 'I don't answer to them any more. I want to help.'

Diljá's disgust did not waver, although her skorrifle remained lowered.

'You are nothing but a weapon. Their weapon. One strange word, one odd gesture, and I'll blow your brains out.'

'I understand.'

'I won't be taking your word for it.' She motioned for him to follow Halla with the bayoneted end of her skorrifle. 'Now move.'

With retreating fire they fell back into the sorcerous highlands, south towards the looming glacier.

Sextán

Sölvi's mother wouldn't listen. He saw it in her eyes – what Amma Dagmar had called the depths of the soul. Elka wasn't there. Not any more. He cried and begged her not to let Ægir take him, but she only patted him on the back and said he needed to toughen up.

She looked at Ægir when she said that. And Sölvi felt so alone and heartbroken he couldn't even bring himself to say anything. Ægir grabbed his shoulder and pushed him towards the door, not too roughly – not in front of Elka – and told him to put on his shoes.

Sölvi knew it wouldn't do to run. There was nowhere to go. And besides, Ægir kept a close eye on him as they walked down to the harbour. Ægir approached a group of men in worn woollen sweaters, reeking of sweat and fish, all of them stupid-looking like Ægir was, brutes who were good for nothing other than toiling like beasts in the field.

Sölvi kept his distance while Ægir talked to the men.

'Come here. Move, boy!' Ægir snapped when Sölvi walked lazily towards them. He didn't pick up the pace and relished Ægir's quiet rage at the blatant disrespect. Ægir's palm snapped across the back of his head. 'You'll keep sharp if you know what's good for you. Ketill here is going to put you on tongue-cutting with the other boys.'

Ketill led him to a long table set with sharp, protruding nails. Vats filled with severed cod heads were lined beside it. A handful of other boys were there, some younger than him. He recognised them from school, but Sævar was the only one he really knew. Sölvi pretended not to see him.

He was given a very sharp knife, and drilled on how to use it. 'If you cut yourself with it, that's because you didn't respect it enough,' said Ketill. He then showed Sölvi how to place a cod head on the nail by its chin and then slice it off. 'When you've filled up most of the nail you put it in your box.'

'What's the pay?' Sölvi spat out arrogantly. 'I don't work for free, you know.'

Ketill snorted. 'You get paid by the half-kilo, rounded down. So get to work, boy. Ægir told me you were lazy and don't think you'll get away with it here. If you slack off, I'll put you on sorting through the guts, separating the livers from the rest.'

'Does that pay by the gram, rounded up?' Sölvi asked impudently, but Ketill was already walking away.

Sölvi's nail wasn't half-filled with cod tongues when he felt as though his mind would melt from boredom. The other boys chatted, trying to sound like big men talking about fishing and who was best at wrestling. They quickly shut up about the latter when Sölvi reminded them who was the reigning champion of wrestling in Heimaey, focusing instead on sickeningly boring talk about who would get a place on a fishing boat first.

The only good thing about this drudgery was slamming the cod's head on the nail and pretending it was Ægir. Not that he'd ever do something like that – he was no brute. Not like that idiot. Sölvi spent his time concocting a plan where he'd get on a boat and tell his mother they were going out for a pleasure cruise, to show her all he knew about sailing and the sea – the goddamn sea she loved so much now, more than him or life itself. Then he'd take them to Reykjavík, and from there to Hafnía where all his dreams would come true. As soon as they got far enough away that this rotten island disappeared below the horizon, he was certain the trance she was under would break.

The child Elka was carrying was conveniently omitted from this fantasy. He was probably just imagining the pregnancy, anyway. Just like he had imagined everything he'd seen in Surtsey.

He made a game of using the knife to poke out the eyes on a cod head. Putting one on the nail, he messed around dissecting it and became oddly fascinated by the anatomy beneath its surface. When the other boys tried to tell him to stop messing around he told them to shut up; he knew how to handle a knife as his father had taught him, and he'd learned how to do it in the royal army.

'You're such a little liar,' Sævar muttered. 'You don't even have a father.'

'Maybe it's hard for you to imagine someone having a father who's not a blockheaded oaf doing something other than hauling slimy fish out of the sea every day to feed his blockheaded children, who boil the entire fish and mash it together with rotten potatoes, bones and guts and everything, because they're too stupid to pick them out, but that still doesn't mean I'm lying.'

That shut Sævar up, but the charged rage emitting from the other boys was palpable. Sölvi had to be careful. But they had seen him slam Hafsteinn to the ground, so they didn't raise their hands to him.

As was right. They knew he was smarter than them and now

they feared he was stronger as well. He could run circles around them all day.

Which is what he did. But at the end, when Ketill saw that he hadn't even filled up a quarter of his box when others had done more than one, he was told he'd be put on liver-sorting the next day.

Sölvi didn't care. Let them see what they thought when they found out he'd burst the gall bladders over their slop of liver. He'd soon be free of this waste of time, and then it would be him teaching Ægir a lesson, not the other way around.

One should respect one's betters.

ᚼ

In the end, the men decided he was unemployable.

'The boy has been ruined by coddling,' they said. 'His mother… The wonderful woman probably meant well, but she's already spoiled him rotten.'

Ægir nodded gravely, agreeing, muttering that Sölvi was no good, but that he could still be steered away from becoming a useless layabout.

Ægir gave him a talking-to, as he later described it to Elka. The man was never much for words. Sölvi hated him more than anything else in the world. He was comforted by the fact that sooner or later, his stupid fishermen wouldn't keep him safe and he'd drown when that dingy little boat of his went down. Or maybe he'd accidentally sail right into a naval mine. Probably likelier, seeing how dumb Ægir was.

As a last resort, they put Sölvi in the care of Styrmir. The huldumaður had lost his hand in a recent accident and now only got some work cleaning the factories and the boats after the working day was over. During the day, he mended oilskin jackets, boots and other workwear. That was what Sölvi was helping him with, to speed things up.

They had spent most of the day working in silence. Something about the huldumaður's dark mood made Sölvi fall quiet, for once. They worked in the back of his house, where Styrmir had a shed with supplies and a worktable.

It was a couple of days later when Sölvi asked him how he'd lost his hand. They were sitting outside by the table in the relatively warm sun, drinking coffee (Sölvi would not admit being too young for it and forced it down without making a face) and eating digestive biscuits dunked into the bitter drink.

'Work accident,' was all Styrmir said.

Sölvi decided not to press the matter. It had been stupid of him to ask.

'And now they won't let you go out fishing any more?'

'That's right.'

Sölvi considered this. 'That's really stupid.'

Styrmir arched an eyebrow. 'Oh yeah? Why's that?'

'You're working two jobs now, aren't you? Someone who can work twice as hard can go out sailing. Not like it's hard.'

Styrmir chuckled. 'You've worked on many ships?'

'No.' His dismissal annoyed Sölvi. 'But my dad has. Anyway, if an oaf like Ægir can do it, it can't be that hard.'

Styrmir laughed at that, but then his face suddenly darkened. 'You don't like Ægir much, do you?'

Sölvi shook his head. 'No. He's a brute.'

'That he is.' Styrmir reached for the coffee pot and refilled his cup. 'He's as brutish as they come.'

'He hits me.'

The wind picked up – a fresh sea breeze tinged with cold despite the summer.

'I know, kid.'

They sat on for a while, chewing on their biscuits softened by the lukewarm coffee. Then Styrmir poured the remains of his cup into the grass and stood up.

'Let's get to it.'

This time, Sölvi didn't mind.

The relentless wind tore at his robes. Kári leaned up against the force and turned his face away, so he could better breathe through the mask. The barren landscape spread out, vast and empty, rendering all distance meaningless – a wasteland of moss and stone. With every step, Vatnajökull claimed more of the horizon.

The seiðmagn tightened its grip on him, pushing in like a toxic cloud.

Through the lenses of his mask the world became a roaring cacophony of vibrant explosions. The stimuli were so frequent, so many and relentless, that he could barely see where he was going, the real world obfuscated by the otherworldly energies raging around him. This was a war zone of the unnatural, the border of the unreal, and he was running deeper into its interior.

They moved in single file, making their way between collapsed piles of rocks barely visible in the monotonous terrain. The náskári soared above, having led them by the safest route back to a cairn path.

A distant rumbling in the distance. The cascading sound of iron hitting stone in waves. The náskári circled down, landing next to the party. He looked ragged and worn, his hertygi stripped of adornment. Leather straps were wrapped around his head, covering one eye with a thaumaturgical lens.

'The iron serpent,' he growled. 'It has our trail.'

'How long?' asked Diljá.

'Err-at half an hour. It gains in speed.'

She considered this.

'The night-trolls. The nest is … what – three kilometres south-west?'

The náskári nodded. 'Follow. I will rouse them from their rest.'

Springing up with the strength of his third foot, he took to the air like a cannonball being fired. They followed him off the cairn path.

The rumbling grew louder. Kári wondered if the Centimotive had weapons powered by seiðmagn, similar to the skorrifles. It was unlikely; such machines would be extremely heavy and could slow the thing down. That wasn't enough reassurance to make him lessen the pace. They sprinted across the black sands, the grimy sheets of ice, scrambled up bare, rocky hills. They ran out into the wasteland like animals being hunted.

From the top of the hill, he looked back and saw the Centimotive furiously tearing across the landscape at tremendous speed. At such a distance, it seemed so much like an insect, the trail of dust left in its wake betraying its true size as its multitudes of steel legs shredded the landscape.

Kári was out of breath and risked enhancing his endurance by drawing in a minor amount of environmental seiðmagn. The energies hit him like a tidal wave, threatening to overpower his entire body and mind, breaking in through the microscopic crack he had opened between himself and the supernatural world. With sheer force of will, he pushed back the seiðmagn, drawing in just what he needed and nothing more, nothing less.

A volcanic hill bulged out from the highlands – a bulbous cone encircled with jagged, tall rocks, the earth splintered with crags and crevices from the raging turmoil which had flooded the land centuries ago. Some of these jagged outcroppings looked odd to him, even to his untrained eye. He realised it wasn't truly rock at all, but night-trolls hiding in plain sight, their rocky skin making them seem part of the landscape as they lay flat and unmoving up against the stone.

They reached the hill and crested it rapidly, cursing under their breath as loose stones ran down the incline in small landslides. Still the night-trolls remained motionless. As they reached the top, they went into the bowl of the crater, then lay flat and overlooked the highlands spread out behind them. The Centimotive was drawing closer.

Under Diljá's command, the left and right flank trained their rifles on those select places that seemed not to fit – a faint mismatch in the coloration of the stone. They held their breath and waited. As the Centimotive approached the hill, antennae flailing as it scanned its surroundings for traps, the centre opened fire. The shots glanced harmlessly off its hull, and it snapped towards the source of the fire.

'Retreat!' shouted Diljá.

Most of the group got to their feet, running across the crater to descend the other side of the hill. Kári and Auður stayed behind, waiting to see if their help was needed.

As the Centimotive started to climb towards the crater, the náskári dived down across the hill's slopes, flying dangerously low and meeting it head-on. Just when a collision seemed inevitable, he dropped a cluster of grenades as he pitched up, soaring just past the black steel carapace before taking to the sky. The remaining insurgents fired on their stone targets as the grenades rolled underneath the Centimotive and burst with thaumaturgical surges.

Sharp peaks dislodged themselves from the outcroppings, glowing eyes appearing amid the natural-seeming formations. Each of them was like a volcanic hill come to life, huge and stooping, its back ending in sharp peaks of hardened lava. The night-trolls rose from their slumber roaring with rage, the sorcerous shots not nearly powerful enough to put a dent in their resilient stone skin. They searched for the source of the violence, seeing the Centimotive wreathed in smoke, temporarily halted by the devastating explosions, and as one they charged it.

The earth shook as they galloped, running on all fours like primates, their fists pulverising the ground like landmines with each resounding step. There were five of them, coming in from each side of the Centimotive, whose crew realised the real danger all too late. The machine started to curl up defensively, but the trolls rushed in, slamming into it with their shoulders so it twisted and turned, rolling over on its side. The night-trolls raised fists like boulders and brought them down on the metallic carapace, denting it visibly with each heavy blow.

Auður pulled on Kári's arm and they ran along with the rest of the party, the earthquake of the violent battle following them as they ran down the hill, out into the sorcerous wilderness.

ᚼ

Lookouts rose from their hideouts like ghosts from the grave at their approach. The náskári had gone in a separate direction once they were safely back on the cairn path, hoping to mislead the Centimotive should it take up the pursuit. They came to a cave entrance, a narrow crack in the lava by a small hill, hiding it from all angles except a direct approach. They were at the roots of Vatnajökull now, the glacier towering over the landscape like a sleeping god. The cave led to a tunnel which seemed to be part of a vast network. It was naturally formed, as evidenced by the uneven walls, but there was something off about how level the floor was, how straight each intersection.

Kári wondered if the náskárar had made these tunnels. They were especially adept with stone and metals in their sorcerous workings, and were known to harvest highland moss to sell in the capital. Perhaps this was one of their safe houses? As he was deep in these meditations, the weak illumination from a lantern revealed a structure that stopped him in his tracks.

The tunnels ended abruptly in pitch-black stone. An ancient-looking entrance, carved out of pure obsidian. Its angular edges glistened menacingly in the light – no wound cut by obsidian could heal in a natural manner. He was led up the steps, uneven and awkwardly made, as if they were built for beings larger than humans. Two braziers were on either side of the black gate, empty of fire for untold millennia.

'I've seen this place before…' he muttered, hesitating before entering the chamber. 'We can't stay here.'

Diljá glared at him, probably wanting to shoot him where he stood for that eerie remark. Auður tightly gripped his arm.

'They've been living here for weeks now. It's completely safe.'

Kári shut up and let Auður lead him on, noticing the others keeping a close eye on him.

The architecture of the hallways was all clear lines and sharp angles, with very few visible seams in the obsidian. The effect made it seem as if they were in a natural pocket, an underground lava bubble that had just happened to form in geometric shapes. But there was no doubting it. The style reminded him of the dig site – the tops of what used to be proud towers – and he again experienced odd, nauseating flashbacks to the dreamlike visions of the skuggsjá.

He had *definitely* been here before. A million lifetimes before. But his body… His body had been—

They entered a hall which served as both the group's quarters and its storeroom: unrolled furs and bedrolls, topped with woollen blankets; rifle boxes, ammunition and the smell of powder; shining bayonets; wooden trunks battered to hell stacked in the corner; linen sacks likely half-full of smoked meat and dried fish, if the wooden crate serving as a cutting board next to it was any indication. He recognised it as having come from the dig site's own supplies. People were resting by the weak light of oil lanterns.

The others stopped here, greeting their comrades and answering their anxious questions at the sight of a seiðskratti. Auður, Diljá and Halla led him onwards into a large chamber, their footsteps echoing in its vastness. The darkness pressed in from all sides, empowered by the obsidian. Their weak light could not reach the ceiling or the edges of this place. As the wall behind them vanished from view, it was as if they had reached the black heart of the world.

Deep within the abyss, a faint light flared. It floated on the horizon; then Kári was suddenly right by it, close to the figures huddled around the glow. The source of it was an opening in the floor, a broad stairway going down. Etchings surrounding the pit were in a peculiar, flowing script that made Kári's mind reel. He had seen them before.

There were three people waiting for them. An armed man wielding a skorrifle, standing next to a pair of young people dressed in rags. They turned, and he recognised them instantly. Both of them were dead.

The siblings.

Móri and Skotta – or so they were called in the newspapers. Traditional monikers for nameless draugar, haunting the place of their demise and thirsty for the blood of the innocent. Haugbúar. *Mound-dwellers.*

The siblings stared at him with eyes deeper than the pitch-black darkness around them. A young man and woman, dressed in rotten woollen tatters, as though they were farmhands who had got lost on the heath, prey to some fell power. The woman carried a knife at her belt – a soldier's dagger. The boy seemed unarmed, but wrapped around his body was a filthy rag, a sheet that radiated a sickening aura of seiðmagn. Both of them were smiling, looking at Kári with unmitigated hunger.

Offering, the boy hissed. *For her. His blood will give her warmth.*

The girl tilted her head, taking a step towards him.

She is cold. She is lonely. She will feast on his secrets. Those embers will stoke the fire of remembrance.

'No,' Halla uttered, holding up a protective hand in front of Kári.

He was too terrified to move, fearing that the slightest flinch would get him torn apart.

'Halla?'

The man next to the siblings had been staring down at the radiance, deep in thought, only looking up when she spoke. His voice broke from the sudden tears. He ran towards Halla and they embraced deeply, whispering to each other, *I thought you were gone, I never stopped thinking of you, I did not dare to hope.* They kissed deeply, and the man took a closer look at Halla, noticing the changes.

'He helped me,' Halla said, gesturing to Kári.

The man took an involuntary step back, reaching for his weapon, as he registered that a seiðskratti was among them.

'What the hell is this *thing* doing here? I've seen him with the command group. What were you thinking, bringing him here?'

'I can vouch for him, Eyvindur.' Auður's commanding tone calmed the flaring tempers. 'We broke Halla out and escaped.'

'I don't trust him,' said Diljá angrily, looking towards the two haugbúar for affirmation. 'I wanted to shoot him where he stood, but Auður here assured me he was a turncoat. No doubt he's going to lead them right back here. He's probably placed a tracking hex on himself or something.'

'Did you truly help her?' asked Eyvindur.

'Yes.'

'*Why?*'

Kári hesitated. That single word had been laden with contempt and suspicion. He gestured to his mask and robes.

'These colours signify that I am a biological seiðskratti. I focus on the body, using seiður to heal it, to change it for the better. I wanted to help her.'

It is a weapon that thinks itself a man, the undead girl said in a hoarse whisper, sniggering hideously. The unpleasant sound echoed through the chamber.

Kári hesitated, weighing the risk he was about to take. There was something off about Eyvindur, how he carried himself. Eyvindur was lithe, but looked deceptively strong. He had been trained. He was handsome with only a hint of an accent; Kári suspected he was from the mainland. His coat confirmed his suspicions. It was well-worn and dyed a muted brown, but the cut was clearly army issue. The man from Halla's file, no doubt.

'You were a soldier as well,' Kári said. 'You know what it means to be their pawn. But now you're here with them, fighting your former masters. Well, I don't want to be a pawn any more. Not after what I've seen.'

'I'm not sure if I can believe that just yet,' Eyvindur said sternly, almost choking on his words as he pushed them through. 'You fucking seiðskrattar.' He glared at Kári, burning him with a look that was pure hatred, refined over years and years of obsession. '*You* did this to her! You fucking abomination, you wrought all this pain upon her!'

'Elskan.' Halla placed a firm hand on Eyvindur's shoulder, calming him down. 'Do you see me losing control of my temper? Let me remind you that it was not yourself who suffered at their hands.' This smothered Eyvindur's rage like an avalanche, replacing it with shame. 'He did help me. He risked everything getting me out, before the agents managed to break me. Why do you doubt my own words?'

Eyvindur sighed, shaking his head. 'I'm sorry,' he said to Halla. 'It's just... he's one of them.'

'I know. But so were you, when I first met you.'

He set his jaw at that, nodding.

We will see what she says, the male haugbúi said, after exchanging a look with his counterpart. His cheeks had completely decomposed, showing the teeth moving as he spoke, the mouth devoid of a tongue, just a black, rotten maw. *Her judgement is our command.*

ᚼ

They walked down, Diljá and Eyvindur with their skorrifles at the ready. Everything here resonated with darkness, making Kári realise that it wasn't a light he'd seen coming from the opening above – but something deeper than the mundane darkness. There was no dust here, no sounds, nothing except the void. At the bottom of the stairs a labyrinth of hallways stretched out before them, and he followed the haugbúar into the depths. On the walls were faded icons, insignia and script that made him dizzy to just glance in their direction.

Jötnar had built this place, millions of years ago. The race that had enslaved the landvættur and destroyed themselves, shattering the world itself in an age of thaumaturgical warfare. How were these ruins so well preserved? Why were they only being unearthed now? How had the jötnar remained mere legend for all this time?

Because they'd never really disappeared. Because they'd engineered it this way.

Kári shook his head clear. This place was getting to him, more than the after-effects of the skuggsjá's vision. The air was laden with an unknowable dormant power, stirring after untold aeons.

Beyond was a smaller chamber which smelled of incense. A small, black elevation was at its end. An altar. On each step was a brass bowl, holding ash remains. A small wooden board displayed a dead bird – a thrush – its wings nailed to the wood, its entrails removed. An eye had been stitched into the cavity. It looked human.

On top of the altar was a cloth similar to the one the male haugbúi had wrapped around himself, steeped in seiðmagn. This one radiated an immense and terrible emotion that fuddled Kári's mind, sending disturbing ripples across waters that should never be disturbed. Resting on the cloth, a faint yellow in the real world, but radiating immense arcane light seen through Kári's thaumaturgical lenses, were a skull, a femur and a spine.

The bones sang. No, they *screamed*. A great and terrible wound had been etched into them, barbed chains that had shredded a tethered spirit down to its corporeal remains, impaled it on white-hot spikes for all eternity.

He recognised this sorcery. A dreadful execution only mentioned in whispers, the worst possible fate to which someone could be submitted. A traitor's death – bound and hanged and tortured for all eternity, with no respite, eternal rest denied to them through a combination of malevolent seiður and svartigaldur.

Except that this spirit had been released from their barbed-wire entanglement, and had chosen to remain by its own willpower.

Kári slowly undid his beaked mask, ignoring his trepidation of revealing himself to the others. The bones' luminescence was too much for him, too beautiful and too painful to bear. He kneeled before the altar, feeling like a child. Ashamed, embarrassed, small. Insignificant. He saw the marks on the bones, the blue spots where demonic influence had affected it, but not truly manifested. He felt the presence watching him, evaluating him.

The haugbúar went to the bowls on the steps, lighting fresh incense and dried highland moss, muttering words Kári had never heard before. He felt the presence sharpen within the bones, as mist gathering into a dark cloud, pregnant with the threat of violence. That sentience latched on to him, as though burning hot hooks into the fabric of his soul, and he was too shocked and too afraid to be able to scream.

𝕬 𝖇𝖊𝖆𝖚𝖙𝖎𝖋𝖚𝖑 𝖜𝖊𝖆𝖕𝖔𝖓, the voice said. 𝕾𝖆𝖈𝖗𝖎𝖋𝖎𝖈𝖊 – 𝖓𝖔𝖙𝖍𝖎𝖓𝖌 𝖇𝖚𝖙 𝖘𝖆𝖈𝖗𝖎𝖋𝖎𝖈𝖊. 𝕿𝖔 𝖊𝖛𝖊𝖗𝖞𝖙𝖍𝖎𝖓𝖌 𝖊𝖝𝖈𝖊𝖕𝖙 𝖍𝖎𝖒𝖘𝖊𝖑𝖋.

Kári felt a movement within himself. Not his body, not his mind – but elsewhere. As if someone was delicately strumming on the tightly wound strings of his fate.

'No. Please.'

There was something wrong with his voice. It sounded multi-faceted, duplicated. It had been weeks since he'd last removed his mask. He dreaded to think just how deeply the mutation had taken hold of him. The siblings finished their ritual, looking expectantly at the bones.

𝕸ó𝖗𝖎. 𝕾𝖐𝖔𝖙𝖙𝖆. 𝕴 𝖜𝖆𝖓𝖙 𝖙𝖔 𝖙𝖆𝖘𝖙𝖊 𝖍𝖎𝖘 𝖋𝖊𝖆𝖗. 𝕳𝖎𝖘 𝖍𝖔𝖕𝖊. 𝕴 𝖜𝖆𝖓𝖙 𝖙𝖔 𝖊𝖆𝖙 𝖙𝖍𝖊 𝖑𝖔𝖛𝖊 𝖎𝖓 𝖍𝖎𝖘 𝖍𝖊𝖆𝖗𝖙. A sound, distant, like howling laughter under a bell ringing maniacally. 𝕲𝖎𝖛𝖊 𝖒𝖊 𝖍𝖎𝖘 𝖑𝖎𝖋𝖊𝖙𝖎𝖒𝖊 – 𝖍𝖎𝖘 𝖒𝖊𝖒𝖔𝖗𝖎𝖊𝖘.

'No, wait, don't—'

They were on Kári before he could blink. They held his arms, their grip tighter than iron vices, the stench of their decay making him retch. He tried gathering seiðmagn, but he was weak and the room was devoid of residual power. Any sliver of seiðmagn was being drained by those bones, which were as unworkable to him as erupting lava is to a blacksmith.

Claws gripped his head, forced it up against the skull, looking right into its vacant eye sockets. The nailed thrush twitched on its wooden board, chirping weakly. The eye stitched into it rolled to look at him.

He couldn't help it. He stared into its depths, the dark of its iris, and he was alone, deep under the surface of the earth, in a ruined empire of obsidian. He was alone and had always been alone, and then he felt a presence next to him.

He could only grasp broken fragments. She wore a moss-green coat and was holding a cat. Its head was like smooth clay, featureless. Its stomach had erupted, emptied like the thrush had been. There was a fire burning inside the woman. A black flame.

She touched his cheek. She spoke to him, and her voice was tender. His fear evaporated. He broke down, every pretence of resistance immediately vanquished. He nodded to her and she pulled him close, her embrace stinging like razor-sharp fangs, ravenous, her heart filled with a burning desire for retribution.

Willingly, he gave in to her. But she did not feed on him, did not drain him of memories and life until nothing remained. She was looking at something he couldn't see. From her flowed a poison, a vicious concoction that surged through his veins.

He became alight with suffering.

She showed him the fear. The torture, the pain. It was all the Crown had left her with – the agents who had broken her within the heart of the Nine. With bitter anger, he recognised Þráinn Meinholt and Hrólfur in the blurred ruin of her memories. Everything else had been stripped away, only small glimmers remaining, fractions that burned with the intense heat of dying stars. She showed him hope. Promises broken. Panic, rage, hatred, the violence permeating the world... that had permeated her.

She filled him to the brim and in turn she drank from the

well of his soul. Everything became searing pain, a blinding brightness.

Kári felt the shift like a storm changing course. The moment when she saw what he had seen, unrestrained by the limitations of the skuggsjá. The possible futures the so-called beings from Laí – the ancient, traitorous jötnar – had worked so hard to scry.

And there, like a towering monolith, stood the revelation of their intentions:

The unhatched moon which was a primordial bull which was a newborn child – three in one manifesting as the abyss beyond the veil. Its name was writ across the stars as they burned:

Mánapjór.

The child which was of this earth, a tether between the real and the unreal – a living bridge. It appeared to him in conflicting revelations: a lumbering titan of a beast crushing the earth beneath its feet, crowned with nine horns as thick as tree trunks; a moon-sized hatchling tapping its pale lunar eggshell to birth itself; a wrapped newborn with too many limbs mewling against its mother's chest.

All of them were one and the same. The moon, the bull, and the child. All were simultaneously three keys and three locks. As one unlocked itself, so did it unlock the others. And with that, a cleansing flood would unmake the earth.

Ancient curses and arcane rituals of unfathomable intricacy held back this final step. Put in place aeons ago, it was an all-powerful machine which held back the flood and warped the supernatural workings of the world with its overwhelming might.

They had unbirthed the universe and placed it back within the world-egg to remake it according to their will. This working placed insurmountable limitations upon the arcane to prevent the bridge from ever being formed. In doing so, it deformed miracles into nightmares, warping and twisting the natural workings of the world into the poisonous well that seiðskrattar and galdramenn drew from today.

But time and wilful sabotage performed by unseen hands had worn it down. The world-egg would break – it was its nature to do so. There was no stopping the tide coming in.

This world was a living tomb. All of them were already dead without knowing it.

Kári cried out from the pain of witnessing again that great unmaking, only now with merciless clarity. Without her help, his mind had not been able to grasp the enormity of time unravelled, had struggled to suppress it. Those dreadful futures seemed to stretch on forever.

At the brink of oblivion, she let him go.

He drifted in a void. Lights flickered around him, like floating algae or roaming stars. Life and light, fading in, fading out. He tried reaching out to her, but she had vanished, retreated back into her paradoxical shell of unlife. He begged her to rid his mind of himself. To drain his sentience away and let him know peace. But there was no answer.

Then, he was lying on his back. His whole body ached, every nerve roaring from longing and suffering. He was crying, sobbing, tears flowing from all the eyes on his face. The undead siblings gazed at him, entranced, and strong hands grasped his shoulders, dragging him out of the chamber.

'Thank you,' said Halla. 'Garún – thank you for your mercy.'

Sautján

The cave network in which they lived was at the top of a massive structure. Having a few quiet moments, Kári accompanied Auður in her exploration of these halls. Hieroglyphics on the walls indicated the possible original shape of the ruin – a kind of pyramid or ziggurat in an unorthodox, asymmetrical form. Navigating it was a hassle, as many paths had collapsed. Just looking at those rough images, trying to unfold and realise the dimensions of that place, was enough to send Kári's mind reeling from vertigo.

He, of course, knew exactly what it had once looked like. If not this place specifically, then another just like it. This was only the outlier of a far larger city, likely buried beneath the crushing mass of the Vatnajökull glacier since the last ice age.

Next to these eroded carvings and the strange, flowing text of these long-forgotten people, he had seen other shapes.

Their near-human appearance was instantly recognisable. Among the depictions of the jötnar, there were a few deviations – an elongated appendage, a morphed head, a broader back, or more limbs than usual.

Further in, the images changed. They bore some resemblance to these first figures, but with each step they became more distanced from their original form. Each of them were an unwinding horror, each unique in an impossible, nonsensical pattern of wings and joints, chitin and beaks and mandibles and feelers, hiding among their mosaic of biological horror hints of hominid anatomy, faint as they might be.

There, in the dark, history was laid bare. Just as the former group faintly resembled humans, the latter horrors were uncannily similar to the beings from Laí. Kári realised that, deep down, he'd wanted to believe that the visions were just that – visions.

In Kári's first attempt with the skuggsjá, the experience had been murky. Vague and dreamlike, altered – but still ringing true. Once he had pierced through the filters put in place by Ingi Vítalín, it had retained that dreamlike feeling. His consciousness had been untethered from time and the physical form. He wondered if this was how gods saw the world – if that was how the landvættur experienced reality.

His last dive into those depths – just before his and Auður's escape – had been different. The future was a chaotic, fractured thing, a torrent in ceaseless transmutation which required immense willpower to piece together in a recognisable pattern. An angle of time not meant for living minds – not mortal ones at least. But the spirit in the bones they called Garún was something beyond that. Just like Ingi, she had shed her mortal shell. She had laid out the intricate pattern of possibilities before him with ease.

The things he had seen still haunted him. Here in the dark of the ruins, he felt the weight of aeons press down upon him. Every living thing was as helpless as insects faced with this grand design of the antediluvian jötnar – the so-called 'beings from Laí' – to accomplish their apocalyptic ritual. Kári told himself that did not mean he and his new allies should give up. A hive of wasps reacts with anger when disturbed. So they must do what they could to try to ensure their survival. Even if it meant that extermination was just as inevitable.

Retreating to a collapsed dead end for some privacy, he studied his own face in the flickering light of an oil lantern. He had borrowed the shaving mirror from Eyvindur, who passed it to him before he even asked for it. Likely Halla had given Eyvindur a nudge.

Eyvindur's relationship with Halla was a beautiful thing to Kári. Resting in the corner of the common room, lying on top of a thin woollen bedroll, Kári had pretended to sleep as he studied them, his mask obscuring his attentions. They were deeply in love. Eyvindur combed her hair as they chatted idly, weaving it into a beautiful Hafnían fishtail braid.

When Kári had helped Halla, he had not tried to turn her back to what was considered normal. Instead, like a woodworker works with the grain and knots of the piece of wood he is handling, Kári had worked with the new form of Halla's body. It was now more comfortable for her to speak, to eat, to move. Eyvindur remarked on her being quicker on her feet, not complaining about aching joints any more, and she'd said it was thanks to the seiðskratti. Eyvindur hadn't responded to that.

Kári was tired. Tired of pretending to be someone he was not, someone he had not been for a very long time, perhaps someone he had never truly been. He had succeeded in avoiding being ostracised by society only to find himself shunned by his closest family. Despite his having done everything he could to fix himself, to appease them.

It surprised Kári how relieved he had felt at the sight of his own face. Seeing all those eyes, accounting for his strange, elongated field of vision, the myriad colours; the odd shape of his mouth; his nose reduced to a slitted stub: all of it would have driven him feverish with anger not so long ago.

Something had come loose in his core, which had triggered a landslide of changes both physical and psychological. He had not seen his reflection for weeks, and by rights it should have felt unrecognisable to him. Instead, he found that the new face staring back at him was more in his likeness than ever. And so Kári strived to push it further into that direction, to become what he felt he was meant to be.

ᚼ

Kári returned to the group carrying his mask. It was clear his appearance unsettled others, even though Auður tried to disguise her apprehension. Only Eyvindur and Halla cared nothing about his condition. Eyvindur accepted the mirror back with a nod.

'You can keep it, you know. I don't mind.'

'That's quite all right, Eyvindur. I think you have more use for it than I do, now.'

They gathered and Auður started to debrief them on what had been happening. The excavation, Kári's vision, the proof writ across the walls of these ruins. The dead siblings stood at the back of the crowd, half-hidden in the weak flickering lights of the lanterns. They'd already heard everything she had to say.

It was a lot to take in. A conspiracy stretching across aeons. Diljá was the one who had the most questions, trying to piece together as complete a picture of the events as possible. In the end, Auður turned to Kári to fill in what had happened during his last dive into the clairvoyant depths of the psychometrical machine.

'The skuggsjá's revelations of the future differed wildly from those of the past.' Kári's voice had a slight tremble, a vibrato that invoked a sense of nervousness in the listener. In a way, it sounded beautiful. 'Before, it was as if viewing a memory filtered through a dream. This... was an unsolvable knot of possibilities. Endless tethers intertwining, breaking off, splitting apart. Through all the noise, one destiny rang more clearly than the others. The unmaking of reality.'

That ancient race – the jötnar, those beings who claimed to be from Laí – commanded supernatural forces in unimaginable ways. They were an empire holding the reins of creation, at least when viewed from this end of history – from a broken world drained of seiðmagn. The jötnar had dived deep into the secrets of the universe and some of them had emerged changed – touched by the endless void that lurks beyond the threshold, an all-devouring dimension of acausality. Through a convoluted and strange ritual, they would clear a path for the great dissolution to spread into this world, like turpentine flowing over a masterwork painting.

They were stopped by a civil war that ended their civilisation, their race, their world. Barriers were put in place, floodgates against the unmaking they hoped to manifest. In doing so, they had altered the workings of reality itself. Except that a select chosen few had survived, through the aeons that followed. The devoted cultists who had accepted the transmundane influence wholeheartedly, becoming as demons themselves. They had endured, stripped of the power they once possessed, more patient than the mountains themselves.

And now, everything was falling into place.

The true work of Ingi Vítalín, the slave to those repugnant creatures. Did Ingi even know what they truly were, whom he served? Or did he naïvely believe them to truly be aliens, bearing him through the cosmos on their disturbing wings? Had the man sacrificed his body and his soul, all because of the ruse these beings had fabricated?

It was the funniest thing Kári had ever heard.

'The nature of the ritual itself is beyond my comprehension.

But what I know is this – the landvættur is key to their success. They aim to use its power to break the restraints upon the world, the only thing holding back the culmination of the ritual. The dormant power is a seal placed on this island. That seal is also the moon – and that which lies in the heart of Öskjuhlíð, underneath the thaumaturgical power plant. At that moment, a vestige will be created on earth. It is…'

It is a child which is the moon which is a bull.

No, he couldn't say that. It sounded too mad, even compared to everything else he was saying.

'It is a bridge between earth and void, linking causal and acausal dimensions. All I know is its name – Mánaþjór. I know it's hard to comprehend. As I said, the complete picture eludes me. But within this being, which is somehow more than itself… is the gateway to the beyond. Once manifested, a chain reaction will be unleashed that spells ruin for us all.'

'Auður, you cannot seriously expect us to believe this nonsense?' Diljá had listened to Kári's explanation stoically, but now her voice was laced with anger. 'These are the ravings of a lunatic. I mean…' She gestured to Kári. 'I'm sorry to say it, but look at him! Whatever that machine did to him, it was unnatural. It ruined him!'

'And what about Halla?' asked Eyvindur. 'Is she mad as well? Is that perhaps why she fights alongside us?'

'That's different,' Diljá snapped. 'She was tortured by *them*.'

That last word was followed by a seething glare at Kári. He bore it.

'You're right,' Kári said. 'That is different. But what you see now was not done by the skuggsjá. Accelerated by it, yes, or perhaps by the thaumaturgical radiation of the landvættur, but I did this to myself.' He swallowed. 'I did what I had to do in order to survive.'

They did not want to prod at that. Or maybe they already knew.

'I know it sounds outrageous,' said Auður. Kári could tell that she was unsettled by what he'd said. A lot of it had been new information to her. 'But I believe him, Diljá. They were using that machine to decipher the future. This entire operation of theirs has reeked of subterfuge from day one – more than usual for Kalmar. Vésteinn is different. Something has changed him. And those things, the so-called "beings from Laí" – you haven't seen them up close. Or heard that man-machine gush about their dreadful plans.' Auður sighed, gathering the facts laid before her, trying to put her conviction in words. 'Say Kári is wrong. Do you really think they still don't have a horrible plan for the machine they're planning to build? I've *seen* the plans. They're going to encase the landvættur in steel, turn it into a mobile power plant. The flying fortress will be like a gnat in comparison.'

'Right,' said Diljá. 'I don't see why the ravings of a lunatic matter. We've always planned to put a stop to this power plant.'

'You can't.' Kári's words echoed in the cave. He was starting to lose his temper and took a moment to calm himself. 'Let's say you succeed. Ruin their devices, kill their soldiers. *So what?* The landvættur is still alive. You stand no chance of putting it down. The jötnar will still be out there, waiting, planning. They've waited for millions of years. Waiting a decade for Kalmar or a century for another empire to gather the resources they need to complete their goal is nothing to them! What you propose is only an inconvenience, a minor setback – in a best-case scenario.'

'All right, *Magister*,' Diljá spat at him. 'What do you propose then, if we have no chance of killing the landvættur?'

Give up, he wanted to reply. He held back, lied to himself that there was a way through this. A future unseen.

'When energy is harvested from the landvættur, it drains it to the brink of death – or at least, as close to death as we can understand it. Just before that moment, when it is on the precipice, the current is reversed. The jolt of thaumaturgical energy kicks it back to life and the cycle is repeated.'

'And?'

'That is when we must strike. We must stop them from bringing it back, and do whatever we can to push the landvættur over the edge of oblivion.'

Diljá took a moment to piece the bigger picture together.

'You idiot. You actually want us to sit here and let them build the power plant?'

'Yes.'

The gathering erupted in outrage.

'There was the proof,' said Diljá, joined in by several others: *He's a spy, he's been sent here by them to mislead us, to trick us into sitting back as they complete their war machine.*

Auður argued back, drowned out by the noise.

Enough.

Styrhildur stepped into the light, flanked by her brother Hraki.

The seiðskratti has spoken to her. She has seen through his eyes.

'She's not lucid,' muttered Diljá. 'I know you care about her. We all do! But she's gone, Styrhildur. She's long gone.'

So are we. Soon, so are all of us.

'That's not the same.'

So you keep saying, said Hraki. *Was she so gone when Halla pulled her from the wreck of the Nine?*

Or when she led Halla to us? Us to you?

'That's enough.' Diljá's voice broke, stifled by a lump in her throat. Styrhildur did not refrain.

Was she lucid when she revealed to you the betrayal of the person you thought you loved? Or is her vision only true when it suits your purpose?

Diljá stormed up and pushed past the dead siblings, heading towards the inner chamber.

'I'll go and talk to her myself!'

ᚼ

They were still very untrusting of him. Kári suspected it was only because of Garún that he was allowed to stay – the exact nature of their relationship to the sentience within the bones was still unclear to him. It reminded him of old pagan myths about the völva, seeresses who sometimes acted as tribal leaders in all but name. Thankfully, Kári was ignored after the meeting, as people talked among themselves in hushed whispers.

Halla and Eyvindur were kind enough to let him sit with them. Auður had followed Diljá to attempt to talk some sense into her, saying that Styrhildur and Hraki were ill-suited to the challenge. The siblings suffered from a severe detachment from the living condition and spent most of their time consorting at the reliquary, as Kári had grown to think of it.

'All of this ancient stuff, all these conspiracies...' Eyvindur stirred a pot over a small fire – thin soup with bits of dried lamb and beets. 'It's a bit too much for everyone to take in. Especially having risked everything to come here and fight for what they believe in.'

Kári changed the subject, exhausted with revisiting that nightmare. Eyvindur was an ex-soldier, hardened and broken by some distant war before he had been sent here, where he had met Halla. His name was really Øyvind, although he preferred the localised version now. He was wanted, first as a deserter and then as a traitor. The Directorate would rip the memories from his mind as soon as they got their hands on him.

Kári learned that he and Halla had been hiding in Rökkurvík, after she'd escaped from Kleppur, the insane asylum. Her family had institutionalised her for fraternising with a foreign soldier. They had been in love and given everything up for each other. But as hard as it had been, they had been happy. That's where they had met Garún and joined the cause.

Halla had been transformed viciously by a seiðskratti under Meinholt's command. She told Kári more about it: how she and Eyvindur had been arrested in a raid on the Forgotten Downtown; how the Directorate of Immigration, working with the Hrímlandic police, had rounded them all up. Recognising Eyvindur as a deserter, both of them now activists and radicals, they had a seiðskratti torture her to make Eyvindur talk.

Kári wondered if it had been Ginfaxi. It likely was. Þráinn Meinholt was the one who'd ordered it, and he kept his sorcerous pets on a tight leash. As Kári explained the agent's presence at the expedition to them, he came to learn more about Hrólfur, his right-hand man.

Hrólfur, the traitor whom they had called 'friend'.

He had been responsible for the deaths of their comrades, manipulating them at every step, stopping dangerous actions, ensuring that everything they did ultimately benefited the powers that be: the wealthy Hrímlanders who owned Innréttingarnar. He had nurtured a relationship with Diljá, and had intended to continue it after the group split apart just before the flying fortress fell. Halla had been the one to put a stop to his schemes. The Stone Giant had liberated her from the Nine and handed Garún's bones to her. It was only through Garún that they had been able to figure out Hrólfur's betrayal.

'He's less than nothing.' Halla's voice was shivering. 'Less than human. He's a fucking monster.' She swallowed forcibly, restraining the turmoil still raging within her.

'We will make them pay for what they did to you.' Kári's words felt weak. 'For everything they've done.'

'We might not be so lucky,' Eyvindur added hesitantly. 'Þráinn is enhanced with seiður or galdur. Likely Hrólfur as well, by now. Both of them will be surrounded by troops at all times. And they keep their pet, the royal seiðskratti, very close.'

'When Auður told us what they were planning... that the Directorate was involved, all of it funded by Innréttingarnar...' Halla was trying to distract herself with work, going over her backpack and making sure everything was in order. 'We couldn't just sit by. Not after everything. Loftkastalinn was a terror – but I often think of what would have happened should it have remained. What it could have done to us, to others, had they ever managed to get it mobilised on the mainland.'

'According to what Auður says, this power plant will be able to refuel a flying fortress such as Loftkastalinn.' Eyvindur poured them each a bowl of the soup. It was meagre, but smelled incredible. 'It'll act as a mother ship to dozens of them. Improved versions, to boot.'

'They've probably already started,' said Kári grimly.

They ate in silence. After a while, Diljá and Auður returned. Diljá looked pale and exhausted. She went to lie down on her bedroll. Auður joined them and finished off the last of the soup.

'We're in agreement. We'll wait for the activation and strike then.'

'They've prepared many stakes already.' Halla's voice was low and soft. She sat by the embers of their fire, stoking it so it didn't go out. She was heating a stone, baking flatbread on top of it. 'How soon until they raise the landvættur on top of it?'

'Months,' said Auður. 'They still have to build the power plant itself. It likely won't be active until the end of the year.'

Each of them silently ran the numbers on this.

'We are low on supplies,' said Eyvindur. 'And we can't risk stealing from them any more. How are we going to keep ourselves fed in the depths of winter?'

'I don't know,' Auður admitted. 'But we'll have to find a way.'

Kári was trying to put his thoughts into order, trying to figure out some solution, when Halla spoke up.

'I lived in a small fishing village when I was a child. Before we moved to the city. We were poor, but we endured. The best part of living there was the beach – a long stretch of black sand, hiding caves in the cliffs. Near the shore were odd columns of stone we called Troll-man, Troll-woman and Sea-cows. The story was that they had all turned to stone as the sun rose. Some folklore nonsense, of course, but still ... it was a beautiful place. We played in small tidal pools and hunted for crabs and sea urchins and weird-looking seaweed.

'We came to the beach one summer morning to find it covered in bodies. Dozens and dozens of whales that had beached the night before. They were pilot whales – black and sleek and so beautiful. It was a tribe of them – families travelling together. Except that something had driven them to swim right up onto the land. Parents and children alike lay there, dead or dying.

'We cried and ran for our parents. Everyone in the village came out to see them. We thought they were going to help the whales, use some seiður or galdur to get them back into the ocean. Instead, my father and the men in the village carved up the whales with spears ending in long blades. My mother and the women butchered the pieces, packing the meat into barrels of sour whey.

'I never went back to play on that beach. It always seemed to me like its black sands reeked of blood.'

She fell quiet, focusing on stoking the fire so it wouldn't go out, flipping a flatbread on the stone. Eyvindur leaned up against her, placing a hand around her back.

'All is hay in hard times,' Kári said in a slow, measured tone. 'That meat must have fed your village for a long time.'

'It did,' Halla said casually. 'It was thanks to the surplus we sold that we managed to move to Reykjavík. I was a child, but I knew we had to do what we must in order to survive. And I still know that today. But that power plant… is like butchering a whale that never dies. Over and over, its meat regenerating every night. It's monstrous. Even if nothing you say is true, Kári – and I don't mean that I don't believe you. I do. As much I want not to. It's just that by itself, without thinking of war and power and everything else – it's despicable. My family did what they needed to in order to survive. And now I will do whatever it takes to do the very same.'

We will end it, sister, said Styrhildur. The siblings were suddenly there, standing right by them without having made a sound. *We used to believe such beautiful things as well, when our blood ran thick and hot.*

Their hubris will be their unmaking, Hraki continued. *And their sins will be tallied up against them.*

III

FLÓÐ

—

FLOOD

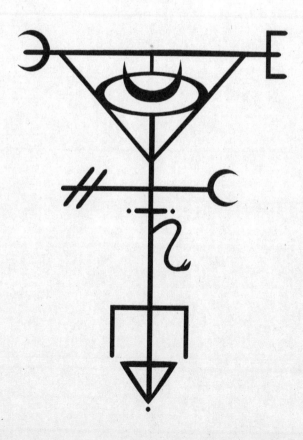

Once, a war was fought between the real and the unreal, what is and what has never been.

A storm descended upon our shores. A storm of our own making. It was met with a tempest of equal measure. This was how we brought the world to ruin.

Those of us who fought against its fury chained it. To life, to earth, to storm, we bound the flood that unmakes reality. The great dissolution was our boon and bane to our successors.

This island is an affront. This island is a curse. This island is violence. This island is nothing but a scab over a deep wound.

This island is a seal. A locked gate.

A wound bleeds, deforming the earth. Infection seeps up between the cracks, welling up from the still-tender cavity.

The barrier will hold. But not forever. An egg is destined to hatch, after all.

Átján

Movement woke Elka. A wriggling eel that circled inside her. A feeling which grew stronger every day. She placed her hand on her stomach and felt the baby move. She could see it poking out through her skin in an undulating motion. Odd that she only recalled this happening in the middle of her third trimester when she had Sölvi.

Her miracle. The treasure from the Deep.

The baby always moved at the same hours of the day. She had realised that it reacted when the tide was at its highest and lowest – when the moon had the most or least influence on the sea. And so the moon pulled and pushed her as well, her body, the ocean within her womb which fed a new kind of life.

The beginning of a new world.

Ægir had given her a book. It was small and worn, bound in unmarked brown leather. He said it was a catechism given only to a select few, those who were in the innermost circle and who had shown that they had the right mindset, the right understanding of the sanctity of the Deep.

Elka devoured the volume, reading it and rereading it, filling her mind with its sacred words. Cradling the bump in her stomach, feeling the Deep move within her, she saturated herself with the sustaining waters of holy scripture.

She worried so about Sölvi. She knew that she had spoiled him, turning him ungrateful and weak-willed. But Vestmannaeyjar would change him. So she prayed to the Deep. Already he was finding the right way forward in life. He had a real chance of becoming a better person than she was.

The storm raged through the night, keeping Elka from sleep. The beginning of the month of Þorri was upon them, fourth of the winter months in the Hrímlandic calendar. The nights were long and the weather fierce, but the light was growing in strength as the solstice was now a full month behind them.

The wind howled, tearing at the house so fiercely that she was certain the roof would fly off it. Hail pounded the iron cladding, a monotone barrage which sounded like an assault. Ægir stirred next to her, turning in his sleep. She held her breath, exhaling softly when he kept on snoring.

Elka did not sleep much these nights. It felt as if the baby was somersaulting within her, squirming and turning like an agitated fish. She had a strange feeling it was either worried or excited. Ultimately, she just wished it would calm down so she could get some rest.

Her stomach was large by only twenty-eight weeks. With Sölvi it had only been an outward curve by this point; now it was as though she was well into her third trimester. Moving as gently and quietly as she could, so she wouldn't wake Ægir, she got up to go to the bathroom.

The floorboards creaked in the hallway, a comforting sound in the noisy storm if she wasn't so worried Ægir would stir. She hoped the storm had masked the noise. Her feet were tired, her hips mildly protesting with each step. She checked on Sölvi as she went down the hallway. Sound asleep. He had become so serious since he started working with Styrmir. Things had improved tenfold at school, and the headmaster kept in touch with Ægir regularly. Still, Elka worried about him. He didn't talk to her, not like he used to, but she knew that was because he was becoming a young man. She couldn't have her baby boy forever. She only wished she had just a little bit longer.

After having gone to the bathroom, she decided it was useless to try to fall asleep during this storm with the baby as agitated as it was. Her tossing and turning would end up with Ægir getting up, too.

She lit a lamp and went into the kitchen, stoking the embers in the stove and lighting a small fire. It was cold, and the warmth that radiated from the iron stove made her feel safe and comfortable. Through the window, she saw strange colours glide through the air, untouched by the gale. The lumbering hills of hardened lava which had almost devoured the village pulsated with a threatening glow, as if it was still molten just beneath the jagged surface. This was becoming more and more common over the last few weeks. A telltale sign it was time to take her medication.

Elka filled a pot with water, as the whistle of the kettle would surely wake Ægir, and brewed a serving of herbal mixture. It was a pregnancy aid from Reverend Bryde. It stank something fierce, a ground-up concoction that looked more like ash than herbs, but it was supposed to soothe pains and help her sleep. She took three capsules with the brew, which usually calmed her and the baby. Instantly the unnatural colours abated and the lava hills dimmed. She put a couple of spoons of precious sugar into the tea and felt so selfish, but it was almost undrinkable without it. With her cup in hand, she went into the study.

When Ægir had proposed to Elka, he had said that he had no desire to keep living like 'a philanderer' and tarnish her reputation as a good woman, and that she and Sölvi should move into his family's house. Not exactly romantic, but still she had been touched. His courting had been refreshingly old-fashioned, and although they now shared a bed, he had shown no interest in more intimacy than that. They had only slept together once. It made her feel as if she had been tricked, even though she couldn't explain how. It was not a subject she was comfortable bringing up. He was not the type of man to talk openly about sensitive matters. It was clear that he cared for her, in his own way.

The house was beautiful and well maintained, despite looking its age with peeled white paint and weathered window frames. Like most houses in Heimaey, it had a name: Hóll. It had three floors, including the semi-basement. The front of the house was reminiscent of an imposing fortress, with two semicircular towers to the east and west, rising one floor above the rest. They protruded out from the house; between them nestled the stairs leading up to the recessed entrance. Hóll had been in Ægir's family for decades. Now, only he remained. The floorboards creaked and the doors fitted poorly into their frames. There had always been plans to bridge the gap between the two towers and make it a proper three-storey house, but time or money had never put the plans into action. Despite its age it had a new roof, including a rain-gathering system with huge tanks. The water ran clear from the taps and was so plentiful Elka could bathe every day if she wanted.

Both Björg and Ægir had insisted that Elka stopped working by the end of summer, even if she felt completely fine. With Ægir's salary, it wasn't as if she truly needed the money, and she found their fretting over her condition endearing. The true nature of the pregnancy was kept strictly secret among the congregation, and was not something they shared with out-siders. Everyone assumed it was Ægir's child. Ægir himself said he had been truly blessed by the Messengers to be given this responsibility. The priest and congregation had spent more time congratulating him than her at the time – as if it was he who had been chosen to carry this miracle of the Deep into the world, and not Elka. She scolded herself for feeling that way, for being so selfish and petty, when she should have felt blessed that a man like Ægir fully supported her and this wondrous miracle that was about to be given to the world.

And she did feel blessed. Despite how he could be, sometimes.

My blood is brine and my heart beats with the rhythm of waves, she repeated to herself during her doubtful moments. Part of the catechisms, the final words of a saint, spoken as her ship crashed into a reef during a fierce storm. *As we are born from the crashing of waves so we must return to the depths of the womb. Blessed be the Deep.*

In the study Elka reclined into an extravagant reading chair, thankful for the back support and firm softness that cradled her perfectly. She placed her feet up on the footstool and rooted around in her basket of knitting supplies, fishing up the dog-eared copy of a romance novel she had been reading in secret when she couldn't sleep. Ægir would lose his temper should he catch her with it, but during these fretful and worried waking hours of the long, dark winter nights she just needed to calm her mind with something comforting. At such times the cryptic religious texts only left her feeling drained and disorientated.

The hot drink soothed her, the bitterness of the herbs muted by the dissolving sugar. Already, it felt as though the baby was calmer, or perhaps it was only Elka herself. Its movements now felt relaxed, her own turmoil settling into a blissful numbness. She leaned back, covering herself with a woollen blanket, falling asleep in the middle of a chapter before she knew it. Outside, the storm raged on, waves breaking on the shore with huge, powerful crashes.

She woke with a gasp, drenched in sweat, to the sound of a child crying. It faded to nothingness as the dream gave way to the real. Glimpses remained, dissolving by the second. The child was stirring within her, coiling like an agitated serpent. She took two more capsules, but after that there was not much sleep to be had.

It was usually the dreams which woke her – her initial moments tinged with rising fear and an undercurrent of anxiety. Vivid, bizarre dreams, which haunted her after waking. Those fragments were as broken shards in her subconscious and felt too dangerous for closer examination. The capsules helped dull their serrated edges, turning them into something wonderful.

Murky images of sunken vessels amid algae-covered ruins of broken obsidian columns. Lights on a dark sea, vanishing as ship after ship went down. Nine massive horns atop a moving mountain, caressed by the gathering storm clouds. The moon mirrored on troubled waves, cracked and shattered in its reflection. A city beneath the sea rising up to the surface, faint glows returning to its darkened windows one by one.

Elka stroked her stomach and hummed a song to her unborn child. Above the island, the waxing moon loomed.

ᚼ

A lot had changed in the nearly six months since Kári fled the excavation. They were situated at the top of a mountain peak, hiding in its rocky terrain, which provided them an excellent view of the entire dig site.

The excavation pit had become a canyon. On its bottom was a confusing mass of machinery, generators and thaumaturgical batteries. From this foundation of steel rose the black spears, obsidian-clad, rising towards the sky, impaling the titanic carcass of the landvættur.

Open wounds, entrails dangling from its burst belly, eyes white and dead. The rough armoured skin peeling off in huge swathes, revealing the disgusting dark grey pinkness of its flesh. The wind carried its foul stench, even at such a distance. The ground beneath the giant was covered in viscera. Tarps covered most of the machinery, ineffectively shielding it from the gore.

Surrounding the would-be power plant, the smaller dig sites had grown larger. They now clearly showed the tops of buildings – towers made from black obsidian or basalt, ancient structures rising from the earth. The shields had been reinforced, now visible to the naked eye as a spherical disturbance in the air – according to others. Kári no longer needed his mask's lenses to see the seiðmagn. The landscape was thoroughly walled off to outside thaumaturgical influence – but the true threat was coming from within. Dead as it might appear, the landvættur was anything but. It still lived, in this repulsive limbo between life and death. It radiated an unwell pallor of bizarre seiðmagn. Calling it 'unwell' seemed unscientific to Kári's mind, but he could not bring himself to think of it in another manner. It was like nothing he had seen.

Everywhere, people were on the move. New materials for the construction had been shipped through the portal, along with a bigger workforce. Rows of cheaply made, army-style barracks lined the eastern side of the main site, their identifying curved roofs of corrugated iron just like those the Crown had built when they first arrived in Hrímland. However, the newly constructed housing indicated a far greater number of workers than those Kári saw deployed. Outside the camp perimeter new mass graves had been dug, adjacent to the one made during the summer. It wasn't only the seiðmagn killing them now – the plague had been borne through the portal by the new labourers.

Several barracks were quarantined with the diseased; corpses were carried out by soldiers in gas masks every other day.

Kári wondered how many workers had died. He told himself there was nothing he could have done for them. It was a lie he despised, but one he felt was necessary for his own peace of mind. People must be desperate to take on this job – the Hanseatic war and its shortages must be devastating in Reykjavík. Thinking back to what he once considered his home, his city, awoke a peculiar feeling. Being what he now was – had been for years; having walked out on his allegiance to the powers that be ... he would never be able to return there.

A liberating thought, strangely.

Halla had vanished as soon as they were out in the open. Two foxes appeared out of nowhere as soon as she ventured outside and tailed her like her own shadow. Their furs shifted with the landscape; each of them had a multitude of tails. The others wouldn't – or couldn't – tell Kári what exactly they were, or how Halla had come by them. Now, she returned to the group, slightly out of breath, neither he nor Eyvindur having spotted her approach. She moved through the barren landscape like nothing else, melding effortlessly into the frigid wasteland.

'It's as we suspected – armed soldiers all around the perimeter. They also have cannons in their fortifications to the north-west and south-east, like you guessed, Eyvindur.'

The foxes scurried around, their colouring shifting as they settled into hiding.

'Did you see what kind of barrels they had?'

She shook her head. 'I can't say. But they are definitely thau-maturgical weapons.'

Kári had cut down his robes for better mobility, using the fabric to shield himself from the cold. They were poorly outfitted for winter. He had traded his beaked mask for the ones they used to obfuscate themselves. These masks were brilliantly simple in their utilisation of seiðmagn. They had applied an ingenious concoction over them – a paste laced with delýsíð. It made their entire form turn into a haze, an incomprehensible outline to the eyes of others. They all had one, which had made them seem like phantoms in the first attack. That said, Kári still kept the seiðskratti's mask on him at all times. It was a necessary filter if one was to draw in any significant amount of seiðmagn, should the need arise.

'And the royal seiðskratti?' Kári asked. Ginfaxi was his prime concern.

'Nothing,' she admitted. 'Can't you feel for him, or something?'

'Not really. But they have obviously been using the portal, and Ginfaxi is the only one there who can operate it – at least when I left. The movement of seiðmagn inside the barrier is strange – structured. Something is manipulating it.' They gave him a tired look. 'It's like looking at a current. You can tell that something is affecting it, but not exactly what that thing is.'

'The power plant.'

'Most likely. Or something else.'

'But they haven't activated it yet?'

He leaned against the rock, again scanning the area.

'No. I don't think so, at least. But everything looks just about ready. We'll have to get Auður out here to confirm.'

Halla settled down on the mossy ground next to them, taking a look at the area with her own binoculars.

'All right. So we wait and study their patterns.'

The next few days were spent monitoring them closely. The soldiers left in the Centimotive every other day, patrolling the surrounding area, using the Centimotive's system to scan for incoming thaumaturgical hotspots or other threats. Either Hrólfur or Þráinn always accompanied them. On the afternoon of the fourth day, it looked as though the power plant was about to be activated, causing some panic among the group. They weren't ready to attack. But an explosion went off in its underbelly. In an instant, soldiers had manned the two main fortifications, the sandbag walls, guarding the Centimotive to make sure they weren't caught off guard.

'If we had used this opportunity,' Eyvindur said, 'we would have been dead before we even got close. Look how fast they are now, how organised.'

'We're going to need a whole herd,' Halla said.

'We just might. Do you think you can get word back to Diljá's group?'

Halla shook her head. 'Not in time.'

'All those workers, however.' Kári thought carefully about what he was about to say next. 'They have no safe place to run. We must be careful when the time comes.'

Eyvindur sneered. 'They're the enemy.'

'No, they're not. They're civilians.'

The ex-soldier turned back to his binoculars. 'Not from where I'm standing.'

Diljá and her team returned to their camp on the evening of the fifth day, accompanied by Bölmóður. The náskári had flown far south to gather food, returning with a dead ram in his claws. Meagre pickings for a group of their number, with each trip being more dangerous – not because of the farmers guarding their livestock, but because of the local tribe of náskárar who considered those lands part of their territory. Twice the tribe had chased him off empty-clawed. He was lucky to have survived the encounters.

The furs Diljá was wearing were frost-covered, making her and the others look like creatures out of myth. It had snowed the previous nights, covering their tents in much-needed camouflage, but the cold had got to them. The seiðmagn had hit them hard. Kári did what he could to heal them, but in many cases the damage was irreversible. He knew many of his alterations would not stick and would likely progress even further. Still, it was that or death. Already it was a miracle they had endured this long.

'They're two days out,' Diljá said.

She was freezing cold, so Kári used seiður to flare up the fire burning in the cave. She gave him a curt nod in thanks.

'How many?' asked Eyvindur. 'There was an accident at the site yesterday. They're now heavily fortified and clearly anticipate an attack.'

Kári pretended not to notice the look of frustration sent his way.

Diljá grinned at this. 'Oh, the twins have wrangled a few.'

'Three?' Halla asked.

Diljá permitted herself a full, satisfied smile. 'A small herd.'

'How many?'

'Depends on how well things go drawing them to the site. Might be up to seven. We'll see.'

Bölmóður went straight back out to rendezvous with the siblings, who were managing the herd. They had decided on the eastern front of the excavation, coming in from the north-east. The cannons would have a limited range at that angle, and Kári and the others would be able to cause massive damage to the barracks before moving on to the centre stakes.

With the ram butchered and cooked, they ate for one last time before gathering their gear for the raid, heading out to their hiding spots on the overlooking mountain.

The next morning, Vésteinn successfully activated the machine.

It started with Kári's hair standing on end, static electricity firing. Halla's foxes scurried into hiding, whimpering. Kári gave the group a signal to brace themselves, and as one they hunkered down into their foxholes. They felt the hum of the generators before they heard the sound – a nauseating vibration that drilled through their bodies.

The landvættur jerked, sending streams of viscera spattering down like rain. Then, the sound ceased. It roared, a booming explosion that resonated through the highlands. It knew what came next.

The world went black and white as energy was unleashed, shocking the impaled landvættur with what must have been the site's entire store of seiðmagn, draining it completely.

The beast roared again. The sound had plagued Kári's sleeping and waking hours since he'd heard it in the skuggsjá. Hearing it now, seeing the divine beast brought back to grotesque non-life after being denied death for so long... it broke his heart. He had never believed in a higher power; the religion of the king's bloodline had always seemed ridiculous and the old ways were long since reduced to mere superstition. But this thing – this creature – was as close to a god as they would ever get on this earth. The old faith didn't seem as nonsensical to him, now.

The wind shifted in a heartbeat. The storm started to gather. The sky turned in an instant, clouds gathering from thin air, thick and dark and booming with thunder. Sleet started to come down in a torrent.

Its eyes lit up, however faintly, however weakly, when compared to its untamed, living glory. Lightning shot around its maw, which started to spew smoke, an engine fired back to life. A barrage of flashes struck down at random, the lightning followed by a cascade of booming thunder.

Through Kári's new vision, the world bloomed into vivid colour, as a geyser of seiðmagn exploded before his eyes, an eruption of sorcerous might so pure, so beautiful, that he felt himself crying tears of joy at its greatness.

Then the power plant sucked the air out of the world.

Or that was what it felt like. As if by the throw of a switch, the flow of power was reversed. The landvættur went limp, its eyes dulled as it spasmed on the spikes, the storm fading to nothing in the blink of a moment. It looked worse than dead.

Later that day, it all happened again. They suffered through it, preparing for what was to come. Bölmóður returned, reporting to them. The siblings would be here early next morning.

Nítján

Escaping a tiny island without getting caught was no small feat.
But Sölvi had been planning this for months. It turned out that
paying attention in school was smart in more ways than one.

There were many caves in Heimaey. The villagers had hidden
in them two centuries before when they had been raided by slavers, outliers from a nation of marbendlar called the Luminous
Armada. It had only been a single ship, but the slavers took
more than four hundred Hrímlanders in total. The roaming
underwater kingdom itself hadn't been close to the shores of
Hrímland, thankfully, or it was likely that few would have
survived. Two hundred and forty-two people had been taken in
Vestmannaeyjar alone, less than two dozen making their way
back a decade later after being retrieved by diplomats.

Sölvi had made a point to go looking for the caves mentioned
in the textbook. Asking adults would be stupid, because they'd
just tell on you, and asking other children would only mean
that your hiding spot became compromised. He'd gone to the
school library, asking politely for a map of Heimaey, telling
the kindly librarian that he wanted to better know the place
his family was from. Only a few caves had been listed there.
He had found old sea maps in Ægir's house, and there a few
others had been marked. Searching for the caves proved to be a

bother; some were only accessible by boat, others flooded at high tide. The best ones were hidden in the landscape, and of those Hundraðmannahellir suited him best. Despite being fairly well known, nobody really went there. It had got its name because a hundred people were supposed to have hidden there during the raids. Now, it would be his hiding spot, before he left this rotten island forever.

Sölvi crawled through the small, well-hidden opening in the ground. It was a while until he entered the cave proper. He lit a match, lighting a lamp he'd stowed away, casting light on his full backpack which held everything he'd need to start a new life. He'd bought new art supplies with the money earned working with Styrmir. He didn't want Ægir to know about it, so he'd asked the huldumaður to buy it for him. It turned out that Bryde was the only one who sold them in town, but Styrmir knew where to get them second-hand. He also wasn't a fan of trading with the priest.

At first, Sölvi had hoped that he and his mother could both hide in the cave from Ægir and whoever came searching, just like people used to do when the raiders came. Then when they gave up and Ægir went out to sea, they'd get on the next ship back to Reykjavík. But he now realised that was a stupid plan – a child's plan. The caves could be used to hide things from Ægir, not Sölvi or his mother. Besides, she was in no condition to be living in a cave. No, he would have to learn to sail a ship and steal one – commandeer it, as they put it in history books.

He'd also learned something else in those books about Vestmannaeyjar. During the eruption, decades before, when the Deep had stopped the volcano (although that hadn't been in the book itself; the teacher made sure they knew who they owed their lives to), only a single person had died. A woman gave birth to a stillborn child. That day was his mother's birthday and Amma Dagmar had left when the eruption started.

Something about that sat badly with him. He knew it was just his imagination messing with him, his own anxieties showing – but Amma Dagmar had said to always trust your gut. But he had no idea how to look further into it.

His gut told him he only had one person he could trust in Heimaey. So he'd asked Styrmir about it during a coffee break on one of the afternoons he spent helping the huldumaður out.

Styrmir had been very quiet after Sölvi told him what he had learned about the eruption.

'That's very sad,' was all he said.

Sölvi considered how to push him on it. In his mind it was almost like a puzzle, seeing where to press to get people to open up. He was getting very good at those puzzles.

'Was the woman a member of the Church?' he asked innocently.

Styrmir's look showed that he obviously hadn't asked innocently enough.

'There weren't that many involved in it at the time. Nobody's ever had to hide their faith around here, however, so it wasn't a secret. Yes, I believe she was a member.'

Sölvi's nerves were betrayed by his hand trembling as he reached for another biscuit.

'She was trying to fulfil their prophecy as well, wasn't she?'

Styrmir didn't say anything. He just nodded, almost imperceptibly.

'What was her name?'

'You shouldn't be worrying about this, Sölvi.'

'I'm not a child.' Sölvi hated how that had sounded. So much like an indignant brat. 'It's just a question.'

'Listen, kid – do you know what happens to people who ask

questions here? Who say the wrong thing to the wrong person?' Styrmir raised the stump that remained of his right arm, ever so slightly. 'Nothing good, that's what. So shut up with the questions. Your mother will be fine.'

He could tell that Styrmir was lying and didn't even believe that lie himself. He tried a different approach.

'Mamma isn't the first one, is she?' he asked.

'I don't know,' Styrmir admitted.

'It was my grandmother, wasn't it? Why did she lie about my mother dying at birth?'

The huldumaður sighed and got up from the table.

'Leave this stone unturned, Sölvi. Never mention this again – to anyone. Do you hear me?'

Sölvi was offended by that. As if he needed to be told such an obvious thing. But Styrmir had all but confirmed his suspicions. Sölvi started to go through the volumes of local tales available at the school library. He found many alluding to the creatures in the Deep, all the way back to the Age of Settlement. A red thread ran through the folklore that stuck out. Stories about women believed to be holy, who had somehow been touched by the sanctity of the depths. Many of them had died while pregnant – sometimes giving birth, other times at sea. These were the saints his mother was reading about in her book – he had stolen a peek at it a few times.

His mother was one of those women. His grandmother had been one as well. Amma Dagmar had escaped and lied about her newborn daughter, hoping that they would leave her be. She'd had the good sense to never return, but failed to instil that fear into Elka.

His fanciful flight from Heimaey had ceased to be a daydream, then. He had to get himself and his mother out of there before it was too late.

Styrmir had been kind enough to show him what was what in a fishing boat owned by a friend of his – a huldumaður, like Styrmir, who didn't mind the two of them snooping around after the catch of the day had been landed. It was good for a young man to learn these skills, after all. A single person could easily go out by himself and catch a respectable haul, should he be lucky. After more than a little begging, Styrmir had finally agreed to ask the owner if he would take Sölvi out one morning. Elka had been quick to approve – which of course meant that Ægir knew about it. A risk, to be sure, but as Sölvi suspected, the thick-headed oaf was smug enough to believe it was down to his scheme to turn Sölvi into an enterprising young man.

It was hard work running the boat; much of it related to fishing properly, which was not something Sölvi particularly cared about. Even so, there were dozens of things to learn. He asked about everything. Sölvi would turn eleven this year. He had to stand on his toes to see out of the pilot house. But it would be fine – it was a small-engined boat.

Sölvi had been wondering if he should tell his mother about the plan. He worried that Elka didn't want to leave at all, and he didn't know if he could make her. Despite everything, she wanted to be with Ægir – even though he hurt her and Sölvi. He had a worse grip on her than the drugs when she used to smoke. She fantasised about a life with her new baby, wanted nothing more than to go every Seiðday to that disgusting church wearing that horrible jewellery, singing hymns about terrifying, awful things. There was no room for Sölvi in that ugly dream. He could see that, even if she didn't. Or if there was, he didn't want any part of it. These islanders were all sick in the head, worshipping monsters who kept their fishing nets full, which was just a backwards way of saying that they worshipped money. He wasn't stupid – he could see how it all lined up. The whole religion was only permitted because it served the fish processing factories' benefit. Styrmir had said as much as well.

Except for that prophecy. That was the only thing Sölvi couldn't rationalise, so he chalked it up to them being mad.

In any case, Sölvi wouldn't be a cog in that ugly machine. He would be free. And if Elka didn't want to go, then Sölvi would simply return to get her when he was rich and educated and powerful. Except it might be too late by then. He felt so powerless at the thought. But no – she was different. She wasn't like those other women from the folklore. As Amma Dagmar had said, they were descended from sorcerer-kings. Elka could take care of herself if he left. He had to believe that with all his heart.

Sölvi tried to make himself comfortable in the cold, damp cave, huddling by the lamplight as he fetched a sketchbook and drawing coal from his backpack. He started to draw to calm himself. He created a nice and peaceful place: a farm under a mountain – far from the ocean – with dogs running and sheep grazing. Then he added a stone tower there, just because he could, like something out of a fairy tale. It was a beautiful dream. One he would realise, some day.

He finally relaxed. He was in control.

ᚼ

'Elka.'

She visibly jumped. She hadn't heard him come in. Something about Ægir's tone made her freeze in place. She continued folding the laundry, not daring to turn around to see him.

'Hæ, elskan. You startled me, I didn't know you were home. I thought you were out sailing today?'

'What is this?'

She knew. It could only be one thing. Her romance novel,

hidden at the bottom of her drawer. She risked a glance over her shoulder, a dreadful feeling settling in as she saw Ægir standing in the doorway like a wrathful thundercloud, a dark and grave look on his face, holding her copy of *The Waking Sands*.

'Oh, that.' She forced a laugh. It didn't sound convincing, even to her. 'It's just a silly thing. Something to make the nights pass quicker when I can't sleep.'

'So this is what you have been reading instead of the catechisms? A book about promiscuity and whoredom!'

'No, not at all! I've barely touched it. I bought it used, that's why it's so dog-eared.' It was hard to hide the panic in her voice. 'Just ... Just throw it away if you want, elskan.'

'Do you know what people would say if they heard that my wife – the woman who has been given the holy task of fulfilling our prophecy – was wasting her time reading smut?'

She stopped folding the laundry. Her hands trembled.

'I am respected in this community, Elka. I was chosen by them as well, when I was saved from a watery grave due to their divine intervention. It is only because of me that you have been given this honour, do you not see that? And this is how you repay me?'

'I'm sorry,' she whispered. 'It won't happen again.'

ᚺ

She'd always known Ægir was cut from a different cloth. She hadn't realised just how far removed from others he was. In the first weeks of their relationship, she ignored those few faults she spotted, dismissing them as minuscule fractures. He was a man who had gone through a lot and found redemption. He was permitted to stand apart from others. Things had altered after Ægir's proposal. Her initial reaction to it was disbelief, feeling unworthy of such a kind and honourable man. After she and

Sölvi moved in, the proposal had mutated into what it truly was – a leash.

But it didn't really matter. What mattered was that she belonged to him. As far as he and the rest of the congregation were concerned, that was the reality of it. She told herself it was good to belong to someone. That meant that you were loved.

She didn't go out of the house much any more.

They said that she was a vessel for the Holy Deep, that her child would change the world. Ægir believed that, too, but still his affection towards her had cooled until it was painful to the touch. His grip on her leash tightened and she was a fast learner. She wasn't a good enough mother, a good enough wife. Bryde had performed the wedding after Mass one day, without much ceremony. There wasn't even a reception afterwards. Ægir said he disliked parties. She didn't mention that they'd met when he'd hosted one for his crew.

Faults spiderwebbed into networks, ground and drifted into deep ravines. A thing believed whole, revealed to be broken. The long, quiet moments spent sitting in the living room on his days off. Refusing to stop and chat when they ran across friends. She found that they had little to talk about and nothing in common. He still refused to touch her, but after marriage she chalked it up to her pregnancy. If she displeased him somehow, his anger flared like a coal fire suddenly revealed, burning with an intense and sudden heat.

The ancient prayers, the hymns and tales of wonder within the holy book, had become her lifeline. Without them she would be lost at sea. One catechism in particular gripped her strongly, a strange and bizarre pull that felt as if it was speaking to her directly. She studied it fervently, turning it into a mantra she recited internally whenever she needed to draw on the strength.

Who are you?

I am a Worshipper of the Deep.

What is the Duty which the Deep requires of you?

The Duty which the Deep requires of us is Obedience and Sacrifice to fulfil our Purpose. So in turn may we be spared from its hunger, so in turn may we find wealth in its bounty.

What is your Purpose?

To be a Vessel for the Deep.

What does the Vessel carry?

It carries an Ocean Within, giving life to the Harbinger of the Last Flood.

Who is the Harbinger?

He is named Andrán and Mánaþjór, Griðungur and Grandröst and Jötuneykur. He is the tether and the gate, the nine-horned beast born of the Ocean Within and hatched from the Night Sky's Roe.

What is the Last Flood?

It is the unveiling of the moon's true visage and the undoing of restraints. It will cleanse the world of corruption as salvation rises from the depths.

Who survives the Last Flood?

True believers will ascend and become Messengers of the Deep. False believers will be cleansed. And so Harmony will be restored.

What is the true visage of the moon?

The Moon lies at the bottom of the Mirrored Deep above. It carries the Ocean Without, the tether and the gate.

She recited the sacred catechism by heart, finding the strength she needed to go on. Inside her, the unborn child squirmed in sync with the words.

ᚻ

Initially Elka had been afraid of her dreams. They had been so unsettling. But now, thanks to the capsules, they felt comforting. As she took the pills and brewed the prenatal concoction, the dreams stretched out into waking life, lending every sharp edge a blurred outline. She knew the daze was muddying her mind, but the medication and the catechisms were the pathway to becoming one with the Deep – becoming a vast emptiness filled with saltwater, hosting a multitude of life within itself.

For there was a hollowness inside her. But it was not the comforting nothingness of the ocean depths – it was a devouring, hungry void. It was a force of destruction, of malevolence, and tried as she had, it kept on following her, like a hateful draugur. Left unchecked, it would hound her to an early grave.

The capsules filled that emptiness; they allowed her burning soul to be quelled by cold waves. Should she neglect to take them, the world flared up with an intensity she'd never experienced before, especially now in the third trimester. She knew that pull of power very well – she had felt it in the factory when she drew on the strength of the sigils with disastrous consequences. For years she had sought to smother it, since the first time she picked up a pipe filled with sorti. But never had it been so strong, so vivid and forceful, making her fear what might happen should she face that vortex unshielded by the medication.

It shamed her to admit this to herself, but she felt a peace in those hazy days that only the otherworldly high of smoking sorti had ever granted her. True bliss, detached from the world and its suffering. Floating in the calmness induced by the medication, she was given the ballast she needed to indulge in dreams of sunken ruins and blessed depths. A side effect of the herbal mixture was making the dreams more vivid, causing her to increase her capsule dosage. All according to Reverend Bryde's advice, of course.

Most nights, sleep only managed to claim her as morning dawned. Usually, she got up after Sölvi had gone to school and Ægir to work, just to put the kettle on and make herself a serving of the brew before going back to sleep. She slept mostly during the day. It made things easier, all being said. As exhausted as she felt, she still got most of her housework done, and when she didn't, Ægir made sure that she knew she was neglecting her duties.

As much as the catechism resonated with her as truly holy words, especially the verses revealing the mysteries of the Harbinger she carried, she had seen in the stories of the saints an unsettling motif. Every saint blessed by the Deep had suffered grave misfortune. These women had survived hardships through grit and unyielding will, all eventually dying for their faith – sometimes poetically, sometimes brutally. Elka identified deeply with the determination of her long-gone sisters of faith, but there her sympathy fell short. This was also a lesson, of this she was certain.

Elka was not going to end up like them.

ᚻ

She woke up with Sölvi lying in bed next to her. She stroked his head, running her fingers through his hair. He had been born with a wild head of hair for an infant. It had been so feathery soft, like down. Now, it was coarse and slightly oily, but that didn't matter. He was still her baby. It grew in a whorl at the back of his head, which always gave him terrible bedhead. She'd had the same type of hair as a child. She smiled to herself as she murmured, eyes still half-closed:

'You need your hair cut, mister. Who let you grow these weeds on your head?'

He couldn't help but chuckle. It was something Amma Dagmar had often said to Elka, and Elka had said it to Sölvi in turn. She opened her eyes properly and noticed that he had been crying.

'Sölvi, what's wrong?'

'Nothing,' he said, wiping his nose on the back of his hand. 'I just miss you so much sometimes.'

'Æ, elskan.' She gave him a kiss on the forehead, hugging him tight. 'You don't need to worry. You'll always have me, even when your baby brother or sister is born. I'll always be your mamma.'

'That's not why I miss you.' He spoke so softly, so tenderly, burying his face into the bed and her body.

'You don't need to miss me, elskan, you can always give me a hug when you want to.'

'I miss the old you. From before here.'

Oh.

'The old me...' She sat up slightly in the bed, wanting to look him right in the eye as she said this. 'She was no good for you, elskan. I think you know that.'

'I don't mean it like that. I mean it more like... when you were yourself. Even then, you were still yourself.'

She smiled, stroking a lock of his hair behind his ear. He really did need a haircut.

'I'm still myself. Just as you are you.'

He threw himself back down, hugging her, snuggling up against her. She went back to stroking his head.

'Can we please move?' he asked. 'We could go back to Reykjavík before the baby is born.'

'You know I can't do that, Sölvi.'

'We can leave now, if you want to. I can get work. Styrmir

419

has taught me a lot of things. I'm learning how to sail a boat, I can practically do it all by myself. I can work and take care of us, until the baby is big enough. Then I can watch the baby while you go to work.'

She almost broke down crying, then and there. But she held it back. She had to be strong – for him.

'No, elskan. That's not what you should be doing. And remember, you should focus on your schoolwork more. So you won't have to break your back slaving at a fish factory like your old mamma. If you work hard, you could be the captain of your own ship.'

'I won't,' he said angrily. 'I'm going to be an artist and sell paintings in Hafnía. I'm going to buy you beautiful dresses and take good care of you and the baby. Then we won't need someone bad like Ægir to take care of us.'

'Hush, now. Ægir works hard to provide for us.'

Sölvi shook his head, slowly. He sat up in the bed, staring at her gravely.

'Whenever he goes out, I make a wish. Like Amma Dagmar taught me. I wish that he would drown. I wish he had drowned all those years ago.'

She had acted without thinking. It had been too much to hear. The slap resounded in the room, which was filled with the quiet between them.

His eyes welled up with tears. She tried reaching for him, to say that she was sorry, to do anything, but he pushed her away and jumped out of the bed, running as fast as he could out of the room.

'Sölvi! Wait, please!'

She got up too quickly and almost dropped on the floor from the vertigo. Her legs felt weak, her arms barely able to stabilise her before she fell over. She had taken three capsules before her nap, not half an hour before.

She heard the front door slam. He was already gone by the time she got to the kitchen window, searching for him outside.

Elka's heart was racing. She grabbed her coat, managing to get her swollen feet into her boots, not even thinking about bothering to do them up properly, and then she went out for the first time in what felt like months, shouting Sölvi's name as she chased after him.

ᚼ

Elka hurried down the street, adjusting the shawl around her head, conscious of the fact that she was trying to disguise herself. Ægir would be furious if he heard about her running around town like a mad woman. Already she was out of breath, her feet ached, her heartburn was getting more intense.

Two militiamen passed her, and she considered asking them for help, but decided against it. She recognised them from church. She forced herself to stop, to think about where Sölvi might have gone. Then she remembered the two children from church. His friends: Sævar and Bára.

Bára's parents lived in a small house on Vestmannabraut. Elka had only talked to them casually at church on a few occasions. She knocked once and the door opened immediately.

'Elka, hæ.' Bára's mother, Hafdís, worked at a saltfish factory. Elka had often passed her going to and from work, exchanging simple courtesies. 'What is wrong? What happened?'

'Is Sölvi here?'

'I don't think so … Bára!' Hafdís shouted into the house, still keeping a concerned eye on Elka.

'Yes!'

'Is Sölvi with you?'

'No!'

'Has he been here today?' Elka interjected, shouting into the house. 'Or do you know if he's with Sævar?'

At this, Bára came over, carrying a home-made stuffed animal. It was a whale – a sacred beast in the canon of the Church of the Deep. Sævar followed shortly after.

'Sölvi isn't here,' the girl said.

'He doesn't want to be friends with us any more,' the boy added.

'What do you mean? Why? What's happened?' Elka noticed that her agitation was worrying the three of them, and forced herself to take a breath. 'Sorry.' She flashed an apologetic smile to Hafdís. 'I'm just a bit tired, that's all.'

'Of course,' Hafdís said, understandingly. 'Bára, elskan, do you know where Sölvi might be?'

She shook her head.

'Do you know where he likes to go to be alone?' asked Elka.

'He goes up to the volcanoes sometimes,' Bára said before skipping back to her room, Sævar following her.

'All right, takk, takk!'

Elka was already heading out, when Hafdís grabbed her by the arm.

'Elka, please, you can't be serious. You're not going to climb up there in your condition. Let me get my coat.'

'Come on now, it's just a big hill, not like it's a proper mountain.'

She tried to get her arm loose, but Hafdís held on to her coat.

'Think of the baby. The wondrous child you're tasked with protecting.'

'I'm going to find my son, Hafdís. I'll be fine.'

She yanked her arm loose from Hafdís's grip. The woman had the good sense to look abashed.

Elka headed to the edge of town, towards the roots of Helgafell. The volcano was a majestic cone, its roots covered in pale grass, black volcanic sand crowning the top. Next to it, to the north, was Eldfell's red form, misshapen in comparison to its older sibling. Faint illumination shone from its crater, spreading all through the lava fields. Flickering like light underwater, just beneath the jagged stone crust that had threatened to engulf the village years before. Elka realised that the lava was still burning hot beneath the hardened surface; the violent force of the eruption had been stalled, not stopped, by the ritual of the Messengers. Streams of eerily coloured and unruly energy flowed from it like smoke. It was the strangest thing – she didn't feel afraid looking at it now. Other times when she'd received mere hints of this vision, she'd been desperate to quell it by taking a capsule or two. Now, it made her feel strong. And she needed to be strong for Sölvi. She saw tracks leading up the muddied dirt road, looking as if they might belong to a child.

She stopped to catch her breath at the end of the road, the slight incline exhausting her quickly. She scanned the landscape, wondering where he had gone next, when she heard footsteps approaching.

Elka's body became very still, her breath instantly glacial in pace, but her heart pounded wildly in her chest. Following her up the road came Ægir, accompanied by three men and two women – her aunt Björg and Reverend Bryde.

'Elka, my poor dear, what are you doing out here by yourself?'

Björg gave her a hug, placing her hand firmly around her waist, guiding her back towards the village.

'Sölvi ran off,' said Ægir. It wasn't a question.

Seeing the look on her face, he directed the other two men to begin their search. He gave Elka a performative smile that was meant to be reassuring. It stuck on his face.

'Elskan, you mustn't overexert yourself like this. Thank the Deep that Hafdís had the good sense to send for me. She said you seemed almost hysterical.'

'I'm fine,' Elka muttered. 'I'm not hysterical.'

'Of course, it's only natural for a mother to worry. Come, let's go home. Ketill and Fúsi are searching for Sölvi, they'll find him in no time.'

'I'd like to go looking for him,' Elka said, even as the priest and Björg guided her home, one on each side, their hands pushing against her back. 'He ran away. Those men are going to scare him.'

'He won't go far, my dear child,' said Reverend Bryde in a soft, soothing voice. 'The Deep is watching over him – as it watches us all. Do not worry.'

Elka stopped trying to resist. It was no use.

At home the women lit the stove, heating water in a kettle. Björg guided Elka to a chair and sat her down. Ægir stood in the doorway, that half-frozen smile still on his face. Bryde pulled a large, familiar tin out of her bag.

'No, I don't want any brew. It makes me feel groggy and I need to find Sölvi.'

'Nonsense, dear. It's medicine, divine medicine. It's a new mixture that I made especially for you. See?' She showed Elka its contents. Inside was a fatty paste, ground herbs mixed into it. 'Crab fat mixed with cod liver oil and varieties of kelp. Just as good used as an ointment, but it does wonders for the body when ingested. It will help with your heartburn.'

Bryde scooped heaped spoonfuls of the lard directly into the kettle, filling the air with a potent fragrance of a reeking shoreline.

Björg sat next to Elka, patting the back of her hand.

'Everything will be fine, they will find Sölvi. Don't you worry, my dear. How is your pelvis? You've had quite a walk, you must be in pain. Are your breasts sore?'

'Björg, please.'

Elka turned her attention to the priest, who was preparing her cup of herbal brew. She hadn't taken any medication since waking up, and she needed to stay sharp if she was to find Sölvi.

'I told you I don't want any of that, Reverend. Maybe later.'

'The kelp was given to us by the Messengers, you know.' The priest put another spoonful directly into her cup, further angering Elka. Bryde smiled. 'It's a most wonderful plant that grows deep beneath the sea, where sunlight does not reach. Miraculously, it can grow almost anywhere. It produces pods somewhat reminiscent of a flower, with black, strange petals. Have you ever seen it?'

'No,' Elka said.

'Oh, I think you have, dear,' said Björg, her voice now laced with resentful judgement. Elka turned to her in confusion, not comprehending what she meant. Or maybe she just didn't want to. 'Although maybe not in its natural form.' She sighed with disappointment.

'The twisted hearts of men turn everything they touch into poison,' said Bryde, stirring the cup with a ticking sound that threatened to drive Elka mad. 'Including the beautiful gifts of the Messengers. Black poison that rots them inside out.'

'Oh, my dear child.' Björg patted Elka's hand again, more forcefully.

'You know that poison very well,' Bryde continued. 'You once nurtured it within you for many years, as you took in its horrible black smoke and submerged yourself in its dreadful dreams. But we... we know how to properly use their wonderful gifts, so the sanctity of the soul can be restored. Haven't I always been kind to you? Didn't the capsules help? Let us help you, Elka. Be a good girl.'

'What are you talking about?' Elka said, horrified. 'Ægir. Please don't make me drink it.' He just stood there, blocking her exit, his face emotionless, as so often when he thought no one was watching. She was on the verge of tears. 'Please.'

'Do as you are told, Elka. It's for the good of the baby.' His voice was unyielding stone.

Bryde lifted the cup to her lips, forcing her to drink it.

'Good, dear, very good. Wonderful. Accept the gracious gifts of the Deep.'

It tasted bitter. Familiar. The rush of the incoming high was like a mother's embrace. She felt herself starting to let go despite herself, that hidden part of herself thankful for the forgetful abyss that overtook her. This would make everything easier.

Except she didn't want things to be easy any more.

Faintly, she registered a wetness running down her legs. Björg and the priest crooned with sounds of surprise and joy.

'Her waters just broke,' Björg said, her voice fading.

The sound of seagulls in the distance.

'Of course they did. Ægir, come help us carry her.'

'Oh my, would you look at that! Like pure silver. Oh! Blessed be the Deep.'

Waves crashing. The sound of tiny stones, rattling against one another. Elka let herself be drawn away from the shore as well. But she clutched that feeling of resistance tightly, refusing to let it go even as the pull of the sea claimed her.

'Blessed be we all.'

Tuttugu

Þráinn bolted up thirty seconds before the alarms sounded. His skin felt as if it was covered with lice, the sourceless smell of iron and sulphur nearly choking him. Something disastrous was coming. The galdrastafur burned cold on his chest, so at least he now knew his hex of foresight worked. Those fucking traitors were making their move, finally. He slept fully clothed these days, mainly because the temperatures at night were so low that the stove in his barracks hardly made a difference – the fucking shortage did not afford them proper insulation. He whipped himself out of bed, stuffing his feet into his freezing cold army boots, shouting for Hrólfur and the troops sleeping in the main dormitory to get the hell up and be combat ready in less than a minute – or he'd shoot them himself. He was not met with opposition.

He banged on Hrólfur's door the same moment as the first klaxon went off. That son of a bitch was as slow as ever. Outside, he strode in the early morning darkness towards the doctor's lodgings. The bastard had an entire building just for himself, having commandeered a Centimotive carriage and fused it with the laboratory housing the skuggsjá. Doctor Vésteinn spent all his time in there with that warped machine, Ingi Vítalín. That *thing* gave Þráinn the chills. He was hoping it would be disassembled once the power plant proved fully operational – maybe put to work as one of the processing units running it.

Vésteinn didn't answer his banging on the door. As he turned to head to the north-east fortification, Hrólfur exited the barracks, a squadron of soldiers filing out after him. His glasses were crooked. Typical. That desk jockey should have taken a post more fitting to his nature. He had never been up for the real work.

'What's going on?' Hrólfur asked dumbly.

Þráinn ignored his question. 'Where is Ginfaxi? Still running the portal?'

'They retired late last night. There's some kind of issue with opening it, apparently.'

'Fucking hell.'

Þráinn scanned the black pillars as he walked. Already squads were taking their place at the points he'd designated as weak spots. Those bastards had got the thaumaturgical shield down once – it wouldn't happen again. He turned to Hrólfur.

'We've got hostiles. Rouse the magister and prepare the worker units for them.'

'What? Really? Just how many are incoming?'

'Stop wasting time with stupid questions and follow your fucking orders!'

'Yes, sir.'

ᚼ

Kári sprinted across the snow-covered ground, slipping on the treacherous terrain and trying not to break his ankle before the real fight started. The power plant was in the process of draining the landvættur of its might. They had to move fast – the alarms were already sounding.

They came in from the north, granting them a good view of

the north-western fortifications as well as the barracks on the eastern frontier. The north-west corner was a fortified hill, a concrete pillbox crafted with seiður from the natural stone, with a double-barrelled cannon on its roof. The soldiers were running to their posts behind barbed wire and sandbag walls, jumping into trenches dug into the hillside. A lot of them were heading towards the most vulnerable pillars holding up the shield. Behind the front line loomed the so-called power plant – the landvættur impaled on dozens of black spears.

He slid down into a ditch where Halla and Eyvindur were already waiting, their skorrifles primed and ready. Kári had refused to carry one.

'What's it look like? Can you break through the barrier?'

He ditched the camouflage mask for the beaked one. Now that the main approach was over, there was work to be done. He examined the seiðmagn in the area, the great, unruly swathes of energy swirling above and around them. A storm was coming in, according to Bölmóður. They could use that to their advantage.

'Aren't the siblings supposed to be here by now?' asked Kári.

'Your guess is as good as mine,' Eyvindur replied.

'We're sitting ducks waiting for them. I could try to upend one of those pillars. They go deep into the ground, but by shifting the earth at the right angle it could be toppled.'

Eyvindur hesitated. 'And you can do that?'

'Yes. I think. At the least, the shield might be weakened.'

'Right. Halla?'

She was crouched, the two foxes lying still next to her. Their fur shifted freely, matching their environment. One was as white as the snow on which it rested, the other as grey as the stone beneath its feet. Where a few of its tails touched yellowed grass, they matched it perfectly. Up close, they did not resemble normal foxes in the least.

'I'm on it.'

With that she was off, the foxes following her like shadows. She ran hunched over at an incredible pace, finding the perfect footing with every step.

'All right.' Eyvindur exhaled loudly, trying to relax, double-checking his rifle. 'Get ready for whatever you have to do, because they'll—'

They came from the east, rising above a ridge like a stampede of mountains. Crashing down on knuckles like boulders, their huge and sharply peaked backs covered in ice and frost. They roared in frenzy, showing jagged, ugly fangs beneath eyes that glinted with uncanny sentience as they chased two tiny figures leading them on, both running breathlessly, robotically, inhumanely. A náskári flew in front of them, cawing and weaving between the beasts' sluggish swings, egging them on. Bölmóður caught an updraught and soared even higher as he approached the site, then banked hard and headed north, regrouping with Kári and the others.

Styrhildur and Hraki led the herd of night-trolls down the ridge, heading right for the eastern side of the excavation site. Kári could hear them whoop and laugh, unable to tell if the voices of the undead siblings boomed clear across the barren earth or if it was partly carried directly into his mind, as when they spoke up close. The sound sent a dreadful shiver crawling down his spine, as though death was out there, calling his name.

And they were the ones on his side.

'I thought Diljá was exaggerating,' Kári murmured to himself.

'Do it now!' Eyvindur shouted, cocking his skorrifle and signalling to the others to prepare to charge.

Kári closed his eyes and released his reservoir of seiðmagn, having let it saturate every inch of his being. He reached into the earth with hands unseen and unfelt, and pushed it away like a brush sweeps away dust.

The earth trembled as the herd of mountain trolls crashed into the fortifications, their basalt shoulders breaking a smaller protective pillar neatly in half, sending it crashing down onto the barracks.

In front of them, one of the main pillars leaned up against another. Kári reinforced the seiður and they slammed together, both crashing down in a cloud of dust.

The thaumaturgical protective shield collapsed from the combined attacks. Seiðmagn flooded freely into the area, crashing down as it filled up this vaccuum, mixing violently with the unearthly seiðmagn from the landvættur. The landvættur twitched visibly on its spikes, its own energy readings flaring up before Kári's eyes.

Eyvindur fired and a volley of shots followed from the others. Out there in the lava fields, Halla joined in from her hidden vantage point.

A whirling sound diverted their attention to the concrete bunker, where the cannon was rotating, a light flaring up on the end of its barrel.

'Not bad, kuklari.' Eyvindur grinned. 'Now we take that fucking cannon!'

ᚻ

The night-trolls were as tall as buildings, crashing down on the site like crazed, agitated rams. They charged through the barracks, sweeping away the buildings in an avalanche of destruction – a sentient natural disaster that changed direction faster than the highland winds.

Magister Ginfaxi had sliced their hand open, drawing a sigil of blood in the grimy snow. Just behind him, guarded by soldiers firing in all directions, a squad was setting up the mortars for the canisters holding the uncolours.

Þráinn screamed at the soldiers, tried to get their commanders to get in fucking formation and focus fire upon those animals, to form a protective circle around the mortars – their only hope of survival. A unit ran out to try to divert the trolls' berserk rage away from the power plant, which was pathetically compromised and out in the open. Half of the team went flying from a lazy sweep of a troll's arm, the other half splattered from a resounding one-two as the beast's boulder-like fists came crashing down on them. The skorrifles barely put a dent in the night-trolls' skin, naturally resilient against seiðmagn.

'She's here!' Hrólfur was panicking, aiming his skorrifle wildly, making the soldiers yell in anger at his lack of discipline. 'Diljá is out there, I know it! They're coming to kill me!'

Þráinn pushed the barrel of Hrólfur's gun down, grabbing him by the collar.

'Get a grip,' he spat in the man's face, 'or I'll do the job for her.'

Thaumaturgical shots whistled past them, from the terrorists taking cover in the rocky field to the north. Those two undead freaks were hiding somewhere in all the chaos. Þráinn hadn't been sure at that distance, even with his augmented vision, but he was fairly certain those two hadn't been wearing the same kind of thaumaturgical camouflage as the others. Those clever masks Garún had invented.

He smiled to himself. They had grown arrogant. Good.

Ginfaxi raised their hands, standing still amid thaumaturgical gunfire and the wanton destruction of the night-trolls. The seiður charged through the air, which became thin and artificial, an overpowering mechanical scent making all of their noses bleed.

'Go for the alpha,' Þráinn said, wiping blood from his face as it kept streaming. 'The big one, with the birch tree on its back.'

Ginfaxi reached out an open hand towards the mountainous night-troll.

They closed it.

The troll's chest imploded, its ribs breaking with sickening cracks like steel beams snapping, and with a whimper the monster collapsed onto the ground, sending earth and stone flying.

The herd stopped, their rage chilled to cold embers in a moment. One of the trolls approached the fallen alpha, ignoring the thaumaturgical fire that barraged its stone shell, prodding it with its stone-pillar hand.

They cried out, sounding like slowed-down whales, the voices of earthquakes and avalanches making their grief heard. Then, they turned towards Þráinn and Ginfaxi, the phalanx of soldiers around them. The soldiers fired at the nearest one as the night-trolls charged.

The air around them was thick, warped with the density of seiðmagn. One of the soldiers fell down, spasming. Another made the mistake of stopping to check on him. He couldn't have known it, but he was already as good as dead.

'Meinholt,' Ginfaxi hissed, reeling in the middle of the bloody circle. 'I need some time to—'

'There is no fucking time.'

Ginfaxi's passive mask turned slowly towards him.

'Only fire one,' the magister commanded the soldiers.

Þráinn glared at the mortar squad. 'Ignore this fool. Fire all the fucking mortars! Now!'

'Yes, sir!'

Þráinn grabbed Ginfaxi by the shoulder and pulled them from the circle, dragging the seiðskratti along in a retreat. His hand felt as if he had dipped it into liquid nitrogen, but pain was something Þráinn was used to ignoring. Ginfaxi was weak, barely able to keep themselves upright as they contained the forces surging through them. Þráinn risked a look back. The soldiers ran for cover behind a building as a night-troll approached at a hobbled gallop. The mortar team held its position, knowing that survival was dependent on them. Two smoking arcs fired up from the mortars; the third malfunctioned and didn't go off.

The troll crashed into the mortar team, which would prove its undoing. As it rendered the soldiers to pulp, it shattered the last remaining canister. The uncolour erupted from its confines with alarming speed, unlike the two small unnatural orbs now floating in mid-air. It latched on to the night-troll, pulling the giant towards it with ease, sprouting more tendrils by the second.

The uncolour fed vigorously. The troll's stone skin cracked, crumbling to gravel, which broke apart like clumps of ash when it hit the ground. There was no resisting it. The light in the troll's eyes faded and went dark as it crumbled, leaving behind a scattering of broken stone, like a landslide come to rest far away from the roots of its mountain.

The tendrils started to spread above, the much larger uncolour on the ground already having latched on to several nearby soldiers, draining them of life.

'Rein the things in!' Þráinn commanded.

'You idiot,' the seiðskratti hissed. 'Do you not recall how many seiðskrattar we needed to wrangle these things when we raised the barrier? Do you realise what you have done?'

'I did what I had to do, Magister. Now you'd better do your part.'

Ginfaxi struggled to contain the monstrosities. They were failing.

'I need Magister Völundur. Fetch Vítalín and his pet as well – the one he calls Kaíamí. We'll need the Laí if we are to gain control over these things.'

ᚻ

The beam of energy shot from the cannon with a blinding flare, rendering the world into a bright green nothingness. Then sound flooded into Kári's ears as a deafening explosion went off, its shock wave knocking the snow from the rocky fortifications beneath the cannon.

The concentrated seiðmagn hit the approaching night-troll, blasting a hole neatly through it, the stone turning in an instant to liquefied lava. The troll oozed molten rock, falling as it ran, crashing to the earth and grinding to a halt before it hit the barricades.

Kári cursed. He thought he had correctly guessed the cannon's capabilities. It must have a dedicated thaumaturgical engine – which meant imprisoned minds. He had to bring that thing down. The second cannon fired in the south-east, just out of sight behind the massive iron spikes of the power plant, its beam still reducing everything to that green-white brightness, blasting off into the sky. It had either missed, or completely pierced a night-troll through.

They needed to act fast. Those cannons, the three uncolours spreading before them. He didn't know which was the worse scenario: Ginfaxi and Vésteinn being tied up controlling those things, or if those hostile masters of the arcane would have free rein to wreak havoc. All in all it was clear that, with the forces the enemy had at their disposal, this attack would spell defeat if it was prolonged. Kári knew that he would be no match for Vésteinn or Ginfaxi, their militaristic training outmatching his own on an instinctual level. He wasn't quite sure what Auður could do with galdur, but he just hoped that she would be able to turn the tide in their favour.

They were under ceaseless fire, the thaumaturgical shots piercing through the shield Kári had thrown up with alarming frequency. It was growing weaker by the minute, demanding increasing effort on his part.

He nodded to Eyvindur, who fired and then got up with Kári, dashing towards their nearest cover – a jagged outcropping of stone, where centuries before the lava had collected into a cracked crest. A few shots surged through the air above their heads, but with their allies giving covering fire they reached their destination untouched.

Eyvindur reloaded, fired, reloaded. The cannon was already flaring up again. Kári adjusted his position, ducking and reflexively diverting the bullet aiming for his head, sending it up into the air. Close. But it took more than a few soldiers to bring down a seiðskratti.

Even if he was an academic.

The cannon was now drawing in seiðmagn from its surroundings, forming a well in the thaumaturgical atmosphere. They must have drained their batteries already, or they were struggling to get resupplies in.

'Brace yourself!' Kári shouted.

The ex-soldier didn't respond, just kept firing.

Kári reached to the open skies, the torrent of seiðmagn around them. With small, minute fluctuations of will, he set off a chain reaction, a cascade of movements that gathered momentum, bringing together a vast mass of wild, hectic, destructive seiðmagn. It fell and crashed onto the path of least resistance, tracing the funnel he had created.

It poured into the engines of the cannon, overflowing it like lightning repeatedly striking a conductor.

The cannon burst in a phosphorescence of hypernatural colours, reducing the hillside to an ugly crater. He heard the screaming of soldiers, knowing what kind of malformed wounds had manifested on those unfortunate enough to survive.

Ahead, Halla came out of hiding, breaking through the enemy lines. She charged a couple of confused soldiers, goring one on her shoulder's horn, stabbing the other with her bayoneted rifle, barely breaking stride as she kept on running.

They followed her into a hellish war zone.

ᚼ

Bölmóður circled above the landvættur, eyeing a good spot below him. His cargo thrashed in the grip of his claws, cursing into the wind. He pulled his krummafótur closer to himself – the strongest of his three legs – using the other two claws to better adjust his grip.

'Err-at wise for any prey to thrash.'

Auður looked up at him angrily.

'I'm not fucking prey! And find a damn landing spot already!'

The duffel bag tied around her was filled with the rest of their explosives. One lucky shot and it would all be over.

'As þérr wish't.'

He scanned the western side of the dig. The soldiers had all rushed to their fortifications on the eastern front, just as planned. They had not banked on Kalmar being desperate enough to unleash three of those alien things, however. Their plan was unravelling.

The náskári plunged down like a meteor, silently appreciating Auður's restraint in letting out a panicked scream. He slowed their descent at the last moment with a powerful beating of his wings, dropping Auður safely. They were in a clear area, between rows of tents. He could hear coughs coming from within. The landvættur towered above them.

Turning the corner, they came upon a pair of soldiers running towards the battle. Bölmóður crouched and leaped forward, impaling one of them on his ironed beak like a thrown spear – or a bolt from a ballista. He pinned the soldier down on the ground, and before the other could even raise his skorrifle, Auður muttered a short incantation rendering the man blind. He panicked, firing widely into the air. Bölmóður crushed the pinned soldier's skull with ease and eviscerated the blinded man with a fling of his head.

She nodded to the korpur. He nodded back. They ran to the steep slopes leading into the pit, towards the heart of the power plant.

ᚼ

The world had dissolved into smoke and screams. Hrólfur was panicked, running past dead soldiers smashed into paste by the trolls, slipping on their pulverised entrails. He held on to his skorrifle like a lifeline. Diljá had to be there, had to be one of them, hunting him.

He had been weak and stupid. He should have had her sent to the Nine when he had the chance, should have demanded that the Directorate drop the undercover operation entirely. But his supervisors stood to gain too much by having him as a plant at the heart of political dissent in Reykjavík. After Garún's insane stunt, they were not about to take any chances.

But he also hadn't pushed them to remove him. He had been arrogant, addicted to the power, the deception of his love for Diljá which had almost become real to him.

Or, well. What was love, anyway? Diljá had been nice. Kind. Comforting. A perk of the job, one he'd hated to lose.

Plus, he totally had a thing for blondes. And the fact that she was a huldukona made it even more exciting, the taboo factor really getting his blood pumping.

He caught movement out of the corner of his eye. Had that been a fox?

That distorted, psychotic laughter resounded again, drilling into his mind, and the night-troll roared in response. It was making him and the soldiers shit themselves with fear, driving the trolls crazy as well. He had to find those two undead monsters and take care of them, once and for all.

The siblings had long been a thorn in their side. He had tried. Oh, how he had tried to get his hands on them. But they had gone into hiding after Trampe's assassination – deep hiding – and when they returned everything had turned ugly. He had been lucky Þráinn had found him before them. Apparently, they had broken into his apartment only an hour after Þráinn retrieved him, rushing him to the safety of their base in Rökkurvík. Even now, he agonised over how they had managed to find him out. He hadn't seen Diljá since then, seven years before.

A group of soldiers behind fortified sandbags almost fired on him as he came sprinting through the dark smoke.

'Your command, sir?'

A snot-nosed kid clutching a rifle looked to him for orders, as he collapsed behind the sandbag wall, trying to catch his breath. Was he in command? The others looked to him expectantly, their faces covered with soot or ash or blood.

'We, uh…' He tried to get a grip on himself. 'They're going for the shark, the power plant. The cannons will take out the night-trolls. Fall back to the power plant, and—'

A bullet stopped him mid-sentence, the young soldier before him collapsing as his neck exploded in a twisting flower of flesh and teeth. Hrólfur ducked as the soldier hit the ground, dead, his body still transforming, and then he spotted those two psychopaths standing out in the open.

Grey-skinned, bared teeth and bone, hair matted and tangled, their clothes decomposed and worn through. And their eyes. Unblinking. Unfeeling. Mocking him, mocking life, mocking his miserable existence.

Hraki and Styrhildur.

Móri and Skotta.

The disciples of that terrorist who had almost doomed them all – the crazed, selfish bitch who hadn't hesitated to court otherworldly and incomprehensible powers to do her bidding. By the king, it had felt good to watch the royal seiðskrattar and galdramenn execute whatever shell remained of Garún after their interrogations, tethering her spirit to this world to suffer eternally. Even if he'd had night terrors for years afterwards, it had been well worth it.

Fucking literal ghosts from his past chasing him. Why the fuck hadn't he taken that nice, cosy desk job in Hafnía?

'Fire!'

Hrólfur unloaded his skorrifle, his hands trembling as he tried to reload quickly. The new bolt action system was a huge improvement on the old design, but it jammed so easily that he suspected the weapon was faulty. That, or someone hadn't maintained the rifle well enough for him. Did he have to do everything?

They returned fire, splitting off in separate directions. Some of the shots found purchase, but to his horror they seemed to have no effect. Were those shits immune to seiðmagn as well? How the hell was that possible?

'Retreat!'

He was running before he issued the command, praying that they weren't so vengeful, so stupid and petty like that bitch

Garún, that they'd risk losing the battle just to chase him and have their little revenge.

To his relief, he kept on running. The sounds of the battle behind him diminished into the murky smoke. Ahead, a flash of sickly emerald light as the cannon fired. For a moment its beam lit up the sky, and he saw the molten glow of a severed night-troll collapsing, its lower body still, stupidly, standing upright.

They could still win this. They could still survive.

That's when he noticed that his squad of soldiers wasn't following behind him.

His knee exploded with pain and he fell over, his face dragging on frozen gravel. He was screaming, or he thought so. He turned and saw his tibia jutting from the wound, blood running in streams from its centre, which was forming into the shape of a double-spiralled conch.

Then she was there. She aimed the skorrifle directly at his face. She looked like a different person – unrecognisable, but it was undoubtedly her. Diljá reached out to him, breaching his non-existent defences, reading his emotions mercilessly.

'Diljá, I can explain, it's not like it seems!'

'It is,' she said, reloading the chamber of her skorrifle.

'No, no, it's not—'

'I won't rip your mind out of your head, like you did to Garún. I'd rather not have anything of yours living within me, even if it's only your pathetic memories. But I can read you easily, now. Not like last time.' Her voice trembled, her pain rising to the surface.

He started to speak, but she shot him right in the stomach. He watched as a tiny cluster of fingers grew from his entrails.

'I was afraid to dig deeper. And you masked the ugly truth behind the sickness and lies you called love, and you made me...'

She stopped, unable to hold back, breaking into tears from her pent-up anger, screaming at him as she stood over his pathetic, broken body, unleashing all the hatred she had for him and people like him.

'You made me betray everything that matters in this world! Because you care about nothing!' She spat in his face. Hrólfur was bawling, pleading with her to show him mercy. 'You care about nothing because you are fucking nothing.'

She pulled the trigger. His voice was silenced as his head burst, leaving behind a growing field of blood-red and fuchsia clovers.

It didn't make Diljá feel any better. As she had known.

Then again, that hadn't been the reason why she had done it.

ᚼ

A strange luminescence was in the air, not from the floodlights or the slowly rising sun, but from the discharged and shredded seiðmagn around them, merging with the gathering storm of the landvættur.

A night-troll approached the pit beneath the landvættur, guided there by the siblings' taunts. It started to glow. Cracks formed in its shell, growing wider as the stone split and oozed. The sharp peak of its back burst, erupting in a cloud of ash, and the night-troll collapsed, melting into a heap of sputtering magma.

Kári traced the source of the seiðmagn to a robed seiðskratti in the heart of a vortex. They were barely twenty metres away. The seiðskratti was surrounded by terrified soldiers, covering behind stone pillars thaumaturgically grown from the earth in tactical patterns.

Magister Völundur. Doctor Vésteinn.

Kári saw, in a moment, a weaving of deception that shrouded Vésteinn. It had always been there, hidden in plain sight – but now, perhaps due to his transformed sight, it stood out like a broken bone. Pulling mentally at the illusion, it unravelled before him, revealing that every bone in Vésteinn's body was coloured blue from the taint of demons. At some point, maybe years ago, Vésteinn had seen beyond the veil as he reached too far and returned transformed. There was nothing visually different about him. But Kári saw as clear as day. He looked monstrous.

And he had seen Kári.

'I thought you had died already, Magister Kvalráður. You repulsive mutant.'

The air was charged with crackling seiðmagn, the storm coming in fast. Kári analysed the currents and realised Vésteinn was single-handedly controlling one of the uncolours.

Through the smoke, he could see Ginfaxi surrounded by soldiers, wresting control of another uncolour. By him was Ingi Vítalín and a jötunn, the one called Kaíamí, which was likely controlling the third. The uncolour under Vésteinn's control undulated and stretched towards the approaching dissidents, who fired ineffectively at it. Vésteinn drew in power, overflowing his body recklessly.

'Do not fear, it will be quick – you'll make a fine processing unit!'

A sudden barrage of thaumaturgical gunfire burst on Kári's shield, sending him reeling. He was off kilter, strained from the exertion, when Vésteinn's attack hit him a moment later.

Pressure.

Overbearing, crushing. Light bending as reality caved in, time becoming a murky slog.

He resisted, fluid and weaving, diverting the relentless force that threatened to bear him down.

Blood on his tongue, breathing in the acrid smoke mixed with the lush scent of the highland moss in his mask. He let the force channel through his body, letting go of all semblance of control as well. After all, what did he have left to lose?

During his struggle with Vésteinn, the soldiers ceased firing, one by one. The area around them was dissolving, the raw energies of making, unmaking and remaking the physical world clashing together, ending up in a meaningless dissolution. Vésteinn endured, shielded against the torrenting seiðmagn, looking like a malevolent sorcerer from ancient legend.

Kári was about to give in and Vésteinn felt it, a predator seeing only its bleeding prey, when an explosion went off beneath the landvættur. It triggered a cascade of smaller explosions, as thaumaturgical batteries burst with tremendous force.

Vésteinn reined in his seiðmagn, bringing it effortlessly under his iron will. He swatted Kári away, sent him flying from the unsuspected rush, crashing into the rubble of the barracks. The doctor floated down into the dig, crackling with the unruly force he had consumed, looking for the perpetrators.

How strange, Kári thought to himself – his last thoughts before everything blacked out.

In that last moment, it had looked as though Vésteinn's shadow was writhing around him. As though it was alive.

ᚼ

They were being picked off like vermin. There was a thing out there, hunting them, moving like a ghost, striking from the shadows with the strength of a hundred men. Two demons accompanied it, in the guise of animals with a multitude of tails. They tore the throats from men's necks in a single leap, too fast for their best marksmen. Hrólfur was already lost in the frenzy, and Þráinn had no intention of going to look for him.

They had done everything in their power to stop the siblings, but they had been found wanting. The siblings were already dead. Their bullets pierced the siblings' flesh, but the seiðmagn did not affect it. Bayonets severed rotten tendons and muscles, but those things were not truly what kept the siblings walking. Their bodies were both corporeal and ethereal. They were liminal, untouchable. The second cannon had stopped firing. It was broken or neutralised. Þráinn had actually breathed a sigh of relief when the explosion sounded from the power plant, thinking that this was it – it was time to cut their losses and get the hell out of there. Someone had to write a report on this shit show, and he didn't intend to be a casualty statistic in it.

That was when that fucking ghost and its beasts started going after them during the retreat. Whatever it was, it was out for blood. He tried calling to Ginfaxi for help, but the seiðskratti was struggling to maintain control over the uncolour, just barely keeping it from running rampant. How Ingi and the thing from Laí were managing, he had no idea.

Those few that had survived holed themselves up in the Centimotive. Þráinn prepared it for launch, the growing storm of seiðmagn causing its systems to go haywire despite its defences.

'Well?' Þráinn glared at the engineer, who was pacing, racking his brain trying to figure something out. 'Why isn't this fucking thing starting?'

'I tried,' he said. 'It's not responding – something is wrong. I need Ginfaxi.'

He sent out the rest of his squad. Finally, the soldiers returned with the magister, only three of them having survived. They carried the dormant seiðskratti on a stretcher between them, strapped into it. There was no way to accurately gauge injuries from their robed and masked form, but it was clear Ginfaxi was barely alive. And now at least one uncolour was unchained.

Fuck.

Still, the seiðskratti could get the job done. With Ginfaxi

as a catatonic focal point, they connected him to the machine. Hopefully Vésteinn would survive. At least Innréttingarnar had copies of all his schematics for the power plant. Þráinn had made sure of that.

The engine hummed back to life.

'We have to get the hell out of here.'

'Without Magister Völundur?' some no-name lieutenant dared to ask.

'Vésteinn can take care of himself.' The soldier was visibly shocked that Þráinn used his real name when the seiðskratti was masked and robed. 'We're done here.'

'What about the workers, sir? They're sheltering in the south-western fortifications. And then the patients – we should send for them, try to evacuate as many people as we can carry.'

'By all means, you can fuck off straight to hell if you want! Just spare me another second of your whining over saving some fucking peasants!'

The man didn't move.

'That's what I thought.' Þráinn turned to the engineer. 'Get me the hell out of here.'

The soldiers locked the doors and strapped themselves in.

The Centimotive moved.

ᚺ

Kári tried to get up from where he lay in the concrete, shattered wood and torn corrugated iron. Pain was a distant feeling, but everything felt broken. A rusted metal rod was sticking through his thigh.

He tried to prise himself off it. He moved an inch or so before almost blacking out. He was losing a lot of blood.

This was not how he would die. Not like this.

Everything had fallen to smoke, lit by the grey darkness of

a winter sunrise. The thaumaturgical storm surged above them. A burst of explosions, bringing several more spears crashing to the ground. He looked up.

Off-yellow ichor tainted with rotten blood spilled from the open wounds of the landvættur. Lightning crackled in the clouds above, its eyes starting to glow on its slumped head. More spears fell, sending showers of rotten purulence flowing down as they detached from the god-beast.

Using the last of his resources, Kári mended broken bones, healed the ruptured arteries in his leg. He soothed his pain, trying to bring clarity to his mind.

Suddenly he was lifted up by a strong, gentle force. The world was so fractured, so confusing, that he didn't initially understand what was happening. Then he saw Halla's face and relaxed, safe in her arms. He let her carry him to safety.

Dazed, half-dreaming, he saw winged creatures take to the sky. They looked so beautiful – a nightmare come to life. One of them clutched a steel crate in its claws. Ingi Vítalín was being saved by his grotesque angels.

Good riddance.

ᛡ

Doctor Vésteinn Alrúnarson had never felt more alive.

He had spent decades amassing power and knowledge, using it to build miraculous engines, machines that would revolutionise and improve the world. But that had never been his true aim, nor the stuff of his dreams.

In the ancient world, arcane masters had reigned supreme. The laws of nature as they are now understood are only so because of the will of these ancient lords. Much power had faded from the world. Except here in Hrímland, for some unfathomable reason, the island of his birth.

And he would claim that power. He would bring about the rule of that long-forgotten world, ushering in a new era of miracles unimagined. In his heart, he had always disowned the stupid, ugly word used to describe learned masters such as himself – seiðskratti. A demonic thing who used seiður. He knew what he was, truly. He knew his birthright.

He was a seiðkonungur: a sorcerer-king. He wielded the powers of the divine – he was all-knowing and all-powerful.

This world was made for him.

All that displeased him, he would destroy.

All that disappointed him, he would remake.

He listened eagerly to the urging of the living shadow from the beyond, that noble being with eyes of silver void which had sought him, recognising his true potential. Since then he had been drunk on its promises of power, of realising a destiny greater than anyone could imagine.

As his flesh boiled with charged seiðmagn and untamed galdur uttered by that viscous shade, Vésteinn's eyes melted away to leave all-seeing sockets behind. Scrambling out of the pit, he saw Professor Thorlacius trying to flee the scene of her betrayal.

He was feeling very displeased.

ᚴ

The wind howled, tearing through the land. The sky was heavy with thunder, lightning sparking within the heart of the gathering clouds, flashing in unnerving colours.

The landvættur sagged as more spikes fell to the ground. Less than half a dozen remained, leaving the gigantic shark-like beast floating in the air, slack and weak like a beached whale. It oozed bodily fluids. Smoke lazed out of its mouth, growing darker, thicker by the minute.

Freezing hail and sleet started coming down like artillery

fire. On the ground, the remaining workers, arcane initiates and injured soldiers huddled together inside a concrete bunker, all pretence of fighting having stopped when the Centimotive abandoned the site. Their cannon's batteries had given out in the thaumaturgical disturbance, which had been a blessing as the other bunker was now a smouldering crater.

The terrorists had stopped chasing them, but now the un-colours lurked in the sky with no one left to rein them in. They searched with their alien senses for prey. One had slithered into a building through a collapsed wall, feeding mercilessly on the defenceless patients inside.

They were rightfully afraid. They knew they were going to die.

ᚺ

Underneath the landvættur, a sorcerer-king burst open the chest of the last night-trolls, sending a spear of living shadow through its beating heart. The shield around him flickered as the two dead siblings ran circles around him, hiding among the smoke and the fire of the ruined machines, the wild, unleashed seiðmagn thick and cloying, sparks of lightning flashing as the storm gathered in strength.

Failure was an unavoidable part of the scientific method. Such was the nature of experiments. This setback, although major, did not displease Vésteinn. This fire would serve as the forge in which his next attempt would be made. Already, he was that much closer to perfection. The landvættur would live, after all. He had all the time in the world. The voice in the recesses of his heart urged him on.

But first he intended to stamp out these vermin once and for all.

Despite the aid of the shadow, the undead terrorists eluded

him. They were never where he expected, and when his attacks found purchase, it appeared as if he had done no damage at all.

Cheap tricks. That was how vermin endured.

He would show them how a king thrived.

He would show them power.

Auður had almost made her way out of the pit when he set off a small landslide, sending her crashing back down. Alerted to his presence, she started to utter those weak, laughable incantations. How pathetic – was this all a so-called master of galdur could do? With a flex of his will, the shadow silenced the words in her throat. She stared back at him in terror, and he was delighted by it.

The last of the spears fell to the earth, becoming scrap iron and obsidian shards as Vésteinn became a living vortex of arcane energy. Unreal colours flared up; the sounds of the storm were muted. Visible streams of seiðmagn were drawn into his core, where he amassed an energy that could eradicate the entire area, the siblings and Thorlacius reduced in an instant to pure nothingness.

Above him, the landvættur had been unchained, the last of its impaling spikes fallen.

Its eyes were now glowing bright with life and destruction and the boundless rage of the tempest, lightning cracking between its rows of jagged teeth. It floated freely in the air, circling like a predator. Drawing in the chaotic energies, it gathered up a thaumaturgical storm.

He saw Auður's despair at the sight. She had actually believed they stood a chance of killing a god. The very idea made him cackle with fervent laughter.

He spread out his arms and looked upon that primordial titan, the fire that would stoke the engines of his empire-to-be. The shadow urged him on to bathe in that divine power; by drenching himself in it, he would ascend to higher realms than even the lords of old. Beneath his mask, he smiled, empty eye sockets burning with lust for power.

A storm never ceases to be. It only fades in and out, sometimes only seeming like nothing at all. But the heart of the storm always endures.

The landvættur was the storm – and the storm was the landvættur. Neither lived, neither died. For the first time in millennia upon untold millennia, it soared freely. For the first time in this age of the world, it roared with anger.

And it struck the diseased and defiled earth beneath it.

Tuttugu og eitt

Pain awoke Kári, a deep pain reaching within the marrow of his bones. He realised someone was gently shaking him awake. It was Halla.

'I'm sorry.' Her voice was gentle, like soothing balm. 'We need your help, Kári. It's Styrhildur – she's dying. For good, this time.'

The world came into sharp focus. Kári quickly registered that his own injuries, painful and multiple as they were, were not life-threatening. They had made it back to their base. Dazed, he looked over his allies. Just under a dozen left. They had lost more than three quarters of their people.

Halla, Eyvindur and Diljá were there. Auður was sleeping, heavily bandaged. He'd have to see to her, check her wounds. Styrhildur was lying on the stone floor on the thin linen bedroll.

Kári stood up, slowly and painfully. His hand went to his face and he found it bare. He panicked a moment, wondering from old habits what had happened to his mask. The mask was lying next to him. Burned, partly melted, black with soot. One lens broken. It felt good, seeing that. Only having his own face to hide behind.

'Vésteinn, he … What happened?'

Halla told him what she had seen as they retreated. Bölmóður and Auður had set the charges. Hraki and Styrhildur had then kept Vésteinn busy, hoping to make an end of it. But their attacks had made no impact.

'Auður was trying to get out, but he was messing with her. He intended to have fun before he killed her. Bölmóður was engaged by a group of soldiers. The uncolour was after him as well, but it got distracted as it found a way into the remaining cannon bunker. It was full of people. Anyway … he got to Auður just before the final charges went off.'

'So we did it?' asked Kári. 'Auður succeeded in bringing it down?'

His heart sank seeing their reaction alone. Worse had come to the worst.

The landvættur had been unleashed.

'How? We attacked at the right moment. It was drained of power, on the verge of death. The power plant hadn't yet shocked it back to life, I'm certain of that.'

'We don't know,' said Eyvindur. 'Auður is better educated to say what went wrong. Maybe we underestimated it.'

The landvættur had gathered its power, unleashing it on the site below. Bölmóður had got Auður out of range, both of them suffering severe burns from the thaumaturgical explosion. Hraki had been incinerated, along with Vésteinn. From what they gathered from Bölmóður, the madman had just been standing there with arms outstretched, laughing as the divine beast above brought destruction down upon them. They found Styrhildur on the edge of the blast radius.

Hearing this, Kári wanted to give up. Why bother trying, now? He forced himself to get up to take a look at Styrhildur. To try to help, however he could.

He couldn't. That much was obvious at a glance.

She was almost cleaved in two. A huge chunk of her midsection and lower ribs was missing. To his horror, he realised that her spine was severed at the bottom. Still, she breathed in rapid bursts, startling him every time as she fell deadly quiet in between. Her skull was fractured, almost caved in from behind. One dead eye looked up, the other staring, unblinking, ahead at nothing at all.

'I can't – I don't know what to tell you. This is beyond me.'

'We know,' Diljá said. Her shoulder was wrapped up, blood seeping through the bandages. 'This isn't why we need you. She is gone.'

'*I have a request.*'

Kári jumped as Styrhildur grabbed his hand. It was freezing cold, so much that it hurt him.

'*She spoke – to me. Before. She foresaw this, in broken fractures. One way or another, it would have happened. Inevitably.*'

Diljá picked up a black cloth sack, unfolding it, revealing Garún's bones. The bones that had spoken to him – that had reached into his mind – in that makeshift chapel deep in the earth.

'*These bones – this body. Make us whole again. Heal us.*'

Styrhildur looked bizarrely human as she spoke. Everyone looked at Kári expectantly, hoping that this man with the shifting face could perform a miraculous heresy in the midst of an apocalyptic storm.

It's impossible, was what anyone would have said. It's unethical; it's wrong; these bones are tainted with an unworldly sentience, the flesh beyond the reach of death; the very idea is ridiculous, dangerous, unprecedented. All of this and so much more is what Kári would have said himself. Once.

That person had died in Svartiskóli. That person had been nothing but a mask.

Strange and unusual seiðmagn filled the area. The landvættur was starting to mutate the surrounding nature. Kári touched the bones, feeling the sentience within them reach out to him, Styrhildur reaching out to him as well. Of course – he chastised himself for only realising now – both of them were huldumanneskjur. He held the skull in one hand, placing a hand on Styrhildur's damp forehead with the other, letting the bones and Styrhildur reach out to him, and through him to each other. Although he could not speak this unspoken language back, he felt some kind of consensus form.

He focused on the two, making himself imagine them as one. Trying to cut through his preconceptions and realise a new kind of being. Something not stitched together, not two parts united, but a unified, single whole.

Drawing in the wild seiðmagn, Magister Kvalráður started his great work.

ᚼ

The landvættur was easily tracked. They had come across a wide trail of bloody viscera on their way back to the ruined excavation site. It streaked across the landscape to the west, as they'd suspected. Straight towards Reykjavík, to what lay buried beneath Perlan.

The landvættur belonged to a lost age, where seiðmagn ran free and unrestricted. Now it sought to make this world more suitable for its survival, by shattering the age-old working that constrained and warped the supernatural forces. Even without Vésteinn binding it to his machines, it innately desired to play its part in the unmaking of the world, unwittingly clearing the path for that fell ritual of the void-worshipping jötnar. Climbing to a higher vantage point, Kári could see the god-beast in the distance.

Circling the overcast sky was the living dead god of the storm, conjuring up an ever-growing tempest. It was still a mockery of its former majesty. Except...

It was burning with anger. With bottomless hate. That was all that remained after centuries of torture. It would reclaim its power to unleash untold destruction upon the face of the earth. It would become an eternal storm that never waned, only grew.

It was calling out. The storm had a rhythm to it, a pulse. Kári did not doubt that on the other side of the country, something was responding beneath the hill of Öskjuhlíð.

They returned to the ruined site, taking shelter in one of the minor dig sites, in the top floor of a black tower the archaeologists had been unearthing. Kári quietly surveyed the sorcerous turmoil through an open window.

Screaming wind and lightning roared through the desolation. The fallen spikes of the power plant lay strewn around the vast central crater, black ends of broken spears. Smoke rose from chemical fires still burning; the ground was littered with smaller craters and straggled corpses, most of them withered husks. Those buildings that still stood were deathly silent. In the knowledge of what fate awaited those sheltered within, they were more macabre than the ones reduced to shattered concrete and debris. On their approach, they saw that the uncolours had merged into one, enormous being. Kári and the others had only moved in when it drifted off to seek further prey.

May all good vættir help those who cross its path, Kári thought to himself.

The protective pillars were weaker on the smaller site, but mostly undamaged. The antediluvian building also acted as a shield against the energies raging outside, testament to the esoteric mastery of the jötnar who had built it. Kári was exhausted, completely drained after performing the strangest and most difficult seiður he had ever done.

But done it he had. He had replaced Styrhildur's spine and skull with that of their fallen comrade, the one they had called Garún in living life. Something peculiar had occurred. He had threaded nerves back together, seamlessly stitching and regrowing the flesh, but ultimately he had worked on a level beyond the corporeal. He was stitching their two broken spirits together, merging the injured and broken souls into one.

When he had finished, a new being lay before him. Neither alive nor dead – not really anything mortals could describe. She had opened her eyes and scrutinised him closely. The determination of her presence, her will, bearing down on him, was almost more than he could bear.

Then, she softened. And something truly living and kind flared up in her eyes, something he had never seen in Styrhildur as a haugbúi. Although she looked like Styrhildur physically, there was an altogether new manner about the being the two of them had become. The others noticed this as well as a sharp, expectant silence descended upon the room. She smiled as she looked at her own hands. She had cried and laughed, and her family had cried with her, as the storm that wanted to break the world raged outside.

They hadn't known how to address her – or, rather, *them*. She had asked to be called Styrrún.

Halla returned from her scouting, vaulting lithely through one of the tower's windows.

'They're all dead,' was all she said.

With that, they headed out to investigate the ruin.

Most of the barracks had been used as dormitories for the ill. Each was overcrowded, all the people reduced to grey, withered husks after the uncolour had breached the walls. The healthy soldiers and workers who had remained had blocked themselves into a fortification beneath the southern cannon. The uncolour had melted through the stone roof, feeding on everyone within. Kári realised that if it were not for the plague having made its way through from Rökkurvík, they never would have stood a chance with their assault – even with the rampaging night-trolls. The western side would have been too heavily guarded for Auður and Bölmóður to infiltrate without being spotted.

The Centimotive was gone. Halla said she had seen Þráinn escape in it with a small squad of troops. She had been picking them off, one by one, but the rampaging uncolours had prevented her from fully finishing the job.

That and saving me, Kári thought but kept it to himself.

There was no trace of Ginfaxi.

They gathered their own dead and piled stones on top of the bodies, the ground too frozen to dig. There were many of them, people Kári had barely recognised at first glance. They had given their life because of his ominous prophecy. And now the rest were about to do the same.

Keys found on the dead guards gave them quick access to the carriage holding the portal to Rökkurvík. Within, Kári and Auður studied the environment carefully.

'I don't think this is something I can help you with,' she said.

'I think you're right. I'll try to figure it out.'

She was feeling better, after Kári had attended to her and Bölmóður's wounds, as well as the others. Still, the explosion had caused severe damage. Most of the left side of her body would be scarred with burn marks. But to the relief of both of them, the spiral pattern he had found on her months before had faded. Getting out of the excavation had relieved her from whatever that strange curse had been.

'I'm going to see to something,' she said as she headed outside.

He didn't need to ask what she meant. She was going to destroy the skuggsjá.

Kári studied the gate closely, focusing his multitudes of eyes to try to see beyond the mundane front of the physical door, to see the framework that led to another dimension. His vision shifted, and to his surprise he felt his eyes adjusting to the task.

Styrrún was suddenly standing next to him. She was holding a human skull. It glowed a tainted blue, thick with the presence of a single-minded demon. Protective runes and sigils covered its surface.

'*We had a knack for this type of thing.*' Her voice sounded faintly like two women speaking in unison. '*But that was a long time ago – when the Forgotten Downtown was a wild dimension, fractured in nature.*'

'From what I gather, they've sealed it shut except for their own exits and entrances.' Kári gestured to the skull. 'How does this work?'

'*The noisefiend within the audioskull speaks through music. Static is what led us to discover several ways in and out of Rökkurvík. Try it, Kári. See if it can guide you as it did us.*'

She placed headphones on him and plugged the cord into the audioskull's forehead. Instantly a strange and paranoid tune started – modern-sounding electronic music with a deep, grim bassline. He approached the door, and sure enough, he started to hear a faint crackle.

Investigating the arcane trappings woven tightly around the gate, Kári let the music guide him towards finding a way through.

ᚴ

Sölvi crawled out of the cave, his limbs stiff. It was so early that it was still night. It had been freezing cold in the cave; he had packed a woollen sweater but it wasn't nearly enough. At least it was only for a night. He chewed on some dried fish and tried to think of a plan.

As soon as he'd made his way to the cave, he had wanted to go back. He'd run off without thinking, leaving Elka alone with Ægir and Reverend Bryde. She shouldn't have slapped him, but he hadn't even given her a chance to apologise – maybe to make things right with them again. That night had been difficult, not only because of the cold. Instead of giving up, he decided that this was their last chance. Maybe now his mother would listen to his pleas of escaping Heimaey – maybe he could ask that they just take a short trip to Reykjavík, just him and her. Ægir would never let her go, he knew that. He'd spun up dozens of plans that night, some of them hopefully naïve, others more realistic.

The sky was clear, the stars were still out in total abandon. The town's lights were brightest down by the harbour, where they had installed lots of new electric lamps and floodlights. The village itself still used fish-oil lamps. This would make it easy to sneak around, until he got to the harbour.

The fishing boats would head out in an hour and a half. It would be difficult to get on one of them without anyone noticing. No use worrying about that now – he'd gauge the risk when he got there.

With the boats moored, that meant Ægir would be at home. Still… there was a chance Sölvi's mother hadn't slept through the night. He could knock on the window of the study, where she was probably wide awake and reading. He had to try to talk to her, he knew that, but playing the conversation out in his head… he knew how it sounded. He wished he had stolen that folklore book from the library, to try to offer some proof of his outlandish-sounding theory. To him, all these dreadful stories about those poor holy women who had suffered misfortune caused by the sea drew up a frightening picture when aligned with Elka's book about the saints. A picture which his mother and grandmother fitted into. But he knew that to Elka – to most adults – things like that were chalked up as coincidences and superstition. He had no proof except for a bad feeling, and that didn't amount to much. Maybe adults were just so used to feeling bad all the time that they forgot it could ever be otherwise. But maybe Elka would listen. He had to try, futile as it might be.

Ægir's house was dark. There was no light in the study, no sign of movement within. He opened the back door and found the house empty. There was a mess in the kitchen, water spilled on the floorboards. Someone had brewed something foul in the kettle. It stank worse than fermented skate, the smell burning its way into his nostrils.

Sölvi didn't like this. Maybe she was still out looking for him. If so, then where was Ægir? Could she be at Aunt Björg's house? Reverend Bryde's? The church?

He walked down to the pier, heading straight to where the small boat was berthed. The one he'd worked on time and again. His mind felt clouded and unclear, busy with elusive thoughts. It was as though his feet moved of their own accord. He just wanted to leave this place. He could start by preparing the boat before he found his mother.

'Hey, kid!'

He froze, then remembered that, no, to others he wasn't running away from home; to others he was supposed to be here and everything was fine. He turned around to find Styrmir sitting atop a pile of fish tubs, smoking a cigarette. He looked haggard.

'What are you doing here, Sölvi?' asked Styrmir.

'Going to the factory to get some extra work before school. I'm saving up for new watercolours.'

'You're a good liar, kid. But not that good. I'm also not stupid.

Don't think I don't know why you've been so interested in learning how to steer a ship.'

Sölvi considered his options. There wasn't much point in lying.

'But you still helped me?'

'That's right. It's a good skill to have, out here. And who knows what the future holds.'

'I'm leaving.' Sölvi decided to trust the man. He was the only one who treated him like a grown-up. 'But Mamma isn't home. Nobody's home. I don't know where she is.'

The huldumaður got up, tossing the cigarette into the harbour.

'Yeah. I know. Listen…' Styrmir looked around. The harbour was still quiet, only a couple of fishermen preparing their nets some distance away. 'Ægir and the priest took your mother yesterday. They went out on Ægir's ship.'

'What?' Sölvi's heart sank. His mouth felt dry.

'I think they took her to Surtsey. My guess is that the baby's coming.'

'I have to go and get her.'

'Just because you've had a few lessons, that doesn't mean a kid like you is ready to sail on his own. You'll crash on the rocks, drown swimming to shore, or die any of the dozen other ways you can mess things up taking the ship out alone. Assuming that I even let you, that is.'

'Then come with me. Help us.'

Styrmir snorted. 'Right. A one-armed man and a little boy against that brute.'

'So go and get your gun. You do have one, right?'

Styrmir's look darkened. 'That's not a toy, Sölvi.'

'I know. It's just to scare Ægir off. I know you also think the Church is bad. They're rotten to the core. Are you really going to just stand here and do nothing about it, just like everyone else on this island?' Sölvi was doing his very best not to let his temper get the better of him. He softened his tone and decided to risk going even further. 'Are you going to let them hurt her like they hurt you?'

Styrmir gave him a dark look. Sölvi's heart pounded in his chest. He'd assumed a lot of things in that last sentence – but he had a feeling his words rang true.

Then Styrmir headed towards the boat and started to undo the moorings.

'What are you waiting for, kid? Give me a hand, for crying out loud.'

463

Tuttugu og tvö

The soldier was dozing at his station when Kári stepped through the gate. The man got up so hurriedly to salute that his metal chair fell over, hitting the concrete floor with a clang. A confused look crossed his face as he registered the different colours of the seiðskratti's robes, then registered the completely ruined mask.

'You're not Magister Ginfaxi.'

Auður Thorlacius stepped through the gate behind Kári and uttered a short incantation. The man was reaching for his rifle, leaning up against the wall, but froze in place. The others followed shortly after. There were ten of them now. Bölmóður had decided against following them through this unnatural portal. Besides, a náskári wouldn't exactly be inconspicuous here. The korpur had taken flight on the trail of the landvættur.

'This isn't like before,' remarked Eyvindur, with his hands on his knees, pale and sweaty.

'*It's the distance*,' Styrrún stated.

All of them felt sick, a sense of wrongness impacting their very sense of being. The others had shifted between Reykjavík and Rökkurvík before and it had never been this bad. This man-made portal stretched the limitations of dimensional geography to breaking point. Only Styrrún seemed unaffected. She approached the paralysed soldier with an unnerving stillness.

'*The portal to Reykjavík,*' she asked him in a calm tone. '*Where is it?*'

The soldier stared at the undead with terror in his eyes.

'Go to hell,' he spat forcibly through his gritted teeth.

Auður spoke a word. The man collapsed to the ground.

They were in a bare, windowless room, the only entrance a heavy steel door right in front of them. The gate was the bottom two steps of a staircase ripped out of an ordinary home, each polished step creaking as a person stepped through. The Directorate had not accounted for anyone else being able to infiltrate their gate. That single soldier was its only defence to speak of. Auður risked opening a crack on the door. The street outside was bathed in crimson light.

'It's as you described,' she said to Styrrún.

'They did that when they arrived,' said Halla, pulling a large cloak from Eyvindur's backpack. He helped her wrap it around her body, so she wouldn't be spotted immediately as one of them. 'We overheard some soldiers talking when they rounded us up. They did something to the sky to seal up the cracks in reality.'

The Forgotten Downtown had changed drastically since most of the others had been there. Then, eerie hrævareldar had trailed the empty muddied roads, their flickering flames leading people to their doom. It had been a dark, foreboding place, filled with crumbling houses which no one had ever built or truly lived in. This place had appeared out of nowhere, a sombre reflection of the small town Reykjavík had once been.

Now, the empty, dark sky was covered with a grid of burning lights, like miniature red suns. Brutalist architecture had replaced the traditional houses, with their windows darkened and boarded up by squatters. Kári followed Auður out of one of those big concrete blocks, this one only housing the portal. Others were windowless edifices of heavy stone. Prisons or offices for the Directorate, in a place beyond the laws of the Kalmar Commonwealth.

The road was empty. Following the side of the building, they came to an intersection.

'*This is familiar to us*,' whispered Styrrún, pointing to a vacant foundation where a house had been torn down. '*That used to be a bar. We used to live nearby.*'

They crossed the intersection, following another concrete block devoid of doors or windows. The red light was dim, bathing everything in deep shadows. They went to the other side of the street, hiding behind a rotting wooden fence in a cluster of empty yards, the houses that had once stood there reduced to ruined heaps of wood and corrugated iron. Styrrún put on the headphones, checking the noisefiend.

'*Nothing*,' she replied. '*This place is dead.*'

'Keep listening. Where did they breach?' asked Auður, looking to Eyvindur and Halla.

'Not sure,' Halla replied. 'We were in hiding at the time.'

'Kári – you got anything? We're sitting ducks out here.'

There was an odd formation to the seiðmagn here. It appeared to contain and arrange itself into neat patterns.

'There is no natural source of seiðmagn here,' he said. 'It's all ... imported, I think.' Its purpose eluded him. 'I need more time to analyse it.'

'Well, we don't have any.'

Kári tried to focus, to analyse the intent behind the sorcery. It was a grand weaving of seiður, encompassing this entire plane. It was thoroughly and deftly crafted. He started to get a sense of seiðmagn in clusters – a condensed power.

'There, that smaller building.'

He indicated a lone bunker, near the shores of a stagnant

mire. Its surface was like glass, untouched by wind or living things, reflecting the reddened sky back with perfect clarity.

Keeping low, they made it to the building unseen.

'Where the hell is everyone?' remarked Eyvindur. 'I expected this place to be crawling with soldiers.'

A single steel door was the only entrance. Auður placed a hand on it, softly speaking words that sounded like no language a living being had spoken. With her left hand, she drew a galdrastafur on the door in white chalk – a long, vertical stroke, impaled by lines down its entirety. A chilling thought invaded Kári.

Are those words and symbols the remnants of the ancient tongue of the jötnar?

The door trembled as the galdrastafur was completed and Auður's incantation finished. A burning metallic smell rose from it, along with acrid smoke across its outline, irritating their lungs so the others had to cough. Kári's mask protected him from most of it and Styrrún did not have to breathe. The door gave in easily when Styrrún pushed it, and she rushed inside with the same unnatural speed Styrhildur and Hraki had moved with in the heat of battle.

Muted sounds of struggle, a crash. Someone cried for help, shut off mid-word. As things fell silent once more, Kári followed Styrrún inside.

He discovered an office, lit by fluorescent lights. A dead soldier was lying on his back, blood rapidly leaking from his slit throat. Rows of neat desks, piled high with papers, the walls lined with metal filing cabinets. One desk had been overturned, papers spilling everywhere. Styrrún stood behind it over a man in plain clothes, wiping the blood off her knife. More such bodies lay around the place. They had been completely defenceless, apart from the one soldier. Kári averted his gaze from the slaughter.

Eyvindur glanced at one of the desks as they quietly made their way through the room.

'Surveillance reports,' he whispered. 'All over the city, it looks like.'

At the far end of the building was a staircase leading down. Following it, they entered a corridor lined with doors. Each was coated in obsidian, the door frame as well.

'It's here,' said Kári. 'A condensed source coming from each room.'

He went to the nearest one, feeling the muted radiation of seiðmagn emitting from it. The door was locked, but Halla, tired of sneaking around in this ghost town, charged it with her shoulder and broke it off its hinges.

The small room was empty. The walls were clad in obsidian, except for a blank spot at the far end. In that space was a sigil radiating dense waves of seiðmagn. It was shaped like an open eye, drawn with impeccable precision, surrounded by a chain of smaller arcane symbols.

Styrrún hissed, '*Those fucking bastards.*'

Before Kári could ask her what she meant, she had walked up to the symbol and placed a flat palm on it. A shudder went through her body and her head twitched. He could feel her activating the thaumaturgical symbol – it was a ritualistic key of some sorts. Not daring to interfere in any way, he and Auður waited tensely for something to happen. Eyvindur and Halla looked crestfallen – did they know what this was?

After a brief moment, she slid her hand off the wall. She turned to them with a look of fierce contempt, tinged with regret.

'*They found the sigils. We remember having to move fast – we didn't have time to ruin them properly.*'

'Your graffiti network,' said Auður. 'The spying sigils Garún invented.'

Styrrún nodded. '*They've made improvements to it. This is the key rune to a certain set.*'

'There are similar signatures in the other rooms,' said Kári dryly.

'*There must be spying sigils all over the city.*'

'What are they made of?' he asked.

'We used to help tagging them,' said Halla. 'Before … well, before everything. Delýsíð mixed in clear spray paint.'

'*Why haven't we found any traces of them in Reykjavík?*' They didn't have the answer to that. '*We can't have them watching over our every move.*'

Eyvindur reached into his backpack, pulling out a spray can. Styrrún blacked out the sigils, one by one, draining the last of their meagre stores of delýsíð-laced paint.

The masks they wore, these monitoring sigils: Kári was baffled at the ingenuity of what – in all fairness – were mere kuklarar. And Garún had managed to do all of this, apparently without compromising herself or the other untrained members of her group. She would have made a fine seiðskratti, in another life – in another world.

Meanwhile, two people stood guard by the door upstairs, while the others searched for anything that could help. One of them gestured to a locked steel cabinet, which Halla easily broke open, revealing a skorrifle and several charges of ammunition batteries. After a while, a pile of papers revealed a schematic of the new layout of Rökkurvík.

There were three large buildings assigned to confinement. The place where they had entered the Forgotten Downtown was one of four gates, the only one completed so far. A clearing had been made around a spot marked TD-Gate Alpha. Clipped to it was a small sheet, filled with dates and specific times marked as departure and arrival.

'This is it,' said Auður. 'It's got to be.'

'All right, so now what?' Kári said. 'We step through there and enter the innermost sanctum of their base in Reykjavík?'

'*No, Magister,*' said Styrrún coldly. '*We tear down the metaphysical walls they have built around this place. We liberate Rökkurvík from the Crown.*'

ᚼ

The deep waters of the night were filled with stars, the darkness cradling the full moon in its nurturing embrace. The sky was vast and infinite, tattered dark clouds gliding rapidly across it as if wanting to escape.

The stars were rocking in the deep.

Elka was on a boat. The waves lapped against its hull as it landed on a rocky shore. Elka tried to sit up, but Björg pushed her gently, but firmly, back down.

'Shhh, shhh.' A beatific smile. 'Your waters broke, you mustn't move. Think of the baby. Rest now, my darling. Rest.'

'My waters,' she slurred. 'They broke?'

Breaking waters and crashing waves. Why wasn't she feeling any contractions?

'That's right, my dear. It's time for our wonderful miracle to come into the world.'

Arms carrying her. Ægir. There were no stars in his eyes, only the Deep. No – it was nothing. Absolutely nothing at all.

Terror crept up on her through the haze. Her head tilted and she saw the priest. Bryde was wading through the waves following Ægir, a boat at anchor on the sea behind her, the rowing boat left on the shore like driftwood.

'Where are we?'

Her body felt strange. As though she did not inhabit it, but was lying very far down inside it, trapped deep in a well.

'The island,' Ægir said. 'Surtsey.'

'Where is Sölvi? I was looking for him, he—'

'Be quiet,' he commanded. 'Save your strength for what is to come.'

The birds circled above them, quiet and brooding. Through the drug-thick haze, she could see their shapes for what they truly were in the moonlight. Trapped souls. Girls who had fallen for sweet words and kind gestures, girls who had been crushed by the insanity and the pressure of the descent into the depths.

That's what destroys you, down in the Deep. First the cold. Then the dark. Finally the overbearing pressure from everywhere at once. It will break you. And if you panic, and kick your way up to the surface too fast, your brain becomes alight with air and you die as your mind expands too rapidly.

Elka faded in and out like the waves. They were ascending. A mountainous hillside, covered in tiny, greenish plants, primal and primitive forms of life clinging to the bare rock in spiralling formations. Again, she thought she saw the glow of hot lava in some of the twisted geological shapes on the mountainside, but it couldn't have been. It had been even longer since Surtsey was formed.

A contraction, faint, distant. Barely managing to pierce through the fog. She started to breathe slowly, methodically. As she calmed herself, she could feel it moving. Slithering around and around itself inside her, turning somersaults, its myriad tendrils moving in agitated excitement.

Above them, the moon.

Watching.

Waiting.

Elka furrowed her brow. *How strange*. It was as if a silver thread was dangling from the moon – leading right towards her, a thing so delicate it seemed to be made from nothing at all. She tried to focus, to reach up her arm to grasp it, but she was too weak.

Oddly shaped stone cairns were piled up at the top of the mountain. Except they weren't stones, they were the Messengers. Standing still and grey and frozen, their wings unfurled and arms stretched out, with multitudes of hands displaying strange gestures, each of them a different symbol, a different key. She felt the pattern they made mirrored inside her, turning and roiling. An elliptical spiral swallowing itself, pierced with straight lines like spears, forming a new and familiar sign.

Keys upon keys upon keys.

No wonder, since everything around her was locked. Soon, everything would be unlocked.

The island.

The moon.

The egg.

Her womb.

Everything would unravel.

The Messengers from the Deep started to sing as Ægir laid her down on the stone altar at the centre of the spiral. This place was unfamiliar to her. Ægir joined them in song, as did Björg frænka and Reverend Bryde. Elka had the stark realisation that none of them seemed to be people at all. They were as marionettes, dancing according to an unseen hand. As they sang, she noticed the things inside their mouths, crawling up their throats now that it was safe to show themselves. Pale parasites clicking their mandibles, stretching out their feelers, singing with their hosts.

Lying on her back, breathing in sync with her odd, irregular contractions, she saw a great and beautiful being fly down from the stars. A Messenger of the Deep, soaring through the air. In its claws it cradled a machine.

'How wonderful,' the machine cooed in a mockery of human speech, as the carrier took its place in the spiral, spreading its wings and locking its chitinous limbs in place. 'We made it in time for the hatching.'

They sung a wordless hymn, in an ancient language laden with power. They gave praise to the opening of a gateway to all-encompassing nothingness, the final peace which would serve as the end of suffering. There would be nothing but chaos and the void, as had always been intended, and their ancient, drawn-out war with self-deluded pawns serving that mindless hunger that is life, would finally come to its inevitable conclusion.

All things would cease to be. At long last the great chain of existence would be broken, and they would all transcend consciousness to become one with the untamed nothing in the raw chaos lurking behind the world.

Listening to the song, Elka could not help but see *everything that was* through their eyes – life was a cursed thing, a prison made of pain and suffering. Soon, they would all be no more – they would never have been, as time unravelled its hateful tapestry. Her contractions grew stronger. It felt as though the island was quaking with her in sympathy.

The Emissary of the Deep suddenly loomed over her. His skin was the alabaster of the moon, eyes filled to the brim with nothingness, night-black horns tangled and gnarled like the bare branches of winter trees.

'The blood of the jötnar flows strong within you. Claim the power that is yours by birthright.'

The words of that transcendent tongue flooded into Elka, filled her soul like water suffocates a drowning person. He spoke with the voice of the sea and the earth trembled in sync with her contractions.

'No more pain. No more needless suffering. Unmake it all, Elka.'

He smiled with sharp teeth and took her hand in his own vastly larger one, making her feel as if she was a child again. He held it tightly, giving her something to squeeze as the contractions worsened.

'Bring the Last Flood into this world.'

They sang and Elka stared into the void behind his eyes, clenching his hand, feeling the life within that was about to come and alter the world. The silver thread was clearly visible to her now, reaching all the way down from the moon to her stomach. A lunar umbilical cord.

'Be welcome, my dear child,' she whispered. 'Be loved, and be welcome.'

ᚼ

Lárus had much preferred being a beat cop in Reykjavík. He had worked hard through the years, kept his head down and retained the good sense to stay out of trouble. It took a certain type of instinct to know when not to ask questions about something that was none of your business. Lárus was proud of that knack of his, almost a sixth sense of knowing when to intervene and when to pretend all was well. It had paid off, resulting in him being promoted to the rank of inspector.

He'd had a good thing going, before that son of a bitch Meinholt dragged him into this shit. Þráinn was an absolute bastard, but Lárus hadn't minded working for him to begin with. Those little side projects, as Lárus had thought of them, paid very well and were not restrained by all the usual paperwork of his normal job. It was a nice change of pace to not have to worry about some boss yelling his head off for not following protocol.

Þráinn Meinholt cared for results – nothing else. And Lárus was a man who got results. Except he had apparently done such a good job of becoming the agent's favourite that he had ended up posted to this miserable place.

The Directorate of Immigration was an adjacent entity to the police. Commissioner Kofoed-Hansen was the head of both institutions, which meant that co-operation between the two was so common they were only separate in name. Intelligence, counter-intelligence – Lárus knew that all of it was necessary in the modern world, but it was something he wanted nothing to do with. Disappearing people into the Nine had been unpleasant, although he had no particular sympathy for the dissidents who had suffered such a fate. Being a criminal was one thing, being a traitor was something else. Still, he found himself longing for his days walking the beat, salt-covered icy streets under his worn boots, breath steaming in the air, always knowing where to stop on the route to get a complimentary hot drink and a kleina or two.

Nobody sold pastries in Rökkurvík.

He stomped his feet, out of habit more than anything, pacing around outside his guardhouse. It was quite cramped, consisting of a small desk and chair, a sheet on the wall detailing the scheduled arrivals and departures. Through a bulletproof window he could monitor the ritual circle. It was bordered by a ring of curved obsidian pillars, looking so much like the unnatural maw of some hideous beast. In its centre was a gap in reality, visible only because the light curved peculiarly around it. Approaching the obsidian circle made Lárus feel nauseous; it was saturated with volatile seiðmagn, but at a safe distance it had little to no effect. Watching it for hours on end was bad enough.

The portal was in the middle of a muddy field where a royal seiðskratti had forcibly pierced through the membrane between dimensions years ago, during their raid on Rökkurvík. That had been an exciting time. Too bad they had torn down the abandoned house they'd used as a makeshift base to start with. Would have been much nicer than this crummy concrete cupboard.

He was on twelve-hour shifts for a week at a time, getting a week in the real world off duty. It was barely enough to get the dread of this place out of his mind, and then he was back in this hellhole again. Lárus couldn't imagine how those drug addicts and outcasts had managed to live here for months on end. He supposed they didn't, really. Rumours were that most people who fled to this place had died here, either from the hrævareldar, substance abuse or plain old depression. The place wore down the soul like nothing else.

Lighting a cigarillo, he convinced himself that, all things considered, things weren't so bad. He had a job, the pay was good. The Directorate had a direct supply of goods through the Atlantean armada; being high on the priority list had its benefits. Like tobacco. Reykjavík had steadily become a ghost town these last few months, as the streets emptied and shops shut down. Soon enough it and the Forgotten Downtown would mirror each other well enough. A man such as Lárus would only get a job digging mass graves for the plague victims, these days. And then he'd be lying in one soon enough. He drew in deeply of the thick smoke, savouring it. No, this wasn't that bad, all things considered.

He checked his wristwatch. There should be a squad arriving any minute for departure to Reykjavík. Pen-pushers from the surveillance office, scheduled for departure at 23:45, just before midnight. Midnight – the notion of it was laughable in a place like this.

A seiðskratti came walking up the road. They carried

themselves proudly, as all those inhuman bastards did, but there was something off about them. Their colours were unfamiliar to Lárus, and as the magister approached he saw better how worn and dirty their robes were, their mask a ruined mess.

'Officer,' the seiðskratti said. 'I'm here to address a problem with the portal's interdimensional manifestations.'

'Er...' Lárus didn't know what the hell they were talking about. 'I see, Magister. I wasn't notified you were coming in.'

'Orders directly from Agent Meinholt. It is of the utmost urgency.'

'Ah, right.' He gestured to the dishevelled regalia. 'You from the excavation or something?' The seiðskratti didn't respond. Lárus was about to push the magister for an answer, but something made him feel uncomfortable with the idea. 'Your magisterial title, please? For my logbook, you see.'

'Magister Helvaki.' The seiðskratti hissed at his blatant insolence.

'Ah yes... and your order?' Lárus chuckled stupidly as he jotted it down. He found it better around these types to play to their prejudices and act more stupid than you were. Put them off guard. 'I'm very sorry, Magister, I'm not familiar with the meaning of the colours of all your, uh... clothes—'

'Regalia,' Magister Helvaki spat.

'Yes, very sorry, sir – Magister. Your regalia.'

'Interspatial thaumaturgy, of course. With a focus on trans-dimensional anomalies, if you must know my specialisation as well. Officer.'

Lárus beamed, trying to hide his alarm with a mask of compliant inferiority.

'Yes, Magister, thank you very much, thank you, please – I'll disturb you no longer.'

Putting out his cigarillo beneath his boot, he strolled casually to the guardhouse, making sure not to look in a hurry. The seiðskratti turned to the portal, approaching the circle cautiously, studying the seiðmagn they allegedly saw as clear as northern lights in winter.

Lárus was no idiot. He had done his homework. That was no interspatial thaumaturgist – they were a biothaumaturgist. What the hell was a biological seiðskratti doing out here, messing with the gate? Inside the guardhouse, he checked his watch. Five minutes to twelve. The surveillance agents were late. Something was wrong.

Sitting at his desk, Lárus couldn't help but feel as though he was being watched. He reached under his desk for a flask of hot coffee, making sure to keep an eye on his surroundings out of the corner of his eye. He felt as if he saw movement out in the dark crimson edge of the field. Behind a half-collapsed wall, long neglected and in need of being properly torn down.

Something was definitely wrong.

He huffed in pretend annoyance and got up slowly, acting as if his aching knees and fat belly were a bigger hindrance than they really were, and picked up a cup from a shelf. The silent alarm was right next to it. He pushed it, hiding the movement as he reached for the cup.

Sitting back down with the cup visibly in hand, he wore the satisfied smile of a lazy cop about to enjoy his coffee break. Inwards, he was seething with frustration. His skorrifle was up against the wall behind the door. He had no chance of picking it up without arousing suspicion.

Outside, the magister had raised their hands, starting to affect the gate with seiður. The portal's vortex had started to change, as the fractured light was bent in different ways. Lárus side-eyed the rifle. Those bastards had better get here fast, before he was forced to take drastic action to stop that sorcerous psychopath.

Still, Lárus sat as calm as ever, sipping his coffee. He hadn't got this far by throwing himself into the line of fire.

A squad of five soldiers appeared, heading right for the portal. Lárus breathed a sigh of relief. Finally. He put down his cup and pushed his chair back in a hurry, intending to go out and shout at the idiots that this seiðskratti didn't belong here at all, when he found, much to his surprise, that he could not move.

Or well – that wasn't entirely accurate. Lárus knew he could move. Nothing had changed his bodily functions: his musculature – even his breathing – was exactly the same, if slightly more accelerated due to his rising panic. It was more as though he did not *want* to move.

With a pained look, he stared at the necklace he had taken off halfway through his shift. It lay on his desk, neatly piled up, placed halfway behind a photograph of his family. It was something Meinholt had demanded a select few of them wear – an extremely expensive artefact. The skull of an arctic tern, a sigil cast in bronze-coloured metal over the cranium. It annoyed Lárus tremendously, causing his chest to break out in a red, allergic rash by the end of each shift. Probably a reaction to the metal alloy, he'd initially thought, but it didn't even help to keep layers of clothing between it and his skin. If he wore it at all times as he was supposed to, the rash would be cracked and bleeding by the end of the working week, not even properly healed by the time his next shift started.

He'd asked Meinholt about it, and the agent told him to cease his whingeing. Cases like this were a common side effect of the powerful – and expensive – enchantment bound into the bone. A minor annoyance was nothing compared to supernatural protection, Þráinn had said. It was the equivalent of body armour.

Lárus stared longingly at it now.

Outside, three of the soldiers approached the seiðskratti.

Apparently, the thaumaturgical confluence surrounding the gate was getting intense. They halted several steps away from the obsidian circle, skorrifles held carelessly, not nearly readied enough for coming to answer a goddamn alarm bell. Lárus cursed them. Lazy Kalmar fucks. The other two headed to the guardhouse, waving to Lárus with a strange look on their faces when he didn't respond. He tried to send them a goddamn signal with the intensity of his stare. One said something to the other, who laughed in response.

Fucking idiots.

Shadows shifted everywhere. A profound sense of vertigo overtook Lárus, as well as the soldiers outside, who reeled as if they were losing their balance. The gloom deepened, crimson light fading to even further dimness. The portal started to flicker in and out of existence, an optical illusion his brain failed to process. The soldiers looked up to the sky, now truly alarmed, shouting at the seiðskratti to cease.

'Lárus!' one of the soldiers shouted in the doorway. 'Who the hell is that seiðskratti?'

'Kill ... them!' he managed to spit out, the hex on him momentarily wavering.

The world plunged into pitch-black nothingness. The hold on him ceased and he threw himself to the floor, reaching up to his desk to fumble around for the necklace. He put it on, his chest already starting to hurt from its radiance, but what a wonderful feeling it was.

'Kill that fucking seiðskratti!' Lárus commanded.

They were already aiming their guns at the magister, shouting at him to desist. Lárus got up to fetch his skorrifle, seeing that the only source of light was now a dim pulse coming from the magister at the centre of the gate, which had been rendered imperceptible – or, he thought with dread, it simply wasn't there any more.

'Just shoot the fucking bastard!'

He charged past the two idiots, so used to being commanded by anyone in those bird-masks that they were genuinely too conditioned to fathom that one could be anything but a figure of authority.

Lárus aimed and fired. The thaumaturgical shot was eviscerated in the torrent of seiðmagn raging around the gate. Immediately, a barrage of sorcerous gunfire lit up the dark, hitting two of the soldiers by the portal. The third stood as immobile as stone, no doubt caught in the same hex that had its cold claws in Lárus. Hideous growths sprouted from their wounds. Lárus and the other two went behind the guardhouse for cover, firing back from each side.

The ground had started to shake in rhythmic pulses. The seiðskratti rose off the ground, the seiðmagn around him running in visible, hypercoloured currents. Lárus fired at his attackers, crouching behind that collapsed wall as he'd suspected, but he was unable to see anything in this goddamn night. The sky above them had darkened once more, the red lights vanished.

'Focus fire on the seiðskratti! He's sealing the portal!'

They all shot, but the result was the same. The seiðskratti diverted their bullets, absorbing their power into his working.

'Helvítis djöfulsins andskotans!' Lárus cursed. 'Where is the backup?' he demanded.

'We thought it was a false alarm, sir,' a soldier said, firing another wasted shot at the magister. 'Surely more must be heading here now!'

'Fire on my command, aim for his chest!'

'Yes, sir!'

They shot on Lárus's order. The seiðskratti coiled up, hit by at least one shot directly in the chest. Writhing in pain, the magister trembled as they focused on finishing the ritual.

'Again!'

'Y—'

The soldier gurgled on his own blood, his throat spraying blood all over the woman suddenly standing over him. The other one rushed her with his bayonet. The full weight of his body should have sent her flat on her back, but instead she only stumbled and took the brunt of the attack with ease.

She wasn't alive. It was her. Skotta. The undead terrorist. Lárus did the only thing that had proved to work for him in situations such as these.

He ran.

Tripping over something in the darkness, he fell flat on his face into the mud. How the hell did this fucking place have such muddy paths when it never rained? He cursed this godforsaken shithole, the stupidity of soldiers, fucking seiðskrattar and goddamn traitorous undead.

Hitting his knee on a ruined wall and biting back another curse, afraid the sound would give him away, he caught a glimpse of a faint light in the distance. Just around the corner of one of the concrete blocks. Fucking finally – backup.

He sprinted towards the light, turning the corner, already shouting warnings about what was happening, where the insurgents were—

He stared directly into a blue-white fire, hovering over the earth. It flickered with cold flame, radiating a different kind of warmth – an unspoken promise of safety, of pleasure, of happiness and fulfilment. It seemed so warm... and he was so very cold.

Numbed, he took one step forwards. Then another. The light retreated, leading him on.

He followed it eagerly.

ᚴ

They entered Reykjavík in a courtyard, crawling out of a broken cellar window onto overgrown grass. All around them were apartment buildings, sealing off the yard. The complex looked empty, most of its windows dark. Rubbish bins were filled with unclaimed refuse; a bicycle was overturned on the grass, its wheels missing. The moon shone full, glimpsed through the heavy, overcast sky. Even this much light was jarring after the gloom of Rökkurvík. The frost-tinged wind was picking up.

Kári crawled across the grass, clutching his malformed wound, exhausted after the exertion of tearing up the portal's intricate working. It had been masterfully made, but thankfully ruining something was easier than trying to operate it. He drew in deeply from the residual seiðmagn of the real world, trying to restrain himself despite the rising panic. The wound on his stomach had grown a cluster of soft, bright orange tendrils, feeling like a slug to the touch, with two bloodstained ivory tusks jutting from the centre. He'd managed to stop the bleeding and stitch up the internal injury. After the gate collapsed, the others had dragged him to shelter, but the malevolent seiðmagn had taken root in him. He was shaking from pain and the existential vertigo of having gone through the gate.

Styrrún and Diljá were already there. Diljá scanned the place in a panic, expecting anything, while Styrrún listened calmly to the audioskull. She had found the fissure between realities quickly with its help. The cracks between dimensions had manifested rapidly back into existence as soon as the Crown's seiður had been undone. Diljá dragged Kári up against a leaning fence, the wood whitened and untended.

'You're injured,' she said.

'Just give me a moment. Are we safe?'

'*Safe enough, according to the noisefiend,*' Styrrún replied.

'Then let me work in peace.'

Kári calmed his breathing, hands on either side of the grotesque wound. The spongy orange growth undulated, the tiny feelers trembling of their own volition.

Accept this, he demanded of himself.

Focusing internally, he worked on healing torn organs, ripped veins and muscles into new forms – more suited to what had now grown on him, become part of him. He gritted his teeth, hissing through them, so intense was the pain. He worked with the new pattern, wanting to cement it in place so the mutation would not spread further.

In the end, he felt he could do no better. He relaxed and flooded himself with dopamine. Hopefully, that would be the end of it.

Only Auður was suffering intensely from the effects of the shift; the others were used to it from years before, during their temporary exile to Rökkurvík. The six of them were all that was left of their group, now. Two had died in the skirmish against the soldiers by the portal; another pair were killed as they held back incoming hostiles as Styrrún figured out how to activate the portal in a ruined house.

'Are you good to move?' asked Diljá. Kári nodded. She looked at him contemplatively. 'We could have used someone like you from the beginning. We've lost many to a single shot.'

'I'm afraid I wouldn't have been of much use at the time.'

She offered him a hand and he took it. It stung like hell getting up. But he could move – if he kept himself stabilised with a constant flow of seiðmagn.

They were in the centre of Reykjavík's downtown area, on the north-eastern side. Checking the street, they found it empty of people. Heading towards Hverfisgata, the main commercial road that looped all around the city, they found the real answer to the emptied streets. Numerous posters covered the walls, declaring the entire city on lockdown by the order of King Jörundur the Ninth of his name, as decreed by Loretz Engel Gyldenlöve, stiftamtmaður of Hrímland. The harbours were shut as well, to prevent any further influx of disease. Other posters declared that due to the ongoing war effort, rationing was now enforced for all goods. Similar propaganda declared that farmers unwilling to submit their goods to rationing by the Kalmar Commonwealth would be arrested for conspiring with the enemy.

'Shit,' Diljá breathed.

'This means we'll likely only come across armed patrols on our way,' said Halla, adjusting the cloak around her. 'They'll recognise us in an instant.'

'We have safe houses,' said Eyvindur. 'We can go there, rest and regroup. Contact the others who stayed behind.'

'*There is no time for that*,' said Styrrún coldly. '*You saw the landvættur's trail back there, how far it had come in a matter of hours. The safe houses are too far from the city centre, contacting others will—*'

Their debate was interrupted by a sudden noise, as a squadron of biplanes rushed overhead, flying dangerously low.

'They must have launched from the armada out in the bay,' muttered Eyvindur.

Air-raid sirens started to sound all over the city.

Styrrún looked up at the darkening clouds, gathering in strength. The light of the moon was smothered by the oncoming storm.

'*They were heading east. It's already here.*'

ᚼ

People rushed out into the streets as the sirens started, remembering all too well when last they sounded and demons had entered their lives. They ran frantically for cover. This was a storm warning like no other. The soldiers and police officers were too busy frantically trying to muster under this unprecedented event, the thaumaturgical storm already becoming fierce and uncontrollable.

Kári and the others slipped through the chaos unnoticed, heading up towards the nearby hill of Skólavörðuholt. Once the split church tower of Haraldskirkja had stood there proudly, looming over the city – now instead ruled the coarse and misshapen figure of the Stone Giant.

A small crowd of people had gathered by the feet of the being, called the southern landvættur in heathen myths. They worshipped it and prayed for salvation from war, disease, starvation. As ever, the unshapely stone stood dormant, weathering the storm.

'Do you think this will work?' Kári shouted over the wind to Auður.

'It better!'

'And if it doesn't?'

He did not like how she looked at him then. Like someone facing death.

'Then you well know what I must do.'

He had already known her answer when he asked. It had been made abundantly clear from the debate on how they could possibly stop the landvættur, before they had gone through the portal to Rökkurvík and set upon this path. No one will be an unbeaten bishop, the saying went – but Kári doubted the sentiment of working hard to achieve your goals applied when it came to invoking the primordial or the malign.

Knowing full well how futile it was, he still wanted to object to Auður's plan should this fail. But he didn't. Faced with complete annihilation, what could he have said? No words could bridge that chasm.

The crowd of worshippers parted as they came running, panicking as they saw the ghostly visage of Styrrún. Freezing rain came down, soaking them to the skin.

Auður Thorlacius had studied the Stone Giant intently. She had been able to gain some glimpse of the tremendous power sealed within it, but never been able to access it. Styrrún looked upon the silent being contemplatively. She had never said what exactly she would do in this moment – how she would do the impossible and breach the ethereal barrier that sealed off the imprisoned being within.

Closing her eyes, standing firm as the raging wind tore at them, she reached out to the Stone Giant.

ϟ

The landvættur approached the city gates, a furious tempest following in its wake.

Biplanes swarmed around it, rattling with gunfire. They smoked and fell like flies around the rotting beast, struck by the raging thunderstorm, the wind battering them so wildly and unpredictably that they span out of control, crashing down to the earth. Seiðskrattar and galdramenn had manned the wall, chanting incantations, drawing in seiðmagn, readying themselves for the ordeal that was to come. They had trained for this, ever since the Stone Giant had torn through their defences as if they were nothing. The approaching storm came like a crashing wave, overwhelming them with unruly seiðmagn. A few seiðskrattar fainted, conquered by the sudden onslaught. The others stood firm, humming with transmundane and sorcerous power.

Thaumaturgical cannons trained their sights on the god-beast as the remaining biplanes retreated.

As one, they unleashed everything they had at the approaching titan.

It disappeared in an explosion of arcane power, a use of force so overwhelmingly dangerous that it had not been attempted in recorded history. A dozen cannons fired volley after volley; galdramenn recited the ancient poetry, ceasing only when they were on the precipice of the abyss, knowing that heavily armed and reinforced soldiers acting as fail-safes were ready to take them out at the slightest sign of demonic possession; seiðskrattar pushed themselves beyond the limit, knowing they would not return from this ordeal whole, a few of them bursting in a thaumaturgical explosion as the flow of seiðmagn overloaded their bodies.

Lightning flashed within the resulting smoke, its toxic fumes merging with the thick clouds, forming an impenetrable wall.

The landvættur dived out of the bank of clouds, roaring. It unleashed massive lightning bolts from its maw, spewing smoke that fell in thick streams. The seiðmagn gathered within the seiðskrattar turned berserk. The resulting explosions took out a sizeable chunk of the battlements, destroying the finest masters of the arcane the Crown had to offer. The landvættur soared over the ruined threshold of Reykjavík's walls, continuing its hateful rampage on the city. It decimated buildings with ease, its blood burning like acid where it fell. Its raging winds tore off roofs; lightning struck rapidly and fires soon broke out in multitudes. Finding little resistance now, the landvættur moved onwards into the city.

ᚼ

The song was at its crescendo when Elka screamed at another contraction, squeezing the Emissary's hand so tightly it hurt. His hand remained as firm as stone. She could see shadows swirling around him, which was impossible – it was the dark of night. Another contraction and all such thoughts were pushed to the back of her mind, buried in adrenaline and pain. With every contraction the song changed. The stone beneath her had changed shape, turning into a bowl.

A vessel for an ocean.

Elka didn't have to phrase her desire, as the Messengers approached her, lifting their hands and conjuring streams of saltwater. It was freezing cold and pure – an abyssal sea that had never felt the touch of daylight, easing her pain as she was bathed in the healing waters.

Her heart rate slowed. Another contraction was coming.

The island and the moon trembled with her ensuing pain, aching in anticipation.

Across the face of the lunar surface, a delicate, tiny crack had started to form. A canyon dozens of kilometres wide, hundreds of kilometres long.

The horned Emissary looked upon it with unrestrained delight.

ᚼ

The Stone Giant remained motionless.

Styrrún had fallen to her knees, pushing the limits of her innate ability to reach out to others and read their emotions, silently calling out to the sentience within for help, for it to gather the will needed to act, to move, to do *something*.

'*Sæmundur!*' she screamed at the silent rock. '*You can't do this to us!*'

'We're out of time!' Auður pointed at a nearby automobile – an older model. 'Eyvindur! Get that thing started!'

He and Halla ran over to it. She shattered a window effortlessly and he jumped in the driver's seat, getting to work on starting the engine.

'Styrrún!' Auður shouted. 'I told you trying to rouse the Stone Giant was useless! I told you Sæmundur was long gone – if it really is him in there!'

'He tore down the Nine, Auður! He broke down the walls! He can do it again, if he just—'

Auður marched up to Styrrún and grabbed her by the shoulders.

'He's fucking gone, Garún! He was a piece of shit, and if you don't remember that, then I know Styrhildur does! He killed my mother! He was ruthless and selfish! For fuck's sake, he turned the flying fortress into a fucking vortex of demons!'

Styrrún broke Auður's grip on her.

'And you want to bring it back! What does that make you?'

'I'll do whatever it takes to stop this from happening.' Auður's teeth chattered from the driving rain, but still she sounded grimly determined. 'Not a single weapon exists that isn't monstrous by nature. All that matters is who wields it. You've seen what Kári has seen. You know what happens if we fail to bring down the landvættur.'

The automobile's engine started.

'Once we believed that any price was worth paying. We learned the hard way just how high a toll that price entails. What use is saving a world where innocents pay in their own blood for salvation? A cursed weapon can only bring misfortune upon those who wield it. Go, if you truly believe the end justifies the means. We'll be here. We won't stop trying until the very end.'

'I'm staying with you,' said Diljá.

She reached out to Styrrún when she shook her head solemnly in response. They communed silently through depths unknown by the others waiting impatiently. Diljá's face changed. She looked crestfallen.

'*This path we must walk alone, sister.*' Styrrún took Diljá's hand in her own and placed something in it. '*For luck, you said all these years ago. We treasured it dearly. Now go.*'

'I'm not going with them.' Diljá looked back at Auður and the others. 'Conjuring that thing is my biggest regret. I don't repeat mistakes.'

Auður darkened with anger at her words. They got in the automobile and sped off.

The bracelet gleamed in Diljá's hand. It had been made by her mother. A gift to Garún. The silver was delicate as hoarfrost, precious stones luminescent with an inner light. The symbol of the Mountain Built from Sunlight, Láternýð, was at the centre. The mask of hope and solidarity.

Diljá gave Styrrún one last hug. There was nothing else to be said. She headed towards Starholt. Whatever was going to happen, it would spell tragedy for every living person in the city. She had to go and help her friends, her people, in whatever way she could.

Styrrún stood behind, out in the rain. She turned her gaze to the Stone Giant, reaching out to someone who was long lost in the vastness of the endless firmament.

ᚻ

The forest on Öskjuhlíð was barricaded by the wind, bending the tall conifers to the point of breaking. Perlan sat on top of the hill, a wonder of steel and glass, its dome shining from countless lights within. Approaching from the east was the landvættur, eyes and maw glowing with destructive energies, heading right towards the power plant.

Speeding towards the hill, the auto crashed through a fenced gate, powering up a muddy service road. A tree had fallen across the road so they got out and ran. The landvættur roared, drowning out the air-raid sirens and the storm.

Auður led them down a trail, easily missed in the darkness, heading into the forest. The air was thick with seiðmagn. No transformed beasts crossed their path – all of them were hiding within their burrows, hoping to wait out this storm.

They exited into a clearing, the rails leading from Svartiskóli up to the power plant right in front of them.

Auður pointed up the hill. The obsidian confinement was just ahead. The wind was so strong that they struggled to keep themselves standing. Drawing in seiðmagn, Kári found the strength he needed to power on, while Auður gasped for breath to chant a few words of power. Halla supported Eyvindur, lagging behind as she helped him fight on. Kári yelled at them to keep their distance, and to his relief they did so. Whatever was to come, they wouldn't be of much help.

Kári and Auður powered on towards the structure. In the clearing around the pyramid, they saw the city stretch out, fires raging across it, diminished by the torrential rain but still blazing regardless, more lightning striking every moment. As they reached the perimeter of steel poles surrounding the pyramid, they saw the landvættur soar over Perlan, circling it like a shark on the hunt. It amassed its power, lightning shooting erratically from its mouth, trailing thick dark clouds that magnified the storm. The blue-tinted bones of animals and humans were welded to the poles, forming a spiral shape with several arms reaching out from the central pyramid. Made from obsidian and covered in gold-inlaid galdrastafir and sigils, the pyramid had no obvious entrance.

Auður placed her hand on the black stone and spoke to it. It vanished, leaving behind a darkness as thick as the obsidian itself. They took one last look back towards the city. The Stone Giant stood as motionless as ever.

'I'm going in alone,' she said.

'When should I go in after you?'

'You don't.'

'What if you don't come back?'

'Then this is goodbye.'

Professor Auður Thorlacius walked into the tenebrous nothing.

The landvættur amassed its power over Perlan. Lightning struck the glass dome, once. Then again, and again. Systems started to fail in a cascading wave, lights flickering and then going out.

Kári believed in no gods. He wished he knew what to pray to.

ᚴ

Styrrún stood at the feet of the Stone Giant in the fierce gale winds. She placed her hand on its moss-covered stone.

'Do something right in your life, for once.'

A sleeping, dulled sentience within the rock stirred, weighed down by the all-encompassing might of the universe. She could feel it, hope rising in her chest. It slipped back, falling into the bottomless depths of ennui that had imprisoned it.

She cursed into the relentless gale and beat futilely against the unyielding stone.

The raging landvættur slammed into the roof of the power plant, shattering the glass. It rose up, ignoring the fresh cuts on its diseased flesh, and it gathered the storm inside its heart. Eyvindur and Halla pleaded for Kári to retreat, to get to shelter.

He told them to go – he would wait for the professor. The wound in his stomach squirmed and grew, making him nauseous.

Behind the thick clouds, pregnant with lightning and seið-magn, the surface of the moon cracked even further. An egg hatching.

On the turbulent sea, a small boat dropped anchor at the shores of Surtsey. An inflatable raft was thrown overboard.

Elka cried out.

She pushed harder.

Ægir's skin drooped, waxen. He looked very much like the drowned man he was fated to be, when his ship sank and the Deep claimed him.

An unsettling discharge cracked through the air in Reykjavík. The real felt thinned, diluted and weak – exposed for the fragile veil it was. Kári felt it and knew Auður had succeeded. He looked up and over the city, and saw a horror beyond the realm of actuality.

A colossal, bloated thing, writhing flesh and hateful steel intertwined in one, incomprehensible nightmare.

The demonic flying fortress known as Loftkastalinn.

Its massive tentacles tasted the air, its corpulent eyes jittering around frantically. It trembled with joyous exhilaration. Its chimneys, turned to bone and flesh, spewed out a terrible black smoke, descending rapidly on the city despite the raging weather. A vast pair of lips separated slightly, a crack that spread across the width of the demonic fortress, revealing rows upon rows of gargantuan human teeth.

Kári watched with awe at the landvættur drawing in all its gathered power, a titan from a long-lost era summoning its dying breath. The dark fortress started to move towards them, when explosions burst upon its surface.

The armada stationed in the bay was firing at it.

The great demon shifted its course, heading towards its delectable targets. More flesh, more steel, to corrupt and disfigure. Kári cried out in anger, his voice lost in the booming thunder.

Out of the corner of his eye, he saw a figure exiting the black pyramid. She was smiling, her eyes not turned to void – but something beyond nothingness. With sight beyond sight, he saw Auður's bones infested with transmundane corruption. She saw it, too, admiring her hands with a cold joy that spoke of terrors to come. The dreadful sight was too much for Kári. He turned and ran for his life.

The landvættur emitted a melancholy cry, through and into the storm raging around it.

The thing at the bottom of Öskjuhlíð responded.

A blast of energy was expelled from the landvættur's maw, bursting through Perlan's dome and layers of machinery, pulverising and melting its iron into slag, ploughing into those still waters at its base, breaching the arcane protections and multitudes of wards with ease. Still the landvættur kept on, even as flame and lightning broke through its stomach, flared through its exposed ribs, burning away flesh and consuming it from within.

Above Surtsey, above Reykjavík and Heimaey, above Hrímland and the planet itself, the moon trembled with cosmic force as something within it started to hatch in earnest.

The songs of the Deep wove a powerful incantation, one not heard on earth for untold ages. Reality flexed, became concave, ripped from the duress.

The moon was so close that Elka could touch it. She reached out a hand and stroked its surface, felt the thumping heartbeat resonating from within, its glowing silver umbilical cord coming down to her.

To her baby.

She sunk deeper into the birthing pool, bracing for the final push.

Elka screamed. And she pushed.

Lightning struck relentlessly as the thaumaturgical storm was expunged by the landvættur's dying breath into the earth, filling the dormant egg laid within Perlan with pure, primal chaos.

The landvættur shattered the world-egg buried within Öskjuhlíð.

And simultaneously, the child of the Deep, named Harbinger, Andrán and Mánaþjór, Griðungur and Grandröst and Jötuneykur, was born into this world.

Buildings trembled and collapsed as waves of powerful earthquakes went off, and in the distant mountains of Hrímland, vast plumes of smoke started to rise from long-dormant volcanoes. From the hypocentre of the burning crater a shift began to spread, a chain reaction of transmutation.

ᚻ

Kári felt the change wash over his broken body, face down in the singed grass. The blast had sent him flying to the ground; his back was scorched and several bones were broken, but he still lived. For the first time in this age, untainted seiðmagn flooded into the world like a sigh of relief. Reflexively, he drew it in to gather the strength needed to look back at the devastation and witness that fountain of sorcery come to life, erupting into the aether, re-forming and rearranging the laws of reality as it spread. As he mended his broken body, he found it shifting, responding like a wilted flower blessed with summer rain. The ivory tusks jutting from his stomach wound grew and spiralled together as the mutation developed uncontrollably. Then, as the clouds parted momentarily, letting the moonlight through, he witnessed another miracle.

As the child drew its first breath and let out a cry with breath-taking euphony, the moon cracked its shell, an unreality beyond nothingness writhing its way out like a thing alive.

The Pale King looked upon his age-old work unfolding, a prophecy older than mankind at long last fulfilled. There was no smile on his face, no satisfaction whatsoever. This was foretold – it had always been inevitable. He looked upon his great work with profound elation over what was now to come.

Elka placed the child on her chest, its feelers wrapping instinctively around her. A tendril wrapped itself around her finger, the grip surprisingly strong, and she wept with joy and relief. Looking down into its silvered eyes, she saw herself within those minuscule mirrors, yet it was more than just a reflection.

She felt the toxins numbing her senses evaporate, realising that it was by her doing they were cleansed from her body. Without realising it, she had drawn in that power she feared within her to ease the birth. Slowly, the hypercoloured currents of seiðmagn revealed themselves in all their majesty as her vision cleared, the island itself glowing with its latent power, and she wasn't afraid any more. The hideous beings before her – Ægir and the other humans who willingly played as puppets... all of them were weak compared to her. Elka knew who she was – and she was done with running away from that person.

She wept with joy as the child's harmonious voice cried out into the night.

Tuttugu og þrjú

Sölvi had run off as soon as they landed in Surtsey. He knew they were up there, at the top of a mountain. Where the silver thread was tethered to the moon. Styrmir called after him to wait, but he ignored him. He hadn't been able to see the tether. It was Sölvi who had to go.

The boat had almost capsized when another earthquake hit them close to the shore, the waves turning the sea unruly and vicious. It was pure luck that they hadn't both died. In that moment Sölvi saw what half the peoples of the world saw unfold in the night sky.

The moon had broken apart as an enormous crack appeared on its surface, splitting it down the middle. Huge chunks had broken off, each the size of a country. In that moment, it was as if something pushed its way out from the inside. A hatchling in an egg, not quite managing to break through. Sölvi's mind could almost perceive it, nearly comprehend it, but in an effort to survive, it stubbornly refused.

The sight broke something in Sölvi's soul. The world was not as it seemed. Everything was a lie. As he ran up the hillside, with those glowing, spiral-patterned plants all around him, those monstrous birds frantically crying above him, he cried. Everything was coming to an end.

His mother was lying peacefully in a stone-shaped bowl filled with water, a small baby crying on her chest. By her stood what he knew were the Messengers from the Deep. Ægir, Bryde and Björg were also there, grovelling in joy or terror, looking like wax figures of their usual selves. Sölvi saw their weakness laid bare and ignored their wretched forms.

'*Sölvi.*'

A giant as pale as the moon itself spoke to him, horns gnarled and entwined like the cold, uncaring night sky. Sölvi avoided looking him in the eyes. He did not want to know what it looked like, that void beyond. Before him stood the one they called the Emissary of the Deep. But Sölvi knew better. He knew what that thing truly was.

A sorcerer-king.

He ran to his mother, collapsing next to her in the pool.

'Sölvi!' she said happily, smiling as she hugged him close.

He cried, blathering about how angry he was, how afraid he had been, how horrible everything had become.

'Oh, elskan, please … please don't cry. Please don't be worried, everything is fine.'

She looked dreamily down at the infant resting on her chest. Sölvi now saw what it really was. A thing born on the threshold, belonging both to this world and the abyss beyond. An anchor, a tether, a bridge.

'*Isn't it beautiful?*' the Pale King said, a living shadow coiling around his body like black fire. '*Do you realise how fortunate you are to witness this sacred moment?*'

Sölvi turned away from the horrible thing, looking at his mother.

'Mamma, we have to go. Styrmir is here – we have a ship. Please, please, please, Mamma, please come with me. Please don't stay here.'

'Everything is fine, Sölvi,' she said, smiling. 'Everything is just perfect as it is.'

Within the moon, something pushed. Trying to break through. There were no stars visible around it, as though black ink had been spilled over the firmament.

Sölvi tried to calm himself, to think how he could reach his mother. She looked gone – so far gone, more than ever before. More than when he had found her, dazed on a sofa, eyes unseeing some distant reality, a dream that he could never reach. He wept and she stroked his cheek, pulling him in for another embrace.

Elka hushed him softly and made him look her in the face. There was a different look there now. Something he had never seen before.

'I'm sorry, Sölvi. I won't let anyone harm you – ever again. You don't have to be afraid – these things surrounding us are nothing but shades. I can see that now. Broken things that need to attach themselves to real, living things – parasites.'

She looked down at the newborn child, and he did so as well – at his tiny brother or sister lying peacefully on his mother. Its silver eyes met his and he knew that this was no shadow. This was a real, living thing. And as his grandmother had said, real, living people make their own destiny.

'This reminds me of you,' Elka said softly. 'Everything changed when you came into my life – for the better.' She kissed him on the forehead. 'I swore then to do everything I could for you. And although I might have stumbled, I intend to keep that promise.'

A delicate tether was right next to the flesh and blood one that connected the newborn's small body to Elka. She followed the lustrous, silvery umbilical cord all the way up towards the moon, where the world was slowly coming to an end.

It didn't strike her as bizarre in the slightest. She had always known it would come to this.

She grabbed it and ripped it apart with her teeth.

'No!' the Pale King shouted, his shadow flaring up in anger.

A look of utter, inhuman contempt darkened his face. The umbilical cord flailed, withering and growing fainter, more intangible. The Messengers from the Deep shrieked, raising their many wings in agitation, claws and tentacles poised for attack.

'You worthless idiot.'

The pale giant approached, the darkness strengthening around him. Sölvi threw himself up against his mother, who held him close.

'Do you believe yourself to be capable of thwarting fate itself? We will mend your pathetic attempt at disruption and resume our great work – as if nothing had happened. A fate worse than death awaits the both of you for that.'

He stopped as Elka rose from the pool, holding the child in her arm, the other wrapped protectively around Sölvi. Sölvi could feel warmth radiating from her – a strange sensation causing light to flare around them, tinted with colours not of this world.

'Are you threatening my child?' she asked calmly.

'Step aside, vessel,' the Pale King spat. 'You face one who has held the reins of the universe in his hands. Hand over the Harbinger.'

Elka held Sölvi and the child closely. The newborn's heart beat along with hers, the flesh umbilical cord still connecting them. Sölvi could feel the air thicken with something he had never felt before.

'Don't look, Sölvi,' she said, and he buried his face in her side.

A thing can be broken in many ways. It is usually only with sheer determination that anything can be so thoroughly broken that it can never be made whole again.

Sölvi was thankful his mother refused to let him see what

happened next. Hypercoloured flashes lit up the darkness behind his shut eyes. The sounds he heard in that moment would haunt him for the rest of his life.

ᚺ

The Stone Giant loomed over Styrrún as the world ended around her. Loftkastalinn, the great demon of flesh and steel wreathed in smoke, manifested in the sky like an old nightmare come to life. A semblance of sorrow washed over her, seeing that Auður had succeeded in her last, desperate resort. She was not surprised as it moved away from the approaching landvættur, gleefully wreaking havoc on the teeming life of the city and the armada stationed in the bay. When she had lived as Garún, she had thought that evil could be tamed for good.

Such callow dreams had been extinguished long ago.

She looked up at the silent edifice of rock. Inside was Sæmundur, dormant in his idiotic slumber, teeming with power that could reshape the foundations of reality. The Stone Giant had remained deaf to her pleading.

A confusing tirade of memories washed over her. Garún's memory had been ripped to shreds by the Directorate's agents, leaving her with only broken fragments and a cold-burning rage that refused to diminish. Fused with Styrhildur's mind, although rendered apathetic and callous from undeath, a new kind of clarity had revealed itself.

This world was doomed. As were all worlds, everywhere. A great betrayal of life was not needed, there was no need for esoteric rituals millennia long to unmake the universe. Reality was destined to unmake itself by design; it was by nature a fell ritual ending in cold, stark nothingness. Given enough time, all would become a clear and empty void that would not stir with life ever again.

The moon cracked above. The shock wave of Perlan igniting in a thaumaturgical blast of unreal colours shattered every window in the vicinity. Still, Styrrún stood unmoved, pondering the so-called landvættur before her.

Everything comes to an end. Why bother resisting that immovable force?

Except that Styrhildur and Garún had ended, had died in their own way, and still they stood here as one – as something new. Remade from broken shards and ruined memories, two lives woven together into something more – something greater – than they had been before.

So it could be for the world. Perhaps not this one – not yet, at least. Things must first break before they can be reforged, die before they can be reborn. Apathy was not an option – had never been an option. That had been Sæmundur's downfall – that, and his hubris. A refusal to care for anything except himself – the guiding light which had led him down the path of a practitioner of svartigaldur, resulting in this failure of a man. She would not wield such tools so carelessly. She would not let herself be consumed by that black flame.

'*Please*,' she asked the silent giant, reaching out her hand in a last attempt. '*Please give us what we need.*'

A movement in the stone, sending a small landslide of moss-grown rocks and gravel crashing to the paved cobblestones. The Stone Giant bowed down, leaning towards her with monumental lethargy.

Biðja – to ask, or to pray. She did both before the imprisoned monstrosity, and the uneven rock at its head spread apart like an organic thing to reveal a limp arm no longer human, covered in rough scales and rows of mismatched teeth like mountain ridges down the forearm. The hand was cluttered with digits, each different and useless, a glazed-over, multi-irised eye in the centre of the palm.

She reached out for the hand and grasped it tightly.

The shock of transcendent revelation hit her like lightning. Gritting her teeth, forging her wilful determination and rage into a tool, she grounded the Stone Giant's might in herself.

But unlike Sæmundur, she did not let go. She did not wholly accept that tantalising offer of godlike might and comprehension. Sæmundur tried to pull away, tried to shield himself from the pain and suffering that was life itself, but she would not allow him that cowardly luxury. With a trembling head, she turned towards the moon and saw a thin silver cord leading down from it towards the earth. She could feel everything, everywhere at once, from the minutest of atoms to collapsing stars on the other end of the galaxy.

A tug on the silver cord made it tremble. With her heightened senses, she felt a distant burning might sever it.

The world shook from the recoil.

Everything inevitably comes to an end. She saw that within a tempest of shifting futures, as time unwound before her in maddening clarity. But that great dissolution would not happen at this moment.

Everything was about to change. It was time for her to let the cards fall where they may. She would not become a new tyrant, a dread overlord dictating the order of the world to suit her liking. Instead, she desired to create – to mend something ruined.

Looking in a direction neither of this place or time, she stared into another world. A broken fragment of reality, a shattered vista that had long ago been reduced to nothing by an apocalyptic unmaking.

A fire she had thought extinguished was relit within her. It was time to make something new.

And she stepped through into that place, dragging the feeble-minded giant with her.

ᚺ

The boat cleaved through the waves as morning winter light tinted the sky a faint pink. Sölvi sat next to his mother, who held him and the baby close, whispering to both of them that everything would be all right – she would never let anyone hurt them.

They passed the islands of Vestmannaeyjar. Dark smoke rose up in a vast cloud from Heimaey. The dormant volcano had erupted with brutal force, having been unnaturally held back for decades. The Wanderer, a massive piece of the volcano that had halted just by Skansinn, had reignited with a ferocity of a magnitude greater than before. As the lava started to flow wildly, it had finally crashed into the fortress, rendering it instantly a ruin. Now, nothing remained. The harbour had been sealed off by the lava flow. They watched the catastrophe unfold in silence. It was nothing compared to what lay ahead.

They were now more visible, as the morning light etched their outlines clearly against the sky. Vast plumes of smoke rose to blot out the fading stars, while violent fires were visible on a few of the mountains, even from their distance.

On the Hrímlandic mainland ahead, every volcano in sight on the southern coastline was erupting simultaneously.

The Mist Hardships had begun.

IV

MÓÐUHARÐINDIN
—
THE MIST HARDSHIPS

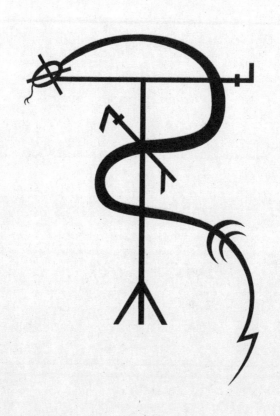

They say that once the world was wild with sorcerous power. That when the earth still lived, in ceaseless transmutation, the ancient poetry was sung pure and untarnished.

They also say that the earth is dying.

The evidence of its final hours is laid bare for all to see: only a handful of places are left in the world where the raw, living lifeblood of creation runs free. When those last embers are extinguished, when those final wells run dry, will there be any magic left in the world? Or will we live out our lives on a husk, a cooling corpse, never knowing what wonders it once held?

Some say that the earth is dormant.

Returning from that dreamless coma will be a rude awakening. Atrophied muscles once more in motion, a mind calmed by an aeon-long emptiness boiling with a cacophony of thought and emotion.

Broken chains leave deep wounds. A renewal of such nature can be naught but painful.

Stories are the lies you must tell yourselves in order to survive. There are far too many things left unsaid. Only one thing is certain:

With painful gasps, the earth draws breath once more.

Tuttugu og fjögur

Ten years later

The northern mountains were unchanged, capped with snow in the early spring as if unwilling to relinquish the calm and dread silence of the winter dark. Silent and majestic, they brought a sense of calm to the lone traveller making his way along the ancient cairn path, the once overgrown and disused trail now beaten into a single-file track threading its way between isolated bastions of civilisation – such as they were in the remoteness of Hrímland. The wanderer wore a fine woollen coat and tall leather boots, both worn from years of trekking from fishing village to fishing village, turf house to turf house. A wooden trunk was strapped to his back; the load was heavy and his posture was bent. His face was covered by a coarse grey scarf to spare him the sting of the cold and the ashen, toxic air carried from the still-active volcanoes. Sölvi Helgason made his way down into the fjord.

Over the years the north country had become something re-sembling home. These mountains knew him and he knew them. On many a night they had been his only companions, as he lay beneath bright summer skies, or sheltered from a blizzard by digging into frost-hardened snow. At those times loneliness set upon him, bittersweet in the summer and suffocating in winter. But with the mountains he was never truly alone. Most of his paintings reflected this, with the mountains either as the work's main focus or always looming in the background, watching.

Coming down from the frostbitten peaks and plateaus, the span of ceaseless white turned to flecks on the slopes, eventually receding to the yellow-dead colours of spring. Eyjafjörður stretched before him, a long and beautiful fjord littered with small farmsteads on each side, many of them now abandoned due to the hardship and death caused by the eruptions. He headed west, towards the peninsula of Tröllaskagi. Rare was the traveller who made their way across those ancient mountains, carved by ice ages long past, rumoured to be infested with rampant trolls once again, which is what had originally given the peninsula its ominous name.

Before him stretched the sea, dull green beneath the overcast sky. He walked all the way down to the cliffs, making a small detour to stand there and look out over the fjord's vastness, watching the white-frothing waves beat against the stones, breaking over small outcroppings in sudden fury. Polishing them down from jagged edges to smooth stone. The man didn't fear the sea any more. Now, he celebrated each wave and fearlessly rejoiced in that furious war of shore and sea.

The books weighed heavily on his back; his small library accounted for much of his travelling weight. Sölvi put down the old, beaten wooden trunk with relief. It was fitted with straps and cleverly made canvas bags and pockets to hold other earthly possessions. Despite the weight, it was as light as a feather to him – for what could be more valuable than knowledge and art? Could a traveller carry supplies more necessary to survival than that? On his aching back was no dead weight, but the wisdom of the ancients – a fountain of knowledge, immortal artworks that would outlast everyone who lived.

Opening the trunk, Sölvi fetched a small painting he had received as a gift. Most of his possessions were such treasures, heirlooms given in gratitude for his help. The work had been an ugly portrait of a boat, lacking both craftsmanship and artistry. A dull vision made by a dull person. He assembled his travelling easel and attached the painting to it as securely as he could. The wind beat the artist and his work savagely but, muttering a short verse and cutting a simple sigil-cross in the ground, he diverted the gust around him, reducing it to a pleasant breeze. Painting over the ugly boat, he captured the view before him – as seen through his own vision, filtering it through his sensitive, artistic soul, elevating the mundanity of reality.

The dull green turned a weathered emerald, streaked with blue to bring out the mysteries of the sea. Not as that hideous cult had seen it, but as a free man would see it – a thing of beauty, promise and freedom. The pathway to the uncharted world – the road to civilisation. The mountains became as mighty lords and ladies, benevolent guardians of the farmsteads littering their lower slopes, with friendly smoke now curving up from every chimney. Here were no cold hearths, no collapsed roofs and mouldy beds. A single wooden house stood out in the fjord, the manor of Dauðsmýri – thus named even if it was nothing more remarkable than any two-storey house in a fishing village of moderate prosperity. Through him, it was given an air of regality, its roof vibrant red instead of rust-spotted, the corrugated iron dressing every wall in pristine white. A refuge from what this harsh land offered for those of higher sensibilities. Here was a place where book-learning could fill your food bowl so high the lid couldn't even be properly shut.

Deciding his work was at least good enough for the madam's

easily manipulated standards, Sölvi dipped his brush in a translucent varnish and painted a symbol on the back of the canvas. Muttering to himself, he could feel the working take hold – a particularly clever hex of his own making. Satisfied, he packed up his belongings and shouldered the heavy trunk, carrying the still-wet painting to the haven that awaited him.

Behind him, a strange shape ascended the mountains. It was gaunt and alabaster white, its limbs too long, its back stooped and its head heavy with a crown of pitch-black antlers. Sölvi did not need to look back to know it was there. It was always there.

Often he had partaken of the generosity of the madam of Dauðsmýri. He was thankful news travelled slow – the volcanic flows, toxic gases and turbulent thaumaturgical storms hindered travel between the eastern provinces and the north, limiting the number of the madam's guests who made their way from there. It made his visits that much more thrilling.

Dauðsmýri was located square in the middle of a mire, rust-red and vast. Once, it had been named after the colour of the water, but after the mists descended its name had changed. A suggestion of a path snaked through the tall grass, and Sölvi had to take great care not to slip and fall knee-deep into the water, potentially damaging the painting. The mire had been quite properly drained, the madam frequently said; all of this had once been green pasture. But the mire had returned when the hardships began, and had become immune to any efforts to restrain it. Then the mists came, and long-forgotten dead left in that mire centuries ago rose from their wet graves. Sölvi knew why the mire could not be contained, but he wasn't about to offer that knowledge to the madam. Even he would not want to anger a vættur by upsetting their domain.

Managing to get through the mire without any major mishaps, though his tall boots were quite splattered with fresh mud, he smiled and waved as the front door opened and the voluminous skirts of the madam of Dauðsmýri came out to meet him.

'Good day, my lady!' he shouted merrily.

'Oh! Master Gyldenlöve, I was hoping it was you!' said the woman in shrill excitement. 'How wonderful to see you!'

Her once noble dress was showing its years, much like the lady herself, its skirts so plentiful it made it hard to move in. It was the kind of thing an upper-class lady would have worn several years before, Sölvi understood. Saving the madam's collection of dresses had been a high priority when she and her husband evacuated the ruined capital a decade ago.

'Stefanía!' she shouted into the house. 'Get out here and help Master Gyldenlöve with his luggage!'

'That will be quite all right, madam,' chuckled Sölvi, knowing all too well that displays of chivalry were a huge soft spot of hers. 'Trouble not your maid to assist me with such trifling matters. I would much appreciate her efforts being directed into putting the kettle on, if you would be so kind.'

The madam nodded, shouting again into the house for the maid to prepare coffee.

Such a shame that turn of phrase hasn't faded, ruminated Sölvi as he placed his heavy burden by the steps leading up to the front door. Coffee had become more precious than gold in Hrímland.

It hurt to think back on the last time he had tasted it. He quickly buried that memory deep, back where it belonged.

He walked up the stairs and bowed ceremoniously, taking the madam's outstretched hand and kissing it in a gentlemanly fashion. She giggled like a maiden, but he had eyes only for the shining rings on her plump fingers. A few of those and he might be able to buy himself passage to the mainland – not that he'd ever happened upon a ship crossing the Atlantean.

One day.

The madam of Dauðsmýri eyed the painting he was carrying, covered with linen cloth now that it had dried well enough.

'Another one of your masterpieces, I trust?'

'I will show you inside, madam. While I was taught by my father that hauteur was an unseemly trait, I daresay I do not risk offending his efforts to make a humble man out of me by saying it is one of my very best works – completed here in Eyjafjörður, as well.'

She beamed at hearing this.

He was led inside by the giggling madam. She had always been called 'madam'; her husband was also only known by his title, and both took grievous offence to anyone who used their given name. Her title gave off an air of the mainland, with it being a loan word from Nordic. Sölvi suspected that the fine ladies of Kalmar did not use this title in such a manner, that it in fact might have a very indecent association abroad – but he'd rather bite off his tongue than point this out to the lady herself.

The house was old and rickety, its floorboards worn and creaking. It had once been grand enough and still was lovingly maintained, in a way. It was only the lack of supplies, craftsmen, and what counted for real currency these days that held them back. A silver chandelier, polished religiously, loomed over the foyer. A wide, carpeted stairway led up to the first floor, the maroon rug faded from sunlight and threadbare from years of use.

'How wonderful to see you in such good health, madam. I trust my salves worked well?'

'Oh, yes, they were a miraculous wonder!'

She patted her red cheeks, flushed with rouge. She must have rushed to apply make-up before coming to see him, which was reassuring. Word of his reputation had still not reached her ears.

'Superb. I will be sure to mix further ointments, from freshly gathered herbs on my travels around the mountains.' In truth, the salves were quite useless. But they did smell nice enough. 'I tell you, my lady, there exists no finer nature than the Hrímlandic wilderness – resplendent in beauty and overflowing with beauteous gifts, much as yourself.'

She blushed even more deeply and lightly patted his arm, using the opportunity to grasp it.

'Master Gyldenlöve, I know full well I am no blooming rose!'

He struggled, trying to recall the botanical texts he had glanced through years before. He had been more interested in the illustrations found within them rather than the text itself. Sölvi had never seen a real rose in his entire life – but Master Gyldenlöve surely had.

'Ah, but the rose that has bloomed already is much the more beautiful. Well preserved, its beauty lasts forever.'

'Oh, hush, now. You make an old woman feel even older with remarks such as these. Your magisterial training is wasted on the likes of me – you should be out there doing the Commonwealth's work.'

'That I am, my dear madam, do not worry about that,' he reminded her. 'I've seen many a wondrous thing, both natural and supernatural, on my travels. All logged and dutifully studied for the benefit of the king himself. And your husband's treatments... how are they progressing?'

A flicker betrayed her shift in mood. 'Quite well, I think. We administer the medicines as per your instructions each night. But...'

She drifted off, not knowing how to phrase her thoughts. Sölvi gave a thoughtful nod.

'You're not seeing any visible change yet. Do not worry, madam. The inner must heal first before the outer reflects it. It's worked for many others before.'

'I know, of course – please take no offence. I do not mean to question your admirable reputation.'

'None taken. The journey to healing is a hard one. Stay the course and you'll find your way there.'

Now beaming again, she led him into the dining room, where the maid was laying out a table – a veritable feast in Sölvi's eyes. Soft-boiled eggs, cold liver sausage, a porridge with a large bowl of cinnamon sugar next to it, salted meats and smoked fish, rye bread and butter. Real sugar. She was pulling out all the stops. An intoxicating scent rose from a shining silver pot the maid brought in with a great show of reverence, making Sölvi freeze in pure astonishment.

'Is that actually ... coffee?'

Sölvi was so stunned that he missed his opportunity to drag out the madam's chair as she sat down at the table, his façade of manners falling for a moment.

'Only the best for the prestigious scholar. Please, sit.'

He did so, entranced by the smell of real coffee – strong, black coffee.

The scent took him back in an instant. He'd last had coffee with Styrmir in Vestmannaeyjar, when he was just a child. The smell was too overwhelming for him to smother the recollection. A lump rose in his throat, refusing to give way as he tried to swallow it down.

'Madam, I hope you don't mind me asking ... but how?'

She gave him a cunning look. 'It shames me to admit that this country life has been hard on me – and I know, Master Gyldenlöve, me, of all people! Truly, country living is the most pure and wholesome way to live, but to be deprived of so many things one once took for granted, starved of any news of the outside world ... Well, that is only one of the ways your visits have become a blessing to this household, Master Gyldenlöve.

I keep regularly in touch with an old friend, the vicar in Dulvík – Reverend Hákon. You see, he used to be a man of means – or ... well, his family was. His brother, Þorlákur Árnason, was quite the character. Coming from a humble upbringing, he worked his way up to have several companies and enterprises.'

'So he was a member of Innréttingarnar?' risked Sölvi.

'Rightly so! Yes, he and Sheriff Skúli were the most daring of the entrepreneurs in that wonderful organisation. Their works have so improved the quality of life for everyday Hrímlanders – all of Dulvík's fishing industry was established by Þorlákur. He passed away in the ... travesty that befell Reykjavík, sadly.'

'How sad,' said Sölvi, placing his hand over hers in a presumptuous show of compassion. She gave him a look and he pulled it back, flustered. 'It was such a horrible affair.'

'Yes, indeed,' she said, her tone now cold. Lingering on the disaster that had ruined her had been his mistake. 'Anyway, to my surprise Reverend Hákon said that he had got word of a ship coming in carrying some rare goods – designated for the civil servants of the Crown still upholding their duty.'

'Of course.'

She was momentarily distracted. 'I do hope the captain will deal with those awful heathens in Dulvík – not to belittle your efforts in any way. The poor priest says he gets barely a soul to church these days. They're all gathering around that devilish plant.'

Sölvi ignored that last comment, a retread of older conversations. When the mists descended on Dulvík, they had brought ruin. Livestock and people were felled by their poison; the village was temporarily abandoned. When the mists lifted and the people returned, things had changed, as in Dauðsmýri – but more drastically so. The madam believed Sölvi could help them get rid of what the mists had grown, and he had happily kept her on the hook for months. He struggled to decide how to enquire further about the ship without revealing his intentions. Where was it heading next? He ached at the unbidden thought that rose up strongly in him – a desire to let everything go, to burn every bridge, to forget about all the pain the last decade had brought him, and just leave. Never to come back to this desolate island, abandoned by all gods. It might be his only chance.

He noticed by the look on the madam's face that her mood had soured. Sölvi had not been able to mask his eagerness. That was the way with all these faux-nobilities that infested the countryside like vermin on a dunghill. They hoarded every advantage, every connection, every gram of privilege. She knew she was better than all of the common folk – even Sölvi, with his backstory of prestigious pedigree. He suspected she now only humoured him by pretending to believe it. At first he'd been greeted as a blessing – a learned man of Kalmar who promised to cure her husband and eradicate Dulvík's enthralling bloom. He knew his story barely held water when put under serious inspection. But they were desperate for a saviour. Unfortunately, he felt they didn't deserve to be saved.

It was not in Sölvi's nature to be outcast or servile. It was below him to bow to the whims of stupid and ignorant people. He was born for something greater – to study all knowledge, to create immortal artworks, to amass a fortune, to travel the world, free and independent, to struggle and emerge victorious, to fight and triumph, to rule and issue commands.

'I wonder if the captain was a companion of my father,' he said, trying to take back control of the conversation. 'I assume it was a Kalmar captain?' She nodded in affirmation, holding whatever knowledge she had of the ship closer to her chest than her pearls. 'My father, as I'm sure I've told you, served for quite a while in the Kalmar navy. A captain himself. He led many a naval battle against the enemy in the Great War.'

'Oh, yes, you have mentioned this before. Where was he stationed?'

A man came thumping down the stairs, thankfully sparing Sölvi from having to concoct a lie that might not accurately reflect his previous narrative.

Rows of four eyes lined the man's face above his mouth, making his head unnaturally elongated, with a triangle of three more eyes sprouting at his chin. The third pair of eyes from the top were pitch-black, as though liquid swirled within them.

Sölvi had made a point of never batting an eyelid when seeing the bailiff. Keeping his composure neutral was proving to be increasingly challenging. Every time was more unsettling than the last, as more changes manifested in the madam's husband.

No one knew what had happened to the bailiff. Anyone who asked was punished, directly or indirectly. Some said he had been attacked by demons in Reykjavík and was now only masquerading as a man. Others said he had been normal when he fled the city, but had been transformed when he met two other men on his way north – that he, a sheriff and a magistrate had melted together into one, horrific mess when lost in the mists. Others said it had been done in a fell ritual, to consolidate their power.

Whatever the truth, the bailiff and the madam had definitely been of some importance in Reykjavík and had rushed here to claim the vacant throne of the county's king – which was no understatement, as the couple certainly thought of themselves as royalty. From where Sölvi stood, they were more akin to vermin, decorated with stolen feathers. No doubt their wilful hiding of their names indicated a troubled past.

The bailiff shook Sölvi's hand firmly, the smile and multi-tudinous eyes not obscuring his brooding look at finding the traveller in his house once again.

'Sólon,' he said. 'You're back.'

'Bailiff. Indeed, my travels have been most enlightening – as I was just informing the madam.'

'No doubt.' He spoke this time with an entirely different voice. He had three varieties in total, which had likely given birth to the rumours surrounding his condition. Sometimes he shifted mid-sentence, which had a most uncanny effect. The man sat down with a huff. Sölvi decided not to let the slight pass unmentioned.

'And I would prefer it if you used my full name when addressing me, as befits my standing. Magisterial Master Sólon Crymogaius Benedicti Gyldenlöve.'

'Wasn't your name shorter the last time you were here?' the bailiff grumbled.

'I merely shortened it for your convenience. Simply Magister or Master Gyldenlöve will suffice, should it prove too long for you.'

The bailiff attacked the spread with fervour and the madam gave Sölvi an apologetic look, offering him a plate of cold liver sausage, which he accepted amicably. She never betrayed a hint of outright disgust at her husband's appearance. Her thin veneer of courtesy did that for her.

'Master Gyldenlöve, did you find any remedies for our problem in Dulvík? Exorcisms, or some kind of pesticide which will kill that cursed plant? Even svartigaldur is not too dire a measure to be considered.'

'I've made several enquiries. I have high hopes of them yielding results the next time I make my way back.'

'Do you hear that, dear?' The madam dropped another spoon-ful of sugar into her cup. 'We'll be rid of this horror in no time.'

The bailiff grunted with disappointment. 'By then it might be too late. The people are losing their faith in the king and the Ancestral Throne. That demonic weed is fomenting disorder in the county.' He put down his fork in distaste and his voice shifted. 'It does things to people – their minds. As a *man of Kalmar* surely you must be worried hearing this. And no doubt, travelling for your *research*, you have no doubt come across similar circumstances – if not worse.'

The sardonic emphases didn't go unnoticed. As always, Sölvi ignored the remarks.

'Deviations of this sort are part of my research, dear bailiff, as you know. All my findings must be kept secret by nature, as per my agreement with the Crown.'

The bailiff huffed. 'At least the captain was more forthright in his travel descriptions.'

Hearing this worried Sölvi, but he couldn't resist taking the bait after the bailiff's belittling attitude.

'Oh? You met the captain yourself?'

The bailiff didn't respond, a grimace passing over his face like a dark cloud.

'So, how long are you staying this time?' he asked as he poured himself a cup of coffee.

'Not long. I must see to some business in Dulvík. Perhaps you could tell me where I might approach the captain of the ship which brought you these delicacies? I have important documents that must make their way to the mainland as soon as possible.'

'Huh. I would have thought the royal university, or whoever it was sponsoring you, would have arranged for such a thing.'

'Quite right – and they did. But my findings have been quite more considerable than I expected. My stay in Hrímland will have to be prolonged, I suspect, and so it would be best for me to write to them post-haste to ask for more funding, as well as deliver some of my research notes.'

The bailiff considered this. He'd initially hoped Sölvi could rid him of the thing in Dulvík – and with it the cult around it – but this supposedly esteemed guest had proven to be more than useless, nothing but tall tales and empty promises. Not to mention the fact that this penniless scholar, who preyed on their good nature and loyalty to Kalmar, might then actually end up covering at least some of the extravagant lifestyle he had demanded. The prospect of being rid of this leech was obviously more than a little enticing.

'The ship is still in port, so you're in luck. Captain Tordenskjold is a great naval hero.'

'I believe my father mentioned him once or twice in my youth,' said Sölvi, weighing up how he might proceed without shooting himself in the foot. 'Although my papers should be more than satisfactory, I fear it might still be a hassle to acquire a private audience with the captain.'

The bailiff eyed him suspiciously with several pairs of eyes. The swirling of the black orbs shifted.

'Your father?'

'My adoptive father, of course.' Sölvi struggled not to betray his nervousness.

'We would be more than willing to write you a letter of introduction,' said the madam. 'Wouldn't we, dear?'

'Yes...' said the bailiff grudgingly. 'Of course.' He cleared his throat. 'And the... other treatment?'

Sölvi dabbed his lip with a napkin. 'The doses are already prepared, of course. Ointments and elixirs, infused with purified gemstones laden with restorative power.'

The madam placed a comforting hand on the bailiff's arm, smiling sweetly through her disgust.

Sölvi's heart was rushing from the deceit as much as the coffee. He'd had a few cups too many, unwilling to let a single drop of the brew go to waste. The bailiff and the madam indulged him by supplying more than was perhaps healthy. They also had trouble restraining their indulgence. Every Hrímlandic home, rich and poor, usually served a herbal brew of wild thyme. It was supposedly good for the digestion and preventive against the year-round Hrímlandic cold, but Sölvi hated it. It was a crude drink for crude people, tasting of bitter dirt. So it was no wonder that his fellow countrymen, who worshipped the dirt above all, who could see no higher beauty or purpose in this world, were so fond of it. Coffee was something else – sophistication and culture, a cup filled with the warmth and light of distant shores, where the sun shone warmly the year round and a free man could go where he pleased.

Their business being adjourned, Sölvi showed the madam the new painting, and as he'd expected she was enthralled by it – quite literally. She gushed about his transcendent artistic vision, his pure way of seeing the beauty of this land. Sölvi agreed, biting back bitter comments about Hrímland.

These pawns masquerading as kings can keep it, he thought. *Let them have all of it, like ravens feast upon a half-rotten ram.*

Excusing himself, claiming weariness from his travels, he retired to the master bedroom. This was the main reason the bailiff was so sick of his presence, as the madam had demanded that such a learned and noble guest could not be housed in any room other than the grandest available. Sölvi had demurred weakly, raising only the minimum of protest to keep up a façade of courtesy. He might not be of any bloodline that these people acknowledged, but he knew that he was of more noble birth than anyone else in this godforsaken country. Whenever he could, he would get his due.

He dozed for an hour on the huge, soft bed, not bothering to undress or wash before throwing himself on the clean white linen. Reluctantly, he rose at twilight and assembled his easel and paints, familiar with how he wanted his artist's studio – or so he thought of the room when he was there – to be set up.

Only stopping briefly to go down to supper, at which he reminded the bailiff of the letter, he went back upstairs to continue working by candlelight. Late that evening, he asked the maid to bring him another pot of coffee and something to eat, and to have a bath prepared for him.

He felt like a king. Doubtless, one would have to search far across Hrímland to find a person surrounded by more extravagance than he now had. Halfway through a painting of a peculiar cluster of flowers he had come across, referring to his sketchbook to refresh his memory, he went to the bathroom and soaked in the warm water for what felt like hours. His blistered feet, hardened by countless miles of walking in the wilderness, were thankful for the reprieve. His joints ached, worn and sore from carrying his burden over mountains and untouched valleys. He breathed a sigh of relief. Soon, this life would be his – truly his. That letter would be his ticket out of here.

ᚻ

Afraid that Captain Tordenskjold would depart, Sölvi went to Dulvík after breakfast the next morning. The madam lent him one of their horses – a fine steed, a red roan stallion which had shed its chestnut winter coat, revealing the pale grey beneath. Its head remained brown, its mane tinted with red. A beautiful horse, the pride of Dauðsmýri, explained the madam. The horse was named Glanni.

Sölvi wasn't too keen on the name. It was a word for a reckless person, or a rogue, connotations he wasn't too keen to be associated with. Still, he took the horse without remark. The people of Dulvík would know that only a prestigious person would ride into town on such an esteemed stallion.

Most Hrímlandic fishing villages are cold and depressing places. A cluster of shacks and turf houses, monuments to the poverty and hardship that characterises daily life in Hrímland.

Dulvík was no exception.

It was a sizeable village, true enough, though still nothing more than a collection of ramshackle houses, an occasional building of acceptable standards, built by wealthy shipowners.

One structure stood out like a skuggabaldur in a henhouse. Located on the outskirts of the village, upon a hill overlooking the area, was a wide manor house on two floors that was split into southern and northern wings. It had been a school that had showed its age before it fell to ruin, clad with corrugated iron that should have been replaced decades ago. In front of the manor was a gravel yard with rusted playground equipment, overrun with wild weeds. The manor was of such high craftsmanship that it felt bizarrely out of place compared to the architecture of the other village houses.

Except for the fact that a gigantic plant had burst through its roof. A massive bulbous growth culminated in a crimson bloom eclipsing the main building. Stems and vines as thick as tree trunks broke through windows and doors. It swayed gently in the breeze. A few white tents had been put up in the adjacent fields, from which the growing cult that worshipped it operated. *Harmless*, Sölvi thought half-heartedly, knowing full well what turns peculiar religions might take given enough time to grow. In any case, it was a clear threat to the bailiff's already weak hold on the village. Who in their right mind would worship a distant and negligent Kalmar king, when a manifestation of the divine had grown on their doorstep?

On a full moon when the northern winds blew in, the people of Dulvík barricaded their doors and windows as the plant released a cloud of spores into the air, which were carried far away by the strong ocean gales. A few radical believers often ventured out on such nights. They were never seen again.

Sölvi paid the plant no mind. Such things were commonplace, even if no two incidences were alike. There did not exist a place in Hrímland which had been untouched by the changes wrought by the eruptions. He rode into town, head held high, basking in the awe the villagers had for the gentleman scholar's arrival.

The pier and harbour were proportionally many times larger than the small village would normally require. It was now bereft of many of its fishing vessels, but a few still lingered, rusting and poorly maintained.

A large ship was docked, an ironclad frigate that made the other vessels look like scrap iron, with large cannons mounted at front and back, as well as a harpoon that was far too big to be used on any whale. Significant damage had been done to the starboard hull: huge perpendicular tears in the metal, as if from enormous claws; corroded and melted metal in splotches all over the deck. The tall tales of sea monsters plaguing the Atlantean were obviously true.

The name *Vindhund* proudly decorated its side. Sölvi's Nordic was rusty, but to any Hrímlander the name was obvious: Wind-Hound. Despite the name, the warship looked fast and sleek, built to prioritise speed over all else. Likely it was intended to outrun the monsters instead of fighting them head-on.

'You there, soldier,' he said in accented Nordic to one of the guards at the gangway to the ship. 'I am Magister Sólon. I wish to speak to Captain Tordenskjold.'

The soldier had been prepared to tell him to get lost, but the magisterial title made him hesitate.

'Do you have any papers, Magister?'

Sölvi reached into his satchel and tossed a ragged bundle of pale leather to the soldier, who caught it with a start. He unfolded it to see the ruined mess of a beaked mask. He looked upon Sölvi with dread.

'Here are my papers.' With the man sufficiently intimidated, Sölvi gracefully handed the soldier a letter, which the man accepted with a trembling hand. 'Take this to the captain. And hurry!'

The soldier snapped to and almost bolted up the gangway and boarded the ship.

Sölvi leaned back in the saddle, making himself comfortable. His little stunt had not gone unnoticed by the other soldiers at the pier. He felt the way they had elevated him in their minds as a person of importance, a superior officer. This would be a cakewalk. The soldier returned and bade Sölvi to follow him. He tethered his horse to a nearby stack of pallets and boarded the ship, straight-backed and chin up.

His confident manner wavered when he entered the gloom of the captain's quarters and was faced by a severe man sitting behind a desk stacked with maps and papers. Next to him stood a fully robed royal seiðskratti.

The iron door shut behind him with a clang. It sounded like a sentence being carried out. Sölvi wanted to bolt, now dreadfully aware of the seal-bone amulet hidden behind his shirt, carved with a dark reddish-brown symbol coloured by his own blood. Þekkur was a galdrastafur of charm and likability. Sölvi had slightly modified it, finding its intended effect to be rather limited in scope, symptomatic of whatever peasant kuklari had come up with it long ago. He had amplified the symbol's power considerably, with twisting branches laden with runes of power, a smooth curve multiplied within itself on the stave's side. Not that it had been easy – he'd burned many a bridge behind him out east, experimenting with the adjustments.

Another object hung around his neck, encased in a small wooden capsule – a shining cord of silver, not having faded or decomposed at all in the decade since it was severed. A piece of ethereal flesh, as pale white as the moon.

The moon.

He shuddered to think about that cracked shell in the sky.

The captain turned over the forged mask in his hand, inspecting it carefully before his eyes turned to Sölvi like the soot-black maws of cannons.

'*Magister,*' the captain said calmly. 'Please sit.'

Sölvi couldn't help but eye the seiðskratti standing next to him. They looked frail, worn-out and hunched over, as if merely standing there was causing them pain. Their back was hunched, a hump rising from their shoulders beneath their clothes. They wore deep crimson robes, set with arcane runes and sigils Sölvi had never seen before. His mind immediately went to speculating their esoteric meaning. The mask eyed him through the red lenses, the beak eerily still.

It was as though the seiðskratti was made of stone. Sölvi sat down opposite Captain Tordenskjold and started to introduce himself when the man interrupted him.

'The bailiff has told me much about Sólon Gyldenlöve – the king's bastard. Although I hesitate to believe a single word that monster says. The so-called madam especially was quite enthusiastic about this scholar sent on a mission by King Jörundur's decree. Apparently to investigate the supernatural anomalies of Hrímland for the Royal University.'

Sölvi gulped. 'Ah, yes. That is indeed my mission here, Captain

Tordenskjold. I have the papers to prove it, as well as my pass-port.'

This last lie was said with utmost confidence. Believe the lie, and it becomes truth. So many people spent their lives believing lies, after all. It was a fundamental aspect of human nature, in Sölvi's opinion, and he intended to leverage that to his advantage at any turn. The letter of introduction was lying open on the captain's desk. Sölvi had taken great care to read it beforehand without disrupting the wax seal. He wondered if the tampering had escaped notice.

Captain Tordenskjold reached out a hand. Sölvi reached into his satchel and handed the other documents to Tordenskjold, who started to read them closely.

They were his finest work yet. Copied with razor-sharp preci-sion, down to the royal stamp and the university's emblem, based on examples found in an old bookshop in Skuggafjörður which was selling off the possessions of their former sheriff. They had executed the man for draining the county dry by raising the tithe, year after year. Stealing the books from the shop had been easy work.

'Magister Ginfaxi,' the captain said lazily as he read on, holding up the ruined mess of pale leather. 'What do you make of this mask here?'

'A pathetic forgery,' hissed the seiðskratti. 'Of our most sacred item, no less. An idiot could see it for what it is – scraps of bleached sheepskin cut and stitched by a child.'

'Indeed. And a capital offence, at that.'

Sölvi considered feigning offence but decided against it. Instead, he sat calmly – cooly – feigning being in control. The sweat on his forehead betrayed him.

'The same, however, cannot be said of these papers. You could take this to Hafnía and I daresay they'd reprint your diploma in

a heartbeat. As would be the case with me, were it not for this …
unusual statement of character. In your passport, of all places.'

Sölvi arched an eyebrow. 'Oh? I think you'll find the statement to be fully accurate.'

The captain leaned over the papers and read out loud.

'"The county magistrate of Northern Múlasýsla makes it
known that Master silver- and goldsmith, painter and scholar
m. m. Magister Sólon Crymogaius Gyldenlöve requests of me
today a passport from Northern Múlasýsla for the eastern,
southern, and northern quarters of Hrímland for various necessary business. Among his other errands, he intends to stay in
some counties on this journey as a scholar, one who is greater
than other scholars, and healthier in both soul and body, as he
has long since earned himself fame in the northern and eastern
quarters with his exceptional knowledge of sciences as well as
most crafts and of all metals, cloth and wood; also for inventions
and various knowledgeable and inventive arts, but above all for
diligence, zeal, industry, flights of fancy, original imagination and
capacity, both in taste, emotion and beauty in all literature and
arts, as well as regarding manhood, prowess, wrestling, vitality
and gymnastics, walking and rigour, swimming and sprinting."'

Sölvi sat stone-faced under the reading, blushing at all the
right points as the captain read on.

'You embarrass me by quoting the magistrate's words,
Captain. I did not ask him to add this to my passport, but he
was adamant on making my better qualities clear to whoever
read these papers.'

Tordenskjold barked out a short laugh. 'It goes on to say that
you've saved dozens of people from drowning at sea with your
athleticism and bravery, your many virtuous characteristics, your
scientific intentions in studying the natural sciences, as well as
how anyone should house you and lend you money with no

532

worry of being repaid, as your one-man expedition is funded by the king himself.'

'Yes, well. The magistrate—'

'The magistrate must have been so distracted from this virtuosic rambling that he managed to spell his name wrong at the end.' Tordenskjold suddenly leaned in, menace now dripping from every word. 'Just who the hell are you, Sólon? A Hanseatic spy?'

Sölvi struggled to find the right response. He risked being caught; no, he was far beyond that – already snared in a trap without means of escape.

'Captain Tordenskjold, you misunderstand. Indeed, it might seem that things are out of order, and they are – just not in the manner you suggest.'

'Well? What am I misunderstanding, *Magister*?'

'I... Uh, yes... Indeed, I am not an educated seiðskratti. In the traditional sense, that is. But I am trained in the higher arts, I assure you. Perhaps not to magisterial standards...' He glanced at the seiðskratti, afraid that this would rouse their ire. Magister Ginfaxi remained motionless. 'But I am not a mere kuklari. As for my papers, the originals were lost on my travels. I am indeed on a mission to catalogue the anomalies of Hrímlandic nature for the Crown, but I was sent by the University of Supernatural Sciences – what remains of it, at least.'

'Svartiskóli, huh?' Tordenskjold eyed him warily. 'And who there signed off on your little scientific trip?'

'Doctor Vésteinn Alrúnarson.'

He burst out laughing at this. 'You've got some fucking guts, kid, I'll give you that. Doctor Vésteinn!' The laughter ebbed, replaced by a threatening air of malice as Tordenskjold's face darkened. 'I doubt a man dead for a decade signs off on any academic ventures. I warn you – one more lie, and Ginfaxi here will turn your body into a piece of abstract art. Do you understand me?'

Sölvi hesitated, then nodded.

'I said – do you understand me?'

'All right, yes! Captain,' he added.

'I don't think you do. Per!'

A soldier opened the door and peered in. Tordenskjold gestured to Sölvi.

'Take him to the brig and let him weigh his options overnight. Send someone to the bailiff's house to fetch his belongings.'

Sölvi did not resist as the soldier manhandled him and slapped a pair of handcuffs around his wrists.

In the panic of the moment, one thing stood out as odd. He had heard that seiðskrattar could see any manner of seiður or galdur in their vicinity. Why hadn't Ginfaxi said something about the charm around his neck? The eyes of the seiðskratti followed him closely as he was led out into the depths of the ship.

Interesting.

Tuttugu og fimm

Pale mist covered the valley, submerging the withering fields in a layer of thick, blue-tinted smog. The sun shone blood-red through the fog; its rays were weak and the weather was unseasonably cold. It looked as if yet another bleak summer was on the cards.

Þráinn Meinholt approached what remained of the village of Fagerdal, still smoking from the previous night's bombardment. Dense mountainous forest surrounded the cluster of simple houses, with a small stream running through the settlement. It must have been idyllic, if impoverished, before the barrage. The survivors were detained in the camp, fewer than two dozen of them left. Mostly elders and children. Perhaps the adults had perished or fled. The last remaining stragglers were still being rounded up from nearby farmsteads, and he had already sent out several squads to comb the forests for people in hiding.

The flying fortress had struck without warning the previous Óðday. In contrast to previous engagements with the Dark Fortress, as it was commonly called, it had not razed Fagerdal to the ground. According to what he had managed to piece together so far, the bloated monstrosity had positioned itself above the village and emitted some kind of sound – music, according to some witnesses. Þráinn doubted that was the right word to describe it. Entranced, the villagers had not fled. The specifics of what had happened next were unclear. Investigation was still ongoing as to the effects on the survivors, most of whom looked human to the naked eye. But through the thaumaturgical glasses their transdimensional influence was clear; most of them had several bones burning with the blue light of demonic manifestation.

The ones who had not needed a device to detect their transmutation were already dead, the carcasses burning brightly in blazes scattered around the area.

He had lost too many men cleansing the village of the corruption. Loftkastalinn had been gone for some time before their arrival. That small blessing was thanks to his intentional misreading of the maps, delaying them by several hours. His unit, I-Company of the 5th Scanian Infantry Brigade, was shipped up north to defend the Commonwealth against the flying fortress. Infantry companies had learned quickly to never engage with Loftkastalinn still present. They dealt with its aftermath, killing off transmundane manifestations or purging corrupt villagers. Þráinn had survived too much, come too far since his fall from favour, to get killed fighting an unbeatable enemy in defence of a worthless place. As things dragged on, most of their time was spent fighting ever-increasing peasant rebellions.

The military operation was supposedly intent on ridding the world of this atrocity. But Þráinn suspected the ultimate goal was instead to rein it back under the Crown's control. It had been their most formidable weapon once, after all, so why should they not attempt to reclaim it through some insanely elaborate ritual of svartigaldur? That's what he would have done, anyway. To his frustration, he was kept in the dark of all such schemes.

Þráinn Meinholt had always been a neatly oiled cog in the great machine of the Commonwealth. Now he was reduced to a smaller working part, a fact he worked tirelessly on rectifying. He had command of Ida Company, but no autonomy. From the top of a muddy hill overlooking the village ruins, he pored over maps of the region on a folding table.

'Lieutenant, we've finished scouring the woods,' reported Staff Sergeant Holmskjer. He looked worn out, his uniform dirt-stained and filthy.

'How many?'

'Seventeen, sir.'

'That's it?'

'We are positive we have apprehended all fugitives, sir.'

'All right. You have a few hours until we move out again. Execute the infected. Standard disposal – remember to salt the earth over the graves this time.'

'Sir.'

Holmskjer wasn't happy hearing this. Everyone was running on empty, with several days having passed since they'd had a decent amount of rest. He knew better than to let his frustration show with Þráinn, ending the discussion by saluting and making himself scarce.

In Hrímland, Þráinn's foreign last name had been a source of prestige. Here, it was cause for suspicion. Meinholt sounded Hanseatic in origin, which it likely was, a surname from the southern parts of the Commonwealth where the uprising had led to a bloody, drawn-out war. His accented Nordic did him no favours either. As such, he stood out everywhere and was frequently met with mistrust.

It was only when people got to know him that they learned they had been way too forgiving. That initial, prejudiced dis-approval quickly turned to active resentment.

News had been radioed in the previous night of recent sightings of the fortress. Having updated their map with the information, he still could find no rhyme or reason to its manifestations, neither in place nor time. Sometimes, Loftkastalinn would not strike for months. Some theorised it was retreating to whatever fell dimension it had sprouted from, appearing only sporadically, but that sounded a bit too hopeful to Þráinn's ears. He was of the school that believed it more likely teleported itself to distant regions of the world, remote lands that were nothing but a vague suggestion on their maps. The Dark Fortress had manifested itself in the world. It would not leave again so readily.

In the years since its first appearance, rumours had spread via the trade routes of unspeakable calamities, terrible demons serving a great dread emperor, all believed to be related to the omen of the broken moon.

That moon was visible now, low on the bright horizon, shaded with the pink hues of a northern sunset. A corpse strung up in the sky, a banshee heralding the impending death of all things. In the last years of the Hanseatic War a decade before, people had suffered from famine and plague – a mere sample of what was to come as the moon fractured and the mists descended upon the mainland.

Calculating the long-term after-effects of the meteorites crashing to earth had been difficult. The immediate destruction caused by the impacts was clear enough – the tides became weaker and erratic, causing catastrophic floods. Thankfully, the moon had not broken completely, only cracked, causing huge parts of it to either crash into the earth or go into orbit. Reports from Rundetårn claimed that it was only a matter of time until those mountain-sized fragments in orbit would come crashing down. The years-long volcanic eruptions in Hrímland had also upset weather systems across the Commonwealth, and it was hard to estimate if the impacts had played a part in that. Regardless, the drastic effects were as clear as day across the known world: droughts and heatwaves; summers turned cold under an obscured crimson sun; frequent hailstorms severe enough to kill livestock; poisonous mists that withered crops in the fields and slowly poisoned the workers who tilled them.

A soldier disrupted Þráinn's spiralling train of thought, handing him a telegram. Þráinn unfolded it and resisted cursing in frustration, keeping his manner cool. Any show of weakness would spread like an infection among the troops.

```
UPRISING IN MEDELPAD STOP
PROCEED TO ÅNGE C ASAP STOP
REPORTED HERESY SUBDUE AAC STOP
ATTWO HRM KJIX
```

This missive was directly from the royal office.

'According to the will of His Royal Majesty, King Jörundur the Ninth', the abbreviated signature stated.

They had to get out there immediately.

In the first years of the Hrímlandic eruptions, harvests had failed catastrophically. The mists had poisoned crops, livestock and people alike; the altered tides caused flooding and tsunamis in places that had never before experienced them. Peasants had resorted to taking up arms, believing they could better survive by overthrowing their rulers. Maybe they were right. Maybe hanging people for heresy and kukl was counter-intuitive when those same people stood a chance of saving an entire harvest in such dire straits. But that was none of Þráinn's business.

It had been easy but messy work to put them back in their place to begin with. After those initial years, the reports of heresy increased drastically. Further driven to desperation and bolstered by the sudden increase in environmental seiðmagn, the farmers had started to blatantly rely more and more on their little peasant rituals to get the crops to grow. Worse was that when the mists lifted, things were not as they had been before. As it stood now, these uprisings could be a nightmare to deal with. Even a single kuklari was like a walking bomb waiting to go off. There had been a dozen of them in the last village Ida Company had dealt with. It was only a matter of time before they got unmanageable.

'Subdue at all costs…' Þráinn muttered to himself.

Shit.

Ida Company was already exhausted and might be verging on mutiny themselves.

Yet again, he wished he had been allocated a galdramaður. Volatile as they were, galdur did not require any energy source to operate. Such scholars were exceedingly rare these days. Most of those chosen few had died in the Hanseatic War, with many promising students lost as Reykjavík fell. Although it was true that ambient seiðmagn was on the rise – for the first time in recorded history, no less – Kalmar still had no thaumaturgical power plants on the mainland. The meagre flow of seiðmagn had never been enough to warrant it. That meant no skorrifles and no machines like the Centimotive. His seiðskratti was only working at half the capacity they would have been in Hrímland.

Þráinn rifled through his maps to find the province of Medelpad. He had barely heard of the place. Ånge was a municipality there, with a city of the same name. At a forced march, they were still five days out. His men were already exhausted; the surviving and untainted wounded had barely been seen to. There was a military base not far from the city. It was small, but should still be sizeable enough. It was a good idea to head there first. He wondered why the base's garrison hadn't been able to deal with this themselves. Were they already overrun? Why the hell was Ida Company being dragged into this shit?

But bemoaning his current situation wouldn't help anything. This was the reality he was faced with. He waved the staff sergeant over.

'Holmskjer, are you familiar with Ånge city?'

'Not really, Lieutenant. I've passed through there plenty of times, mostly to change trains. Never stopped for more than a few hours. It's just a junction town.'

'We have orders to march there immediately. Sounds like some peasants decided it was high time to stage an uprising.'

Holmskjer failed to mask his frustration.

'Lieutenant, with all due respect – the men are exhausted, we're low on supplies, we still haven't got enough gas masks for our troops.'

'I'm well aware, Staff Sergeant. The order comes right from Hafnía – by decree of the king. I expect I don't have to explain to you what that means?' Holmskjer nodded. 'Good. You have one hour to prepare the company.'

'Sir.'

↯

The strong breeze wasn't enough to provide any respite from the fumes. The mists never cleared up. They sunk down heavily, smothering the earth. Marching under the darkened sun, the worn-out members of Ida Company made their way towards Ånge. With only two trucks, filled with their supplies, most of the company was reduced to walking. Except Þráinn, who had been issued a horse. It had its own gas mask, or it would likely be already dead.

They stopped a few wagons that came across their way. They questioned families who had piled their carts with their most valued and necessary possessions, fleeing a conflict that had spread through the countryside like wildfire, eventually reaching

Ånge. Reports were grim. The insurgents were using kukl to aid them in combat. Situated deep inland, in the heart of the Commonwealth's Crown Lands, the military presence there had been at a minimum. Þráinn questioned the families about the base he had seen on his map, but most were not familiar with it. Only one farmer recognised it and said it had been a highly restricted industrial site, not a military base. He'd worked for them clearing the forest a few years back, when it was built.

Odd that Þráinn's orders from the Crown hadn't mentioned the base, if they were truly defenceless. Maybe that responsibility fell to another company located closer. He put it away for now; there was no reason to expect any kind of support from there, although it might be wise to retreat towards the base, should it come to that. He used to like planning contingencies for failure, working for the Directorate. Anticipating the worst had been something of a knack of his, until the excavation had been utterly destroyed on his watch. There was no room for failure now.

The years had not been kind to Þráinn Meinholt. Volcanoes had erupted on the voyage back to a ruined Reykjavík, the North Atlantean fleet destroyed by a fell force. Some of the shipwrecks were alive, remade into disturbingly familiar horrors to anyone who had witnessed the demonic transformation of Loftkastalinn.

He was court-martialled when he returned to Hafnía. The charges against him were diverse, as the Crown sought a scapegoat to pin the catastrophes on. On the journey to the mainland, he'd foreseen this and cooked up a narrative where the eruptions were mostly to blame for the expedition's failure, as well as hinting at suspicions of demonic corruption among key members. They had not believed him. He was going to be executed.

Then, Loftkastalinn had manifested itself in the heart of the Commonwealth. It had appeared above the fortress-city of

Vordingborg in Sjáland, reducing it to ruin in half a day. After that it had headed east, into the Hanseatic archipelago. Military opposition on land, sea and air did nothing to slow it down. Kalmar had decided to bolster their own defences, leaving their once-rebellious city states in Hansa to defend themselves. After weeks of destruction, it had vanished once more, and people breathed a sigh of relief.

Then it had appeared far up north, in the forest of Norrland. Since then there was no knowing when and where it would strike.

It was strange, but Þráinn owed his life to the so-called Dark Fortress. Left to rot in a cell, unaware of what was happening, he'd been brought out to review blurry surveillance photos of the fortress. Walking its mutated battlements was the clear shape of a lone human-looking figure among the warped manifestations of the void. A person immediately recognisable to him.

Auður Thorlacius.

Þráinn's story was considered proven by her appearance, although he couldn't give the Crown answers as to how and why she was there. He was cleared of all charges, although that did not mean his reputation was unscathed.

His years of hard work and climbing the ladder had been reduced to ashes in an instant. The Hrímlandic Directorate of Immigration had been dismantled following the ruin of Reykjavík. Innréttingarnar had been declared bankrupt and its properties seized by Skattestyrelsen, Kalmar's Ministry of Taxation. There were far more important things to focus on than a sorcerously toxic island in the northern reaches of the Atlantean Ocean.

But Þráinn was still a government man. Thanks to a shortage of officer candidates, he had been promoted to the military rank of lieutenant, responsible for a company of just under one hundred soldiers. All in all, he had worse pay and fewer men under his command than he had when he was a Directorate agent.

The soldiers took turns with the gas masks to try to mitigate the effects of the toxic mist, others using whatever cloth scraps they could to cover their mouth and nose. Officers each had a mask and were forbidden from sharing it, as per command's orders. Grunts could be easily replaced as long as the company's officers were all in place. They passed empty fields, covered with withered spring crops that had barely sprouted. Farmers worked with cloth masks, spreading fertiliser, herding gaunt sheep or cattle out to yellowed pastures.

Þráinn wasn't surprised by the revolt. Things had been much the same in their time in Norrland, and apparently all over the Commonwealth. He just didn't understand what the revolt wanted to accomplish. Things were just as fucked with a new king on the throne. It wasn't as if a change in government would stop the volcanoes from erupting or reforge the moon.

The attack came when they were a day out from Ånge. Following a dirt road on a humid, peculiarly hot day, with thick forest cover on each side, they were flanked from the front and rear of the line. Appearing from the trees like phantoms came people armed with hunting rifles and foresting axes, knives and various farming tools. He even saw one man wielding a goddamn scythe, as sharp as if death itself held it, cutting off a soldier's leg at the knee as though he was reaping barley.

Ida Company was utterly spent, and the situation quickly developed into a chaotic skirmish. Þráinn looked around for his seiðskratti, not finding the pale mask anywhere in the fray.

'Ulv Squad, battle formations!' he barked. 'Fix bay—'

One of the trucks exploded in viridian fire. The flames extended upwards in a stream, an unnatural emerald pillar of flame. Þráinn's horse panicked and reared up. He pulled at the reins, tried to keep himself in the saddle, but something hit him hard in the head and sent him crashing to the ground.

Blood streamed down his forehead, stinging his left eye and obscuring his vision. A stone had hit him, evidenced by many more bombarding them as slingers let loose from the foliage. His horse had bolted, already lost in the frenzy.

A man roared and charged him, swinging a rusty axe overhead. Þráinn's heart rate slowed, his pupils dilated, and everything snapped into sharp focus. He rolled out of the axe's way, the blade driving itself deep into the earth where his chest had been moments ago. Springing up to his feet, he drew his knife and drove it into the man's throat, already turning as blood sprayed from the artery to slash at another attacker behind him – a woman with a soldier's rifle. He parried the bayonet away as if it was a branch, sending her off balance, and followed up with an elbow to her head before he stabbed her in the chest. His strikes were so forceful, and his senses so sharp, he could hear the bones snapping in her skull.

'Retreat!' he screamed over the melee, his voice booming as if he were speaking into a megaphone. 'Fall back!'

Rifles were fired as some manner of order was established for a moment. They were outnumbered. He saw his men being cut down like sheep in autumn. A glimpse of red, and he spotted Magister Hrælögur, their hands raised in strenuous sorcerous channelling. A circle of soldiers surrounded the seiðskratti, rifles aimed and firing at any who approached. Stones ricocheted off an invisible shield surrounding the magister.

A flow of seiðmagn rushed out around the royal seiðskratti – and then they burst apart in a thaumaturgical blast that sent soldiers flying. Hypercoloured streams of energy rippled through the air, crackling loudly as the overflow of seiðmagn rippled through the aftershock of the explosion like smoke in the wake of flames. In the woods, Þráinn caught a glimpse of emerging figures. Men and women, their foreheads, chests and arms covered in inked sigils: galdrastafir, runes and esoteric symbols mixed together in a chaotic weave, conflict upon conflict that still somehow managed to work together. There were dozens of them – kuklarar. Peasant meddlers in the occult who had just killed his seiðskratti and turned one of the trucks into a pile of molten metal.

'For Fagerdal!' one of them shouted.

The rebels roared in one voice, echoing the war cry. A small part of Þráinn registered that at least he now knew why they'd only found older people and children in the village.

The world moved in slow motion, blood drops trailing like flower petals lazing down a clear stream. They weren't going to succeed in retreating. This was a massacre.

A second of analysis was all it took for Þráinn Meinholt to turn tail and abandon his duty. Sprinting into the thick forest, decimating those few solitary stragglers that were unfortunate enough to be in his way, he left Ida Company to die on their own.

Tuttugu og sex

The brig stank of old blood and sweat. It only had two holding cells, the doors made of solid iron bars. At least Sölvi had been given a bucket. That was something. The room was lit by a single light bulb from the corridor, which had no porthole. He idly played with the pieces of chalk in his pocket, marvelling at the captain's arrogance in not searching him. Although, it annoyed him to admit, it probably didn't matter. He wasn't too keen on experimenting with kukl somewhere in the bowels of a ship. Things could go really wrong, really fast.

He still wasn't about to sit here idly, waiting for whatever doom the captain had planned for him. He chalked a stave of protection underneath the bare bed, then took off his coat and drew a similar sigil inside the back. Not much, but it would have to do. Bored after merely an hour waiting, he started sketching in his pocketbook, taking to the steel walls when even that began to bore him.

Sölvi often found himself returning to the same imagery these days. A cascading waterfall, streaming down in multiple tiers. Splitting apart, joining again, the flow of water captured in a moment that through him still felt alive and moving. A solitary traveller at the bottom of the waterfall, turning away, his back straining from the weight he carried. Up above on the cliffs, partially obfuscated by watery mist, a similarly hunched-over figure, its limbs gaunt and elongated, its head weighed down by a crown of thorns.

'You are quite the talent, Sólon Gyldenlöve,' hissed a quiet voice.

Sölvi started and dropped his chalk, the sound of it splitting so loud that it seemed to echo. He stared at the seiðskratti, who had slithered into the room without making a noise. He knew how loudly you had to shut the door that led to the brig; it needed to be slammed in order for the locks to properly engage.

'When Captain Tordenskjold heard about you from that grotesque bailiff and the so-called madam, I knew we had to get hold of you. As a courtesy, we decided not to inform the bailiff who you really are – Sölvi Helgason.' The magister's pale mask measured him calmly, then turned towards the artwork that encompassed an entire wall. 'A variation on a theme, I see. Your journals were interesting – although not for the reasons I was expecting.'

'I'm sorry to disappoint, Magister.'

'Not at all. You've travelled our newly remade island quite extensively, never stopping in the same place for more than a few nights, it seems. On our travels there's barely been a place unmarked by your lies and swindling.'

'My research demands that—'

'Oh, please,' Ginfaxi interrupted. 'Can we be done with that charade? Do not treat me like some dull-witted turf house farmer.'

'All right.' Sölvi risked an upfront approach, for a change. 'What do you want from me?'

'The captain wants to have you arrested for vagrancy and fraud. He could have you sentenced as well.'

'On whose authority?'

'Don't be foolish. This island still belongs to the Commonwealth. As a high-ranking officer in the Kalmar military, he is fully within his rights to try you himself – under a state of emergency. A state we have been in for a decade, now.'

'I see. But there are no prisons in Hrímland.'

'No suitable ones, at least.'

'So he will be forced to take me to Hafnía.'

Ginfaxi shook their head, leaning on their staff as they shifted their weight to their other side. The magister was obviously in deep and constant pain.

'Don't sound so overjoyed at the prospect, son. A Hafnían prison is a hellhole.'

'It can't be much worse than this place.'

'Perhaps. But they'll never let you stay. You'll get shipped back where you belong as soon as you've served your sentence.' Ginfaxi reached out and touched the cell door. The lock clicked from his touch. 'I would like to propose an alternative. Follow me.'

The seiðskratti exited without checking to see if Sölvi followed. After the door shut behind them, Sölvi checked his cell's door. It was unlocked.

He followed. It was not as if he truly had a choice.

ᚼ

Sölvi did not know exactly how a royal seiðskratti's chambers should look, but whatever he had imagined did not match the reality of Ginfaxi's cabin. There were no tomes, no sigils or runes, no bones or esoteric materials. It was spartan, neat and tidy, the cot made and not a speck of dust or filth showing. Sölvi's journals were piled up on the solitary desk in organised stacks.

Ginfaxi motioned for him to sit. He obeyed, leaning back in the seat in order to try to make himself feel relaxed and in control, even though nothing was further from the truth. He wondered if his charm had any effect on Ginfaxi.

He doubted it.

The seiðskratti sighed and sat on the edge of their cot, slowly, like an old man with aching joints. They looked defeated, hunched over and exhausted.

'Tell me, Sölvi – in honesty... what do you know of the landvættir?'

Sölvi suffocated the rising nervousness evoked by that word.

'You mean the Stone Giant?' he asked, hoping he didn't sound too simple.

Ginfaxi laughed softly. 'Yes. For example. From what I gather, you are somewhat infamous. We've collected quite the report about you on our journey through the eastern fjords. One note-worthy trait was how particularly unwilling you are to admit your own shortcomings – especially of an intellectual nature.'

'My academic work might have some shortcomings, but if you truly read it you know of the value it has to those with the capacity to comprehend it.'

'As you say. Well, as a learned man, how familiar are you with the four landvættir of Hrímland?' The seiðskratti didn't bother waiting for a response. 'According to the old heathen ways, vættir, the nature spirits of the land, were worshipped as minor gods. Among them, the four landvættir were considered the mightiest.'

Ginfaxi reached to his desk and opened a drawer, pulling out a few worn sepia photographs. He handed them to Sölvi.

The first faded photographs showed a temple made of ancient-looking wood, set on crumbling stone foundations that seemed even older. The building was oval in shape, with a low domed roof. Sölvi flicked through the pictures, amazed by the magnificent workmanship and variations in style and materials used for each sculpture. He went through them again, meticulously this time, soaking up the details of each grainy photograph.

Then came four close-ups, each depicting a different column located outside the temple. On top of each column was a fantastical being, with a plethora of unique and strange vættir depicted beneath them. The first was roughly cast in strange-looking metal, perhaps the skrumnisiron of the náskárar – a monstrous bird of prey digging its talons into the horde of avian vættir beneath it, looking ruthlessly out over its domain.

Sölvi held back a laugh. The depiction of the northern land-vættur couldn't have been further from the truth.

The second was also cast in metal, the light reflecting off it with an unsettling sheen. It flowed in smooth lines, making it seem as though the sculpture wasn't solid at all, but liquid that had been captured in this state for only this specific moment. It showed a long, scaly wyrm, the vættir beneath it so vile and contorted Sölvi thought they might be demons instead of nature spirits.

A solid basalt column made up the third sculpture, chiselled in lines so sharp it could have been cast in concrete. The brutal and dominating form of a horned bull jutted out of the pillar – manifested violence itself frozen in place. A shiver ran down his spine.

Sölvi recognised the fourth easily. The Stone Giant, a roughly man-shaped thing made from lava rocks and obsidian. It was uncomfortably close to his memory of the giant itself, having seen it a few times in his youth, back when Reykjavík had been a city teeming with life. It alone stood solitary among the landvættir, with no lesser beings beneath it. Ginfaxi explained in a droning voice as Sölvi looked through each photo.

'The landvættur of the north – the Great Eagle, also called Gammur. The landvættur of the east – the Wyrm, also called Dreki.

The Bull of the West, named Griðungur. And the southern landvættur you know – the Stone Giant.'

'Where was this taken?'

'In the old heathen temple of Landakot. It used to be in the city centre. Who knows if it still stands? It saw some use after the Stone Giant attacked Reykjavík. A cult rose around it shortly after its appearance. The authorities regularly raided the temple, of course, but I don't think they tore it down.' Ginfaxi permitted him a moment to take in the artworks before continuing. 'What do you know of the Great Eagle, Sölvi?'

'This one?' He held up the first photograph. 'The landvættur of the north, you said.'

'Correct.'

He shrugged nonchalantly. 'Never heard of it. Never heard of any of them, to be honest.'

'Except the Stone Giant?'

'Well, of course I've heard of that one. I said so, previously.'

'I don't believe you,' said Ginfaxi gently.

Sölvi shrugged. 'All right.'

'Tell me, Sölvi, why did you come up north?'

'I burned every bridge out east. It was time to move on to pastures new. You know as much, from the sound of it.'

Ginfaxi was still leaning on their cane as they sat, switching hands as they tried to make themselves more comfortable.

'Your notes are quite thorough. Quite remarkable, really. You've noted down every piece of folklore you've encountered, it seems.'

'I took my duty seriously, even though my papers were ...' *Forged*, he almost said. 'Not yet officially authorised. I knew my studies would be precious to a learned individual – not that there are many around these parts.'

'No. I suppose not. I found it odd that there were visible gaps in your notes. No mention of rumours about a powerful being recently come to light, said by some to be the long-lost northern landvættur. Rumours we've encountered in every quadrant of Hrímland so far. Apparently, people make quite the pilgrimage to seek it out. They say it can heal any wound, no matter how grievous. But whoever sets out by themselves is not able to find it. A powerful vortex of obfuscation shrouds it. Only those who are accompanied by a shepherd – or so they call him – can make their way to the landvættur. A lone wanderer, disguised as a beggar, an artist, a scholar, a farmhand, who invites those found worthy to seek comfort from their suffering.'

Sölvi laughed. 'Well, you would know not to place a lot of trust in rumours. If you step out of this hunk of metal, you'll see that weird things are happening everywhere. Inexplicable things that spread tall tales like wildfire. I've heard of this so-called shepherd, of course, but my notes only account what I believe to be credible and valuable. Not fairy tales.'

'I see. Only truth, as appraised by your scholarly education.'

'That's right!' Sölvi couldn't help raising his voice. 'I've worked hard to educate myself in this fucking intellectual wasteland. Do you know how hard it is to come across readable books? Let alone books worth reading?'

'I don't,' said Ginfaxi quietly. 'But I can imagine what a torture it must be for a mind such as yours to find itself in such circumstances. The seed of a magnificent flower cast onto barren ground.'

Sölvi fell quiet. He knew the seiðskratti was toying with him – but he found it hard to disagree.

'They said *you* lead people to the Great Eagle, Sölvi. Those you find worthy of its attention. Those in need, with nowhere else to go, who have nothing but still give freely to help others. But they say a lot of things about you. They also call you a liar, a thief, a good-for-nothing crook who hasn't done an honest day's work in his life.'

'Menial tasks are for menial minds,' muttered Sölvi.

'There we agree.'

'But I don't know anything about this so-called shepherd of yours.'

Ginfaxi sighed again. It was the sound of something giving way, like an obstruction breaking loose from the flow of a stream.

'You are right to remain suspicious of my motives, Sölvi. The captain is here to find the landvættur and harness it for the might of the Commonwealth. They've tried to do so before, with disastrous results.' Their voice fell quiet, still seeming to echo from a great depth, a darkness impenetrable by light. 'I was there. Years ago, I witnessed the culmination of their hubris. Deceit upon deceit, caring naught for the prices paid or lives lost, like fuel cast into the fires of their empire. I considered myself a mechanism in their machine, and I believed that made me important. Indispensable.' They scoffed, spitting out the words as they spoke. 'Nothing could have been further from the truth.'

'The storm-shark,' said Sölvi slowly. 'You were there.'

'I was.' Ginfaxi's mask remained unreadable, unmoving. 'How do you know about that?'

Sölvi bit his tongue. He'd let his curiosity get the better of him and had showed his hand.

'There are a hundred stories about that out east. I never gave them any credit until now. What was it like?'

Ginfaxi seemed to accept his lie. 'It was terrible beyond imagining.'

'But you're still here. You're still their mechanism.'

'Yes,' they admitted. 'I am. But no longer. Do you know what is happening on the mainland?'

Sölvi shook his head, desperate for any news.

'The world is changing,' Ginfaxi continued. 'Awakening. As the eruptions go on in Hrímland, clouds of ash obscure the sun – deadly mists descend upon the land, killing crops and cattle in droves. There is a famine there, too. All across the Commonwealth. But something else is changing as well. Seiðmagn is returning to the world. Right now it is only a trickle, a slight flow of power where there was none before. Just as in an arid desert, that meagre flow is bringing forth drastic changes to all life.'

Ginfaxi reached up to their mask, hesitating for a moment. Then they started to slowly undo the buckles.

'In every fishing village, on every farm, there are kuklarar. Perhaps they are talented people such as yourself, or perhaps they are only hacks. It does not matter. For generations they have performed empty and mostly ineffectual rituals in the hopes of better crops, safe sailing, stronger herds and safe travels. And now these people are starving, serving an empire that has treated them like cattle themselves for far too long. Kalmar has dozens of seiðskrattar – but they have thousands of kuklarar. People will rise up. The weak flow of seiðmagn is not enough for a royal seiðskratti to work at their full power – not for long, at least – but it is enough for an army of kuklarar to do small miracles.'

'The Crown has entire armies. Machines and weapons and—'

'Yes. They do. Maybe they will quell the fire. Despite still having barely recovered after the war against the Hanseatic Islands. But I will not bet on it. *The world is changing.*'

'Why are you telling me all of this? What does it have to do with anything?'

'Because I want you to know that I have no intention of helping Captain Tordenskjold find the landvættur and enslave it. Instead, I am asking you to help me – not *them*. Even though I do not claim to be deserving of anyone's help.'

'Help you with what?' asked Sölvi.

Ginfaxi's beaked mask hung loose on their face. They took it off and placed it gently on the table. A pallid, gaunt face stared at Sölvi, with sunken eyes and clammy skin. Their hair was mouse-grey and thin, their sharp eyebrows lending the face a look of determination like steel. Ginfaxi smiled mirthlessly, their eyes unaffected.

Sölvi knew that this was a sacred moment, or perhaps treachery to whatever code the royal seiðskrattar upheld. Usually skilled at reading people, Sölvi struggled to read Ginfaxi now that they were unmasked. Their entire manner was eerily still, their body language signifying a deep level of exhaustion. Overall, Sölvi felt a deep sense of something that felt like loss, or perhaps regret. Or maybe it was just fear of dying and an inkling of the acceptance of that fate.

'Things were wrong long before the eastern landvættur – the so-called storm-shark, as you put it – broke free of its tethers. But that venture was emblematic of the problems we face. People died in droves working on that dig. A few accidents, at first. Then the mutations. As we got more replacements in, they brought the plague with them. I thought I was above them. People were treated worse than animals. I thought I was safe behind my mask. All along, a much more insidious kind of infestation was taking hold in me.'

Ginfaxi got up slowly and unfastened their robes. Beneath, an adjusted linen shirt covered the body, cut open at the back.

A small mountain of crystal jutted out from their upper back. It was clouded like ice, laced with imperfections, containing within itself a shimmering that caught the weak light in such myriad patterns that it looked as if it was moving. At the roots, up against the skin, the crystal was tainted with dark crimson – veins reaching out from the body into the growth, fading from a deep red to faint, pink hues, eventually ending in a clear whiteness. The centre was the highest, uneven as it still was, the ends jagged and rough like formations found in nature.

'Seiðmagn?' was all Sölvi could think to ask.

'In some regards, yes. In others, no.'

'So, you mean—'

'My bones are clear of any infestation,' Ginfaxi interrupted gruffly. 'Although... I fear that transdimensional influence has played some part in this, even though I do not fully comprehend how.'

Sölvi didn't really know how to respond to that. He knew nothing about demons and their ilk. He tried to incorporate as little of galdur as he got away with in his kukl.

'It looks like a mutation caused by seiðmagn to me,' he offered. 'Or... well, as alike as any two can be.'

'Maybe. It started during that excavation. I stupidly ignored it, although I can't even begin to explain why.'

'I understand. Some things are too awful to face.'

'Something like that.'

'Do you mind if I take a closer look?'

Ginfaxi turned slightly and Sölvi got up to inspect the mutation more closely. It was not one solid growth, as he'd first suspected. It had grown in a circular pattern – no, a spiral, strangely elongated.

A symbol uncomfortably familiar to Sölvi.

'What did it look like, to begin with?'

'It was something that appeared on several people working the dig. A spiral shape that appeared somewhere on the body, like a rash or an infection. The spiral had a certain occult affiliation to the work being done there. After... Well, after everything went to hell, it started to worsen. Small, jagged points pierced the skin. In the years since, nothing I've tried has managed to stop it or even slow it down.' Ginfaxi shrugged on the robes again. 'Listen. I know I have not been a good person. I let myself become a mechanism for violence, all in the name of my own pursuit of power, of excellence. I have severed myself from humanity. From empathy, is perhaps a phrasing that better fits. If there is anything I can offer you, then name it. I will do anything I can to give you what you want in return for your help in healing this wound. But I will not try to force your hand. I've had enough of coercion.'

Sölvi considered this. Ginfaxi could be his ticket away from Hrímland. Maybe not on this ship, but who knew what a royal seiðskratti was capable of? But then there was the matter of the storm-shark.

Whether Ginfaxi was deserving of forgiveness wasn't his to decide. He knew that. In either case, he'd make sure Ginfaxi would keep their end of the bargain.

'Not like you give me a lot of choice,' he said eventually. 'I am your prisoner, after all. And you've taken everything I own.'

Ginfaxi seemed genuinely startled by this, as if they had not realised the position Sölvi had been put in.

'I'm so sorry. I will let you go, no matter what. Regardless of whether you help me or not, I will tell Captain Tordenskjold you don't know anything and that your crimes are not worth the effort.'

'And he will believe you?'

'He will. He will assume I was ... persuasive in my questioning.'

'Huh. And how will he let you, his thaumaturgical weapon, out of his sight?'

'That will not be a problem.'

ห

They disembarked with no interference. They passed soldiers, and even the captain himself without Tordenskjold so much as sparing a glance in their direction. Sölvi had gathered his possessions back in his trunk, with nothing out of place. It felt surreal to walk past all these people like ghosts, who still moved out of their way.

'Don't think that you can replicate this trick,' Ginfaxi said as they walked out of the village, towards the mountains. 'The officers all have little trinkets. Some of them, such as the captain, have been thaumaturgically enhanced.'

'Then how...?'

Ginfaxi gave him a knowing glance, cocky even when obscured by their mask.

'Who do you think crafted that seiður?'

'Ah. Right.'

Although they seemed frail, Ginfaxi had no problem keeping up with Sölvi as they ascended the steep incline, heading up a mountain valley, carved by long-vanished glaciers in a distant era. He could feel the seiðskratti drawing in the abundant seiðmagn to sustain themselves, and decided to say nothing. He knew it to be dangerous, but Ginfaxi was a learned magister and must have known what they were doing. Even if that was not the case, it beat having to drag them through the difficult terrain that lay ahead.

Sölvi knew he shouldn't trust the seiðskratti. The red-robed royal seiðskrattar were widely feared, and even though he had never met one himself, he had heard plenty of stories. None of them were good.

But he had been told that didn't matter. Good or bad, a healer's job was to heal. Recalling that lesson, his conscience stung at the

559

thought of the bailiff and his wilful neglect of aiding him. That man had changed on the outside, but still remained the same rotten monster within, Sölvi reminded himself. Ginfaxi might be different – or so he hoped. He wasn't afraid that Ginfaxi could bring any harm to him or his family. Powerful as the seiðskratti might be, they were as nothing compared to the power resting up in the mountains.

His little brother, waiting beneath the glacier.

Tuttugu og sjö

They made good time. Ginfaxi ate little and slept even less, which meant that Sölvi got a larger share of the supplies than he'd expected. A couple of days out, Sölvi asked Ginfaxi to take off the regalia, as the seiðskratti called it. Other people might be alarmed by it, he explained. With some reluctance, Ginfaxi packed away the mask and robes that had served as their outward self for so many years. Sölvi gave them some of his extra clothes to stave off the cold. Snow still lingered up on the highlands, in large patches here and there.

'Anyway, what's your real name?' Sölvi asked, trying to lighten the mood and take the seiðskratti's mind off feeling so vulnerable. This had a reverse effect on the magister.

'Ginfaxi,' they said in a heavy, final tone.

'Right, yes.' Sölvi considered his words carefully. 'I understand – it's none of my business, obviously. Except… the people we are about to meet won't take kindly to meeting someone with what is obviously a magisterial name.'

'It could be a name from some remote village.'

'They'll know.'

Ginfaxi considered this. 'Eir,' they said.

'Eir it is. It means "copper", right?'

'In the grammatical masculine form, yes, it does. But there

561

is also an archaic feminine form that means "peace".' Ginfaxi rubbed their hands together, trying to warm themselves. Without the regalia, seiður was no longer a crutch to lean on. 'I've never much cared for the tradition of choosing a masculine magisterial title.'

Three days out, they passed a herd of sheep grazing a hillside. The flock scurried away as they approached, the leader sheep standing firm as they passed by. The horned sheep had odd, curving spikes growing down their spine.

It was late that afternoon that Ginfaxi finally noticed they were being followed. A pale shape trailing far behind.

'It's nothing,' said Sölvi. 'Ignore it. It won't – or, well, can't – do us any harm.'

'What is it?' asked Ginfaxi, unable to obscure the fear in their voice.

'A manner of draugur, so to speak. But a powerless one.'

'It's dead?'

'Maybe. I wouldn't say it's alive, at least. It's a shadow, nothing more. A shell of whatever it once was.'

Ginfaxi stared at the pale shape, barely visible at this distance. It lurked half-hidden behind a mountainside boulder. Its pitch-black horns weighed down its stick-thin alabaster frame. Of all the strange things found in the world, it looked like a thing out of myth.

'And what did it used to be?' Ginfaxi asked.

'I'm not quite sure,' Sölvi admitted, turning his back on the thing following them and continuing on his way without a worry. 'Whatever it was, it was powerful. So powerful that I'm not certain it's even capable of dying. But it is capable of being broken, and that's what it's become. A wretched, broken thing. It follows me at a distance, never daring to approach.'

'Why?'

'It believes I'm carrying something that will help it. Something taken from it a long time ago.'

'And are you?'

Sölvi smiled, shaking his head. 'I don't think anything in this world can help this wretched thing.'

'You know what happened to it.'

It was a statement, not a question. Sölvi considered this for a while, weighing how much he should say.

'I do, although I didn't see it with my own eyes. And I'm glad I didn't. My mother broke it. Years ago. She tore its spirit apart. This is all that's left. A toothless wolf that cannot even starve to death.'

Growth gave way to a rocky desert, cold and uninviting. A few blades of grass clustered together here and there. Tiny purple flowers grew between them, sometimes out on their own. They looked so weak, alone against the vast desert. Still, they survived. A couple of days passed before Ginfaxi discovered another being on their trail. Two of them, to be exact.

'Those are too big to be foxes,' they whispered, trying to catch a proper look at the things scurrying between cracks and crevices in the jagged terrain. 'They've been following us for hours.'

'I know,' said Sölvi, shifting the weight on his back. 'Don't worry. They belong to a friend. It means we're getting close.'

This visibly worried Ginfaxi far more than the horned being. Sölvi thought he knew why, but decided not to say anything. To the seiðskratti's credit, they kept marching on.

'You certainly are carefree for a man trailed by strange things out in the highlands,' Ginfaxi said after a while. 'One would think a vagabond would practise more caution.'

Sölvi decided to say nothing about the distant shadow up in the sky, which had been keeping an eye on them for days. Ginfaxi was worried enough.

'One would think,' Sölvi laughed.

It was a few hours later that the seiðskratti visibly jumped when a woman suddenly stood up from the top of a rocky hill ahead, where she had been lying out of sight. Sölvi waved to her and she started to descend.

'Don't worry,' he muttered to Ginfaxi. 'She's a friend.'

The woman strode towards them, straight-backed and proud. She wore woollen clothes, cleverly designed to accommodate her severe mutations. Her height and the spike jutting from her shoulder gave her an intimidating appearance, but her bright smile was warm and inviting. What did tarnish her seemingly carefree demeanour was the old rifle hanging from her shoulder.

She whistled and the two fox-like things tailing Sölvi and Ginfaxi came running out of hiding, sprinting around her as she approached. Their fur shifted rapidly, settling into an iridescent sheen of frost as they ran too fast for the camouflage to keep up with the changing surroundings. Each had several bushy tails and they were larger than wolves.

'Rarely seen are white ravens!' the woman said. 'And who is this poor soul you've dragged along?'

'Halla!'

Sölvi ran towards her and they hugged. She towered over him, like an adult hugging a child. Sölvi gestured towards Ginfaxi.

'This is Eir, who I'm taking to the glacier.'

As he turned around to introduce Ginfaxi, he noticed the seiðskratti's fearful look. They had gone even paler than usual.

'Please, do not worry,' said Halla. 'I mean you well.' That didn't seem to calm Ginfaxi in the slightest. 'Listen,' she continued, suddenly on edge, 'if you're one of the farmers down by Grjótá, I don't know anything about any missing sheep.'

Sölvi could suddenly feel the rush of seiðmagn flowing towards Ginfaxi, like a wave being pulled back to the sea. He could see that Halla had felt something as well; a dark look crossed her normally jovial features. Sölvi turned slowly to Ginfaxi, arms out in a calming motion.

'Eir – please. There is no need to be afraid. She's a friend. Please don't give into fear.'

He saw the uncertainty written plain on Ginfaxi's face. Halla had retreated a few steps, resisting the urge to reach for her rifle, which would inevitably break the tension with disastrous results.

Slowly, Sölvi felt the flow of seiðmagn slow and ebb. Ginfaxi went limp, suddenly looking as if they could barely stand up. Sölvi hesitantly placed a hand on their shoulder. Ginfaxi was avoiding looking at Halla.

'Sorry about that,' they said.

Halla forced a laugh. 'I understand your trepidation, friend. Come along now. And don't mind my little cretins that have been following you around. They're here to keep us safe. Like Bölmóður, up there in the sky somewhere.'

This prompted Ginfaxi to look upwards, spotting the náskári in the distance, soaring lazily on high-altitude wind currents, the sun glinting off his ironed beak.

'How did I miss that?' Ginfaxi muttered.

'Don't worry – he's on our side. Bölmóður has saved our hides more often than I care to count.'

Halla went back up the hill she had been camping on, retrieving a butchered reindeer carcass from it. She carried it easily across her shoulders, as if it weighed nothing at all. They followed Halla through the windy landscape – barren rock with a few tufts of grass fighting against the erosion. In the distance the glacier waited, a white burden crawling over the mountains, bleeding glacial rivers in strong currents of cold, muddied water, flecked with minute icebergs like body parts. They crossed one such river on a long bridge made from stone, grown out of the earth in twisting, wild patterns – a lava flow that had immediately hardened, with no other thing in the landscape resembling it. It was just wide enough for one person to cross, and a rope had been stretched across its length for travellers to grasp. The rock still felt warm under their feet.

It got colder the closer they got, caused by air currents coming off the great, dormant arctic giant before them. The glacier loomed over the landscape, a sleeping giant laid flat over the earth, lethargically transforming it beneath its colossal weight. A small patch of green stood out in the bleak region, where a copse of low birch trees grew. As they approached, they saw children playing, tending to a few animals – horned sheep similar to the ones they had passed several days before. The children came running, cheering as their mother returned home safely, clustering around Sölvi and the newcomer excitedly. All of them were mutated in some way.

'Sölvi, what did you bring us?' a girl asked, her back and shoulders lined with bone outcroppings like clusters of broken glass.

'Yeah, Sölvi, show us the treasures!' shouted a boy who ran circles around them, his legs scaled and ending in asymmetrical claws, with a mouth that stretched back just below his earlobes.

Sölvi put down his trunk and popped it open, barely managing to stop the children from rummaging through it like a pack of wild animals. He fished out bags of rock candy and trinkets: an old compass, paper and coloured pencils, various tools for crafts and woodworking. They accepted his gifts eagerly, and he reminded them that they were for all of them – they had to share.

He'd kept a close eye on Ginfaxi during the whole exchange. The seiðskratti kept their face as impassive as the mask they used to wear. A poor choice in deception, Sölvi thought to himself.

The other people he'd brought in the past had all been shocked, even after meeting Halla. Most had seen their fair share of mutated people, but never like this. An entire family, thriving, healthy and happy. If Ginfaxi wanted to keep playing the role of Eir, they should have feigned surprise.

Here, in the place he loved the dearest, surrounded by laughing children, Sölvi was doubtful of having brought Ginfaxi. Perhaps this had been a grave mistake. Sölvi knew well what the seiðskrattar truly were. They were people who willingly turned themselves into weapons. They took the wondrous and deformed it into brutality through their workings. One of them had tortured Halla – but another had saved her as well. People could change if they found the strength within themselves to do so. That was the real reason he'd given Ginfaxi the benefit of the doubt.

Everyone deserved a second chance. A lesson his mother had often repeated, although he found it difficult to take to heart.

Eyvindur stepped out of the turf house, greeting Halla with a hug and a kiss, ecstatic at the quarry she had brought home for them. He looked worn-out but healthy, a man who had lived a hard but satisfying life. The shadow of hard living that lined the faces of many Hrímlanders was not found on his brow. He was carrying a half-woven basket made from reeds he'd been working on.

Ginfaxi grabbed Sölvi's arm as Halla went with Eyvindur to finish butchering the reindeer.

'All of these people are mutated,' they hissed. 'You said the landvættur was capable of healing mutations.'

Gently but firmly, Sölvi removed Ginfaxi's gaunt hand from his arm.

'And that much is true,' he said. 'Look at them. They are all healthy – thriving, even. You saw how strong Halla is, how happy the children are. Their mutations are not malignant, they are not progressing. I never said you could become your old self again. Only that you would get the help you need.'

He could see the seiðskratti retreating into themselves at hearing this. After some hesitation, they followed him into the turf house in sullen silence.

The house was a ramshackle building, made from earth and stone, green grass covering the roof to make it blend almost seamlessly with the landscape. A Hrímlandic home, as they had been made for centuries since settlement. It was, by any measure, a hovel – even for a turf house. Halla led them into the earthy darkness so they could rest, eat and catch up on the outside world. Ginfaxi remained mostly silent. Neither Halla nor Eyvindur bothered them with many questions. They trusted Sölvi to only lead the worthy here, and knew from experience that those pilgrims cared little for sharing their painful pasts unless they volunteered the information.

Coming here always felt like coming home to Sölvi. He envied the children of growing up wild and free, even though it was a hard life far removed from the allures of civilisation which tantalised him so. But who needed paintings and cathedrals, philosophy and literature, when you had the great expanse of the highlands where every hardy flower was a masterpiece, the grandeur of the eternal and all-knowing mountain ranges were your backdrop, and the serene, transcendent solitude of the glacier was on your doorstep?

Sölvi knew that wouldn't be enough for him. He tried telling himself it was, and sometimes he even believed it for a moment. But he would always want more – the world, nothing less. Even so, Hrímland had always been his greatest source of inspiration, proven by countless sketches and paintings of its ethereal nature. Seen with his eyes, the hostile and bleak landscape could be shown in its true light. Through an artist, the harsh land became untethered from the strife and hardships of the beings trying to survive there, seen for only its beauty. Beauty was a useless thing here, like all art. But to Sölvi, it was the most vital thing in existence. Without it, the act of living was meaningless.

He did not know if Ginfaxi would keep their word and help him get off this island once and for all – especially if the treatment they had imagined wasn't what they'd expected. But in some strange manner, it did not really matter. Sölvi had a destiny – a fate already woven. He knew he was a great artist and that he would find a way to fulfil his purpose. Perhaps this was his stepping stone to the grand adventures found in foreign lands – perhaps not. It did not matter. He knew it would happen, one day.

His sibling had told him so.

ᚼ

Þráinn ditched his uniform on the outskirts of the forest. In the deep of the night, he sneaked into a remote farmhouse and stole fresh clothes. The family did not hear a sound as he rifled through their wardrobes in the same room they slept in. An old trick from his days spent as an agent for the Directorate.

Every miserable village he passed through had seen fighting. The insurgents now patrolled the streets, with not a soldier of the Crown in sight. The number of capable kuklarar in their ranks were far higher than he had witnessed before. Whatever defensive forces each place could muster had been severely lacking when faced with such force and numbers. Their militia were heavily armed with a mismatched assortment of peasant weaponry and stolen military equipment. Wagons and automobiles had been repurposed for the rebellion, either heavy with loot or the rabble that served as their troops.

This was way more serious than his briefing had indicated. Its phrasing had made this sound just like every minor revolt he'd quelled over the years. Did Hafnía know what was happening? They had perhaps already lost the entire province. From what he'd gathered by eavesdropping, a fair number of the soldiers had deserted. Þráinn knew Kalmar was stretched thin, but allowing this to happen in the heart of their own homeland would never have crossed his mind.

The civilian clothes permitted him to blend in fairly seamlessly. His weapons were all Kalmar equipment, which could have been looted from fallen soldiers. That still likely marked him as an insurgent soldier just wandering around by himself. Should he be submitted to a thorough search, they'd find his papers – which he needed if he was to return to military command.

Ånge was a small industrial city, built around an intersection of railway lines. A place of this size would have a sizeable garrison, but even that had not been enough to stop the assault. Ruined buildings littered the outskirts, blown apart by thaumaturgical blasts and mortar shells. Occasional wrecks of armoured automobiles blocked the road. The fighting had not reached the city centre, which suggested that Kalmar's forces had marched out to meet them. That arrogant mistake had cost them the city.

He had to get into radio contact with headquarters. Somewhere there must be a pocket of resistance that had held out, a place where a counter-attack was being mustered. Þráinn used seiður to mask his passage, a fairly intricate huliðshjálmur that rendered him inconspicuous in crowds and obscured him from any casual thaumaturgical manner of detection. The city seemed shut down; every shop was barricaded and guarded by rebels. There was nowhere to buy food, people lined up in the central square to receive meals and supplies. The insurgents were organised and had already set up some kind of allocation system, based at the town hall. Þráinn was starving, but he would not risk queueing up like the rest of them. His only chance was that army-run industrial site, just outside of Ånge.

He was almost caught as he headed out of the city. A patrol squad came across his way, different from the others. Each soldier was outfitted with a single thaumaturgical lens affixed in makeshift helmets or glasses, stolen from the masks of presumably dead seiðskrattar. His little trick of sorcerous obfuscation made him stand out like a roaring bonfire. One of them shouted at him and Þráinn bolted into an alley, just barely managing to lose them in the crowd. He got out of the city as fast as he could.

He kept off the main roads as he continued on his way to the army base he'd seen on the maps. If any place had held out it would be there, but having seen the scale of the rebellion he feared that the base had already fallen. Either he'd get shot on approach by the neurotic garrisoned military, or by the insurgents ransacking the place. He wasn't sure which of the two possibilities was more favourable.

Distant explosions sounded as Þráinn ascended a steep hill where he might gain a decent view of the base. He sprinted up, utilising his sorcerous enhancements to improve his stamina, even though he knew the crash would hit him hard. He hadn't eaten properly in days. Columns of black smoke were visible as he crested the top. His worries were confirmed as the base came into view.

It was overflowing with insurgents. Two gates had already been breached and reduced to rubble. Several buildings were on fire. Gunfire spattered across the base in vibrant, sorcerous colours. The soldiers were retreating to a concrete hub at the base's centre. The layout was peculiar, from what Þráinn could tell. It was a research facility, if he had to guess. Likely based underground for the most part.

A large gate opened at the central hub. A shining black machine exited, its hull gleaming in the light. Shots ricocheted off its carapace. Þráinn's heart skipped a beat, as he thought it was the Centimotive – *his* Centimotive. He had last seen it when they docked at Hafnía on a ship crewed by battered, broken souls. As he had lost his career, so had he lost that magnificent machine.

But this was a different beast altogether. It walked on long, multi-jointed legs like an arachnid; its bulbous centre was armoured with heavy plates. It raised itself up high and a cannon appeared from its top, glowing with ethereal light as it started to draw in the surrounding seiðmagn.

Þráinn realised he had seen this machine before – one of the many schematics Doctor Vésteinn had drafted at the initial phase of the excavation. The doctor had dubbed it the Arachnomotive – a version of the Centimotive outfitted for war, akin to what a tank was in comparison to a train. Þráinn seethed at the Crown's audacity, to rob him of the credit of bringing the raw materials they needed to make this miracle of war into a reality. Without him, it would have taken them decades of work to catch up with Vésteinn's secretive research.

Mortar shells were fired, hitting the Arachnomotive without so much as making it reel. Lightning burst within the smoke as the cannon reached its limit and fired at the insurgents that had breached the eastern gate.

The explosion was so bright Þráinn had to shield his eyes. It flared up silent, smokeless, the sound wave hitting him several seconds later than a normal explosion of this magnitude would have. The eastern gate was wiped out, leaving only a crater of molten concrete and twisted earth in its place. The wounded survivors crawled and retreated into shelter. Þráinn was glad he was not able to see the thaumaturgical havoc being wrought upon their bodies.

A tremor shook the earth, making him almost lose his footing. The trees shivered from the impact. With a dread suspicion, he fished out his thaumaturgical goggles and surveyed the battle-field.

The seiðmagn was a crackling torrent, but swathes of it were being reined in to a current running around the Arachnomotive. The insurgents had spread out thinly, surrounding the central hub and the machine guarding it. Streams of seiðmagn flowed between them, forming a net that grew more intricate by the second. Þráinn realised he had again vastly underestimated the number of kuklarar among the fighting force. There must have been dozens – perhaps as many as half of their total number. All of these weak, would-be seiðskrattar were working together in unison to channel the seiðmagn into a counter-attack.

Fools, he thought. The machine was coated in obsidian-infused steel. They had no hope of breaching its defences.

The ground burst apart at the Arachnomotive's numerous legs, like landmines going off. It lost its footing and crashed down. Þráinn laughed. The impact wasn't nearly enough to cause any significant damage to it. Already, its undamaged spider-like legs were working to raise it back up.

His laugh was cut short when a massive spike burst out of the earth through the machine's core. It was hardened metal, shaped into a metallic point. It visibly twitched, and scores of smaller spikes burst from it, shredding the machine apart. It exploded in a blinding display of hypercoloured energy.

'Don't move,' said a voice behind him.

Þráinn tensed up, coiled like a steel spring. He listened closely and heard nothing. No rustle of fabric or creaking of leather, fingers tightening around a trigger, boots bracing against the ground. They'd obfuscated their passing quite thoroughly, to be able to sneak up on him like this.

'Turn around and raise your hands – slowly.'

Þráinn did as he was ordered. He could not hide his surprise when he found himself faced with five barrels of skorrifles. The insurgents were heavily armoured in stolen military gear, each with at least one thaumaturgical lens in their helmets. He recognised them – the patrol squad that had spotted him in Ånge. Their leader was clearly the woman who had spoken to him. A navy-blue band was wrapped around her upper arm, marking her as some sort of officer.

'This is a mistake,' he started. 'I'm one of—'

'Shut the hell up. We know who you are, Meinholt.'

Not good.

He studied the other soldiers, not even risking turning his head. The leader laughed at him.

'Surprised? I'd imagine so. Turns out the company you left for dead weren't too keen on dying for a tyrannical cause. Especially when their coward of a commander made a run for it.'

One of the other soldiers chuckled darkly. Þráinn didn't recognise him, but the man was looking at him with unrelenting hatred.

'They'll do much worse than hang you for this, traitor,' Þráinn growled at the man.

'I'd spend my energy on worrying what's going to happen to *you*, you piece of shit.' The man spat on the ground.

There were five of them. Despite his sorcerous enhancements, he would not be able to take them all down. But he might be able to run for it.

His vision exploded into dark blotches when he was hit on the head from behind. Þráinn fell, convulsing, helplessly throwing up as the others who'd sneaked up on him from behind let loose with their thaumaturgical seizure-truncheons, beating him into oblivion.

Tuttugu og átta

They ate well that night – reindeer stew with potatoes and swede, seasoned with thyme. The children badgered Sölvi for stories, and he obliged them. He told them how he'd outwitted a troll; about the magical forest that had grown in the north-east; how he had chanted a draugur back into their grave and refused the hand of the fairest maiden in the village as a reward; how he had been made a king of the vættir living inside the realm hidden behind a remote waterfall up in the mountains. Each story was accompanied by a painting, one for every child to keep. There was some truth to each one, but telling the children about the reality of things was too much for Sölvi. A story isn't any worse for being a half-truth.

Ginfaxi ate little and spoke less. Sölvi could now see how they tried to mask the pain caused by their mutations. He hoped Ginfaxi could find the respite they so deeply wanted – that seeing this family living happy and free out here would give them hope.

After dinner, Sölvi went outside with Halla and Eyvindur to talk in private. Ginfaxi retreated to their bed early, looking more exhausted now they were in a safe haven than they had been out in the wilderness.

Sölvi shared a few precious cigarettes with the couple and

spoke quietly of developments in nearby provinces: new, strange entities that grew from the rampant seiðmagn coursing through the land; petty grievances that escalated into feuds; the hardships of life on a barren island dominated by lawlessness and shortage.

It wasn't all bad news. A few places had managed to use the seiðmagn to their advantage. The farm of Dysjarholt had seen a variety of new plants growing in their vicinity after the mists lifted, located in a secluded valley where the climate had inexplicably become more temperate. Sheer desperation had caused a few farmers to band together and try to establish a presence there, but the lethal wildlife and new diseases had wiped most of them out. The ones who'd survived had made it back with a few seeds. Through a clever use of seiður they had cultivated them into new, wondrous fruits and vegetables that could thrive despite the cold climate. Sölvi had brought a few with him, along with the knowledge of how to grow them – knowledge traded for stories, paintings and poems with the remote farmers on the edge of the world.

A beating of wings almost put out their cigarettes as Bölmóður landed. The náskári shared his latest report with Halla. Since Sölvi was last here, Bölmóður had managed to establish an alliance with a nearby tribe of náskárar, called Territory-of-the-black-sands. The northern landvættur was a holy being to many náskárar, who believed the Great Eagle to be the primordial hatch-mother of all náskárar. According to myth, all tribes had once been united under the landvættur's banner. Their skrumnir felt a powerful presence at the glacier and believed it to be the Eagle. That had been enough for the hersir and the rest of the Territory-of-the-black-sands to pledge allegiance. Word was already spreading among the other tribes.

'They misunderstan't the nature of that which sleeps beneath the glacier,' said Bölmóður. 'Err-at the Great Eagle. They can-at know what sleeps here.'

'So you lied to them?' asked Eyvindur.

'Err-at lie. *Ixarggk'graakt* believed he sensed the Great Eagle. Did-at correct, as the Great Eagle does in truth nest within the ice.'

'So their … ixa … I mean, the …'

'*Ixarggk'graakt*,' growled Bölmóður. 'Or skrumnir, as you say't.'

'Yes,' Eyvindur said dumbly, ignoring Halla's and Sölvi's sniggering. 'Their skrumnir. I don't think it's a good idea to hide things from them. What if only the skrumnir came here?'

Bölmóður clicked his ironed claws together in contemplation with an unpleasant sound.

'*Ixarggk'graakt* sees further than his beak,' he admitted. 'It shall be considered.'

ᚺ

Black sand drifted across the ice in wide strokes, contrasted by light streaks of grey with thick black veins like soot. The sun reflected harshly off the glacier, making Ginfaxi and Sölvi squint. Hrímlandic terrain was so empty and vast that distances became warped when overlooking it. This was even more amplified on the vacant whiteness of the glacier. Bright blue light shone within cracks in the ice – ravines that stretched down into a strangely illuminated, quiet realm of death. Sölvi led Ginfaxi on in a criss-cross pattern, constantly deciphering the minute and great changes in the ice since last he'd found a safe path through.

Eventually they came across a narrow gorge. Worn ropes ran down the sheer, icy cliff, nailed to the top on large iron spikes. Sölvi pulled the ropes up and tied one around himself, the other around Ginfaxi. Abseiling down was easy enough, despite his small backpack of supplies. Ginfaxi struggled, physical strength not being their forte. Eventually, by taking it slowly, they made it down to a dark stone sill, where a black tunnel stretched out before them.

'What is this place?' asked Ginfaxi once they'd caught their breath, studying the brickwork intensely. They risked a glance further down the gorge, seeing sporadic stonework jutting from the ice before all faded into darkness. They muttered to themselves in horror. 'This is – I've seen this…'

'There's an entire city beneath the ice, we think,' said Sölvi, tactfully ignoring the strange comment. 'Don't worry, it's completely safe. It's stood for who knows how long under the crushing weight of the glacier. Whoever built it really made it to last.'

He lit an oil lamp and started down the tunnel. The seiðskratti followed shortly.

An ancient, still cold permeated the ruins, more piercing than on the surface. It settled deep into their bones. Ginfaxi stopped occasionally to take in the strange glyphs and etchings on the walls, but Sölvi did not slow his pace. A faint glow started to illuminate the tunnel. It grew in strength as they progressed further into the ancient city.

'Can you feel it?' Ginfaxi asked. 'The landvættur… I can feel it like a second heartbeat.'

Sölvi did not respond. The severed cord hidden within his necklace echoed that same, intangible surge.

The tunnel ended abruptly at a vast, open chamber. Tall edifices of stone formed a circular plaza, roofed by a jagged dome of ice. Sunlight filtered through the glacier, bathing the area in a diffused, blue-tinted light.

In the centre of the square was a vast tree, the trunk thick and knotted, resembling a woven rope. Above, the canopy spread out wide and bristled with foliage. The white bark was marked with carved runes in concentrated patterns, dark red from the sap. Its roots were gnarled and spread out, grasping the impenetrable stone floor tightly. As Sölvi and Ginfaxi approached, it became evident that the tree was actually made of bone, like clusters of tusks entwined around themselves in a dense coil. What initially seemed to be red sap colouring the markings was dried blood. The foliage was in all the splendour of autumn, wild yellow to orange to a vibrant red, the leaves holding an almost metallic, glistening sheen.

Ginfaxi jumped as something stirred by the gnarled roots of the osseous tree. An enormous serpentine being revealed itself, coiling around the trunk. It had no scales, but pale, tough-looking flesh, and bared vertebrae jutted from its back. The being slithered around the trunk of the tree and turned to face the travellers. The snakelike body ended in a humanoid upper figure: torso, two arms, a head. From its back stretched two useless wings with feathers the same colours and sheen as those on the leaves.

Sölvi grabbed Ginfaxi firmly when the seiðskratti made to run. The being took a long look at them. Then Sölvi approached it, dragging Ginfaxi along behind him.

The snake-man's head was too big for the human torso it sat upon, bloated to twice the expected size. It was covered in eyes. Brown and blue, purple, green and yellow, some glowing iridescent. They varied wildly in size and shape, their pupils in a chaotic disorder: large, slitted, split and in various multiples crowding the irises.

'Sölvi,' the being said in a chiming voice that reverberated through the chamber. 'Welcome back.'

Sölvi placed the supplies he was carrying on the ground. Ginfaxi stared downwards like a beaten dog. The being stretched its serpentine body to get a closer look at them.

'This is Eir,' Sölvi started, and the snake-being laughed.

'No, dear Sölvi. It is not.' Despite having no visible mouth, their countless eyes communicated sheer mirth in the wrinkling of their eyelids. 'Hello, Ginfaxi. It's been a long while.'

At the mention of their magisterial name, Ginfaxi dared to look the creature in the face.

'So it really is you.'

'Yes. It is.'

Calming their breathing, Ginfaxi studied the environment closer. They traced the coiling body around the tree, down to where it sprung from within the cluster of tree roots. There, hidden deep beneath them, was the hint of a withered bottom half of a body. The tree had sprouted from its stomach.

'My injury grew from last we met – as you can clearly see.' The being gestured towards the tree of bone growing out of the body's abdomen. 'A seed was planted within me. When I realised what was truly happening to me, I stopped trying to fight it. I nurtured it instead.'

'You're the so-called landvættur of the north?' spat Ginfaxi angrily. '*This* is the Great Eagle? I'm disappointed, Kári. I never took you for a charlatan, deranged as you might be.'

Kári laughed like a cascading waterfall. 'That title is perhaps too grand for me. But yes, I am the one who heals the unfortunate souls who find their way here. I help them see themselves for what they are fated to become in a transformed world unchained from its tethers. The story that's been woven around me helps others trust me and accept their fate – but you know well that I am not the landvættur you no doubt sensed on your approach. Have you truly come here to seek healing? Or to once again attempt to enslave a living god to your pathetic machines?' Kári's eyes glared at the seiðskratti with a cold

ALEXANDER DAN VILHJÁLMSSON

ruthlessness. 'I think you'll find your attempts will prove even more disastrous than your previous venture.'

Ginfaxi deflated at this. 'That is not why I am here.'

Sölvi had remained quiet up to this point. He knew that this confrontation would be difficult.

'Ginfaxi was part of an expedition to find the landvættur,' said Sölvi. 'But they convinced me they wanted no part of it. I believe them. They want to be healed, Kári. Made whole again, before the fracture within them tears them asunder.'

'I'll find no help here,' muttered Ginfaxi. 'Only an expedited death. This was a mistake.'

Kári settled his serpentine form down, coiling up so he was at Ginfaxi's height.

'It's the spiral, isn't it? I can see it turning within you. Unravelling your being.'

Ginfaxi said nothing.

'A new world is awakening, Ginfaxi. The world as it was – as it should always have been. We have been living out generations on a decaying corpse. For whatever reason you choose to believe, you have been appointed a new purpose in this world. I cannot foresee what it is. I can only help you find the way there – if you'll let me.'

Ginfaxi looked up at Kári's unrecognisable form with tears in their eyes.

'You'd have me become a monster? A grotesque thing like you?'

Kári was not unkind when he responded. 'You have been a monster for a long time, Ginfaxi. Perhaps it is time to become something different.'

'You're mad.'

Sölvi left them to talk. Not everyone was prepared to accept what the winged serpent had to say. It was up to Ginfaxi now.

He itched with the desire to know more about their past – but he let that go for now. Everyone had something they wanted to forget, to leave buried. He would not be the one who pecked at those still-healing scars.

Several dark openings led out of the chamber. He headed down one, through which a warm wind blew. The air became humid as he walked, the carved passage giving way to a natural tunnel. With every step the presence that permeated this place grew stronger, almost unbearably so. The only sounds came from his own breathing and droplets that fell lazily from stalactites. After a long while, a faint echo became audible, rising in volume as he proceeded. A woman's voice singing a sombre lullaby. His heart racing, he entered the cave where his brother slept.

The lake was still and vast, and smelled of sulphur. Steam rose from its surface. A light shone from its depths, emanating from something huge sleeping at the bottom – the landvættur, resting, growing. Sölvi could faintly feel his brother stirring, dreaming whatever dreams a god in metamorphosis dreamed.

A woman sat by the shores of the lake, singing to the dark stillness. Elka turned as Sölvi approached. Her face lit up at the sight of him and they ran to each other, mother and son embracing within the darkness of the earth.

Tuttugu og níu

Þráinn started awake and thrashed as he tried to get up. His arms and feet were chained in iron and he fell face down on cobblestones. His head throbbed. Waves of nausea still lingered, following his beating with the seizure-truncheon. Someone cursed, and then a guard pulled him roughly to his feet and pushed him back on the bench where he had been sitting unconscious. Blurred vision returned to Þráinn, with the realisation of what had happened – was happening – to him.

He was in a prison cell with several others, all chained as he was. Soldiers and civilians alike in muddied and torn clothes, splotched with blood, bruised and beaten. At a glance, he recognised all of them as Kalmar loyalists. The guard told him to shut up and be quiet or he'd be left on the filthy floor next time.

He spent an unknowable time in that dungeon. They were fed stale bread and water. The prison block was vast, but the prisoners there only occupied one quarter of the available space. The facility was heavily used, with grime covering every surface and the stale smell of fear in the air. He was certain he was being kept within the military facility. Þráinn wasn't sure why the base required this amount of prison space. Maybe the garrison had been dealing with rebels and heretics for a long while.

The other prisoners chatted occasionally to each other in low voices. The guards didn't seem to mind. The rebels had overtaken a huge part of the province, according to the hushed gossip. A man who claimed to be a clerk at the local governor's office said that uprisings were happening elsewhere, all over the heartlands of the Crown.

Þráinn's thoughts wandered frequently to the Nine, the Directorate's old prison. The memories rose unbidden and refused to remain buried. As bad as this was, it still paled in comparison to the operation he'd had going there. He tried to find comfort in this. It could be worse – far worse. He still had a chance to get out of this alive.

They were let out after a few days and put to work clearing away rubble from the collapsed buildings. The fallen military base was now being used as a base of operations for the insurgents. The place buzzed with activity. Craftsmen had set up shop and worked tirelessly, repairing armaments and organising stolen loot. Soldiers trained in sloppy formations.

The work was back-breaking but repetitive. It provided ample opportunity to monitor the surroundings. The place was heavily guarded, but the rebels' schedules were lax. There were obvious gaps in the patrols and their visual area. These people were not trained soldiers, at least not most of them. Most likely the high command who managed this mess had some training, but the average grunt was just another village idiot.

Occasionally, everyone went on high alert. Þráinn could see it from how a semblance of discipline infected the rebels. They perked up, cleaned their ragtag uniforms, kept their weapons in check. He eventually did figure out what exactly was causing this shift when a group of higher-ups came to inspect the wreck of the arachnid-machine they had downed. Half of them were dressed up in what counted as their military command, if Þráinn was to guess. The others were a mismatched bunch, laden with talismans and rune-covered clothing. Each wore a unique mask or helmet, not always obscuring the face, but it was clear from where they had drawn their inspiration.

Would-be seiðskrattar. Or so these kuklarar saw themselves. The sight made him furious. Did they really think that by covering themselves in charms and nonsensical markings that they could hold a candle to a truly learned magister? Idiots.

The mundane military staff were obviously intimidated by the kuklarar. From the way they carried themselves, it was clear that they were the real leaders of the movement, the officers reduced to mere administrative purposes.

He averted his gaze when they walked past his work site. One of them lingered and watched him and his fellow prisoners for a while. She was dressed in a scaled emerald cloak, wearing an old sallet. The helmet was round with a long tail at the back, lending it an angular, ferocious shape. A red lens had been welded into the visor's eye slit. Countless fetishes of bound bone and wooden charms hung from her clothing, which was well-worn and utilitarian. She left and he breathed a sigh of relief. There had been something very uncomfortable about the way she was studying them.

Guards grabbed him from behind as his shift ended and everyone else was herded back to their cells. A black bag went over his head and everything went dark.

ᚽ

Excruciating pain woke Þráinn. He looked down and saw the bloody mess on his chest, the intense pulsing that was the source of his pain. He struggled against his restraints, screaming in agony and frustration.

They had branded him. A galdrastafur had been burned into his entire solar plexus, a sigil that nullified his sorcerous enhancements. They could just as well have cut out his tongue, or severed an arm. The loss was as unbearable as the pain. Cold sweat covered his body and he shook uncontrollably.

'I told you he was a freak. He was glowing like the goddamn sun.'

He looked up. It was the woman who'd led the group who'd captured him. She wore a smug smile. Next to her was the kuklari who'd spotted him. She'd taken off her helmet and placed it on the table in front of him. Next to it were various instruments – ones he did not wish to dwell further upon.

'I read your report, Kaleva. You saw the seiður he was using, not his enhancements. You're not ordained yet, remember.'

Kaleva grimaced. 'Yeah, yeah. But I was right, Skymning. You remember that.'

The kuklari grunted. Þráinn started to laugh, gritting his teeth through the pain.

'What's so funny, Lieutenant?'

'Ordained?' He took a quick few breaths, suffered through another hateful laugh. 'You fucking heretics think you're worthy of titling yourselves magisters?'

'Don't you worry about that. Those enhancements – who gave them to you? How was the ritual performed?'

He didn't answer them. Then Kaleva went for the tools.

It did not take long to get him to talk. Stripped of the protection from his enhancements, he was as vulnerable as a newborn.

He gave them everything. His name, his rank, the movements of Ida Company, how he'd come to be on the mainland. He tried to hold back regarding his work for the Directorate – but that meagre resistance was broken as well. He despised himself for being so weak, so afraid. During his time, he had tortured countless prisoners. None who had something to hide had broken as easily as he did. But then again, he also knew what happened to those who held out. There was only one place that grit led to, and the prospect of that was even more terrifying than the reality facing him now.

They dressed his wounds after the session. Fed him, gave him clean clothes. He was led back to a solitary confinement cell, soundproofed but not lightless. Still, it was not as bad as the worst of the Nine. These minimal decencies which had been afforded him only made him that much more scared of what lay ahead. To him, it seemed like a good tactic to wear someone down. Give them respite, just so you can break them all over again.

It never came to that. He was already broken. Next time they brought him out, he was led to a large meeting room, filled with the higher-ups. Rebel officers and those strange kuklarar like Skymning, each bearing a Nordic pseudonym like her. They had already gleaned how to perform their own sorcerous enhancements from his descriptions – although he did not doubt that trial and error would result in grotesque and brutal missteps. Now they grilled him about the excavation, the Centimotive, the thaumaturgical power plant in Perlan, as well as the thing named Ingi Vítalín.

He tried to barter, bolstered by not being in a torture chamber for the interrogation. He asked for freedom, a clean slate – anything that would result in his walking out of here alive. To his surprise, his demands were easily met. He would be set free when they got all the information they wanted. They even threw in a horse and a few basic supplies.

Þráinn told them everything. Although he was no scientist like Doctor Vésteinn, who had designed the actual machinery, he knew a great deal about how it worked in principle – especially the Centimotive. He had been there as a representative of Innréttingarnar, to ensure that their investment paid off. His access level had been high.

A few of the kuklarar drilled him with tough, technical questions. How were the brains extracted? What sensors allowed them to manipulate the machines? How could they still channel seiðmagn? What measures were in place to keep them compliant? Why had Ingi Vítalín not been given such restraints? What kind of person was a good candidate for becoming a cognitive unit?

He did not have all the answers they wanted, but they were still satisfied. Catching a glimpse of the papers they were eagerly comparing, speaking in hushed tones, he realised they already knew quite a lot about things. There were some gaps they needed filled in – and he was perhaps the link they had been missing.

'And the mists?' asked Skymning.

'What about them?' Þráinn was perplexed by the question. 'Even the Crown wasn't stupid enough to actually put the blame for the Hrímlandic eruptions on me, although they would have loved to.'

The sallet obscured most of Skymning's face, leaving part of the lower half exposed. With a slight visible frown, Þráinn understood that he'd given the wrong answer to the question she had truly asked.

Þráinn ate well that night. He was moved to a different cell that felt more like an ordinary room. He could see out over the courtyard through the barred window.

They had cleaned up the wreckage of the Arachnomotive and laid it out neatly. Engineers were crawling around its insides, welders fused together broken plates, vast supplies of obsidian and iron were being hauled in.

His wound was healing up nicely. The mark looked terrible

ALEXANDER DAN VILHJÁLMSSON

and would leave an ugly scar. Still, he reminded himself, it was better than the alternative.

And it was definitely better than he deserved.

ᚼ

The next day, Kaleva and Skymning came by with a couple more questions. After that, they had Þráinn taken out of his cell to inspect something. Following stark hallways, he was led into the depths of the compound, eventually opening up to a factory floor. He was awed by what was waiting there.

It was a thaumaturgical power plant. Smaller than Perlan, but still more than enough to supply several companies with thaumaturgical weapons. The kuklarar worked alongside white-clad scientists – turncoats. It seemed as though the place had been nearly operational when the insurgents attacked. He was taken deeper into the confines, past several security checkpoints. The air grew colder, sterilised and dead.

Glass-paned walls revealed laboratories that were being scoured, workers going methodically through piles of documents. In the dimness beyond were glowing vats, filled with viscous liquid. Within were things either dead or kept in suspension. The few he could glimpse clearly at their rapid pace resembled alien plant life, others living stone or abhorrent protozoa, with clusters of wild appendages and perplexing sensory organs. There were also several chambers filled with blue-tinged vapour. The abominations grew more nightmarish with each step they progressed through that bleakly lit hallway. Þráinn now understood Skymning's question the night before.

'They were weaponising the mist,' he muttered numbly to himself.

Skymning didn't spare him a glance as she replied.

'You must be disappointed to have been left out of the loop, Lieutenant.'

At last they entered a nearly empty room. Only a few kuklarar were working here. A cold shiver ran down his back as he witnessed an even more dreadful horror than the laboratories he had passed. It was an extraction chamber.

Just a glance at the people assembled there told Þráinn that they had not been able to turn or capture the scientists in charge of this operation. Likely, most of those had been fully trained seiðskrattar, and had either not gone down without a fight, or managed to escape. Only one device was fully completed, but the rebels were struggling to operate it.

A bare chair was fused to a convoluted mess of cable and steel. Dials and gauges clustered around a printout machine, which would vomit a confusing mess of lines when a patient was being operated on. From it rose a metallic arm ending in a four-pronged claw, its palm lined with serrated edges. In the middle of the blades was a long steel needle, glistening in the light.

Þráinn had been there when Ingi Vítalín had been reborn – as the machine had put it. Kaleva and Skymning asked about the machine and he replied to the best of his knowledge. He had been part of the selection committee for the Laían ambassadorial position, and so he knew a lot about what the procedure entailed. Including what they had withheld from Ingi.

Kaleva kept a cool smile throughout his replies. Skymning jotted down notes, along with the others. When they were satisfied, Þráinn sensed that his purpose had been fulfilled.

'I'll be wanting that horse now,' he said to Kaleva.

'Right you are.'

Her smile intensified, and she glanced at the other scientists. Out of the corner of his eye, he glimpsed them nodding in response.

Deep down, he had known. But it had been nice to pretend.

He struggled as they strapped him into the chair. He did not know what he was screaming at them as they fired up the device, but as Skymning injected him with a sedative it all receded into a deep haze. Þráinn looked up at the metal claw above him, its mouth filled with serrated edges and a lethal point. He prayed to whatever god would listen that he would not be himself on the other side – but he knew that would not be the case unless they messed up the procedure.

Ͱ

A strange feeling woke him. Not pain, this time. Deep in the obscured recesses of his mind, Þráinn was relieved by that.

Different restraints held him back now. Something unfelt, but all-encompassing. He felt as if he was submerged in a lukewarm void, at the bottom of a great abyss. The pressure was intense and relentless.

An urge awoke in him. A command he was driven to comply with. He acted without thinking, a reflex he could not suppress. He sensed others around him – unknowable and distant things that were tied to him through a thread he could not control or fully comprehend.

Together, acting as one, they woke the machine that housed them. Glimpses of the world were passed through him – sensors for light and movement, currents of seiðmagn and performance levels of countless bits of machinery. The information was meaningless, a blurred haze his limited consciousness could not grasp. Comprehension had not been allocated as his task.

Instructions were punched in, and he responded like a puppet on a string. *Move to the south-east. Expect hostiles.* Enslaved within the repurposed Arachnomotive, what remained of Þráinn Meinholt set to work doing the rebels' bidding.

ᚻ

Ginfaxi was deep in conversation with Kári when Sölvi and Elka headed back to the chamber. Sölvi decided not to disturb the pair. Whatever Ginfaxi would decide was up to them now. He followed Elka through one of the tunnels to her chambers. It had been some kind of living area before, possibly a simple home. Melted candles crowded the carved sills of the stone room, while Sölvi's paintings covered the dreadful glyphs on the walls. Simple furniture decorated the room: a bedroll of sheepskin furs, a few of Eyvindur's woven baskets, a birchwood trunk and an almost-full bookshelf. It had the bare necessities a place needed to be called a home. A hearth had been made from rocks fused together with seiður, and Elka summoned a bright-burning flame within it that needed no physical fuel to burn. She still didn't like using her gift, which came to her as easily as flight to an arctic tern. They cooked together from the supplies Sölvi had brought.

She had not aged a day since they left Vestmannaeyjar. As Sölvi had grown into a young man, it seemed time could not touch Elka. Soon he would catch up with her apparent age. He told her about Ginfaxi's offer – the slim chance he had to get away from Hrímland and see the world. The idea of Sölvi's leaving saddened Elka, but still she remained supportive.

'What about people who need Kári's help?' he asked. 'How will they find their way here without help?'

'You've planted the seeds – now leave them to grow in peace. Ours is not the harvest, only the sowing. People must make their own way in this world, for better or worse. It is up to them now to find the Eagle of the North.'

He laughed at this, scooping up the last spoonful of stew. His mother looked at him disapprovingly.

'That title is no misnomer, Sölvi.' Elka's tone brooked no argument. 'Beneath the glacier, your sibling is changing during his tranquil sleep. So is Kári transforming into something greater than himself.'

He knew better than to argue. Many times before, her words had proven to be prophetic. That was, after all, why they'd made their way up north to begin with. Usually it took him far longer to see just how she had been speaking truth.

When the meal was done, Sölvi cleaned the wooden bowls in a basin while Elka brewed tea.

'I will not stay here for much longer,' she said as she stirred the dried herbs in the iron kettle. Sölvi ceased his scrubbing. 'Recurring dreams have become more frequent, extremely vivid in these last weeks. Your sibling's sleep grows restless. We will head west when he awakens – Griðungur does not belong in the north. Nestled somewhere in those oldest of Hrímlandic fjords lies a mist-touched place made for him. Where I'll go after that, I do not know.'

Sölvi nodded to himself as he resumed scrubbing diligently. Similar feelings had pulled at him in the early morning, between waking and sleep. He had not wanted to admit it to himself, but he had known Elka would say something like this during his visit to the glacier. He also knew that it would be his last.

'We'll find each other then,' he said with confidence that was mostly bluster, focusing on the work at hand. There was no such doubt in Elka's voice when she replied.

'We will.'

Ginfaxi approached him early next morning. They had decided to stay with Kári and explore their options.

'I can't go on pretending that nothing is wrong. Maybe I can help others, like Kári does.'

'Maybe,' was all Sölvi said.

There was no way of knowing how Ginfaxi could end up.

They gave him their regalia as a parting gift, as well as a charm that would help disguise Sölvi as Ginfaxi on the ship. It was a convoluted working of seiður, bound in bone taken from Kári's tree. Sölvi was awed by it – his own work was now revealed for the kukl it was. Ginfaxi also briefed him on how best to deal with Captain Tordenskjold and where to go once the ship reached Hafnía.

It took a lot out of Ginfaxi to hand over the regalia. Despite that, they showed no little hesitation when giving it up. The mask had been their face for most of their life, Sölvi knew. He took it with what he hoped was suitable reverence and then he said his goodbyes.

Elka escorted him all the way back to Halla and Eyvindur's place at the roots of the glacier. She rarely went down there and claimed to need the fresh sunlight, unfiltered by the ice. On the way, she decided to stay a few days this time. Days filled with the laughter of children, hands dirty from hard work, breathing in the fresh air – it did wonders for a tired soul.

As they approached the homestead, Sölvi spotted the Pale King half-hidden behind dark outcroppings of rock, standing out like a lost ram against the black sands. It knew to keep well away from the glacier. It bolted away as soon as it saw who was accompanying Sölvi.

'Does he give you any trouble?' Elka asked, with only a slight hint of worry.

'No. He just watches at a distance.'

'I tried to end it, all those years ago.' She sighed. 'This old draugur should be tailing me, not you.'

'Don't worry. I'm fine – and I will be fine.' He patted his chest, where the necklace holding the piece of silver thread lay beneath his coat. 'I'll be keeping this for a while longer. It seems to keep that thing occupied. I don't want to give him a moment's peace for his mind to settle.'

She nodded. 'Takk, my dear Sölvi.'

Sölvi didn't look back as he left. If he didn't look back then he could imagine her always there, just behind him, waiting for him to come back home. It wasn't goodbye. It was just a slightly longer journey than usual.

He donned the regalia as Eyjafjörður came into view, over-looking Dulvík at a distance from the mountain slopes. The world was transformed when seen through the mask's lenses, with a great torrent of seiðmagn gently swirling out from the gigantic crimson flower that had grown out of the ruined manor. The mysterious components within the beak had a rich, earthy scent, each breath invigorating him in strange ways he did not fully comprehend.

The *Vindhund* was still docked, the damage to its hull now fully repaired. The soldiers looked upon him with fearful respect, tripping over themselves to get out of his way. Captain Tordenskjold was waiting up on deck for the seiðskratti.

'Well?' the captain growled. 'Is it there?'

'Just another thaumaturgical deviant,' said Sölvi, trying as hard as he could to mimic Ginfaxi's detached tone. 'The boy naïvely believed it to be a landvættur. He has paid for his mistake.'

Tordenskjold cursed. 'Another damned wild goose chase. They'll have our heads back in Hafnía if we return empty-handed.'

'Captain, I remind you that our secondary mission is to find a landvættur. Our primary goal is to gather information on Hrímland. And our information is clear as day – Hrímland is a scorched wasteland. With the rise in seiðmagn across the continent, there is little reason to invest in this backwater. At least Kalmar can now be fully made aware of that fact and summarily focus its efforts elsewhere.'

'If you say so.' The captain gave him a look. Sölvi started to sweat. 'That kid's really dead?'

Sölvi inclined his head slightly. 'That is a somewhat philosophical question. Rest assured that he won't be a further nuisance to anyone.'

Tordenskjold gestured to the trunk Sölvi carried on his back. 'Why did you bother bringing his garbage back?'

'I'd like to go over his notes. There might be something useful there, still.'

'If you say so.'

They departed the next day, threading through the north-western fjords as they completed their tour of Hrímland. Many villages had been left to ruin, some of them now unrecognisably strange sites: clusters of gleaming crystal formations; tundra jungles filled with unnerving sounds; new mountains like nothing formed by the natural world, crafted by the still-erupting volcanoes. Those villages still populated had mostly been overtaken by cults worshipping whatever bizarre thing had manifested there. They seemed to be doing well – at least seen from a distance.

The soldiers were not keen to investigate these places further. From what Sölvi could gather, such peculiar changes were happening on the mainland. It was not as intense compared to what was happening in Hrímland, but a foreboding sense of things to come lay over the crew. They whispered about distant places, some close to home, that had become unrecognisable after the mists lifted.

Sölvi eased into his new role with little difficulty. Seiðskrattar were notoriously arrogant, so finally he found a natural outlet for his own haughtiness. He lied through his teeth when some thaumaturgical insight was needed, and no one there was learned enough to challenge him. Rarely was any kind of actual seiður needed. Ginfaxi had been right – Tordenskjold was unsettled by the supernatural sciences and resented leaning on them for minor things. It was a serious fault for a captain with a seiðskratti at their beck and call, as the sorcery might have provided a huge advantage, but now it worked wonderfully in Sölvi's favour.

On the open sea, seiðmagn was more limited. Still, Ginfaxi had used their resources heading here to stave off the sea monster that had attacked the ship, as well as diverting the winds and currents for a quicker escape. Sölvi would not dare to even pretend attempting such feats. As Hrímland sunk below the horizon, he retreated to his cabin and feigned a supernatural malady. He was in luck, as the ship encountered no storms or malignant beings on its way.

Finally, the great city of Hafnía came into view. Sölvi was dumbfounded by the vastness of the metropolis, with its numerous towers and throngs of people. He still recalled Reykjavík vaguely, but even from a child's perspective where everything seemed bigger than it actually was, Hafnía towered over the fallen capital of Hrímland.

The captain was worried. A naval blockade guarded the city, with smoke rising from the distant east. He told Sölvi to get ready for war – the capital was under attack.

Soon after they docked, messengers arrived with orders. Rebels had stormed through the mainland over the previous months, and now they stood at the gates of Hafnía itself. It was said they had a great metallic construct that tore mercilessly through the Crown's forces, as well as a legion of heretic kuklarar.

Ginfaxi's orders were to report to the front immediately. Sölvi's luggage was hauled to an automobile, which would drive him directly there. Tordenskjold was so relieved to see the last of the seiðskratti that he spared no thought to Sölvi's actions, so he was not suspicious that Ginfaxi had brought all of Sölvi's belongings as well.

Sölvi got into the automobile. Only a single soldier was driving. As they entered the hustle and bustle of the city, it proved easy to knock the soldier out with a few well-chosen words of power. Sölvi took off the mask and headed the opposite direction, towards the west. He ditched the car on the outskirts of the city and, with some trouble, managed to trade it in for a horse.

He headed out west along with many of the citizens who were abandoning their homes, heading away from the oncoming war. They moved against a steady rush of troops coming to defend the Commonwealth.

He took out a map from his bag, a fine leather satchel given to him by Ginfaxi. He had spent considerable time studying the map in the seiðskratti's cabin. It charted the entire continent. South of Hafnía was another city, called Fenvangur in Hrímlandic. It was easy enough to buy the ferry passage south, with all the money Ginfaxi had left him. From there he could travel easily by land. He had read about it voraciously over the years – a place of high art, masterful music, philosophy and literature.

Sölvi smiled. The weather was calm and the sun warm, less hostile than up in the distant north. Life teemed everywhere, with insects and animals he had only read about in books. As night fell he stopped at a roadside tavern and ate the best meal of his life – deer and roasted vegetables. He practised his Nordic by telling tall tales of his journeys and gathering any piece of useful information he could find. The locals were worried about the changes wrought by the mists. The news calmed Sölvi, although he played along with the villagers' trepidation. As the evening went on he retreated to his private room and painted voraciously all the new and strange things he had seen.

His soul was alight – soaring, finally free of the fetters that had restrained it his entire life. Opportunity waited, promising finer and more spiritually rich experiences than he had ever dreamed of.

He knew that many hardships lay ahead – grief and toil and struggle. In this moment, Sölvi welcomed the prospect, for it meant that there was much to be won – joy and triumph and peace. So it was for all who lived in a world awakening, all who found their bonds severed. This was the dawn of an age of dreaming manifested in the real, of miracles and rebirth. He intended to seize that renewing fire with all his strength and wield it with his own hand.

With ardent determination, he dipped the brush in vibrant paint and set to work.

ᚼ

Far to the north, where the mainland met the waves in sandy dunes, a pale shape crawled from the surf, its slumping form crowned with obsidian. It collapsed on the water's edge, ever on the threshold of all things, momentarily exhausted. Algae covered its grimy alabaster skin, with seaweed hanging from its horns. It stared longingly at the warm lights of inland homes, sensing the distant sounds and smells of life.

The broken thing waited. It could do nothing else but watch and pray for an apocalypse that must inevitably come to pass. It arched its back, its heavy head falling listlessly backwards, to look longingly at the broken moon. It lamented those tragic fragments of an egg still unhatched, the nightmare of being not yet ended. Deprived of power, the only thing in the world it had cherished, it warmed itself with half-remembered memories of long-vanished glories and imagined events that might have come to pass.

It would wait till the oceans dried and the skies darkened, if needed. One day, new pawns would present themselves. The gate would stand open once more.

So it was written, so it will be done.

Þrjátíu

The fishing boats were coming in. Diljá headed to the pier to help with offloading the day's catch, which would then be processed and hung to cure on rafters. Styrmir waved to her from his boat, tossing a painter to her as he docked. They chatted about everyday things, the weather and happenings in the village. Diljá told him that the encroaching fungal forest had been cleared and that the hunters had got a few kills. The meat was being salted, the chitin was enough for a handful of new knives and other tools. Styrmir was happy hearing that, as he had worried people would want to send another scavenging group into the ruins of Reykjavík.

Diljá set to work gutting the fish. She treasured these small, everyday moments like gems found within mundane rocks. It had taken a lot of hard work to make them reality. As the repetition of work set in, her mind drifted. It was not easy to let go of the past.

Things had fallen apart before Diljá made it to Starholt a decade earlier. She'd struggled to reach her old home, pushing against throngs of panicked people. Her family had not seen her for years. All of them were terrified. In a flurry of confused communication, they had reached out to one another. They fled Reykjavík as everything collapsed around them.

The appearance of the Stone Giant and the downfall of the flying fortress were still vivid in people's memories. Their worst fears were realised as Loftkastalinn appeared again, and with it madness and despair spread like the plague that had devastated them for months.

That was when the moon shattered.

They had run through frenzied streets, harrowed by fire and demonic shadows. A sea of people had breached the dam that was the city walls, flooding out across the country, leaving their lives behind in a desolation ruled by waking nightmares.

Still, during restless nights, those memories surfaced should she wake in the dead of night, clinging to her until the sunrise banished them.

As Reykjavík fell, the people of Huldufjörður had evacuated. The huldufólk and huldumanneskjur who lived there had hurried to gather their meagre belongings as the unimaginable manifested and the refugees came flooding out of the city. It had been Diljá's first instinct to head to the village for shelter, but she and her family had reached the same conclusion as the Huldfirðingar as the devastation unfolded. Huldufjörður was far too close to Reykjavík.

Refugees had spread in every direction. Diljá and her family had joined those who put out boats and crossed over to Suðurnes, the peninsula-turned-island. Out in the distance, they had watched the futile fight of the armada against the demonic fortress. The fortunate ironclads sank. The others became new terrors that had stalked the Atlantean Ocean ever since. The refugees had hurried to make landfall on Suðurnes, lest they fell prey to these new horrors.

A single thought surfaced among each of the huldufólk and huldumanneskjur, in varying degrees of intensity: Was this what it had been like when their world-that-was collapsed? For long centuries huldufólk had survived in Hrímland, but their ancestral myth had never been forgotten. Their world had perished and they had fled to another. Now, that cruel fate seemed to be repeating itself. Except now there was nowhere else to run. The sins of this world had become too great for it to bear. All peoples truly felt as though the end of all things was upon them.

Diljá didn't have it in her to tell them that they were not imagining it. She was glad she didn't. The sun kept rising each morning, much to her bewilderment – even to this day.

The refugees who had ventured to Suðurnes ended up taking many more people on their already crowded boats, during their flight. Some people had wanted to abandon the additional refugees, but Diljá and others had refused to take any part in it. Not for the last time, she had witnessed groups of people fracturing over irreconcilable world views.

Suðurnesjamenn were starving peasants who had for generations warred with one another in a ceaseless chain of blood feuds. Among the refugees from Reykjavík were some humans who feared or despised huldufólk and huldumanneskjur. Tensions were high. All had faced a simple choice: adapt or die. Most had found the strength of mind required to let their hatreds die.

That didn't mean it had been easy, Diljá reflected as she eviscerated a twin-tailed cod. But they had got there eventually, through unrelenting dedication. Strange, how most people needed things to burn for something new to take root.

Suðurnes was an island of barren lava fields, equally hostile in ways natural and supernatural. Cairns marked a few relatively safe paths through the volatile thaumaturgical zones, but only the desperate relied upon them. The eruptions were especially bad here, where a row of long-dormant volcanoes awoke fiercely as one. The living lava fields of Reykjanes, already treacherous, awoke with the excessive flow of seiðmagn. They had lived as nomads, fishing as they sailed along the coastline, only rarely venturing inland.

Hard years passed. Many who had lived through the sorcerous upsurge, the ashen blight and the toxic mists, fell to plain old famine. As supplies ran out and people got desperate, some had risked eating the strange plants and animals they found after the blue-tinged fog vanished. They had known a terrible fate awaited them. Many had thought it better to starve to death. But to their surprise, no ill had come to those who partook of the bounty. They had risked further inland exploration, and very few people had succumbed to the sorcerous mutations – even off the cairn paths.

Many survivors had struggled to find a place to call home. Villages that could sustain a population did not take kindly to more mouths to feed. Their group split countless times, as some managed to find a place to settle, while others kept on moving. Eventually, Diljá was part of the group that risked heading back towards Huldufjörður.

Slowly, they had realised that this was no apocalypse. It was the painful rebirth of a long-lost world once again drawing breath. Not all were willing to accept that. The unknown is sometimes more terrifying than a familiar threat. But Diljá could feel the change affecting the earth reflected deep within her – even though she never could let go of her fear that the end had only been postponed. Despite that, she, too, had let new things take root in the desolation of her heart. She had nurtured that seedling of hope with the utmost care.

Today's catch had been processed, the pier crowded with people working together on gutting and salting, laying fish out to dry on fields or hanging fish heads to rafters. As she looked over the crowd finishing their work, gossiping about this week's happenings or moaning about the weather, she had a hard time distinguishing between the humans, huldufólk or hulduman-neskjur.

Diljá wiped her bloody hands on her smock, cleaning and sharpening the knives before sheathing them at her belt. Styrmir asked her a few things about the next day's undertaking, then went to see to his boat. A significant part of their fishing fleet were old vessels from Vestmannaeyjar. According to Styrmir, Eyjamenn had also spread all over the country after their island burned. Not many had survived. He had joined up with a group of like-minded people and found his way here. Fishing was their lifeline, and they had proven to be a boon to the village. Their knowledge of everyday fishing hexes was invaluable.

As she made her way home, carrying a bucket full of fish guts, Diljá marvelled at the transformation the village had undertaken since it was reclaimed. During its previous incarnation, it had been nothing but a loose gathering of ramshackle buildings, mostly made from cast-off corrugated iron and driftwood. After years of neglect and harsh conditions it had been reduced to ruins, with the fungal forest encroaching upon it when they arrived.

Houses had been rebuilt from salvaged ruins, fortified with metal looted from wrecked ironclads which had run aground. Turf had been harvested and rocks gathered, as in the Age of Settlement, but new methods were also invented. Chitinous insect shells had been stitched together, some big enough to roof an entire house.

The lava fields around Huldufjörður were now overgrown with strange plants, low and gnarled, with towering toadstools and mushroom caps that emitted clouds of thick spores. Nothing useful for building, but a food chest when it came to feeding the village. Regularly, hunting groups ventured into the spore-fog to hunt game. New kinds of fish filled their nets just off the shore, although none dared to venture too far out to open sea where monsters roamed.

Diljá's home was a simple cottage – neatly stacked lava stones and turf, roofed with a single moss-grown carapace. Tiny clusters of mushrooms sprouted here and there – she'd have to take care of that before it got out of control. She tossed the bucket of fish guts into the enclosure next to the house. The muddied ground was crawling with rotsugur – bloated larvae as large as cats. Sensing the refuse, they wriggled towards their food. Nothing in the new forest could be tamed – not yet, anyway – but these creatures who fed on carcasses and rotted undergrowth had turned out to be suitable livestock. They yielded fatty meat, very bland in taste, but new recipes were always being discovered and shared. All is hay in hard times. Diljá picked one of the fat grubs up and put it on the roof of her house, where it immediately started devouring the lichen and fungus growing on the shell. She'd have to remember to put it back down later in the week.

That night, she prepared her gear and went over yellowed maps of the city. Just before dawn, she led a small group of people towards the unguarded city walls of Reykjavík.

Diljá had never been formally chosen as a leader. The part had grown on her as naturally as leaves in the spring. She had become as ballast to the group of people surrounding her. Without her, they would have been cast adrift.

Cold wind blew between the empty, ruined buildings. The scars of desolation marked the streets. Demons still lurked within the shadows, but did not venture past the city limits.

People who could reach out took point as scouts, communicating without words or gestures. Their chitin armour was light, treated to deflect a sharpened blade. Behind them followed a group in heavy, sand-coloured carapace armour, looking like knights out of a legend. Wielding claw-blades, nets and harpoon guns, they had as a team brought many a demonic abomination down.

Diljá and Styrmir scouted well together. They were dead silent and overly cautious, with an uncanny sense of danger lurking down a silent alley. By now, relatively safe routes had been mapped out in Reykjavík, but they were not to be relied upon. She suspected that small groups of people still lived here among the horrors. She'd seen various signs that squatters had temporarily taken residence during her exploration of the city. She doubted anyone could survive in this hell without becoming one of the monsters roaming it. Hopefully they had only been travellers passing through.

It reminded her of Styrhildur and Hraki, who had resorted to hiding in a place that turned people into living ghosts. No one deserved such a fate.

At midday, the group reached their destination – an elementary school, overgrown with ivy and thorned birch. Quickly securing the school, they went to work finding books that were undamaged enough to read. The school's library was still severely incomplete. Through a window on the third floor, she could see the nacreous crystal formations rising from the crater atop Öskjuhlíð.

Only once had she had a good enough vantage point to inspect their source closely through her binoculars. The towering crystal pillars had grown in chaotic clusters from the corpse of the landvættur. Little remained of its body where it had died, self-immolating to wipe Perlan off the face of the earth. The resulting explosion and fire had burned down much of the forest on Öskjuhlíð. The new one had grown seemingly overnight, and was rapidly overtaking the abandoned city ruins. The thick forest was filled with sounds of species unknown to them.

The luminescent crystals were milky white, shining like

mother-of-pearl. Huldfirðingar called it Perlan – the Pearl. A much more suitable name than that sorcerous machine-monstrosity that had once claimed the hill as its throne.

Diljá always noticed the absence of the Stone Giant from the derelict skyline of Skólavörðuholt. Every time, she wondered what had become of her friends. Each day, ordinary life in Huldufjörður made her think of Styrhildur and Garún. They would have loved what had been formed there. It was a small community, but it was what they had always dreamed of. What they had fought and died for. She said a quick prayer to any god that was listening, that her friends were at peace.

The book haul was decent enough. Unspoken in the air was the frequently brought-up idea that they should send a group out to Svartiskóli to harvest its untold secrets. They had sent out an expedition years before, but they had never returned. With Svartiskóli so close to Öskjuhlíð, deep within the forest, few were willing to attempt it again. The depths of that green metropolis remained unplumbed.

Thanks to careful navigation, they all made it back home unharmed. That was not something to be taken for granted. In the evening, Diljá took part in categorising the books for Huldufjörður's school.

Mass had not resumed in the church of Hamar after the re-clamation of Huldufjörður. The cathedral within the stone pillar, a remnant of the fallen world of hulduheimar, was instead used as a classroom. A strange collection of knowledgeable people had survived. Underneath the ancient altarpiece of Adralíen-toll, students learned about fishing and agriculture, carpentry and ironwork, along with natural sciences. The history, philosophy and literature of all the peoples of Huldufjörður was taught in equal measure, to their best capability. Diljá occasionally taught a class covering various subjects, such as leadership, politics and defensive skills. It gave her a welcome respite from managing the everyday issues of the town. A collection of poems surfaced in this haul. It wasn't quite something well suited for her, but it drew her attention. So much of their focus had been on something practical – the knowledge needed to survive. Leafing through the collection of classics, she knew she had to study it intensely and make up a class or two. Knowing how to survive wasn't enough if you didn't have a reason to live. For some people, this could be the first step in finding out what that meant to them.

Some time later when teaching, she noticed one of the children staring out of the window. The moment reminded her of Garún, who had shared with Diljá how she spent those long hours at Mass growing up, looking out at the beautiful fractures of a shattered reality. Mirages that could never be touched. When Diljá asked the girl what she saw, she described similar landscapes – but altered from what Garún had described.

There was also a figure, the girl said, moving among the ruins of hulduheimar, painting in the gaps between the broken pieces. The figure was glowing like the sun and moved like a dancer. The girl felt as though the being was painting a new home for them, free of strife and suffering. The being had reached out to the girl and she had known that one day, that great work would be complete and then the pathways through the worlds would once again be opened.

Diljá had been unsettled, hearing this at first. It was as if ghosts out of myth had come to haunt them – had vestiges of that dreadful civilisation survived, hunting once more for fresh souls to lure into their world? Suddenly, the tranquil vistas of dreamlike ruin seemed laden with threat.

One afternoon a few years later, while she was preparing the classroom, she had glimpsed movement through the sunlit windows. A figure made from shimmering starlight moved between clouds, filling and forming them like a living paintbrush. The vision had only lasted for a moment. Just before it faded, the being had looked back and flashed an enigmatic smile.

The warm smell of summer filled the room, despite the cold and wet early spring outside the church. Diljá remained still, as if frozen in time, fighting back tears that she couldn't let overwhelm her. The peace was shattered when the children flooded in with laughter and excitement, taking their seats, ready for the day's lesson.

With a heart filled with gratefulness, Diljá set to work.

Núll

The world existed in broken fragments. Skies ripped to shreds, time unravelling into delirious vortexes, light fracturing and falling in nonsensical ways. Night and day melded into one. The world was a mausoleum of memories, moments frozen and looping. Things ruined, things constantly being destroyed, things as they were moments before the apocalypse crashed like an unstoppable wave.

She moved between these fractures by paths unseen. Styrrún had tethered herself to the Stone Giant, channelling its arcane might through her like a leashed thunderstorm. Back in the real world left behind, she had seen countless futures unfolding, timelines constantly shifting and diverging. Here, in this desolation, time had no meaning. She existed perpetually teetering on the precipice of destruction.

Endless variations of wonders and catastrophes intertwined. The bleached bones of an unmade dimension. Remnants of the huldufólk's long-extinguished home.

The part of Styrrún that was Garún recognised some of these places. As a child, she had spent many hours staring out of the window of Huldufjörður's church and caught glimpses of the fallen world. A ruined city of silver and glass in the desert, its architecture defying gravity and geometry alike. The city sang.

Mountains like nothing found in the world she had been born in, broken and shattered as if the gods themselves had cleaved them apart. Great dead forests, a boiling sky of liquid darkness above where living lightning trailed through.

A step, a shift, and she and the giant were on a plateau, overlooking a wave of fire that swept over the land, looping back repeatedly, killing the denizens of towns and farms and cities over and over again.

Temples of Adralíen-toll simultaneously defaced and pristine. Powerful masters of the arcane arts facing off against a senseless horde of void-worshipping nobility, their once graceful dignity tarnished by their debauched appetites. Despairing refugees making a run for the collapsing gateways into other worlds, families separated as some were halfway through, others taken by the all-devouring void. A father, seemingly frozen as he was destroyed by the great unmaking, reaching out a hand to his family passing through, shouting for them to run. Nothing could be done to save any of them. All of this had already happened, a long time ago. This was a world of echoes.

Grief overwhelmed Styrrún. She could still hear the screams on the wind, feel the pain in the air, see the wounds of the earth bleeding as if freshly made. Simultaneously a miasma of the surreal permeated everything. Nothing felt real – because it wasn't. Not any more.

The Stone Giant loomed beside her every step of their journey through the desolation. A useless, lumbering beacon of trans-cendent might in a world bereft of substance. She felt no pity for Sæmundur. His own hubris had led him down this path. Willingly, he had walked into the hungering maw of oblivion, only to find himself in an ingenious and ancient trap. Instead of ascending, he had taken the place of the prisoner locked within the stone. Although he had inherited the power that remained within the confines, Sæmundur was unable to wield it. He was the architect of his own misfortune. Many others had suffered for the fulfilment of his great plan – as others had suffered for Garún's actions, she reminded herself.

All of that suffering would be for something – had to be for something. Styrrún set to her work.

With raw emotion as her blade, she methodically butchered the primordial titan. The Stone Giant did not make a sound or single movement. Nothing could permeate its mind-prison of apathy. Raw, cosmic power welled from its carcass, which could not die by any measure understood by mortal beings.

Styrrún was as one, but simultaneously not. They were two made whole again. The part that was Garún felt elated. This was who she was at heart – an artist. This shattered mirror was a vast canvas laid out before her. Styrhildur provided a different perspective – a deep and profound desire for harmony, love, empathy. Many things that had been worn away in Garún's heart over the course of her life.

From the Stone Giant's skull she forged a new sky, fusing it with the world-fragments that remained. The brain was scattered and spread across the fuming black sky, binding it together, restraining its form into dark grey clouds and thunderstorms charged with a new kind of arcane energy. From the giant's beheaded corpse a fountain erupted, a roaring waterfall that cascaded into the world and filled it with bitter waters. The flesh was butchered into the shape of continents and archipelagos, letting the blood run over the earth and weather it down, like the rough strokes of a brush. She tore out the giant's spine and femurs, teeth and ribs, and cast them into new mountains, more impossible and stranger than the faint reflections that still remained. Smaller pieces were scattered as boulders and hills; grains became pebbles and dust turned to black sand.

The storm and the water raged across the mercurial earth, dancing to Styrrún's will as she drew in the Stone Giant's power that still raged like an unrelenting sun. She laughed from the sheer joy of pure creation.

She cut his hair and laid it across the earth as new forests, which mixed together with those rotten, diseased woods that remained. And from that primordial fusion, forged in the thaumaturgical storms, life arose. With the utmost care, Styrrún guided it, culling and nurturing it in equal measure. Many great cities fell to the green inferno, while others would become foundations of new, shining beacons of art and beauty.

With a flick of her wrist, Styrrún extinguished the old sun, that bloated red god burning angrily in the sky, and from the Stone Giant's eye she cast a new celestial sphere upon the firmament, blue-white and hopeful. The other eye was ignited and cast into the planet's core, as kindling for the roaring furnace of its heart, burning dark purple with the radiant sorcery of a newborn world. The remnants of those who had lived faded as reality was stitched back together, thread by thread, woven from the Stone Giant's unravelling spirit.

With a few words whispered in the language of creation, revealed to her through the giant, Styrrún spoke to the new sorcery and bound it together with life in perfect harmony. A pact was made with all things, derived from the huldufólk's innate ability to sense one another. All things that were – stone and mountain, sea and forest, every living being – reached out to each other innately, seeking equilibrium, balance and understanding. Here were no hunters and no prey, no oppressors and no oppressed. Unity settled over the world, which had not been born from chaos like so many others, but painted into existence with a quiet compassion.

A great binding of blood and echoes. A new reality forged

from broken fragments and suffering, with none of the hunger of the old one. Styrrún worked for an eternity, stuck outside time itself. As the Stone Giant was bound and its undying power sealed within the world, the immense temporal workings resumed their function.

The artist-goddesses who were bound as one worked on joyously, fading with each stroke of their brush, until they became as faint as the shimmering constellations in the night sky when time resumed its flow once more. One by one, fires of the old gates linking this world with others were reignited. With an unseen hand, their work went on, never tiring, never faltering, waiting for those who are lost to find their way home.

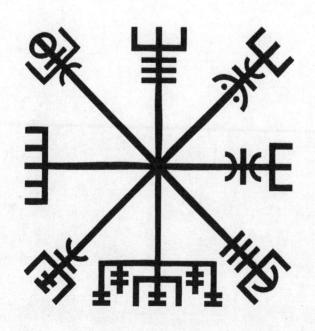

Credits

Alexander Dan Vilhjálmsson and Gollancz would like to thank everyone at Orion who worked on the publication of *The Storm Beneath a Midnight Sun*.

Agent
Jennifer Jackson

Editor
Brendan Durkin
Áine Feeney

Copy-editor
Steve O'Gorman

Proofreader
Gabriella Nemeth

Editorial Management
Áine Feeney
Jane Hughes
Charlie Panayiotou
Tamara Morriss
Claire Boyle

Audio
Paul Stark
Jake Alderson
Georgina Cutler

Contracts
Anne Goddard
Ellie Bowker
Humayra Ahmed

Design
Nick Shah
Rabab Adams
Joanna Ridley
Helen Ewing

Communications
Will O'Mullane

Finance
Nick Gibson
Jasdip Nandra
Elizabeth Beaumont
Ibukun Ademefun
Afeera Ahmed
Sue Baker
Tom Costello

Inventory
Jo Jacobs
Dan Stevens

Production
Paul Hussey
Fiona McIntosh

Operations
Sharon Willis

Rights
Susan Howe
Krystyna Kujawinska
Jessica Purdue
Ayesha Kinley
Louise Henderson

Sales
Jen Wilson
Victoria Laws
Esther Waters
Frances Doyle
Ben Goddard
Jack Hallam
Anna Egelstaff
Inês Figueira
Barbara Ronan
Andrew Hally
Dominic Smith
Deborah Deyong
Lauren Buck
Maggy Park
Linda McGregor
Sinead White
Jemimah James
Rachael Jones
Jack Dennison
Nigel Andrews
Ian Williamson
Julia Benson
Declan Kyle
Robert Mackenzie
Megan Smith
Charlotte Clay
Rebecca Cobbold